Teen Health

Course 2

Teen Health

Course 2

Mary Bronson Merki, Ph.D.

GLENCOE

McGraw-Hill

New York, New York
Columbus, Ohio
Mission Hills, California
Peoria, Illinois

Meet the Author

Mary Bronson Merki has taught health education in grades K–12, as well as health education methods classes at the undergraduate and graduate levels. As Health Education Specialist for the Dallas School District, Dr. Merki developed and implemented a district-wide health education program, *Skills for Living,* which was used as a model by the state education agency. She also helped develop and implement the district's Human Growth, Development and Sexuality program, which won the National PTA's Excellence in Education Award and earned her an honorary lifetime membership in the state PTA. Dr. Merki has assisted school districts throughout the country in developing local health education programs. In 1988, she was named the Texas Health Educator of the Year by the Texas Association for Health, Physical Education, Recreation, and Dance. Dr. Merki is also the author of *Glencoe Health,* a high school textbook adopted in school districts throughout the country. She currently teaches in a Texas public school where she was recently honored as Teacher of the Year. Dr. Merki completed her undergraduate work at Colorado State University in Fort Collins, Colorado. She earned her masters and doctoral degrees in health education at Texas Woman's University in Denton, Texas.

Editorial and production services
provided by Visual Education Corporation, Princeton, NJ.

Design by Bill Smith Studio, New York, NY.

Send all inquiries to:
Glencoe/McGraw-Hill
15319 Chatsworth Street
P.O. Box 9609
Mission Hills, California 91346-9609

ISBN 0-02-652566-6 (Course 2 Student Text)
ISBN 0-02-652567-4 (Course 2 Teacher's Wraparound Edition)

Printed in the United States of America.

3 4 5 6 7 8 9   QPK/LHP   03 02 01 00 99 98 97 96

Health Consultants

Unit 1
Your Total Health

E. Laurette Taylor, Ph.D.
Department of Health and Sport Sciences
University of Oklahoma
Norman, Oklahoma

Howard Shapiro, M.D.
School of Medicine
University of Southern California
Los Angeles, California

Unit 2
Social and Public Health

Richard Papenfuss, Ph.D.
University of Arizona Health Sciences Center
Tucson, Arizona

David Sleet, Ph.D.
Injury Center
Centers for Disease Control and Prevention
Palo Alto, California

Unit 3
Fitness and Nutrition

Kathleen Morgan Speer, Ph.D.; R.N.
Children's Medical Center of Dallas
Dallas, Texas

Peter Wood, D.Sc.; Ph.D.
Center for Research in Disease Prevention
Stanford University
Palo Alto, California

Unit 4
Your Physical Health

David Allen, M.D.
Infectious Disease Consultants of North Dallas
Dallas, Texas

Mark Dignan, Ph.D.; M.P.H.
The Bowman Gray School of Medicine
Wake Forest University
Winston-Salem, North Carolina

Unit 5
Avoiding Substance Abuse

Pamela Luna, Dr.P.H.
RIMS–Healthy Kids Regional Center
California Department of Education
Riverside, California

Prevention Materials Review Unit
National Clearinghouse for Alcohol and Drug
    Information
Rockville, Maryland

Unit 6
Safety and the Environment

Sharon Gonzales, M.A.; R.N.
West Windsor–Plainsboro Middle School
Plainsboro, New Jersey

Diane Imhulse
National Safety Council
Itasca, Illinois

Teacher Reviewers

Unit 1
Your Total Health

Essie E. Lee, Ed. D. Professor Emerita
Hunter College New York City
Professor Community Health Sciences

Lynn Westberg
Health Education Department Head
Kearns High School
Salt Lake City, Utah

Laura Williams
Health and Science Teacher
Memphis City Schools
Memphis, Tennessee

Unit 2
Social and Public Health

Martha R. Roper
Health Teacher
Parkway South High School
Manchester, Missouri

Brenda C. Wilson
Director of Health Education
Iredell Statesville Schools
Statesville, North Carolina

Unit 3
Fitness and Nutrition

Raynette Evans
Director of Health, Physical Education, and Athletics
Bibb County Public Schools
Macon, Georgia

Robin GrayBallard
Health Educator
Suva Intermediate School
Montebello Unified School District
Montebello, California

Ed Larios
Department Chair
Health and Physical Education Department
Burlingame High School
Burlingame, California

Unit 4
Your Physical Health

Randall F. Nitchie
Health Specialist
Osseo Public Schools, District #279
Maple Grove, Minnesota

Ann Orman
Science/Health Teacher
West End Middle School
Nashville, Tennessee

Unit 5
Avoiding Substance Abuse

Beverly Berkin
District Chairperson, Health Education
Cold Spring Harbor School District
Cold Spring Harbor, New York

Dona Carmack
Health Educator
Burlingame High School
Burlingame, California

Claudia Thorn
Coordinator, Staff Development
Prevention Education Center K–12
Sacramento County Office of Education
Sacramento, California

Unit 6
Safety and the Environment

Ed Hedges
Health Education Teacher
Central High School
Phoenix, Arizona

JoCyel Rodgers
Health Teacher
Glencrest Middle School
Fort Worth, Texas

Liz Clark, M.S.
Connections Consulting
Three Rivers, California

Contents

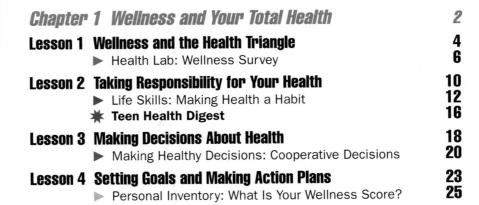

Unit 1
Your Total Health

Unit 2
Social and Public Health

Unit 4
Your Physical Health

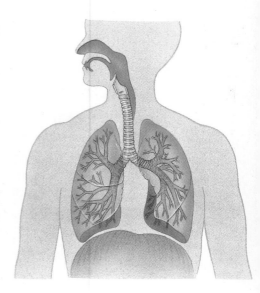

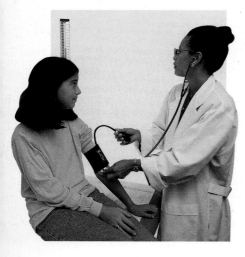

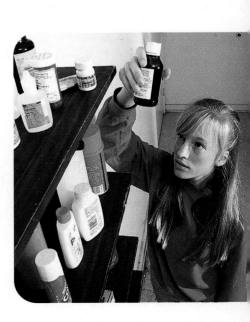

Unit 6
Safety and the Environment

Features

Health Lab

Life Skills

Making Healthy Decisions

Personal Inventory

People at Work

Teens Making a Difference

CON$UMER FOCU$

Health Update

Sports and Recreation

Myths and Realities

Unit 1
Your Total Health

Chapter 1
Wellness and Your Total Health

Student Expectations

After reading this chapter, you should be able to:

1. Explain the concept of wellness.
2. Recognize how your attitudes and behavior affect your level of health.
3. Explain how to make responsible health decisions.
4. Recognize how setting goals and taking action affects self-esteem.

I think this is the busiest time of my life. It's hectic, but I really enjoy what I'm doing.

Mom got a new job, and in a way I did, too. When I come home from school, I have an hour to myself before my little brother and sister get home. If the weather's nice, I like to spend that hour riding my bike or jogging. On really cold or rainy days, I listen to music or start my homework.

When Lisa and Joey get home I'm in charge of them until Dad gets home from work. We do our homework together so I'm right there if they need help. Mom leaves me instructions for starting dinner. While I'm doing that, Lisa and Joey set the table and feed Sammi (she's our dog).

When Dad arrives, he and I finish cooking dinner. After dinner, everyone else cleans up while I do my homework. Then I usually talk on the phone or read for awhile until it's time to go to bed. Even though there's a lot to do, I feel like I'm helping out by pitching in.

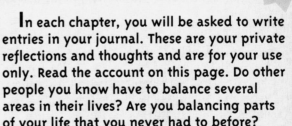

in your journal

In each chapter, you will be asked to write entries in your journal. These are your private reflections and thoughts and are for your use only. Read the account on this page. Do other people you know have to balance several areas in their lives? Are you balancing parts of your life that you never had to before? Start your private journal entries on wellness and total health by answering these questions:

▶ Do you consider yourself healthy?

▶ How happy are you about the choices and decisions you make about your health?

▶ Do you have any behaviors, related to health, that you would like to change?

When you reach the end of the chapter, you will use your journal entries to make an action plan.

Wellness and the Health Triangle

This lesson will help you find answers to questions that teens often ask about being healthy. For example:

▶ **What does being healthy really mean?**
▶ **What do I need to know to be healthy?**
▶ **What is the difference between health and wellness?**

Words to Know

health
wellness

What Is Health?

What is your definition of health? Many people think that being healthy is not being sick. Others think that if a person is in good physical shape, that person is healthy.

Take a closer look and you may see that being healthy involves more than physical well-being. Do you know students who are always getting into fights? Would you call these people healthy? What about a person who seems unhappy no matter what he or she does? Being in good physical shape is important. Yet there is much more than that to good health.

You make choices every day that affect your health. You decide what to eat, who will be your friends, and how to spend your time. Do you know which choices lead to good health and which do not? This book will help you learn to recognize the choices that are best for you. It will also give you the chance to look at your health habits now. Then you can decide whether you need to change any of your behavior to become a healthier person.

| Exercising is one choice you make that affects your health.

The Foundations of Health

Besides physical health, your total health picture includes your mental/emotional health and your social health. In other words, being healthy also means feeling good about yourself and getting along with others. **Health** is *a combination of physical, mental/emotional, and social well-being.* **Figure 1.1** explains more about these three sides of health.

The Health Triangle

The three sides of your health are connected, like the sides of a triangle. Each side affects the other two sides. For example, being physically tired or being hungry can make you grouchy. Being depressed for a long time can make you feel physically weak and run-down. Experiencing problems in getting along with others can make you feel bad about yourself.

Being healthy means having a balanced health triangle. It is not hard to have a balanced health triangle. All you have to do is decide to take action to keep each side of your triangle healthy.

Figure 1.1
The Health Triangle

The three sides of health combine to form the health triangle.

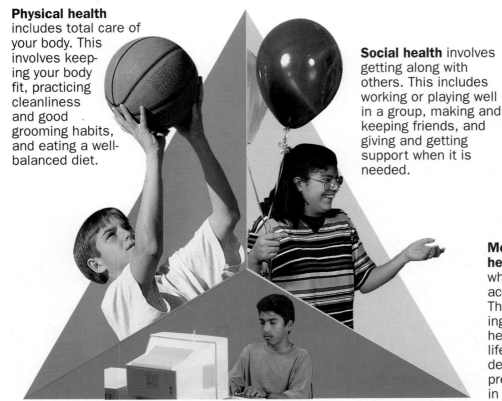

Physical health includes total care of your body. This involves keeping your body fit, practicing cleanliness and good grooming habits, and eating a well-balanced diet.

Social health involves getting along with others. This includes working or playing well in a group, making and keeping friends, and giving and getting support when it is needed.

Mental and emotional health includes liking who you are and accepting yourself. This involves expressing emotions in a healthy way, facing life's problems, and dealing with its pressures or stresses in a positive way.

Q & A

This Is Health?

Q: Roland, who's 14, brags that he's never been sick a day in his life. He spends hours in front of the TV. He loves junk food, hates fruits and vegetables, and laughs at people who exercise. I say he's not as healthy as he claims. Am I right?

A: Yes, you are right! Roland's health triangle is not balanced. He may find, in the future, that his choices start to affect his health.

Each side of your triangle is equally important to good health. By working to keep the sides balanced, you will be on your way toward becoming a healthy person. **Figure 1.2** shows what can happen if your health triangle is not in balance. When one side becomes more important than the others, the other sides suffer.

The following scenarios describe the health triangles of three teens. Do any of them sound like yours?

■ Jordan has lots of friends. He spends most of his time getting together with them. They play video games, go to the beach, or watch movies. Jordan has never been very good at sports or school, and he does not try to change that.

■ Tamara has a few close friends and sees them primarily on weekends. She is busy most weeknights with basketball practice and homework. Geography is her favorite subject.

■ Aaron does not spend much time with friends or family because he has soccer practice on weeknights and baseball games on weekends. His grades, which used to be good, are slipping and his parents are annoyed because he's not doing his chores.

Practicing *good* health habits helps you balance your health triangle. It also lessens your chances of illness and helps you stay well. Good health habits include:

■ choosing the right foods.

■ avoiding tobacco, alcohol, and other drugs.

■ taking part in a regular exercise program.

■ learning ways to handle stress.

■ getting along well with others.

HEALTH LAB
Wellness Survey

Introduction: Why should teens be concerned about staying healthy or becoming healthier than they are now? The answer is easy. Prevention is easier than cure. It takes much more time and effort to cure an illness than to keep the body well. Also, more serious health problems can occur as a result of poor health choices.

Objective: With one or more classmates, develop a health survey to give to a sample of

Figure 1.2
Three Health Triangles

Match these triangles with the scenarios on page 6. Which of these triangles are unbalanced? What needs to happen to make them balanced again?

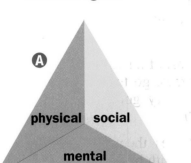

A

physical   social

mental

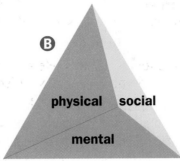

B

physical   social

mental

C

physical   social

mental

What Is Wellness?

Wellness is *an overall state of well-being, or total health.* It is a way of life. It involves making choices and decisions each day that promote good health.

Decision Making for Wellness

What kinds of decisions do you make every day that affect your health? The way you spend your time and the foods you choose to eat are two decisions. After school, do you practice a musical instrument, review your Spanish vocabulary, ride your bike, or do you just watch television? Do you eat fruit or yogurt for an after-school snack, or do you eat potato chips, cake, or candy?

The everyday decisions you make will affect your health for years to come. Of course, watching television one day a week after school or having candy for one afternoon snack will not harm your health. Daily habits have a long-term effect on you.

Your Total Health

The Mind-Body Connection

The three sides of total health affect one another to such a large degree that some physicians have begun to give the following advice to people who are scheduled for major surgery:

► Think one happy thought every hour, or as needed, for each of the three days leading up to the surgery.

► Take an extra-large dose of visits from family and close friends the day before the surgery is scheduled.

students in your school. Use the survey to find out how aware students are about the following:

► their physical, mental and emotional, and social health

► the choices affecting their health triangle

Materials and Method: On a sheet of paper, list questions to see how much students know about their physical, mental/emotional, and social health and the choices they make that affect their health triangle. A few sample questions are: Is getting plenty of sleep essential to good health? Are there good ways and bad ways to

express your anger? Do you need to know how to communicate with others to be healthy?

With the help of your teacher, make copies of the survey and distribute them to your classmates. Ask the students to return the survey to your teacher.

Observation and Analysis: Tally the responses in the surveys. Write an article about the results of the survey for the school newspaper.

The Wellness Continuum

The wellness continuum shown in **Figure 1.3** is a scale that shows a person's level of wellness, from a low level to a high level. People on the left side of the continuum, the low level, usually rely on someone else to help them maintain their health. People on the right side of the continuum, the high level, are usually responsible, have a high level of self-discipline, and have personal goals.

Maintaining Your Wellness

The people on the right side of the continuum accept responsibility for maintaining their own health. However, the level of wellness for most people is not high. The levels usually cluster around the midpoint on the continuum. Why do you think this is so? On what point of the continuum do you fall? What steps can you take to improve your position on the health continuum?

The choices you make regarding your health will influence your level of wellness for the rest of your life. Can you think of choices you make that help you to maintain your wellness? Can you think of areas that need improvement? What can you do to work toward maintaining a high level of wellness for yourself?

in your journal

Make a list of all the people you know who are at least partly responsible for good health choices you have made. For example, who helped you decide to have regular dental checkups? Then make a list of your own behaviors that may have led to good health habits in others. Write the lists in your journal.

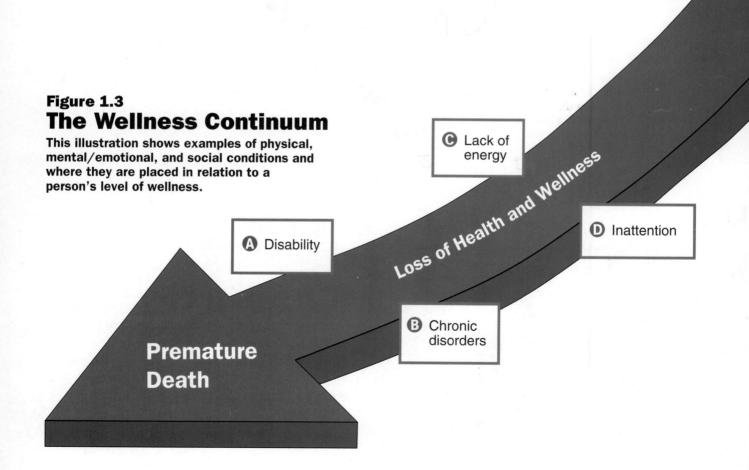

Figure 1.3
The Wellness Continuum

This illustration shows examples of physical, mental/emotional, and social conditions and where they are placed in relation to a person's level of wellness.

C Lack of energy

Loss of Health and Wellness

A Disability

D Inattention

B Chronic disorders

Premature Death

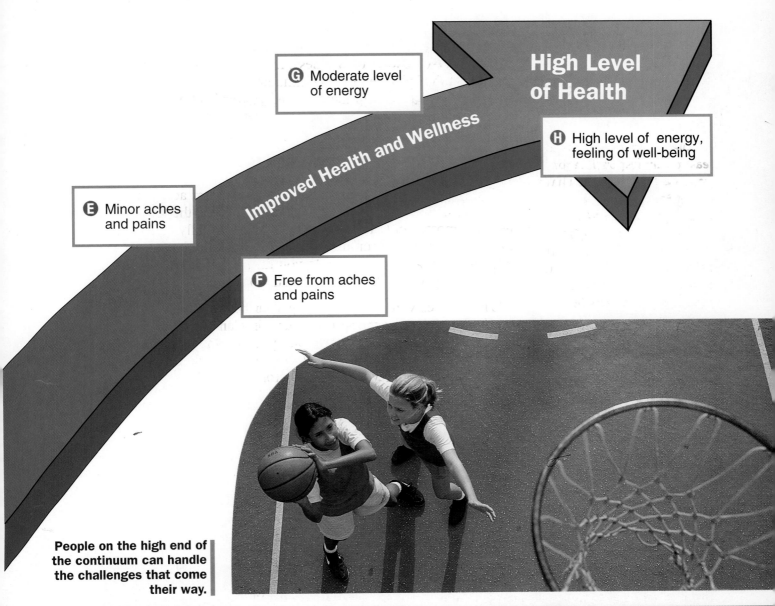

G Moderate level of energy

High Level of Health

Improved Health and Wellness

H High level of energy, feeling of well-being

E Minor aches and pains

F Free from aches and pains

People on the high end of the continuum can handle the challenges that come their way.

Using complete sentences, answer the following questions on a separate sheet of paper.

Reviewing Terms and Facts

1. **Vocabulary** Define the term *health*. Use it in an original sentence.

2. **Compare and Contrast** Use your own words to explain the difference between health and wellness.

Thinking Critically

3. **Describe** List three signs of a person whose health triangle is not balanced.

4. **Suggest** What are some ways that you can improve your position on the wellness continuum?

Applying Health Concepts

5. **Personal Health** Draw your own health triangle. If your triangle is balanced, make a list of recent choices and decisions you have made to keep the three sides equal. If the triangle is unbalanced, list specific ways you can help balance it.

Taking Responsibility for Your Health

This lesson will help you find answers to questions that teens often ask about taking responsibility for their health. For example:

► How do heredity, environment, and available health care affect my health?
► Is my environment healthy?
► How do behavior and attitudes affect my health?
► How can I develop habits to improve my health?

Words to Know

heredity
environment
behavior
attitudes
lifestyle factors
health education

Factors That Affect Your Health

The health choices you make every day are a major factor in your total health. In addition to your choices, other factors affect your health. They are heredity, environment, and available health care (see **Figure 1.4**).

Figure 1.4
Influences on Your Health

The three factors that affect your health are heredity, environment, and available health care.

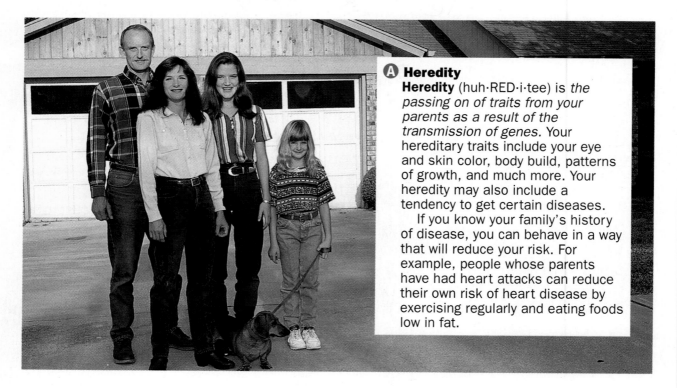

A Heredity
Heredity (huh·RED·i·tee) is *the passing on of traits from your parents as a result of the transmission of genes.* Your hereditary traits include your eye and skin color, body build, patterns of growth, and much more. Your heredity may also include a tendency to get certain diseases.

If you know your family's history of disease, you can behave in a way that will reduce your risk. For example, people whose parents have had heart attacks can reduce their own risk of heart disease by exercising regularly and eating foods low in fat.

B Environment

Environment (en·VY·ruhn·ment) is *the sum total of your surroundings*. It includes the place where you live, the school you attend, and the people you see often.

Where you live can be very important. If you live in a warm climate, for example, your skin may be exposed to more hours of sunlight. You can, however, behave in ways that minimize your risk of overexposure to the sun. You can learn how to protect your skin and eyes from the sun's damaging rays.

The people in your environment can affect your health choices, both positively and negatively. For example, if you see many of your friends trying out for sports teams at school, you may become interested in trying out as well.

C Available Health Care

Available health care, the third factor, is determined by where you live. A person living in a major city will probably have more doctors and clinics to choose from than a person in a small town.

To get the most out of available health care, you need to have regular health maintenance such as immunizations, dental checkups, and physical examinations. Keeping up on current health care information can also help you choose the best ways to promote and protect your health.

Although you have little or no control over these factors, the way you behave has an effect on them. Your **behavior** is *the way you act in many different situations and events in life.* Your behavior can have a positive or negative impact on any or all of the factors. Since you can control your behavior, you need to do everything you can to make health choices that are best for you. **Figure 1.4** shows how behavior is linked with the factors that affect your health.

Taking Control

Taking control of your health depends on more than just recognizing healthy choices. Your personal **attitudes** (AT·i·toodz)—your *feelings and beliefs*—also play a role in how well you take care of yourself. You need to believe that making good choices and developing good health habits can affect your health.

Your attitude also includes the way you feel about yourself. If you like who you are and feel that other people like you, you will want to take care of yourself. You will want to be at your best in all areas. To ensure that you are at your best, you will make choices that protect and promote your health.

Your parents are a good source of information and advice on staying healthy, but only you can take the necessary action to be healthy.

LIFE SKILLS
Making Health a Habit

A first step toward improving yourself and your total health is to know yourself. Take an honest look at your behavior. Do you see yourself as a responsible person? Do you feel that adults should give you more responsibility? Do you show that you are ready for it? There are ways that you can demonstrate your readiness. For example:

► If you see something that needs doing, do it without waiting to be told.

► Do your schoolwork and turn it in on time.

► Do your household chores without having to be reminded.

► Follow through on your promises.

► Show up on time.

► Finish tasks that you start, and clean up after yourself.

You can also improve yourself by practicing the lifestyle factors listed in **Figure 1.5** on page 14. Are all of those factors part of your present daily routine? If not, try the following:

► Identify a habit you want to start. On a piece of paper, write it down four times. Next to the habit, write at least two benefits you could gain from making it part of your routine.

► Practice the habit at least four times in the next week. Each time, circle one of the times you wrote it on your list. Also circle the benefits you got from practicing the habit.

Steps to Responsible Health

Taking care of your health is mainly your own responsibility. The list that follows shows the three basic steps you should take in accepting responsibility for your health.

- **Find out how much you know about your health.** This means knowing at any time your health level on each of the three sides of your health triangle. You can determine this by taking a self-health inventory such as the one on page 25.

- **Get good, reliable information on how to stay healthy or improve your health.** Breakthroughs in health are happening all the time. By reading magazines or newspapers, you can keep up-to-date on events that could affect your health.

- **Take action.** This means setting realistic goals for yourself. If you decide you want to lose weight, do it gradually, following a sensible, safe eating plan. Taking action also means becoming actively involved in your total health. Eating a bowl of high-fiber cereal and fruit each morning is not enough if you are going to snack on sweets the rest of the day. Working to maintain a high level of wellness is a full-time job.

Shaping Your Future

What habits affect your health? After studying many different types of people over the years, health experts have identified certain habits that can make a difference in people's lives. Those who practice these *life-related habits,* or **lifestyle factors,** appear to live longer and be happier. **Figure 1.5** on page 14 illustrates these habits. How many of them do you practice regularly?

Science Connection

Choosing with Care ACTIVITY!

Some athletes believe that products such as bee pollen and ginseng root will give them extra strength and power. However, beliefs such as these have been challenged by scientists in the fields of medicine and nutrition. Look through current magazines for advertisements of "health" products. List the ones that may not stand up to scientific scrutiny.

Follow-up Activity

Think about the times you demonstrated responsibility in the past week. If responsibility is still lacking, choose one of the suggested ways for showing you are responsible. Record the number of times you perform that particular action during the next week.

Then select a healthy behavior you would like to make part of your life. Practice making it a part of your daily routine. Evaluate your progress at the end of a week.

Figure 1.5
Lifestyle Factors
Positive lifestyle factors like these can affect your health now and for years to come.

Social Studies Connection

Where in the World?

Many diseases in the United States are referred to as "lifestyle diseases." Heart disease, diabetes, arteriosclerosis, high blood pressure, and some types of cancer have been linked to poor eating habits, sedentary living, and unhealthy work environments. Select two countries in different parts of the world and research the presence or absence of similar lifestyle diseases in those locations. Also identify the factors that contribute to the presence or absence of the diseases.

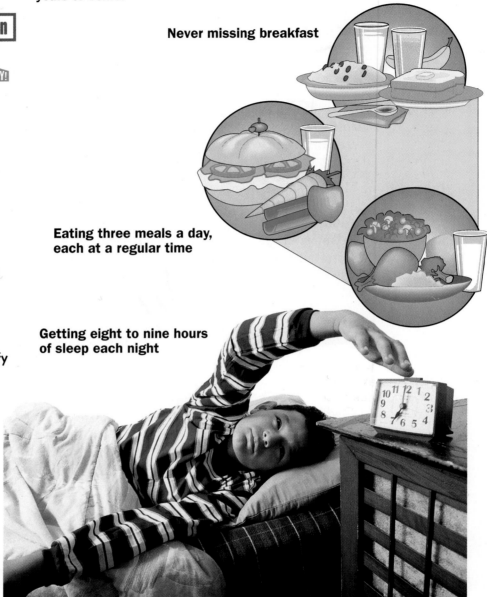

Never missing breakfast

Eating three meals a day, each at a regular time

Getting eight to nine hours of sleep each night

Staying Informed

Because good health is part of a happy, satisfying life, learning how to get and stay healthy should be an important part of your life. That is why health education is so important. **Health education** means *providing health information in such a way that it influences people to change their attitudes and take positive actions regarding their health.* The goal of health education is to help people live long and productive lives.

Health education is more than just learning health facts. It can help you gain the tools you need to maintain and improve your total health and wellness. You can use health facts you learn in all areas of your life.

Staying at a recommended level of weight

in your journal

What types of health education are you exposed to? How has this education influenced you to take positive actions toward your health? In your journal, write a paragraph that answers these questions.

Doing vigorous exercise for 20 to 30 minutes at least three to four times each week

Avoiding tobacco, alcohol, and other drugs

Review
Lesson 2

Using complete sentences, answer the following questions on a separate sheet of paper.

Reviewing Terms and Facts

1. **Vocabulary** Which of the following terms are factors affecting your health that you *can* change: *heredity, behavior, environment, attitudes, lifestyle factors?*

2. **Give Examples** What are three steps you can take toward more responsible health habits?

Thinking Critically

3. **Synthesize** Imagine you live in a town that has many hills. Give an example of two health habits—one good, one bad—that you might develop on the basis of this environment.

4. **Analyze** Look at the list of lifestyle factors in **Figure 1.5.** Choose one and think of ways you could help someone develop it as a personal health habit.

Applying Health Concepts

5. **Personal Health** Find out what kinds of diseases can be passed down through generations of a family. Choose one of the diseases, and read current information about the medical advances being made to combat the disease. Report your findings to the class.

6. **Consumer Health** Prepare a survey of the available health care in your community. Report your findings in the form of a pamphlet.

CONSUMER FOCUS

Wading Through the Confusion

Water is important to the body. It also is important to business. For example, there are dozens of different kinds of bottled water displayed at most supermarkets and other food outlets. Bottles are labeled *spring water, mineral water,* or *sparkling water.* Look around and you will see all kinds of advertisements urging you to drink a particular brand.

As a consumer, it helps to know what the differences are among the bottled waters. *Spring water,* or natural water, is drinking water that comes from an underground spring or a bored well. This type of water may undergo some treatment, such as filtration, but generally nothing is added to it.

Mineral water has a certain amount of dissolved solids. These solids are minerals that have been added or that occur naturally.

Sparkling waters are carbonated drinks that are often flavored. They are usually considered substitutes for soft drinks, not drinking water.

When purchasing bottled water, you should make sure that the bottler is a member of the International Bottled Water Association. This association is not regulated by the federal government, but it requires its members to test for more than 200 contaminants.

Meridian Market

Natural Spring Water

Water Source: Pine Valley Spring
Pine Valley, CT

50.7 FL. OZ. (1 QT. 18.7 FL. OZ.)

Although safety is important, taste is also an important part of deciding which kind of bottled water to buy. Before you decide to purchase bottled water, read the information on the label.

The Spirit of the Boston Marathon

An active body can carry you many miles and many years. Just ask John Adelbert Kelley. He knows all about the benefits of staying in good health. The 86-year-old Kelley has run the Boston Marathon 61 times!

Mr. Kelley is known as the heart and soul of the Boston Marathon. He first ran in 1928, but was unable to finish. He tried again, without success, in 1932. It was not until 1933, however, when he was 25 years old, that he completed the race (in slightly more than three hours). During the next 58 years, Kelley finished in all but two marathons, and placed first in 1935 and 1945.

Once, when the grand old man of the marathon was asked if he would retire from running, he gave this answer: "When the time comes to quit, it will be with regrets because I've had a lot of fun and won a lot of races and associated with the swellest bunch of athletes in the world." That was in 1942. In 1994, Kelley still believes that a distance run is "a very serious thing" that takes a lot of work.

People at Work

Community Health Educator

Laura is the director of community health education for a small hospital in her hometown. She has a college degree in public health and has worked as a health educator for ten years. Laura decided to apply for the director's position five years ago. Since becoming a director, she has worked hard to provide interesting programs for patients, their families, and other community members.

Laura's main objective is to teach people of all ages how to promote health and prevent illness. She especially likes holding "talk-ins for teens." Health-related subjects such as nutrition and first aid are covered. The programs are so popular that there is always a waiting list.

Health Update

Cycle with Care

Taking risks is a part of many activities that you do each day. However, you do not have to take unreasonable risks.

According to the National Safety Council, hundreds of bike riders under the age of 15 are killed each year in accidents. There are several ways to reduce the chances of becoming a statistic.

Start by wearing a safety helmet. (In some states, such as California, it is the law!) A helmet can reduce the risk of head injury by as much as 85 percent. Practice basic safety rules, such as: (1) looking left, right, and left again before entering traffic; (2) riding close to the curb on the right side of the road; (3) obeying traffic signs and lights; and (4) using hand signals for right and left turns. If you must ride in the dark, remember to wear reflective tape or clothing and have a light and reflectors on your bike.

Teens Making a Difference

Rapping for Health

Omar is part of a school-sponsored rap group. His group is called "Rappin's Right." They write the words and perform for teens, their parents, and some community groups.

There are six boys in Omar's rap group. Last year they signed a pact with their principal to use rap as a positive force. Their goal is to get teens excited about healthy behavior, rather than about behavior that could damage their health. At first, Omar and his friends thought they would be laughed at for using their rap to point out the positive. That did not happen, though. In fact, a lot of people have asked about joining their group.

Rappin's Right hopes to be part of next summer's local health festival. The group has a positive message about good health and cannot wait to share it with the entire community.

Making Decisions About Health

This lesson will help you find answers to questions that teens often ask about decisions. For example:

► **Are all risks bad?**
► **How can I learn to make better decisions?**
► **How do my decisions affect my health?**
► **How do my decisions affect other people?**

Words to Know

risk behavior
precaution
decision making
values

Cultural Diversity

Opposites Attract

ACTIVITY!

The ancient Chinese principles called yin and yang say that conflicting forces are part of the natural order. For example, opposites, such as hot and cold, are necessary in order to appreciate each one.

Yin and yang can be compared to differences of opinion or opposing points of view. These differences often help people arrive at balanced decisions that are mutually agreeable.

List some differences of opinion that you had to weigh to arrive at a decision about a situation.

Decisions Come in All Sizes

An important part of good mental health is being able to face problems and work on finding solutions to them. We all have problems, some of them major, some of them minor. Decision making can be used to solve many of these problems. Knowing how to make decisions is an important skill to develop. **Figure 1.6** illustrates some of the major decisions that teens face.

Figure 1.6
Major Decisions

A teen might ask himself or herself questions similar to these when facing major decisions.

Should I get a part-time job? What type would I like?

Should I get training after high school? What kind of training should it be?

Should I go to a party where there will be alcohol and drugs?

Should I participate in a sports program? Which one?

Examining the Risks

Many actions you take involve risks. A **risk behavior** is *the possibility that an action may cause injury or harm to you or others.* When you take a risk, you expose yourself and others to possible danger. For example, if you decide not to wear a helmet when you ride your bike, this would be considered a risk behavior.

You cannot avoid all risks. You take a risk whenever you cross the street or climb the stairs. However, reasonable risks such as these are not likely to injure you or someone else.

Risky Situations

Unreasonable risks carry with them the likelihood that someone will get hurt now or in the future. The best way to lower the risk is to avoid risky situations. For instance, do not pick a fight with someone you disagree with. Instead, express your feelings in a calm manner and walk away before the conflict turns violent.

Taking Precautions

You can cut down on the risks you take by planning ahead and taking precautions. A **precaution** is *a planned action taken before an event to increase the chances of a safe outcome.* For example, learning to ski can be a high-risk activity. However, you can make it less risky by using safe equipment and by taking ski lessons.

Before making any major decisions, think about the risks involved. Then ask yourself these questions:

■ Are they necessary risks?

■ If the risks are reasonable, what precautions can I take to increase my chances of a safe outcome?

■ If I am taking risks to show off or to feel important, what could I do instead to feel better about myself?

This teen's mountain climbing is a risk behavior because she could injure herself while doing it.

Six Steps of Decision Making

Whenever you must make a major decision, it helps to know as much as you can about the decision-making process. **Decision making** is *the process of making a choice or finding a solution*. It involves a series of steps you can follow. **Figure 1.7** illustrates these steps. Which of these steps do you use in making decisions?

Figure 1.7
The Decision-Making Process
Making a major decision will be easier if you use this six-step process.

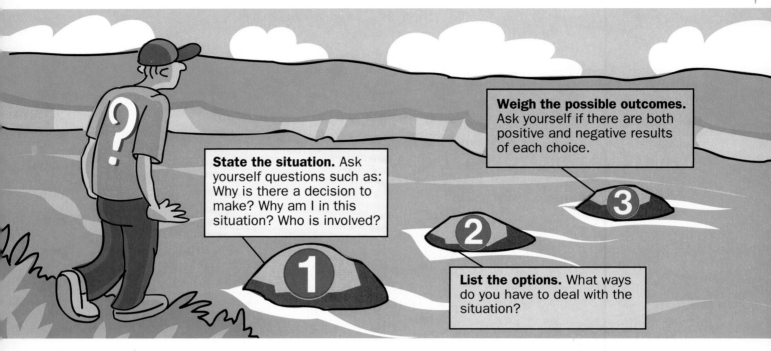

State the situation. Ask yourself questions such as: Why is there a decision to make? Why am I in this situation? Who is involved?

List the options. What ways do you have to deal with the situation?

Weigh the possible outcomes. Ask yourself if there are both positive and negative results of each choice.

MAKING HEALTHY DECISIONS
Cooperative Decisions

Kim has been chosen to be in the school play. If she accepts the part, she will have to attend practice for one hour every day after school for three weeks. Kim is very happy about being chosen. She loves drama and hopes to be an actress.

Kim's mother also is happy about the good news. However, she has a problem with Kim's required practice time. She is a nurse and works a twelve-hour shift on Mondays, Wednesdays, and Fridays. She counts on Kim to pick up her five-year-old daughter, Lee, from kindergarten after school on the days that she works. On those days, Kim looks after Lee and prepares part of the evening meal. Their mother returns home from work about 7:15 p.m.

Kim really wants to be in the play, but her mother depends on her to look after Lee. Should Kim tell the drama teacher she cannot be in the play? If she accepts the part, who will pick up Lee from kindergarten and look after her? Kim and her mother decide to use the steps in decision making to help them solve their problem:

❶ **State the situation**
❷ **List the options**
❸ **Weigh the possible outcomes**
❹ **Consider your values**
❺ **Make a decision and act**
❻ **Evaluate the decision**

Evaluating Your Decision

After you have made the decision and taken action, reflect on what happened. You might ask yourself the following questions:

■ What was the outcome? Was it what I expected?

■ How did my decision affect each part of my health triangle?

■ How did my decision affect the way I feel about myself?

■ What effect did my decision have on others?

■ What did I learn? Would I take the same action again?

in your journal

How can you apply what you have learned about decision making to your own life? Think about some of the situations you face at home and with your friends. In your journal, apply the six steps to your decision making.

Make a decision and act. Use everything you know at this point to make a decision. You can feel good that you have prepared so carefully.

Consider your values. Values are *the beliefs and ideas that are important to you and to your family.* They should serve as guidelines for making decisions.

Evaluate the decision. You may decide that your decision was the right one, or you may choose to act differently.

Follow-up Activities

1. Apply the six steps of the decision-making process to Kim's story.

2. Along with a partner, role-play a scene in which Kim turns down the offer to be in the play. Have her share her feelings in a dialogue with the audience.

3. Role-play a scene in which Kim and her mother work together to create a course of action that satisfies both of them.

Practice Makes It Easier

It helps to practice decision making ahead of time. For instance, think about some of the problems that you or your family face. Go through all six steps to come up with a healthy solution for each problem. This can help you prepare for times when major decisions come your way.

The more you practice the steps of the decision-making process, the easier decision making becomes. Do not hesitate to ask your parents and other people whose judgment you respect for their suggestions. In time, the practice will prepare you so you will be able to make wise decisions on your own.

If you practice using the decision-making process, you will be prepared to make healthy decisions that are right for you.

Lesson 3

Review

Using complete sentences, answer the following questions on a separate sheet of paper.

Reviewing Terms and Facts

1. **Vocabulary** What is the difference between a *risk behavior* and a *precaution?*

2. **Give Examples** What are four real-life examples of major decisions that teens often make?

Thinking Critically

3. **Suggest** Identify a major decision teens might have to make. Suggest some precautions that they could take to reduce the risks involved in the decision.

4. **Analyze** Think of a decision you have made in the past year. Compare your process with the steps given in this lesson. Which of these steps did you use? Which did you not use? How might the outcome have been different if you had used all six steps?

Applying Health Concepts

5. **Growth and Development** Write a conversation a teen might have with himself or herself in which the teen decides whether or not to smoke a cigarette. Use the steps in the decision-making model. You might tape the conversation to share with the class.

Setting Goals and Making Action Plans

This lesson will help you find answers to questions that teens often ask about goals. For example:

▶ **What is a goal?**

▶ **How does setting goals affect my self-esteem?**

▶ **Why do I need to set goals?**

▶ **How can I achieve my goals?**

Why Set Goals?

How do you feel about your life? Do you believe that life is something that happens to you, or do you believe that life is something over which you have some control?

You can help give your life direction by setting goals. A **goal** is *something you aim for.* Reaching any goal takes planning and effort. Goals are important to your **self-esteem,** or *the way you feel about yourself.* People who set goals and achieve them feel better about themselves and about their lives.

If you do not have any goals, ask yourself why. Are you afraid of failing or afraid of being made fun of? Then ask yourself how you can remove the obstacles that keep you from setting goals and working to achieve them.

Your Total Health

The Whole Picture

Goals that you set for one area of your life often lead to the achievement of goals in other areas. For example, if you work to reach a goal to be on the swim team, you probably will achieve some fitness goals, too. If you make the team, you may reach goals such as increasing your circle of friends and managing stress better.

Andre Agassi is an example of a person who sets goals and works to achieve them. Are you that kind of person?

The Importance of Goals

Your goals are important because they keep you focused and on track. They help you identify what you want out of life. They also help you use your time, energy, and other resources wisely.

Some goals, such as completing a homework assignment, are short term. Others take longer to achieve. Earning enough money to buy a new bike is a long-term goal. Finishing school and learning to play a musical instrument are also long-term goals.

Both long-term and short-term goals are important. For instance, suppose you wanted to run 5 miles in a race sponsored by your community's park district. The race is two months away. To attain this long-term goal, you need to set some short-term goals. These are like stepping-stones that you could manage one at a time.

Figure 1.8 shows all the short-term goals you could set to help you reach your long-term goal. You might set short-term goals of exercising fifteen to thirty minutes every day and of changing your diet to prepare yourself to run the race. By running the race, you will achieve your long-term goal and boost your self-esteem.

in your journal

Choose two long-term goals you would like to achieve. For each long-term goal, set a few short-term goals that will help you achieve the long-term goal. Write your goals in your journal.

Figure 1.8
Short-Term and Long-Term Goals

This teen set a series of short-term goals that helped him achieve his long-term goal. Have you ever used a process like this to set and achieve goals?

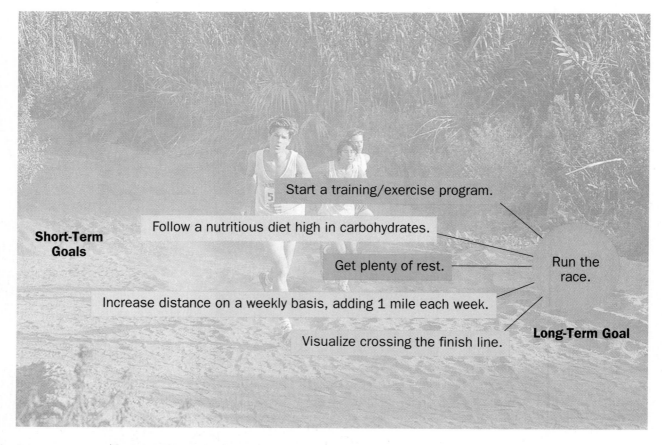

Short-Term Goals

Start a training/exercise program.

Follow a nutritious diet high in carbohydrates.

Get plenty of rest.

Increase distance on a weekly basis, adding 1 mile each week.

Visualize crossing the finish line.

Run the race.

Long-Term Goal

Personal Inventory

Although some factors may be out of your control, your level of wellness is mainly up to you. This is because you are in charge of your attitudes, goals, and decisions.

On a separate sheet of paper, write yes or no for each statement below. Your answers can help identify goals you need to set to improve your level of wellness. Total your number of yes responses. Compare your score with the ranking at the end of the survey.

1. I generally like and accept who I am.
2. I deal with stress in positive ways.
3. I eat a healthy breakfast every day.
4. If I have a problem with someone, I try to work it out.
5. I do at least 20 minutes of aerobic exercise at least three times each week.
6. I express my emotions in healthy ways.
7. I share my thoughts and feelings with others.
8. I stay within 5 pounds of my weight range.
9. I can accept constructive criticism.
10. I use a seat belt whenever I ride in a car.
11. I get at least 8 hours of sleep at night.
12. I enjoy being alone at times.
13. I do not use alcohol or illegal drugs.
14. I feel that I communicate well with others.
15. I refuse to ride with drivers who have been using alcohol or other drugs.
16. I have at least one hobby that I enjoy.
17. I do not use tobacco.
18. I work well in a group.
19. I have at least one or two close friends.
20. I say no when people ask me to do things that might threaten my health or safety.

Check out your score. Give yourself 1 point for each yes. A score of 16–20 is very good. A score of 11–15 is good. A score of 6–10 is fair. If you score below 5, you need to look seriously at the choices and decisions you make each day.

Making an Action Plan

Setting goals is a skill that you can use in all areas of life. It is a process that gives you direction, a framework within which to work, and a timetable for completing the work. **Figure 1.9** shows the steps one teen used to improve her goal-setting skills and, as a result, her self-esteem. Following these steps can be a big help to you when you set your own goals.

in your Journal

Think of two short-term goals you want to reach this week. Use the steps for goal setting to plan how you will reach one of these goals. Write your plan in your journal.

Figure 1.9
The Action Plan Process

The process of setting goals is easier if you follow the six steps this teen did.

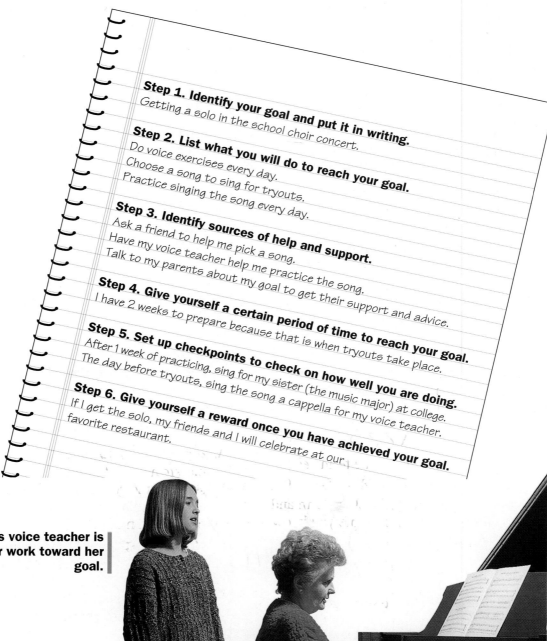

Step 1. Identify your goal and put it in writing.
Getting a solo in the school choir concert.

Step 2. List what you will do to reach your goal.
Do voice exercises every day.
Choose a song to sing for tryouts.
Practice singing the song every day.

Step 3. Identify sources of help and support.
Ask a friend to help me pick a song.
Have my voice teacher help me practice the song.
Talk to my parents about my goal to get their support and advice.

Step 4. Give yourself a certain period of time to reach your goal.
I have 2 weeks to prepare because that is when tryouts take place.

Step 5. Set up checkpoints to check on how well you are doing.
After 1 week of practicing, sing for my sister (the music major) at college.
The day before tryouts, sing the song a cappella for my voice teacher.

Step 6. Give yourself a reward once you have achieved your goal.
If I get the solo, my friends and I will celebrate at our favorite restaurant.

This teen's voice teacher is helping her work toward her goal.

Whether you achieve your goal or not, you deserve a treat for working hard toward reaching it.

Making a Difference

Having goals can make a difference. Goals can help you get control of your life. Goals can prepare you to face whatever comes along in your life, and they help boost your self-esteem.

Having goals can also make a difference to the people around you. By having a focus in your life, you raise your self-esteem. In turn, you enhance your relationships with family and friends and widen the circle of people you know. In this way, you make a difference in the lives of others as well as in your own.

Review  Lesson 4

Using complete sentences, answer the following questions on a separate sheet of paper.

Reviewing Terms and Facts

1. **Vocabulary** Define the term *self-esteem*. Use it in an original sentence.

2. **Give Examples** List short-term and long-term goals that people you know set and achieve.

Thinking Critically

3. **Suggest** What are some goals that you could set to improve your level of health?

4. **Analyze** List the different groups to which you belong. Choose one group and list the goals, formal or informal, of the group.

Applying Health Concepts

5. **Growth and Development** With a classmate, create a mural depicting some of the community's or school's goals. Display and discuss the completed mural.

6. **Health of Others** Find examples in newspapers, magazines, and books about people who achieved goals that made a difference to themselves and to others. Share your examples with the class.

▶ Health is a combination of physical, mental/emotional, and social well-being. (Lesson 1)

▶ The three sides of your health triangle should be balanced. (Lesson 1)

▶ Wellness involves making choices and decisions that promote and protect total health. (Lesson 1)

▶ Heredity, environment, available health care, and your behavior—which includes your health choices—are factors that affect total health. (Lesson 2)

▶ Accepting responsibility for your health includes learning as much as you can about your health, getting good health information, and taking action to promote and protect your health. (Lesson 2)

▶ Lifestyle factors, or habits, are important in shaping your future health. (Lesson 2)

▶ Decisions come in all sizes. Many major decisions involve risks. You can minimize risks by avoiding risky situations and taking precautions. (Lesson 3)

▶ You can use the six steps of decision making to make healthy decisions. Practicing decision making can prepare you to make real decisions. (Lesson 3)

▶ A goal is something you aim for that takes planning and effort. Goals keep you focused and on track as you work to achieve them. (Lesson 4)

▶ You can use an action plan to carry out your goals. Goals can make a difference in your life and in the lives of others. (Lesson 4)

Using Health Terms

On a separate sheet of paper, write the vocabulary term that best matches each definition given below.

1. An overall state of well-being, or total health (Lesson 1)

2. The passing on of traits from your parents as a result of the transmission of genes (Lesson 2)

3. The sum total of your surroundings (Lesson 2)

4. Feelings and beliefs (Lesson 2)

5. The act of making a choice or finding a solution (Lesson 3)

6. The beliefs and ideas that are important to you and to your family (Lesson 3)

7. The way you feel about yourself (Lesson 4)

Reviewing Main Ideas

Using complete sentences, answer the following questions on a separate sheet of paper.

1. What are the three sides of health? (Lesson 1)

2. What is wellness? (Lesson 1)

3. What are three factors over which you have little control that affect your health? (Lesson 2)

4. What two things can you do to get the most out of available health care? (Lesson 2)

5. What is behavior and how does it relate to factors that affect your health? (Lesson 2)

6. What three things can you do to show that you are accepting responsibility for your health? (Lesson 2)

7. List four lifestyle factors that make a difference in your level of health. (Lesson 2)

8. What is a risk behavior? (Lesson 3)

9. What are the six steps in decision making? (Lesson 3)

10. What is a goal? (Lesson 4)

11. Why is goal setting important? (Lesson 4)

12. What are the six steps to follow when setting goals? (Lesson 4)

Thinking Critically

Using complete sentences, answer the following questions on a separate sheet of paper.

1. **Give Examples** What are some ways the other two sides of the health triangle are affected when one side is neglected? (Lesson 1)

2. **Analyze** How might heredity and environment affect a person's health? (Lesson 2)

3. **Evaluate** What are some ways parents and teens might work together to make lifestyle factors a regular part of teens' lives? (Lesson 2)

4. **Analyze** Why is it important to keep your and your family's values in mind when making decisions? (Lesson 3)

5. **Hypothesize** Why is it helpful to practice decision making ahead of time? (Lesson 3)

6. **Give Examples** What are some examples of how teens' self-esteem can affect the goals they set? (Lesson 4)

7. **Analyze** How might some of your goals make a difference to yourself and to others? (Lesson 4)

8. **Explain** How does setting short-term goals help people to achieve long-term goals? (Lesson 4)

Your Action Plan

Balancing Your Health Triangle

To balance your health triangle, you need to set a goal. Look back through your private journal entries for this chapter. What choices and changes do you want to make?

Once you have decided what your long-term goal will be, write it down. Make sure your goal is achievable. Next, think of a series of short-term goals you could take to achieve your long-term goal. Write these down. If your long-term goal is to make a *B* in a course you got a *C* in, a short-term goal might be to study that subject one hour each night.

Plan a timetable for accomplishing your short-term goals. Check with your schedule to keep yourself on track. When you reach your long-term goal, reward yourself and celebrate.

Building Your Portfolio

1. Read a magazine article or book about a person you admire. List the lifestyle factors that are a part of this person's life. List examples of how the individual's attitudes influenced his or her life. Include the lists in your portfolio.

2. Create a full-page, full-color magazine advertisement for a teen magazine. Feature one or more ways that teens can make a difference by setting and carrying out their health goals. Include your advertisement in your portfolio.

In Your Home and Community

1. Create a "Teen Help" bulletin board in your classroom. The board should contain names, addresses, and phone numbers of people and places teens could turn to whenever they need help with their physical, mental and emotional, and social well-being. You might look in the telephone directory under the words *mental*, *emotional*, *youth*, and *crisis*. Your school librarian or teacher may also be able to help you locate names of sources.

2. Ask a parent or other adult at home to tell you about an important decision he or she had to make as a teen. Find out how the decision was made and why he or she believes it was the right choice.

Chapter 2
Looking and Feeling Good

Student Expectations
After reading this chapter, you should be able to:

1 Explain how to have healthy skin, hair, and nails.

2 Describe how to take care of your mouth and teeth.

3 List ways to care for your eyes and ears.

Discuss the importance of good foot care and good posture.

Mirror, mirror, on the wall, who's the handsomest of them all? Well, today I think it might be me. I'm looking good. Nice face. Nice smile. Nice hair.

Uhmm . . . I wonder if Shannon would like me better if I parted my hair on the right. Let's see. No, better leave it the way it is. Can't risk having my hair stick out.

Okay, time to check out the old mouth. Anything disgusting caught between my teeth? Nope, clean as a whistle.

Uh, oh . . . What's this on my chin? Maybe it's a whisker. I hope. I hope. Oh, it's a pimple, and it's going to be bigger than Mt. Everest! Now what'll I do? I can't go anywhere looking like this!

Okay, okay. Don't panic. Calm down. Let's see. I could put some pimple cream on it. No, no . . . that only makes it more obvious. I know. I'll put a bandage on it. I'll tell Shannon I cut myself shaving. That's it.

Well, mirror, I have to get out of here. My sister wants to take a shower. See you later.

in your journal

Read the account on this page. Does it sound familiar to you? Do you worry about your appearance? This chapter will show you how to feel good about your looks. Start your private journal entries on looking good by answering these questions:

► In general, how do you feel about your appearance? Do you like how you look?

► How do you think others see you?

► Are good health and appearance related?

When you reach the end of the chapter, you will use your journal entries to make an action plan.

Healthy Skin, Hair, and Nails

This lesson will help you find answers to questions that teens often ask about their skin, hair, and nails. For example:

▶ How can I make sure I don't have body odor?

▶ Why does my face break out?

▶ Why do some people have naturally curly hair?

▶ How can I have better-looking fingernails?

Words to Know

epidermis
dermis
subcutaneous
    layer
melanin
pores
sebum
dermatologist
follicle
dandruff
head lice
cuticle
keratin

Your Skin

Your skin is a body organ like your heart or brain. In fact, it is the largest organ of all. Your skin is on view to everyone you meet. That is why it plays such an important role in your appearance.

Your skin performs several important functions for your body. **Figure 2.1** describes these functions.

Figure 2.1
The Skin's Functions

Besides having a great effect on your overall appearance, your skin performs many important functions.

A **The skin is a shield against water.** Like a formfitting raincoat, your skin keeps out water when you swim or take a bath.

B **The skin is a defense against germs.** That is why people badly burned in fires have such a high risk of infection. That is also why you need to administer first aid for open cuts.

C **The skin helps control body temperature.** Blood circulation beneath the surface of the skin increases or slows down depending on your internal temperature. If it increases, perspiration is released through your pores, and your skin cools. If it slows down, sweating stops and body heat is conserved.

D **The skin works as a sense organ.** Nerve endings in the skin let you know when something touches your body. They let you feel different textures. They also allow you to tell the difference between hot and cold and to feel pain as a way of protecting you.

The Parts of the Skin

Your skin has two main layers, an outer layer and an inner layer. The *outermost layer of skin* is called the **epidermis** (e·puh·DER·mis). The *thick inner layer of skin* is called the **dermis** (DER·mis). Below the dermis is *a layer of fat tissue* called the **subcutaneous** (suhb·kyoo·TAY·nee·uhs) **layer. Figure 2.2** describes the parts of the skin.

Many layers of cells make up the epidermis. As new cells are manufactured deep down, old ones at the surface are shed. This process of making and replacing cells is continuous. Through shedding, you replace your outer skin about once a month. If you live to be 70, you will wear more than 800 new coats of skin!

Q&A

"Pruny" Skin

Q: Why do my hands and feet get all wrinkled and pruny after I've been in the water for a while?

A: Because the skin on the palms of your hands and the soles of your feet contains no oil glands to keep water out.

Figure 2.2
The Skin

The skin is made up of an outer layer, a thick inner layer, and a layer of fat tissue.

Ⓐ **Epidermis**
The cells in the deepest part of the epidermis produce **melanin** (MEL·uh·nin), *the substance that gives the skin most of its color.*

Ⓑ **Dermis**
The dermis contains blood vessels, nerve endings, hair follicles, and two types of glands. Oil glands produce oils that keep the skin soft and waterproof. Sweat glands secrete perspiration, which is released through **pores,** or *tiny holes in the skin.*

Ⓒ **Subcutaneous Layer**
The subcutaneous layer has fat cells and connects the skin to bone and muscle.

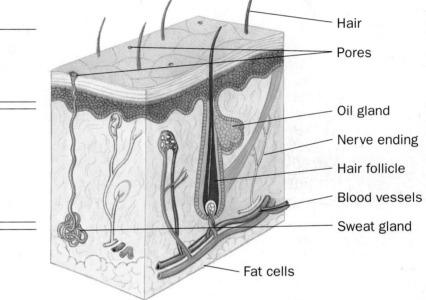

Hair
Pores
Oil gland
Nerve ending
Hair follicle
Blood vessels
Sweat gland
Fat cells

Taking Care of Your Skin

Your skin is a vital organ of your body. Good health habits, along with good grooming, promote healthy skin. Proper skin care should be part of your daily routine.

■ Take a bath or shower every day. During the early teen years, the sweat glands become more active. The best way to care for your skin is to keep it clean. Daily bathing or showering with soap will rid your skin of bacteria and excess oils.

■ Apply deodorant or antiperspirant daily. Sweat glands are numerous under the arms. Any bacteria there may act on perspiration and cause an unpleasant odor. Deodorants and antiperspirants cover up the odor, and antiperspirants help the area remain dry.

Acne

A skin problem common to teens is acne, in which oil glands produce great quantities of *a whitish, oily substance* called **sebum** (SEE·buhm). Eventually sebum clogs the pores, causing the problems shown in **Figure 2.3**. If the condition is serious, you may want to see a **dermatologist** (DER·muh·TAHL·uh·jist), *a doctor who treats skin disorders*. You can also practice the do's and don'ts in the list below.

Diet does not *cause* acne, but certain foods may contribute to it. If the condition worsens after a person eats a certain food, it would be wise not to eat that food for a while.

Figure 2.3
Types of Acne

Whiteheads, blackheads, and pimples are three common types of acne.

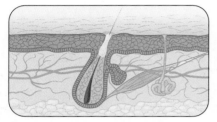

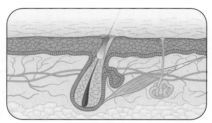

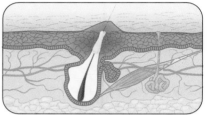

Ⓐ A *whitehead* is a pore that is plugged with sebum.

Ⓑ A *blackhead* is a pore that is plugged with sebum and darkens because it becomes exposed to the air.

Ⓒ A *pimple* is a clogged pore that has become infected and filled with pus. The skin becomes red and inflamed at the site of the pimple.

in your journal

You have just read some ways of taking care of your skin. Now use your journal to help you evaluate your skin. For a period of one week, keep a record of how often you bathe, wash your face, use deodorant, and protect your skin from the sun.

DO'S

- Wash the infected area at least twice a day, morning and night, with a mild soap and warm water.

- Use acne-fighting preparations recommended or prescribed by your doctor.

- Get lots of exercise and rest.

- Eat a well-balanced diet.

DON'TS

- Avoid using heavy or greasy creams or makeup.

- Avoid rubbing areas affected by acne.

- Avoid picking or squeezing pimples, which can spread the infection and result in a scar.

- Avoid touching the infected areas with your fingers.

Other Skin Problems

Other skin problems are caused by different types of germs:

- **Warts** are small growths on the skin caused by a virus. Report any changes in the color or size of a wart to your doctor.

- **Boils** are skin infections accompanied by swelling, redness, and a buildup of pus. Boils are caused by bacteria.

- **Cold sores** are caused by a virus called herpes simplex I. The blisters appear as small sores on or near the lips and usually go away in 10 to 14 days. They can spread if scratched or broken.

What Causes Sunburn?

If you have ever spent much time in the sun, you know that it affects people differently. Some people tan easily. Others burn when they are in the sun without proper protection.

Sunburn is caused by ultraviolet (UV) rays, or the light rays that come from the sun. Concern about exposure to UV rays has grown in recent years. In addition to causing sunburn, UV rays make the skin age and wrinkle faster, may lead to skin cancer, and an eye condition called *cataracts* (KA·tuh·rakts).

To help people protect themselves from dangerous UV rays, the National Weather Service now predicts the next day's *solar-hazard rating* in its daily weather reports. Officially called the Ultraviolet (UV) Index Forecast, this rating is given for 58 cities. The rating ranges from 0 to about 15 with *0* being a minimal health risk and *10 and over* being a very high health risk. **Figure 2.4** lists the ranges, risk of harm from sun exposure, and warnings that comprise the UV Index.

Even on overcast days, the UV rays of the sun can damage your skin.

Figure 2.4
The Ultraviolet Index

Pay attention to the solar-hazard rating for days when you will be out in the sun, and follow the appropriate warning on the index.

Solar-Hazard Rating	Health Risk and Warnings
0 to 2	**Minimal risk** Most people can stay in the noon sun up to 1 hour without burning.
3 to 4	**Low risk** Fair-skinned people may burn in less than 20 minutes during the middle of the day. Wear a sunscreen, hat, and sunglasses.
5 to 6	**Moderate risk** Fair-skinned people may burn in less than 15 minutes. Use a sunscreen with a sun protection factor (SPF) value of at least 15, a hat, and sunglasses.
7 to 9	**High risk** Fair-skinned people may burn in less than 10 minutes. Use a sunscreen with an SPF value of at least 15, a hat, and sunglasses. Limit time spent in the midday sun.
10 and over	**Very high risk** Fair-skinned people may burn in less than 5 minutes. Avoid sun exposure between 10:30 A.M. and 3:30 P.M. Use sunscreen with an SPF value of 20 to 30, and wear sunglasses and protective clothing.

Your Hair

The hair that you see is made of dead cells. **Figure 2.5** shows that its roots are in the dermis, housed in *small pockets* called **follicles** (FAHL·i·kuhlz). As new hair cells are formed, old ones are forced outward through the surface of the skin and die.

Hair takes its color from melanin. Hair color is inherited, or passed on to you by your parents. The shape of the hair shaft determines whether your hair is wavy, curly, or straight.

Taking Care of Your Hair

For healthy hair, your daily routine should include the following:

- Brush your hair once a day to remove dirt and to move oils down the hair shaft. The oils make hair shiny and attractive.

- Wash your hair frequently with a gentle soap or shampoo. Let your hair dry by itself. The heat from electric blow dryers can rob your hair of oils, making hair ends rough and dry. Dyes, permanents, and hairspray can damage hair as well.

Figure 2.5
The Hair

The part of the hair that you can see is the hair shaft. The hair follicle and root are imbedded in the skin.

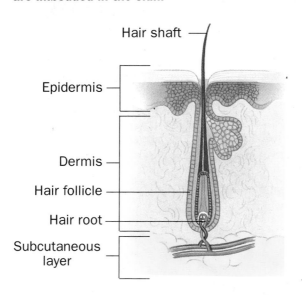

Hair shaft

Epidermis

Dermis

Hair follicle

Hair root

Subcutaneous layer

LIFE SKILLS
Protecting Yourself from the Sun

*M*any people used to think that sunshine was good for you. People with deep tans were thought to be "the picture of health." Research has shown otherwise. Medical authorities now know that prolonged exposure to the sun is harmful.

Experts say that more than 80 percent of a person's lifetime sun exposure occurs before the age of 18. This means that warnings of prolonged sun exposure have special urgency for teens. What's more, as the earth's ozone layer continues to shrink, sunlight will become even more dangerous. The ozone layer helps prevent the sun's harmful ultraviolet (UV) rays from reaching the earth.

If you are planning to spend time outdoors, play it safe. It can make a dramatic difference in your skin appearance for years to come. You can take several actions to protect your skin from the sun.

▶ Avoid being in direct sunlight between 10:00 a.m. and 2:00 p.m. This is when the sun's rays are most intense.

▶ Apply sunscreen generously to all exposed skin. Sunscreens are oils, lotions, and creams that filter out the sun's UV rays. Choose a waterproof sunscreen with a sun protection factor (SPF) of 15 or higher.

Hair and Scalp Problems

Dandruff (DAN·druhf), a common scalp problem, is a *flaking of the outer layer of dead skin cells:* It is usually caused by a dry scalp. Often, a person can control dandruff by washing. Sometimes a special dandruff shampoo is needed. If the problem persists, see a doctor. You may have a skin infection.

At times, an itchy scalp is caused by **head lice,** *parasitic insects that live in the hair.* Head lice are very common and very easy to catch from someone else. That is why you should avoid sharing brushes and combs with other people. You can control head lice by using a medicated shampoo. Also be sure to wash all bedding, towels, and clothing that have come into contact with the scalp. Others in the family also may need to be treated at the same time. If left untreated, head lice can lead to infection.

Your Nails

How do your fingernails look? Are they usually dirty or clean? Do you bite your nails, or are you careful about trimming them? Good nail care is important for your appearance and total health.

Fingernails and toenails, like hair, are dead cells that grow out of living tissue located in the dermis. Around the nails is *a nonliving band of epidermis* called the **cuticle** (KYOO·ti·kuhl).

Taking Care of Your Nails

Caring for your nails means trimming them and using plenty of soap when you wash to clean underneath the nails. If your hands are very dirty, use a gentle brush under the nails and around the cuticles. **Figure 2.6** on page 38 shows additional ways to keep your nails healthy and looking their best.

Figure 2.6 on page 38

► Wear sunglasses that filter UV rays and protective clothing. Wear a hat with a wide brim that shades your face and neck. If you are working outdoors, wear long pants and a long-sleeved shirt.

► Beware of reflected light. Surfaces such as water, sand, cement, and snow (light-colored surfaces) can reflect harmful radiation.

► Bring a big umbrella to the beach, or seek a shady area. Realize, however, that the umbrella by itself will not guarantee protection.

► If you wear makeup, use moisturizers, lipbalms, and creams that contain sunscreen ingredients.

► Be careful even when the sun is not shining. On cloudy days, 80 percent of the sun's rays still penetrate the clouds.

You might think you can get a safe tan by using a sunlamp or by going to a tanning salon. Sunlamps and tanning salons, however, will expose you to dangerous long-wave UV rays and should never be used. You could use a self-tanning lotion to give yourself the appearance of a tan for a few days, but beware that self-tanners do not take the place of sunscreen.

Follow-up Activity

Young children tend to spend even more time outdoors than teens. Plan a way to teach young children about protecting themselves from the sun. You might prepare a picture book or present a puppet show. Be a role model for younger brothers or sisters by protecting your own skin from exposure to the sun.

Nail Problems

The nails on your fingers and toes contain **keratin** (KEHR-uh·tin), *a substance that makes nails hard.* Sometimes minor problems can affect nails. *Hangnails* are splits in the cuticle along the edge of the nail. Once you have carefully cut away the splintered edge, the cuticle will grow back in several days. An *ingrown toenail* occurs when the nail pushes into the skin on the side of the toe. This can happen when toenails are cut too short. If the toe becomes red and inflamed, infection may have set in. This sign is your cue to see your doctor.

Figure 2.6
Caring for Your Nails

The basic tools to use when caring for your nails are a cuticle stick, nail clippers, and an emery board.

A Use a cuticle stick to push back the cuticle. First soften the cuticle with warm water. This makes it easier to push back the cuticle. You can also apply a cuticle remover.

B Use a nail clipper or small scissors to trim your nails. Fingernails should be slightly rounded at the ends. Cut toenails straight across, with the nail at or slightly beyond skin level. If you cut the nail any shorter you risk infection.

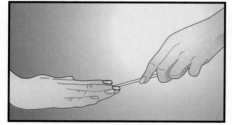

C Use an emery board or nail file to help round out the ends of your fingernails. An emery board also smooths out rough edges.

Lesson 1 Review

Using complete sentences, answer the following questions on a separate sheet of paper.

Reviewing Terms and Facts

1. **Vocabulary** Define the term *subcutaneous layer.* Use it in an original sentence.

2. **Recall** What is a *hangnail* and how should it be treated?

Thinking Critically

3. **Analyze** Your classmate Ted starts sunbathing as soon as it gets warm. It seems he has a tan most of the year. He says that "a little sun" is good for you. What do you think?

4. **Hypothesize** What are some ways teens treat their hair that might not be "sensible"? Explain your answer.

Applying Health Concepts

5. **Consumer Health** Check the labels of several acne medications. Note the ingredients they have in common. Write an advertisement about a "new" product. Identify the ingredients in the product that will make it effective in controlling acne.

6. **Personal Health** Prepare a video on how to give yourself a manicure and a pedicure. Follow the directions for nail care in this lesson. Present the video to the class.

Healthy Mouth and Teeth

This lesson will help you find answers to questions that teens often ask about their mouth and teeth. For example:

▶ **Why do I get cavities?**

▶ **What is the right way to brush and floss my teeth?**

▶ **How can I keep from having bad breath?**

Your Mouth and Teeth

When you smile, you make yourself and others feel good. Clean teeth and gums and a fresh breath enhance your smile. Make tooth care a part of your daily grooming. This lesson will tell you how.

The Jobs of the Mouth

Your mouth, teeth, and tongue are responsible for some actions that are very important to your health. These include tasting, digestion, and speech. The list below explains these actions.

- **Tasting.** You taste by means of sensitive areas of the tongue called taste buds. When food touches the taste buds, a signal goes to the brain. The brain identifies the food as either sweet, sour, salty, or bitter.

- **Digestion.** Digestion starts in your mouth. Your teeth tear and crush the food. Saliva in your mouth moistens the food and starts to change it chemically before you swallow it.

- **Speech.** All the consonant and vowel sounds you make are determined by precise placements of the tongue, lips, teeth, and other parts of your mouth.

Your mouth and teeth not only affect your appearance but also allow you to taste and digest food and speak.

As long as they are healthy, teeth that have spaces between them or that slightly overlap are part of a person's uniqueness. In your journal, describe how your teeth and a friend or family member's teeth affect that person's smile.

The Teeth

In addition to helping you chew food, your teeth help shape and structure your mouth. They also contribute to your appearance.

Parts of the Tooth

A tooth is a living structure. **Figure 2.7** shows the three main parts of the tooth: the crown, the neck, and the root. Each tooth also contains the following types of **tissue,** or *groups of cells:* enamel, dentin, pulp, and cementum.

The area around the tooth is the **periodontium** (pehr·ee·oh·DAHN·shee·um). This is *a structure made up of the jawbone, the gums, and connectors called ligaments.* It supports the teeth.

Types of Teeth

Usually the mouth has room for a total of 32 teeth. Each tooth has a specific name and function (see **Figure 2.8**).

Figure 2.7
The Tooth

The tooth is made up of many parts.

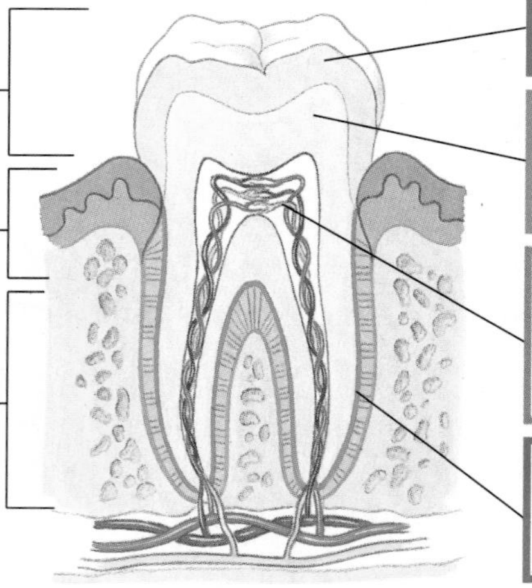

A The **crown** is *the part of the tooth visible to the eye.*

B The **neck** is *the part of the tooth between the crown and the root.*

C The **root** is *the part of the tooth inside the gum.*

D **Enamel** (ee·NA·muhl) is *the hard material that covers the crown of a tooth.*

E **Dentin** (DEN·tin) is *bonelike material surrounding the pulp of a tooth.*

F **Pulp** is *soft, sensitive tissue containing nerves and blood vessels deep within the root of a tooth.*

G **Cementum** (se·MEN·tuhm) is *thin, bonelike material covering the root of a tooth.*

Figure 2.8
The Types of Teeth

Each type of tooth has a specific function.

A **Incisors** (in·SY·serz), the eight center teeth, cut into and tear food.

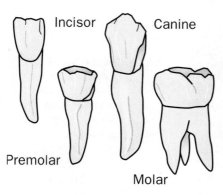

Incisor Canine

Premolar

Molar

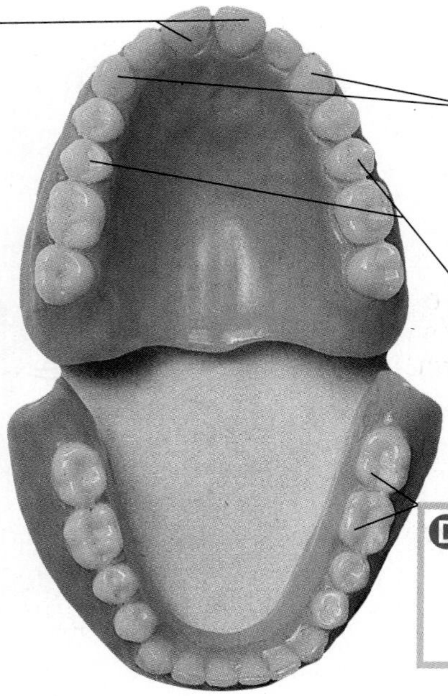

B **Canines** (KAY·nynz), four pointed teeth next to the incisors, grasp and tear food.

C **Premolars** (PREE·moh·lerz) are the eight short teeth between canines and molars.

D **Molars** (MOH·lerz), the twelve stubby teeth in the back of the mouth, do the major work of chewing.

What Causes Tooth Decay?

Good, regular oral health is necessary for healthy, clean teeth. Regular brushing after eating and before bedtime is essential. Flossing is also important because you often miss hard-to-reach spots with your toothbrush.

If teeth and gums are not cared for properly, problems can result. One of the most common problems is tooth decay. In fact, about 98 percent of all Americans have or have had cavities. Yet tooth decay is also one of the most preventable diseases in the United States.

Figure 2.9 shows how healthy teeth develop cavities. If left untreated, cavities grow larger and larger. A tooth may eventually become so decayed that it needs to be removed.

Figure 2.9
The Process of Tooth Decay
When teeth are not cared for properly, tooth decay follows this process.

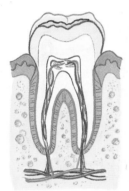

Ⓐ Air, food, and bacteria in your mouth form a sticky film called **plaque** (PLAK) on your teeth. Plaque combines with sugar to form acid. If not removed, plaque hardens into **tartar** (TAR·ter).

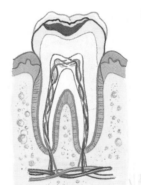

Ⓑ Acid under the plaque or tartar eats a hole, or cavity, in tooth enamel.

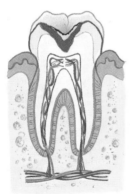

Ⓒ The decay spreads to the dentin.

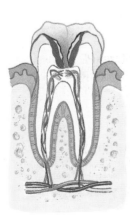

Ⓓ The decay then spreads to the pulp, where it exposes a nerve. Air hitting the exposed nerve causes your tooth to ache.

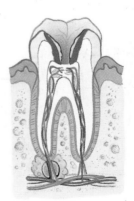

Ⓔ If the decay is not stopped, it moves into the roots and *pus collects in the bone sockets around the tooth.* This very painful condition is known as an **abscess** (AB·sess).

Proper Brushing Technique

Figure 2.10 shows you how to brush your teeth properly.

Figure 2.10
How to Brush Your Teeth

If you brush your teeth properly, you can prevent tooth decay.

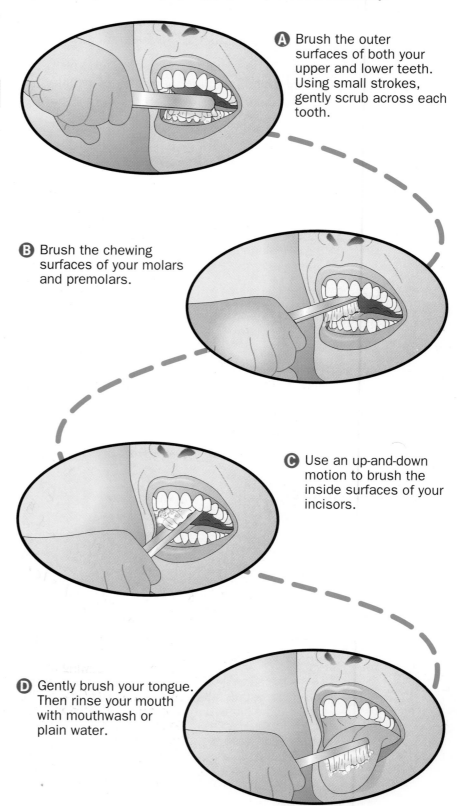

A Brush the outer surfaces of both your upper and lower teeth. Using small strokes, gently scrub across each tooth.

B Brush the chewing surfaces of your molars and premolars.

C Use an up-and-down motion to brush the inside surfaces of your incisors.

D Gently brush your tongue. Then rinse your mouth with mouthwash or plain water.

Q&A

Buying a Toothbrush

Q: I never know what kind of toothbrush to buy. Can you help me?

A: Buy a soft or medium-soft toothbrush. A brush that's too stiff may not get into crevices. It also may cause your gums to bleed. Buy a toothbrush with a small head so you can get at every tooth. Be sure to change toothbrushes regularly. Bent or frayed brushes are ineffective.

Proper Flossing Technique

Figure 2.11 shows you how to floss your teeth properly.

Figure 2.11
How to Floss Your Teeth
If you floss your teeth properly, you can prevent tooth decay as well as gum disease in hard-to-reach spots.

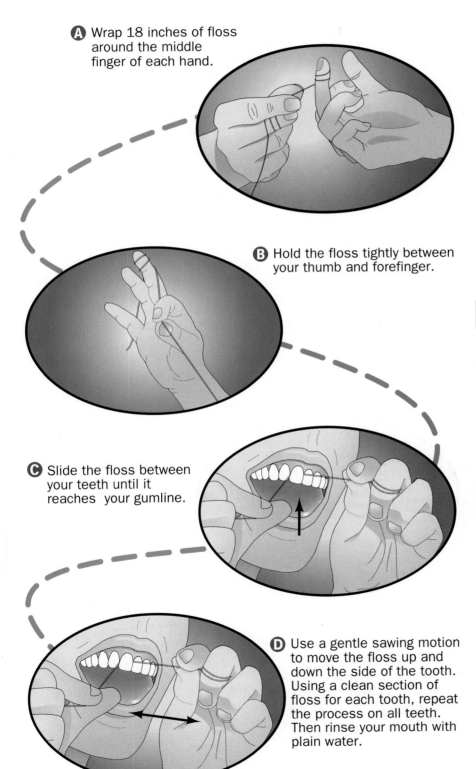

Ⓐ Wrap 18 inches of floss around the middle finger of each hand.

Ⓑ Hold the floss tightly between your thumb and forefinger.

Ⓒ Slide the floss between your teeth until it reaches your gumline.

Ⓓ Use a gentle sawing motion to move the floss up and down the side of the tooth. Using a clean section of floss for each tooth, repeat the process on all teeth. Then rinse your mouth with plain water.

Your Total Health

Sugar Free, Cavity Free ACTIVITY!

A diet low in sugar not only keeps your teeth healthy but also helps you to control your weight. Cut out magazine pictures of foods you should eat to keep your teeth healthy and your weight under control. Create a collage with them.

Taking Care of Your Teeth

Dentists in the United States recently reported a sharp decline in tooth decay among young people. Some even predict that tooth decay will disappear in the United States in the next 20 years. You can help meet that goal by following sensible dental care.

- **Brush your teeth after eating.** Bacteria work rapidly, so you must remove food particles within minutes after eating.

- **Floss between your teeth.** Dental floss can reach food particles and plaque that cannot be reached with a toothbrush.

- **Reserve starchy foods and foods high in sugar for mealtimes.** Mealtime beverages and saliva production help rinse the mouth of acid-producing sugar.

- **Have regular dental checkups.** A dentist and dental hygienist can clean your teeth and spot signs of tooth decay and gum disease before they become serious problems.

Other Problems

Other problems of the mouth and teeth can result from poor oral health or heredity. **Gingivitis** (jin·juh·VY·tis) is a common disorder in which *gums become red and swollen and bleed easily.* It is caused by improper dental care, plaque, or misaligned teeth. If gingivitis is untreated, it can lead to a more serious gum disease called *periodontitis* (pehr·ee·oh·dahn·TY·tis).

Another problem called **malocclusion** (ma·luh·KLOO·zhuhn) is *a condition in which the teeth of the upper and lower jaws do not align properly.* It may be caused by heredity, thumb sucking, or tooth loss. Orthodontists treat malocclusion by recommending braces or other appliances to help align teeth.

in your journal

You have just read about ways to keep your mouth, teeth, and gums healthy. Use your journal for a week to write down everything you eat, the times you eat, and the times you brush your teeth. At the end of a week, write a paragraph evaluating your dental habits. Do you brush and floss after eating? Do you eat a healthful diet?

HEALTH LAB
Attacking Plaque

*I*ntroduction: Bacteria-forming plaque constantly lurks in your mouth. It waits for a chance to build up on your teeth and harden. If you do not defend your mouth against this enemy, it will soon destroy your teeth. A toothbrush, toothpaste, and dental floss are weapons you can use to attack plaque. However, you must use these weapons effectively to keep plaque under control.

Objective: This experiment will show you how effective you are as a plaque fighter and how you can improve your plaque-fighting techniques.

Materials and Method: You will need these materials: toothbrush, toothpaste, dental floss, water, mirror, and food coloring. (Note: Instead of the food coloring, you might use disclosing tablets. These are available from a drugstore.)

Brush and floss your teeth the way you normally do. Then mix the food coloring with water and swish it around in your mouth. Spit it out like mouthwash. Now look at your mouth in the mirror. The places where color sticks to your teeth indicate areas that need more brushing and flossing. Continue the procedure until no color appears in your mouth.

Bad breath, or halitosis, is a condition caused by tooth decay, eating certain foods, or using tobacco. Good oral hygiene can control bad breath. However, if it is caused by tooth decay, the cure involves treating the underlying problem.

Using complete sentences, answer the following questions on a separate sheet of paper.

Reviewing Terms and Facts

1. **Explain**   How does the sense of taste work?

2. **Vocabulary**   Which of the following terms refers to a gum problem: *gingivitis, dentin, malocclusion?* Describe the problem.

Thinking Critically

3. **Evaluate**   You have a friend who brushes his teeth "in record time." You noticed that he brushes only the outer surfaces of his teeth. He says that he brushes after every meal and, therefore, doesn't have to brush more carefully. What do you think?

4. **Suggest**   List ways you can care for your teeth when brushing them is not convenient.

Applying Health Concepts

5. **Personal Health**   Create a poster or puppet show that demonstrates the brushing and flossing techniques described in this lesson. Present it to a preschool class.

6. **Personal Health**   Visit your dentist. Ask for any brochures or other printed information about caring for your teeth. Bring them to class. Form small groups and discuss them. Could you improve the way you care for your teeth? Write a short paragraph explaining what you have learned.

Observation and Analysis:

What did you learn about your skill in removing plaque from your teeth? Do you need to improve your brushing and flossing techniques? Plaque that you were unable to remove has hardened into tartar. A dentist or dental hygienist will need to scrape the tartar off your teeth.

Remember that the best time to attack plaque is after eating. That's when the bacteria in plaque reacts with sugar to form the acid that destroys enamel and irritates gums. You will never win the war against plaque, but you can do a great deal to keep it from defeating you.

Teen HEALTH DIGEST

People at Work

Hair Stylist

As a young girl, Deanna Metcalf enjoyed combing and arranging the hair of her ten brothers and sisters. Now, as an adult, Deanna has turned her talent for styling hair into a successful career.

After graduating from high school, Deanna went to beauty school for a year. She learned how to cut hair, give perms, tint and color hair, and do manicures. She also learned how to treat hair and nail problems.

To become a licensed beautician, Deanna had to pass a written exam. She also had to demonstrate her ability to give a perm and a haircut. Since hairstyles are always changing, Deanna frequently takes classes to learn the latest styling and cutting techniques.

Deanna works in a beauty shop at the mall. People frequently walk in and want a haircut without having an appointment. Deanna usually turns "walk-ins" into repeat customers, which helps build her clientele.

Deanna enjoys being able to use her skill and creativity to help people look and feel their best. She also enjoys the relationships that have developed over the years with her steady customers. Still, when her brothers and sisters visit, she sometimes has the urge to cut their hair.

Myths and Realities

Chocolate Update

For years, teens were warned that "chocolate will make your face break out." Numerous studies now show, however, that chocolate does not cause acne.

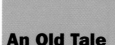

An Old Tale

Do you like being frightened by horror movies? Imagine you are watching this scene. On a dark, moonless night, cemetery workers dig up a body buried 100 years ago. When they open the coffin, they discover a skeleton with long hair and fingernails!

Horror movies perpetuate the myth that hair and fingernails continue to grow after a person dies. Actually, nothing grows after death. The skin does shrink, however, giving the impression that growth has occurred.

Sports and Recreation

Right Shoe, Right Sport?

Are you "into" sports? If so, you need to be careful about the shoes you wear. Most foot problems are caused by wearing the wrong type of shoe.

So how do you go about choosing the right kind of shoe? That depends on the sport you choose. For a sport such as basketball, a high-top shoe may help prevent ankle strain. A low-top shoe may have additional support and the ability to absorb the shock produced by pounding the ground during such sports as running and aerobics.

Whichever shoe you choose, remember that price is not as important as fit. Your shoes should be wide enough so that you can wiggle all your toes when standing. However, they should not be so wide that your foot can slip from side to side.

Teens Making a Difference

Traveling Tooth Show

"Remember, always brush your teeth after meals," says Sparkle Plenty. "That's right," adds Sturdy Enamel. "You don't want Mr. Tooth Decay to make holes in your teeth."

Sparkle Plenty and Sturdy Enamel are hand puppets. Lori Williams and Janey Lynch, students at Highland Middle School, created the puppets to teach young children how to care for their teeth. Sparkle is a girl puppet, and Sturdy is a boy puppet.

Lori and Janey got the idea for the puppet show after studying dental hygiene in health class. The girls made the puppets and props, wrote a script, and built a portable puppet stage. Lori provides the voice and movements for Sparkle Plenty, and Janey operates Sturdy Enamel.

The girls' first show was for students at nearby Garfield Elementary School. The show was such a big hit that soon other schools in the area were requesting a performance. Now Lori and Janey regularly visit several elementary-school classes, using Sparkle Plenty and Sturdy Enamel to teach children about proper dental care.

CON$UMER FOCU$

All the Right Words

Advertisers have a way with words. They know how to use words to create interest in their products and to make consumers want to buy them. This skillful use of language is especially apparent in ads for personal grooming products.

Advertisers choose words that form images in people's minds. Instead of saying that a certain toothpaste will whiten your teeth, the advertiser might say that the toothpaste will make your teeth "look like pearls."

Advertisers sometimes make up new words to influence consumers. A certain hair spray, for example, possesses *volumizing, luminizing,* and *detangling* capabilities. Advertisers are prone to using exaggerated language. A certain mascara will give you *mega*lashes, or a soap will make you feel *fantastically* clean.

Advertisers make promises in a way that cannot be challenged legally. A certain acne cream may "help" fight blemishes. The ad does not say the cream ever wins the fight.

The language of ads can be enjoyable to read or hear. Be careful, however, not to accept the words at "face value."

Healthy Eyes and Ears

This lesson will help you find answers to questions that teens often ask about their eyes and ears. For example:

► How can I keep from getting eye infections?
► How do I know if I need glasses?
► How can loud music damage my ears?
► What is the right way to clean my ears?

Words to Know

lens
cornea
pupil
iris
aqueous humor
sclera
optic nerve
retina
eustachian tube
vestibule
semicircular
   canals
cochlea
auditory nerve

Your Eyes

Your eyes are your windows to the world. People with full vision gather about 80 percent of their knowledge through their eyes. Your eyes can distinguish shapes, colors, movements, and light.

The Structure of the Eye

In humans, the eye is similar to a camera. It has an opening to let in light and can focus depending on what is being viewed. Your eye is nearly round and rests in a bony socket in your skull. Eyes work together, yet they are independent of one another. Each eye is made of several parts. **Figure 2.12** shows the parts of the eye.

Figure 2.12
The Eye
The eye has many parts, each of which has a specific function.

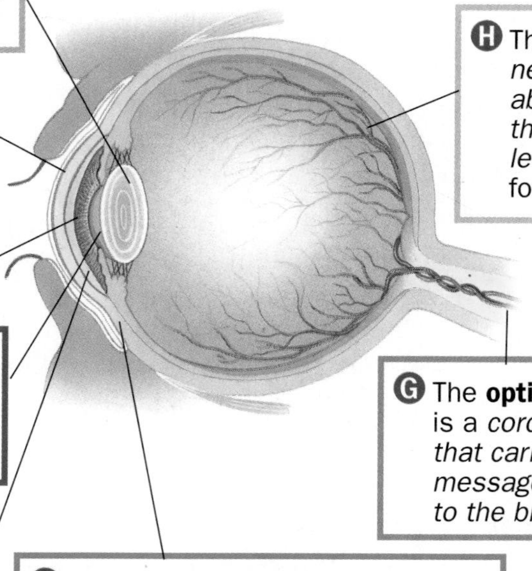

A The **lens** (LENZ) is the *structure that allows light to come together in the inner part of the eye.*

B The **cornea** (KOR·nee·uh) is a *clear, almost round structure that lets in light.*

C The **iris** (EYE·ris) is the *color of the eye seen from the outside.*

D The **pupil** (PYOO·puhl) is a *dark opening in the center of the iris.* It controls the amount of light entering the eye.

E The **aqueous** (AH·kwee·uhs) **humor** is the *watery fluid between the cornea and lens.* It helps maintain pressure within the eye.

F The **sclera** (SKLEHR·uh) is the *tough outer covering*—the white of the eye. It protects the eye.

H The **retina** (RE·tin·uh) is a *network of nerves that absorbs light rays after they pass through the lens.* It is responsible for vision.

G The **optic** (AHP·tik) **nerve** is a *cord of nerve fibers that carries electrical messages from the retina to the brain.*

How the Eye Sees

The eye does not "see" objects. Instead, it sees the light that objects reflect or give off. **Figure 2.13** shows how the eye sees.

Figure 2.13
How the Eye Sees
Sight is a process that occurs when light enters the eye.

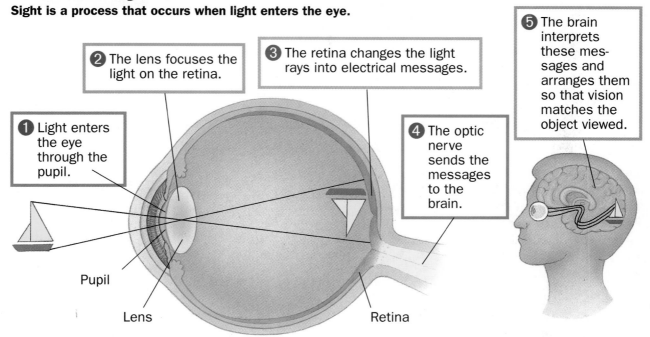

❶ Light enters the eye through the pupil.

❷ The lens focuses the light on the retina.

❸ The retina changes the light rays into electrical messages.

❹ The optic nerve sends the messages to the brain.

❺ The brain interprets these messages and arranges them so that vision matches the object viewed.

Pupil

Lens

Retina

How the Eye Sees Color

Within the retina are millions of nerve endings that contain pigments, or colors. These pigments change when light comes into the eye. Some of these nerve endings distinguish objects in shades of black, white, and gray. These endings are known as rods, and they are used by your eye in dim light. Rods are also used by the eye to perceive motion. Other nerve endings, the cones, distinguish the colors red, blue, and green and their different shadings. Your eyes mix these colors just as you would adjust the color on a television set. Rods and cones send messages to the brain, which interprets the information.

in your journal

Healthy eyes are important to your sense of well-being. Have you ever had an eye problem, such as an eye infection or an eye injury? Perhaps you just had something in your eye, such as an eyelash, that irritated it. How did it affect you and your daily activities? Write a short paragraph about your experience.

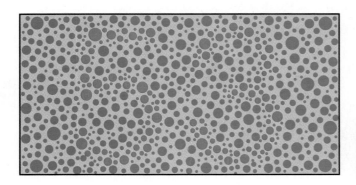

Can you see the number in this box? If so, your color vision is fine. If not, you may be red/green color-blind.

Taking Care of Your Eyes

Your eyes are a vital part of your body. For this reason, you should follow these hints to protect your eyes:

Although any sunglasses are better than no sunglasses, some types are more effective in blocking UV rays. If possible, buy ultraviolet-absorbent sunglasses. Look for labels that state "blocks 99 to 100 percent of ultraviolet light." Choose sunglasses that meet the standards of the American National Standards Institute (ANSI). For more information, read recent magazine articles on how to buy sunglasses. Then share your findings with your classmates.

- Read and watch television in a well-lighted room. Shine the light from your reading lamp on what you are reading and not in your eyes. Sit a comfortable distance from the television set.

- Take breaks from using your eyes for long periods of time. Just close your eyes for a short time.

- Avoid exposing your eyes to direct sun or other bright light. When you are outside, wear sunglasses that offer protection from ultraviolet (UV) rays (see **Figure 2.14**). Over the years, exposure to UV rays can damage the lens, retina, and cornea.

- Avoid rubbing your eyes, which irritates or gets dirt in them.

- Keep sharp objects away from your eyes. Beware of pointed sticks, BB guns, and bows and arrows. Avoid throwing sharp items toward another person. Never play with fireworks.

- Wear protective goggles or glasses when engaging in an activity that could cause an eye injury.

- Wear protective equipment when playing such contact sports as baseball and hockey.

- Make sure any towels or washcloths you wipe your eyes with are clean. Diseases such as pinkeye (conjunctivitis) can be spread easily by soiled or dirty towels.

- Be careful not to touch the eyeball when applying eye makeup. Avoid makeup that is old, dirty, or belongs to someone else.

Figure 2.14
What to Look for in Sunglasses
Not all sunglass lenses are created equal. You should keep these differences in mind when purchasing sunglasses.

Ⓐ Sunglasses should block 99 to 100 percent of both UV-A and UV-B radiation.

Ⓑ Sunglasses should screen out 75 to 90 percent of visible light.

Ⓒ Sunglasses should have gray, green, or brown lenses that are of good quality.

Ⓓ To determine if sunglasses are dark enough, try them on in front of a mirror. You should not be able to see your eyes easily.

Getting an Eye Checkup

An eye checkup by an optometrist (ahp·TAHM·uh·trist) or an ophthalmologist (ahf·thuhl·MAHL·uh·jist) also helps you maintain healthy eyes. If you wear glasses or contact lenses, you should have your eyes checked once a year. If not, an eye examination every two years is sufficient. An eye checkup includes the following:

- **Examination of each eye.** The cornea, pupil, and lens are checked to see if they are clear.

- **Vision check.** Your vision will be determined by the size of the letters you are able to read on the eye chart. If you already wear glasses or contact lenses, your prescription and the fit of your glasses or contact lenses should be checked.

- **Glaucoma check.** Glaucoma (glaw·KOH·muh) is a disease in which the fluid in the eye does not drain properly. Pressure builds up and, if untreated, destroys the optic nerve. Checkups can detect this disease, which is treated with eye drops or pills.

- **Cataract check.** A cataract is a clouding of the lens that may cause some loss of vision. If one is found, an operation can fix the problem. Most cataracts result from aging.

Treating Problems of the Eye

The main job of the eye is to focus images for you. Many people have vision problems, such as farsightedness, nearsightedness, and astigmatism, because their eyes do not focus perfectly. **Figure 2.15** describes these problems, which can be corrected with eyeglasses or contact lenses. The type of lenses suggested by a doctor depends on the condition of your eyes. Today, many people can wear contact lenses, which float on the cornea, to correct a vision problem.

Q & A **?**

Eye Exam

Q: I think I have an eye infection. My eyes are full of mucus when I wake up in the morning. They're red and they itch like crazy. What should I do?

A: You need to see an ophthalmologist, a medical doctor who specializes in eye diseases. If you just want to have your vision checked, you could go to an optometrist. An optician, by the way, makes and sells glasses and contact lenses prescribed by an ophthalmologist or an optometrist.

Figure 2.15
Problems of the Eye

Farsightedness, nearsightedness, and astigmatism are common eye problems that involve focusing.

Farsightedness
is a condition in which you can see far objects clearly, but close objects appear blurred. This occurs when the visual images come to a focus behind the retina.

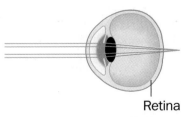

Retina

Nearsightedness
is a condition in which you can see close objects clearly, but distant objects appear blurred. It occurs when the visual images come to a focus before they reach the retina.

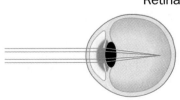

Astigmatism
(uh·STIG·muh·tiz·uhm) is a condition in which images are distorted or blurred because of an irregularly shaped cornea or lens. In this case, visual images do not meet at a single point in the eye.

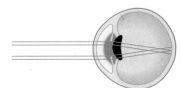

The Structure of the Ear

Your ears allow you to experience the sounds of everyday life. They also help your body keep its balance. Your ears go deep into your skull. **Figure 2.16** shows the parts of the ear.

Figure 2.16
The Ear

The ear has three main parts: the outer ear, the middle ear, and the inner ear.

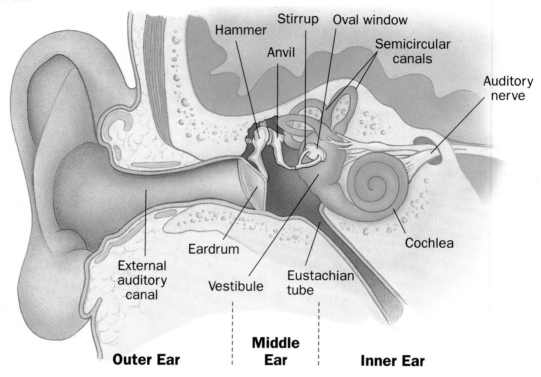

Hammer · Stirrup · Oval window · Anvil · Semicircular canals · Auditory nerve · Cochlea · Eardrum · External auditory canal · Vestibule · Eustachian tube

Outer Ear | **Middle Ear** | **Inner Ear**

MAKING HEALTHY DECISIONS
Lowering the Boom

Jeff Orner asked Matt to be his partner in a neighborhood yardwork business. Matt gladly accepted the offer. He was looking for a way to make money and to keep busy during the summer.

Jeff provides all the equipment the boys need: rakes, pruning shears, shovels, and boom box. Boom box? Yes, one of those large, portable radios with a four-way speaker system. When the volume is on maximum, the whole neighborhood is alive with the sound of Jeff's music.

Jeff likes to have the radio on full-blast while he works. He says that rap and heavy-metal music energize him and help him work harder. He doesn't

think the noise is a problem for his customers, because most of them are not home when he does the yardwork.

Jeff's boom box makes Matt feel uneasy. He learned in health class that all that noise is not good for anyone's ears. On the one hand, Matt would like to tell Jeff to turn the radio off, or at least lower the volume. On the other hand, Matt doesn't want to risk making Jeff angry.

Matt doesn't know what to do. Then he remembers the decision-making process he learned in health class. Matt decides to try it out.

The **eustachian** (you·STAY·shuhn) **tube** *allows air to pass from the nose to the middle ear so the air pressure is equal on both sides of the eardrum.* While not actually part of the middle ear, this tube stretches from the back of the nose to the middle ear.

The inner ear contains three parts. The **vestibule** (VES·ti·byool) is *a baglike structure lined with hair cells that are essential to your hearing.* The **semicircular** (SEM·i·SER·kyuh·ler) **canals** are *responsible for your balance.* The **cochlea** (KOK·lee·uh), *a snail-like structure,* is *made up of three ducts filled with fluid and more than 15,000 hair cells. The nerves in the cochlea carry messages to the brain.* These nerves *form a vast network,* which is called the **auditory** (AW·di·tor·ee) **nerve.**

Hearing is a complex process. **Figure 2.17** shows the steps.

Figure 2.17
The Steps in Hearing
Every time your ear hears a sound, these five steps occur.

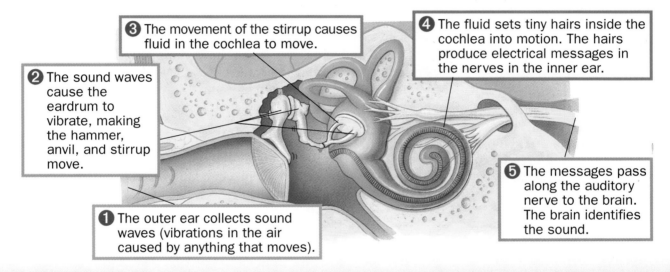

❸ The movement of the stirrup causes fluid in the cochlea to move.

❹ The fluid sets tiny hairs inside the cochlea into motion. The hairs produce electrical messages in the nerves in the inner ear.

❷ The sound waves cause the eardrum to vibrate, making the hammer, anvil, and stirrup move.

❺ The messages pass along the auditory nerve to the brain. The brain identifies the sound.

❶ The outer ear collects sound waves (vibrations in the air caused by anything that moves).

❶ **State the situation**
❷ **List the options**
❸ **Weigh the possible outcomes**
❹ **Consider your values**
❺ **Make a decision and act**
❻ **Evaluate the decision**

Follow-up Activities

1. Apply the six steps of the decision-making process to Matt's problem. Compare your outcome to the solutions of your classmates.

2. Research the relationship between loud noise and hearing loss so that Matt has some facts to present to Jeff.

What Is Balance?

When you learned how to ride a bike or roller-skate, you also had to learn how to balance yourself. Balance is the feeling of stability and control over your body. As noted, the semicircular canals in the inner ear control balance.

Fluid and tiny hairs fill the canals. The hairs are connected to nerve cells. When you move or change position, the fluid and hairs move, sending messages to the brain. The brain receives the messages and tells your body how to adjust or change to meet the new situation. Sometimes the canals send too many or too few impulses to the brain, which can result in balance abnormalities. Two such common problems are *vertigo,* or dizziness, and motion sickness.

Taking Care of Your Ears

The ability to hear makes your life more enjoyable. You can take care of your hearing in several ways.

■ Avoid loud sounds, which can damage nerve cells in your ears and cause permanent hearing loss. Turn down the volume on your radio and television. Keep the volume low when you use a personal cassette player or other device with speakers close to the ear, or when you are in a closed car.

■ Wear hearing protection, such as ear plugs, when you are exposed to loud noises. See **Figure 2.18** for some examples of noises that are dangerous.

■ Use a wet washcloth to clean your outer ear. Avoid sticking a cotton swab into your ear canal.

■ Keep all sharp objects out of your ears.

■ Wear earmuffs or a hat that covers your ears in cold weather to protect the outer ear from frostbite.

■ See a doctor if you have an ear infection or other ear problem. Allow a doctor to remove a buildup of wax in your ears.

This teen is taking care of his ears by wearing hearing protection and by turning down the volume of sound.

Figure 2.18
Decibel Levels of Common Noises

The decibel measures the loudness of sound. Constant exposure to sounds over 70 decibels can harm your hearing. Serious damage occurs with exposure to sounds over 120 decibels.

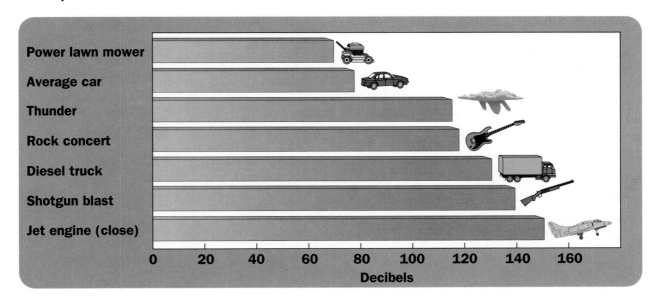

Review Lesson **3**

Using complete sentences, answer the following questions on a separate sheet of paper.

Reviewing Terms and Facts

1. **Vocabulary** Define the term *astigmatism.* Use it in an original sentence.

2. **Recall** How do the semicircular canals in the inner ear help you to maintain balance?

Thinking Critically

3. **Analyze** Your friend Michael never wears sunglasses, even when he is at the beach. He says the sun does not hurt his eyes. What do you think?

4. **Explain** How is the process of hearing like a chain reaction?

Applying Health Concepts

5. **Health of Others** Write a brief guide for teens about protecting their eyes. Display it on a bulletin board.

6. **Personal Health** Look for examples of harmful noise levels at home. Perhaps you have a noisy vacuum cleaner, or a family member has the volume on the television or stereo turned up high. Make a list of the examples you find. Then discuss with family members what can be done to reduce noise pollution in your home. Summarize your findings in a short paragraph.

Healthy Feet and Posture

This lesson will help you find answers to questions that teens often ask about their feet and posture. For example:

► **How can I select the best-fitting shoes?**

► **Why do I get corns and blisters?**

► **Why do adults always want me to stand up and sit up straight?**

Words to Know

callus
corn
blister
bunion
athlete's foot
fallen
   arches

Taking Care of Your Feet

Your feet are really marvels of engineering! They support your weight, act as shock absorbers, and help you maintain good posture. Feet and posture go together to make you feel and look good.

However, when shoes do not fit right, they can hurt your feet and affect your mood. In fact, ill-fitting shoes and socks cause most foot problems. You can prevent problems simply by wearing shoes and socks that fit your feet comfortably. **Figure 2.19** explains what to look for in shoes.

Your feet are enclosed inside shoes most of the day, so they perspire. This perspiration can cause the buildup of bacteria. To prevent this buildup, wash between your toes and scrub away dead skin from the heel and ball of your foot. Then be sure to dry your feet thoroughly.

Feet swell during the day. As a result, shoes that fit in the morning may be too tight in the afternoon. If possible, switch to another pair of shoes during the day to relax your feet.

When you buy a new pair of shoes, it is important to make sure they fit correctly.

Some Foot Problems

Proper foot care can eliminate or reduce many of the following uncomfortable foot problems.

- A **callus** is *a hard, thickened part of the skin on the foot.* It results from your foot rubbing against the inside of a shoe. Calluses are often found on the ball of the foot.

- A **corn** is *an overgrowth of the skin at some point on a toe.* It usually appears where the toe rubs against a shoe. Corns can be painful. If they thicken too much, a doctor must cut them away.

- A **blister** is *a fluid-filled pouch on the skin.* Like a corn, a blister is usually caused by an ill-fitting shoe. Blisters usually are painful.

- A **bunion** (BUHN·yuhn) is *an inflammation in the first joint of the big toe.* Tight shoes can cause discomfort.

- **Athlete's foot** is *a problem caused by fungi growing in the warm, damp areas of the foot.* Redness and itching usually appear between the toes. Athlete's foot is contagious. It can be treated with powder or medications.

- **Fallen arches** is another name for *flatness in the bottom of the feet.* Muscles and connective tissues in the arches weaken. The best relief for flat feet is wearing shoes that support your feet well.

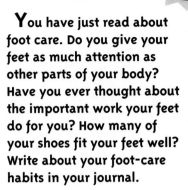

in your journal

You have just read about foot care. Do you give your feet as much attention as other parts of your body? Have you ever thought about the important work your feet do for you? How many of your shoes fit your feet well? Write about your foot-care habits in your journal.

Figure 2.19
What to Look for in Shoes

You should look for these qualities in shoes.

A A fit that is not too tight or too loose

B No binding or pinching

C Enough room to wiggle your toes

D Good support to the heel and ball of your foot

E No rubbing, or chafing, of your feet

How to Build Good Posture

Posture is the way you carry yourself. It involves standing, sitting, and walking. You can work to improve your posture by following the guidelines in **Figure 2.20.**

Figure 2.20
Correct Posture

Your posture has an effect on your overall appearance as well as on your health.

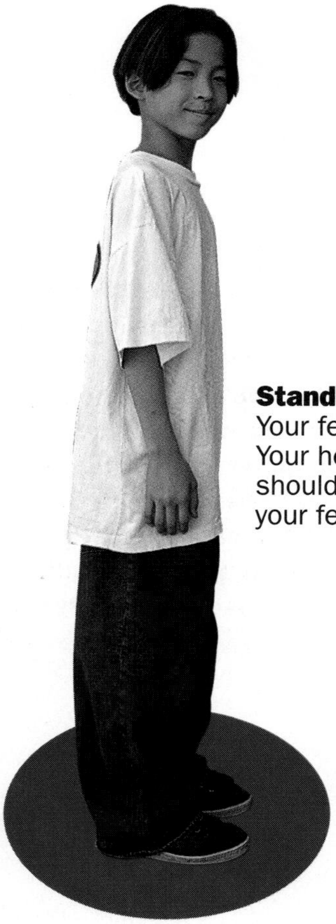

Standing:
Your feet are the key to good posture. Your head, upper body, and lower body should be balanced on the balls of your feet.

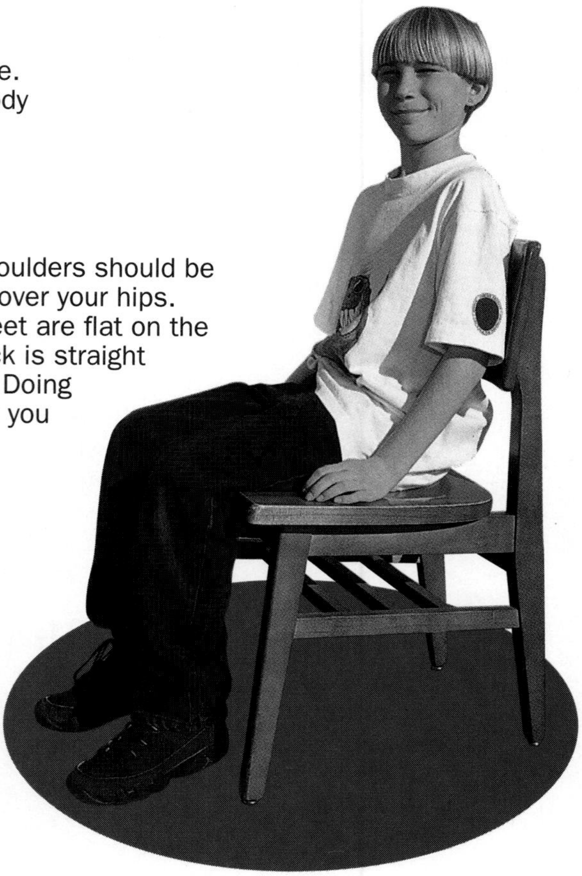

Sitting:
Your head and shoulders should be balanced directly over your hips. Make sure your feet are flat on the floor and your back is straight against the chair. Doing this can also help you stay alert.

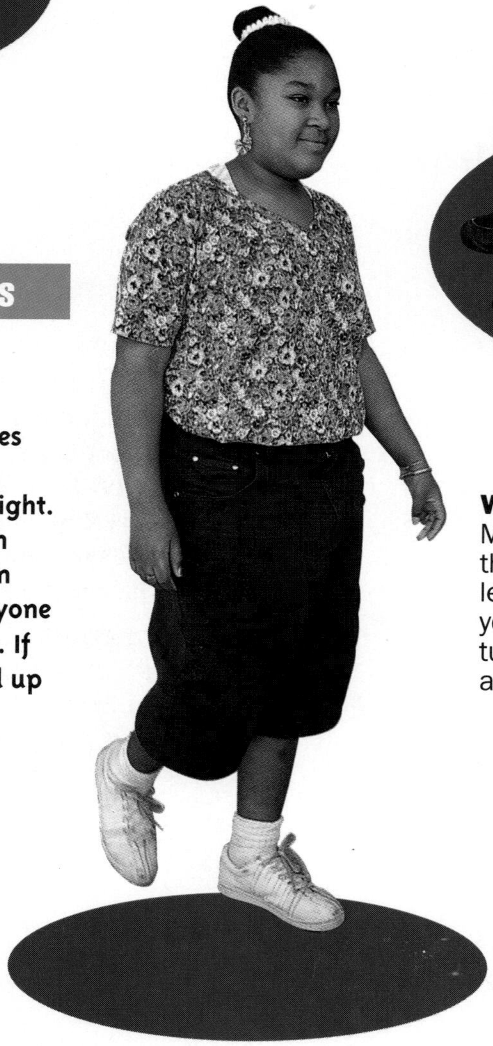

Teen Issues

Stand Up and Be Counted

Tall teens are sometimes uncomfortable or self-conscious about their height. Because of this, they lean over or slouch, which can harm their posture. Everyone grows at a different rate. If you are a tall teen, stand up and be counted as the special person you are.

Walking:
Make sure your body is balanced over the balls of your feet. Use your upper legs to move your body forward. Hold your shoulders back in a natural way, tuck in your stomach, and allow your arms to hang freely at your sides.

Here are some easy ways to improve your walking posture.

- Keep your back straight when rising from a chair.

- Keep your feet parallel to one another when walking. Your toes should not point in or out.

- Wear comfortable walking shoes. Walking shoes should be almost flat. High-heeled shoes throw off your balance, creating stress on your ankles and the arches of your feet.

Having Good Posture

Now that you know what good posture is, you have to practice it. Posture can tell as much about you as the appearance of your hair and skin. It can reflect your attitude and affect your health. In fact, poor posture is one of the more common causes of backaches. Good posture is important because it

- helps you move, stand, and sit with ease.

- helps you save energy because you can move more easily.

- allows your internal organs to function properly because you are not hunched over.

- distributes pressure so it does not put added stress on your back.

- helps your bones and muscles grow properly.

- makes your figure and body build look good.

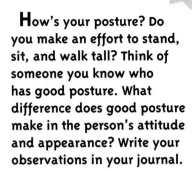

in Your Journal

How's your posture? Do you make an effort to stand, sit, and walk tall? Think of someone you know who has good posture. What difference does good posture make in the person's attitude and appearance? Write your observations in your journal.

Review

Lesson 4

Using complete sentences, answer the following questions on a separate sheet of paper.

Reviewing Terms and Facts

1. **Describe** What are the characteristics of comfortable shoes?

2. **Vocabulary** What is the difference between a *callus,* a *corn,* and a *bunion?*

Thinking Critically

3. **Synthesize** Your friend wants to buy a pair of shoes that are just the right style, just the right price, and just a little tight in the toes. What advice would you give your friend? Why?

4. **Persuade** What advice might you give a friend who stoops because he or she is self-conscious about being tall?

Applying Health Concepts

5. **Personal Health** Along with a classmate, evaluate one another's posture. Then help each other practice the tips for good standing, sitting, and walking posture. Write a short paragraph about what you learned about your posture and any changes you have made to improve it.

6. **Consumer Health** Look through catalogs and magazines for pictures of shoes that can lead to back pain or injury. Cut out and paste the pictures on poster paper. Title your poster.

Chapter Summary

▶ The skin is the largest organ of the body. It protects internal organs from water and disease, helps control body temperature, and acts as a sensory device. (Lesson 1)

▶ The hair and nails consist of dead cells that have grown out of living tissue located in the inner layer of skin. (Lesson 1)

▶ Proper care of the skin, hair, and nails is essential for a healthy appearance. (Lesson 1)

▶ The mouth, teeth, and tongue aid in tasting, digestion, and speech. In addition, the teeth help shape and structure your mouth. (Lesson 2)

▶ Immediately after you eat, bacteria in plaque combines with the foods in your mouth to form acids that can lead to tooth decay. (Lesson 2)

▶ Good dental habits and a healthful diet can help prevent tooth decay and bad breath. Take care of your teeth by brushing after eating and before bedtime. Regular flossing also helps keep your teeth clean. (Lesson 2)

▶ The eye is a complex organ through which people with full vision receive most of their information about the world. (Lesson 3)

▶ Good eye care includes regular eye exams. Most common vision problems can be corrected with eyeglasses or contact lenses. (Lesson 3)

▶ Your ears help you hear and also maintain your balance. (Lesson 3)

▶ The ear can be permanently damaged by loud noises, foreign objects in the ear, and infections. (Lesson 3)

▶ Feet support your weight, act as shock absorbers, and help maintain posture. (Lesson 4)

▶ Posture affects your appearance and your health. You can work to improve your posture when standing, sitting, and walking. (Lesson 4)

Using Health Terms

On a separate sheet of paper, write the vocabulary term that best matches the definition given below.

1. Tiny holes in the skin (Lesson 1)

2. A doctor who treats skin disorders (Lesson 1)

3. Hardened plaque (Lesson 2)

4. A condition in which the teeth of the upper and lower jaws do not align properly (Lesson 2)

5. The tough outer cover, or white, of the eye (Lesson 3)

6. The part of the inner ear that is responsible for balance (Lesson 3)

7. Flatness in the bottom of the feet (Lesson 4)

Reviewing Main Ideas

Using complete sentences, answer the following questions on a separate sheet of paper.

1. What are some do's and don'ts in dealing with acne? (Lesson 1)

2. Describe proper care of the nails. (Lesson 1)

3. What are the three main parts of the tooth? (Lesson 2)

4. How can you keep plaque from building up on your teeth? (Lesson 2)

5. Describe how the eye sees. (Lesson 3)

6. What is the difference between farsightedness and nearsightedness? (Lesson 3)

7. Describe how the ear hears. (Lesson 3)

8. What are five ways of taking care of your ears? (Lesson 3)

9. What are four problems that can be lessened by good foot care? (Lesson 4)

Thinking Critically

Using complete sentences, answer the following questions on a separate sheet of paper.

1. **Evaluate** Why are the sweat glands the body's built-in air-conditioning system? (Lesson 1)

2. **Hypothesize** Why do you think that diet does not cause acne? (Lesson 1)

3. **Analyze** Which is more important—brushing your teeth within minutes after eating or brushing your teeth with the proper technique? Explain your answer. (Lesson 2)

4. **Analyze** Why is it important to floss your teeth even if you brush after every meal? (Lesson 2)

5. **Hypothesize** Why do you think you have two sets of teeth—your baby teeth and your permanent teeth? (Lesson 2)

6. **Give Examples** What might be some symptoms of eye problems? (Lesson 3)

7. **Hypothesize** What factors might contribute to significant hearing loss among teens and young adults? (Lesson 3)

8. **Give Examples** How might foot problems such as corns or blisters affect posture? (Lesson 4)

Your Action Plan

Choose a personal grooming task that you would like to improve. This will be your long-term goal. Look back over the entries you made in your private journal for this chapter for ideas. Perhaps you want to get into the habit of flossing your teeth once a day. Performing the task each day will be your short-term goal.

To help you meet your long-term goal, it's a good idea to create a system for checking on your progress. For instance, put a calendar in your bathroom. Every time you floss your teeth, make a tally on the calendar. After a while, flossing will become a natural part of your day and you will no longer need the calendar. Once you have reached your long-term goal, reward yourself.

Building Your Portfolio

1. Pretend you are the director of an agency that hires teenage models. You look for teens who radiate good health rather than teens who are just beautiful or have a muscular body. Write an advertisement that describes the type of teen you are seeking. Add the advertisement to your portfolio.

2. Proper care of the skin, teeth, eyes, and ears begins in childhood. Look for newspaper and magazine articles and brochures that inform parents and other caregivers about hygiene and proper care for children. Add these resources to your portfolio. If possible, use the information to teach a good health habit to a young child.

In Your Home and Community

1. Conduct a dental clinic for younger students. Teach them how to clean their teeth well. Demonstrate proper brushing and flossing techniques. Show them the proper type of toothbrush to use.

2. Identify sources of noise pollution in your community. For example, freeway noise or noise from a nearby airport may be a source of concern for neighborhood residents. Keep informed of the issues involved by reading newspaper accounts. Contact community and government groups to see what action they might be taking to reduce noise levels. If possible, join in the action.

Chapter 3

Your Mental and Emotional Health

Student Expectations

After reading this chapter, you should be able to:

1. Identify the traits of good mental health.
2. Explain the benefits of a positive self-concept and high self-esteem.
3. Identify healthy ways of meeting your emotional needs and communicating.
4. Describe ways of dealing with stress.
5. Identify major mental disorders.
6. List sources of help to solve problems.

I've been feeling really tired lately and I've been pretty crabby with my family. My mom thought it might be a good idea for me to have a checkup. I wasn't surprised when the doctor said I looked "just fine."

The problems I have don't stand out like a rash or a broken bone. My problems are my thoughts and my feelings. I try to smile and act like everything is fine at school, but inside I'm a mess. I worry about all kinds of things—like about how I look and what people think of me. A lot of my friends know what they want to do when they grow up. I don't have a clue.

I know that it's normal to worry some of the time, but worrying too much might be a sign of a mental disorder. So how much worrying is too much? I really would like to talk to someone about my feelings, but I'm embarrassed. I started to talk to my dad once. Before I could say anything he told me how grown up I looked. Somehow, I lost my nerve. I guess I didn't want to appear like a kid to him. Maybe I should try someone else. I'm confused because I used to have more confidence in myself than I do now.

in Your journal

Read the account on this page. Do you ever feel that people do not take time to appreciate the inner you? Do you, too, have thoughts and feelings that cause you to worry? Start your private journal entries on mental health by answering these questions:

► In general, how do you feel about yourself? Identify your strengths and weaknesses.

► Do you worry about how to help a friend or relative who might be troubled?

When you reach the end of the chapter, you will use your journal entries to make an action plan.

What Is Mental Health?

This lesson will help you find answers to questions that teens often ask about mental health. For example:

► **How can I tell if I have good mental health?**
► **How can I develop good mental health habits?**
► **What shapes my personality?**

mental health
personality
values

in your journal

Review the signs of good mental health. For the next three days watch for examples of these signs in the behavior of yourself and others. Write these examples in your journal.

Mental Health

The three important parts of good health rely on one another for total balance and strength. All parts are equally important. Two sides of your health triangle are physical health and social health. The remaining side is mental and emotional health. **Mental health** is *your ability to deal in a reasonable way with the stresses and changes of everyday life.* When you have good mental health, you like yourself and accept yourself as you are. Some qualities common in people with good mental health are listed in **Figure 3.1.**

Signs of Good Mental Health

■ You have a positive outlook on life and welcome challenges.

■ You accept your limitations and set realistic goals for yourself.

■ You feel good about yourself and others.

Figure 3.1
The Benefits of a Positive Outlook

Ⓐ Having a positive outlook leads to making an effort.

Ⓑ Making an effort leads to encouragement from others.

- You can usually accept disappointment without overreacting.

- You act responsibly in your work and in your relationships.

- You are aware of your feelings and are able to express those feelings in healthful ways.

- You accept honest criticism without anger.

If you showed all the qualities of mental health all the time, you would have perfect mental health, but no one does. These qualities are goals you can achieve. Like physical health, there are many different levels of mental health, and everyone's mental health has its ups and downs. Don't worry if you aren't showing all these qualities at all times. You can, however, improve your overall mental health by developing good mental health habits. Look at the next section, Tips for Developing Good Mental Health. Which of the tips do you find the easiest? Which do you need to improve?

Tips for Developing Good Mental Health

Understanding Others

- Accept other people as they are. It isn't fair to judge everyone by your own background and behavior.

- Focus on other people's strengths, not their weaknesses.

- Consider other people's feelings.

Understanding Yourself

- Focus on your strengths.

- Accept things about yourself that you cannot change.

- Work to improve things you can change.

- Don't dwell on failures and disappointments.

- Learn from your mistakes.

© Encouragement from others leads to success.

D Success strengthens your positive outlook and leads to efforts in new areas.

Lesson 1: What Is Mental Health?   **65**

Personality and Mental Health

Just as no two snowflakes are alike, no two people are exactly the same. Each person is an individual with a **personality,** which is a *special mix of traits, feelings, attitudes, and habits.* You may have heard a person described as having no personality. This can never be. Everyone has a personality. Your personality is everything about you that makes you the person you are.

Factors That Shape Your Personality

Many factors influence the development of your personality. The three most important factors are heredity (the passing-on of traits from your parents), environment (all of your surroundings), and behavior (the way you act in the many different situations and events in your life). Behavior is the factor over which you have the most control. Study the examples in **Figure 3.2;** then, think of one specific example of each factor that describes you.

To some extent, each factor will continue to shape your personality throughout your life. Some factors, such as heredity, are beyond your control. No one gets to choose her or his inherited traits. Much of your environment is also beyond your control. Most young people live where the adults in their family choose to live.

Figure 3.2
What Shapes Your Personality?

Heredity	Environment	Behavior
Height	Community	Caring for yourself
Skin, hair, and eye color	Family and friends	Caring for others
Body type	Experiences	Reflecting your values

Teen Issues

Snap Judgments ACTIVITY!

We all give and receive impressions of one another at first meetings. Some people rely too much on first impressions in their opinions of others. They make snap judgments from visible personality traits about people they just met. These judgments usually are based on a bias about certain physical or cultural characteristics.

The next time you meet someone new, take the time to get to know the person before you decide if you like him or her. Isn't that the way you want to be judged?

How you behave toward other people is an important factor in shaping your personality.

What you do have control over, however, is how you will deal with your inherited traits and your environment. The final decision about how you act is yours. You decide if you will focus on your strengths or weaknesses. You decide if you will work to improve those situations that can be changed. Your behavior is your choice and your responsibility. A big part of who you are is up to you.

The Factor You Control

Behavior is the way you act in the various situations of your life. It is the factor of your personality over which you have the most control. Your behavior is based on your **values,** which are *beliefs and ideas about what is important in your life.* Most of your values are learned from your family, and to a lesser extent, from your friends. How you behave reflects those values. If good health is important in your life, then you will behave in a manner that reflects this. You will actively take good care of your mind and your body. You will choose behaviors that promote good health. You will not take risks that endanger your health or the health of others.

Your heredity, environment, and behavior have combined to shape the person you are today. To some extent, they will continue to shape your personality throughout your life.

Your family teaches you about values through their actions and behavior.

Review

Using complete sentences, answer the following questions on a separate sheet of paper.

Reviewing Terms and Facts

1. **Vocabulary**   Define the term *mental health.* Use it in an original sentence.

2. **Recall**   What are the three factors that shape personality?

Thinking Critically

3. **Apply**   List at least five specific examples of good mental health qualities.

4. **Describe**   Give examples of two times in the last week that your personal behavior demonstrated good mental health habits.

Applying Health Concepts

5. **Growth and Development**   Role-play the following situation. You and a friend play on the same sports team. Your friend makes an error that causes the team to lose. You confront your friend angrily, upset him or her, and end up not speaking. Discuss with your classmates alternative responses to the loss of the game. Replay the situation using more healthful responses.

6. **Personal Health**   Examine an aspect of your physical surroundings, such as your bedroom, the place where you study, or the outside area around your home. How does this place affect your mental well-being? What can you do to improve the space? Share your ideas with your classmates.

Lesson 1: What Is Mental Health?   **67**

Building Positive Self-Esteem

This lesson will help you find answers to questions that teens often ask about liking oneself. For example:

▶ **Why do I feel the way I do about myself?**

▶ **How does self-concept differ from self-esteem?**

▶ **How can I feel better about myself?**

Words to Know

self-concept
self-esteem

 in your journal

Write a description of yourself in your journal. Tell how you think you usually feel, think, look, and act. Mark your calendar to reread what you have written in three weeks. Do you still think it is accurate? Add your answer to your journal.

How Do You See Yourself?

Imagine for a moment that you are about to enter a room to meet some people for the first time. You ready yourself at the doorway, pull open the door, and walk in. Describe the person (you) that these people are about to meet. Are you confident, fun to be with, intelligent, honest, well groomed, happy, healthy, organized, or creative? Are you sincerely interested in other people? Your description paints a word picture of how you view yourself and how you believe others view you. This *view that you have of yourself* is called your **self-concept.**

Your self-concept could be realistic, which means that you have a pretty accurate awareness of the strengths and weaknesses of your personality. Some teens, however, have an unrealistic self-concept. They dismiss their strengths and focus only on their "faults," usually exaggerating them. Think back to the Tips for Developing Good Mental Health on page 65. Which of the points listed would you associate with having a realistic self-concept?

Focusing only on what you perceive as your "faults" makes them seem greater than they actually are.

How Self-Concept Develops

The self-concept that you have today has been in the making for a long time. It was built gradually from your experiences with other people. In general, people who are given support, encouragement, and love tend to develop a positive self-concept. People who are neglected, spoken to harshly, frequently criticized, and discouraged tend to develop a negative self-concept.

Your self-concept began in your early years, but it keeps developing as you grow. Remarks that your family, friends, and teachers make and ways in which they act toward you can reinforce, or strengthen, the view you have of yourself. **Figure 3.3** illustrates how various experiences contribute to your self-concept.

Thanks for mowing the lawn, Tom. That was a great help.

Figure 3.3
Shaping Your Self-Concept

What kind of reinforcement—positive or negative—does each of these messages represent?

- Your older sister calls you clumsy when you spill the juice.

- You join two friends at lunch, but they ignore you.

- Your teacher shakes her head during your oral report.

- The coach gives you a thumbs-up sign.

- Your friends wait for you to catch up and walk with them.

- Your teacher smiles encouragement when you give your report.

HEALTH LAB
The Qualities You Admire

Introduction: "I wish I had Rosa's confidence." "Everyone likes Garrett. I wish I was more like him." Have you ever made statements like these? Most people admire certain qualities in others. Do you look for and admire qualities in others that you also have, or do you most admire qualities that you do not have? You can find out by carrying out the following experiment.

Objective: Look for evidence during the next week that tells you if you have any of the six qualities that you most admire in others.

Materials and Method: List eight to ten qualities that you admire in others. Examples are being a good listener, keeping secrets, and being reliable.

When you complete your list, circle the six qualities that you most admire. Clip three sheets of notebook paper together, and fold them in half. On each half page, write one of the six qualities. During the next week, look for signs that you have, or don't have, each of the qualities. Every time you have any evidence, either way, write it down under the appropriate quality heading.

Observation and Analysis: At the end of the week, ask a classmate to help you analyze your observations. Remember to weigh the evidence fairly. For example, returning a library book a day late does not mean that you are not reliable. However, breaking your word might. Do you have the qualities that you most admire in others?

The Power of Your Words ACTIVITY!

As a teen, you know the effect others have on your self-concept. At the same time, remember that you are reinforcing the self-concepts of others. Make an effort to say and do things that help friends and family members improve their self-concepts. If you see people doing something kind, compliment their behavior. If you like a meal at home, say so and thank the person who made it. Keep a list for a week of all the times you have said or done something positive to reinforce someone's self-concept. Remember that your words have power.

Self-Concept and Self-Esteem

Closely tied to your self-concept is your self-esteem. **Self-esteem** is *the way you feel about yourself.* Self-esteem refers to confidence and pride you have in yourself. The way you feel about your body, your mind, your emotions, and your interactions with others are all part of your self-esteem. **Figure 3.4** lists the types of behavior that indicate self-esteem.

Figure 3.4
Behaviors That Indicate Self-Esteem
Where do you fall on the self-esteem continuum?

Low self-esteem is often linked to an unrealistic self-concept. For example, people who overlook their strengths and exaggerate their weaknesses in their own minds will probably not feel very good about themselves. In other words, people who do not like or respect themselves have low self-esteem.

Like your self-concept, your self-esteem is formed in part by messages, both positive and negative, that you receive from other people. Your self-esteem is also formed by messages that you send yourself. The messages you give yourself are sometimes powerful enough to change the meaning of messages from others. Have you ever received a compliment that you were unable to accept? Perhaps the more the person praised you, the more you rejected the praise. If you have had this experience, you have let your own negative messages override the positive ones from someone else. What incident can you recall when your own positive messages lessened the sting of negative messages from another person?

Self-Esteem and Your Health

Probably no single factor has a greater impact on your total health than your self-esteem. People with high self-esteem are more likely to practice good health habits than people with low self-esteem. People with high self-esteem are also more likely to avoid harmful behaviors, such as overeating, abusing alcohol and drugs, and refusing to take personal safety measures.

Because people with high self-esteem like themselves, they take good care of themselves. Their health, safety, and appearance are important. They try to accept and learn from fair criticism, and they are able to ignore mean remarks. Having high self-esteem lets you accept the negative incidents in your life as exceptions, not the rule. People with high self-esteem generally act responsibly toward themselves and others. People with low self-esteem do just the opposite. They tend to believe that all experiences are negative.

Were you ever feeling down when suddenly something really positive happened that made you feel great for the rest of the day? Everyone's level of self-esteem changes from day to day and sometimes from hour to hour. Although your self-esteem goes up and down, it usually falls within a specific range on the self-esteem continuum. Which of the signs of high and low self-esteem in **Figure 3.4** do you think describe you most of the time?

Improving Your Self-Esteem

When your self-esteem is high, you are usually happy with yourself and get along well with others. You are able to bounce back quickly after a loss, and your total health seems to get a boost. For these reasons, having high self-esteem is a worthy goal. There are several actions you can take to help you reach the goal of high self-esteem. **Figure 3.5** on the next page describes some of these actions. What other items would you add to the list?

in your journal

Your behavior can sometimes trigger just the response you do not want. For example, if you want more freedom at home, acting irresponsibly will convince your parents that you are not ready for more personal freedom. Think of two recent incidents, one that resulted in the desired response and one that did not. Describe both incidents in your journal.

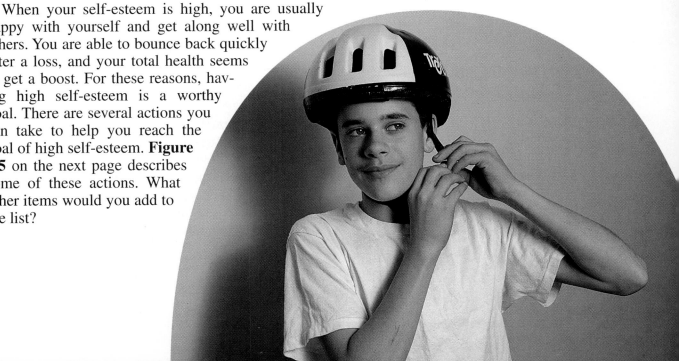

Wearing a helmet when riding a bicycle is an example of a personal safety measure.

Keeping a realistic self-concept and raising your self-esteem takes effort. Although some people always appear confident and happy, everyone has occasional self-doubts and personal concerns. The teen years are usually times of changing self-esteem levels. Temporary periods of unrealistic self-concepts and low self-esteem seem to happen frequently, but usually they do not last long. Teens who feel unloved, unimportant, and unworthy most of the time, however, should talk about their feelings with an adult family member, clergy member, school counselor, or coach.

Figure 3.5
Working Toward High Self-Esteem
Here are some suggestions for raising your self-esteem.

A Focus on your successes.

B Send yourself positive messages.

C Set realistic goals for yourself.

D Ask people for help when you need it.

E Learn from your mistakes.

Lesson 2

Review

Using complete sentences, answer the following questions on a separate sheet of paper.

Reviewing Terms and Facts

1. **Vocabulary**   What is the difference between *self-concept* and *self-esteem?*

2. **Give Examples**   List three ways to improve self-esteem.

Thinking Critically

3. **Explain**   How and when does a person's self-concept develop?

4. **Analyze**   Why do people with generally high self-esteem have times in which their self-esteem is low?

Applying Health Concepts

5. **Growth and Development**   Think of a common problem that affects a teen's self-esteem. Draw a cartoon strip that shows what teens with this problem do to feel better about themselves.

6. **Health of Others**   Write down the number of times during the day that you reinforced someone else's self-concept. Perhaps you smiled at someone, complimented a friend on a job well done, or invited someone to join an activity. Include any negative reinforcements you may have given.

Understanding Your Emotions

This lesson will help you find answers to questions that teens often ask about emotions. For example:

▶ **Does everyone have the same emotional needs that I do?**

▶ **How can I satisfy my emotional needs?**

▶ **How can I express my emotions in healthy ways?**

▶ **How can I deal with my anger?**

Your Emotional Needs

There are certain things that your body just cannot do without for very long. These needs, which include food, water, and sleep, are called basic physical needs. If these needs are not met, your physical health will suffer.

You have another set of basic needs called your **emotional needs.** These are *needs that affect your feelings and sense of well-being.* Emotional needs play an important role in your mental health. Meeting your emotional needs is as important to your total health as meeting your physical needs.

Although people have different specific emotional needs and demonstrate their emotional needs in different ways, everyone shares three basic needs. Study the list of basic emotional needs on the next page. How do you exhibit these three needs?

Words to Know

emotional needs
emotion
hormones

in your journal

Emotional needs mean different things to different people. Before you read any farther in the text, write in your journal what you think your most important emotional needs are.

Helping your team and being appreciated make you feel worthwhile.

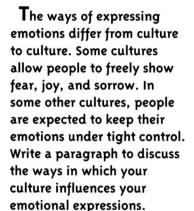
Basic Emotional Needs

- **The need to love and be loved.** You need to feel that you are cared for and that you are special in someone's eyes. You also need to feel that way about others.

- **The need to belong.** You need to know that others like you and accept you as part of a group. The first group that most people belong to is their family.

- **The need to feel worthwhile.** You need to feel that you make a difference in the world—that you are making a contribution. When you help another person do something or come up with a useful idea, you are contributing.

Meeting Emotional Needs

Just as you regularly seek food, water, and sleep to meet your basic physical needs, you are also always striving to meet your emotional needs. The urge to meet emotional needs is strong and constant. In fact, most people are not even aware that they are taking actions to satisfy those needs.

People with good mental health seek out positive ways to meet their emotional needs. **Figure 3.6** shows how the emotional needs of one teen were met and helped her feel better.

Here are some other positive ways to meet emotional needs.

- Offer to help out with chores around the house that are usually someone else's responsibility.

- Take time out to ask family members how their day went, and really listen to their answers.

- Organize a fund-raiser or join an interest group, such as a science club or music group at school. Do your best to help make the club activities successful.

- Volunteer to help at a local nursing home or hospital, or help a neighbor who has special needs.

- Pitch in and help a local or national charitable organization meet its goals. What additional ways can you think of?

Figure 3.6
Meeting an Emotional Need

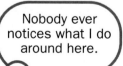

Nobody ever notices what I do around here.

Thanks for helping me study last night. I really aced the test.

Wow, he noticed. I guess I'm okay after all.

What Are Emotions?

Another factor influencing your mental health is your **emotions,** or *feelings*. Your emotions are a natural part of being alive, and they influence everything you do. Emotions affect your behavior. For example, if you are afraid of being hurt, you tend to practice good safety measures. If you like someone, you will probably act in likable ways toward them.

During your teen years, changes in your body cause your emotions to shift suddenly. You have probably noticed times when you are feeling happy, and then suddenly, for no apparent reason, you feel blue. These sudden emotional shifts are related to the production of **hormones** (HOR·mohnz). Glands produce hormones, which are *chemical substances that regulate many body functions.* Sudden emotional shifts are nothing to be alarmed about. For most people these shifts are part of being a teen.

Kinds of Emotions

Some people believe that certain emotions are bad, wrong, or unhealthy. In themselves, emotions are neither good, bad, right, wrong, healthy, nor unhealthy. Emotions carry no moral value. How they are expressed is another matter. People with good mental health seek healthy, responsible ways of expressing their emotions.

An important part of learning how to express your emotions is learning to be aware of them. This is not always as easy as it sounds. Sometimes people confuse one emotion with another. This is especially true of the emotions fear and anger.

Fear

Everyone has fears. Some fears are helpful. The fear of danger makes you careful around fire and alerts you to look for traffic before stepping into a street. Not all fears are helpful, however. Some fears can keep you from doing the things you need or want to do. For example, you may want to join the track team, but fear of failing prevents you from showing up for the tryouts. Sometimes fear may even damage a relationship. One way to deal effectively with unhelpful fear is to recognize it for what it is. Once you admit fear, you are on the way to coping with it.

Teen Issues

Gloom Busters

Everyone feels down sometimes. Still, it is not fun to feel this way, so the next time the gloom sets in, take action. Try the following:

▶ Push negative thoughts from your mind.

▶ Avoid dwelling on past or future problems.

▶ Invite a friend to join you in a walk, a bike ride, or a swim.

▶ Start a new project or tackle a job around your home.

The teen years are sometimes like a roller-coaster ride of emotions.

Primary Emotions

Red, yellow, and blue are primary colors. All other colors are combinations of these three basic colors. There are also primary emotions. They are anger, fear, sadness, acceptance, disgust, happiness, and surprise. All other emotions are combinations of these.

Anger

Anger is an emotion that can be expressed in a variety of ways. Often people express their anger by saying things they really do not mean. People may say things like, "I hate you!" and "I never want to see you again!" when what they mean is "I'm angry with you." When you are feeling angry, try to take the following steps.

- Pause for a moment and take a deep breath.
- Admit your anger to yourself.
- Try to focus on what it is that has made you angry.
- Try to think of the words that will express your true feelings.
- Tell the other person how you feel.

Handling Emotions in Healthy Ways

The way you handle your emotions has a lot to do with your personality. Your tendency to be short-tempered or always to look for the good in everything will affect the way you handle your emotions. You learned ways to handle your emotions from watching others. Although you may not have even been aware of it, you learned some of the same ways of dealing with emotions that your family members use.

In some families, members are very open and talk frequently about feelings. Some other families do not say much but communicate how they feel by smiling when they are pleased, or by slamming doors, remaining silent, or crying when they are displeased. No matter what has influenced a person's way of dealing with emotions, everyone can learn healthy ways to deal with and express them.

Communication

Everyone responds to situations and shows emotions differently. Because human emotions are so complex, it is important to learn how to communicate them effectively. Communication is not an easy skill to learn, but it is a vital one. With practice, you can become better at understanding what other people are feeling and at letting others know what you are feeling.

Feelings of sadness are normal, and usually temporary, after a disappointing event.

Conflict Resolution

Good communication skills are especially helpful during conflicts, or disagreements. **Figure 3.7** shows some tips for communicating effectively when you are trying to resolve a conflict.

Using these rules does not guarantee that the problem will be solved. Communication is a two-way street, and the other person has to cooperate. Many times, however, all it takes to start heading toward agreement is for someone to make the first positive move.

in your journal

In your journal, briefly describe a situation in which you became angry because of something another person did or said. Tell if the conflict was resolved. If it was, tell how you went about resolving it.

Figure 3.7
Stating Your Case Effectively

A State your view of what happened and tell how you feel. Tell the person how your anger involves him or her.

B Think about the words you are using. Start your sentences with "I." Attacking the other person with "you" statements usually makes things worse.

C Pay attention to your gestures, facial expressions, and your body language. Make sure your body language is sending the same message that your words are sending.

D Listen respectfully to what the other person has to say. Try to understand the other person's point of view and feelings.

Review

Lesson 3

Using complete sentences, answer the following questions on a separate sheet of paper.

Reviewing Terms and Facts

1. **Vocabulary** Define *emotions* and use it in an original sentence.
2. **Recall** When can fear hold you back?

Thinking Critically

3. **Apply** List examples from your daily life that show how you have met each of the three basic emotional needs in the last two days. List one example for each need.

4. **Summarize** What are three communication rules to use during conflict resolution?

Applying Health Concepts

5. **Health of Others** Imagine that you are angry with a younger sibling for wearing your favorite shirt without permission. Role-play ways in which you can express your anger without negatively affecting your sibling's self-concept.

BUY!

BUY!

BUY!

Teen HEALTH DIGEST

People at Work

Music Therapist

Sal Marino has been a music therapist for six years. "I love my job," says Sal. "Music has always been part of my life. When I started college, I was torn between studying music or psychology. Luckily, one of my teachers told me how to combine both my interests into a very satisfying career.

"As a music therapist, I use music to help people with their mental and emotional problems. Some of my patients are suffering from harmful stress. I show them that playing music can bring relief. Some of my patients cannot express their emotions in healthful ways. For example, I have several patients

who have trouble expressing anger in a healthful way. I often teach people with this problem to play the drums. Being a music therapist is different from being a music teacher. The point of my job is to make people feel better. How good the music sounds isn't really important. How good the patient feels is."

CON$UMER FOCU$

Self-Image Bait

Advertisements aimed at teens imply that if they wear certain clothing, drink certain beverages, eat certain foods, and use certain personal grooming products, they will feel good about themselves and be popular. Many even go so far as to make it seem that if teens use a particular product, they will get the boyfriend or girlfriend they want.

By encouraging self-doubt, the messages in these ads create a problem and then offer a solution. Many teens have a shaky self-image to start with. Ads like these take advantage of this lack of confidence to undermine the consumer's self-image even more. The ad hints that your looks are in need of improvement and that you do not have enough friends. Don't let ads undermine your self-image or self-confidence.

Teens Making a Difference

Teen Mentors

In 1994, about 160 students who attended Bloomington North High School in Bloomington, Indiana, participated in the Teen Mentors program. Teen Mentors began in 1990, when five students decided to establish a program that matched elementary school students with teen "buddies."

In the beginning, the program's focus was on tutoring. Teen Mentors met with their elementary-school buddies every two weeks to review homework problems. Over time the program evolved into more of a big brother/big sister program.

Today, Teen Mentors meet with their buddies once a week throughout the school year to help with homework, play games, or talk. The mentors and their young buddies are finding the program a huge success.

Health Update

Hope Can Help

Research carried out by Martin Seligman, Ph.D., a psychologist at the University of Pennsylvania, and other researchers suggests that having hope helps in difficult situations. New studies identify hope—the feeling that you can improve the situation—as a powerful force.

In a study carried out at the University of Michigan, students who had little or no hope suffered twice as many colds, sore throats, and other illnesses than the students with high hope. Lack of hope is also thought to contribute to clinical depression.

Experts suggest that hope can be nurtured. Even if you have only a little hope, you have a nugget of strength on which you can build.

Myths and Realities

Are Beliefs Deadly?

Can hopefulness prolong the lives of terminally ill patients? Can hopelessness shorten lives? Research from the University of California suggests that hope makes a difference.

California sociologist David Phillips tested the effect of resignation by looking at the intensity of belief. He found that people who believed that it was their "fate" to get a certain disease died up to five years earlier than others with the same disease but without those beliefs.

Our beliefs and wellness are closely related. People whose religious beliefs include refraining from tobacco and excessive alcohol use, as well as sexual promiscuity, have a decreased risk of lung disease, alcoholism, and sexually transmitted disease. Even those people who, because of heredity, may be predisposed to a certain illness can decrease the risk of getting that illness by working to maintain a healthful lifestyle, including eating a balanced diet, getting plenty of rest, exercising, and reducing stress. Those who resign themselves to their fate and who do not take an active role in maintaining good health increase that risk. The message is that positive thinking may not only keep you healthier but also keep you alive longer.

Managing Stress

This lesson will help you find answers to questions that teens often ask about stress. For example:

▶ **How does stress affect me?**

▶ **What circumstances in my life might be causing me stress?**

▶ **How can I cope with the stress in my life?**

Words to Know

stress
distress
stressor
adrenaline
fatigue
physical fatigue
psychological
  fatigue

in Your journal

Consider the sources of stress in your life. List them in your journal. Write why you think each is causing you stress. Write down the signs of stress you notice in yourself.

Stress in Your Life

Stress is a familiar term. You probably hear it mentioned almost every day. Most often, stress is mentioned in a negative way, as something to avoid. **Stress,** however, is only *your body's response to changes around you.* Those responses can certainly have a negative effect. Feeling nervous and maybe having an upset stomach because you are worried about an upcoming event are definitely not pleasant. *Stress that keeps you from doing the things you need to do or causes you discomfort* is called negative stress, or **distress.**

Some stress is considered positive. Positive stress helps you to accomplish and reach goals. The stress that makes you feel excited or challenged by an activity is an example of positive stress.

Like stress, changes in your life might also be labeled either positive or negative. Winning a race is usually considered positive and losing a race negative. Your body, however, cannot tell the difference. Because your body responds to every change, any change—positive or negative—causes stress. The Personal Inventory feature on page 81 lists some life changes that cause stress. How many of these events have you experienced lately?

Positive stress can challenge athletes and motivate them to work hard toward meeting a goal.

Personal Inventory

Stress and the effect it will have on people is difficult to measure. What causes one person a great deal of stress may hardly affect another person at all. The following chart gives values in "stress points" to certain life changes. Accumulating between 150 and 299 stress points in one year increases a person's chance of getting sick. Whether sickness will actually occur depends on the person. It is not the amount of stress that is important, it is how you respond to it.

Rank	Event	Stress points	Rank	Event	Stress points
1.	Death of a parent	98	17.	Father or mother losing a job	69
2.	Death of a sister or brother	95	18.	Being seriously sick or hurt	64
3.	Death of a friend	92	19.	Arguing with parents	64
4.	Divorce or separation of parents	86	20.	School troubles with teacher or principal	63
5.	Failure in one or more school subjects	86	21.	Discomfort and concern about weight, height, acne	63
6.	Getting arrested	85	22.	Going to a new school	57
7.	Repeating a grade in school	84	23.	Moving to a new home	51
8.	Family member's alcohol or drug problem	79	24.	Change in physical appearance due to braces, glasses	47
9.	Starting to use alcohol or drugs	77	25.	Arguing with sister or brother	46
10.	Loss or death of a pet	77	26.	Beginning to menstruate (girls)	45
11.	Family member's serious illness	77	27.	Making a decision about smoking	45
12.	Making choices about sexual relationships	75	28.	Having someone, such as a grandparent, move in	35
13.	Losing money you've saved	74	29.	Mother's pregnancy	31
14.	Breaking up with girlfriend or boyfriend	74	30.	Beginning to go out on dates	31
15.	Quitting or being suspended from school	73	31.	Making new friends	27
16.	Pregnancy of a close friend	69	32.	Marriage of a sister or brother	26

Stress and Stressors

Stress is a natural part of everyday life. The *triggers of stress* are called **stressors.** It isn't just major events that cause stress. Stress is caused by everyday irritations and pleasures.

Your body responds to most stressors by getting ready to act. This response is called the "fight-or-flight" response because your body prepares to fight the stressor or flee from it (see **Figure 3.8**). One part of this response is the release of **adrenaline** (uh·DRE·nuhl·in). This hormone *increases the level of sugar in your blood, which gives your body extra energy.*

Figure 3.8
The Fight-or-Flight Response
When your body responds to a stressor, certain physical reactions occur.

A More blood is directed to your muscles and brain.

B Your heart beats faster.

C Your muscles tighten up and are ready for action.

D Your senses sharpen. You become more alert.

E Your air passages widen so that you can take in more air.

F The level of sugar in your blood increases, which gives you extra energy.

Stress and Fatigue

Once the stressor is gone, your body's response usually stops. However, if the stress is great or if it lasts long enough, the response may continue. After a time, your body can become exhausted. **Fatigue,** or *extreme tiredness,* then sets in.

There are actually two types of fatigue. **Physical fatigue** is *extreme tiredness of the whole body.* It usually occurs after vigorous activity. Muscles may be overworked and sore, and your body feels tired all over. When this happens, you need rest.

The other type is **psychological** (SY·kuh·LAH·ji·kuhl) **fatigue,** or *extreme tiredness caused by your mental state.* This type is brought on by stress, worry, boredom, or depression. Activity, such as exercise or doing a project, can help this kind of fatigue.

LIFE SKILLS
Time Management

People who manage their time well are better able to control this major source of stress in their lives.

To rate your time-management skills, answer the following questions with *yes* or *no.*

► Are you almost always in a hurry?

► Do you leave tasks or chores incomplete?

► Do you feel as if you are working hard but not accomplishing much?

► Do you not have enough time for rest or for personal relationships?

► Are you regularly late with assignments and for appointments?

► Are you overwhelmed by demands?

► Do you often try to do several things at once?

► Do you have trouble deciding what to do next?

If most of your answers are yes, your time-management skills need improvement. Try putting the following tips to work in your life.

1. **Set priorities.** Decide which activities are obligations and which are choices. Of the activities that are choices, decide which are most important to you.

2. **Make a schedule** (see **Figure 3.9**). Decide when you will do each activity. Try to be realistic about how much you can do, and leave time for relaxing. If you need to drop some activities, check your priority list.

3. **Learn to say no.** Most important, know your limitations and when to say no.

Follow-up Activity

After three weeks, take the time-management quiz again. Have any of your answers changed? What else can you do to better manage your time?

Figure 3.9
Managing Your Time

Sunday	Monday	Tuesday	Wednesday	Thursday	Friday	Saturday
29	30	31	1	2	3	4
Picnic with friends	Photography club after school	Baby-sitting for neighbor from 6:00 to 8:00 p.m.	Marching band tryouts	Trumpet lesson after school	Movie night with Aunt Celia	Grandma's 80th birthday party

Planning for Health

Serious and long-lasting stress can cause illness. By being ready for changes and planning for them whenever possible, you can reduce stress and the chance of becoming sick.

Coping with Stress

Everyone feels stress from time to time, but not for the same reasons. You might feel stress over not being asked to join a new club at school. Your friend might not give it a second thought. It is also important to know how to handle stress when it comes. **Figure 3.10** lists some tips for handling stress. Which do you use?

Figure 3.10
Tips for Effective Stress Management

Plan Think ahead to avoid the stresses of cramming for tests, turning in homework late, and dealing with mountains of chores.

Redirect Your body reacts to all stress by making adrenaline, which raises your energy level. Rechannel all that extra energy into something worthwhile.

Relax Try imagining yourself in a quiet, peaceful place, such as under a tree by a lake. As you relax, try to empty your mind of troubling thoughts.

Talk Just talking things out with another person can relieve stress. People who aren't directly involved can often see solutions to your problems that you cannot.

Laugh Spend time with people who enjoy a good laugh. See a funny movie after an especially stressful day. Laughter relieves stress.

Lesson 4 Review

Using complete sentences, answer the following questions on a separate sheet of paper.

Reviewing Terms and Facts

1. **Vocabulary** What is the difference between *stress* and *distress?*

2. **Recall** List some tips for improving time-management skills.

Thinking Critically

3. **Compare** Explain how positive and negative stress are similar.

4. **Analyze** Your friend tells you she is feeling very tired. She says she is so worried about some problems at home that she can't think of anything else.

What kind of stress is she feeling? What can she do right away to relieve her stress?

Applying Health Concepts

5. **Health of Others** Interview ten people about how they handle stress. You can interview family members, teachers, classmates, and friends. Ask them to suggest one tip for coping with stress. Share the tips with your classmates.

6. **Health of Others** Watch for signs of stress in family members. Try to find out what is causing them stress. What can you and they do to relieve their stress?

Mental Disorders

This lesson will help you find answers to questions that teens often ask about mental health problems and mental disorders. For example:

▶ **What is the best way to deal with my problems?**

▶ **How can I tell if my mental problems are serious?**

▶ **What causes depression?**

▶ **What should I do if I suspect a friend is thinking of suicide?**

Words to Know

defense
  mechanism
neurosis
anxiety disorder
psychosis
schizophrenia
clinical depression
suicide

Facing Problems

Life is filled with events that create problems and cause stress. Some problems can be solved easily. A misplaced notebook might cause stress only until you find it. Other problems, such as a death in the family, last longer.

Regardless of the problem, the way to deal with it in a healthful manner is first to face up to it. If you are having trouble dealing with a problem on your own, ask for help. For some problems, such as drug use, there are professionals who can help. **Figure 3.11** offers information on how to handle problems.

Figure 3.11
How to Handle a Problem

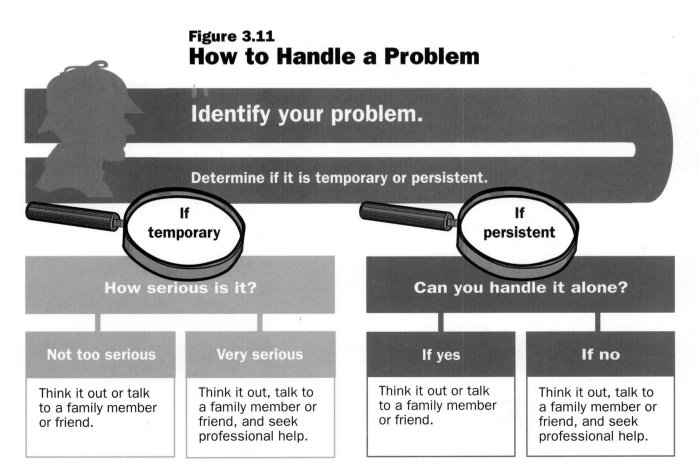

Identify your problem.

Determine if it is temporary or persistent.

If temporary	If persistent
How serious is it?	**Can you handle it alone?**

Not too serious	Very serious	If yes	If no
Think it out or talk to a family member or friend.	Think it out, talk to a family member or friend, and seek professional help.	Think it out or talk to a family member or friend.	Think it out, talk to a family member or friend, and seek professional help.

Defense Mechanisms

The fight-or-flight response is your body's reaction to stress. Your mind also reacts to stress. These reactions, called **defense mechanisms** (duh·FENS MEK·uh·nizms), are *short-term ways of dealing with stress*. Defense mechanisms allow you to set aside a certain amount of stress until you are better able to face the problem and deal with it (see **Figure 3.12**). When used as a temporary solution to problems, defense mechanisms can actually help people. However, if you use them as a permanent substitute for facing the problem, your mental health could be harmed. There are several types of defense mechanisms. Which of the following defense mechanisms are familiar to you?

■ **Denial** is a refusal to accept reality. Ted's parents are getting a divorce. Ted refuses to accept that his dad is moving out and acts like everything is fine with the family.

■ **Rationalization** is justifying behavior, ideas, or feelings to avoid guilt or to obtain approval or acceptance. Marlene says she did not finish her homework because she was busy helping her grandmother with her food shopping.

■ **Repression** is blocking out unpleasant thoughts. Kahlil has a lot of homework to do tonight, but he does not even think of it when he agrees to go out with his friends.

■ **Displacement** is having bad feelings toward someone not really related to the cause of the problem. Wynona had an argument with her friend that left her hurt and angry. Later, at home, Wynona yelled at her sister for no reason.

■ **Projection** is blaming someone else for your problem. Will got up late, spilled his juice on his shirt, could not find his homework, and finally missed his bus. While these were his problems, he blamed his mother for everything.

Did You Know?

Automatic Relief

Defense mechanisms can kick in automatically to bring you relief from stress. In other words, you may be using defense mechanisms without being aware of it.

Figure 3.12
Examples of Defense Mechanisms
Identify the defense mechanism at work in each situation.

Pete's more popular than me because you give him everything.

You have to tell Lisa that you were hurt by what she did.

No, no. It's not a problem.

Understanding Mental Disorders

In everyone's life, there are times when he or she feels that life is difficult to deal with. Feeling anxious, angry, fearful, or blue from time to time is natural. When these feelings continue for a long time or make a person feel out of control or unable to deal with life, they could signal a mental disorder.

Causes of Mental Disorders

The causes of mental disorders can be divided into two general categories. They are physical causes and emotional causes.

Physical causes

- Injury to the brain
- High fevers
- Certain drugs
- Certain illnesses

Emotional causes

- Neurosis (anxiety, phobia)
- Psychosis (paranoia, schizophrenia)
- Other (clinical depression, manic-depressive disorder)

Neurosis

Everyone has, at some time in life, felt fear or been anxious about something. When *a fear gets in the way of a person's ability to function in daily life,* that person may suffer from *a condition* known as **neurosis** (noo·ROH·sis). Neurosis can cause physical symptoms, including uneven breathing, a speeding-up of the heart, muscle pain, and sweating.

All mentally healthy people experience some form of anxiety, or fear, from time to time. For these people, the anxious feelings pass and do not really affect their ability to deal with life. Anxiety disorders, however, do affect that ability. The problems called **anxiety disorders** are *disorders in which real or imagined fears keep a person from functioning normally.* Sometimes the anxiety is over something specific, such as being in a crowd. Sometimes the anxiety disorder is general. When a person has an unreasonable, exaggerated, and long-lasting fear of something, he or she has a phobia. Each type of phobia has its own name. Acrophobia (ak·ruh·FOH·bee·uh) is an abnormal fear of being in high places. Zoophobia (ZOO·uh·FOH·bee·uh) is an abnormal fear of animals.

Psychosis

Sometimes problems are so severe that the victim's view of the world becomes distorted. When this happens, the person is said to suffer from **psychosis** (sy·KOH·sis). This is *a condition in which a person is not able to function in the real world.*

Science Connection

Foods to Calm ACTIVITY!

Low-fat proteins tend to stimulate you whereas carbohydrates tend to calm you down. Foods that put your brain in high gear include low-fat milk, skinless chicken, and beans. Foods that help soothe your mood include bread, pasta, and cereals. Check your moods with your diet for a few days. Write your observations on a sheet of paper. What connections do you see? Discuss your answer in class.

There are many types of psychosis. The most common type is **schizophrenia** (skit·zoh·FREE·nee·uh), which means "split mind." Schizophrenia is *a serious disorder in which people turn inward and often completely lose touch with reality.* Schizophrenia may be caused by an imbalance of brain chemistry.

Other Mental Disorders

- **Clinical depression.** Feeling sad and lonely once in a while is perfectly normal. In a few days, the sad feelings usually pass and things seem to brighten. Someone who experiences *feelings of sadness or loneliness and a feeling of hopelessness that continue for more than a few weeks* may be suffering from **clinical depression** (KLI·ni·kuhl di·PRE·shuhn).

- **Manic-depressive disorder.** When a person has extreme mood swings for no apparent reason and on a regular basis, she or he may suffer from manic-depressive disorder. Manic-depressives sometimes take unnecessary risks during their high periods.

- **Hypochondria.** A person who is really well but constantly feels aches and pains and worries all the time about having a serious disease suffers from hypochondria (HY·puh·KAHN·dree·uh).

Seriously Troubled Teens

The teen years are full of changes—in the body, in feelings, in relationships, and in responsibilities. These changes cause stress, which sometimes becomes more than a person can cope with alone. If that happens to you, ask for help. There is nothing wrong with needing help with mental problems. Most people need help sometime. People who do not get help suffer more than they need to.

Suicide

Each year thousands of teenagers attempt suicide. **Suicide,** *intentionally killing oneself,* has been the second-leading cause of death for people between the ages of 15 and 19 since 1986. Suicide is a serious matter and threats of suicide should never be ignored. The best thing to do is to get help immediately.

Sometimes there are warnings that a person is thinking about suicide. If you notice any of the following signs in someone, try to get the person to talk to someone who can help. If he or she will not, tell an adult why you are worried about that person. It is important to get help before it is too late.

If a friend has problems that are overwhelming her, urge her to talk to a concerned adult or professional counselor.

Q&A

Eating Disorders

Q: My friend hates food. She practically never eats. Even when she has food, she seems to just play with it. She is getting thinner and thinner, yet she says she needs to lose weight. What's going on with her? Does she have a mental disorder or an eating disorder?

A: Both. Eating disorders such as anorexia nervosa, in which a person refuses to eat, have long been regarded as emotionally based mental disorders. Eating disorders are dangerous and lead to serious physical illness and even death. Get some help for your friend now. Tell an adult why you are worried about her.

The Warning Signs of Suicide

- Statements such as "They'll be sorry when I'm gone" or "I wish I could sleep forever"

- Avoiding activities involving friends or family

- Low level of energy

- Taking greater risks than usual

- Loss of interest in hobbies, sports, job, or school

- Giving away prized personal possessions

- A past history of suicide attempts. Eighty percent of suicides have attempted suicide before.

What the Numbers Mean

Every year, between 300,000 and 600,000 teens attempt suicide. Nearly 5,000 succeed. Most teens who talk about suicide or attempt it are really pleading for help. They do not really want death—they just want their troubles to go away. When anyone attempts suicide, he or she is choosing a permanent solution to a temporary problem.

Although most teens who attempt suicide do not really want to die, many do. That is why it is important to seek help for yourself or a friend when problems seem overwhelming. Remember that you are never alone. With the help of a concerned adult or a professional counselor, you can find solutions to your problems. You can prevent suicide.

in your journal

Imagine that you write an advice column for teens. You receive a letter from a teen who says he is beginning to think that suicide is the only solution to the stress he feels. In your journal, write an answer to that person.

Review
Lesson 5

Using complete sentences, answer the following questions on a separate sheet of paper.

Reviewing Terms and Facts

1. **Vocabulary** Which of the following is a condition in which a person is not able to function in the real world: *neurosis, psychosis, clinical depression?* Describe each one.

2. **Recall** Name five mental disorders.

Thinking Critically

3. **Apply** Choose two defense mechanisms. For each, describe how the mechanism could be helpful for a short period but harmful for an extended period.

4. **Compare** Explain how the behavior of someone with normal anxiety is similar to that of someone who has an anxiety disorder.

Applying Health Concepts

5. **Health of Others** Imagine that you have a friend who daydreams all the time. Write a note telling that person what advice you have for him or her.

Sources of Help

This lesson will help you find answers to questions that teens often ask about where to get help for mental health problems. For example:

▶ **How do I know when the situation is serious enough to ask for help?**

▶ **Who can really help?**

▶ **What responsibility do I have for friends in trouble?**

in your journal

Is it easy for you to ask for help with problems? Why or why not? Write your answer in your journal.

Knowing When to Go for Help

Everyone needs help in solving problems at one time or another. Being able to ask for help is a sign that you are growing up. It shows that you are capable of deciding which problems or parts of a problem you need help with and which you can solve yourself.

Figure 3.13
Warning Signs

■ Suspecting that everyone is against you	■ Aches and pains that seem to have no medical cause
■ Continually feeling sad	■ Feelings of hopelessness
■ Sudden or extreme changes in mood	■ Trouble sleeping or frequent nightmares
■ Trouble concentrating or making decisions	■ Taking extreme or unusual risks
■ Does not take care of self	■ Loss of appetite

Teens who are mature are not afraid to ask for help in solving problems.

With mental and emotional health problems, knowing when to seek help is largely a matter of paying attention to warning signs. Paying attention to these signs could actually save a life. **Figure 3.13** shows some warning signs that often signal serious problems. Naturally, no one warning signal is a sure sign of a serious problem. On the other hand, any one signal may be a symptom of an unhealthy buildup of stress. If you experience—or see in another person—any of the warning signs over a period of days or weeks, something may be seriously wrong. It is time to go for help, just to be on the safe side.

Knowing Who Can Help

Talking out your problems with someone will not make them vanish instantly. It will, however, reassure you that you are not alone. This is often the first step in solving the problem. There are a number of people you can turn to when you or someone you know has a serious emotional problem (see **Figure 3.14**).

Language Arts Connection

Help in Any Language ACTIVITY!

Needing help from time to time is a universal need. There are dozens of ways to say "help me" both with and without words. In Spanish, it is ayúdame. Work with a partner to compile a list of different ways to ask for help. Ask people from different cultural backgrounds to tell you how to ask for help in their native language. Don't forget sign language.

Figure 3.14
Sources of Help

Identify your problem.

Decision to get help

Parent or Other Family Member. Families are built-in support systems. A **support system** is *a network of people available for help when needed.* A parent, older brother or sister, or grandparent, can be a great source of help. These people care about you the most.

Mental Health Professional. These people are specially trained to deal with mental and emotional problems. Your family doctor or school counselor can help you find the program for you.

School Nurse. Nurses are specially trained to understand and deal with the problems of teenagers. They can give you real help and will respect your privacy.

Priest, Minister, Rabbi, or Other Clergy Member. The leader of your church, synagogue, or mosque may be a good person to talk to. Members of the clergy are educated in counseling people with emotional problems.

Teacher or School Counselor. A teacher or guidance counselor that you like and trust could be a friend when you are in need.

Hot Line. Teen hot lines are *special telephone services that teens can call when feeling stress.* Some hot lines are answered by teens; others are answered by adults. Both groups are trained to listen to and help teens experiencing a crisis.

Figure 3.15
What to Do if Someone Talks About Suicide

Listen. Let the person talk. This lets your friend know that you are there for him or her. Your calmness can also be a source of comfort to your friend. Do not, however, promise to keep the discussion secret.

Talk. Never challenge the person to carry out the suicide threat. Tell your friend that his or her life is very important to you. Point out that this bad time will pass. Urge your friend to come with you now to get some help. Tell your friend that you will stick by him or her.

Troubled Friends

Figure 3.15 explains what to do if someone you know talks about suicide. However, there may be times when you feel that it takes all of your time and energy to keep your own stress under control. What is your obligation to your friends or sisters and brothers? Are you supposed to get involved with their problems too? Are you responsible for their health and safety? These are questions that everyone must answer for himself or herself. Consider the following points when answering them.

MAKING HEALTHY DECISIONS
Deciding Whether to Tell

*M*ason and Steve have known each other since second grade. From the start, they got along well and have always run with the same crowd. For years each has considered the other to be among his closest friends.

Somehow, this year things have begun to change. For one reason or another Mason hasn't seen as much of Steve as before. Lately, Mason has made a special effort to invite Steve to join in some activities. Steve always seems to have a reason not to go. When they do run into each other, Steve seems different to Mason. Once a generally happy, easygoing guy, Steve now always appears sad.

As Mason became more and more aware of the changes in Steve, he decided to talk to him. Steve confided that he just could not shake his sadness. He said he started feeling sad a few months ago because of some problems at home, but now he does not even know why he feels sad.

Mason suggested that Steve talk to a counselor at school or to a teacher, but Steve refused. "There's no point. I can't be helped. It's just hopeless," said Steve. When Mason offered to talk to someone for Steve, Steve got angry. "Mind your own business," shouted Steve. "If you want to stay my friend, you'd better not tell anyone about how I feel."

Everyone who is mentally and physically capable must take responsibility for his or her own behavior. Even if you help a friend, the final outcome is your friend's responsibility.

Another consideration is how you feel when you need help. The golden rule to treat others as you would have them treat you still makes a lot of sense. Perhaps no one needs immediate help more than people thinking of suicide.

Review

Using complete sentences, answer the following questions on a separate sheet of paper.

Reviewing Terms and Facts

1. **Recall**   When may a warning sign signal that a person has a serious problem?

2. **Vocabulary**   Define the term *support system*. Use it in an original sentence.

Thinking Critically

3. **Interpret**   One of your friends has been acting irritable for a couple of weeks. You have noticed that he hasn't been eating much and that he seems suspicious of you. Should you get involved? If so, what should you do?

4. **Summarize**   Describe what you would do, and not do, if a friend threatened suicide.

Applying Health Concepts

5. **Consumer Health Figure 3.14** on page 91 lists possible sources of help. For as many sources as possible, list the names of people you know whom you would recommend as people to go to with problems.

Now Mason does not know what to do. He is worried about Steve and thinks Steve might need help, but he is not sure. He is sure that he does not want to lose Steve's friendship. He decides to use the step-by-step decision-making process to make up his mind:

❶ **State the situation**
❷ **List the options**
❸ **Weigh the possible outcomes**
❹ **Consider your values**
❺ **Make a decision and act**
❻ **Evaluate the decision**

Follow-up Activities

1. Compare Steve's behavior with the warning signs in **Figure 3.13** on page 90. Could this information help him make a decision?

2. Apply the six steps of the decision-making process to Mason's story.

Chapter Summary

► Personality is shaped by heredity, environment, and behavior. (Lesson 1)

► The view that you have of yourself is your self-concept. (Lesson 2)

► Self-esteem results from believing that you are competent and worthy of happiness. (Lesson 2)

► Everyone has three basic emotional needs—the need to love and be loved, the need to belong, and the need to feel worthwhile. (Lesson 3)

► During the teen years, changes in the body cause emotions to shift suddenly. (Lesson 3)

► Every change in your life causes some stress. (Lesson 4)

► Developing good time-management skills can help you control stress in your life. (Lesson 4)

► Defense mechanisms are short-term ways of dealing with stress. (Lesson 5)

► Everyone needs help from time to time in solving problems. (Lesson 6)

Using Health Terms

On a separate sheet of paper, write the vocabulary term that best matches each definition given below.

1. Your ability to deal in a reasonable way with the stresses and changes of everyday life (Lesson 1)

2. A special mix of traits, feelings, attitudes, and habits (Lesson 1)

3. The way you feel about yourself (Lesson 2)

4. Chemical substances that regulate many body functions (Lesson 3)

5. Your body's response to changes around you (Lesson 4)

6. Extreme tiredness caused by your mental state (Lesson 4)

7. Short-term ways of dealing with stress (Lesson 5)

8. A fear that gets in the way of a person's ability to function in daily life (Lesson 5)

9. A network of people available for help when needed (Lesson 6)

Reviewing Main Ideas

Using complete sentences, answer the following questions on a separate sheet of paper.

1. What are seven signs of good mental health? (Lesson 1)

2. What are two ways to develop good mental health habits? (Lesson 1)

3. How does having a realistic self-concept compare with having an unrealistic self-concept? (Lesson 2)

4. Why do people with high self-esteem generally take better care of themselves than do people with low self-esteem? (Lesson 2)

5. How can personality influence the way you handle your emotions? (Lesson 3)

6. Describe what happens to you during the fight-or-flight response. (Lesson 4)

7. What are five tips for effectively managing your stress? (Lesson 4)

8. List and explain at least three defense mechanisms. (Lesson 5)

9. What are the physical and emotional causes of mental disorders? (Lesson 5)

10. What are five good sources of help for mental and emotional problems? (Lesson 6)

Thinking Critically

Using complete sentences, answer the following questions on a separate sheet of paper.

1. **Give Examples** What parts of your environment can you control to help your mental health? (Lesson 1)

2. **Synthesize** What could you do to raise a friend's or a family member's self-esteem? (Lesson 2)

3. **Hypothesize** Why might some attempts to communicate be unsuccessful, even when you follow all the tips for effective communication? (Lesson 3)

4. **Compare and Contrast** How can you tell the difference between physical and psychological fatigue in someone else? (Lesson 4)

5. **Give Examples** How can you identify a phobia? (Lesson 5)

6. **Evaluate** What defense mechanisms do you use most? (Lesson 5)

7. **Explain** Why should you never dare or challenge a person to carry out a suicide threat? (Lesson 6)

8. **Hypothesize** Do you think a person might say he or she didn't want help when he or she was really hoping someone would help? Explain your answer. (Lesson 6)

Your Action Plan

Most teens have periods of low self-esteem and other problems that worry them. There are probably aspects of your mental and emotional health that you would like to improve. To improve your mental and emotional health, you need to set a long-term goal.

If you are having trouble thinking of a goal, review your private journal entries for this chapter. What do they tell you about yourself that you didn't know before? Once you've established what your long-term goal is, write it down. Make sure your goal is realistic.

Then, think of a series of short-term goals, or things to do to gain your long-term goal. Write these down. Plan a schedule for checking your progress. Ask a family member or a friend to help you judge your progress. Be proud of your success.

Building Your Portfolio

1. Interview students about how they manage stress. Ask about specific incidents and how they dealt with them. Take notes and write a short summary of any of the ideas *you* could use to help you manage stress. Keep these ideas in your portfolio.

2. Ask as many people as possible to recall something someone else did to brighten their day. Tell them it could be as simple as a smile or as spectacular as a surprise party. List the responses and analyze them. What kinds of things show up the most? Put your analysis and the list in your portfolio.

In Your Home and Community

1. Choose a family member and give him or her a specific day to be special. On that day, go out of your way to build up the family member's self-esteem by just being nice to him or her. Spend time with the person, listen, and show that you care. Choose a different family member each week.

2. Would you like to help younger kids feel better about themselves? Ask a counselor or teacher in your school to help you start a teen mentor program. Be sure to agree on some goals and rules before the program gets going.

Unit 2
Social and Public Health

97

Chapter 4
Your Social Health

Student Expectations

After reading this chapter, you should be able to:

1. Explain how to build healthy relationships with other people.
2. Identify and practice important communication skills.
3. List different kinds of families and describe ways that families are changing.
4. Describe the role that friendship plays in social health.
5. Discuss dating practices and marriage patterns.
6. List and describe the roles and responsibilities of parents.

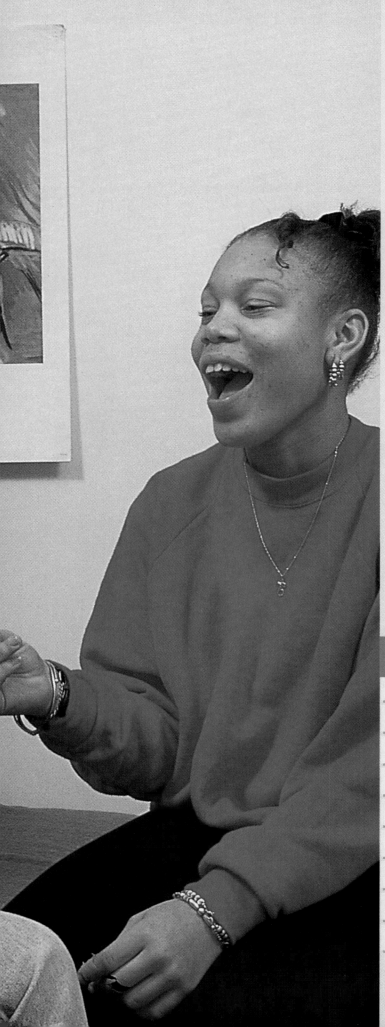

NO TRESPASSING! That's what the sign on the outside of my bedroom door says. I put it there to keep out my little brother.

I like to come in here, shut the door, and listen to music. My parents don't like my music. They think it's just noise. I've tried to explain it to them, but they won't listen.

It seems like there are a lot of things these days that are hard to talk to my folks about. Now my friends are different. I can talk to them about anything. I wish I had my own phone. Then I could talk to my friends anytime in private, here in my own room. It's so much easier to explain things to someone my own age.

Sometimes I do need to talk to an older person, though. Luckily for me there is one adult I can relate to. My mom's sister Theresa is great. She seems to understand what it's like to be my age. I can talk to her about things I can't talk to my parents about—like how I feel about some of my friends, and why I want to be more independent. She doesn't always agree with me, but she's good at listening and at explaining things. I want to be like her when I'm older.

in your journal

Read the story on this page. Does it sound familiar? Are your relationships changing? Start your private journal entries on social health by answering these questions:

► In general, how do you feel that you get along with other people?

► What would you like to change about your relationship with family members?

► What do you like about your friendships? What do you dislike?

When you reach the end of the chapter, you will use your journal entries to make an action plan.

Building Healthy Relationships

This lesson will help you find answers to questions that teens often ask about relationships. For example:

► How can I learn to get along better with others?

► What should I do when I disagree with what someone says?

► What's the secret of being a successful team player?

Words to Know

social health
relationships
communication
compromise
cooperation
tolerance

What Is Social Health?

Two sides of your health triangle are physical health and mental health. The third side is social health. **Social health** is *your ability to get along with the people around you.* When you have good social health, you work well as a member of a group. You also know how to make and keep friends and how to offer and get help when it is needed. People with good social health

■ can accept differences in other people.

■ get along with family members.

■ meet people easily.

■ have at least one or two close friends.

■ can accept other people's ideas and suggestions when they are working in a group.

■ can make friends with people of both sexes.

■ continue to take part in an activity even when other people disagree about what to do.

Taking part in a group project at school helps you build your social skills.

Social Health and Relationships

Your social health is tied directly to your relationships with other people. **Relationships** (ri·LAY·shuhn·ships) are *the connections you have with other people and groups in your life*. These connections are based on how you relate to, or act toward, others. Your life is full of relationships. **Figure 4.1** shows some of them.

Building Healthy Relationships

Most people do not relate to everyone in their lives in exactly the same way. How you act with a brother or sister, for example, may be very different from how you act with a parent or teacher. You may have a very close relationship with one friend, and more casual relationships with other friends. You may choose not to have any kind of friendship with some people if their values are very different from your own. What is important about all your relationships is that they be as healthy as possible.

You can build healthy relationships by learning three key skills of social health. They are *communication, compromise,* and *cooperation.* These skills will help you get along with others.

in your journal

The list on the facing page identifies the characteristics of good social health. Which of those characteristics do you feel you already have? Which do you need to work on? What other qualities do you think contribute to good social health? Write your responses in your journal.

Figure 4.1
Balancing Relationships

It's not always easy to find the right balance among all the different people in your life. Most people experience conflicts from time to time.

Communication

Communication is *the exchange of thoughts, ideas, and beliefs between two or more people.* By communicating, you get to know people. Communication also enables you to share your thoughts and feelings and have a good time with people. Communication also helps you solve problems. You will learn more about developing communication skills in Lesson 2.

Sometimes disagreements occur between two people or groups of people. **Figure 4.2** gives some rules for good communication when these disagreements occur.

No Way!

It is important to learn to compromise, but it is just as important to learn never to compromise about matters you believe in strongly. Suppose someone tries to get you to do something you believe is wrong. When you are faced with this situation, the right response is not to compromise. The right answer is to say, "No way!"

Compromise

Have there ever been times when you wanted to see a movie and your friend wanted to play video games but there was not enough money for both? Do you remember how you handled the problem? At such times, compromise might be the answer. **Compromise** (KAHM·pruh·myz) is *the result of each person's giving up something in order to reach a solution that satisfies everyone.* Compromise is also known as "give and take."

Compromise can take many forms. Consider the choice between a movie and video games. The compromise might be that your friend gets to choose the activity this time and you get to choose next time. It may be that the two of you decide to do something completely different. Whatever form the compromise takes, it helps a relationship run smoothly. It also accomplishes something that arguing never will: it leads to positive action.

Figure 4.2
Communication Tips

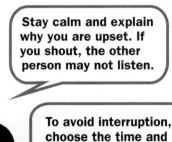

Stay calm and explain why you are upset. If you shout, the other person may not listen.

To avoid interruption, choose the time and place carefully.

Concentrate on the main problem and avoid raising side issues.

After you have spoken, give the other person a chance to respond.

Cooperation

Cooperation is *working together for the good of all.* Another name for cooperation is *teamwork.* Suppose you and a friend are working together to make a science display for the school fair. In order to have the project ready on time, you decide to share responsibilities. By cooperating with each other, you reach a solution. For example, you might design labels and captions while your friend collects samples. Together, you and your friend assemble the display. That's cooperation!

Working as a team builds stronger relationships. To be a good team player, you need to be willing to work with and listen to others. You also need to have a helpful attitude.

Acceptance of Individual Differences

People of many different races, religions, and cultural groups live in the United States. Part of good social health is tolerance of all these individual differences. **Tolerance** (TAHL·er·ens) means *accepting and respecting other people's beliefs and customs.* It helps you recognize that different people have a right to express themselves in ways that may be different from your own. At the same time, you recognize that people are more alike than they are different. Tolerance helps you get along with others.

A person with good social health also shows tolerance of people of all ages. Disagreements sometimes arise between people of different generations. Teens may have difficulty getting along with older adults because they have different ways of talking, dressing, and acting. You need to be willing to accept all people and to develop an understanding of their point of view.

Caring and Respect

You can show tolerance within your family, too. Good social health includes respecting family members. That means listening to your parents' point of view and learning how to communicate your opinions. It means being considerate and polite. It means not teasing your brothers or sisters about mistakes they make. When you have good social health, you can accept family members—faults and all—because you care for them.

Cultural Diversity

"Getting to Know You" ACTIVITY!

Learning about the customs and beliefs of various groups of people helps develop tolerance. The more you know about other people, the easier it is to understand and accept them. Get to know another cultural group by attending an event such as the following:

► Cinco de Mayo
► Passover seder
► Kwanzaa observance
► Native American powwow
► Vietnamese New Year celebration
► A neighborhood block party

Take photographs and share them with your classmates.

Learning about other people's beliefs and customs is an important step toward accepting individual differences.

Belonging to a Group

Have you ever stopped to think about the number of groups to which you belong? You belong to your family, to your class at school, and to your circle of friends. You may be part of a club, a team, or a religious group. Certainly you are a member of a very large group known as society.

The health of each group depends on the social health of each of its members. Each member shares an equal responsibility for maintaining the health of the group. By the same token, the health of every member is affected by the overall health of the group.

You can see how this works if you think about a soccer team. Each member of the team is responsible for showing up for practice, staying healthy, and playing as well as he or she can. That way, the whole team benefits. When the team plays well together, each member benefits. Similarly, when one member lets the team down, the whole team is affected and may not play as well as usual. When the team plays badly, everyone suffers.

Lesson 1

Review

Using complete sentences, answer the following questions on a separate sheet of paper.

Reviewing Terms and Facts

1. **Vocabulary** Explain in your own words what *social health* means.

2. **Recall** What is the term that means "accepting and respecting other people's beliefs and customs"?

3. **Explain** What are some ways of showing respect for members of your family?

Thinking Critically

4. **Compare** Use real-life examples to explain the difference between compromise and cooperation.

5. **Illustrate** What are some ways that teens and older adults can demonstrate greater tolerance toward one another.

6. **Analyze** List the different groups to which you belong. Identify one way you keep one of those groups healthy and one way it keeps you healthy.

Applying Health Concepts

7. **Health of Others** Pretend you are the leader of a group that is planning a community project, such as cleaning up litter in a park, conducting a recycling campaign, or planning a food drive. Decide what tasks are involved and make a plan to show how members of the group can cooperate to meet the overall goals of the group. If possible, carry out your plan.

8. **Growth and Development** Create an illustrated guidebook to cultural events, customs, traditions, organizations, festivals, and historical landmarks in your community. Include specific dates and locations of the events.

Developing Communication Skills

This lesson will help you find answers to questions that teens often ask about communicating. For example:

- ▶ **How can I learn to communicate better?**
- ▶ **Why are some people easier to talk to than others?**
- ▶ **What is body language and what do I need to know about it?**
- ▶ **How do I say no to my friends without offending them?**
- ▶ **How can I persuade my friends to make the right decisions?**

Words to Know

verbal communication
active listening
body language
eye contact
refusal skills

The Importance of Communicating

The foundation of any relationship is the ability to communicate. People need to communicate to start a relationship and to keep a relationship strong. Communicating helps you get to know other people. Sharing interests, experiences, feelings, and concerns helps people grow closer together.

Talking is the main way most people communicate. Talking is a form of verbal communication. **Verbal communication** means *using words to express thoughts, ideas, beliefs, and wants.*

Just talking to another person does not guarantee good communication. The listener may be daydreaming and may not actually listen to what the speaker is saying. The speaker may be talking too fast for the listener to follow along. Good communication is a skill. It needs to be learned and practiced.

Communication skills don't just happen. They need to be practiced.

Speaking Skills

Communication is a two-way street—giving and receiving messages. Speaking is the giving part. Good communication involves speaking clearly and carefully. Developing speaking skills takes practice. Here are some tips for improving your speaking skills.

- **Avoid nonstop talking.** Find a balance between sharing your experiences and letting the other person talk. If you do all the talking, the other person may become bored and tune out.

- **Think before you speak.** Avoid embarrassing yourself or hurting the other person by saying something you will later regret. Allow your message to go through your brain before it comes out of your mouth.

- **Be positive.** No one likes to listen to someone who's grumpy all the time. Try to be cheerful and enthusiastic—unless, of course, you have a serious problem to discuss.

- **Be aware of your listener.** Make sure the other person understands what you are saying. Ask for feedback from time to time.

- **Be direct.** Say what you want to say. Be direct about your values and about what's important to you.

- **Be creative.** If your listener doesn't understand you the first time you say something, express the idea in a different way.

A Conversation Tip

You may have less of a problem communicating with family members and friends. Communicating may be more difficult with a person you are just getting to know. For example, you might say, "Do you play basketball?" The other person might reply "No" and that's the end of the conversation! Instead of asking questions that require only a yes or no, ask open-ended questions (see **Figure 4.3**).

Figure 4.3
Conversation Starters

Ask open–ended questions that encourage communication.

For example, you might say, "What hobbies do you have?" Open-ended questions encourage the other person to say more. In the process, the person will reveal information you can use to keep the conversation going—"Oh, yeah? I play the guitar, too."

Listening Skills

Listening is the receiving part of communication. Good communication requires active listening. **Active listening** means *hearing, thinking about, and responding to the other person's message.* Don't just sit back and absorb the sound waves. Make a real effort to understand what the person is saying. Here are some tips for improving your listening skills.

■ **Pay attention.** Concentrate on what the other person is saying. Give the speaker your undivided attention. For example, don't try to watch TV and listen at the same time. Don't be thinking about what you're going to say next.

■ **Provide feedback.** Let the other person know you're listening by nodding your head, asking questions, or saying to him or her, "Then what happened?"

■ **Let the person finish speaking.** She or he will be better able to explain if there are no interruptions.

■ **Stay calm.** Even if you're hearing something you don't like, stay calm instead of getting angry. Breathe deeply.

■ **Keep an open mind.** Listen even if you disagree. Accept that other people will not always think the same way you do.

in your journal

Look at the lists of speaking skills and listening skills. From each list, choose one skill that you need to work on. Write it in your journal. Over the next week, concentrate on improving those skills. Record your progress in your journal.

What movies would you recommend?

Who's your favorite rock group?

I heard you went to Alaska. What was it like?

Social Rules

Different cultures have different ways of showing social courtesies. For example, in some cultures it is customary to shake hands upon meeting. In others, people hug each other when they meet. Ask members of your community to give you other examples of cultural courtesies and share them with your classmates. Why is it important to know about these social rules?

Body language sends powerful messages. If these two teens were applying for a part-time job, who do you think would be chosen?

Body Language

"I'm okay," you say bravely, but your friend knows you are really feeling scared. Your body language—drooping shoulders, downcast look, and trembling lip—gives you away.

Body language is *a form of nonverbal communication.* Without saying a word, people can send messages by the way they hold their bodies (posture), by the expressions on their faces, by the gestures they use, and by the clothes they wear.

Speakers and listeners need to be aware of body language. Body language can be a sign of a person's true feelings, as in the example above. Some body language, such as smiling and nodding, encourage communication. Other forms, such as frowning and crossing arms tightly across the chest, discourage communication.

A special type of body language is eye contact. **Eye contact** is *direct visual contact with another person's eyes.* You can use eye contact to show that you are sincere or listening carefully. In the United States, eye contact is acceptable, but in some cultures, it is seen as a sign of rudeness.

MAKING HEALTHY DECISIONS
Deciding to Say No

*C*hristy plays goalie on her school's soccer team. Her coach asked her to join a traveling soccer team this summer. At first, Christy was excited at the thought of being on the team. She loves playing soccer. Being able to play during the summer would help improve her skills. Traveling around the state would be fun.

There's a problem, however. Christy has already made a commitment for the summer. The McGuires, who live across the street from Christy, are going away for a month. Christy has promised to feed their cat every day, mow the lawn weekly, and water the houseplants. The McGuires have agreed to pay Christy $20 a week for her work. Christy is looking forward to earning some money. She has been

saving for a new bicycle, and that extra money would give her what she needs.

So now Christy is confused. Should she tour with the team this summer or honor her commitment to her neighbors? She decided to use the step-by-step decision-making process to help her evaluate her options and make a decision:

❶ **State the situation**
❷ **List the options**
❸ **Weigh the possible outcomes**
❹ **Consider your values**
❺ **Make a decision and act**
❻ **Evaluate the decision**

Refusal Skills

To develop relationships, you need to be open to the ideas and wishes of other people. However, sometimes friends and acquaintances want you to do something that you do not want to do. Maybe you don't have the time. Maybe it's something that goes against your values or your family's values. Maybe you're just not interested. You might be afraid to say no, fearing that he or she might not like you anymore or might not include you in future activities. You might be afraid of hurting his or her feelings.

Refusal skills are helpful for these situations. **Refusal skills** are *communication strategies that help you say no effectively.* Using these skills will help you be true to yourself. You can say no without feeling guilty or uncomfortable. Other people will respect you for being honest about your needs and wants.

No thanks. I'm not interested.

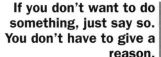

If you don't want to do something, just say so. You don't have to give a reason.

Follow-up Activities

1. Apply the six steps of the decision-making process to Christy's story.

2. Along with a partner, role-play a scene in which Christy turns down the coach's offer to be on the traveling soccer team. Have her use refusal skills.

3. Now role-play a scene in which Christy explains to the McGuires that she cannot keep her promise. Think about suggestions she can make for helping them deal with the problem she has created.

Teen Issues

Setting Priorities

Knowing your short-term and long-term goals can help you say no to activities that don't fit your plan. Make a list of your goals for this week. Then, if a friend asks you to hang out at the mall on Saturday afternoon, consider how doing so will affect your goals.

How to Say No

When you need to say no to someone, you need to show that you mean what you say. Here are some suggestions you can follow to build your refusal skills.

- **Be honest.** Tell the other person exactly how you feel about the situation. You can explain your decision if you like, but you are not obliged to give an explanation.

- **Be friendly and polite.** Don't insult or yell at the other person.

- **Match your tone to your message.** If your voice sounds wishy-washy, the other person might try to change your mind. Sound firm when you say no.

- **Use eye contact.** This will show that you mean what you say.

- **Offer an alternative.** Suggest something—a different time, a different activity—that would be more acceptable to you.

Lesson 2 Review

Using complete sentences, answer the following questions on a separate sheet of paper.

Reviewing Terms and Facts

1. **Recall**   What are six ways of improving speaking skills?

2. **List**   Give five tips for being an active listener.

3. **Vocabulary**   What is body language? Give some examples of ways people communicate using body language.

Thinking Critically

4. **Analyze**   Choose someone you consider to be a particularly good communicator. Identify the skills that person uses to communicate so well.

5. **Describe**   Give examples of body language that might indicate a person is not listening attentively.

6. **Synthesize**   A friend is participating in a walkathon for a local charity. He asks you to pledge two dollars for every mile he walks. You don't have any extra money right now. How can you say no without making your friend angry?

Applying Health Concepts

7. **Growth and Development**   Every day for the next week, make an effort to say something positive to family members, teachers, or classmates. Keep a log of your positive statements. At the end of the week, write a paper describing how giving positive reinforcement can affect people's emotional health.

8. **Personal Health**   Pretend you wrote a best-selling book on communication skills. Give the book a title and write a summary of how the book can help improve these skills and why they are important for success. Create and illustrate the book's cover.

9. **Health of Others**   Make a videotape that demonstrates the impact of nonverbal communication. Tape the body language of family members and friends, and narrate the tape explaining how body language sends messages. Ask the audience to interpret each person's message from his or her body language.

Social Health and Your Family

This lesson will help you find answers to questions that teens often ask about families. For example:

► **What makes families different from other groups?**
► **What are some ways my family helps me?**
► **What are some ways I help my family?**
► **How are families different today from the way they used to be?**
► **Whom can I turn to if I have family problems?**

Words to Know

**family
couple family
nuclear family
single-parent
   family
extended family
blended family
stepparent**

The Importance of Families

Humans are social beings. Each of us needs to feel that he or she belongs. Most of the time, this need to belong is satisfied by groups. In your lifetime, you will belong to many groups.

The first group to which we belong is the **family,** *the basic unit of society.* All societies in the world are made up of families. It is within the family that you share experiences and develop lifetime bonds. Being part of a family means acquiring values, building traditions, and feeling the comfort of belonging.

In your family, you also begin to develop social skills. Through your family, you form a sense of who you are. Through your family, you also learn to care for and share with others.

Your social health starts with your family. Family members have been influencing your values and attitudes since you were born.

The Family

Members of a family have special emotional bonds with one another. The family provides for and nurtures its members. It is also responsible for guiding its members and teaching them right from wrong. You learn your values through your family.

Family Roles

In most societies, different family members have different roles, or jobs. In our society, it is the job of the adults of the family to supply food, clothing, shelter, and medical care for the rest of the family. The adults are also responsible for teaching the children right from wrong and helping them grow. Children, in turn, take on more responsibilities as they grow older. In doing so, they learn how to succeed as adults.

Kinds of Families

There are many different kinds of families in our society. **Figure 4.4** shows five of the most common family structures, but many others exist as well. It is not unusual in our society for family structures to change many times. For example, single adults, or adults who are not married, are also part of a family—the family they grew up with.

Also, when people do not live close to other family members, they may look upon close friends as almost a family group. Thus, family structures are very flexible and have many variations. Every family has special characteristics that each member can enjoy.

Figure 4.4
Kinds of Families

Families today come in many shapes and sizes.

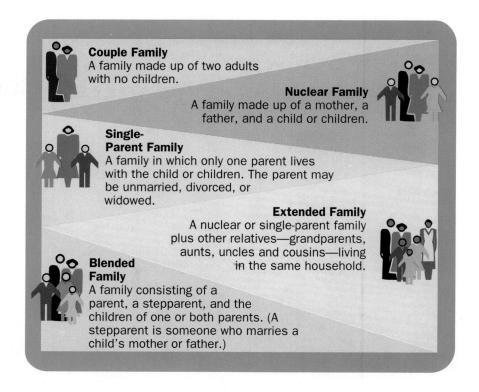

Couple Family
A family made up of two adults with no children.

Nuclear Family
A family made up of a mother, a father, and a child or children.

Single-Parent Family
A family in which only one parent lives with the child or children. The parent may be unmarried, divorced, or widowed.

Extended Family
A nuclear or single-parent family plus other relatives—grandparents, aunts, uncles and cousins—living in the same household.

Blended Family
A family consisting of a parent, a stepparent, and the children of one or both parents. (A stepparent is someone who marries a child's mother or father.)

Changing Families

In recent years, many major changes have taken place in family structure, roles, and lifestyles. These changes affect the idea of "family" in our society. They have also affected the ways children in our society are cared for.

Trends Affecting Families

Some of the ways American families have changed include the following trends of recent years:

- **more smaller families.** Married couples these days are having fewer children. Some of them feel they have time and energy for only one or two children. Other reasons for smaller families include the expense of raising a family and concerns about overcrowding the earth.

- **more single-parent families.** One-quarter of the families in the country are now headed by one parent, usually the mother. **Figure 4.5** shows how the number of single-parent families has been increasing in recent decades.

- **more dual-career families.** In more and more families, both parents have jobs outside the home. One reason for this is the expense of supporting a family. Another reason is that some parents like their jobs and want to keep working after they have children.

These trends have changed the ways families operate. Today, many parents take their children to child-care centers during the week. Many communities offer after-school activities and other support programs for families.

With more single-parent and dual-career families, teens often have to do more to help at home.

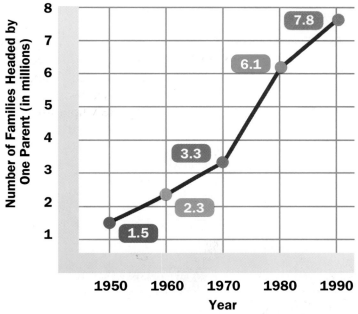

Figure 4.5

Changing Families in the United States

Number of Families Headed by One Parent (in millions)

- 1950: 1.5
- 1960: 2.3
- 1970: 3.3
- 1980: 6.1
- 1990: 7.8

Year

Source: U.S. Department of Commerce, Bureau of the Census, Current Population Report, Series P-20 Household and Family Characteristics Table I, 1993

Strengthening Families

Living in a family brings many joys. It also presents certain challenges. For a family to be healthy, it must respond to these challenges. If one family member is troubled or does not get along with another, the family as a whole suffers.

Strong family relationships depend on communication and shared values. In healthy families, members feel free to express their thoughts and feelings. Yet they listen to and value what others have to say.

Sharing celebrations and traditions strengthens family bonds. What traditions does your family observe?

Dealing with Family Problems

All families have problems from time to time. Good communication within the family can help members deal with many of their problems. For serious problems, such as those listed below, people may need to seek outside help.

Separation and Divorce When parents can no longer get along, they may separate and divorce. Divorcing parents may argue over the care and custody of the children. Family members must adjust to new living arrangements. The divided family may have less money to live on.

Illness A serious illness or accident can disrupt family life. Family members may need to spend a great deal of time caring for the ill or hurt person. Medical bills may drain the family's finances.

LIFE SKILLS
Improving Family Relationships

*D*o you sometimes get the feeling that you just don't sit down and *talk* with your family anymore? Busy schedules, outside interests, and rushed meals can keep families from spending time together. You can do something to change that and to improve relationships within your family.

Suggest that you have regular family meetings. Just like a student council or 4-H Club, family members can meet to talk about one another's activities, plan events such as weekend outings or vacations, and discuss problems. Family meetings can improve communication and keep the family healthy.

Discuss the idea with your family members and get their help. Together, you can decide when and where to have the meeting. Choose a time that is convenient for everyone. Choose a place free of distractions so that everyone will focus on the conversation. Make sure everyone agrees to turn off the TV during the meeting. Some families hold meetings around the dinner table after sharing a meal together.

Suggest that everyone make notes about items they want to talk about at the meeting. You could start a list and place it on the refrigerator door. That way,

Unemployment   A parent may lose her or his job. If that parent provided the family's main or only income, the family may have to change its way of living. Also, an unemployed parent may feel additional stress and may need extra emotional support.

Substance Abuse   A family member may become dependent on, or addicted to, alcohol or other drugs. Other family members may live in constant tension, never knowing how the addicted person will act. The addicted family member may cause problems by not carrying out responsibilities.

Abuse of Family Members   A family member may mistreat another family member. The abuse may be physical, such as hitting, slapping, or choking, or it may be emotional, such as taunting or being cruel. Sexual abuse occurs when one person forces a sexual act on another.

Running Away

Serious family problems can cause teens a great deal of stress. Some teens react to family problems by turning inward. They don't feel like talking to anyone or being with anyone.

Some teens try to get away from a problem by leaving home. Running away often leads to other problems, however. Runaways usually have no place to live and no money for food. Some runaways turn to crime. Many become the victims of crime.

The key to getting help is talking about the problem. Teens need to talk with someone they trust. That could be a parent, another family member, or a person in the school or community.

Neglect

Another type of abuse is neglect. Neglect occurs when adult family members fail to provide adequate food, clothing, or shelter for children. Neglect also means failure to meet children's emotional and social needs.

Running away is never the best solution. Do everything you can to urge a friend to get help from a trusted adult.

other family members can add to the list. Everyone will know ahead of time what topics will be discussed.

The family will need to agree on guidelines for the meeting. For example: Everyone is given a chance to speak his or her mind; Everyone is encouraged to express her or his opinion; No one laughs at or puts down the ideas of another person.

Try to stick to a time limit for your meeting. This will encourage everyone to get down to business. Besides, no one likes to sit through meetings that run too long.

Try to have family meetings on a regular basis. Your family will look forward to this time together.

Follow-up Activity

Take a look at the way you and your family communicate. Do you think you set aside enough time to talk things over? Can you think of some ways of improving communication within the family? If so, make a plan like the one described above. Talk it over with your family. Then make it happen.

Community Counseling

Listed below are some of the people in the community that troubled teens can turn to.

- **Teachers, school guidance counselors, social workers.** They want to help students solve problems and succeed.

- **Peer counselors.** Some schools and religious groups train young people to help peers with problems.

- **Religious leaders.** Ministers, priests, rabbis, and mullahs are trained to counsel people.

- **Doctors, nurses.** Medical workers in clinics can help with health problems.

- **Youth leaders.** Leaders of groups such as Scouts, 4-H, YMCA, and YWCA are ready to help.

- **Crisis center volunteers.** These people offer emergency help.

- **Support group leaders.** In support groups teens can talk with others with similar problems.

> There is always someone who will listen to you. Don't hesitate to call if you think you need help.

Lesson 3 Review

Using complete sentences, answer the following questions on a separate sheet of paper.

Reviewing Terms and Facts

1. **Vocabulary** What is the difference between an extended family and a blended family?

2. **Recall** What three trends have changed families?

3. **List** Give four examples of people teens can turn to when they and their families are troubled.

Thinking Critically

4. **Analyze** What makes your family different from any other group you belong to?

5. **Explain** What are some ways that your community has responded to changes in American families?

6. **Hypothesize** If a friend told you she was having problems at home or was planning to run away from home, what organizations could you refer her to?

Applying Health Concepts

7. **Growth and Development** With a group of classmates, compile a list of traditions and rituals that families might share. Then discuss your list. Which of the traditions and rituals does your family take part in? Which would you like to have your family practice? Why? How could each of the traditions enhance a family's sense of unity?

8. **Health of Others** Make a list of local sites, events, and outings appropriate for families that include teenagers. Work with classmates to plan, make, and display posters advertising two or three of your choices.

Social Health and Your Friends

This lesson will help you find answers to questions that teens often ask about friends. For example:

▶ **What makes a good friend?**
▶ **How can I make new friends?**
▶ **What are some good ways of dealing with peer pressure?**

Words to Know

reliable
sympathetic
peers
peer pressure

Friendships

Everyone needs friends. Friends provide us with companionship, and they can be a source of help when we have a problem. Friends are people with whom we can share a common interest or hobby. We cooperate with our friends to get jobs done better and faster. In short, good friendships are important to our social health.

Tips for Making New Friends

Making new friends is sometimes hard, but it is not impossible. Just remember that making friends is a skill that gets better with practice. **Figure 4.6** on page 118 tells you some ways you might try to make friends.

Sharing a hobby or interest with a good friend makes it even more enjoyable.

Qualities of Good Friends

You may have known some of your friends for as long as you can remember. Others may have entered your life just this year. No matter how you met them, or how long you have known them, four qualities are generally true of all good friends:

■ **Loyalty.** Good friends stick by you. They like you for who you are. They are there when you need them.

■ **Reliability.** Good friends are **reliable**—*able to be counted on.* Have you ever stood outside a movie theater after the picture started, waiting for a friend to show up? A reliable friend will do his or her best to keep dates and promises.

■ **Sympathy.** Good friends are usually *aware of how you are feeling,* or **sympathetic** (sim·puh·THE·tik). Most friends will share your happy times, but *good* friends will also share your bad ones. Has a classmate ever comforted you when you were sad? If so, then that person is a good friend.

■ **Caring.** Good friends care for and about each other. A friend who cares can accept the other person's weaknesses as well as strengths. Caring friends will value each other's feelings as much as they do their own.

Remember, good friendship points in both directions. It is important to have good friends, but it is just as important to *be* a good friend to others.

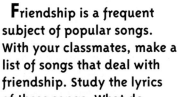
Figure 4.6
Tips for Making New Friends

Ⓐ Start a conversation with someone in your class.
Ask a question or give a compliment. At the very least, you'll have classwork to talk about.

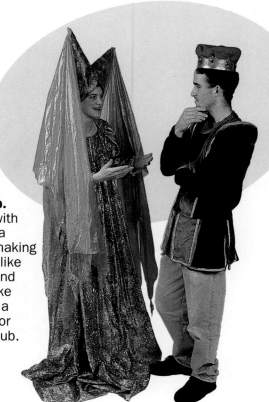

Ⓑ Join a club or group.
Meeting someone with similar interests is a good start toward making a new friend. If you like biking, join a weekend biking club. If you like acting in plays, join a local theater group or the school drama club. Take part in school activities.

Recognizing Peer Pressure

During your teen years, your friendships take on a special role. Your friends and classmates are your **peers,** or *people your age who are similar to you in many ways.* As a group, your peers have certain attitudes and beliefs. **Peer pressure**—*influence to go along with these beliefs and to try new activities*—may come from the group, either directly or indirectly. This kind of pressure can be hard to resist. There are two types of peer pressure, positive peer pressure and negative peer pressure.

Positive Peer Pressure

Positive peer pressure is what you feel when others your age inspire you to do something worthwhile. If you see your friends working hard at a team sport, their enthusiasm may be catching. You may find yourself exercising more often and practicing a sport in which you are interested.

Your peers can have positive effects on you in other ways. As a young teen, you are becoming more independent. You are making your own decisions more often. This can be scary. Growing up is less frightening when you have your peers to support you. You can try out your ideas on your peers and get their reaction. If you are not sure of yourself, your peers can help give you confidence.

in Your Journal

Study the tips for making new friends. If you want to make new friends, use your journal to say how you will do that. If you have someone particular in mind, write down ways you could start a conversation with that person.

C Offer to help someone. If someone in your class is having difficulty with math or needs help fixing something, offer to help. By reaching out to others, you let them know you want to be friends.

D Volunteer to work on a committee or project. Join classmates who are helping with a recycling effort or decorating the gym for a school dance. Working together forms bonds among people.

Negative Peer Pressure

Negative peer pressure is what you feel when others your age try to persuade you to do something you don't want to do. This might be using tobacco or other drugs, including alcohol. It might be doing something dangerous or illegal or something that hurts other people. You may also be pressured to try something you feel you are not ready for and that goes against your values.

Dealing with Negative Peer Pressure

As you grow into a young adult, it is important for you to develop your own identity, one that is separate from that of the group. When someone challenges what you believe in, it is important for you to know how to stand your ground and what you can do to resist negative peer pressure.

One way to deal with negative peer pressure is to avoid getting into difficult situations. That way you prevent problems from occurring in the first place. You also need to ask yourself, "Is this something I need or would I be better off doing something else?" Think about your values, too. Ask yourself, "Am I being asked to do something that goes against my beliefs or my common sense?"

If you do find yourself in a situation in which you need to resist negative peer pressure, you can act in a number of ways. **Figure 4.7** shows some of the refusal skills you can use.

Figure 4.7
Closing the Doors on Negative Peer Pressure

A **Get out of the situation.** There is no need to defend your position. If you wish, state your reasons clearly, and then leave.

B **Don't agree to "meet the person halfway."** It is your right to say no. Giving in a little is still giving in.

C **If the person persists, make up an excuse.** Say anything that will end the conversation.

D **Suggest some alternatives to the behavior the other person is suggesting.** Create a little positive peer pressure of your own.

E **If all else fails, walk away.** That's certain to end the debate.

Using complete sentences, answer the following questions on a separate piece of paper.

Reviewing Terms and Facts

1. **Vocabulary**   Use the word *reliable* in a sentence to show that you understand its meaning.

2. **Recall**   What is positive peer pressure?

3. **List**   Give three examples of ways to deal with negative peer pressure.

Thinking Critically

4. **Compare**   Look up the words *friend* and *peer* in a dictionary. In what ways are peers and friends similar? In what ways are they different?

5. **Apply**   Gina's family just moved to your community. What advice would you give Gina on making new friends?

6. **Interpret**   Think about the saying: "One rotten apple spoils the barrel." What do you think this saying means? How might it apply to peer pressure?

Applying Health Concepts

7. **Growth and Development**   Write an advertisement for an "ideal" friend, stating the qualities you look for. Include the activities and interests you would like to share with the friend. Display the ad anonymously on a bulletin board. Do other ads list similar requirements?

8. **Personal Health**   Working with a classmate, think ahead of a situation in which your peers might try to pressure you into doing something you don't want to do. Plan how you would use refusal skills. Develop a skit and role-play it for the class.

HEALTH LAB
Recognizing Peer Pressure

Introduction: To belong to a peer group, you may feel that you have to think and act the way the group does. This is called peer pressure. Peer pressure may influence your choice of clothes and the way you spend your time. It may also influence your decisions about alcohol, tobacco, and other drugs.

Peer pressure is everywhere in society. All age groups must deal with peer pressure, but it is especially common among young teens. Learning to recognize peer pressure will help you decide whether to go along with the group or to act as an individual.

Objective: During the next week, observe the peer pressure around you. Try to identify one example of peer pressure in each of these areas:

► in your life and the lives of your friends.

► in the lives of your family (parents or brothers and sisters).

► on television or in other media.

Materials and Method: You will need a sheet of paper for each observation. Divide the sheet into two columns. Head the columns with the words *Observation* and *Analysis.* In the Observation column, write just the facts—who, when, where, and what. If possible, include quotes from the people involved to give an idea of their thinking. In the Analysis column, write your interpretation of the event. Answer questions such as these: In what way was peer pressure involved? Was the pressure positive or negative? Did the person handle the pressure correctly? If not, what should the person have done?

Observation and Analysis: At the end of the week, share your observations and analyses with a group of your classmates. See how many different situations of peer pressure the group identifies. Discuss consequences of giving in to negative pressure and ways of resisting it.

Teen HEALTH DIGEST

Teens Making a Difference

Helping the Homeless

Alesha Hersch and Troy Rowe are eighth-graders at Lincoln Middle School. Earlier this year the local chapter of the American Red Cross chose Alesha and Troy to lead the Garlock Team Project. This project, funded by the Garlock Company, was established to involve young people in planning and carrying out volunteer community services.

Alesha and Troy chose homelessness as their area of service. They thought of ways they could use the money from the Garlock Company to make life easier for the homeless families in their community. They decided to make personal care kits.

First, Alesha and Troy enlisted ten teen volunteers to negotiate with local merchants for the best prices on toothpaste, shampoo, and other items. Then, other volunteers packed the items in colorful gift bags. The teens delivered 250 personal care kits to families living in a local shelter.

Troy explained why he got involved in the Garlock Team Project. "I think everyone has a responsibility to help." "Besides, it was fun," Alesha added.

People at Work

Family Therapist

Dr. Jane Taylor works many evening and weekend hours. Those are the most convenient times for the people who want her advice.

Dr. Taylor helps families deal with the stresses of divorce, substance abuse, and violence. Once a week she brings together all the members of a troubled family to talk about their problems. She observes how family members interact with one another and suggests ways they can get along better.

Besides her work as a family therapist, Dr. Taylor conducts workshops on effective parenting. She also writes a weekly column on parenting for the local newspaper.

Dr. Taylor has a degree in clinical psychology. Earning a doctoral degree required four years of college and four years of graduate school. To open a practice in her state, she also had to pass a licensing exam.

Dr. Taylor says that a genuine concern for other people is the most important quality for a family therapist. Patience is essential, too, as it may take a long time for a hurting family to heal. Dr. Taylor believes that healthy families are essential for a healthy society. She is committed to doing her part to keep American families strong.

CON$UMER FOCU$

Jumping on the Bandwagon

Advertisers use peer pressure to persuade you to buy their products. Consider an ad for a soft drink that shows teenagers playing volleyball on the beach. Everybody is having a great time and, of course, drinking the soft drink. The advertisers want you to think that if you drink this soda, you, too, will be part of the "in" crowd.

Using peer pressure to sell products is known as the *bandwagon technique.* The expression "Everyone's jumping on the bandwagon" means everyone is eager to become part of the trend. The technique plays on people's fears of being left out of a group. When you see this type of advertising, decide if the product is right for *you* before jumping on the bandwagon.

Myths and Realities

Smiling Is Good for You

Did you know that a smile— even an insincere smile—is good for your physical health? When you smile you set off a healthful chain reaction. Smiling forces you to breathe through your nose, which exerts pressure on muscles in your face. This pressure forces cooler blood to a special region of your brain, which releases endorphins throughout your body. Endorphins are natural body chemicals that make you feel good.

Of course, smiling is great for your social health, too. Most people prefer being with someone who smiles. What's more, your sunny smile may cheer up someone who is feeling blue.

Teens Making a Difference

Peer Mediation

Meg and Teri sit in a conference room at Dakota Heights Middle School. They were arguing loudly in the cafeteria. In a few minutes Gina joins them.

"Okay guys," begins Gina, "let's figure out how to solve this problem. Meg, let's hear your side first. After that, you'll get a chance to talk, Teri." Gina listens to both girls. She asks a few questions. After talking the situation over for a while, Teri and Meg agree to a solution that satisfies them both.

Gina is one of 21 specially trained peer mediators at Dakota Heights. Peer mediators help other students resolve conflicts before it becomes necessary for school authorities to become involved.

Peer mediation programs are becoming popular in schools across the country. School officials find that the programs are helpful in easing tense situations. "Lots of times students will talk more freely to a peer mediator than to an adult," says Gina.

Dating and Marriage

This lesson will help you find answers to questions that teens often ask about dating and marriage. For example:

▶ **Do most people my age feel more comfortable going out in a group?**

▶ **What do I need to think about before I go out?**

▶ **Why do people marry? Why do some marriages succeed while others fail?**

Words to Know

socializing
group dating
responsible dating
love
commitment
divorce

As you begin to spend more time with your friends, you'll have a chance to practice and improve your social skills.

Changing Relationships

During adolescence, your relationships with other people begin to change. You depend less on your parents and other adults to make decisions for you. As you grow in knowledge and experience, you begin to make more decisions for yourself. For example, you begin to decide who you will spend your time with and how you will spend that time.

As a child, you may have had a limited circle of friends. Perhaps you played just with the children in your neighborhood. Now your circle of friends and acquaintances is expanding. By being with different people, you practice your skills at **socializing** (SOH·shuh·ly·zing), *getting along with and communicating with other people.* You become aware of your strengths and weaknesses. You learn how to express yourself and how to work out differences of opinion with others.

Dating Relationships

Dating can help you learn more about relating to people of the opposite gender. It can help you learn about yourself as well.

Not all teens your age want to date or feel ready to date. Some teens have other interests they prefer for the time being. Some teens are shy, and the idea of dating makes them nervous. It is a good idea to date only when you're ready. If anyone pressures you into dating, you probably will not have fun.

Going Out in Groups

Group dating, *going out with male and female friends at the same time,* is popular among teens. There may be an equal number of boys and girls, there may be more girls than boys, or there may be more boys than girls.

Going out in a group is a good way to ease into dating. Many young people are more comfortable going to parties, movies, and dances in groups. You do not have to worry about making conversation with one person. You can get used to being with people in a social situation. What's more, going out with the group can be a lot of fun. **Figure 4.8** shows ways to have fun with a group.

Figure 4.8
Activities to Do with a Group

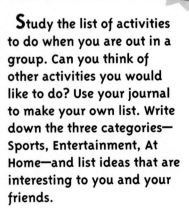

Sports	Entertainment	At Home
bowling	dancing	board games
roller-skating	spectator sports—football, baseball, basketball	backyard games—croquet, lawn darts, badminton
swimming		
volleyball	picnic	video rental
ice-skating	amusement park	pizza party
bicycling	fair	potluck supper
tobogganing	movies	
hiking	youth center activities	

Cultural Diversity

Matchmaker, Matchmaker ACTIVITY!

Dating is not practiced in some cultures because parents arrange the marriages of their children. They might use the services of a matchmaker to find a mate for their son or daughter. In other cultures, adult chaperones accompany young men and women on dates. Look in an encyclopedia or ask people you know for more information on interesting dating and marriage customs around the world. Share your findings with your classmates.

in your journal

Study the list of activities to do when you are out in a group. Can you think of other activities you would like to do? Use your journal to make your own list. Write down the three categories—Sports, Entertainment, At Home—and list ideas that are interesting to you and your friends.

Individual Dating

When you go out with a group, you may begin to develop special feelings about one person. You may want to spend more time with that person alone rather than with the group. Whether you are with a group or with one other person, you are responsible for your behavior. **Responsible dating** means *being trustworthy, showing respect for the other person, and thinking ahead about the consequences of your actions.*

You can be responsible and show respect for your date by choosing an activity that both of you will enjoy. Use good communication skills. Be honest with yourself about your feelings for the other person. Go out with someone because you want to. Sometimes teens spend time with certain people to win the approval of their peer group. Go out with someone because you want to get to know that person and have fun.

Physical attraction for another person can be very strong. You will be faced with decisions about the way you express your affections with a person you care for. It is easier to decide on what limits you will set before you are in a situation that is hard to control.

Parents are often involved in teens' experiences, especially during the early teen years. They are often concerned about issues of safety and responsible behavior. Curfews and other limits that parents set show their love and concern for their children. You can show your respect by following family rules.

When parents set rules about dating, they are showing their love and concern.

Marriage

"I do" are words most American adults say at some time in their lives. Statistics show that at least nine out of ten Americans marry. Marriage is a serious decision that is not to be taken lightly.

Reasons for Getting Married

Most people get married because they are "in love." **Love** is *a strong emotional attachment to another person.* By getting married, people demonstrate their desire to live with and care for each other throughout their lives.

People get married for other important reasons. Most people feel that marriage provides a stable environment in which to raise children. Many people enjoy the companionship and comfort that marriage brings. As a contract, marriage entitles the partners to certain financial benefits as well.

Factors Affecting a Marriage

While love is important in a marriage, love is often not enough to keep a relationship strong and healthy. Many other factors affect whether a marriage will be successful. One of the most important of these is emotional maturity. Emotionally mature people bring commitment, effort, compromise, good communication, and understanding to a marriage. A **commitment** (kuh·MIT·muhnt) is *a pledge or a promise.* Emotional maturity includes understanding someone else's needs and feelings and being able at times to put the other person's needs ahead of your own. Emotionally mature people are better prepared to make a marriage work.

Teen Marriage

Teenage marriage, as a rule, does not work. Only one out of four teenage marriages lasts. Why do the other three fail? There are several reasons for this high rate of failed marriages.

- **Most people are not ready to get married during their teen years.** Teenagers are just beginning to learn about themselves and to discover what they want from life. Most do not yet know enough about themselves to choose a partner for life. Most are not emotionally mature enough to make a lasting commitment to someone else.

- **Most teenagers are not ready to be parents.** Many teenagers get married because of an unplanned pregnancy. The responsibility of a baby is often more than the young couple can handle.

- **Most teenage couples do not have enough money.** Teenage couples are likely to have a hard time supporting themselves. Stress from money problems often breaks up a marriage.

Three out of four teen marriages fail. Most teens are simply not ready for adult responsibilities.

Divorce

A marriage that does not work is likely to end in divorce. **Divorce** is the *legal termination of a marriage.* For a child, it means one parent moving out of the family home. At some point, it may also mean getting used to a new stepparent and new brothers and sisters as part of the family.

Divorce is usually very stressful. Afterwards, many family members go on to live happily and healthfully. The keys are communication and adjusting to change. By talking about their feelings, either among themselves or with an outside professional, family members can learn to adjust to their new lives. Both parents need to comfort their child, who may be frightened and unsure of the future. The child, in turn, needs to understand that she or he is not to blame for the divorce. Divorces happen because adults are no longer willing to stay married.

in your journal

Use your journal to analyze a successful marriage. Choose a couple you know who has a happy marriage. Write down their names. Then complete the statement: "I think their marriage is successful because . . ."

Even if a teen's parents decide to divorce, it is important to maintain a healthy relationship with both parents.

Lesson 5 Review

Using complete sentences, answer the following questions on a separate sheet of paper.

Reviewing Terms and Facts

1. **Vocabulary**   In your own words, explain what is meant by the term *responsible dating.*

2. **Recall**   What is the failure rate for teen marriages?

3. **List**   Give three reasons why teen marriages generally fail.

Thinking Critically

4. **Analyze**   What are the advantages of group dating over individual dating?

5. **Evaluate**   How does emotional maturity help a marriage succeed?

Applying Health Concepts

6. **Growth and Development**   Write a skit in which one teen asks another teen to go to the movies and he or she refuses. Write it so that the teen shows respect when he or she says no. Write several different last lines to your skit, showing different ways a person can handle the disappointment of being turned down.

7. **Health of Others**   Talk to adults you know who have been divorced. Ask them to identify resources within the family and community that they used to help them through the difficult time.

Parenthood

This lesson will help you find answers to questions that teens often ask about parenthood. For example:

▶ **What does being a parent involve?**
▶ **What special challenges do single parents face?**
▶ **Why are teens discouraged from becoming parents?**

Words to Know

parenting
responsibility
single parent

Parenting Roles and Responsibilities

Parenthood can be one of life's most wonderful experiences. Most parents find great joy in loving and caring for a child. They watch excitedly as the child grows and develops over the years. When the child becomes a healthy, well-adjusted adult, they feel a great deal of satisfaction.

A parent is the father or mother of a child. However, there is a difference between being a parent and parenting. **Parenting** means *meeting a child's physical, emotional, social, and mental needs.* Many people, including grandparents, aunts and uncles, and teachers, use parenting skills. When you take care of younger brothers or sisters or baby-sit the neighbor's children, you are likely using parenting skills.

Parents get great pleasure from seeing their children grow and change.

Parenthood can be rewarding; it can also be hard, demanding work. Effective parenting requires knowledge of child growth and development. It requires teaching, counseling, and nursing skills. It requires personal qualities such as patience, understanding, and a sense of humor. As the list below shows, people who become parents must fulfill a large number of responsibilities. A **responsibility** is *a duty or an obligation expected of you.*

Parents' Contract

Although parents do not sign a contract as such, by having children they take on a number of responsibilities. If parents were to sign a contract, it might state the following:

We, the parents, agree to do the following for our children:

- **Take care of their physical needs.** We promise to give them nutritious meals and snacks, clean clothes, and adequate shelter. We will see that the children get plenty of rest, enough exercise, and good medical care.

- **Take care of their emotional and social needs.** We promise to love them. We will help them feel accepted and valued. We will teach them right from wrong and how to get along with others.

- **Take care of their mental needs.** We promise to stimulate their thinking and learning. We will help them get a good education. We will teach them how to make decisions and solve problems so they can become independent adults.

Besides taking care of their children's needs, parents must make time for themselves as individuals as well as for their partners. They must look out for their own physical, emotional, social, and mental well-being. Being a good parent takes work!

Single Parents

As you read earlier, a **single parent** is *someone who raises one or more children without a partner in the home.* The single parent may be unmarried, divorced, or widowed.

Single parenthood is more common now than in the past. Between 1960 and 1990, the percentage of children under the age of 18 living in a one-parent family rose from 10 percent to 25 percent.

Raising a child is especially challenging for a single parent, especially a teen single parent.

Studies indicate that soon 50 percent of all children will spend some time in a one-parent household. Although most single parents are still women, an increasing number of single fathers are raising their children alone.

Many single parents do a good job raising their children. Raising children alone, however, is not easy. If the parent must also work outside the home to support the family, the amount of time he or she can spend with the children is limited. Single parents have no partner to help discipline the children. They have no partner to help with chores around the house or share financial responsibilities. They may become tired and frustrated trying to do everything by themselves. Single parents generally have less time to take care of their own needs and interests.

Teen Parenting

In the United States each year, more than 500,000 babies are born to teens (see **Figure 4.9**). About 70 percent of those babies are born to unmarried teens. Many unmarried teen mothers choose to keep their babies rather than give them up for adoption.

Under the best of circumstances, parenthood is a challenging task. Teen parents generally lack money, education, and emotional maturity. As a result, raising children is more challenging for teen parents than for older parents.

Consequences of Teen Parenthood

Teen pregnancy and parenthood can present health risks, financial problems, and emotional stress. Teen parents may also find themselves with fewer choices in life.

Q & A **?**

Baby Love

Q: I know a girl who wants a baby so she'll have something to call her own—something she can love and that will love her back. What do you think of this?

A: Many teens have the mistaken idea that a baby will satisfy their emotional needs. Loving a child is a one-way street. Young children are not yet capable of returning love in the way an adult might. Your friend is setting herself up for a major disappointment.

Figure 4.9
Births to Women Under Age 20, 1981–1991

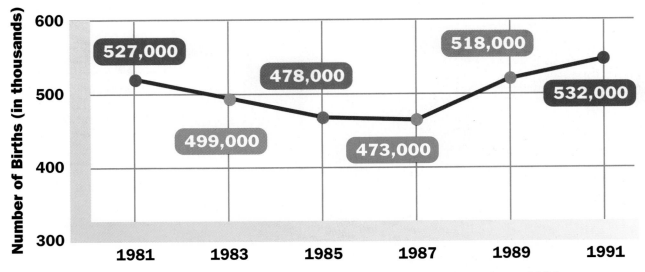

Source: National Center for Health Statistics, 1994; Alan Guttmacher Institute, 1994

Fewer Choices

Oftentimes, teen parents must put aside their plans for education and a fulfilling career. They may have to drop out of school to take care of their child. They may have to quit school to earn money to support their child. Teen dropouts usually find it hard to go back to school, complete their education, and graduate.

Teens without a high school diploma have a limited choice of jobs and little chance of a well-paying job. Teens who continue in school may find it difficult to take care of a baby and study.

Health Risks

Teen pregnancy and parenthood create health risks for the young mother. In the teen years, the young female body is still developing and may not be completely ready to support and nourish an unborn child. The pregnant teen may not get enough nutrients for herself and her baby, which can harm both of them.

Teen pregnancy and parenthood create health risks for the child, too. Teen mothers may not know how to take care of themselves during pregnancy. Only 50 percent of teen mothers, for example, seek prenatal care within the first three months of pregnancy. As a result, children born to teen mothers are more likely to have low birth weight, which can lead to health problems. These children are also more likely to have physical and mental handicaps. Raising a child with health problems is costly and stressful.

Helping Hands

Fortunately, many schools and communities provide help for pregnant teens and teen parents. **Figure 4.10** shows some of the services they offer.

in your journal

You have been reading about the problems teen parents face. Since there are so many of these problems, why do you think so many teens become parents? Use your journal to write your thoughts about this.

Figure 4.10
Help for Teen Parents

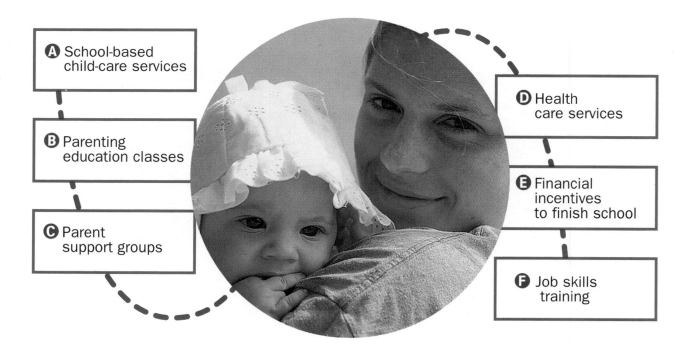

Ⓐ School-based child-care services

Ⓑ Parenting education classes

Ⓒ Parent support groups

Ⓓ Health care services

Ⓔ Financial incentives to finish school

Ⓕ Job skills training

As children of teen parents grow older, they continue to be at risk for health problems. Many teen parents cannot afford to take their children to the doctor. The children do not get shots and other care they need to stay healthy. Also, teen parents may live in run-down housing, which risks accidents and disease.

Financial Problems

Raising a child costs a great deal of money. **Figure 4.11** shows just some of the items that parents need to buy. Teen parents have difficulty meeting expenses. Constantly worrying about money causes great stress. Teen parents may find themselves falling into a cycle of poverty from which they cannot escape.

Emotional and Social Stress

During adolescence, teens struggle to discover who they are and where they fit into the scheme of things. Many teens have all they can do to cope with the normal anxieties of adolescence. Adding the responsibility of caring for a baby creates even more pressure.

Parenting is a time-consuming job. Teen parents will have less time to spend with their friends, or they may be too tired for other activities. Many teen parents eventually become frustrated and re-sentful of the limits on their personal freedom.

Figure 4.11
Items for Baby

In the first year alone, parents need to buy hundreds of dollars' worth of items.

Review

Lesson 6

Using complete sentences, answer the following questions on a separate sheet of paper.

Reviewing Terms and Facts

1. **Vocabulary** Use the word *responsibility* in a sentence to show that you understand its meaning.

2. **List** What are the three types of needs in children for which parents are responsible?

3. **Recall** What kinds of problems do teen parents face?

Thinking Critically

4. **Explain** How do you use parenting skills? How does this differ from parenthood?

5. **Hypothesize** What factors enable parents to practice effective parenting skills?

6. **Analyze** If parents fail to take care of their own needs, how might this affect their children?

Applying Health Concepts

7. **Growth and Development** Observe young children and their parents in a public place such as a park, playground, or shopping mall. Notice instances in which the parent uses effective parenting techniques. Keep a list of these techniques and share your findings with your classmates.

8. **Health of Others** Set up a debate that explores the rights and responsibilities you believe teenage males have when their sexual partner becomes pregnant. How—if at all—does the role of the father-to-be differ from that of the mother-to-be?

Chapter Summary

▶ Social health is the ability to get along with the people around you, which includes respect for individual differences. (Lesson 1)

▶ Communication, compromise, and cooperation help build healthy relationships. (Lesson 1)

▶ Effective communication depends on using good speaking and listening skills and paying attention to body language. (Lesson 2)

▶ Refusal skills help you say no to people who want you to do something that goes against your interests or values. (Lesson 2)

▶ Types of families in the United States include couple, nuclear, single-parent, extended, and blended. (Lesson 3)

▶ Families may need outside help to solve serious problems. (Lesson 3)

▶ Teens troubled by family problems should talk to a parent or another adult. (Lesson 3)

▶ Good friends are loyal, reliable, sympathetic, and caring. (Lesson 4)

▶ Peer pressure *is* the influence people your age place on you to look, think, and act like them. It can be positive or negative. (Lesson 4)

▶ Dating is a way to get to know members of the opposite gender. Group dating is a good way to begin dating relationships. (Lesson 5)

▶ When people marry, they make a lifelong commitment. Most teens are not ready for such a commitment. (Lesson 5)

▶ Parenthood is a challenging and rewarding task. Parents have the responsibility to provide for their children's physical, emotional and social, and mental needs. (Lesson 6)

Using Health Terms

On a separate sheet of paper, write the vocabulary term that best matches each definition given in the following list.

1. Your ability to get along with the people around you (Lesson 1)

2. The exchange of thoughts, ideas, and beliefs between people (Lesson 1)

3. Communication skills that help you say no effectively (Lesson 2)

4. Able to be counted on (Lesson 4)

5. Influence to go along with the beliefs of other people your age (Lesson 4)

6. A duty or an obligation expected of you (Lesson 6)

Reviewing Main Ideas

Using complete sentences, answer the following questions on a separate sheet of paper.

1. What are some of the characteristics of people who enjoy good social health? (Lesson 1)

2. What does it mean to compromise? (Lesson 1)

3. How does using good speaking and listening skills help to keep relationships healthy? (Lesson 2)

4. How do people communicate their feelings nonverbally? (Lesson 2)

5. What are some factors causing American families to change? (Lesson 3)

6. Who are some people a teen might talk to about family problems? (Lesson 3)

7. How can you tell the difference between positive peer pressure and negative peer pressure? (Lesson 4)

8. What are some ways to resist negative peer pressure? (Lesson 4)

9. What are some advantages of going out in a group? (Lesson 5)

10. What are some reasons that teen marriages often fail? (Lesson 5)

11. Why is it a good idea for teens to delay parenthood until they are older? (Lesson 6)

Thinking Critically

Using complete sentences, answer the following questions on a separate sheet of paper.

1. **Compare and Contrast** Are popularity and good social health the same thing? Why or why not? (Lesson 1)

2. **Give Examples** What are some ways a school might foster tolerance among students from different cultural backgrounds? (Lesson 1)

3. **Hypothesize** When might a teen need to use refusal skills with someone other than a peer? (Lesson 2)

4. **Give Examples** List ways that families you know have changed over recent years. (Lesson 3)

5. **Compare and Contrast** What is the difference between loyalty and reliability? (Lesson 4)

6. **Analyze** How can a teen be an individual and still be part of the peer group? (Lesson 4)

7. **Hypothesize** What are some concerns that children whose parents are divorcing might have? (Lesson 5)

8. **Analyze** How might living in an extended family make parenting easier? (Lesson 6)

9. **Evaluate** Why is teen parenthood particularly challenging? (Lesson 6)

Your Action Plan

Improve Your Social Health

You can make an action plan to improve your social health. First, you need to set a long-term goal. Look back through your private journal entries for this chapter. What do your comments tell you about areas of your life you would like to change?

Once you've identified your long-term goal, write it down. Make sure your goal is achievable. Making new friends is a realistic goal. Next, think of a series of short-term goals, or what you will do to achieve your long-term goal. Write these down. Plan a schedule for reaching each short-term goal. When you reach your long-term goal, reward yourself.

Building Your Portfolio

1. Arrange to interview an older adult or a person from a different cultural background. Plan some topics to talk about such as friends, jobs, and hobbies. Practice good speaking and listening skills during the conversation. Ask the other person for permission to tape-record the conversation, and then include the tape in your portfolio.

2. Write a short play about teens and negative peer pressure. You might base the play on something that happened to a friend. Set the scene and then have a teenage character use refusal skills to get out of an unhealthy situation. Ask your classmates to act out the play. Place a copy of your play in your portfolio.

In Your Home and Community

1. Volunteer to be your family's historian. Put photos of family events in an album or a scrapbook. Include stories about the funny, unusual, or special family events. You and your family will have fun together looking through the album.

2. With your classmates, write a manual, or handbook, to guide student behavior in your school. Include rules of conduct for the cafeteria and halls and rules of conduct for school dances and other events. The handbook should promote healthy social behavior in your school, including respect for all adults and students. You might present your handbook to the administration and student council for schoolwide use.

Chapter 5

Conflict Resolution and Preventing Violence

Student Expectations

After reading this chapter, you should be able to:

1. Define abuse and explain why it happens.
2. Explain how violence in society affects people.
3. Identify ways to resolve conflicts nonviolently.

The news frightens me. Every time I turn on the television, I see terrible stories about guns, gangs, rapes, and murders. In the past, stories like these happened to people I didn't know, people who lived far away. Now, these awful stories are on our local news, too, and they're getting closer and closer to home.

Last week, two students in my best friend's class got in a bad fight at school. The police even came to break up the fight. One of the guys was hurt so bad that he had to go to the hospital.

For the rest of the week, everybody was really uptight at school. Both students met with the Peer Mediation Leadership Team yesterday. They seem to have handled their differences for now.

I don't understand why people have to get violent when they're angry. Don't they know that it doesn't solve anything? Can't they find other, healthier ways to deal with their anger?

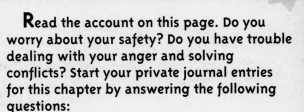

in your journal

Read the account on this page. Do you worry about your safety? Do you have trouble dealing with your anger and solving conflicts? Start your private journal entries for this chapter by answering the following questions:

▶ Are you ever concerned about your personal safety?

▶ Do you worry about the safety of your family members or friends?

▶ Do you know of organizations in your school or community that help teens and family members deal with their anger and solve disagreements in nonviolent ways?

Dealing with Abuse

This lesson will help you find answers to questions that teens often ask about abuse and violence. For example:

► **What is abuse and why does it happen?**
► **How does abuse affect a person?**
► **What can be done to prevent abuse?**
► **What help is available for abused and troubled people?**

Words to Know

abuse
victim
battery

What Is Abuse?

You may find it difficult to understand how anyone can abuse a child, a family member, another relative, or a stranger. However, abuse in the United States is a significant problem. See **Figure 5.1** for some alarming statistics on abuse.

Abuse (uh·BYOOS) is *the physical, emotional, or mental mistreatment of another person,* and it can take several forms. Abuse may be physical, emotional, sexual, or a result of neglect. It can cause obvious physical wounds such as bruises, scratches, broken bones, or burns, or emotional wounds such as anger, sadness, and fear. Abuse can happen in all kinds of families—from the richest to the poorest, from the most well educated to those with no schooling at all. Abuse can happen anywhere—in the largest cities and in the smallest towns. The effects of abuse are long lasting.

Wherever abuse occurs, and whatever form it takes, abuse always does damage. It is a crime to abuse another person. This is so important that physicians and teachers are required by law to report suspected cases of abuse. Abuse is never the fault of the **victim,** *the person against whom a crime is committed.*

Figure 5.1
Abuse Statistics

The incidence of abuse in families is evidence of the number of troubled families in our society.

Reported cases of child abuse and neglect in the United States —2.9 million
In an average year in this country, 2 million women are severely assaulted by male partners.
Number of elderly abused or neglected—1 in 25

Types of Abuse

There are four major types of abuse. They are physical abuse, emotional abuse, sexual abuse, and neglect. Anyone in a family may be the victim of abuse: a child or adolescent, a husband or wife, a brother or sister, or a grandparent.

Physical Abuse

Physical abuse is mistreatment that results in injury to the body. In some cases, physical abuse results in burns, bruises, and broken bones. In severe cases, the victims of physical abuse die. The most common form of physical abuse is **battery,** *the beating, hitting, or kicking of another person.*

Emotional Abuse

Emotional abuse is the use of words and gestures to mistreat another person. It also occurs when love and affection are withheld from a child. Angry words, threats, constant teasing, or criticism are examples of emotional abuse. When people are treated this way, they end up feeling worthless and helpless. This condition is known as loss of self-esteem.

Sexual Abuse

Sexual abuse is any sexual contact that is forced upon a victim. It is a very serious crime. The abuser is often someone the victim knows and trusts, such as a parent, stepparent, older brother or sister, or family friend. When sexual abuse occurs between family members, it is called incest.

The victim of sexual abuse may feel guilty that somehow he or she is responsible for what has happened. However, no matter who the abuser is, sexual abuse is *never the victim's fault*—it is always the abuser's. The person who commits sexual abuse needs professional help. One way to get that help is for the victim to talk to a trusted adult—someone who can assist in arranging for the counseling that is needed.

Neglect

Neglect is the failure to meet the basic physical and emotional needs of a person. Young people need proper food, clothing, and housing to help them grow and develop. They need love and encouragement to help them feel safe and secure. Children who do not have these needs satisfied are neglected.

Teaching young children about child abuse is one way to help prevent it.

Causes of Abuse

Your Total Health

Stemming the Tide of Abuse ACTIVITY!

Many cases of abuse are related to alcohol or drug abuse. See chapters 14 and 15 for more information on where to get help if someone in your family has these problems. Organizations like Alcoholics Anonymous help people to stop drinking and reduce the chances that they will abuse someone else. Find out about organizations in your community that offer help to alcohol and drug abusers. Share your findings in class.

All families have problems from time to time. An important key to dealing with these problems is communication. In a healthy family, members learn how to express emotions in a nonviolent way. Often the cause of abuse is that the person does not know how to control his or her own frustrations and emotions, or does not know how to handle problems in a positive way.

In some families, problems are too serious to be solved within the family. People who abuse others often do not intend to do harm. They usually are hurting badly themselves. In addition, they do not have the emotional skills to deal with their frustrations and problems. Here is a list of some of the reasons why people may become abusive.

- The person was abused as a child
- Alcohol or other drug abuse
- Unemployment and poverty
- Illness
- Divorce
- Feelings of worthlessness
- Emotional immaturity
- Lack of parenting skills
- Inability to deal with anger
- Lack of communication and coping skills

MAKING HEALTHY DECISIONS
Deciding to Report Abuse

*J*enny is Tasha's best friend. She knows that Tasha's father drinks too much, and when he does, he gets really mean. Several times Tasha has told Jenny about her father's "fits"—how he hollers, throws things, and once put his fist through a door.

This afternoon, in the locker room, Jenny noticed some awful bruises on Tasha's back and arms. At first Tasha explained the cause as a "skating accident." Later, though, she confided to Jenny that her father had beaten her. This was not the first time either. Tasha made Jenny promise not to tell anyone.

Jenny has to make a decision. She knows that it is important to report abuse. She is afraid that the next beating may be worse. Still, she does not want to break a promise to her best friend. To help her choose the best solution, Jenny will use the step-by-step decision-making process.

1. **State the situation**
2. **List the options**
3. **Weigh the possible outcomes**
4. **Consider your values**
5. **Make a decision and act**
6. **Evaluate the decision**

Signs of Abuse

A child who has been beaten may show signs of physical abuse such as bruises, burns, scratches, or broken bones. The signs of emotional abuse, sexual abuse, and neglect are more difficult to recognize. Some of them are listed here.

- Frequent absences from school
- Poor grades and lack of interest in school
- Dirty or neglected appearance
- Extreme shyness, sadness, or fear
- Aggressive behavior toward others
- Inability to communicate

Effects of Abuse

Abuse is always harmful. It causes damage to the abuser and the victim. Some teens try to escape from abuse by leaving home. Running away, however, often leads to other problems. Runaways usually have no way to support themselves. They have no place to live and no money for food. Life on the street is rough. Some runaways turn to crime. Many runaways become the victims of crime.

People who were abused as children generally have low self-esteem, a high level of stress, and other problems. They often find themselves in abusive relationships as adults, and they sometimes become abusers themselves. However, with help, people can break the cycle of abuse.

Cultural Diversity

"Space Invaders"

Personal space refers to the space you need between yourself and another person to feel comfortable when you are talking. People from some cultures feel comfortable with less distance between them. People from other cultures may feel comfortable only with greater distances between them. They may feel that people who stand too close are invading their space and showing disrespect. Think of ways to maintain your personal-space comfort zone. If you feel that someone is trying to get too close, or is touching, patting, or grabbing you, you have a right to ask them to stop. If they do not, walk away or yell for help.

Follow-up Activities

1. Apply the six steps of the decision-making process to Jenny's dilemma.
2. Imagine that you are Jenny. Write a diary entry for the day she decides what to do.
3. With a classmate, role-play Jenny telling Tasha that she cannot keep her promise and why.

Sexual Harassment at School **ACTIVITY!**

Sexual harassment is any unwelcome sexual comment, contact, or behavior. This includes jokes, looks, notes, touching, noises, or gestures. Sexual harassment is a type of sexual abuse. It can happen to boys or girls. Find out if your school has a policy for dealing with sexual harassment.

There are many different types of community programs available to help teens break the cycle of abuse.

Breaking the Cycle of Abuse

The longer abuse continues, the greater the damage will be. Abuse can be stopped. The key to breaking the cycle of abuse is reporting it and talking about it. If someone has been abused or is in danger of being abused, it is important for that person to tell someone, such as a family member, a teacher, a school nurse, a doctor, a counselor, or another adult he or she trusts. The victim may be afraid to tell, however, for fear that the information will break up the family, that the abuser will go to jail, or that no one will believe him or her. If a friend is being abused, it is important to encourage him or her to get help.

Where to Get Help

What kind of help is available for abused children and troubled families? Some of the community programs that deal with and prevent abuse are described here.

Police department. This is the place to call for help for someone who is in immediate danger of being hurt. In many communities, the emergency number for the local police department is 911. Dial 0 for the operator if you are not sure how to reach the police department in your community.

Local hospital. This is the place to get emergency medical treatment if you are injured, hurt, or seriously ill.

Crisis hot lines. These are telephone services that parents and abused children can call to get help.

Family violence shelters. These are places where families in danger of abuse can stay while they figure out what to do. Counselors at family violence shelters help families find solutions to their problems.

Family counseling programs. These are programs to help family members identify their problems and work together to solve them. School guidance counselors, youth counselors, and hospital social workers also provide support to family members on an individual basis or as a group.

Support or self-help groups. In these groups, people have a chance to talk with and listen to others with similar problems. Some support groups are for victims of abuse, and some are for abusers. For example, Parents Anonymous is for parents who have abused their children or are afraid they might. Members encourage one another as they learn to understand and change their behavior.

Home health visitors. Some communities arrange for nurses to visit families to help them improve their parenting skills.

About Hot Lines

Some people, teens and adults alike, may feel embarrassed talking about their problems to people on telephone hot lines. They might feel as though they are opening up their private lives to strangers. However, the people who work at these places are kind and caring. They have special training to help people in trouble. They know what to do. The information is kept confidential, and the caller does not have to give his or her name.

Review Lesson 1

Using complete sentences, answer the following questions on a separate sheet of paper.

Reviewing Terms and Facts

1. **Vocabulary**   Define the term *battery*. Use it in an original sentence.

2. **Give Examples**   Identify some of the signs of abuse.

Thinking Critically

3. **Synthesize**   Suggest ways in which a teen could help a friend who is being abused.

4. **Explain**   Why is it important for victims of abuse to report the crime? Describe why reporting abuse may be difficult for the victim.

Applying Health Concepts

5. **Health of Others**   Use the local telephone directory to find out about the counseling centers, support groups, and telephone hot lines in your area that offer help to victims of abuse. Make a poster that tells other teens this information. Obtain permission to hang the poster in the school hallway or lunchroom.

6. **Health of Others**   Role-play a situation in which a friend tells you that she or he is being abused. Include ways to help the friend.

2 Dealing with Violence

This lesson will help you find answers to questions that teens often ask about violence and violence prevention. For example:

▶ **What are the causes of violence?**

▶ **What can I do to protect myself so I do not become a victim?**

▶ **How can I help to prevent violence in my school?**

Words to Know

homicide
prejudice
hate crime
gang

Violence in Society

The images of violence are all around us—from music lyrics to the daily news reports. Grim stories of beatings, stabbings, gang wars, and family abuse are reported on the news and glorified in the movies. Violence is a major public health problem in the United States. **Figure 5.2** shows how frequently violent crimes are committed in the United States.

Some people blame the increase in violence on television. By the age of 18, the average teenager has watched 22,000 hours of television. That is slightly more than three hours a day. Because some television programs glamorize violence, they may lead people to believe that violence is an acceptable way to settle disagreements.

Other people blame the increase of violent acts on the breakdown of the family, the decline in moral values, and the availability of weapons. Whatever the cause, there are many factors that contribute to the violence in society. In the end, we are all victims—either directly or indirectly.

Figure 5.2
Violent Crime Watch

Violent crime is a problem that affects everyone in our society.

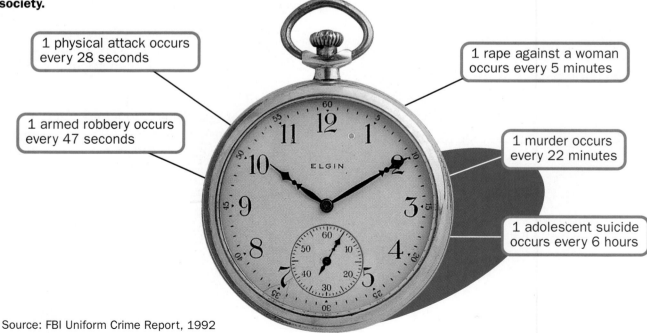

1 physical attack occurs every 28 seconds

1 armed robbery occurs every 47 seconds

1 rape against a woman occurs every 5 minutes

1 murder occurs every 22 minutes

1 adolescent suicide occurs every 6 hours

Source: FBI Uniform Crime Report, 1992

The Victims of Violence

Who are the victims of violence? Each and every one of us is a victim of the violence in society. To solve this problem, communities, schools, and individuals need to work together.

In the past, an argument might lead to a shouting match or a fistfight. Today, the results may be more tragic. Simple arguments or disagreements might end in gunfire, stabbings, and possibly death. The fact is that violence today is more serious and more random than in the past. Random violence is committed for no particular reason and against anyone who happens to be around at the time. As a result, innocent people may be the victims of violence. Long after the violence has occurred, the victims and their families experience prolonged emotional trauma. In addition, victims may undergo the stress of testifying at long, costly legal trials.

Perhaps you have not been a direct victim of violence. However, you still have felt the impact of violence. Every year, crime in the United States costs an estimated $674 billion. This includes police protection, prisons, lost lives and wages, and medical costs. Even within some schools, security measures have been initiated to prevent violent acts. Locker searches, metal detectors, and security in schools increase costs to schools and communities.

Teens and Violence

The majority of teens are not violent and they do not commit crimes. However, teens are twice as likely as other age groups to be the victims of violence. In fact, the second leading cause of death of all people between the ages of 15 and 24 is homicide. A **homicide** (HAH·muh·syd) is *a violent crime that results in the death of another individual.*

Teens are also more likely than any other age group to commit violent crimes. In fact, more than half of all crime in the United States is committed by young people between the ages of 10 and 20. What drives these teens to commit such crimes?

Did You Know?

How Many Violent Crimes?

According to the FBI, nearly 2 million violent crimes were committed in 1993. These included murders, robberies, burglaries, rapes, and carjackings.

in your journal

Do you know someone who has been the victim of a violent crime? In your journal, describe how you felt when you heard about the crime. Could the victim have prevented the crime? Explain your response.

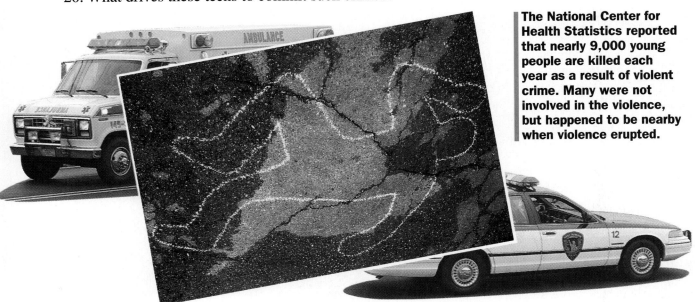

The National Center for Health Statistics reported that nearly 9,000 young people are killed each year as a result of violent crime. Many were not involved in the violence, but happened to be nearby when violence erupted.

Causes of Violence

People who commit violent acts usually have not learned how to deal with their feelings. Other factors that contribute to violence are discussed below.

Anger

Anger is a normal emotion. Learning how to control it is the most important step in preventing violence. Here are some ways to control your anger.

■ Count to ten before you say or do anything.

■ Talk to someone you trust and respect about your feelings.

■ Exercise to get rid of some of your pent-up feelings.

■ Channel your energy into a worthwhile activity.

■ Find a nonviolent way to deal with the situation.

Prejudice

Prejudice (PRE·juh·duhs) is *an opinion that has been formed without careful consideration.* Prejudice is often based on a person's gender, race, religion, or country of origin. Prejudice sometimes leads to **hate crime,** which is an *illegal act against someone just because he or she is a member of a particular group.*

Possession of Weapons

An important relationship exists between access to weapons and the rise in violent crime. As anger increases during a dispute, a weapon may be used as an easy solution. See **Figure 5.3.**

LIFE SKILLS
Protecting Yourself

*P*eople who commit violent crimes seek out people who look vulnerable. You can reduce the chances of becoming a victim of violent crime by learning to protect yourself. The following tips will help you to stay safe.

In General:

► Do not look like an easy target. Stand up straight and walk with a confident stride.

► If someone bothers you, use direct eye contact and a forceful voice and say "Leave me alone," or shout "Fire!"

► If you are being attacked, get away any way that you can.

Figure 5.3
Causes of Gun-Related Death Among Young People

When young people use guns, the result is often death.

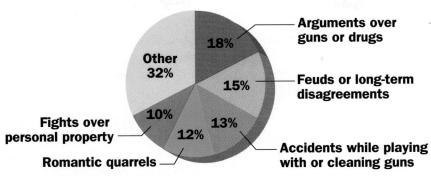

- Other 32%
- 18% — Arguments over guns or drugs
- 15% — Feuds or long-term disagreements
- 13% — Accidents while playing with or cleaning guns
- 12% — Romantic quarrels
- 10% — Fights over personal property

Source: Center to Prevent Handgun Violence

in your journal

Think about a time when you felt really afraid. How did your body react? Did your hands turn cold? Did you tremble? Did the hair on the back of your neck stand on end? Use your journal to write about your reactions to the fear you felt.

Peer Pressure

Many teens want to be accepted by a group and will take part in any conflict to show loyalty to the group. Sometimes, pressure from the group causes a teen to do something that goes against his or her own values.

Alcohol and Other Drugs

Alcohol and other drugs can contribute to violence. Substance abuse makes people act in unpredictable and dangerous ways. It can also prevent a person from making good decisions and judgments. Half of all violent crimes are committed by people under the influence of alcohol or other drugs.

Outside:

▶ Do not walk alone at night or near alleyways. Walk in lighted areas.

▶ If you think someone is following you, go into a store or other public place.

▶ When entering your house, make sure your keys are ready so you do not have to fumble for them at the door.

▶ Do not hitchhike or ride in a car with strangers.

▶ If someone wants your money or jewelry and you are in danger, throw your purse, wallet, or jewelry away from you. Then run in the opposite direction.

Inside:

▶ Avoid entering an elevator alone with a stranger.

▶ At home, keep the doors and windows locked. Do not open the door for someone you do not know. Do not tell strangers on the phone that you are home alone.

Follow-up Activity

Using these tips as a checklist, examine the way you protect yourself in general, on the street, and in your home. In what areas are you safety conscious? In what areas do you need improvement? Make an action plan to keep yourself safe.

Taking action can help to boost your self-esteem and make you feel that the violence in our society is not a hopeless situation. Write to the lawmakers about the violence in your school or community, or describe a personal experience if you have been a victim. Urge your representatives to introduce and pass laws that prevent violence and help victims of violent crime. You can write to your state senator at the U.S. Senate, Washington, DC 20510 or your state representative at the U.S. House of Representatives, Washington, DC 20525.

As a way to remember loved ones and friends who have been victims of violence, people in a community can work together. They can help to make their neighborhoods safer.

Gangs and Gang-Related Violence

A **gang** is *a group of people who associate with one another because they have something in common.* Although teen gangs are not all alike, many are involved in criminal activities. Most of the crimes involve some type of violence, intimidation, drive-by shootings, robbery, gang warfare, or rape.

Young people join gangs for many reasons, including the need for companionship, racism, poverty, boredom, anger, lack of family support, and peer pressure. However, there are many safer, non-criminal alternatives to joining a gang.

- If you are lonely or bored, look for a youth group, sports team, or church group in your neighborhood.

- If you are being harassed by gang members and are scared, get help. A family member, community group, school counselor, or police officer can give you support and help protect you.

- If peers are pressuring you, band together with other teens to start a community group that works for positive change.

Stopping and Preventing Violence

Although violence in America is on the rise, communities and individuals are working together to eliminate the risk factors and reduce the incidence of violent crimes. Here is a list of what some communities are doing to make their neighborhoods safer.

- More police on the streets
- Stricter gun laws
- Nighttime sports programs
- Improved lighting in parks and playgrounds
- Neighborhood Watch programs
- Teen curfews
- Tougher punishments for violent crimes

Violence and You

Figure 5.4 on page 149 shows how many students and teachers are victims of violence. Do you, like other students, feel that you would learn more in school if you felt safer? If that is true, then there are many ways that you can work with others to help make your school a safer place.

Figure 5.4
Violence in School

The violence in schools does not always involve physical harm. Often, it is shoving, threatening notes, physical threats, or insults.

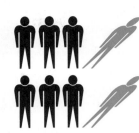

1in4 Students
1in4 Teachers

say that they have been victims of violence on or near school property.

Toward Safer Schools

Principals, school board members, teachers, parents, and students are working together to stop violence in the schools. Here is a list of what some schools are trying.

- Stricter dress codes
- No expensive jewelry
- Ban on beepers
- Locker searches
- Video surveillance cameras
- Metal detectors
- Security guards
- Drug- and gun-sniffing dogs
- Peer mediation programs
- Violence prevention programs

Schools are also trying to eliminate some of the causes of violence by teaching respect for others and providing counseling.

Review

Lesson 2

Using complete sentences, answer the following questions on a separate sheet of paper.

Reviewing Terms and Facts

1. **Vocabulary** Which of the following terms are illegal acts: *homicide, hate crime, prejudice?* Describe each one.

2. **Give Examples** Identify ways in which peer pressure might lead a teen to do something she or he would not ordinarily do.

Thinking Critically

3. **Hypothesize** Why do you think some young people join gangs?

4. **Analyze** Do you feel safe at school? What steps do you take to protect yourself? In what ways do you help to protect the safety of others?

Applying Health Concepts

5. **Health of Others** Organize a group to brainstorm ways to prevent school violence. Attend a student council meeting. Share your group's ideas with the students.

6. **Consumer Health** Find out about movie ratings and warnings on record albums, tapes, and compact discs. Evaluate the need for them, and share your findings in class.

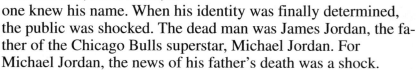

Teen HEALTH DIGEST

Sports and Recreation

Hitting Home

In 1993 a man was found shot in his car on a country road. He was a victim of random violence and, for a while, no one knew his name. When his identity was finally determined, the public was shocked. The dead man was James Jordan, the father of the Chicago Bulls superstar, Michael Jordan. For Michael Jordan, the news of his father's death was a shock.

Since then, Jordan has made some major changes in his life. He retired from basketball. Hoping to make something positive out of the senseless loss of his father, Jordan has begun to speak to young people about the dangers of guns and violence.

Myths and Realities

Abuse and Violence

There is a lot being said about abuse and violence these days. Can you separate the facts from the stories? You may be surprised when you read the following statements.

Myth: Abusive parents hate their children.

Reality: Not so. Parents who abuse their children may do so because they do not know healthy ways to express their anger and frustration. Many abusive parents were abused children themselves.

Myth: Having a gun is the best way to protect yourself.

Reality: No. Having a firearm actually increases your chances of being killed.

Myth: Most murders are committed by strangers.

Reality: Over half of all homicides are committed by people who know their victims.

CON$UMER FOCU$

Safety Guaranteed

There are many products and devices being sold today that offer protection from crime. Are they really "crime proof"? These products include locks for the steering wheels of cars, theft tracking devices, alarm systems for cars and homes, and pocket-sized canisters of pepper gas to deter potential attackers.

Some of these products are very expensive. In addition, having an anticrime device may give you a false sense of security. Do not rely on the product alone to protect you. Take the necessary precautions to stay out of harm's way, read the directions and warning labels carefully, and use the item only as directed.

People at Work

Police Officer Works with Gangs

Steve Garcia has a dangerous but important job. As a police officer in a high-crime area of a major city, he has been assigned to a gang control unit. His job is gang intervention—becoming involved with gang members and working with them to control violence in their community. "This is a tough business," he says. "The odds aren't good. There are about 15,000 police officers and more than 100,000 gang members. Gangs will protect their turf at all costs, and they don't care who they have to blow away in the process."

Officer Garcia continues, "That's why I feel like I have to do this job, despite the danger, because so many innocent people are getting killed. Last week a four-year-old boy died in my arms. That's a picture you don't forget."

To become a police officer, Garcia had to be 21 years old and a U.S. citizen. He had to be in top physical condition and have good vision. He attended the police academy for six months of training. He also took college classes in criminal justice, the psychology of gangs, and the role of drugs in gang activities.

"The drug trade plays a big part," he says, "but so do poverty, family breakups, and the weapons on the street. There's a lot of strain in this job, but somebody has to do it. Some of the gang members are so young. Underneath—way underneath—they're just scared, neglected kids."

Once a week, Garcia works in a special gang prevention program with third graders. He goes into schools to teach youngsters about the dangers of peer pressure, gangs, weapons, and prison life. "The best hope is with the younger ones," he says. "Sometimes I take the kids headed for trouble to visit the prison. I'm encouraged when they realize that they will end up here if they continue their behavior."

Teens Making a Difference

Talk Show Host

Tamara Morris, a student from Wilmington, Delaware, is committed to straight talk about teen issues. Recently, she became the host of a cable television talk show for teens. On the show—called "What's Up?"—Tamara leads discussions with students about the issues that most affect their lives.

"We talk a lot about violence in the schools," she says. "Kids say the situation at home plays a big part."

Tamara goes on, "Some kids come to school with anger or rage over something that happened at home. It's bottled up until they get to school, and then the violence erupts."

Tamara believes in helping other people. Every morning, she serves breakfast to homeless people at a local church. She speaks to teens about staying in school and stopping the violence. She also writes a newspaper column.

Tamara served on a mayor's task force making suggestions about ways to stop youth violence. She hopes to become a lawyer and go into politics, where she believes she can continue to make a positive change in the future.

Conflict Resolution

This lesson will help you find answers to questions that teens often ask about resolving conflicts. For example:

▶ **What makes me really angry?**

▶ **How can I recognize when a situation may be building toward an argument or a fight?**

▶ **How can I stop an angry situation before it gets to the fight stage?**

▶ **How can I help others to avoid fights?**

How Fights Begin

Disagreements begin for all kinds of reasons. Your brother borrows your baseball mitt without first asking. A girl insults another girl's boyfriend. A teen accuses a classmate of stealing his athletic shoes. The causes are endless.

Sometimes, the reason for a disagreement may seem unimportant. Yet a small quarrel may result in a nasty, even deadly, fight. When fights occur, it is usually because the people involved do not know healthy ways to settle their differences. Disagreements do not have to end in violence. In this lesson, we will examine causes of fights and nonviolent ways to deal with conflict.

Teen Issues

Fight Stoppers

If one approach fails to stop a disagreement, try another.

▶ **Do something creative and unexpected.** For example, write a friendly note on a lunch bag.

▶ **Offer the other person a way out of the conflict** by proposing a truce or a compromise.

▶ **Apologize for your part.** This step may break the ice.

This is my sweater. I told you not to go in my closet!

I didn't have anything to wear!

Disagreements are a natural part of life. The way you handle them, however, determines whether or not you learn from them.

Arguments

Arguments occur when people are not communicating well or when they are disrespectful of one another. When arguments get out of hand, fights may result. Here are some of the most common reasons for teen arguments.

- **Property.** Teens may not respect one another's property. They may use items that belong to someone else without getting permission ahead of time.

- **Jealousy.** Young people may feel jealous when they are not included in certain activities or when a boyfriend or girlfriend notices someone else.

- **Territory.** Teens may not want others to cross the boundaries that make up their neighborhood.

- **Values.** Teens may refuse to do something that goes against their values, such as lying, cheating, or stealing.

Hurt Pride

Sometimes, fights begin because someone's pride has been hurt. A teen may do something hurtful such as insult a family member, spread a rumor, or ridicule another in public. Often, the injured party feels hurt or angry, and responds by fighting back.

Peer Pressure

Fights also begin when teens encourage others to "fight it out." They may stand on the sidelines, heckling and cheering the fighters. This behavior only worsens the situation. Once a crowd has gathered, the chances for settling the problem peacefully decrease substantially. In fact, the crowd may exaggerate the problem and make the fight more serious than before.

Revenge

One mean act or insult can start a chain of events in which the victim wants to get even. He or she may recruit family or friends to get involved in the conflict. As the need for revenge grows, the fighting may become more intense and more dangerous.

Acts of revenge are common among rival gangs when one of their own members has been harmed. Because gangs frequently use weapons, a minor misunderstanding can result in violence, such as a stabbing or a shoot-out.

Prejudice

Sometimes, people refuse to accept others who are different. Their feelings are usually based on an opinion about people with a particular skin color, religious or political belief, nationality, or other difference.

People who are prejudiced may single out someone from the group and harass, intimidate, or threaten him or her. He or she may retaliate alone or with others who support his or her position. As a result, fights or dangerous gang warfare may occur.

Preventing Fights

It is not always easy to avoid fights, but it is possible. Like a balloon that is inflated too much, anger can build up inside you until the pressure makes it explode. However, you can learn healthy ways to keep conflicts from reaching the explosion stage. The best way to prevent fights is to recognize conflict early, control your anger, and ignore some conflicts. When you are unable to avoid a conflict, using nonviolent methods can help you resolve the problem in a peaceful way.

Recognize Conflict Early

There are usually signs that a problem exists. For example, there may be name-calling, insults, threats, or shoves. The key to preventing fights is to recognize the signs early and deal with them before they reach the danger stage. It is easier to resolve a conflict peacefully when you are still in control of your emotions.

HEALTH LAB

Mediating a Conflict

Introduction: In some schools, when students have a conflict they cannot resolve on their own, they sign up to meet with a student mediator, or a neutral third person. Usually, adults are not present at this meeting. The mediator takes the students through the following steps to resolve the conflict.

1. Emphasize neutrality and assure the participants that everyone will cooperate to reach a satisfactory solution.

2. Set guidelines for the meeting. For example, there should be no name-calling, insults, swearing, or interrupting.

3. Allow each person to give her or his side of the situation without interruptions. A mediator should listen carefully but does not react. Ask people to repeat or make their points clearer when necessary.

4. Help the participants brainstorm solutions that will feel right to both sides.

5. Have both sides promise to abide by the agreement.

Objective: During the next week, observe conflicts around you that would benefit from mediation. Consider examples of these conflicts in your own family, among your friends, or in the news.

Control Your Anger

The first step in managing your anger is recognizing its early signs so you can stay in control. The body usually reacts to anger with physical changes such as increased heart rate and breathing, sweaty palms, flushed face, stuttering, and a high-pitched voice. By being alert for these signs, you can try to resolve the conflict peacefully or ignore it altogether.

To manage your anger, find a way to relieve pent-up feelings that works for you. Some suggestions follow. If, however, you feel really angry, find someone such as a school counselor or health care professional who can help you sort it out.

■ Walk, jog, swim, or shoot some baskets.

■ Listen to quiet music.

■ Take a long bath or shower.

■ Pound a pillow.

■ Talk it out with a good friend.

■ Have a good cry.

■ Sit quietly for half an hour or so.

Ignore Some Conflicts

Some issues are not worth your time and effort. For instance, if the other person is a stranger or someone you will never see again, it is probably best to just walk away. If the other person is someone you care about, you need to communicate your feelings in a calm and reasonable manner.

Material and Method: You will need one 3-by-5-inch card for each conflict you are observing and a long strip of paper. On each card, write *Observation* on one side and *Analysis* on the other. On the *Observation* side, write the facts—the words, gestures, facial expressions, or actions of the people you are observing. On the *Analysis* side, write how these behaviors make it more or less likely that the conflict will be resolved. Select one of the cards and imagine you are the mediator in that conflict. Divide the strip of paper into frames and create a mediation "cartoon" for this conflict. In a series of drawings with dialogue in cartoon balloons, take the argument through the mediation process.

Observation and Analysis: At the end of the week, share your observations, analyses, and cartoon with your classmates. Find out what other solutions they might suggest.

Use Nonviolent Confrontation

Nonviolent confrontation means resolving your conflict by peaceful methods. With nonviolent confrontation, you settle matters without angry words or looks, threats, punches, or weapons. The benefit of nonviolent confrontation is that the argument is likely to be settled so that both parties are satisfied. See **Figure 5.5** and try some of the following guidelines.

- Carefully plan what to say, stay calm, and stick to the subject.
- Pick the right time and place.
- Confront the other person when he or she is alone.
- Be a good listener; do not interrupt.
- Be sensitive to body language, or any nonverbal communication.
- Be positive; avoid insults, blame, sarcasm, accusation, and threats.
- Be willing to compromise.
- Leave the area if there is a weapon present.

Helping Others Avoid Fights

Friends can help one another to avoid fights by showing disapproval of fighting. For instance, they can refuse to spread rumors and ignore people when they talk badly about others. Advising friends to do the same is a good way to help them stay safe.

When people you know and care about are starting to argue, you can help without getting hurt. You can assist by sharing what you know about neutrality, mediation, and negotiation.

Q & A

Oh, Brother!

Q: My brother is having a big feud with another guy at school. They always fight in the locker room. Things are really heating up. Now my brother wants me to back him up when they meet after school to fight it out. What should I do?

A: Don't get caught in the middle of someone else's battle, even your brother's. Tell him that fighting will only make it worse. Urge him to talk with a peer counselor or mediator at school. Suggest that he use some of the skills you've learned about nonviolent confrontation.

Figure 5.5
Two Approaches to Conflict

The teen in the pictures on this page and the next one is reacting differently to a problem. Why does one promote settling the conflict while the other makes it worse?

Hey, you can't cut in line.

- **Neutrality** (noo·TRA·luh·tee) is *not taking sides when others are arguing.* Avoid fights and urge others to do the same.

- **Mediation** (mee·dee·AY·shuhn) is *resolving conflicts by using a neutral person to help reach a solution that is acceptable to both sides.* Many people use mediation to resolve disagreements.

- **Negotiation** (ni·goh·shee·AY·shuhn) is *the process of discussing problems face-to-face in order to reach a solution.* Negotiation involves talking, listening, considering the other point of view, and compromising.

Toward a Win-Win World

People often think of situations in terms of winning and losing. In relationships, win-lose thinking can lead people to feeling angry or cheated.

Mediation is a way to turn a win-lose situation into a win-win situation. Many families, schools, and communities are using mediation as a way to prevent violence. When people resolve their differences peacefully, both sides, as well as society, benefit.

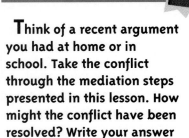

in your journal

Think of a recent argument you had at home or in school. Take the conflict through the mediation steps presented in this lesson. How might the conflict have been resolved? Write your answer in your journal.

Review — Lesson 3

Using complete sentences, answer the following questions on a separate sheet of paper.

Reviewing Terms and Facts

1. **Give Examples**   List three causes of fights.
2. **Vocabulary**   Compare and contrast the following terms: *neutrality, negotiation.*

Thinking Critically

3. **Suggest**   How can you manage your anger before it gets out of control?

4. **Recall**   How does mediation result in a positive situation for all people involved in a conflict?

Applying Health Concepts

5. **Health of Others**   Do some research on Mohandas Gandhi and Martin Luther King, Jr., and their commitment to non-violence. Share your findings in class.

6. **Personal Health**   List your own signs and symptoms of anger, and decide at what point you are likely to use poor judgment. What steps do you need to take before you reach this point of anger?

In a hurry? Sure, you can go ahead of me.

Chapter Summary

► Abuse is the physical, emotional, or mental mistreatment of another person. (Lesson 1)

► Abuse is a crime and it is never the fault of the victim. (Lesson 1)

► The four main types of abuse are physical abuse, emotional abuse, sexual abuse, and neglect. (Lesson 1)

► People who abuse others usually lack the skills to deal with their own frustrations and problems. (Lesson 1)

► To break the cycle of abuse, the victim and abuser need to get help. (Lesson 1)

► Today, violence is more serious and more random than it was in the past. (Lesson 2)

► People who commit violent acts usually have not learned how to deal with their emotions. (Lesson 2)

► Some factors that contribute to violence are anger, prejudice, possession of weapons, poor coping and communication skills, peer pressure, and alcohol and other drug abuse. (Lesson 2)

► Alcohol and other drugs make people act in unpredictable and dangerous ways that often result in violence. (Lesson 2)

► Fights happen for many reasons, including arguments that get out of hand, hurt pride, peer pressure, revenge, and prejudice. (Lesson 3)

► Fights can be prevented by recognizing conflict early, controlling your anger, ignoring some conflicts, and using nonviolent confrontation. (Lesson 3)

Using Health Terms

On a separate sheet of paper, write the vocabulary term that best matches each definition given below.

1. The person against whom a crime is committed (Lesson 1)

2. The beating, hitting, or kicking of another person (Lesson 1)

3. The failure to meet the basic physical and emotional needs of a person (Lesson 1)

4. A violent crime that results in the death of another person (Lesson 2)

5. An opinion that has been formed before careful consideration (Lesson 2)

6. Not taking sides when others are arguing (Lesson 3)

7. Resolving conflicts by using a neutral person to help reach a solution that is acceptable to both sides (Lesson 3)

8. Discussing problems face-to-face to find solutions (Lesson 3)

Reviewing Main Ideas

Using complete sentences, answer the following questions on a separate sheet of paper.

1. What is neglect? (Lesson 1)

2. List some causes of abuse. (Lesson 1)

3. How can you tell if someone is being abused? (Lesson 1)

4. What should you do if you suspect someone is being abused? (Lesson 1)

5. How does television contribute to violence? (Lesson 2)

6. List the causes of violence. (Lesson 2)

7. What is a gang? (Lesson 2)

8. What are some alternatives to joining a gang? (Lesson 2)

9. What are schools doing to prevent violence? (Lesson 2)

10. What are the most common things that teens argue over? (Lesson 3)

11. What is the benefit of nonviolent confrontation? (Lesson 3)

12. What methods can you use to help others avoid fights? (Lesson 3)

Thinking Critically

Using complete sentences, answer the following questions on a separate sheet of paper.

1. **Compare and Contrast** What are the similarities and differences between physical abuse and emotional abuse? (Lesson 1)

2. **Apply** Why is it important to report all types of abuse? (Lesson 1)

3. **Classify** Several places where a victim of abuse can receive help were listed in this lesson. Which of these places were for immediate and short-term help and which were for long-term help? (Lesson 1)

4. **Synthesize** Why do you think random violence is increasing? (Lesson 2)

5. **Analyze** What effect does peer pressure have on violence? (Lesson 2)

6. **Explain** How does neutrality affect a conflict situation? (Lesson 3)

7. **Summarize** Explain the importance of each step in the mediation process. (Lesson 3)

8. **Apply** Think of a recent disagreement you had with someone. Explain how negotiation helped that situation or could have helped it. (Lesson 3)

Your Action Plan

Staying safe means taking certain steps to reduce your chances of becoming involved in fights or becoming a victim of crime. To make an action plan to increase your chances of staying safe, you need to set a goal. Look back through your private journal entries for this chapter. What do they tell you about the choices you can make to keep yourself from becoming a victim of violence or abuse?

Once you have set a goal, write it down. Make sure your goal is something you can achieve.

Next, write down the short-term steps you will take to reach your goal. To resolve your conflict, you could start by reviewing the steps in Lesson 3.

Now, plan a timetable for taking the steps that will help you achieve your goal. When you reach your goal, reward yourself and feel good about your accomplishment.

Building Your Portfolio

1. Write a story in which a teen helps a young abused child who lives next door. Be sure to include how the teen found out and what he or she did to help. Place a copy of your story in your portfolio.

2. Find articles in newspapers and news magazines about disagreements between workers and management or between athletes and team owners. Describe how negotiation was used to settle these disputes. If negotiation failed to resolve the situation, identify the cause of the failure. Write a one-page paper about one of the disputes. Place a copy of your paper in your portfolio.

In Your Home and Community

1. With several classmates, create a manual for preventing fights and taking a conflict through the mediation process.

2. Collect free pamphlets that contain information about places where victims of abuse and violence can go for help.

3. Find out if there is a crime watch, Neighborhood Watch, or other community program near you. Check your local library or police department for this information. If there is no community program in your area, write to the National Crime Prevention Council for tips on how to start such a program. The address is 1700 K Street NW, Washington, DC 20006-3817.

Chapter 6
Consumer Choices and Public Health

Student Expectations

After reading this chapter, you should be able to:

1. Describe the major benefits of being a wise consumer.

2. Explain how to comparison shop, and name some influences on your consumer choices.

3. Describe the American health care system and the types of health services available to consumers.

4. Identify and avoid quackery, and describe how to handle problems with health goods or services.

5. Tell how government agencies, public health laws, and voluntary organizations promote good health.

Have you heard of people having "bad-hair" days? I've had a bad-hair life! From the day I was born, my hair has been superfine and straight as a stick.

I saw an ad for an amazing product called Magic Hair in a teen magazine. The ad said that scientific research had found a way to give people thicker, stronger hair in just days.

I decided to try Magic Hair for myself. All I had to do was send my payment, either $6.95 for a three-month supply, or $11.95 for a six-month supply. Mom always says it's cheaper to buy in quantity, so I ordered the six-month supply.

After waiting nearly two months, I finally got my order. There it was—a plastic jar of colorless gook—my ticket to fuller, more luxurious hair.

That evening, I used Magic Hair. When my hair dried, it didn't seem any different, but I figured I needed to try the product a while longer. After two weeks, my hair still wasn't better. I was really disappointed. I wasted 12 bucks, and I still had wimpy hair!

in Your journal

Read the account on this page. Have you ever been disappointed with a product you bought? Start your private journal entries on consumer choices and public health by responding to these questions:

▶ Do you plan your purchases or buy on impulse?

▶ What influences your spending choices?

▶ What do you do if you buy something that is broken or defective?

When you reach the end of the chapter, you will use your journal entries to make an action plan.

1 Building Healthy Consumer Habits

This lesson will help you find answers to questions that teens often ask about their consumer decisions. For example:

▶ **How can I be a wise consumer?**

▶ **What are the benefits of improving my consumer skills?**

▶ **What government groups protect consumer rights?**

Words to Know

consumer
goods
services

Where Does Your Money Go?

Who is a consumer? You are. So are all of your friends. All together, you and your friends and all other teens buy millions of dollars' worth of products. A **consumer** (kuhn·SOO·mer) is *anybody who purchases goods or services.*

Some of the items you buy—such as music tapes, CDs, food, and clothes—are **goods.** These are *products that are made and purchased to satisfy someone's needs or wants.* You also buy services. **Services** are *activities that are purchased to satisfy someone's needs or wants.* You may pay to hear a concert or to have someone cut your hair. You are also a health consumer. **Figure 6.1** shows some health goods and services you might buy.

Some of the goods and services you buy are not as clearly related to your health, but they still affect it. Sunglasses are an example. You may think of sunglasses as a type of product you buy for

Figure 6.1
Consumer Goods and Services
Which of the health-related items shown here is a service?

their looks, but sunglasses are a health product. Some protect your eyes from the sun's harmful ultraviolet rays, whereas others do not. To make healthy consumer decisions, you need to know which product is best for your health. You can get information from many sources to help you learn the facts about sunglasses and other health products.

How to Be a Wise Consumer

- Use your money wisely to get the most out of what you spend.

- Buy useful goods and services—ones that will help you maintain a high level of health.

- Buy safe goods and services, and stay away from goods and services that will harm you.

- Know what to do if you have a consumer problem.

Consider what happened to Natalie. She bought some deodorant to keep her underarms dry. When she applied the deodorant, her skin turned red and began to itch. Natalie knew that she was allergic to an ingredient in some health care products. She should have looked at the label for that ingredient. When she did not, she was not using good consumer skills. If she had read the label, she might not have bought the deodorant. She would have saved herself some money—and spared herself the rash!

Why Be a Wise Consumer?

Being a consumer also means building your consumer skills. These help you choose health products and services wisely. Being a wise consumer benefits you in four ways.

- **You can promote and protect your health.** When you purchase useful goods, you can improve your health. When you buy safe products, you lessen your risk of harm.

- **You can save time and money.** By shopping carefully, you have the best chance of choosing products that work for you. That means you will not waste your money on products that do not work. It can also mean that you will not have to spend more money later trying to fix a problem caused by an unwise purchase. Natalie, for instance, may now have to buy some medicine to clear up the rash.

- **You can build your self-confidence.** As you use your consumer skills well, you become more sure of yourself. This helps build self-esteem, which can carry over to other areas of your life.

- **You protect your rights.** Each of us has certain rights as a consumer. Many groups work with consumers who have problems. You can turn to them for help and advice when you have a problem, but the best defender of your consumer rights is you.

in Your Journal

Do you consider yourself a wise consumer? If so, list the traits that make you wise. If not, list two steps you can take to build your consumer skills.

Wise consumers read product labels when choosing health products.

The Rights of Consumers

Many groups have worked hard to establish rights for consumers. The list below summarizes those rights.

- **We have the right to safety.** We have the right to purchase goods and services that will not harm us.

- **We have the right to choose.** We have the right to select from many goods and services at competitive prices.

- **We have the right to be informed.** We have the right to truthful information about goods and services.

- **We have the right to be heard.** We have the right to join in the making of laws about consumers.

- **We have the right to have problems corrected.** We have the right to complain when we have been treated unfairly.

- **We have the right to consumer education.** We have the right to learn the skills necessary to help us make wise choices.

Consumers have the right to return products that are not fresh.

MAKING HEALTHY DECISIONS
Being a Wise Consumer

*M*itch has been shopping around, looking for a mountain bike for weeks. Most of them are too expensive for his budget.

Yesterday, his friend Matt called and told him that the Cycle Center is going out of business. Matt said that all bicycles are on sale for 30 percent off. That sounded like a good deal to Mitch.

When Mitch went down to the Cycle Center, he found that one of the models he likes was within his price range. His mother reminded him that if the store goes out of business, Mitch won't have anywhere to go if he has a complaint or needs a repair.

The bicycles are selling fast, so Mitch needs to decide soon. His mother suggested that he use the step-by-step decision-making process to make up his mind.

❶ **State the situation**
❷ **List the options**
❸ **Weigh the possible outcomes**
❹ **Consider your values**
❺ **Make a decision and act**
❻ **Evaluate the decision**

Consumer Protection

Consumers are not completely on their own. Governments at all levels have agencies that are concerned with protecting consumer rights. The federal government has a number of agencies concerned with ensuring that products are safe and that their benefits are represented accurately.

■ **Consumer Product Safety Commission (CPSC).** This organization makes sure that appliances, toys, and other products are safe. It can ban products it finds dangerous and can order manufacturers to notify people who have already bought the product with the problem. The CPSC requires that medicines be sold in child-resistant packaging.

■ **Food and Drug Administration (FDA).** The FDA is responsible for the safety and purity of cosmetics, medicines, and all foods, except for meat and poultry. It requires that labeling be accurate and complete. It also decides whether a medicine should be sold by prescription from a doctor or whether it is safe to sell it over the counter.

■ **Food Safety and Inspection Service (FSIS)** of the Department of Agriculture. The FSIS oversees the safety of meat and poultry. It inspects meat-packing plants.

■ **Federal Trade Commission (FTC).** The FTC regulates the advertising of products and services in newspapers and magazines and on radio and television. The goal is to prevent advertisements from presenting false or misleading information.

Your Total Health

Cold Remedies

In 1992, Americans spent $805 million on the top six cold remedies. Cold medicines are among the hundreds of health-related products that Americans purchase each year. What others can you think of?

Did You Know?

Two Sides of the Same Coin ACTIVITY!

Every consumer right comes with a responsibility. Think of the consumer responsibility for each of the rights on page 164. For example, along with the right to safety goes the responsibility to use products as directed. Make a poster or sign for each responsibility.

Follow-up Activities

1. Apply the six steps of the decision-making process to Mitch's story.

2. If Mitch decides to buy the bicycle, do you think he is being a wise consumer? Why or why not?

3. Along with two or three other students, role-play a scene in which Mitch explains his decision to buy the bike.

Consumer Education

Consumer rights have another side: consumer responsibilities. One is to exercise your rights. This starts with consumer education.

Many publications evaluate and report on products. However, you the consumer must do some research to benefit from these studies. Many consumer organizations can help you if you have a problem with a store or a manufacturer. However, you the consumer must know about and use these organizations. It all comes down to this: the educated consumer is the best-protected consumer.

Government agencies test many products for safety and effectiveness. Consumer organizations conduct tests on different brands or models of the same product. Doing some background research before you buy will help you make wise consumer choices.

Lesson 1 Review

Using complete sentences, answer the following questions on a separate sheet of paper.

Reviewing Terms and Facts

1. **Vocabulary** What is the difference between *goods* and *services*?

2. **List** Name the four ways in which being a wise consumer benefits you.

Thinking Critically

3. **Analyze** Some people believe that the right to be an informed consumer is the most important right of all. Explain why that could be true.

4. **Give Examples** Consumers expect people who sell goods and services to treat them honestly. How can they act honestly in turn? Give examples.

Applying Health Concepts

5. **Consumer Health** Take an inventory of health-related goods in your home, such as hair products, deodorants, and first-aid supplies. Based on what you have learned in this chapter, decide which products may have been a waste of money. Make a list of the products and summarize your findings.

6. **Consumer Health** With a group of classmates, look for newspaper and magazine articles that give advice on spending money wisely. Put together a collection of these articles, then discuss them. Which ones are really helpful? What tips do they offer on spending money wisely? Which articles are less useful? Why?

Lesson 2

What Influences Your Choices?

This lesson will help you find answers to questions that teens often ask about the purchases they make. For example:

- **How do I know I'm getting the best buy for my money?**
- **What influences me to buy certain goods and services?**

Words to Know

comparison shopping
warranty
discount store
coupon
generic product
tradition
advertising

Shopping Around

Al thought it would be easy to buy a pair of glasses. However, when he and his mom went shopping, they had to make some choices. Should they buy glass lenses or plastic lenses? How can they decide from among the different kinds of plastics, coatings, and tints that are available?

Like Al, you may need to choose from among several products or services that do the job. Good information will help you choose. You can get information by talking to family members or friends. You can read books or magazines that publish ratings of products or services to learn which are well regarded.

Shopping for Goods

Comparison (kumn·PEHR·i·suhn) **shopping** is *a method of judging the benefits of different goods or services.* Comparison shopping helps you get the best value for your money. **Figure 6.2** shows the factors to consider when you comparison shop.

Figure 6.2
The Factors in Comparison Shopping

Price	Features	Quality	Convenience	Warranty
Staying within a certain cost range is important to most people.	The characteristics of a product are important.	Quality includes how well a product is made, how well it performs its job, and how long it will last.	The labor-saving features of a product affect many consumer decisions. The store's location may also make a difference.	A **warranty** is a *written promise to handle repairs if the product does not work.*

How to Comparison Shop

Figure 6.3 shows an example of comparison shopping. In addition, you can use comparison shopping to find the best place to make your purchase. Ask yourself these questions: Which store offers the best price for the product I want? What are the store's return policies? How helpful are the salespeople? Is the store's location convenient? This is particularly important if return visits are needed for adjustments or repairs. For convenience, many people opt to make purchases through the mail.

Figure 6.3
An Example of Comparison Shopping
After you have gathered information about different products, you can make a chart like this one to see similarities and differences at a glance. Al made this chart to compare glasses. If you know that Al plays a lot of basketball, which factors do you think are important?

Options	Price	Features	Quality	Convenience	Warranty
Glass lenses	$60 to $75	Heavy; more likely to shatter than plastic	Resist scratching	Varies	None
Regular plastic lenses	$60 to $75	Lightweight	Need scratch protection	Varies	One year
High-index plastic lenses	$100 to $150	Thinnest plastic; filter UV rays	Very durable	Varies	Lifetime
Polycarbonate lenses	$80 to $95	Almost unbreakable; filter UV rays	Need scratch protection	Varies	Lifetime

Shopping for Services

Before buying new glasses, people need to have their eyes checked. They can choose between two kinds of doctors. An optometrist (ahp·TAHM·uh·trist) examines eyes, diagnoses vision problems, and prescribes eyeglasses and contact lenses. An ophthalmologist (ahf·thuhl·MAHL·uh·jist) is a medical doctor, who provides the same services as an optometrist but can also prescribe medications and perform surgery.

When Al started complaining about blurry vision, his mother took him to Dr. Rodman, an ophthalmologist associated with their health insurance plan. Al's parents think the doctor gives thorough examinations, and her hours are convenient for them. They also like the way she takes time to answer their questions.

Shopping for Price

Different stores charge different amounts for the same products and services, as illustrated in **Figure 6.4.**

- **Discount stores** are *stores that offer few services but have lower prices.* Most discount stores have fewer salespeople than full-price stores and may look less fancy.

- **Coupons** (KOO·pahnz) are *slips of paper that offer savings on certain brands of goods.*

- **Generic** (jeh·NEHR·ik) **products** are *goods sold in plain packages and at lower prices than brand name goods.* Buying generic products makes sense if they are equal in quality to brand name items.

Figure 6.4
Comparing Stores' Prices

Have you ever compared a product in two different types of stores? Why is it less expensive in one store than the other?

HEALTH LAB
Generic or Brand Name Products?

***I*ntroduction:** Generic products can cost a lot less than brand name products. Sometimes the only difference is in the fancy packaging of brand name products.

Objective: Compare prices, ingredients, and other features between generic and brand name products.

Materials and Method: Make a comparison chart with vertical columns for "Name of Generic Product" and "Name of Brand Name Product"; and with horizontal columns for "Price," "Ingredients," and "Other Features." Go to the drugstore or grocery store and compare three different products. Make sure the generic and brand name products are supposed to be the same. Write down all the information in the chart, placing in the "Other Features" column any "extras" that make one product more desirable than another.

Observation and Analysis: After completing your chart, which of the three products would you buy—the generic ones or the brand name ones? Give reasons for your selections. Do you believe that it is wise for consumers to buy generic products? Why or why not?

The Influences on What You Buy

Your consumer decisions are yours alone. You will decide which goods or service you want, but many factors influence you. Those influences include cost, tradition, advertising, peers, and salespeople. You have already learned how prices affect your choices. The other factors are explained below.

Tradition

Tradition (truh·DI·shun) is *the usual pattern of thought, behavior, or action.* Many consumer decisions are based on tradition. Your food choices, for instance, are strongly influenced by the kind of food your family buys and eats.

Advertising

The main influence on your consumer choices is **advertising.** This is *a format for sending out messages (or advertisements) meant to interest consumers in buying goods and services.* Billions of dollars in advertising are spent each year on television, on radio, in newspapers and magazines, and on billboards.

Ads give information. They also try to persuade you to buy a specific product. Different appeals are used to convince you that a product or service will make you healthier, happier, or more popular. Wise consumers get the information they need to make a purchase without being deceived.

This advertisement is trying to convince consumers to buy a specific brand of suntan lotion. Do you think it is effective? Why or why not?

Peers

Your friends and images of teens in the media can strongly influence your consumer decisions. You want to do things your friends are doing. This can mean wearing the latest styles or joining in their activities. Your health, however, is affected by your health decisions—not anyone else's. If friends pressure you to do something that is not good for your health, decide to resist their influence and stick by your decision.

Salespeople

Salespeople can give good information about a product, but they sometimes pressure buyers. To resist sales pressure, give yourself time to make a decision. Use the decision-making process. Also, ask questions. The answers may be useful in helping you make a wise consumer choice, or they may reveal that the salesperson does not know much about the product.

When you get help from a salesperson, ask questions and give yourself time to make a decision.

Review

Lesson 2

Using complete sentences, answer the following questions on a separate sheet of paper.

Reviewing Terms and Facts

1. **Vocabulary**   Define the term *warranty*. Use it in an original sentence.

2. **Recall**   What are the five factors that influence what consumers choose to buy?

Thinking Critically

3. **Apply**   Leona wants a new exercise bike. What are some things she should consider *before* she begins comparison shopping?

4. **Suggest**   Cindy wants to purchase expensive cosmetic products she has seen advertised in teen magazines. What advice would you give her?

Applying Health Concepts

5. **Consumer Health**   Choose a health product that many teens buy, such as sunglasses, contact lenses, or blow dryers. Look in consumer magazines for ratings of different brands of the product. Do the magazines include useful tips on what to look for and what to consider when purchasing these items? Share the information you find with your classmates.

6. **Consumer Health**   Identify sources of consumer information in your school and community. Which do you think would be most useful to you? Are there any resources specifically for teen consumers?

Choosing Health Services

This lesson will help you find answers to questions that teens often ask about health services. For example:

▶ **Where should I go if I get sick or if I am injured?**

▶ **Why do I need to have health insurance?**

▶ **How do I shop for health services?**

health care
   system
primary care
   provider
specialist
health care facility
health insurance
preferred provider
Medicare
Medicaid
health
   maintenance
   organization
   (HMO)

The Health Care System

Molly fell off her bike and bumped her head. Several weeks after the accident, her head still hurt and she was not sleeping well. Her mother took her to see the family's regular doctor, Dr. Kim. After examining Molly, Dr. Kim sent her to Dr. Miller, a specialist in treating people with head injuries.

When Molly went to see Dr. Kim, she entered our country's health care system. A **health care system** includes *all the medical care available to a nation's people, the way they receive the care, and the way the care is paid for.* The health care system in the United States includes primary care providers and specialists.

Who Provides Health Care?

Doctors play a vital role in the health care system. However, a wide range of other people provide health care. Nurses, dentists, dental hygienists, optometrists, pharmacists, and physical fitness instructors are just a few examples of people other than doctors who work in the health care field.

Some people receive health services at a community clinic. In some areas, these clinics are located in schools.

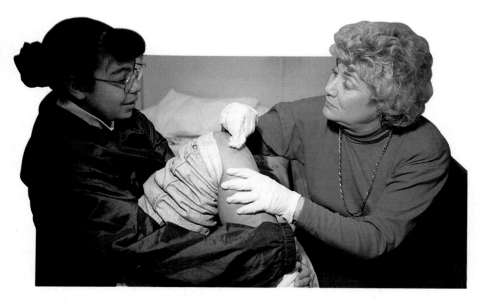

Primary care providers are *the doctors and other health professionals who provide medical checkups and general care.* Patients with more serious conditions or conditions that require specialized equipment may see a specialist. **Specialists** (SPE·shuh·lists) are *doctors trained to handle particular kinds of patients or health matters.* Midlevel practitioners are a relatively new kind of health care professional. Some common ones include nurse practitioners and physician's assistants. They help to keep health costs down by performing many of the routine medical tasks that doctors used to perform. Workers in the health care system have three main goals. They are shown in **Figure 6.5.**

in your journal

Make a list of the people who provide you and your family with health care. Beside each name, write what the person does for you or others in your family.

Figure 6.5
Health Care Goals

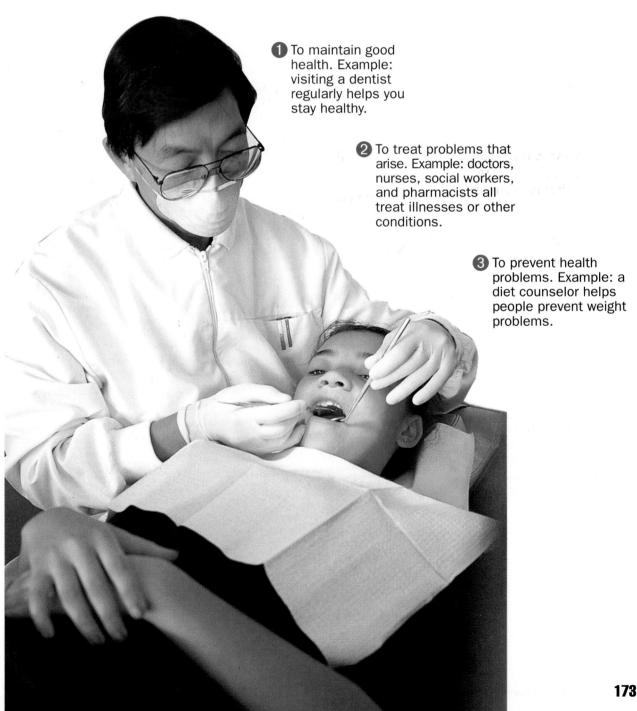

❶ To maintain good health. Example: visiting a dentist regularly helps you stay healthy.

❷ To treat problems that arise. Example: doctors, nurses, social workers, and pharmacists all treat illnesses or other conditions.

❸ To prevent health problems. Example: a diet counselor helps people prevent weight problems.

Types of Health Care Facilities

A **health care facility** is *a place where you can receive health care.* The two basic types are facilities for inpatient care and facilities for outpatient care.

Inpatient Care

Patients need inpatient care when they cannot care for themselves, require treatment that cannot be given on an outpatient basis, or are not in stable condition. Examples are major surgery or a medical condition that may worsen without warning. Patients stay at the facility as long as necessary. The two main types of inpatient health facilities are hospitals and nursing homes.

Outpatient Care

Outpatient care is provided for less serious conditions or simple operations. Examples are treating sprains, putting stitches on serious wounds, extracting teeth, and performing some minor surgery. Patients come to the health care facility, get the treatment they need, and leave for home on the same day. Facilities that provide outpatient care include doctors' offices, clinics, and hospital outpatient clinics.

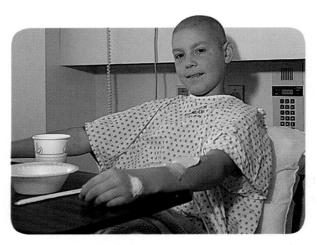

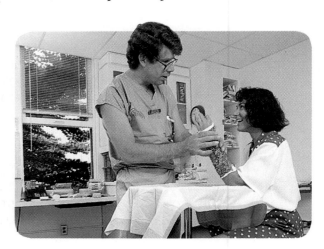

Patients receive either inpatient care or outpatient care depending on their conditions and the types of treatment they need.

Health Insurance

Health care in the United States is costly. In 1990, national health expenditures totaled over $666 billion. Americans might spend thousands on a single medical test, surgery, or a hospital stay. Costs continue to increase each year because of high-technology equipment, organ transplants, the AIDS crisis, and insurance fees that doctors and medical facilities must pay.

Health insurance is a way to ensure that many of these medical expenses can be paid. **Health insurance** (in·SHUR·ens) is *a plan in which private companies or government programs pay for part of the medical costs, and the patient pays for the rest.* **Figure 6.6** shows the breakdown of the different types of medical insurance coverage Americans have.

Private Insurance

Many private companies sell health insurance to consumers. In return for a monthly premium, or fee, the company agrees to pay a portion of the insured person's medical bills. The consumer pays the rest. Some insurance plans require consumers to go to preferred providers. **Preferred providers** are *doctors approved by the health care plan.* They keep their rates within a certain range.

Consumers may purchase private insurance as part of a group or as individuals. Group insurance is sold primarily through places of employment. The employer may pay all or part of an employee's premium as a work benefit. In individual health insurance programs, people pay the premium themselves.

Millions of Americans do not have health insurance. Some are unemployed; others have jobs but their jobs do not include health insurance. In most cases, private insurance is too expensive for them, and they may be ineligible for government programs.

Government Programs

The federal government has two insurance programs for the general public. **Medicare** (MED·i·kehr) provides *health insurance to people 65 years old or older.* People who receive Social Security disability benefits are also eligible, even if they are younger than 65. Medicare covers the costs of hospital care. Patients must purchase additional insurance to pay doctors and other costs.

The other government insurance program is **Medicaid** (MED·i·kayd). It provides *health insurance to people who are poor.* People with low incomes and dependent children, people with high medical costs in relation to their income, and people with disabilities usually qualify for Medicaid.

Obtaining Health Services

Health services are available in most communities in a variety of forms. Those forms include private practices, group practices, clinics, and health maintenance organizations. However, many people receive health care insurance through their work. Increasingly, the type of health services they receive is determined by the insurance program. In many programs, for example, participants must choose doctors from a list of preferred providers.

Figure 6.6
Medical Insurance Coverage

In 1992, Americans' health insurance coverage was broken down into these categories.

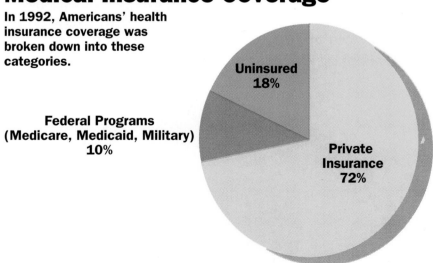

Uninsured
18%

Federal Programs
(Medicare, Medicaid, Military)
10%

Private
Insurance
72%

Source: Center for Health Statistics, 1992 National Health Interview Survey

Private Practices

Primary care providers and specialists may be in private practice. Molly's primary care provider, Dr. Kim, is in private practice. She has her own office and works for herself. When you see a doctor or other health professional in private practice, you are billed for each visit. You pay only for the services you receive.

Group Practices

Often two or more doctors join together to offer health care. They work in a group practice. Doctors in group practice share office space, equipment, and staff. They often consult with one another on the care of their patients. Groups may include a number of doctors with different specialties, or the entire group may specialize in the same area, such as the care of children.

Clinics

Primary care providers and specialists may work for clinics. Clinics provide care for people who are sick or injured. They may operate as part of a hospital or school. Some clinics are run by a group of doctors or community organizations. Clinics often receive government funding to help pay for some of the care given to patients who cannot afford it.

Health Maintenance Organizations

A health maintenance (MAYN·te·nuhns) organization is like a clinic in many ways. A **health maintenance organization (HMO)** includes *many different types of doctors who give health care to members.* You can receive medical care, dental care, and eye care through the HMO.

They are different in several important ways, however. HMOs stress preventive medicine in an attempt to reduce the high cost of medical care. HMOs charge members a yearly or monthly fee. In return, members receive medical care—from routine checkups to major surgery—for little or no additional cost.

Members must choose a primary care physician who belongs to the HMO. In most cases, they are limited to specialists and hospitals that are part of the HMO. To see a doctor outside the HMO, members must get approval.

A health maintenance organization may have a central location where members receive medical care, dental care, and eye care.

Trends in Health Care

Our country's health care system is changing every day. Several trends have developed that aim to improve the quality of health care or reduce its cost.

■ **Birthing centers.** These facilities offer several benefits over the traditional hospital setting. They are homelike, and they involve the entire family in the delivery. They are also significantly less expensive than hospitals.

■ **Computerized health technology.** This program collects health information on computer. It will allow people to answer their own health questions and will provide visual images of complicated medical procedures.

■ **Health centers.** These centers meet the needs of people who are not covered by other health care supports. Some meet the needs of adolescents whereas others serve all the people who are part of a particular community.

■ **Hospice care.** This care for the terminally ill combines loving care with techniques for pain and symptom management. Hospices provide for patients' physical and emotional needs.

■ **National health care.** This proposed program of the U.S. government would regulate medical costs and provide access to health care to all Americans.

Review — Lesson 3

Using complete sentences, answer the following questions on a separate sheet of paper.

Reviewing Terms and Facts

1. **Vocabulary**   Which of the following terms are types of physicians, and which are types of health insurance? *primary care provider, Medicare, specialist, Medicaid, health maintenance organization, preferred provider?*

2. **List**   What are the three main goals of workers in the health care system?

Thinking Critically

3. **Apply**   Luis' grandmother recently broke her hip. She lives alone and cannot care for herself while her hip heals. What type of health care facility would be best for her? Why?

4. **Analyze**   Would you prefer to go to a doctor in a private medical practice or one who belongs to an HMO? Explain your answer.

Applying Health Concepts

5. **Personal Health**   Write a list of suggestions on how to prepare for a visit to the doctor. Along with a classmate, role-play a visit to the doctor.

6. **Personal Health**   Find out what health-related services and screenings are offered at your school. Share your findings in a written report.

Teen HEALTH DIGEST

Teens Making a Difference

Pet Therapy

The newest health workers at Sunnyside Care Center have four legs and bark. They are dogs that belong to sixth and seventh graders from nearby Poplar Bridge Middle School. Every week the students bring their pets to the nursing home. They encourage the elderly residents to talk to the dogs and stroke their fur.

The staff at Sunnyside say that the dogs have a beneficial effect on the residents. The elderly people seem to perk up whenever the dogs come to visit, and they seem happier and more relaxed afterwards. Staff members believe that being able to feel something warm and alive has a positive effect on the residents.

People at Work

Consumer Safety Inspector

Joe Fransen is a consumer safety inspector for the state department of health. He routinely inspects businesses that produce or sell food, drugs, and cosmetics. Whenever there is a sudden outbreak of illness among a group of people, Joe becomes part of a special investigative team. Team members work like detectives to track down the source of the illness and prevent its spread.

One recent case involved 30 eighth-grade science students who went on a field trip to a planetarium. On their way back to school, the students stopped for lunch at a fast-food restaurant. By late afternoon, nearly all of the students were experiencing fever, chills, vomiting, and diarrhea. Joe's team found that undercooked hamburger meat at the restaurant made the students sick.

Joe has a college degree in chemistry and biology. To get his job with the health department, he had to pass a special examination. After he was hired, he was instructed in laws related to product safety and was trained in inspection procedures. Joe knows that his job helps protect people's health. He especially likes the detective work involved in finding the cause of a mysterious illness.

CON$UMER FOCU$

Testimonials

The television advertisement shows a pro basketball player holding a bottle of Sportade. Drinking Sportade, he says, helps him play better. This ad is an example of a testimonial. In a testimonial, a famous person recommends a product or a service.

The advertiser of Sportade hopes that you will buy this drink because a famous athlete tells you to. When faced with a testimonial, you need to ask yourself two questions: "Is this star an expert on sports drinks, or is he only interested in making money?" The real experts might say that plain water or fruit juice is just as good for restoring energy.

Laws say that a famous person must actually use a product before he or she can give a testimonial. However, no law requires that the person think the product is good! A company may pay a star thousands of dollars to say its product is good, even if he or she does not really believe it.

Health Update

High-tech House Calls

Nowadays most patients travel to the doctor's office or a clinic to get treatment. Years ago, however, the family doctor came to the patient's house. New technology promises to bring back those house calls.

Doctors and nurses will come to patients' homes via two-way videophones. Patients will see their doctor or nurse on a screen. The doctor or nurse, in turn, will perform a visual check of the patient. The patient's videophone will be part of a console with attachments for checking on various conditions. For example, by wearing an arm cuff and pushing buttons, the patient can transmit blood pressure readings.

Experts believe that videophones can reduce the cost of health care. Patients will rent the videophone consoles at a fraction of the cost of nursing home or hospital care. People in rural areas, where getting to a doctor is often difficult, would also find the videophones convenient.

Myths and Realities

More Is Not Always Better

Twelve-year-old Jake had swollen nasal passages and could hardly breathe. He had been treating a sinus infection with a nasal spray decongestant. Instead of using the spray twice daily, as directed, he used it every two hours.

Thirteen-year-old Megan looked as if she had second-degree burns on her face. It turned out she was using four times the prescribed amount of an acne medication.

Both these teens fell victim to the medicine myth that if a little of something does a good job, then a lot of something must do even better. More of something can damage your health. When using health care products, always be sure to read and follow directions carefully.

> **TRI-X Extra Strength Acne Treatment**
> **Directions:** Cover affected area with thin layer one to three times daily as needed or as directed by your doctor.
> **Warning:** FOR EXTERNAL USE ONLY. This product may cause irritation, characterized by redness, burning, itching, peeling, or possible swelling. More frequent use may aggravate such irritation.

Handling Consumer Problems

This lesson will help you find answers to questions that teens often ask about dealing with consumer problems. For example:

► How can I keep from buying worthless products and services?
► What should I do if I have a problem with something I buy?
► What should I do if I have a problem with health services?

Words to Know

quackery
placebo effect
consumer
    advocate
small-claims court
second opinion
license
malpractice

Let the Buyer Beware

A centuries-old saying is "Let the buyer beware." This means that consumers have to watch out for goods and services that do not do what sellers claim they will do. Most products *do* work, and most sellers *are* honest. Some businesses, however, sell useless products. Part of being a wise consumer is knowing how to spot them—and avoid them.

Health and Medical Quackery

Quackery (KWA·kuh·ree) is *the sale of worthless products and treatments claimed to prevent diseases or to cure other health problems.* An example is a miracle "cure" for a disease that does not have a cure such as AIDS. Selling weight-reduction programs that are not healthy is also quackery. A quack is a person who makes dishonest claims about products and treatments to make money. Some impostors pretend to have medical skills when, in fact, they have none.

It is against the law to make false claims about drugs and cosmetics. Yet quackery makes millions of dollars a year by selling products that are not cures. This deception takes advantage of people's desire for fast, easy results or their desire to look better. Perhaps the saddest kind of quackery is the kind that offers false hope to people suffering from diseases that do not have effective treatments. **Figure 6.7** describes some of the most common types of quackery.

Do not always believe the claims made about products in television ads. Ask a physician or pharmacist if you have any doubts about health products.

I'm not a doctor, but I play one on TV.

The Placebo Effect

If a person's health improves soon after taking a quack's remedy, it can be due to the **placebo** (pluh·SEE·boh) **effect.** This means that *the person improves because of a strong belief that the "medicine" is helping and not because of anything that the quack provides.*

How to Spot Quackery

To protect yourself from quackery, learn to recognize signs. Some of the common ones follow.

- Quacks tend to work alone—not in clinics—and to sell their products through the mail or door-to-door.

- Quacks often insist on payment by cash.

- Quacks may claim a "medical breakthrough."

- Quacks may say that the health care system is suppressing the news about their miracle cure.

If you have a question about some product or a person selling something, ask an expert—a doctor, a person at a clinic, or someone in your local or state government.

History Connection

Dr. Johnson's Snake Oil

Quackery has been around for centuries. In the 1800s, fast-talking salesmen traveled in "medicine wagons" from town to town. They put on shows and sold "medicinal" potions between acts. These potions, claimed the salesmen, could cure anything from an ingrown toenail to a broken heart. See if you can find other examples of quack remedies and devices from the past.

Figure 6.7
Common Types of Quackery

Type of Product	Typical Advertisement	Facts
Diet Aids Pills Fad diets	TEEN GIRLS! LOSE WEIGHT FAST! Our Body Shaper program lets you eat all the foods you want. No need for boring exercises. To get started on a totally gorgeous body, send $25 to: P.O. Box 19209, Las Vegas, NV 89109.	A good weight-loss program is based on eating fewer calories and less fat and exercising to burn calories. Losing weight takes time. False diet aids can damage your health.
Beauty Products Acne creams Hair enhancers	HAVING PROBLEMS WITH YOUR SKIN? Our remarkable new formula can erase pimples and blackheads forever. Try a FREE sample today. Just send $10 for shipping and handling to: Med-Sci Formulas, P.O. Box 70443, Detroit, MI 48243.	Many products can help your skin temporarily. No product, however, can make your skin blemish-free permanently. Quack products have not been approved by the government and may actually harm your skin.
Miracle Cures Arthritis Cancer	HELEN LAMAR, HEALER Are you sick or in constant pain? Do you suffer from anxiety or depression? Helen Lamar, a gifted healer, can solve your health problems for as little as $25 per visit. Call today. 555-6900.	Quacks sell worthless products and services, often giving seriously ill patients false hope. Even worse, people who take these so-called cures may delay getting the medically approved treatment that could help them.

Problems with Products

Even the wisest consumer has a problem with a purchase from time to time. It can happen to anyone. What can you do if a problem like this happens?

Figure 6.8 shows how to solve a consumer problem. You can usually go to the store where you bought the product if you have a problem with it. You can also write to the manufacturer to get either a replacement or your money back.

In most cases, these steps are enough to solve the problem. Most businesses depend on their customers being satisfied. They will want to solve your problem to maintain your good will as a customer—so you will come back again.

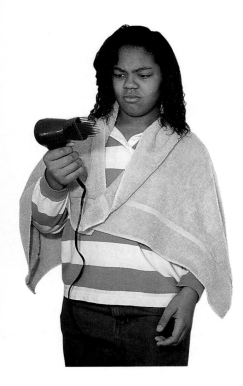

The blow dryer this teen purchased was defective. She took the steps above to solve her problem.

LIFE SKILLS
Evaluating Product Claims

*E*very day, manufacturers bombard you with claims about their products. Take toothpaste, for instance. Toothpaste X contains fluoride, said to strengthen tooth enamel. Toothpaste Y forms an "invisible shield" around your teeth. Which product claims can you believe?

Knowing something about product ingredients will help you evaluate claims. Different brands of the same product generally contain the same basic ingredients. Other ingredients may make the product look, taste, or smell better—and make the product cost more.

All toothpastes, for example, contain a mild abrasive for cleansing the teeth. Toothpaste is really soap for your teeth, and an abrasive is the only ingredient necessary for cleansing. Manufacturers add other ingredients that supposedly improve your teeth. Of all the additives, however, only fluoride has been proven to have beneficial effects.

Knowing something about healthful practices can help you evaluate product claims. You should use personal grooming products as aids and not as substitutes for healthy habits. Toothpaste must be used along with proper brushing, flossing, proper diet, and regular visits to the dentist.

Knowing something about how the body works can also help you evaluate product claims. Bad breath may be due to diseases of the nose, sinuses, lungs, or stomach and intestines. No toothpaste can prevent bad breath that results from these causes.

You can also ask for the opinions of experts. The seal of approval from the American Dental Association (ADA) on a toothpaste can guide your selection. Often you must simply try several products to see which works best for you—regardless of the claims.

Follow-up Activities

1. Choose a personal grooming product you use every day, such as soap, deodorant, or shampoo. Watch for advertisements for this product. Write down the manufacturer's claims. Decide which ones are probably truthful, which claims are exaggerations or half-truths, and which claims are outright lies. Share your findings with your classmates.

2. Research old catalogs and magazines from the early part of this century. Compare the products, the way they were presented, and the claims about them to present-day ads. Share your findings in a two-page report.

Figure 6.8
Solving a Consumer Problem

(1) START. Your new blow dryer is not working properly.

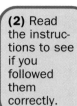

(2) Read the instructions to see if you followed them correctly.

(3) If the blow dryer still does not work, you have a right to complain.

(4) Gather the information you will need to back up your complaint.

(5) Find the sales receipt proving you bought the blow dryer.

(6) Write down what you did, what happened, and why you are not satisfied.

(8b) If you are satisfied with the results, STOP. If not, contact a special consumer group.

(8a) Take the blow dryer to an authorized service center or mail it to the manufacturer for repairs.

(8) Read the warranty that came with the blow dryer. Follow the directions in the warranty.

(7) Decide what you think would be a fair solution. If you want the dryer repaired, GO TO **(8)**. If you want a refund, GO TO **(9)**.

(9c) If you are satisfied with the results, STOP. If not, contact a special consumer group.

(9b) If the person does not agree with your solution, ask to see a manager and explain your story again.

(9a) Tell your story calmly, show your evidence, and offer your solution.

(9) Go to the store where you bought the blow dryer, and ask to talk to someone who can handle your complaint.

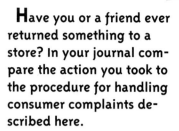

in your journal

Have you or a friend ever returned something to a store? In your journal compare the action you took to the procedure for handling consumer complaints described here.

Language Arts Connection

Letter Perfect

Use the following tips to write a complaint letter.

- Keep the letter short.
- Be firm but polite.
- State the product's name, when you bought it, what you paid, how you used it, and what happened.
- Include copies of related papers, but keep originals.
- Include a request for action—tell the company what you want.
- Include your address and phone number.

Special Consumer Groups

The actions in **Figure 6.8** on page 183 should take care of most product problems. Sometimes, though, more action is required. Different kinds of groups help consumers with problems if taking the usual steps does not produce a satisfactory result.

- **Consumer advocates** (AD·voh·kets) are *people or groups who devote themselves to helping consumers with problems.* These include the Consumers Union and local consumer groups.

- **Business groups** also help consumers with problems. Among the most useful are the Better Business Bureaus (BBB).

- **Governments** at all levels have workers whose job is to make sure that consumers' rights are being upheld. They work in places like the "consumer affairs office."

- **Small-claims courts** are *state courts that handle cases with problems involving small amounts, usually under $3,000.* The consumer and the person or store being sued present their own cases. A judge hears both sides and decides who wins.

You can find the addresses and phone numbers of any of these groups or agencies in your local library or in the telephone book. When you go for help, be prepared to tell the whole story and have documentation to prove your case. Describe your problem, how you tried to solve it yourself, and what happened. Many times, the group or agency can get the problem solved. They know what to do and say to convince a business to act.

Problems with Health Services

In addition to having problems with products and personal services, some people have problems with health services. Sometimes these problems are solved simply by discussing them with a physician or other health care professional or by changing physicians. For example, if someone feels that a doctor does not spend enough time answering questions, he or she can change doctors.

Because this teen could not solve her problem with the blow dryer by going through the usual channels, she consulted a local consumer group.

At other times, however, the question is over the quality of health care. Someone may feel that a doctor did not identify an illness early enough. In another case, a patient may think that a recommended treatment is not really needed.

The first step is to get a **second opinion.** This is a *statement from another doctor giving his or her view of what should be done.* The second doctor may reach a different conclusion or may agree with the first doctor's opinion.

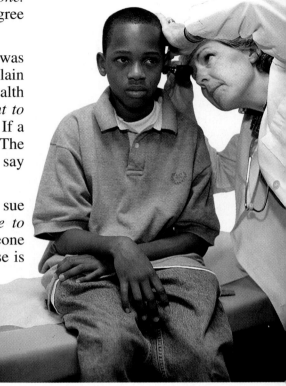

If you have a problem with the care or treatment you receive from a physician, there are many ways to try to resolve it.

A patient who thinks that a treatment already carried out was performed poorly can take a second step. He or she can complain to a state licensing board. These agencies license certain health workers. A **license** is *a document that gives a person the right to provide health care but holds that person to certain standards.* If a licensing board gets a complaint, it will look into the matter. The board may find that the worker did something wrong, or it may say that what the worker did was reasonable.

After taking these steps, the patient must decide whether to sue the doctor for **malpractice** (mal·PRAK·tis). This is *a failure to provide an acceptable degree of quality health care.* Someone making a decision to sue needs the help of a lawyer. If the case is taken to trial, a judge or jury will decide the case.

Review

Lesson 4

Using complete sentences, answer the following questions on a separate sheet of paper.

Reviewing Terms and Facts

1. **Vocabulary** What is the difference between a *consumer advocate* and *small-claims court*?

2. **Recall** What steps can you take to resolve a problem that you have with your physician?

Thinking Critically

3. **Suggest** Your friend wants to spend $12.95 for a cream with a "secret beauty formula." She saw the cream advertised in a supermarket tabloid. What would you say to your friend?

4. **Apply** Michelle's new curling iron does not heat properly. Michelle says she is going to throw it away. What should Michelle do instead?

Applying Health Concepts

5. **Consumer Health** Write a letter to the manufacturer of a health-related product you like. Tell the manufacturer what you like about the product (or suggest how it could be improved). Include the letter and any response in your portfolio.

6. **Health of Others** Make a directory of local groups or persons you can contact for help in solving consumer problems. Distribute your directory to family members, neighbors, and friends.

Public Health

This lesson will help you find answers to questions that teens often ask about public health. For example:

▶ **How do I know the cosmetics, grooming products, and medicines I buy are safe?**

▶ **Who makes sure that the food I eat and the water I drink are safe?**

Words to Know

**public health
ordinance
sanitation**

Government Health Departments

You receive health care from health workers such as doctors, nurses, and dentists. You also receive health care from many agencies of the government. Federal, state, and local governments all provide health services.

Government efforts to keep individuals healthy are part of a larger effort to keep the entire community healthy. These efforts are often referred to as public health. **Public health** deals with *the protection and improvement of community health.*

Public health authorities ensure that the water in public swimming pools is safe to swim in and that the water you drink is safe for consumption.

Local and State Health Departments

All states and most cities and counties have health departments. Although the jobs of these agencies differ from place to place, they all help to prevent and control diseases. Some tasks of local and state governments are listed below.

- Making sure that restaurant and hotel kitchens are clean and safe

- Making sure that garbage is taken away

- Making sure that local water is clean

- Offering health education programs

- Enforcing laws aimed at controlling disease

- Making sure that buildings are clean and sanitary

- Keeping birth and death records and records of diseases

Federal Health Departments

Many agencies of the federal government provide services related to health care. They belong to the Department of Health and Human Services. The agencies are described in **Figure 6.9.**

Q & A **?**

Health Hazard

Q: The water in our city swimming pool seems dirty. The bathrooms and changing areas aren't very clean either. What should I do?

A: Contact your local health department right away. Ask them to test the water in the pool. Also tell them about the dirty rest rooms. Get your friends to call too. This sounds like a dangerous situation.

Figure 6.9
The Main Groups of the Department of Health and Human Services

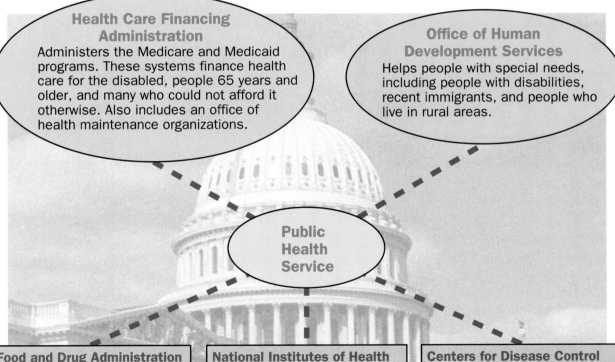

Health Care Financing Administration
Administers the Medicare and Medicaid programs. These systems finance health care for the disabled, people 65 years and older, and many who could not afford it otherwise. Also includes an office of health maintenance organizations.

Office of Human Development Services
Helps people with special needs, including people with disabilities, recent immigrants, and people who live in rural areas.

Public Health Service

Food and Drug Administration (FDA) Makes sure that food, drugs, and cosmetics are safe and pure and that product labels are truthful.

National Institutes of Health (NIH) Researches the causes and cures of diseases. There are 13 institutes. Each one focuses on a major disease or area of health, such as the National Heart, Lung, and Blood Institute.

Centers for Disease Control and Prevention (CDC) Prevents and controls the spread of disease. There are seven centers. The National Center for Infectious Diseases tracks and analyzes epidemics such as AIDS.

Laws to Protect Public Health

Governments at all levels pass laws or ordinances that protect people's health. An **ordinance** (OR·di·nuhns) is *a law passed by a city or town.* **Figure 6.10** shows major federal laws that have been passed to protect your health.

Toward a Healthy 2000

In 1991, the U.S. Department of Health and Human Services set 300 new health goals for Americans as the year 2000 approaches. These national health objectives, titled "Healthy People 2000," will help states or communities identify their most pressing problems and plan ways to improve them. An offshoot, titled "Healthy Youth 2000," targets objectives specific to adolescents. Among its many goals are increasing daily physical activity, reducing the number of youth who drink alcohol and smoke, and decreasing the incidence of sexually transmitted diseases.

Figure 6.10
Federal Laws that Protect Public Health

Food, Drug, and Cosmetic Act (1938)	Prohibits the distribution of unsafe foods, drugs, medical devices, and cosmetics. Forbids false or misleading labeling on such products.
Clean Air Act (1990)	Requires industries to reduce the amount of toxic substances they release into the air. Sets standards for release of pollutants by vehicles.
Clean Water Act (1972)	Prohibits discharge of pollutants into rivers and streams.
Safe Drinking Water Act (1974)	Sets standards by which drinking water is to be judged safe.
Resource Conservation and Recovery Act (1976)	Regulates storage, transport, treatment, and disposal of hazardous wastes. Describes cleanup of contaminated sites.
Labeling of Hazardous Art Materials Act (1988)	Requires warning labels on art materials that contain hazardous substances.

Your Total Health

Legal Protection ACTIVITY!

Choose one or more of the laws in the chart on this page. Write a paragraph to explain how the law affects you. For instance, because of the Food, Drug, and Cosmetic Act, you know that it is safe to use a particular lotion on your skin to prevent chapping.

Dealing with Disaster

Federal, state, and local governments work to help people stay healthy on an everyday basis. All levels of government also safeguard people's health during disasters. Hurricanes, floods, earthquakes, and fires disrupt sanitation systems. **Sanitation** (san·i·TAY·shuhn) means *the disposal of sewage and wastes in ways that protect health.* When sanitation systems are disrupted by a disaster, people are exposed to disease.

Government health workers hurry to the scene of a disaster. They bring food and clean drinking water and immunize disaster victims against disease. They show people how to avoid getting sick. They work fast to disinfect the water supply and clean up contaminated areas.

Nongovernmental Health Organizations

The work of nongovernmental groups is an important source of health services. Such groups as the American Heart Association and the American Cancer Society pay for research into ways to prevent and cure diseases. They help people who suffer from these diseases. They teach the public how to avoid these diseases.

The American Red Cross works to relieve human suffering after disasters such as fires and floods. It collects blood from volunteers and distributes it to people who need transfusions. The Red Cross also offers courses on first aid, safety, and health.

These groups need people's help. They are not governments that get money from taxes. They are not businesses that make money by selling goods or services. They can do their work only if they receive money from people. Many people also volunteer their time to help these groups do their jobs.

Both governmental and nongovernmental health workers help people in a disaster area by providing food and clean drinking water.

Review

Lesson 5

Using complete sentences, answer the following questions on a separate sheet of paper.

Reviewing Terms and Facts

1. **Vocabulary** Define the term *sanitation*. Use it in an original sentence.

2. **Recall** Why are nongovernmental health groups necessary?

Thinking Critically

3. **Investigate** Public health concerns become more critical wherever large groups of people are in close contact. What are some actions your school takes to safeguard the health of students?

4. **Explain** How do state and local health departments promote health in your community?

Applying Health Concepts

5. **Health of Others** Interview the manager of your school cafeteria. Find out what state and local health laws the cafeteria must obey.

6. **Personal Health** Take a class in first aid or cardiopulmonary resuscitation (CPR) sponsored by the American Red Cross.

Chapter 6 Review

Chapter Summary

▶ Wise consumers improve their health and get the most for their money. (Lesson 1)

▶ You have rights and responsibilities as a health consumer. (Lesson 1)

▶ Comparison shopping for goods and services will help you get the best buy. (Lesson 2)

▶ Cost, tradition, advertising, peers, and salespeople influence consumers' decisions. Wise consumers resist these influences and make the best choice for them. (Lesson 2)

▶ Many types of professionals and facilities provide health care. (Lesson 3)

▶ The health care system is set up to prevent health problems, maintain good health, and treat health problems that arise. (Lesson 3)

▶ Some people and companies sell fake health aids. They take advantage of people's desire to be beautiful, lose weight, or be healthy. (Lesson 4)

▶ You can often solve problems with products and services by going back to the business where you bought them. You can also get help from business groups or agencies of the government or take the problem to court. (Lesson 4)

▶ Consumers can get help for certain health care needs from the government. (Lesson 5)

▶ Many groups help people suffering from diseases or disasters. (Lesson 5)

Using Health Terms

On a separate sheet of paper, write the vocabulary term that best matches each definition given below.

1. Anybody who purchases goods or services (Lesson 1)

2. Activities that are purchased to satisfy someone's needs or wants (Lesson 1)

3. A method of judging the benefits of different goods or services (Lesson 2)

4. Sending out messages meant to interest consumers to make a purchase (Lesson 2)

5. A plan in which private companies or government programs pay for part of the medical costs and the patient pays for the rest (Lesson 3)

6. A government program of health insurance for poor people (Lesson 3)

7. The sale of worthless products and treatments claimed to prevent diseases or to cure other health problems (Lesson 4)

8. The protection and improvement of community health (Lesson 5)

Reviewing Main Ideas

Using complete sentences, answer the following questions on a separate sheet of paper.

1. What are the characteristics of a wise consumer? (Lesson 1)

2. List your six rights as a health consumer. (Lesson 1)

3. Identify five factors to use when comparison shopping for a product. (Lesson 2)

4. List three ways to save money on products. (Lesson 2)

5. What are three goals of health care? (Lesson 3)

6. List the forms of health services available in most communities. (Lesson 3)

7. What are some ways to spot quackery? (Lesson 4)

8. List the steps you should take to solve a problem with a health service. (Lesson 4)

9. What three health services are provided by state or local governments? (Lesson 5)

10. How does the Food and Drug Administration protect your health? (Lesson 5)

Thinking Critically

Using complete sentences, answer the following questions on a separate sheet of paper.

1. **Analyze** Some corporations now furnish public schools with equipment and materials that the schools need. In return, schools allow the corporations to advertise their products to students in the school. Do you think this arrangement is beneficial to students or harmful to them? Explain your answer. (Lesson 1)

2. **Evaluate** There are some occasions when comparison shopping is not possible. List two instances when that might be the case. (Lesson 2)

3. **Assess** Do you think that businesses should be required to contribute to their employees' health insurance plans? Explain your answer. (Lesson 3)

4. **Judge** Should people who promote quackery be allowed to advertise in newspapers and magazines and on television? Explain your answer. (Lesson 4)

5. **Analyze** Why do you think the U.S. government passes health-related laws? Do you think laws such as these are necessary? Why or why not? (Lesson 5)

Your Action Plan

If you are like most people, you would like to be a better consumer. You can make an action plan to improve your buying habits. Look back through your private journal entries for this chapter. What do they tell about habits you would like to change? Perhaps you want to take more control of your spending and not depend so much on advertising or friends.

You may want to set a long-term goal for yourself as a consumer. Once you have decided on a long-term goal, break it down into a series of short-term goals. Short-term goals are the steps you take to achieve your long-term goal. As you accomplish short-term goals, you make progress toward reaching your long-term goal. When you have reached your long-term goal, reward yourself.

Building Your Portfolio

1. Find out as much as you can about your own health history. What diseases have you had? What immunizations have you had, and when? Are you allergic to anything? What medications do you take? Have any relatives had serious illnesses? This information will be helpful when you visit a primary care provider. Write a report on your health history and put it in your portfolio.

2. Health care is a growing field of employment in the United States. Look in the employment section of your local newspaper for ads for health care workers. Note the kinds of jobs available and the qualifications. Choose a job in health care that you might like to have. Read more about the job in a career encyclopedia. Write a brief job description and put it in your portfolio.

In Your Home and Community

1. You and your family can have fun and save money by making your own beauty and personal grooming products. Check out a book from the library that tells you how to make hand lotions, facial masks, bath oils, shampoos, and many other products.

2. Volunteer your services at a local health care facility. You might deliver mail, flowers, and gifts to hospital rooms. You might write letters for disabled residents of nursing homes. You might read stories to children who are hospitalized or play games with them.

Unit 3
Fitness and Nutrition

Chapter 7

Your Growth and Development

Student Expectations

After reading this chapter, you should be able to:

1. Describe fertilization, growth before birth, and the birth process.

2. Identify the factors that influence the health of the developing baby and some causes of birth defects.

3. Describe the stages of life from birth through adolescence and the developmental tasks of a teen.

4. Identify the changes caused by aging and list the stages of adulthood.

5. Explain the definitions of death and the stages of dying and grief.

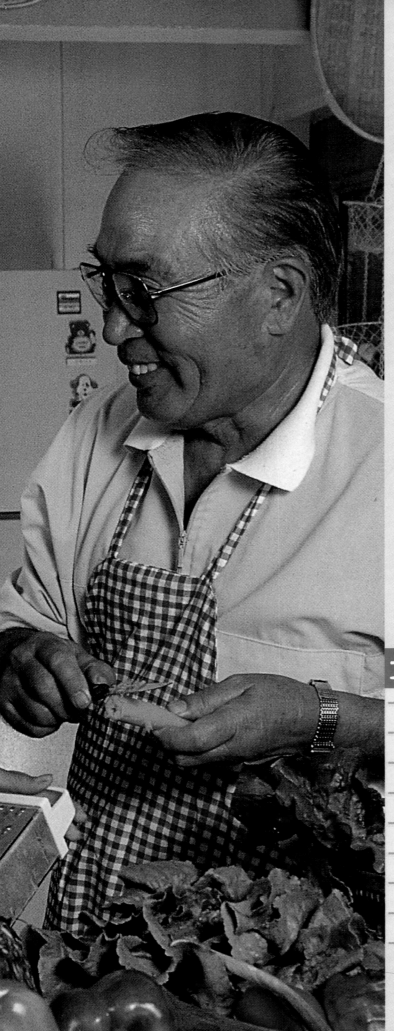

My grandfather is a really neat person. He moved in with us after Grandma died, and it's great having him here. It took everyone a little while to adjust, but we soon got used to each other.

Grandpa loves to cook. He usually makes dinner for us during the week. I like to help him. He has taught me how to make all kinds of dishes.

Grandpa also loves to talk. He talks to me a lot—usually when we're cooking together. He likes to talk about his life and about life in general. One day he told me that a good life is like a good book. It has lots of different characters and chapters. "Always keep the whole story in mind and where you want the story to go as it unfolds," he said. "Some chapters may seem to be written by chance, but most are written by the choices you make along the way."

I often think about what Grandpa said that day. I would like to make my "book" a great story. I want it to be filled with lots of interesting experiences and with caring people, just like Grandpa's "book."

in your journal

Read the account on this page. Are you finding that you think a lot about growing up? Do you wonder what you will write in your "book"? Start your private journal entries on growth and development by answering these questions.

▶ How did your earlier years influence the person you are now?

▶ What kind of adult would you like to be?

When you reach the end of the chapter, you will use your journal entries to make an action plan.

The Beginning of Life

This lesson will help you find answers to questions that teens often ask about the beginning of life. For example:

▶ **How did my life start?**

▶ **What happens during pregnancy?**

▶ **How is a baby born?**

Words to Know

cells
tissues
organs
fertilization
egg cell
sperm cell
uterus
embryo
fetus
placenta
umbilical cord
cervix

Beginning of Life

Life begins with a cell—a tiny bit of matter so small that it can be seen only through a microscope. In an astounding process, that cell grows into many cells, and these cells form our tissues, organs, and body systems (see **Figure 7.1**). Each of us is made up of trillions of cells. Cells are the building blocks of life.

The remarkable process of growth continues throughout life. Everyone grows at a different rate, but there are stages of growth that each person goes through.

Figure 7.1
From Cell to System

Ⓐ Cell
Cells are the *basic units, or building blocks, of life.* Every cell in your body does a specific job. There are many types of cells. The cell shown here is a nerve cell in the brain. Examples of other kinds of cells are blood cells and muscle cells.

Ⓑ Tissue
Cells that do similar jobs form **tissues.** Your body is made up of several kinds of tissue. Nerve cells make up the brain tissue shown here. Heart muscle cells make up heart muscle tissue.

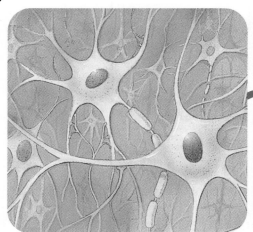

A Single Cell

The body begins with a single cell that is the result of fertilization. **Fertilization** (fer·til·i·ZAY·shuhn) is *the joining together of two special cells, one from each parent.* The *cell from the mother that plays a part in fertilization* is called an **egg cell.** The *cell from the father that enters the egg cell* is called a **sperm cell.** The sperm fertilizes the egg cell. After fertilization, a protective coating forms around the egg cell to prevent other sperm cells from entering. Fertilization takes place inside the mother's body.

Sometimes a newly fertilized egg splits into two complete fertilized eggs, which then copy each other. This produces identical twins of the same gender. If two separate eggs are fertilized at the same time, this produces fraternal (fruh·TERN·uhl) twins. These twins are not identical. They may be two girls, two boys, or a boy and a girl.

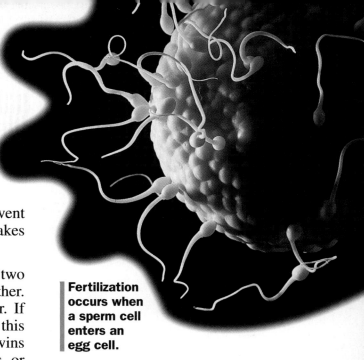

Fertilization occurs when a sperm cell enters an egg cell.

C Organ

Tissues combine into larger structures called organs. These **organs** are *body parts,* such as the brain, shown here. The main kind of tissue in the brain is nerve tissue. The heart is also an organ.

D System

Groups of organs that work together form systems. Your body has several systems, such as the nervous system, shown here. The brain is the main organ of the nervous system. The heart is the main organ of the circulatory system.

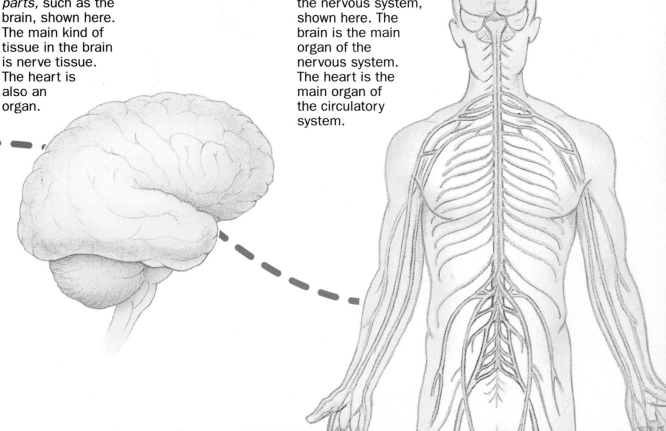

Growth During Pregnancy

The newly fertilized cell attaches itself to the wall of a *pear-shaped organ inside the mother's body. This organ is called the* **uterus** (YOO·tuh·ruhs). *As the fertilized cell begins to divide, it is called an* **embryo.** Cells in the embryo continue to divide and eventually join to make tissues, organs, and systems. *After two months, the developing baby is called a* **fetus.** At the end of about nine months, the baby is ready to be born. **Figure 7.2** shows the development of the embryo and fetus during these nine months.

Figure 7.2
Development Before Birth
How a baby develops during the nine months before birth.

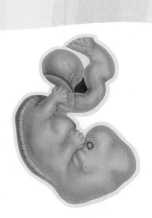

A End of First Month
About ⅓ inch long. Heart, brain, and lungs are forming. Heart begins to beat.

B End of Second Month
About 1 inch long. Skin and other organs are developing. Arms, fingers, legs, and toes are forming.

C End of Third Month
Weighs about 1 ounce and is about 3 inches long. Can open and close mouth and swallow. Fetus begins to move around.

D End of Fourth Month
Weighs about 6 ounces and is 5 inches long. Facial features become clearer. Movement can be felt.

E End of Fifth Month
Weighs about 1 pound and is just under 10 inches long. Eyelashes and nails appear. Heartbeat can be heard.

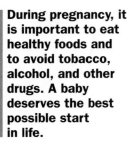

During pregnancy, it is important to eat healthy foods and to avoid tobacco, alcohol, and other drugs. A baby deserves the best possible start in life.

Growth Inside the Uterus

From the start, the developing fetus needs food to help it grow. It gets this food from a *thick, rich lining of tissue that builds up along the walls of the uterus and connects the mother to the baby.* This tissue is called the **placenta** (pluh·SEN·tuh). The placenta also gives the baby oxygen to breathe. The food and oxygen reach the baby through *a cord that grows out of the placenta.* This tube, called the **umbilical** (uhm·BIL·i·kuhl) **cord,** attaches to what will become the baby's navel. The baby's waste travels through the umbilical cord as well. The waste products are then carried away in the mother's bloodstream.

Cultural Diversity

Naming the Baby ACTIVITY!

Choosing a name for a baby is important. In some cultures, parents name babies after relatives. In many Latin American cultures, a baby may receive several names: the family name of the mother and the father and, perhaps, even the place of birth. Babies are sometimes named for qualities their parents hope they will have.

Find out about your own name. Did it come from another language? What does your name mean? Ask someone in your family why you were given your name.

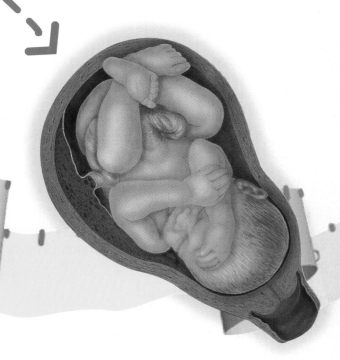

I End of Ninth Month
Weighs 6 to 9 pounds and is 18 to 21 inches long. Body organs have developed enough to function on their own.

H End of Eighth Month
Weighs about 4 pounds and is about 18 inches long. Hair gets longer. Skin becomes smoother.

G End of Seventh Month
Weighs about 2 to 2.5 pounds and is about 14.5 inches long. Arms and legs can move freely. Eyes open.

F End of Sixth Month
Weighs about 1.5 pounds and is about 12.5 inches long. Develops ability to kick, cry, and perhaps hiccup. Fetus can hear sounds. Footprint appears.

Birth

The process started with the joining together of the egg and the sperm cell. Now, nine months later, a baby is born.

By the ninth month, the fully developed baby is ready to be born. Birth happens in three stages.

■ **Stage one.** The first stage begins with mild contractions (kuhn·TRAK·shuhnz). These are a *sudden tightening in the muscles of the uterus.* Contractions cause the muscles of the uterus to shorten. This forces the **cervix** (SER·viks), which is *the opening of the uterus,* to open, or dilate.

■ **Stage two.** By the beginning of the second stage, the cervix has opened to a width of about 4 inches (10 cm). Contractions are now quite strong. The contractions push the baby through the cervix and out of the mother.

■ **Stage three.** In this final stage of birth, several more very strong contractions of the uterus help push out the placenta. If any part of the placenta remains inside the mother's body, she could become ill. The health care professional must make sure that all the placenta comes out.

Lesson 1 Review

Using complete sentences, answer the following questions on a separate sheet of paper.

Reviewing Terms and Facts

1. **Give Examples** List two types of body tissue.
2. **Recall** Identify the main organ of the circulatory system.
3. **Vocabulary** Using your own words, define the term *fertilization.*
4. **Vocabulary** What is the difference between an *egg cell* and a *sperm cell?*
5. **Review** Describe the development of the embryo and fetus during pregnancy.
6. **Identify** What is the function of the placenta?

Thinking Critically

7. **Explain** Cells are often referred to as the building blocks of life. Why is this an appropriate description?

8. **Analyze** A pregnant woman should be careful about what she eats and drinks. Explain why this is important.
9. **Synthesize** Make a list of the main events of pregnancy from fertilization to birth.

Applying Health Concepts

10. **Consumer Health** Find out about classes for preparing expectant parents for childbirth and parenthood. During what month in the pregnancy do classes normally begin? What topics are covered in the classes? Are there different types of classes given in your community, such as early pregnancy classes, exercise classes for pregnant women, childbirth education, baby care classes, and exercise classes for pregnant women? How do they differ?

Factors in Your Development

This lesson will help you find answers to questions that teens often ask about factors in development. For example:

▶ **Why was I born with certain traits such as my hair color and the shape of my nose?**

▶ **Should a pregnant woman continue to exercise?**

▶ **Why are some babies born with birth defects?**

What Makes You Special

Have you ever wondered what makes every person unique? Each person is one of a kind, with his or her own special looks, manner-isms, and personality. A number of factors shape each baby at birth. These factors affect how babies look and how healthy they are. The two most important factors are heredity and environment.

Words to Know

heredity
chromosomes
genes
genetic disorder
environment
prenatal care
obstetrician
birth defects
**fetal alcohol
   syndrome (FAS)**
addiction
rubella

Children inherit certain physical characteristics, such as hair color and eye color, from their parents. Sometimes a child does not look like either parent. Sometimes there is a strong family resemblance.

Teen Issues

Kid Brothers and Sisters ACTIVITY!

Do you have a little brother or sister? If you do, you can make a difference in his or her development. Older brothers and sisters are important people in the lives of children. With your younger brother or sister, make a list of activities you can do together. Then set aside some time each week to do them. Your help will be appreciated by everyone in the family.

Q: I have straight hair, but neither one of my parents has straight hair. How could that happen?

A: Some of the traits you have may be shown by your mother, some may be shown by your father—and some may be shown by neither one. For example, the trait for straight hair can be carried by a parent's genes, but not be visible in the parent.

Heredity

Heredity is *the passing of traits from parents to their children.* The color of children's eyes and the shape of their faces are examples of traits they inherited from their parents. Structures within cells play important roles in heredity. (See **Figure 7.3**.)

■ **Chromosomes.** The *threadlike structures found within the nucleus of a cell that carry the codes for inherited traits* are **chromosomes** (KROH·muh·sohmz). There are 46 chromosomes, or 23 pairs, in most human body cells. One chromosome of every pair is from each parent. A sperm cell or an egg cell each has 23 single chromosomes. A fertilized egg, however, has 46 chromosomes—23 from each parent.

■ **Genes.** The *basic units of heredity* are called **genes**. They are located on chromosomes and carry codes for individual traits, such as hair color, eye color, and height. Children of the same parents inherit different combinations of chromosomes and genes.

Heredity and Genetic Disorders

Most of the time the genes that both parents pass on to children produce a healthy, normal baby. Sometimes, however, the genes carried by one parent lead to unexpected results. When this happens, the baby may be born with a **genetic** (juh·NE·tik) **disorder.** This is *a disease or condition in which the baby's body does not work normally because of a problem with genes.* Sometimes the disorder is obvious at birth. Sometimes it does not surface until the child is a few years older.

Several hundred thousand babies are born each year with genetic disorders. Some of these disorders are mild, others very severe. They can have a serious effect on a person's health. Scientists have

Figure 7.3
Inherited Characteristics

A The photo shows a single cell with 23 pairs of chromosomes. The genes that determine individual traits are located on the chromosomes.

B The diagram shows how one trait, eye color, is passed on to children. If one parent has brown eyes and the other has blue eyes, the baby could have either brown or blue eyes. However, the chances of the baby having brown eyes are three out of four.

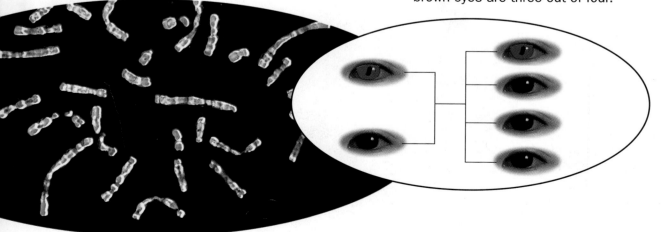

determined that some genetic disorders occur when a cell has more than the usual number of chromosomes. One of these conditions is Down syndrome. However, the cause of more than half of all genetic disorders remains a mystery. Scientists have made many breakthroughs in the last 20 years, and research continues to find ways of preventing and treating many genetic disorders.

Environment

The second factor in the health of a developing baby and a newborn child is environment. **Environment** (en·VY·ruhn·ment) is *the sum total of a person's surroundings*. The environment of the developing baby is the uterus. The baby's health, then, is affected directly by the actions and total health of the pregnant woman.

Care of the Pregnant Woman

Healthy mothers are more likely to have healthy babies. That is why it is extremely important for a woman to begin a program of prenatal care as soon as she finds out she is pregnant. **Prenatal** (pree·NAY·tuhl) **care** includes *a number of steps taken to provide for the health of a pregnant woman and her unborn baby*. One of the most important steps is regular visits by the woman to a health clinic, family doctor, or **obstetrician** (ahb·stuh·TRI·shuhn). This *doctor specializes in the care of a pregnant woman and her developing baby*. The obstetrician will make sure the pregnant woman stays healthy and that her child is developing as it should. When the mother takes good care of her own health and follows the steps listed below, she is giving her baby the best possible start in life.

Steps to Good Prenatal Care

- Visit an obstetrician or other health care professional regularly.

- Eat nutritious foods.

- Get enough rest and participate in moderate exercise.

- Avoid the use of tobacco, alcohol, and all medications and other drugs that have not been allowed by the health care provider. These substances can be very dangerous to the fetus.

Birth Defects

Following these steps to good prenatal care is the best present a mother can give her newborn baby. For example, seeking medical care in the first weeks of pregnancy and continuing with regular checkups will help ensure that problems are identified and dealt with at an early stage. Not following the other steps for good prenatal care—eating properly; avoiding the use of tobacco, alcohol, or drugs—can lead to serious problems in the developing child. In some cases, using alcohol and drugs can result in birth defects. **Birth defects** (DEE·fekts) are *disorders of the developing and newborn baby*. Birth defects may be caused by a genetic disorder or by harmful substances in the fetus's environment. Certain infections can also be harmful during pregnancy.

in your journal

Babies born to very young mothers often have a lower than normal weight. In general, the younger the mother, the greater the risks to the baby's health. Having a baby also causes problems for teenage parents. Write a short paragraph describing how the life of a teenager would change with the added major responsibility of raising a child. Write your paragraph in your journal.

Problems in the Fetal Environment

- **Nutrition.** The baby gets all food from its mother. When a woman fails to eat the right foods during pregnancy, the baby may be born too early or have a low birth weight. These babies have a greater chance of having mental or physical problems. Eating nutritious foods is extremely important for the health of the mother and her developing child.

- **Alcohol.** When a pregnant woman drinks alcohol, it passes through the placenta and enters the developing baby's body. This can lead to a condition known as **fetal** (FEE·tuhl) **alcohol syndrome (FAS),** *a pattern of physical and mental problems that occur in the child of a woman who drinks alcohol during pregnancy.* Women who are pregnant should avoid alcohol.

- **Medications and drugs.** A woman who is pregnant should avoid the use of all medications and drugs—unless she has her doctor's approval. Even drugs that seem harmless, such as over-the-counter cold pills, can affect the developing baby. Illegal drugs can lead to **addiction** (uh·DIK·shuhn), *a physical or mental need for a drug or other substance.* When such substances are taken by a pregnant woman, her baby may be born with an addiction to the drug.

- **Tobacco.** A woman who uses tobacco during pregnancy can seriously harm her unborn baby. Growth before birth can be slowed and the baby may be born prematurely or with a low birth weight. The baby may develop an addiction to nicotine (NI·kuh·teen), a drug found in tobacco. Women who are pregnant should avoid smoking and also try to avoid secondhand smoke from others.

MAKING HEALTHY DECISIONS
Giving Advice

Rachel spots her cousin Maria across the room at a family reunion, and she shouts and makes her way through the crowd. They both start hugging and talking excitedly. It is the first time they have seen each other for several months because Maria moved out of town after she got married. Rachel, who is 14, has always looked up to Maria.

When they sit down to eat, Rachel has a soft drink and Maria takes a glass of wine. Rachel announces that she made the basketball team and asks Maria what's new with her. "I thought you'd never ask," says Maria, "I just found out I'm pregnant, and I'm so happy!"

Rachel has a problem. On the one hand, she respects her cousin's ability to make her own decisions. On the other hand, Rachel knows that Maria will have a better chance of having a healthy baby if she does not drink alcohol during her pregnancy.

What should Rachel do? Should she say nothing, hoping that a glass or two of wine won't matter? Should she tell Maria that even a little alcohol might harm her unborn baby? Rachel uses the step-by-step decision-making process.

❶ **State the situation**

❷ **List the options**

❸ **Weigh the possible outcomes**

❹ **Consider your values**

❺ **Make a decision and act**

❻ **Evaluate the decision**

■ **Infections.** If a mother-to-be has **rubella** (roo·BE·luh), *the disease called German measles,* her baby may be born deaf or have other serious health problems. There is a vaccine that protects against rubella. Some sexually transmitted diseases may also pass from the mother to the baby. These can cause such problems as brain damage, blindness, or even death. It is important for a pregnant woman to tell her doctor about any possible infections so they can be treated.

Using complete sentences, answer the following questions on a separate sheet of paper.

Reviewing Terms and Facts

1. **Give Examples**   List at least two traits we inherit from our parents.
2. **Vocabulary**   Which of the following are the basic units of heredity? *environment, genes, chromosomes, rubella*
3. **Recall**   Identify two causes of birth defects.
4. **Identify**   List three problems in the fetal environment.

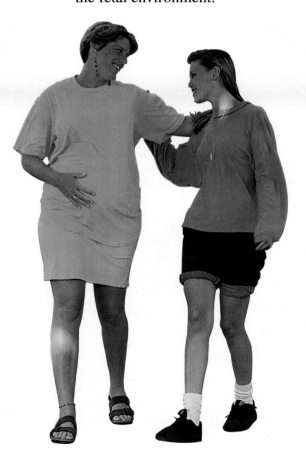

5. **Recall**   Cite two causes of low birth weight in newborns.

Thinking Critically

6. **Explain**   Describe how heredity and environment affect the development of the unborn and newborn child.
7. **Analyze**   Write a list of questions you think a pregnant woman might ask her doctor about what she could do to have a healthy baby.

Applying Health Concepts

8. **Health of Others**   With your classmates, make a poster listing the causes of birth defects. Display the poster in the classroom.

Follow-up Activities

1. Apply the six steps of the decision-making process to Rachel's story.
2. With a partner, role-play a conversation between Rachel and Maria in which Rachel avoids giving any advice to her cousin.
3. Now role-play a conversation in which Rachel tells Maria of her concern and explains why she hopes Maria will not drink during her pregnancy.

From Childhood to Adolescence

This lesson will help you find answers to questions that teens often ask about the ways people grow and develop. For example:

▶ **What changes occur during infancy?**

▶ **What changes will happen to me during adolescence?**

▶ **Why do my moods seem to change more often than they did before?**

Words to Know

infancy
adolescence
hormones
puberty
developmental
   tasks

The Growth Years

The period of life from the first years through the teen years is a time of enormous growth. During these growth years, we learn many skills and form many habits. We also go through many physical, mental, emotional, and social changes.

There are many different theories about the way children develop. Some focus on physical growth. Some look mainly at mental or emotional growth. One important view is that of scientist Erik Erikson, who studied the social and emotional development of individuals from infancy to old age. Erikson believed that people pass through eight stages of development. His theories and those of experts on physical and mental growth are combined in the descriptions of the four stages of childhood that follow. These stages—infancy, early childhood, childhood, and late childhood—are also illustrated in **Figure 7.4.**

Figure 7.4
From Infancy to Late Childhood

Each individual follows his or her own path of development. Some children, for example, walk or talk at an earlier age than others. However, researchers have found that development occurs in roughly the same order in most children. To study growth and development, researchers divide childhood into four stages.

Ⓐ Infancy
During the first months of life, a child begins to move around and to explore the world.

Ⓑ Early Childhood
Walking, running, and climbing stairs are some of the physical skills learned in early childhood. Children of this age are also beginning to do things for themselves and to communicate with others.

Infancy

During the first year of life, the fastest physical growth takes place. The weight of the child triples, and the height increases by 50 percent. During **infancy** (IN·fuhn·see), as this *first year of life* is called, trust develops. If an infant's needs are met in a loving way, he or she learns to trust and feel safe.

Early Childhood

Between the ages of one and three, children learn to walk and talk. They also learn how to control the removal of wastes from their bodies. Children feel proud of their achievements and eager to do more things for and by themselves. Sometimes a child will fail when trying something new, but that is part of learning and growing. If adults offer love and encouragement and accept the child's individuality, they can help the child develop positive self-esteem.

Childhood

Between the ages of three and five, children's arms, legs, and bodies become longer, and they are able to coordinate their movements better. Children of this age enjoy playing make-believe and imitating adults. They also begin to ask many questions. Once again, the way adults respond to a child's behavior is important. When parents encourage these new abilities and questions, they promote the child's self-esteem. However, if parents are impatient with a child's attempts to do things independently, this may make the child feel guilty about starting new activities and decrease the child's self-esteem.

Late Childhood

From ages six through eleven, children grow at a steadier rate than they did when they were younger. Their physical skills improve and their mental skills increase.

Children of this age often spend a lot of time making things. If the child's creative efforts are appreciated and rewarded, pride in her or his work increases. Children who are scolded for getting in the way or creating a mess may begin to feel worthless. A child's success or failure in any of these stages of growth affects emotional development at that stage. By succeeding at later stages, a child may overcome the setbacks of earlier stages and gain self-esteem.

Literature Connection

Growing Over Time ACTIVITY!

You might enjoy reading the novel *Grandma Didn't Wave Back* by Rose Blue. This is a touching story about the close relationship between a young girl and her grandmother, whose memory is deteriorating. With your family, discuss changes that occur over time. Then write about a special relationship you have and describe how it has changed over time.

D Late Childhood
The physical skills of children improve steadily between the ages of six and eleven. Friends are important in building social skills and self-esteem.

C Childhood
Children between the ages of three and five can jump and hop and draw simple shapes. Pretend play helps them develop social skills and practice future roles.

Knowing When to Stop

A growth hormone determines when our bodies stop growing. The pituitary gland, located near the brain, produces the growth hormone. The brain works with the pituitary gland to determine when growth will stop. When the gland stops producing the hormone, the body stops growing.

Adolescence

Next to infancy, the second fastest period of physical growth is adolescence. **Adolescence** (a·duhl·E·suhns) is *the time of life between childhood and adulthood.* It usually begins somewhere between the ages of 11 and 15. Girls often show the physical changes of adolescence earlier than boys.

Perhaps at the start of this school year, you noticed that some of your classmates had grown much taller over the summer, while others looked the same. You may be aware of some changes in yourself as well. Maybe some new hair has begun to appear on parts of your body. These changes are all part of a growth spurt that occurs during adolescence. They are related to the release of **hormones,** which are *chemical substances produced in glands and which regulate many body functions.* These hormones and the changes they cause are preparing you for adulthood.

Growth during adolescence takes place in all three areas of your health triangle. You grow physically, mentally and emotionally, and socially. Keep in mind that there are individual differences in the rate of growth in all three areas.

Figure 7.5
Erikson's Stages of Life

Erik Erikson believed that a person's life could be divided into eight stages of development. Each stage is associated with a developmental task that involves a person's relationship with other people and with the world around. Whether or not a person masters the task of a particular stage, he or she moves on to the next stage of development. If the task was not mastered, it affects the way the individual handles the next stage of development.

| STAGE 1 | STAGE 2 | STAGE 3 | STAGE 4 |

Infancy
Birth to 1 Year
Characteristic of stage: child is completely dependent on others to meet his or her needs
Developmental task: to develop trust—a sense that others will be there to help
If not mastered: mistrust—the sense that one is alone

Early Childhood
1 to 3 Years
Characteristics of stage: child is learning to control own body, to do things on his or her own, and to separate from parents
Developmental task: to develop autonomy—confidence in one's ability to do tasks oneself
If not mastered: shame and doubt—a lack of confidence

Middle Childhood
3 to 5 Years
Characteristics of stage: child begins to make decisions and to think of and carry out projects
Developmental task: to develop initiative—ability to create one's own play
If not mastered: guilt—feeling guilty about the actions one takes

Late Childhood
6 to 11 Years
Characteristics of stage: child explores surroundings and must master more and more difficult skills
Developmental task: to develop industry—interest in making objects and performing activities
If not mastered: inferiority—feeling that one is unable to succeed

Physical Growth

Adolescence begins with **puberty** (PYOO·ber·tee), *the time when you begin to develop certain traits of adults of your own gender.* The exact age at which puberty begins is different in different people. Girls tend to start puberty at an earlier age than boys. No two people grow in exactly the same way.

Physical growth during puberty is rapid. Many girls begin their growth spurt between the ages of 11 and 14, adding about 3 inches in height during those years. Boys tend to start their growth spurt later, between the ages of 13 and 16. They may add 6 to 7 inches in height at that time. Growth for boys and girls often continues for several years after the first growth spurt.

Growth during adolescence is rapid and uneven. Among girls and boys of the same age, there is great variation in size and shape.

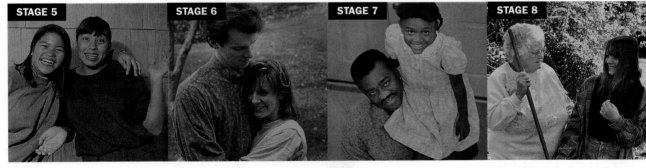

STAGE 5   STAGE 6   STAGE 7   STAGE 8

Adolescence
12 to 18 Years
Characteristic of stage: adolescent searches for his or her identity
Developmental task: to develop one's own identity—a sense of who one is
If not mastered: role confusion—being mixed up over the many roles one plays

Young Adulthood
19 to 30 Years
Characteristic of stage: person tries to develop close personal relationships
Developmental task: to develop intimacy—forming a strong relationship with another person
If not mastered: isolation—being alone

Middle Adulthood
31 to 60 Years
Characteristics of stage: person tries to achieve something in work and is concerned with the well-being of children and community
Developmental task: to develop generativity—the sense that one has contributed something to society
If not mastered: self-absorption—being concerned only with one's own needs

Maturity and Old Age
61 Years to Death
Characteristic of stage: person tries to understand meaning of own life
Developmental task: to develop integrity—feeling complete and satisfied with one's life
If not mastered: despair—feeling that one's life has not been satisfying

Coming of Age

Throughout history, puberty has been marked in many cultures by ceremonies. The Apache, a Native American group, had a ceremony that marked puberty in girls. In the ceremony, each girl who was entering puberty shared a blanket with an old woman. The woman then became the girl's guardian and was sworn to protect the girl for life.

Physical growth during puberty is very uneven. The outer parts of your body—head, hands, and feet—generally grow first. As a result, your hands and feet may suddenly seem too large for the rest of your body. You may feel awkward. Some young people feel unhappy or self-conscious about their bodies during this stage. These developments, however, are perfectly normal.

During puberty, many other changes take place. Boys may find their voices growing deeper. Girls may find that their figures are developing. Some of the other changes are shown in **Figure 7.6.**

Mental and Emotional Growth

Thinking skills develop during adolescence. As a child, you were able to solve only very basic kinds of problems. As an adolescent, you are able to solve more complex problems. You can see degrees in situations and understand other points of view. You can also think ahead to what might happen if you act in a certain way. You understand that you often have a choice. When friends dare you to walk into an old boarded-up house, you can weigh the consequences of accepting or refusing the dare.

During adolescence, your emotions, or feelings, also go through changes. These changes include the following:

- **Mood swings.** You may feel very happy one minute and moody or unhappy the next. Like the physical changes in your body, these mood swings are related to the release of hormones.

Figure 7.6
Physical Changes During Puberty

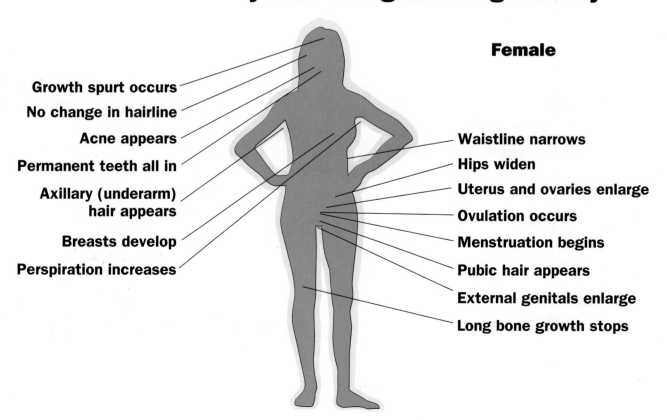

Female

Growth spurt occurs

No change in hairline

Acne appears

Permanent teeth all in

Axillary (underarm) hair appears

Breasts develop

Perspiration increases

Waistline narrows

Hips widen

Uterus and ovaries enlarge

Ovulation occurs

Menstruation begins

Pubic hair appears

External genitals enlarge

Long bone growth stops

- **Feelings toward others.** You may see family and friends in a new way. People around you are no longer just "givers," as they were when you were a child. You now see these people as having needs, just like yourself. Sometimes you are able to help meet the needs of others. You can listen, for example, when a friend has a problem.

- **Increased interest in the opposite gender.** You may begin to feel a desire to spend time with members of the opposite gender. These new feelings can be confusing, even frightening. Having them, however, is a normal part of growing up.

Social Growth

During adolescence, your friends become very important to you, and you want to spend a lot of time with them. At the same time, you will be meeting many new people and forming new relationships. You will also become more aware of other people's needs. These developments are all part of social growth, an important part of adolescence.

Many aspects of social growth are defined by **developmental** (di·vel·uhp·MEN·tuhl) **tasks,** *events that need to happen in order for you to continue growing toward becoming a healthy, mature adult.* Experts have identified nine developmental tasks that are basic to adolescence. They are shown in **Figure 7.7** on page 212.

Going out as a group gives boys and girls the opportunity to get to know members of the opposite gender in a relaxed setting.

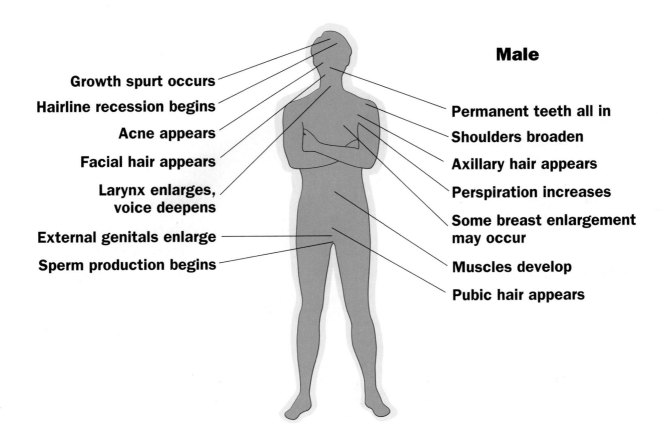

Male

Growth spurt occurs

Hairline recession begins

Acne appears

Facial hair appears

Larynx enlarges, voice deepens

External genitals enlarge

Sperm production begins

Permanent teeth all in

Shoulders broaden

Axillary hair appears

Perspiration increases

Some breast enlargement may occur

Muscles develop

Pubic hair appears

Figure 7.7
Developmental Tasks of Adolescence

The nine developmental tasks of adolescence are important steps in the process you go through to develop into the person you want to become.

Accept your body and its characteristics.

Become more independent of parents and other adults for your emotional health.

Form more mature relationships with people of both genders.

Learn more about who you are.

Develop a set of your own values.

Gain a masculine (MAS·kyuh·lin) or feminine (FEM·uh·nin) view of yourself.

Develop an interest in and a concern for your community.

Get ready for marriage and family life as an adult.

Learn how to solve problems in an adult way.

Personal Inventory

YOUR DEVELOPMENTAL RATE

How successful are you at the nine developmental tasks at this point in your life? The following quiz will help you find out. For each statement, write true or false on a separate sheet of paper.

1. I try to think through problems, looking at all possible solutions.

2. There are several jobs I think I would do well as an adult.

3. I have more adult discussions with my parents or other grown-ups than I used to have.

4. I am able to list my four most important beliefs.

5. I act in a way that goes along with my beliefs.

6. I can describe at least two ways that my life would be different if I were a parent.

7. I am successful most of the time at making male and female friends.

8. I do some things alone or with friends that I used to do with my family.

9. The choices I make promote my overall health and well-being.

10. I know and accept my physical strengths and weaknesses.

11. I listen to other people's ideas even when they are different from mine.

12. I am concerned about local and national problems in the news today.

13. I have one or two close friends with whom I can talk about almost anything.

14. I have an idea of what kind of man or woman I want to be as an adult.

Look at all the statements for which you wrote false. Find the developmental task in Figure 7.7 that each one relates to. These are tasks you will need to work on in the coming years.

During adolescence, your friends and their views become more important than ever. However, you also need to find out who you are, separate from the group. You begin looking, often without knowing it, for an answer to the question, "Who am I?" This search for yourself is a normal part of the developmental tasks that you take on in adolescence.

The choices you make over the next few years will affect your success in these tasks. As you grow throughout your life, your choices will shape how healthy that growth will be.

in your journal

Which of the developmental tasks of adolescence do you think is the most difficult? Which is the easiest? Explain your feelings about these tasks in your journal.

During the next few years, you will be spending a lot of time on your own—at school, with your friends, and pursuing personal interests. This growing independence from parents and other adults is one of the developmental tasks of adolescence.

Review
Lesson 3

Using complete sentences, answer the following questions on a separate sheet of paper.

Reviewing Terms and Facts

1. **Vocabulary** What is meant by the term *infancy?*
2. **Vocabulary** Which of the following is the second fastest period of physical growth? *infancy, late childhood, adolescence, developmental tasks*
3. **Summarize** Describe Erikson's eight stages of life.
4. **Recall** List seven physical changes that occur during puberty.
5. **Recall** List three emotional changes that occur during adolescence.
6. **Review** Cite seven of the developmental tasks of adolescence.

Thinking Critically

7. **Observe** What stages of development do you observe in the infants and children in your family and neighborhood or in the infants and children that you baby-sit?

8. **Synthesize** Recall some of the activities you were involved in during your childhood. Explain how your activities reflected Erikson's stages of life.

Applying Health Concepts

9. **Growth and Development** Create a poster titled "The Tasks Ahead," using pictures and articles from magazines and newspapers that show teens successfully meeting the developmental tasks of adolescence. Include a sentence describing each picture.

10. **Health of Others** Compare adolescence in the 1960s with adolescence today. Interview people who were teens during that time. Find out what were their concerns, their favorite songs, their role models. Tape the interviews and share them with the rest of the class.

Teen HEALTH DIGEST

People at Work

Midwife

Sandy Hall's working hours are never predictable. When you learn that she is a midwife, a woman who assists in childbirth, you will understand why. She delivers babies, and babies are as likely to arrive in the middle of the night as at any other time.

There are two types of midwives—certified and lay. Certified midwives are trained both as registered nurses and as midwives. They may deliver babies in a hospital under a doctor's supervision, in a birthing center, or in a mother's home. The way they practice is regulated by each state.

Lay midwives learn their skills in a midwifery school and test their skills as apprentices under senior midwives. They deliver babies in the homes of the mothers, in their own home, or in private birthing centers. They are usually in touch with a backup doctor and no more than 30 minutes away from a hospital.

Sandy Hall is a lay midwife. She practices in a small town where there is only one obstetrician. Lay midwives also provide their clients with prenatal and postnatal care.

Sandy Hall believes that childbirth is a natural process. Her reward is bringing a new life into the world in a warm, bright, and loving environment.

CON$UMER FOCU$

Do You Believe Everything You Hear?

Have you heard that certain vitamin pills help you grow, help you cope with stress, or slow down the aging process? As a consumer you need to think twice before believing such claims. Research on the effects vitamins have on the body is still ongoing, but if the product sounds too good to be true, then it probably is.

The U.S. Food and Drug Administration (FDA) has placed limits on the health claims that vitamin pill manufacturers can make. The FDA has also approved certain health claims. One of these is that folic acid, a vitamin, can reduce the threat of certain birth defects.

Beware also of claims that more is better. Large doses of some vitamins and minerals can actually make you sick. Your best bet is to stick to a well-balanced diet. If you also want to take dietary supplements, take doses that provide only the recommended daily allowance.

Health Update

Beat the Clock

As a person ages, he or she gradually loses lean body mass, or muscle tissue. At the same time, there is often an increase in fat tissue. One way to slow down these processes is to maintain physical fitness at all ages.

However, growth-hormone therapy may be a way to turn back nature's biological clock. In a Wisconsin study, a dozen men aged 61 to 81 received growth hormones. The therapy helped them reduce the amount of body fat by as much as 14 percent and increase their muscle mass by 9 percent.

If the results of further studies are as promising, this therapy could help millions of elderly people. It could mean stronger, healthier bodies for those whose bodies no longer naturally produce the hormone. Having stronger and healthier bodies may reduce the numbers of injuries and illnesses in older adults.

Teens Making a Difference

The "Senior" Prom

In Gaithersburg, Maryland, the senior prom has taken on a new meaning. Several years ago, students at the newly opened Quince Orchard High School were faced with a problem. How could they have a prom when they did not have a senior class? After a lot of thought, they decided to hold a Senior Citizens Prom.

The first prom was so successful that it has become an annual event. At the first Senior Citizens Prom, there were 80 students and 60 senior citizens. Recently, 400 students and 300 senior citizens came to the prom.

To get ready for the prom, student committees plan a theme, design invitations, and arrange for food and flowers. The students have also learned ballroom dancing. The senior citizens always respond positively and warmly. The Senior Citizens Prom has become so successful that other high schools have written for information about hosting similar events.

Sports and Recreation

The Sky's the Limit

Do birth defects set limits on what a person can do? Ask Jim Abbott. Jim was born with just one hand. His dad thought soccer would be the perfect game for his son, but Abbott wanted to play baseball.

What's more, Abbott wanted to pitch. So he worked out a way of throwing and catching a baseball with just one hand. When he throws, he balances his glove on the stump of his right arm. As soon as he has thrown the ball, he shoves his left hand into his glove. Then he is ready to catch the ball if it is hit toward him.

As a starting pitcher for the 1988 U.S. Olympic team and as a major league pitcher for the New York Yankees and California Angels, Abbott has received a lot of attention from sports writers. "If my story helps someone else with a problem, then it makes what I'm doing all the more worthwhile," Abbott says.

Adulthood and Aging

This lesson will help you find answers to questions that teens often ask about aging. For example:

▶ **What are the stages of adulthood?**

▶ **What happens to the body and mind as a person gets older?**

▶ **What is it like to be an elderly person?**

Words to Know

chronological age
biological age
social age
Alzheimer's disease

 Did You Know?

The Aging of America ACTIVITY!

In the late 1700s, about half the population of the United States was 16 and under. By 1990, fewer than one-quarter of the people in the United States were under 16 and half were 33 or older. Discuss the implications for society of the aging of America.

From Adolescence On

Adolescence prepares you to become a young adult able to be independent and responsible for yourself. As you look to the future, you may think of adulthood as the time when growth finally ends. In fact, young adulthood is the beginning of another stage of life. There are several stages beyond that, too.

Americans today are living longer than ever before. As **Figure 7.8** shows, life expectancy in the United States has increased steadily over recent years.

Figure 7.8
Life Expectancy in the United States

For the years shown, what is the difference in life expectancy between males and females? What do you think might account for the difference?

1970 **1980** **1990**

| 74.7 | 77.5 | 78.8 | **Females** |

| 67.1 | 70.0 | 71.8 | **Males** |

The Adult Years

Like the early years of life, the adult years—the period from the twenties on—are made up of stages.

Early Adulthood

In their twenties, most people begin a career. This is also the time when people start to feel the need to share their lives with another person. For many people, that need is met by marrying and beginning a family.

Middle Adulthood

Advancing in their jobs is a key goal for many people in their thirties, forties, and fifties. People in their middle adult years often gain satisfaction from helping young people. Doing so adds to their feelings of self-worth. Many people get this satisfaction from raising their children.

Late Adulthood

People in their mid-sixties and beyond often look forward to retirement. They also look back on their lives as a whole. If they can feel they have made a contribution, they enter these years feeling good about themselves.

Individual Choices

While most people in our society follow the stages described above, not everyone does. Some people choose to marry later on or not to have children. Others never marry at all. Some begin new careers well into their middle adult years. Others choose not to retire. Each person must do what is best for him or her. Doing so helps that person feel the sense of well-being that comes from living a full and healthy life.

Teen Issues

No Time Like the Present

The teen years are a time to enjoy. There is no reason, however, why you can't enjoy yourself and prepare for your future. Your decisions now will affect the person you become as an adult. You can invest in your future by thinking responsibly when you are faced with tough choices.

Adulthood is marked by different rewards and challenges. You can learn a great deal from the adults in your life.

Most adults marry during the early adulthood stage, but some choose to wait until a later stage.

How Age Is Measured

You have probably heard the expression, "Act your age." You may also have heard certain people described as "looking younger than their years." Actually, age is measured in three different ways. These are described in **Figure 7.9**.

Physical Aging

When you think of aging, you may think of wrinkled skin and gray hair. Actually, physical aging begins when people are in their twenties. Starting in this period and going on through adulthood, the body cells divide and replace themselves more slowly.

Figure 7.9
Three Ways of Measuring Age

Chronological Age
Age measured in years is called **chronological** (krah·nuh·LAH·ji·kuhl) **age.** This is the number of your most recent birthday.

Biological Age
How well various body parts are working determines your **biological** (by·uh·LAH·ji·kuhl) **age.** This age is affected by heredity and by your health habits, exercise, and diet.

Social Age
A person's lifestyle is his or her **social age.** Social age has to do with the activities that society expects you to perform at a particular point in life. As a teen, you are expected to be in school, learning. Later you will be expected to be working, having a family, and helping others in your community.

Other signs of aging include a slow weakening of the five senses and a stiffening of the joints and weakening of the muscles. In addition, there is a loss of calcium in the bones, which causes them to become more brittle.

Although aging is a part of life, the signs differ from person to person. The signs also have much to do with a person's lifestyle. A person who makes healthy choices in diet, rest, and exercise throughout life may show fewer signs of aging.

Mental Aging

Mental aging also depends on the individual. Many people have active and alert minds well into old age. A healthy lifestyle not only reduces the signs of physical aging but can also reduce the signs of mental aging.

Some people, however, suffer from a *form of mental slowdown* called **Alzheimer's** (AHLTS·hy·merz) **disease.** This disorder may strike people in their forties and fifties, but most victims are over 65. People with Alzheimer's lose their memories over a period of time. They may also lose the power of speech and control of body movement. The cause of Alzheimer's disease is not yet known.

HEALTH LAB
The Media and the Elderly

Introduction: Some people have a negative image of late adulthood. They view it as a time of disease and disability. They think of the elderly as helpless individuals living out their later years in depressing nursing homes.

In fact, the majority of elderly people live productive and independent lives. Most live in their own homes. Most can take care of themselves.

Attitudes toward the elderly are in part the result of the way they are portrayed in the media. Newspapers, magazines, and television often highlight the plight of the elderly. They may suggest that most elderly people are forgetful and confused. This lab will help you become informed about media portrayal of the elderly so you can differentiate between what is based on fact and what is a stereotype.

Objective: During the next week, locate and read advertisements and articles in magazines and newspapers that relate to the elderly. Make a collection of clippings of these ads and articles. For each source, ask yourself the following questions:

▶ Does it fairly depict the abilities and activities of the elderly?

▶ Does it stereotype the elderly as being decrepit and helpless?

Materials and Method: You will need a poster board on which to attach your ads and articles. Divide the poster board into two columns: Media Depictions and Evaluation. In the Media column, attach the ads and articles. In the Evaluation column, write your interpretation of how each ad or article portrays the elderly. Does the source depict the elderly respectfully? Does it make assumptions about the elderly that are not based on fact? Does it portray the elderly negatively?

Observations and Analysis: At the end of the week, share your depictions and evaluations with your class. Find out how your classmates feel about the portrayal of the elderly by the media. Discuss the importance of being able to evaluate what you see and read about in the media and to identify portrayals that are stereotypes.

Meeting the Needs of the Elderly

Older people have the same emotional needs that younger people have. These include the need to love and be loved, the need to feel worthwhile, and the need to feel they are making a contribution. Several key factors can help make old age a rewarding and productive stage of life.

- **Having dealt with changes effectively throughout life.** People who learn early in life to accept change often have less difficulty accepting the changes that are part of growing old.

- **Maintaining contact with family and close friends.** Older people who have their loved ones close by tend to adjust much better than those who live alone.

- **Getting involved with younger people.** Some communities keep their older people involved through programs like Adopt a Grandparent. Such programs keep the elderly active and, at the same time, make them feel useful and needed.

Lesson 4 Review

Using complete sentences, answer the following questions on a separate sheet of paper.

Reviewing Terms and Facts

1. **Select** According to the information in Figure 7.8, which have the greater life expectancy—males or females?
2. **Summarize** Describe the three stages of adulthood.
3. **Give Examples** Cite at least three individual choices that people in a certain stage of development may make that may not be part of that stage of development.
4. **Vocabulary** What is the difference between *chronological age* and *biological age?*
5. **Vocabulary** What is meant by a person's *social age?*

Thinking Critically

6. **Illustrate** Create a poster showing the changes that people undergo in the three stages of adulthood.

7. **Analyze** Why might a person's age measure differently based on chronological, biological, and social age?
8. **Evaluate** What benefits might there be for teens who make an effort to know and help some older people in the community?

Applying Health Concepts

9. **Health of Others** Visit a senior citizen center, and talk with participants in several different programs. Make an audiotape of your interviews. Identify parts of the tape that portray positive aspects of your visit. Play your tape for the class.
10. **Growth and Development** In the library, find out about gerontologists, people who work in and study the area of aging. What kind of education is needed for this job? What personal characteristics would be helpful for a career in that field? Write a job description and share it with the class.

Facing Death and Grief

This lesson will help you find answers to questions that teens often ask about death. For example:

▶ **What is death?**
▶ **What are the stages of dying and grieving?**
▶ **How do people cope with a loved one's death?**

The End of Life

Of all the creatures on earth, humans alone go through life knowing that someday they will die. This is not a fact that healthy people spend a great deal of time thinking about. Yet healthy people learn to accept the reality of death as a natural part of the cycle of life. Learning to face this reality becomes a little easier when we better understand the nature of death.

Two Meanings of Death

There is no single definition of death. In **clinical** (KLI·ni·kuhl) **death,** *a person's body systems shut down.* Sometimes people who are declared clinically dead can be brought back to life. For example, a person who dies on the operating table may be saved through the efforts of doctors. Another example is the use of cardiopulmonary resuscitation to revive a drowning victim.

Brain activity is usually considered the difference between life and death. **Brain death** occurs *when oxygen is cut off from all the brain cells.* When the brain ceases to function, a person is said to be medically dead.

Q & A

Declaring Death

ACTIVITY!

Q: How do doctors know when brain death has occurred?

A: A person is considered brain dead when an electroencephalogram shows no brain activity for 24 hours. Find out how an electroencephalograph records brain activity.

In some cases, CPR (cardiopulmonary resuscitation) can revive people who are clinically dead. CPR is an emergency procedure that is used to get the heart beating again and to restore breathing. Learning how to perform CPR can be a life-saving skill. It must be taught by a health care or rescue professional.

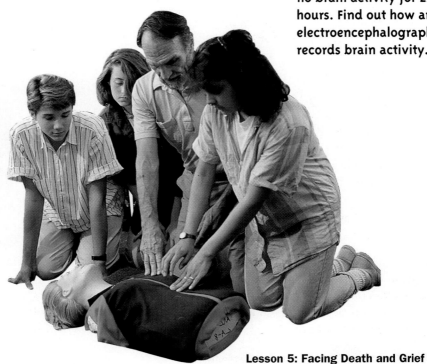

Dr. Elisabeth Kübler-Ross found one emotion to be typical of dying people throughout all the stages of death: hope. The dying patients she talked to all hoped a cure would be found so they would not have to die.

Accepting Death

For some people, the end of life comes peacefully while they are asleep. For others, death comes after a long struggle with a disease. For still others, it is sudden and unexpected.

Elisabeth Kübler-Ross, a noted doctor, has studied the experiences of dying people and their families. Dr. Ross identified five stages that people go through in facing death. These stages are listed below. Not all people experience the five stages. However, they are general guidelines we can use to understand how people experience dying.

■ **Stage 1: Denial**
Refusing to accept that one is dying. Telling oneself "it is all a mistake" and hoping to wake up from this "nightmare."

■ **Stage 2: Anger**
Angrily asking, "Why me?" Often directing the anger toward anyone close by—friends, family members, doctors, nurses.

■ **Stage 3: Bargaining**
Looking for ways to prolong life. Hoping for a medical miracle or praying to be spared in exchange for living a better life.

■ **Stage 4: Depression**
Feeling deep sadness for loss of life and other losses. Realizing that one will not live to keep promises or realize goals.

■ **Stage 5: Acceptance**
Accepting the reality of death and making peace with the world.

The family of a dying person often finds great strength and comfort in the dying person's acceptance of death. In this way, the dying sometimes teach the living about life.

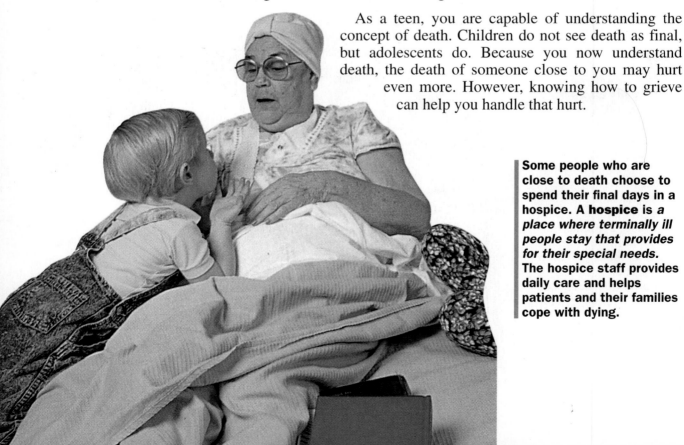

As a teen, you are capable of understanding the concept of death. Children do not see death as final, but adolescents do. Because you now understand death, the death of someone close to you may hurt even more. However, knowing how to grieve can help you handle that hurt.

Some people who are close to death choose to spend their final days in a hospice. A **hospice** is *a place where terminally ill people stay that provides for their special needs.* The hospice staff provides daily care and helps patients and their families cope with dying.

The Grief Process

The death of someone we care deeply about brings out many different feelings. The *sum total of feelings caused by the death of a loved one* is known as **grief.** The length of time that people grieve after a loved one dies varies with the individual. It also varies with the circumstances of the death. When a loved one's death is sudden and unexpected—as in the case of a fatal accident—the grief process tends to take longer.

Some experts have observed that grief has several stages similar to Dr. Kübler-Ross's stages of dying. As with dying, grief reactions vary from person to person. However, five reactions are common.

- **Shock.** Shortly after the death of a loved one, people tend to feel separated from their emotions. They are often numb. If they have any feeling at all, it is an emptiness.

- **Anger.** Sometimes the survivors feel angry. The anger may even be directed toward the dead person for having died.

- **Yearning.** The survivors ache. The loss of the loved one has left a great emptiness in their lives. They wish the loved one could come back, if just for a moment.

- **Depression.** The survivors begin to accept the reality of their loss. The person has died and will not be coming back.

- **Moving on.** The survivors are able to go forward with their lives. They have not forgotten the one who died, but the deep pain over the loss has lessened.

Teen Issues

Shedding a Tear

Some people think that if they haven't cried over a death or loss, they haven't been hurt by it. That isn't true. Grieving can take many forms. When you or someone you know suffers a loss, it is important to let the feelings come. The hurt needs to be expressed in order for healing to begin.

Different cultures deal with death in different ways. Most cultures have rituals that celebrate the life of the person who has died or encourage survivors to recall personal memories. These ceremonies help people cope with the death of a loved one.

Dealing with the Death of a Loved One

Everyone, at one time or another, loses a loved one to death. The one who dies may be a friend, a relative, or a pet. Regardless of the type of relationship, the death of someone close can be a terribly painful experience.

Funeral services, memorial services, and other kinds of services help people deal with their loss. For many people, the service offers an opportunity to celebrate the life of the person who has died. At the same time, the service brings people together to share their grief. Most cultures have special rituals that they observe when somebody dies. These rituals vary from elaborate parades to simple grave-side ceremonies.

Mental health experts have come up with a number of **coping strategies.** These are *ways of dealing with the sense of loss people feel at the death of someone close.* They include the following:

- **Remember what was good about the person.** Focusing on happy times and on ways in which the person was special can help ease the pain.

- **Don't run away from your feelings.** The hurt from the loss is there and cannot be denied. It is best to let the feelings out.

- **Share your feelings with other people.** If nothing else, telling someone else about the hurt you are feeling will remind you that you are not alone.

- **Join a support group.** Most communities have support groups in which people who have suffered a loss can share their pain with others. These groups are usually sponsored by churches, synagogues, and other associations.

LIFE SKILLS
Helping Another Person Cope with Loss

*H*ave you ever had a serious disappointment or lost something that meant a lot to you? Perhaps you lost the friendship of someone close after the two of you had a serious argument. You may have felt very sad when a good friend moved away. Possibly you were depressed because you did not make the basketball team. If you have had such an experience, do you remember how you felt?

The feelings people have after a loss or disappointment are often similar to grief. When someone you care about suffers a loss, there are ways you can help that person cope.

▶ **Let the person set the speed of recovery.** Everyone handles these feelings differently. Some people get over losses quickly. Others do not.

▶ **Let the person decide how you can be the most helpful.** Some people simply need to feel the presence of someone close. Don't insist on talking or giving the person advice when he or she just wants to sit quietly.

Using complete sentences, answer the following questions on a separate sheet of paper.

Reviewing Terms and Facts

1. **Vocabulary** What is the difference between *clinical death* and *brain death?*

2. **Give an Example** Cite an emergency procedure that can revive a person who is clinically dead.

3. **Vocabulary** Write an original sentence of your own using the term *grief.*

4. **Recall** List three coping strategies for dealing with the loss of someone close.

Thinking Critically

5. **Compare** How are the stages of dying and the stages of grief similar and how are they different?

6. **Explain** How do funeral services and other rituals relating to death help those who are grieving?

7. **Synthesize** How might you help a younger brother, sister, or other child you know whose pet hamster had died?

Applying Health Concepts

8. **Health of Others** Research hospice care. Find out when it is used and how it is different from hospital care. Then visit a hospice and talk with staff and patients. How does the staff feel about its work? How do the patients feel about their treatment? If a visit is not possible, find an article about hospice care that includes first-person accounts by staff and patients. Write a report of your findings.

9. **Growth and Development** Look in your library for books or poetry on death and grief. Choose one that seems interesting to you. Read it and write down your thoughts about what you have read. Examples that you might look for include the poem "Death Be Not Proud" by John Donne, and the books *A Taste of Blackberries* by Doris Buchanan Smith and *A Bridge to Terabithia* by Katherine Paterson.

▶ **Respect the person's right to feel sad.** Don't tell the person she or he is wrong or silly to feel bad or that the loss is not important. To her or him, the loss may be very important. The best help is to deal with the grief, not to pretend it will go away.

Follow-up Activity

Think about an experience that a friend or an acquaintance might have had with a loss. How did you help that person cope with it? Do you think you should have handled the situation differently? If so, use the suggestions above to describe what you could have done to help that person cope.

Chapter Summary

▶ The body begins to grow from a single cell, which is created by the fertilization of an egg cell by a sperm cell. (Lesson 1)

▶ The developing body gets its food and oxygen from the placenta, a special tissue that connects the mother to the baby. (Lesson 1)

▶ Two major factors in the health of a developing baby are heredity and environment. (Lesson 2)

▶ Good prenatal care includes regular visits to a health care professional; eating properly; enough rest; enough exercise; and avoiding tobacco, alcohol, and drugs not allowed by a doctor. (Lesson 2)

▶ The growth years include the stages of infancy, early childhood, childhood, late childhood, and adolescence. (Lesson 3)

▶ Adolescents need to take on several developmental tasks in order to become healthy, mature adults. (Lesson 3)

▶ The stages of adulthood include early adulthood, middle adulthood, and late adulthood. (Lesson 4)

▶ Older people have the same emotional needs as people in other stages of life. (Lesson 4)

▶ Death can be defined in two ways: clinical death and brain death. (Lesson 5)

▶ The grieving process includes five stages. (Lesson 5)

Using Health Terms

On a separate sheet of paper, write the vocabulary term that best matches each definition given below.

1. Groups of cells that perform a similar function (Lesson 1)

2. Reproductive organ in which the fertilized egg implants and develops (Lesson 1)

3. The passing of characteristics from parents to their children (Lesson 2)

4. Psychological and emotional dependence on a drug or other substance (Lesson 2)

5. Chemical substances produced in the body to regulate body functions (Lesson 3)

6. Period during adolescence in which males and females begin to develop adult traits (Lesson 3)

7. What society expects you to do at a particular point in your life (Lesson 4)

8. Mental disorder characterized by loss of memory over a period of time as well as problems with speech and movement (Lesson 4)

9. A program or a place that cares for the terminally ill (Lesson 5)

10. Ways of dealing with feelings of loss when someone close dies (Lesson 5)

Reviewing Main Ideas

Using complete sentences, answer the following questions on a separate sheet of paper.

1. How does the developing baby get its food and oxygen? (Lesson 1)

2. What are four important steps a pregnant woman can take for the health of her unborn baby? (Lesson 2)

3. What are environmental causes of birth defects? (Lesson 2)

4. During which stage of development does the fastest growth occur? (Lesson 3)

5. What three types of growth occur during adolescence? (Lesson 3)

6. Describe two physical changes that take place as a person gets older. (Lesson 4)

7. What three basic emotional needs do the elderly share with people in other stages of life? (Lesson 4)

8. List the five stages in grieving. (Lesson 5)

Thinking Critically

Using complete sentences, answer the following questions on a separate sheet of paper.

1. **Summarize** During which stage of birth does the mother first have contractions? During which stage do the contractions help push out the placenta? (Lesson 1)

2. **Evaluate** Why should a woman visit an obstetrician or other health care professional as soon as she suspects she is pregnant as well as throughout the pregnancy? (Lesson 2)

3. **Classify** Susan has turned 13. She feels proud about how her body is changing. Her character seems to be changing, too. She is interested in boys. Last week she offered to help out at a nearby nursing home. What developmental tasks is Susan working on? (Lesson 3)

4. **Summarize** What are some of the changes that occur with aging? What can a person do to slow down the aging process? (Lesson 4)

5. **Apply** What are some ways you might help a friend cope with the death of a friend or relative? (Lesson 5)

Your Action Plan

Make an action plan to help you work toward being the kind of adult you would like to be. Look back through your private journal entries for this chapter. What do they tell you about who you are now and about who you want to be in the future? Then review the developmental tasks of adolescence listed in Figure 7.7. Which tasks do you think you have mastered or are on the way to mastering? Which ones do you need to work on?

Mastering those developmental tasks can help you become the kind of adult you want to be. You can focus on one task at a time or on a few at a time. For example, you might want to think about your values. Do you care about preserving the environment? If so, you might take part in local cleanup campaigns and make an extra effort to reduce waste by reusing bags and recycling bottles and cans.

Building Your Portfolio

1. Create a picture album of Erikson's eight stages of life. Assemble a collection of illustrations (from magazines or family photos) for each stage. The pictures should be related to each stage's developmental task. Write captions to the photos explaining the developmental task and how it is shown in the photo. Add your album to your portfolio.

2. Interview two or three senior citizens in your community who appear to be in good health. Ask them about their interests and activities. Ask them to tell you what helped them live long and healthy lives. Get permission to tape-record the interviews. Keep the recordings in your portfolio.

In Your Home and Community

1. With your classmates, put together a handbook suggesting ways of helping people cope with a loss. Include the three coping strategies and provide several examples of how these strategies can be used. You might make your handbook available in the library or counselor's office for other students to see.

2. Take a survey of the recreational resources in your community. Find out what parks or playgrounds are suitable for use by parents with young children. Make a map that highlights these areas, and briefly describe what is available at each place. Display the map at a local child care center or clinic.

Chapter 8
Reaching Your Fitness Goals

Student Expectations

After reading this chapter, you should be able to:

1. Explain what physical fitness is.
2. Determine how physically fit you are.
3. Design a fitness program to meet your fitness goals.
4. Describe different types of sports that can help you meet your fitness goals.

My name is Maxwell, but I'm Max to most people. Being strong and fit has always been important to me. When I was a little kid, I called myself Muscle Max. I'd put up my arms and stand like Superman and announce my super strength. I have always thought of myself as being pretty strong and fit—until three weeks ago.

I began to doubt my fitness when I almost missed the school bus. Carmen, who lives next door and has known me since I was Muscle Max, is in my class. Well, that day we both got a late start. The bus pulled away just as we were leaving our homes. We both started running. After half a block, I was huffing and puffing and had to stop. Carmen didn't stop; she caught the bus and asked the driver to wait for me. "Give it full power, Muscle Max," she laughed. I laughed too, but the truth was I was on full power.

So I started thinking. How did Carmen become more fit than me? Just what happened to old Muscle Max anyway?

in your journal

Read the account on this page. Who do you identify with most—Carmen or Max? Do you, like Max, find yourself doubting your fitness? Perhaps you are more like Carmen—doing well and working to stay that way. Start your private journal entries on fitness by answering these questions:

▶ In general, are you as fit as you want to be?
▶ Which personal fitness characteristics would you like to improve?
▶ Which personal fitness skills would you like to improve?

When you reach the end of the chapter, you will use your journal entries to make an action plan.

What Is Physical Fitness?

This lesson will help you find answers to questions that teens often ask about fitness. For example:

▶ **What does *being fit* really mean?**

▶ **What is my physical fitness potential?**

▶ **Is exercising really all that is needed to be fit?**

Words to Know

totally fit
physically fit
aerobic exercise
anaerobic exercise

Being Fit

Many people think of fitness as they do health, in only physical terms. They think fitness means being in good shape or being able to play a sport well. In part, fitness does mean those things, but total fitness means a lot more. In addition to its physical part, total fitness has a mental part and a social part. When you are **totally fit,** you are *able to handle physical, mental, emotional, and social day-to-day challenges without feeling exhausted.*

Having good physical fitness is a key part of total fitness. One meaning of the word *physical* is "of the body," and the basis of physical fitness is a healthy body. When you are **physically fit** your body is *ready to handle whatever comes your way from day to day.*

Figure 8.1
Fitness Benefits

Being totally fit gives you physical, mental, emotional, and social benefits.

Increases energy *(physical)*

Sharpens alertness *(mental)*

Increases self-esteem *(mental and emotional)*

Lowers blood pressure *(physical)*

For example, a physically fit person can get through the school day, get at-home chores done, do a good job on homework, and still have enough energy to join in a neighborhood softball game or snowball fight. **Figure 8.1** summarizes some of the benefits of physical fitness. Which are most important to you?

Benefits of Fitness

Being fit keeps your body working at its best to help you feel good and do what you want to do. Fitness benefits the "physical you." Your heart delivers enough blood with each beat to supply your body cells with all the oxygen they need to work well. You don't run out of breath during active work or play. Your blood pressure stays low. Your appetite levels off—you are more likely to take in only the calories you use for energy.

Fitness benefits the "mental and emotional you." Because being physically fit makes you look better and feel better, your self-esteem rises. You find that you like the physically fit *you.* Staying fit also reduces depression and helps you manage the stress in your life. Exercise improves your mood and clears your mind. You may also find that exercise can be a healthy outlet for tension, anger, or frustration.

Fitness benefits the "social you." Being physically fit helps you be at ease with yourself and with others. You have the energy to join in activities with your friends and get the most out of active sports and games. You can meet new people when you participate in organized exercise activities. Organized sports provide a great opportunity for you to work with others toward a common goal.

in Your Journal

The following questions will help you decide whether you need to improve your physical fitness. Write your answers in your journal.

▶ Do you tire easily from physical or mental activities?

▶ Do you often "run out of steam" before your friends do?

▶ Do you have poor posture?

Provides opportunities to meet new people *(social)*

Reduces stress *(mental and emotional)*

Improves muscle tone *(physical)*

Provides opportunities to share common goals *(social)*

Personal Inventory

Most people have a fitness level that is below their potential level. However, there are actions people can take to increase their fitness. How many of the following physical fitness-building actions do you take?

Regular exercise helps develop physical fitness traits.

1. I walk or bike to school.

2. When my friends are trying to decide what to do, I suggest an active game or activity, such as swimming, basketball, hiking, or bike riding.

3. I take the stairs rather than the elevator or escalator when I have a choice.

4. When traveling by bus a distance too far to walk, I get off early and walk part of the way. If I'm being driven, I suggest that we park and walk part of the way.

5. I participate in an active game, sport, or work activity every day, either with others or alone.

Good nutrition helps develop physical fitness traits.

6. Generally, I eat a balanced diet.

7. When I snack, I choose healthful foods such as fruit, rather than sweets or snacks high in fat or salt.

8. I choose portion sizes that are reasonable: not too large, not too small.

9. I never starve myself to lose weight.

Enough rest and relaxation helps develop physical fitness traits.

10. I get eight to nine hours of sleep each night.

11. I take time to sit and rest for a while after a vigorous game or activity.

12. I allow time daily to relax and do nothing.

Give yourself 1 point for each yes answer. A score of 10-12 is very good. A score of 6-9 is good. If you score below 6, your fitness behavior needs work.

Everyone can develop physical fitness—the strength and energy to continue an activity over time without tiring. Of course all people cannot develop those traits to the same level. Each person's body has a fitness potential level, which is the highest possible level of fitness that person's body can develop. Each person has his or her own fitness potential level determined by the body's limitations. Even when those limitations are great, there is room for development. For example, a person who must use a wheelchair can still develop his or her arm strength.

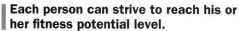

Each person can strive to reach his or her fitness potential level.

Fitness and You

How many statements in the Personal Inventory apply to you? If most of them do, you are probably already committed to being physically fit. If some of the statements do not apply to you, then you may want to make some changes in your lifestyle. Look at the statements you answered with a *no*. Think about what you can do to fit those activities into your day. For example, if you have trouble running for the bus, put some more vigorous activity into your life. If you are too tired to pay attention in school, think about getting more rest and relaxation.

One factor to consider when deciding to raise your physical fitness level is your physical fitness potential. In Lesson 2, you will learn how to determine your fitness potential. Every person's body has limits. Keep your goals challenging, but realistic. Not everyone can break athletic records, but everyone can improve.

Deciding to raise your physical fitness level is only the first step. Actually getting started in a fitness program is the next step. To motivate yourself, review the benefits of physical fitness on pages 230–31. Do these benefits appeal to you? Which of the benefits would you like to achieve first?

Another way to get started with fitness is to get some help. There are a lot of people who can help you improve your physical fitness. Parents, friends, brothers and sisters, teachers, and coaches are a few. The most important person, however, is you. You must take responsibility for your physical fitness. You can ask other people for advice or encouragement. You can ask someone else to join you in an activity. In the end, however, the level of physical fitness that you reach is up to you.

Did You Know?

Awards of Fitness

ACTIVITY!

The Presidential Physical Fitness Award Program was started in 1966. The program, which is designed for young people from the ages of 6 to 17, including students with special needs, increases awareness of the importance of physical fitness. Ask your physical education teacher how you can participate and be a "winner."

What can you do to improve your physical fitness level?

Exercise: A Key to Fitness

Cars, home appliances, and other technologies have removed the need for physical activity to carry out many daily activities. Most people do not get very much exercise unless they make a special effort to do so. Yet, as you have learned, exercise is an important key to fitness. There are two categories of exercises: aerobic and anaerobic. Later in this chapter, you will learn more about how each type of exercise helps you.

A **Aerobic** (e·ROH·bik) **exercise** is *nonstop, repetitive, vigorous exercise that increases breathing and heartbeat rates.* Swimming, running, and cross-country skiing are examples.

B **Anaerobic** (an·e·ROH·bik) **exercise** involves *great bursts of energy in which the muscles work hard to produce energy.* Examples are gymnastics, push-ups, and sprinting.

Lesson 1 Review

Using complete sentences, answer the following questions on a separate sheet of paper.

Reviewing Terms and Facts

1. **Vocabulary** Define the term *totally fit* using your own words.

2. **Give Examples** List at least five ways to increase your fitness level.

3. **Vocabulary** What kind of exercise is vigorous and sustained, and increases breathing and heartbeat rates?

4. **Recall** Give examples of the two categories of exercise.

Thinking Critically

5. **Analyze** Would you describe yourself as physically fit? Every day for one week write down your activities and how you felt at the end of the day. Tell why you would describe yourself as physically fit or not.

6. **Analyze** How might staying fit help you manage stress? Has physical exercise ever provided you with an outlet for tension or anger?

7. **Explain** Describe how one person's physical fitness level may be different from that of another person.

Applying Health Concepts

8. **Personal Health** Make a list of your physical activities during the last week. Which were aerobic? With a partner, think of ways that both of you can increase your aerobic activity.

9. **Health of Others** Survey adult friends, classmates, and family members who exercise regularly. Ask each why he or she exercises. Write down their answers and compare them to the list of benefits of physical fitness listed on pages 230–31. Share your findings with your classmates.

Elements of Fitness

This lesson will help you find answers to questions that teens often ask about physical fitness. For example:

▶ **What are the parts of physical fitness?**

▶ **How can I test my own physical fitness?**

▶ **How can I set reasonable physical fitness goals for myself?**

Determining Physical Fitness

Use your imagination to picture a physically fit male and a physically fit female. Did you picture a young, slim girl and a tall, muscular young man? Perhaps you pictured both as being very skilled at active games and spending a lot of their time playing competitive sports. Many advertisements in magazines and newspapers and on television associate those images with physical fitness. People who match those descriptions may be physically fit, but the truth is that a lot of people who are quite different from those descriptions are also physically fit.

Everyone can develop a level of physical fitness. Some people are short; others are tall. Some people are naturally thin; others have a broader body structure. In addition, some people are naturally good at sports. They seem to be good at every sport they try. Many others have less natural ability, and still others seem to be "all thumbs" at most sports. People of all body types, ages, ability levels, and levels of general health can reach their own potential levels of physical fitness.

The first step in reaching your physical fitness potential is to determine just how physically fit you are now. Physical fitness can be divided into several parts. This lesson explains the major parts of fitness and shows you ways to test yourself for each part. On which parts do you think you will test best?

Words to Know

muscle strength
muscle endurance
flexibility
heart and lung
endurance
body composition

in your journal

Predict your scores on the tests in this lesson. Write your predictions in your journal. Then record your actual scores. How well did you predict?

Whatever your shape or size, you can be as fit as your ability level allows.

Muscle Strength and Endurance

The ability of your muscles to exert a force is called strength. Lifting a weight and pushing a load are acts of strength. *The most weight you can lift or the most force you can exert at one time* are measures of your **muscle strength.**

The ability of your muscles to exert a force over time without becoming overly tired is called **muscle endurance** (en·DER·uhns). Raking a yard takes muscle endurance. **Figures 8.2, 8.3,** and **8.4** show some tests for muscle strength and endurance.

Figure 8.2
Determining Leg Muscle Strength

You can test your leg muscle strength by measuring your ability to do a standing broad jump.

1 Put a piece of tape on the floor or ground and stand behind it with your toes touching the tape.

2 Bend your knees and jump forward as far as you can, landing with your weight on both feet. Mark where you land.

3 Measure from the tape to your landing point to find the distance of your jump. Use the table to rate your muscle strength by comparing the distance you jumped to your height.

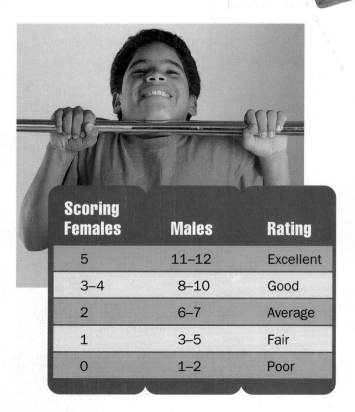

Scoring

Distance Jumped	Rating
About 6 inches more than your height	Excellent
Between 2 and 4 inches more than your height	Good
Equal to your height	Fair
Less than your height	Poor

Scoring

Females	Males	Rating
5	11–12	Excellent
3–4	8–10	Good
2	6–7	Average
1	3–5	Fair
0	1–2	Poor

Figure 8.3
Determining Upper Body Strength and Endurance

You can test your upper body strength and muscular endurance by counting the pull-ups you can do. Find a horizontal bar from which you can hang by your hands without touching the ground or floor.

1 Grasp the bar with your palms facing away. Hang without bending your elbows. Pull yourself up until your chin clears the bar.

2 Lower your body to the starting position to finish one pull-up.

3 Your score is the number of pull-ups you can do in one session. Resting between pull-ups and kicking are not allowed.

Figure 8.4
Determining Abdominal Strength and Endurance

You can test the endurance of the muscles of your abdomen by counting the number of bent-knee sit-ups you can complete in one minute. You will need a partner and a watch with a second hand. During the test, remember to breathe freely. Do not hold your breath. Your partner should keep the time and count your sit-ups.

Scoring Females	Males	Rating
30+	40+	Excellent
24–29	33–39	Good
18–23	29–32	Average
11–17	21–28	Fair
10 or less	20 or less	Poor

1 Lie on your back with your knees slightly bent. Place your hands behind your head. Have your partner hold your ankles for support. Raise your upper body from the floor until you touch one elbow to the opposite knee.

2 Return to the start position to do one complete sit-up. Your score is the number of complete sit-ups done in one minute.

Flexibility

When you move, you bend your body joints and stretch your muscles. *Your ability to move within the range of motion for each joint* is your **flexibility.** People with good flexibility can bend, stretch, and turn their bodies easily. People with poor flexibility feel stiff when they move. You may be more flexible in one part of your body than in another. You can test the flexibility of the major muscles in your lower back and the back of your legs by doing the sit-and-reach test (see **Figure 8.5**).

Figure 8.5
Determining Flexibility

Begin this test by doing some light stretching to protect your muscles from injury. During the test, move smoothly. Avoid quick, jerking motions. Your reach should be gradual and slow.

Sit on the floor with your legs straight in front of you. Your heels should touch a piece of tape on the floor and be about 5 inches apart. Place a yardstick on the floor between your legs so that the 36-inch end points away from your body, and the 15-inch mark is even with your heels. With fingers straight, slowly reach with both hands as far forward as possible and hold your position. Look at the yardstick to see how many inches you reached, which marks your score. Try the test three times. Use your longest reach to find your score.

Scoring Females	Males	Rating
23+	22+	Excellent
19–23	16–22	Good
16–19	12–15	Average
14–16	9–11	Fair
less than 14	less than 9	Poor

Make a line graph of your fitness test scores. For the vertical scale, use poor, fair, average, good, excellent. For the horizontal scale, use the names of the tests. Analyze your scores. Do you have mostly the same score in every test?

Heart and Lung Endurance

Your power to move your whole body over time is called your heart and lung endurance. You can move your body while staying pretty much in the same place, such as when you jump rope. You can move your body while moving from place to place, such as when you walk or run. Either way, *how effectively your heart and lungs work during exercise and how quickly they return to normal after exercise* is a measure of your **heart and lung endurance.** You can get a general idea of your heart and lung endurance by trying the step test shown in **Figure 8.6.**

Caution: Forcing yourself to go on if you become exhausted can be dangerous. People with diseases of the heart or lungs should check with their doctors before trying this test.

Figure 8.6
Determining Heart and Lung Endurance

For this test, you need a step or a sturdy bench about 8 inches high that you can easily step onto without it wobbling or breaking. You also need a partner and a watch with a second hand to time you.

❶ Stand in front of the step or bench. When your partner says "go," step up and down on the step repeatedly. Step up with the right foot, then the left, extending each leg fully. Then step down with the right foot and then the left. Do about 24 steps per minute.

❷ When three minutes are up, your partner should say "stop." Immediately stop and sit down. Do not talk. Have your partner take your pulse on your wrist or on the side of your neck. Your score is the number of heartbeats he or she counts in one minute.

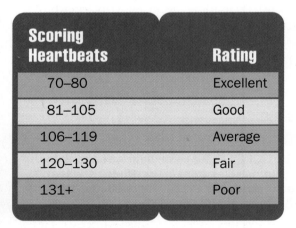

Scoring Heartbeats	Rating
70–80	Excellent
81–105	Good
106–119	Average
120–130	Fair
131+	Poor

Body Composition

Another part of physical fitness is your **body composition,** or *the proportion of body fat in comparison with lean body tissue, such as muscle and bone.* People with too high a percentage of body fat are said to be obese. One generally accepted way to measure body composition, and to estimate obesity, is to find Body Mass Index (BMI). BMI is found by dividing a person's weight by the square of his or her height (see **Figure 8.7**).

Healthy People 2000, a report by the U.S. government, defines overweight for various ages, including adolescent boys and girls whose BMI is equal to or greater than certain numbers. The BMI numbers for being overweight are as follows. Ages 12 through 14: males 23.0; females 23.4. Ages 15 through 17: males 24.3; females 24.8. Ages 18 through 19: males 25.8; females 25.7.

If your BMI falls at or above the limit for your gender and age, you may need to change your diet or exercise habits. Before you take action, talk it over with a parent, fitness instructor, or family physician. There may be other factors to consider.

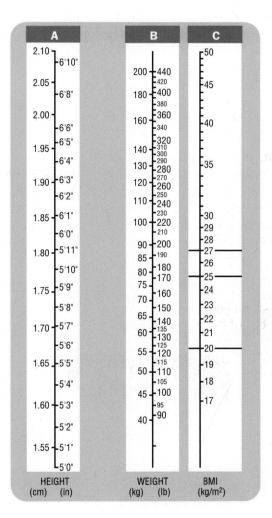

Figure 8.7

Body Mass Index

You can easily find your BMI by using this chart. Mark an x at your height on scale A. Mark an x at your weight on scale B. Use a ruler to draw a straight line through both x's. Make sure the line extends through scale C. The point where the line meets scale C is your BMI.

Your Fitness Level

After completing the tests on the major parts of physical fitness described in this lesson, you should have a good idea of your present levels of muscle strength and endurance, flexibility, heart and lung endurance, and body composition. From the Personal Inventory in Lesson 1, you should have identified your present physical fitness traits. In other words, you know if you have a healthy diet, get enough relaxation and sleep, and exercise every day. Together, this information gives you a data image of your present level of physical fitness. Now it is time for you to decide if you want to improve that image. If you do, you need to set goals and decide how to achieve these goals.

Consider Your Limits

Before you set goals for improving your physical fitness, you must consider your limits. Recall from Lesson 1 that everyone has a physical fitness potential—the highest level of fitness he or she can achieve. Your fitness potential is unique. It is probably higher than that of some people you know and lower than that of some others.

Many factors influence fitness potential. Inherited traits are one factor. Long-lasting illnesses and conditions are other major factors. For example, people with asthma, a lung disorder, often become short of breath when they exercise hard. People with weak body joints or other bone problems are also limited in their ability to take part in certain activities. Before setting goals to improve your physical fitness, it is a good idea to check with your doctor. If you have a long-lasting illness or condition, you should definitely ask your doctor to help you set realistic goals.

Setting Your Goals

When setting your physical fitness goals, keep in mind what you want to improve. For example, if you want to increase your heart and lung endurance, choose exercises designed to give your heart and lungs a workout. You can find out which exercises are best for various parts of physical fitness in Lesson 3. The following guidelines can help you set your physical fitness goals.

■ Set goals based on your fitness test results, your Personal Inventory results, and your personal preferences. Set goals that you really want to achieve.

■ Set goals based on how much time you really can exercise.

■ Set goals that you can reach. Remember your limits. Set short-term goals based on where you are now. If you tested "fair," a reasonable goal is to reach a "good" rating.

HEALTH LAB

Finding Your Target Pulse Rate

*I*ntroduction: To improve your physical fitness, you must make your heart and lungs work at higher-than-normal rates for at least twenty minutes, three or four times per week. At these higher rates, your heart beats faster, your blood flows faster, and your breathing is deeper. Done regularly, working at this higher-than-normal level makes your body stronger and more fit.

Every person has a maximum heartbeat rate, which gradually decreases with age. Your heart cannot beat faster than its maximum rate. Exercise that causes your heartbeat to go above 85 percent of its maximum rate may be dangerous. On the other hand, exercise that does not raise your heartbeat rate to at least 70 percent of your maximum rate won't do your heart and lungs much good.

The heartbeat rate that will safely give you the most benefit out of exercise is between 70 and 85 percent of your maximum heartbeat rate. This rate is called your target pulse rate.

Objective: Follow the directions on the next page to find your target pulse rate.

Using complete sentences, answer the following questions on a separate sheet of paper.

Reviewing Terms and Facts

1. **Vocabulary** What is the difference between *muscle strength* and *muscle endurance?*

2. **Vocabulary** Use the term *heart and lung endurance* in an original sentence.

3. **Recall** List three ways to test muscle strength and endurance.

4. **Recall** What information do you need to evaluate your level of fitness?

Thinking Critically

5. **Evaluate** After testing *poor* on muscle strength and endurance, Kim set a goal to "test *excellent* in three weeks." Kim can exercise three days a week and is in good health. Is this a realistic goal? Why or why not?

6. **Analyze** Suppose you knew that a friend of yours often exercised hard enough to raise his heart rate above the upper number of the target pulse rate range for his age. What advice would you give him? Why?

Applying Health Concepts

7. **Health of Others** Make a list of the parts of physical fitness. Review the tests for each part. As you go through your day at school and around your community, look for people engaged in work and other activities that require a good level of at least one of the parts. For example, a carpenter doing a lot of nailing would require good muscle strength and endurance. Make a poster explaining your findings and share it with your classmates.

8. **Health of Others** With one or two classmates, make up a song that tells the benefits of each part of physical fitness. Perform your song for your classmates.

Materials and Method: To find your target pulse rate, first determine your maximum heartbeat rate. Your maximum heartbeat rate is the number *220* minus your age. Your target pulse rate is a range. Multiply your maximum pulse rate by 70 percent and 85 percent to find the two ends of your range. Check your figures with the chart.

Observation and Analysis: Over the next week or two, take your pulse while exercising. Does your heartbeat rate fall within the range of your target pulse rate? Record your observations and analysis in your journal.

Age	Maximum Pulse Rate	Target Pulse Rate
11	209	146–178
12	208	146–177
13	207	145–176
14	206	144–175
15	205	143–174
16	204	142–173

Teen HEALTH DIGEST

CON$UMER FOCU$

Exercise Machines

Many people buy exercise machines for their workouts. Machines such as stationary bicycles and treadmills provide users with an opportunity to work out indoors during bad weather. People who have busy schedules and little time to go to a gym or exercise class find these machines convenient.

Exercise machines, however, are expensive. They range in price from around $100 to thousands of dollars. Some exercise machines are simple pulley devices for working muscles. Others, such as treadmills, are more complex, often containing many computerized features.

If your family is considering the purchase of an exercise machine, be sure to check it out for comfort and construction. Ask a fitness instructor for advice. Buy only what you need and what you will use.

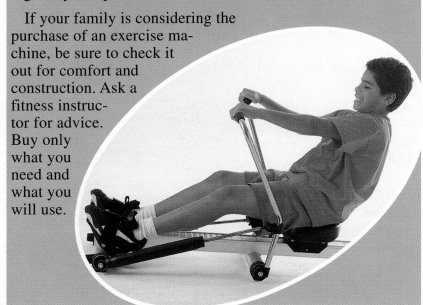

People at Work

Personal Fitness Trainer

After earning a degree in exercise physiology and education, Yvonne Blue became a personal fitness trainer at a large health club. She works with people, usually one at a time, to help them improve their fitness.

To begin, Blue tests each client and talks to him or her about goals. "Once I know where the client is and where he or she wants to be, it isn't hard to develop a fitness program to achieve those goals," says Blue. Planning fitness programs is just the beginning of Blue's work. The real job is supervising the exercise sessions and keeping her clients motivated. Blue compares her role of personal trainer with that of being a good friend. "I have to know when to push, when to praise, and when to just be quiet."

Teens Making a Difference

Bikes for Earning and Learning

In December 1993, eighth-grader Roger Smith of Indianapolis, Indiana, picked up a shiny red top-of-the-line mountain bike at the Earn-A-Bike program shop. Roger and dozens of other teens in Indianapolis and Boston are working hard to earn bikes and are learning some valuable lessons along the way.

Teens like Roger overhaul and repair used bicycles that have been donated to the Earn-A-Bike program. Teens work at the shop with adult volunteers after school and on weekends. During the first few sessions, a teen must learn good work habits in a shop environment: order, discipline, and cooperation. Then he or she may choose a bike to work on. Teens can spend no more than one half of their time working on the bike they are trying to earn. The rest of the time they help someone else. The bike with the least value can be earned after 25 hours of labor. Roger Smith's high-tech model took 110 hours to earn.

In-line Injuries

The Consumer Product Safety Commission is telling all skaters to wear helmets and other protective gear when in-line skating.

The design of the skates—a single row of wheels on each skate—allows in-line skaters to go very fast over a variety of paved surfaces outdoors. With the speed, however, there often comes a fall.

As in-line skating grows in popularity, the number of in-line skating injuries continues to rise. Every year emergency rooms expect more than 49,000 kids to come in for treatment of in-line injuries. About 7,000 of those injuries will be head injuries. Some of them are very serious. That's why people who in-line skate without a helmet and protective equipment are strictly out of line!

Myths and Realities

Gain Without Pain

"**N**o pain, no gain" is a common saying associated with exercise. It suggests that in order for exercise to be good for you, it must cause some pain. A lot of people believe this. It's easy to remember because it rhymes, but it's totally false.

When you use muscles during exercise that haven't been worked lately, it is common to feel some mild discomfort or soreness. Pain, however, is usually sharp, and it hurts.

Pain is a signal that something is wrong. When you feel pain, you should lower the intensity of the exercise until you feel comfortable. If the pain continues, you should stop exercising. If you keep exercising when you feel pain, you could cause serious injury or permanent damage. No pain, no gain is a dangerous exercise myth.

Planning a Fitness Program

This lesson will help you find answers to questions that teens often ask about designing their own fitness programs. For example:

▶ What are the best exercises to help me meet my fitness goals?
▶ How can I find time to exercise?
▶ How often and how hard should I exercise?
▶ How can I keep from being hurt during exercise?
▶ What clothes and shoes should I wear?

Words to Know

warm-up
exercise frequency
exercise intensity
exercise time
cool-down

Choosing the Right Exercise

Once you have set your fitness goals, you can choose the exercises that will help you reach them. In Lesson 1, you learned about two types of exercise: aerobic (vigorous exercise that gives your heart and lungs a workout) and anaerobic (intense, short bursts of activity).

To improve your heart and lung endurance, flexibility, and body composition, you need to do aerobic exercises. For muscle strength, you need to do anaerobic exercises. For muscle endurance, a program that is part aerobic and part anaerobic is most helpful. **Figure 8.8** shows how various activities rate in each area of fitness. Ratings show the benefits of an activity when done for thirty minutes or longer. The highest score possible is 21.

Figure 8.8
How Exercise Activities Rate

You can choose the kind of exercises that will help you meet your fitness goals.

Exercise	Flexibility	Muscle Strength and Endurance	Heart and Lung Endurance
Handball	16	15	19
Swimming	15	14	21
Jogging	9	17	21
Bicycling	9	16	19
Tennis	14	14	16
Walking	7	11	13
Softball	9	7	6

Figure 8.9

An Exercise Plan

Having a written plan makes it more likely that you will follow it.

Sunday	Monday	Tuesday	Wednesday	Thursday	Friday	Saturday
29	**30**	**31**	**1**	**2**	**3**	**4**
•Bike ride 1 hr. Total: 1 hr.	•Gym class 30 min. •Soccer practice 1 hr. •Walk home from practice 20 min. Total: 1 hr. 50 min.	•Tennis or jog after school 40 min. Total: 40 min.	•Gym class 30 min. •Soccer practice 1 hr. Total: 1 hr. 30 min.	•Tennis or jog after school 40 min. Total: 40 min.	•Gym class 30 min. •Walk home from school 20 min. Total: 50 min.	• Soccer game 50 min. Total: 50 min.

When and Where to Exercise

Whatever your fitness goals include, you should plan on doing at least one form of exercise every day. It is also a good idea to balance your activities throughout the week. One way to be sure that you meet your goals is to make a weekly fitness schedule like the one in **Figure 8.9.**

To begin your schedule, write in all the present times you have to be active. For example, if you have gym class two or three times a week, write that on the correct days. If you ride your bike to and from school all or part of the time, put it down. If you take part in an organized sport, make a note of it on your calendar plan.

When you have written down all of the set times you exercise, try to balance your days by adding, subtracting, or rearranging activities. You want to arrange your activities so that you do something every day and so that you are not overloaded on any one day. Fill in light days with exercises and activities that will help you meet your fitness goals. You don't need to have a specific activity for every exercise session. For example, you may want to plan a forty-minute session twice a week when you will either walk, ride your bike, or play basketball with your friends. The time stays the same, but the activity changes to suit your mood or the weather.

Your exercise schedule should help you meet your personal fitness goals and be healthy. The schedule you make up should be right for you. Your friends' schedules may differ from yours.

Exercise Session Stages

Every exercise session should have three stages—the warm-up, the workout, and the cool-down. Every stage is important, and none of the stages should be skipped. Each of the stages is discussed on the following pages. As you study the stages, apply what you learn to your own fitness plan.

in Your Journal

For two days, keep track of how you spend your time. In your journal, make a chart that divides your day up into fifteen-minute segments. As the day passes, note what you are doing during each segment. After two days, analyze your chart. How do you spend most of your time?

Pumping Iron

The best way to develop muscle strength is through weight training. For it to be helpful, however, you must follow some guidelines. If you lift weights incorrectly, you can injure yourself. The weight should be light enough so that no fewer than 10 lifts can be performed. To build strength, the weight should be heavy enough so that no more than 15 lifts can be performed. Get help from a fitness expert such as a coach or a fitness instructor before you start lifting.

Stage 1. Warm-up

A **warm-up** is *a period of mild exercise that gets your body ready for vigorous exercise.* You should warm up at the beginning of every exercise session for five to ten minutes.

During the warm-up stage, your body gradually changes. Your temperature begins to rise. Your heartbeat rate increases. As more blood flows to your muscles, they become more elastic. The more elastic your muscles are, the less likely they are to become injured when you are exercising.

Some physical fitness trainers recommend warming up by going through the motions of your planned activity at a slowed-down pace. For example, if you are planning to run, walk first. If you are planning to shoot baskets, do shoulder stretches.

Stretching exercises such as those shown in **Figure 8.10** are good warm-up exercises that will increase your overall flexibility. Try doing each exercise two to five times.

Caution: Stretching should be an even, gradual pull on the muscles on both sides of your body. As you stretch, you should feel tension but not pain. Overstretching can damage your joints and the body tissues that hold your bones in place.

Figure 8.10
Warm-up Exercises

A Hip stretch
Lie on your back. Relax and straighten both legs. Pull knees, one at a time, toward chest.

B Shoulder stretch
For support, lean against something at about shoulder level. Keep arms straight while moving your chest downward. Keep feet under hips, with knees slightly bent.

ⓒ Calf stretch

Stand close to a wall and lean toward it. As you lean, keep one leg bent and the other extended as shown. Keeping the heel of the extended leg on the ground, move hips forward until you feel a stretch in the calf muscle.

ⓓ Hamstring stretch 1

Keep knees slightly bent as you bend slowly from the hips. Bend until you feel a stretch in the back of the legs.

ⓔ Hamstring stretch 2

Sit on the floor as shown. Bend front leg slightly while keeping other foot next to the inside of the leg. Bend forward until you feel slight tension.

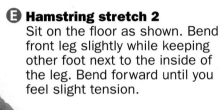

ⓕ Achilles tendon stretch

Lean forward with one leg extended as in the calf stretch. Bend the extended knee slightly, keeping the heel flat.

ⓖ Groin stretch

Sit as shown with soles of feet together. Hold onto feet and pull yourself forward.

Recall the last time you exercised or took part in an active sport. What did you do to warm up? Write your answers in your journal. If you did not warm up, tell why.

Figure 8.11
Factors of Your Workout

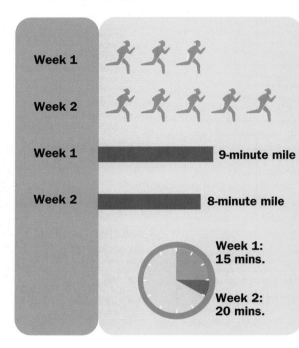

Week 1	🏃 🏃 🏃
Week 2	🏃 🏃 🏃 🏃 🏃
Week 1	9-minute mile
Week 2	8-minute mile
	Week 1: 15 mins.
	Week 2: 20 mins.

Frequency

The number of times you exercise each week is your exercise frequency. Begin by exercising three times the first week. Then increase to five times by the end of the second week.

Intensity

The amount of energy you use when you exercise is your exercise intensity. Intensity is usually measured by your pulse rate. One way to increase the intensity of your workout is to increase the speed—for example, running a mile in nine minutes the first week to running a mile in eight minutes the second week.

Time

The amount of time you spend exercising during one session is your exercise time. Limit your workout to about 10 to 15 minutes the first week. Then, increase your program by 5 minutes the second week.

Stage 2. Workout

In this stage you work to reach your specific fitness goals. It takes a full day for your muscles to recover from exercises that build muscle strength. If you decide to spend time on both muscle and heart and lung exercises during a workout session, do your heart and lung exercises first. For you to benefit from exercise, you must work out often enough, hard enough, and long enough during each session to improve your health (see **Figure 8.11**).

Here are some important points to keep in mind:

■ When starting any exercise program, it is best to begin at a comfortable level and build up gradually.

MAKING HEALTHY DECISIONS
Too Rushed to Cool Down

*E*veryone would describe Meredith as extremely busy. She is involved in student government, is captain of the field hockey team, and bikes every day after school. Her friends often ask, "How do you find the time to do everything?" Meredith always just smiles and says, "Planning."

Meredith rides her bicycle with her friend Mark. Warming up and cooling down have always been part of their exercise sessions together. Lately, however, Meredith has decided to skip the cool-down so that she can fit other activities into her evening schedule.

Following their workout this afternoon, Meredith felt a pain in her calf muscle. She tried to ignore it, saying that a little pain now and then is the price an athlete must pay. Mark knew that Meredith was risking injury by not cooling down. He also knew that Meredith liked doing things her own way. What should Mark do? Should he say nothing, hoping that she will realize on her own that she

- One way to increase the intensity of some exercises is by slowing down. For example, in one exercise you lie on your back while raising and lowering your legs. The more slowly you lower your legs, the greater the intensity of the workout.

- The way to increase the intensity of other exercises, such as sit-ups, is to do them faster than before.

- As your endurance improves, increase the time of your workout by about 10 percent each week.

Stage 3. Cool-Down

The warm-up stage of your fitness session gradually gets your heart and muscles working faster and faster. The workout stage brings them up to top speed. **Cool-down** is *a period of gentle exercise that gets your body ready to stop exercising.*

During the workout stage of your fitness session, your increased heartbeat rate sends more blood than usual to your muscles. Your muscles are stretching. If you stop exercising suddenly, your muscles tighten and blood flow slows down. Blood can collect in your muscles. If that happens, you may not get enough blood flow to your brain and heart. This condition could make you feel ill.

When blood collects in your muscles, something else can occur. Waste made by your body cells during exercise can build up in your blood. This waste can result in muscle pain.

The best way to cool down is to continue the motions of the workout stage at a slower and slower pace. If you have been jogging, jog slower and then walk. If you are biking, go slowly and then get off and walk your bike a little. If you are swimming, do stretching exercises in the water. Cool-down should last from five to ten minutes.

might be risking injury by not cooling down? Should he remind her about the importance of cooling down? Mark uses the six steps of the decision-making process to help him come to a decision:

❶ **State the situation**
❷ **List the options**
❸ **Weigh the possible outcomes**
❹ **Consider your values**
❺ **Make a decision and act**
❻ **Evaluate the decision**

Follow-up Activities

1. Apply the six steps of the decision-making process to Meredith's situation.

2. Along with a partner, role-play a conversation between Meredith and Mark in which he gives her advice.

3. What decision would you probably make if you were Mark? Explain your decision.

Water, Please

Drinking water during exercise will not lead to bloating or cramping during your exercise session. In fact, drinking water can actually reduce your risk of overheating when exercising, especially during hot, humid weather. Drink one or two 8-ounce glasses of water about an hour before you begin to exercise. Then, during exercise, stop for water breaks.

Drinking plenty of fluids helps avoid dehydration.

Safety First

Whenever you exercise, you increase your risk of injury. Following the safety tips below will help you keep that risk to a minimum. A few moments spent to prevent injury can save you recovery time and pain. Better safe than sorry!

- **Choose a safe place.** Exercise on soft, even surfaces, such as a track, grass, or dirt. A soft surface is better for a runner's knees than is a hard surface. The street is not a safe place to exercise.

- **Choose a safe time.** During hot, humid weather, exercise less than you normally do. Hot, humid weather puts an extra strain on your body. You could become dehydrated, or dried out. You could become exhausted. On hot days, exercise in the early morning or early evening.

- **Choose proper, loose-fitting clothing.** The looseness helps your skin to breathe. You will stay cooler and avoid overheating.

- **Wear light-colored clothing and reflective coverings if you exercise outside at dusk or at night.** The light-colored clothes and the reflective coverings will make you visible to drivers.

- **When exercising in cold weather, wear one layer less of clothing than you would otherwise wear.** Because you will be making heat when you work out, you won't need as much clothing as you would if you weren't exercising. Wearing layers allows you to take off or add layers as needed.

- **Wear shoes and equipment that fit correctly and are suitable for the activity.** Speak to a coach or a fitness instructor. Try to get the best that you can. Good equipment and shoes that fit comfortably can protect you from injury. Remember that the best is not always the most expensive.

- **Drink plenty of fluids.** Sweating while exercising removes water from your body. You must keep replacing the lost fluid so that you do not become dehydrated. Water and juice are healthy drinks during exercise. Soda pop is not.

- **Protect your feet and legs.** To prevent injury to your feet and legs, try to land on your heels rather than the balls of your feet during active sports and exercise.

- **Pay attention to signals from your body.** Increase your exercise level gradually. If you begin exercising muscles in a new way, it is normal to feel a little discomfort in those muscles. Feeling pain is not normal. If you feel pain anywhere, stop exercising and see a doctor.

  - **Begin your exercise session by warming up and end it by cooling down.** You will help prevent serious injury by gradually getting your body ready to begin exercising and by gradually getting it ready to stop exercising.

  - **Never exercise when injured.** It is all right to get better by resting. Try alternative activities.

Checking Your Progress

You can check your progress by reviewing your fitness goals and retesting the areas of fitness you want to improve. If you are sticking to your program and not reaching those goals, ask a coach or gymnastics teacher to help you figure out why. Perhaps your goals are not realistic. Maybe you just need more time. Most people do not notice any significant changes as a result of a fitness program for four to six weeks or more.

Even before you reach your fitness goals, you may notice some positive changes of another kind. People who start exercising regularly tend to feel better, sleep better, and have more energy than they did before exercising. After several weeks, you may have less body fat and more muscle. (You may weigh more because muscle tissue is heavier than fat, but you will look trimmer.) You might also feel more confident.

Another way to measure your progress is by measuring your resting heartbeat rate. Your resting heartbeat rate is the number of times your heart beats in one minute while you are resting. The average heartbeat rate is between 72 and 84 beats per minute. A resting heartbeat rate below 72 beats per minute usually indicates a healthy level of physical fitness.

You can check your progress by reviewing your list of exercise goals.

Review — Lesson 3

Using complete sentences, answer the following questions on a separate sheet of paper.

Reviewing Terms and Facts

1. **Vocabulary**   Which of the following is the amount of energy used with exercise: *exercise time, exercise frequency, exercise intensity?*

2. **Recall**   Name the three stages of every exercise session.

3. **Give Examples**   List four stretching exercises that are good warm-ups.

4. **Recall**   Cite at least six safety tips that will help you decrease your risk of injury during exercise.

Thinking Critically

5. **Analyze**   Tom wanted to improve his muscle strength and his heart and lung endurance. He has been lifting weights at the YMCA for a month. Does his fitness program match his fitness goals? Why or why not?

6. **Distinguish**   Helen does weight training three times a week. She warms up and cools down at every session. What part of her sessions will probably help most to improve her flexibility?

Applying Health Concepts

7. **Personal Health**   Make a fitness schedule like the one in Figure 8.9 on page 245. Analyze your schedule with a partner. Are your days balanced? What can you do to improve your schedule? When can you start?

8. **Health of Others**   Find and read an article on fitness routines. Ask two classmates to read the same article. Then discuss the article and write an essay on how it does or does not relate to teens.

Individual and Team Sports

This lesson will help you find answers to questions that teens often ask about individual and team sports. For example:

▶ **What are the advantages of individual sports?**

▶ **What are the advantages of team sports?**

▶ **What do I need to know about sports equipment and facilities?**

▶ **What are the benefits of lifetime sports?**

Words to Know

individual sports
team sports
lifetime sports

Individual Sports

To choose an exercise program that is right for you, you need to ask yourself an important question. Do you prefer to exercise on your own or do you prefer to join a team? To answer that question you need to examine your needs and preferences. Doing so will help guide you toward the best kind of exercise for you.

Many people prefer **individual sports.** These are *sports that you can do on your own or with a friend.* You don't have to be part of a team to take part in individual sports. Examples of individual sports are running, swimming, hiking, skating, and biking. Can you think of other examples?

What are the advantages of individual sports? They are more flexible than team sports. You can do them whenever you feel like it. You don't have to show up at a specified time. Also, you can do them for as long as you wish. For example, you can run for twenty minutes or for an hour. It's up to you.

That's also one possible disadvantage of individual sports. It *is* up to you. You have to find the time and the motivation to take part in your chosen sport. There are no set times and no team members to meet. For some people, that is not a problem. They prefer making their own plans. Others, though, find it hard to stick to an exercise plan if they have to do it on their own. You need to decide which kind of person you are.

Some teens prefer the flexibility that individual sports offer.

Team Sports

Many teens enjoy taking part in **team sports**—*organized physical activities involving skill, in which a group of people play together on the same side.* By joining a team, you sign up for a regular exercise program. You also give yourself an opportunity to make new friends and get to know people better.

There are many team sports including volleyball, softball, soccer, football, hockey, baseball, and basketball. Check out these places in your community for team sports opportunities:

- Local schools
- Community centers
- Local park district
- Teen clubs
- Sport and fitness centers
- Church and synagogue youth programs

Team sports offer a number of advantages over individual sports. Exercising with other people can be fun. When exercise is fun, you are more likely to keep doing it. Team sports can improve your mental and social health as well as your physical health. They provide you with opportunities to be with other people, and to work together toward a goal. Team sports give you a chance to practice your communication skills and to learn more about cooperation and compromise, which are important social skills.

Of course, team sports are not right for everyone. Some teens dislike the discipline of certain team sports. They do not want to commit themselves to regular practices and weekly games. Perhaps their family circumstances prevent them from committing themselves to a team. For these people, individual sports offer a better alternative that still leads to fitness.

Team sports offer opportunities to exercise, make friends, and have fun—three great ways to reduce stress.

Equipment and Facilities

When choosing an exercise program, you should find out about the equipment you will need. Different sports require different equipment. The equipment for some sports is quite expensive. You will need to discuss the cost of equipment with your family before you make a decision.

Some activities require a lot of equipment; others require very little. For example, to do in-line skating safely, you need the skates, a helmet, knee and elbow pads, and gloves, as well as a smooth surface on which to skate. On the other hand, walking requires only good sports shoes.

Sporting goods stores display many varieties of equipment in different price ranges. Check with your coach at school before you buy any equipment. He or she will be able to tell you what is essential and what kind of price you should pay. It may be that the shoes you bought for tennis are just fine for aerobics, too.

The sports you can take part in will also be determined by the sports facilities in your community. You need to find out what facilities are available for sports at local community centers and parks as well as at your school. Some of these public facilities may charge a fee. For example, you may be required to purchase a special badge in order to use the community tennis courts or swimming pool. Private clubs also charge for the use of their facilities. You will need to discuss the cost of using specific facilities with other people in your family.

Cultural Diversity

Bicycling Habits

Most bicycles in the United States are used for sport, recreation, or competition. In most other countries, bicycles outnumber automobiles. In China, for example, bicycles are the main method of personal transportation, and they are used to carry goods as well as people.

LIFE SKILLS
Getting Fit and Staying Fit

This chapter has provided you with information about setting fitness goals. You have learned how to test your fitness and choose exercises that will help you get fit. Staying fit is a different challenge.

Once you reach your fitness goals, you need a plan for staying fit. Variety, balance, and fun are three exercise factors that can motivate you to keep exercise as a regular part of your life.

▶ **Variety.** Everyone gets bored doing the same thing over and over. Put some variety into your exercise program. Don't just do the same activity or set of exercises day after day, week after week. Add a different activity now and then, or change your program entirely every few months.

▶ **Balance.** Don't set up an exercise program that takes too much time or overloads you on one or more days. If your program is too difficult to do, you are less likely to follow it.

▶ **Fun.** The very best way to stay interested in your exercise program is to have fun doing it. Choose activities that you enjoy. Another way to put fun into your exercise sessions is to get a friend or family member to join you.

Follow-up Activity

Look at your exercise schedule and program. Do they have the variety, balance, and fun to keep you exercising all year? Think of at least one way to improve your program and take action!

Canoeing is just one of many forms of exercise that a person can learn when young and enjoy throughout a lifetime.

Lifetime Sports

Research has shown that exercise helps people of all ages be healthier than they would be without it. The most important fitness goal you can have is lifelong exercise. As people age, their exercise opportunities, abilities, and interests change. Most team sports, for example, are played by young people during their school years. You can keep practicing some sports, however, throughout life. *Exercise activities that can be continued throughout life* are called **lifetime sports.** Learning to enjoy these sports now can help you keep fit for life. Canoeing, hiking, dancing, and cross-country skiing are four lifetime sports. Can you name some more?

> ### in your journal
>
> **C**hoose a lifetime activity that you think you are most likely to enjoy. Use your journal to explain how you plan to participate in this activity. List people you know who already do this activity. Make a note to talk to them about equipment needs and local facilities.

Review — Lesson 4

Using complete sentences, answer the following questions on a separate sheet of paper.

Reviewing Terms and Facts

1. **Give Examples**   List three individual sports.

2. **Recall**   Identify two advantages of participating in a team sport.

3. **Recall**   What is the most important fitness goal you can have?

4. **Vocabulary**   Use the term *lifetime sports* in an original sentence.

Thinking Critically

5. **Hypothesize**   What are some reasons that a person might have trouble sticking to an exercise program?

6. **Analyze**   Susan has the opportunity to play basketball on a team or to join a friend for tennis twice a week. Susan, however, has a very busy schedule and sometimes volunteers to tutor students after school. Which sport would be best for her? Why?

7. **Analyze**   Why is it important for teens to learn lifetime sports while they are young?

Applying Health Concepts

8. **Health of Others**   With a partner, make a list of all of the places that provide opportunities to join a sports team in your community. Include on your list information about the hours they are open and fees charged. Share your list with your classmates.

9. **Growth and Development**   Research the details of one lifetime sport. Find information that describes how to do it, where to do it, equipment needed, and cost. Make a poster explaining what you learned. Display your poster in your classroom.

Chapter Summary

▶ Physical fitness, mental and emotional fitness, and social fitness are all part of total fitness. (Lesson 1)

▶ Every person has his or her own physical fitness potential. (Lesson 1)

▶ Exercise is an important key to physical fitness. (Lesson 1)

▶ There are several parts to physical fitness, and each part can be tested to determine how fit you are. (Lesson 2)

▶ It is important to consider your limits when setting fitness goals. (Lesson 2)

▶ Each area of physical fitness is best helped by certain types of exercise. (Lesson 3)

▶ To be healthy for you, your exercise schedule should be balanced. (Lesson 3)

▶ Every exercise session should include a warm-up stage, a workout stage, and a cool-down stage. (Lesson 3)

▶ Many exercise activities require little or no special equipment. (Lesson 4)

▶ The most important fitness goal you can have is lifelong exercise. (Lesson 4)

Using Health Terms

On a separate sheet of paper, write the vocabulary term that best matches each definition given below.

1. Physically able to handle day-to-day challenges (Lesson 1)

2. Type of exercise, such as sprinting, that involves great bursts of energy (Lesson 1)

3. Ability to move joints easily within a range of motion (Lesson 2)

4. The proportion of body fat in comparison with lean body tissue, such as muscle and bone (Lesson 2)

5. How often you exercise every week (Lesson 3)

6. The amount of time you exercise during one session (Lesson 3)

7. Sports that you can do by yourself or with a friend (Lesson 4)

8. Sports that you do with a group of people (Lesson 4)

Reviewing Main Ideas

Using complete sentences, answer the following questions on a separate sheet of paper.

1. What are three benefits of physical fitness? (Lesson 1)

2. Nutrition is one area to consider when you want to develop physical fitness traits. What are the other two? (Lesson 1)

3. List four parts of physical fitness. (Lesson 2)

4. What determines how effectively your heart and lungs work during exercise and how quickly they return to normal after exercise? (Lesson 2)

5. What are three factors that influence physical fitness potential? (Lesson 2)

6. About how long should the warm-up stage last? (Lesson 3)

7. What is the exercise frequency recommended by most fitness experts? (Lesson 3)

8. What length of exercise period is recommended by many fitness experts? (Lesson 3)

9. Why should you drink a lot of fluids during exercise? (Lesson 3)

10. Recall three advantages of individual sports. (Lesson 4)

11. What are three exercise activities that require little or no special equipment? (Lesson 4)

12. List four lifetime sports. (Lesson 4)

Thinking Critically

Using complete sentences, answer the following questions on a separate sheet of paper.

1. **Identify** Mavis jumped rope. Beatrice lifted weights. Who did aerobic exercise? (Lesson 1)

2. **Analyze** Helen scores well on physical fitness tests but does not always eat a balanced diet or get enough sleep. What does this tell you about her physical fitness level? (Lesson 2)

3. **Explain** Nicole does all of her exercising on the weekends. "This schedule is healthy because I have five days in a row to rest up," she says. Is Nicole correct? Explain. (Lesson 3)

4. **Identify** Put each of the following activities in one of three categories: warm-up activity, workout activity, or cool-down activity—playing soccer, calf stretch, walking gradually more slowly, biking, shoulder stretch, lifting weights, swimming slowly. (Lesson 3)

5. **Compare and Contrast** Carl is interested in building skills for lifetime fitness. He has been invited to join a mountain hiking club and a skateboard workshop. Which will best help Carl meet his goal? Why? (Lesson 4)

Your Action Plan

You can make an action plan to raise your physical fitness level. First, decide on a long-term goal and write it down. Look back at your private journal entries for this chapter. You may want to build endurance, reduce body fat, or improve a sports skill. Make sure your goal is realistic.

Next, jot down a series of short-term goals to help you reach your long-term goal. For example, if your long-term goal is to run 5 miles and you can do 2 miles now, a good short-term goal is to run 2½ miles three times a week. Start slowly and gradually increase the distance and frequency of your running each week.

Write up a schedule for reaching both your short-term and long-term goals. If you get off schedule, don't quit. Just rework it to get back on track. Share your accomplishments.

Building Your Portfolio

1. Go to two stores that sell magazines. Jot down the titles of the fitness magazines and describe each cover. Note any statements on the cover that suggest the content of the articles. Make a chart with two columns. Label one *Health* and the other *Appearance*. Then analyze the data. Decide if each cover appeals mostly to people's desire to be healthy or to their desire to be attractive. Write each magazine's title in the appropriate column. In which column are most of the titles? Write a paragraph about what you have learned. Add the summary and chart to your portfolio.

In Your Home and Community

1. If you have access to a video camera, film family members involved in fitness activities. Include parents and grandparents. Ask their permission to show the film in health classes. Ask your audience if watching the film inspired them to participate in physical fitness activities.

2. Volunteer to work with young children in your district's fitness programs. If your area has no programs, ask your coach or gym teacher about starting one.

Chapter 9

Eating Healthy, Eating Well

Student Expectations

After reading this chapter, you should be able to:

① Discuss the impact good nutrition has on health.

② Describe the Food Guide Pyramid and how its use can help ensure a nutritious, balanced diet.

③ Explain how to control weight healthfully.

④ List the steps you would take to help someone with an eating disorder.

I never really thought much about what I ate or how much I ate until a few months ago. That's when my friend Diane made the soccer team. Diane's coach gave her some tips on how to eat for peak performance.

I started to think about what I ate. I figured that if eating right could make you run faster and longer, maybe it could help in other areas too. Maybe eating right could help me get better grades or make me look better.

I know I haven't always eaten the right foods. I have a crazy schedule and am always on the run. If I don't have time for meals, I grab a bag of chips or a candy bar to tide me over. When Mom works late, I usually raid the cupboard before I do my homework.

So, what should I be eating? I know that too much fat and sugar is bad for me, but I'm not so sure what's good. Maybe I should talk to Diane's coach or my health teacher.

in your journal

Read the account on this page. Do you, too, wish you knew what you should eat? Start your private journal entries on healthful eating by answering these questions:

► How much attention do you pay to what you eat each day?

► Do you think that you already have a nutritious, well-balanced diet?

► What influences you to choose one food rather than another?

► If you learned that your diet was not properly balanced, what would you do?

When you reach the end of the chapter, you will use your journal entries to make an action plan.

1 Building a Nutritious Diet

This lesson will help you find answers to questions that teens often ask about healthful eating. For example:

▶ **What can eating the right foods do for me?**

▶ **What influences the choices people make about food?**

▶ **What nutrients do I need to be healthy?**

▶ **How can I use the Recommended Dietary Allowances list?**

Words to Know

nutrition
diet
nutrients
carbohydrates
proteins
amino acids
vitamins
minerals
fats
saturated fats
unsaturated fats
water
Recommended
  Dietary
  Allowances
  (RDA)

Food for Life

Food, along with air and water, is one of life's basic needs. When you go without food for a long time, you feel hungry. This is your body's signal that it needs more food. After you eat, the hunger disappears. Your body has received the fuel it needs to keep going. When that fuel is used up, you will be hungry again.

Although the most important reason for eating is physical, eating is also a social experience. For example, what foods do you associate with sports events, holidays, or picnics? Eating is tied to your emotions as well. Eating to relieve tension or not eating because of stress may result in some unhealthy habits.

Eating the foods your body needs helps ensure proper growth and development. Family background can be a strong influence on your food choices.

By eating healthful foods in recommended amounts, you make sure that you will grow and be healthy. *Eating foods the body needs to grow, develop, and work properly* is called **nutrition** (noo·TRI·shuhn). Good nutrition is one of the main factors in good health. Because you make food choices every day, good nutrition can have a powerful impact on your overall health and well-being.

Good nutrition is especially important in your teenage years. During this time, you are growing faster than you grow at any other time after early childhood. A well-balanced, nutritious diet will provide the fuel you need for energy and growth.

Are You on a Diet?

What do you think of when you hear the word *diet?* Most people think of a weight-loss diet but that's only one type of diet. A **diet** is something we all follow—*it's the food and drink that we regularly choose to consume.* Think of the foods that you eat each day, each week. Think of the beverages you drink. You will begin to get a picture of the diet that you follow. Many factors affect your choice of foods. **Figure 9.1** shows some of these factors.

Figure 9.1
Factors That Influence Your Diet
The choices you make about what to have for lunch are influenced by the region you live in, your cultural background, convenience, and a number of other factors.

Factor	Influences	Examples
Geography	Local products	South: grits, okra Coastal area: fish
Family	Traditions	Vegetarian meals Meat and potatoes meals
Cultural background	Ethnic foods	Vietnamese: rice, fish Mexican: beans, corn, tortillas
Convenience	Time available for food selection and preparation	Choosing easy-to-prepare foods and takeout meals
Cost	Family budget affects choices	Chicken legs or breasts Pasta or steak
Advertising	Creates demand for products	Selecting one brand over another
Friends	Peer pressure	Choosing snack foods or places to go to eat
Personal taste	Preference for some foods, dislike for others	String beans rather than brussels sprouts Beef rather than lamb

The Six Types of Nutrients

Q&A

Vitamins and Energy

Q: I've been feeling tired a lot lately. Would vitamin pills give me more energy?

A: The answer is no. You get energy only from fats, carbohydrates, and proteins. In addition, taking too much of vitamins A and D can be very harmful to your body.

Though you have a diet, you may not have a healthful one. A healthful diet provides the nutrients you need to grow and develop. **Nutrients** (NOO·tree·ents) are *substances in foods that your body needs.* Scientists have found some 50 nutrients, which can be grouped into six main types.

The six types of nutrients are carbohydrates, proteins, vitamins, minerals, fats, and water. Each one plays a vital role in your body.

■ **Carbohydrates** (kar·bo·HY·drayts) are *the starches and sugars that provide the body with most of its energy.* There are two kinds of carbohydrates—simple and complex. Both are important sources of energy for your body. Simple carbohydrates are found in fruit, sugar, and milk. Complex carbohydrates are found in starchy foods, such as breads, cereals, dry beans, potatoes, and other starchy vegetables. They also provide fiber to aid digestion. Health experts generally recommend that you get about 60 percent of the calories you eat from carbohydrates, mainly from complex carbohydrates.

■ **Proteins** (PROH·teenz) are *needed to build, repair, and maintain body cells and tissues,* particularly muscle. They also provide energy. Proteins are especially important during childhood, adolescence, and other periods of growth. Meat, fish, poultry, eggs, milk, cheese, nuts, and dry beans are sources of protein.

Proteins are made up of **amino** (uh·MEE·noh) **acids.** Of the 22 amino acids in proteins, your body can make 14. The other eight, called *essential amino acids,* must come from the foods you eat. Foods from animal sources are *complete proteins*—they contain all eight essential amino acids. Foods from plants are *incomplete proteins*—they lack at least one essential amino acid. It's important to get all these essential amino acids in your diet. Vegetarians can combine plant foods to make complete protein. Beans and rice is one such combination.

■ **Vitamins** (VY·tuh·minz) are *substances needed in small quantities that help regulate body functions,* including helping the body process other nutrients and fight infections. Vitamins fall into two groups—*water-soluble vitamins,* such as vitamin C and many B vitamins, and *fat-soluble vitamins,* such as vitamins A and D. Water-soluble vitamins cannot be stored in the body, so they must be included in your daily diet. Fat soluble vitamins, on the other hand, can be stored in the body until needed, so they don't have to be eaten daily. Since vitamins cannot be made in the body, they must be provided by the diet. Fresh fruits and vegetables, whole-grain breads and cereal products, and fortified milk are rich sources of vitamins. **Figure 9.2** contains more information about vitamin sources.

■ **Minerals** are *elements needed in small quantities for sturdy bones and teeth, healthy blood, and regulation of daily elimination.* Whole grains, fruits, peas, spinach, raisins, and milk are good sources of minerals.

- **Fats** are *a source of energy and are essential for vital body functions.* They insulate the body from temperature changes, cushion body organs, carry fat-soluble vitamins, and promote healthy skin and normal growth. Excess fat is stored in the body as extra weight. Fats can be found in butter and margarine, whole milk, egg yolks, most cheeses, and salad dressings.

  Some fats, such as *fats found in meats and dairy products,* are called **saturated fats.** They tend to be solid at room temperature. Eating too much saturated fat can raise blood cholesterol levels, increasing the risk of heart disease. **Unsaturated fats,** *found mainly in vegetable oils, such as olive, corn, or canola oil, are fats that remain liquid.* Most experts recommend that you choose unsaturated rather than saturated fats.

- **Water** is *the most common nutrient,* making up about 60 percent of the body. It carries other nutrients through the body, helps digestion, removes wastes from the body, lubricates the joints, and keeps the body from overheating. You must constantly replace the water your body loses.

A healthful diet contains the right amount, or balance, of nutrients. That is where the term *balanced diet* comes from. A diet that is out of balance may cause health problems. Too much fat may lead to heart disease. Too little protein hinders growth. You need a variety of foods to get all the nutrients.

Figure 9.2
Vitamins and Minerals: Sources and Functions

Nutrients	Sources	Functions
Vitamin A	Carrots, eggs, liver	Promotes healthy skin, normal vision
Vitamin C	Oranges, tomatoes, leafy green vegetables	Helps muscles, heart function well
Vitamin D	Fortified milk, oily fish, egg yolks	Promotes strong bones and teeth
Vitamin K	Cabbage, spinach, cereals	Helps blood clot
Calcium	Milk, cheese, shellfish, spinach	Needed to build bones and teeth
Fluoride	Fluoridated water, fish	Promotes strong bones and teeth
Iron	Red meat, nuts, dried fruits	Needed for hemoglobin in red blood cells
Potassium	Oranges, bananas, dry beans, molasses	Helps regulate water balance in tissues

Putting Nutrients in Your Diet

Scientists have developed *guidelines for the amount of each nutrient to be eaten each day*. These are called the **Recommended Dietary Allowances (RDA)**. This information is found on food package nutrition labels. **Figure 9.3** can help you use this information to plan nutritious meals.

Figure 9.3
Reading a Nutrition Label

Nutrition Facts

Serving Size ½ cup (114g)
Servings Per Container 4

Amount Per Serving

Calories 90	Calories from Fat 30

	% Daily Value*
Total Fat 3g	5%
Saturated Fat 0g	0%
Cholesterol 0mg	0%
Sodium 300mg	13%
Total Carbohydrate 13g	4%
Dietary Fiber 3g	12%
Sugars 3g	
Protein 3g	

Vitamin A	80%	Vitamin C	60%
Calcium	4%	Iron	4%

* Percent Daily Values are based on a 2,000 calorie diet. Your daily values may be higher or lower depending on your calorie needs:

Calories	2,000	2,500
Total Fat	Less Than 65g	80g
Sat Fat	Less Than 20g	25g
Cholesterol	Less Than 300mg	300mg
Sodium	Less Than 2,400mg	2,400mg
Total Carbohydrate	300g	375g
Fiber	25g	30g

Calories per gram:
Fat 9   Carbohydrate 4   Protein 4

A The stated serving size is the basis of the nutrient content of the food.

B Major nutrients are listed in milligrams or grams and as a percentage of the recommended diet for a person consuming 2,000 calories per day.

C The amount of total fat in a serving is listed with the number of calories supplied by that amount of fat. The amount of saturated fat in the total fat is also listed.

D Dietary fiber and sugar are listed under Total Carbohydrate.

LIFE SKILLS

Reading Nutrition Labels

*B*y law, packaged foods must now carry a Nutrition Facts label so that consumers can make healthful food choices. The labels use Daily Values (DVs) for proteins, vitamins, and minerals. They also list recommended amounts of fat, sodium (salt), carbohydrates, and fiber in your daily diet:

Fat	less than 65 g
Sodium	less than 2,400 mg
Carbohydrate	300 g
Fiber	25 g

The DVs are based on a 2,000-calorie daily diet. The percent Daily Values on the label show how a food's nutritional content fits into a 2,000-calorie diet. For example, if the label tells you that one serving of a food contains 10 grams of fat, the percent DV column will tell you that 10 grams is 15 percent of 65 grams (your total daily fat allowance).

Follow-up Activities

The new Nutrition Facts labels are designed to help you choose foods for a more healthful diet. Using the labels, however, requires some practice. Refer to the sample label in **Figure 9.3** and the information presented here to answer the following questions. (Assume that you eat about 2,000 calories a day.)

1. How many grams of fat does one serving contain? How much of the fat is saturated?

2. What percentage of your total daily sodium allowance does one serving of the product contain? Would the product be a good choice if you were on a low-salt diet?

3. If you ate two servings of the product, how many grams of fiber would you need to obtain from other foods to get your daily value for fiber? Is the product a good source of fiber?

No two people need exactly the same amount of each type of nutrient. For example, teens need more calcium than adults do for building growing bones. In addition to age, several other factors affect the amount you need of each type of nutrient. To be sure that you get enough of the nutrients you need, scientists have set the RDA nutrient levels fairly high. They estimate that a diet that meets the RDA nutrient levels will be a healthful diet for 95 out of every 100 Americans.

Nutrient needs change throughout your life. Four factors affect your nutrient needs.

Ⓐ Age
Children need more nutrients than adults do for growth and activity.

Ⓒ General health
Illness increases the amount you need of many nutrients.

Ⓑ Body size
Larger people need more nutrients than smaller people do.

Ⓓ Exercise
The more active you are, the more nutrients you need.

Review

Lesson 1

Using complete sentences, answer the following questions on a separate sheet of paper.

Reviewing Terms and Facts

1. **Vocabulary**   What is a *diet?* What do people often mean when they use the word?

2. **List**   Identify the six main types of nutrients your body needs for proper growth and development. List a few sources for each nutrient.

3. **Identify**   Which nutrient provides the body with most of its energy?

4. **Explain**   What is the difference between complete protein and incomplete protein? How can people who do not eat meat get complete protein in their diet?

5. **Recall**   What is the most common nutrient? What is the function of this nutrient?

6. **Vocabulary**   What do the initials *RDA* stand for? Explain what information the RDA provides.

Thinking Critically

7. **Analyze**   Too much fat can lead to heart disease and other health problems. Should fat be eliminated completely from your diet? Why or why not?

8. **Evaluate**   What are some ways that advertising and convenience influence your choice of foods in your diet?

Applying Health Concepts

9. **Personal Health**   Find a cookbook at home or in the library. Choose a main course from the cookbook. List all the ingredients. Plan the rest of the menu for that meal. Identify what nutrients are supplied by the foods you chose. Did you plan a balanced meal?

10. **Consumer Health**   Go to the supermarket and compare the nutrients contained in several different breakfast cereals. Based on your comparisons, decide which product is the best choice for a healthful breakfast. Write a brief summary and analysis of your observations.

Making Healthful Food Choices

This lesson will help you find answers to questions that teens often ask about healthful eating. For example:

▶ How can I plan a balanced diet?

▶ What are nutritious snacks?

▶ What's unhealthy about eating foods with a lot of fat?

Words to Know

Food Guide
　Pyramid
fiber
cholesterol
caffeine

Teen Issues

Ching! Ching!

If you're like most teens, your snacks often come from vending machines. Be aware that many vending machine snacks are high in fat. One study found that the fat content of the 30 most popular vending machine snacks averaged about 45 percent. The recommended amount of fat in the diet is 30 percent or less of total calories.

The Food Guide Pyramid

The easiest way to make sure that you are eating a balanced diet is to use the Food Guide Pyramid (see **Figure 9.4**). The **Food Guide Pyramid** is *a guide to daily food choices from five groups of healthful foods.* The basic idea behind the food pyramid is that all foods can be part of a healthful diet if they are eaten in the right proportions. The pyramid illustrates these food choices graphically. At the bottom is the large base of carbohydrates that should form the bulk of your diet. At the top in the small triangle are fats, oils, and sweets; these should be limited in your diet.

To get the most benefit from using the Food Guide Pyramid, keep the following tips in mind:

■ **Pay attention to serving sizes.** It is just as important to eat the right amount in each serving of food as it is to eat the right number of servings in a meal.

■ **Keep meats lean.** Before cooking, remove skin from poultry and all visible fat from meat.

■ **Read the labels on dairy products.** Choose skim, or 1 percent, milk and nonfat or low-fat yogurt and cheese.

■ **Use whole-grain or enriched grain products.** Check package labels, and choose these more nutritious breads and cereals.

■ **Cook it right.** The way food is prepared really matters. Broiled foods have less fat than fried foods; steamed vegetables retain more vitamins than vegetables cooked in water.

■ **Consider nutritive values.** Certain foods supply plenty of nutrients for the calories. The foods at the tip of the pyramid do not and should be used sparingly or not at all.

■ **Consume sufficient complete proteins.** This is a special challenge for some vegetarians. Sources of complete proteins are combinations of legumes and grains, eggs, or dairy products.

Figure 9.4
The Food Guide Pyramid

Foods within each group of the pyramid supply similar nutrients. By eating the suggested number of servings from each group, you automatically eat a balanced diet. Because each food group contains a variety of foods, it's easy to find a number of healthful choices that appeal to your taste.

in your journal

Are you eating a balanced diet? In your journal, make a list of everything you eat and drink each day. After three days, review your diet.

Fats, Oils, and Sweets
Foods: Butter, margarine, cream, salad oil and dressing, dips, desserts, sugar, jam and jelly, candy, soft drinks
Nutrients: few or none

Milk, Yogurt, and Cheese Group
Foods: Milk, cheese, yogurt, ice cream
Nutrients: vitamins A, D, and B$_2$, proteins, calcium, and phosphorus

Meat, Poultry, Fish, Dried Beans, Eggs, and Nuts Group
Foods: Beef, pork, veal, lamb, liver, chicken, turkey, fish, shellfish, eggs, beans, nuts, peanut butter
Nutrients: protein, B vitamins, iron, and phosphorus

Vegetable Group
Foods: Green beans, broccoli, leafy green vegetables, cabbage, carrots, corn, potatoes
Nutrients: fiber, carbohydrates, vitamins A, C, and K, calcium, iron, and magnesium

Fruit Group
Foods: Citrus fruits, apples, bananas, peaches, pears
Nutrients: fiber, carbohydrates, vitamins A and C, magnesium, and potassium

Bread, Cereal, Rice, and Pasta Group
Foods: Whole-grain or enriched breads, cereals, rice, pasta
Nutrients: carbohydrates, fiber, B vitamins, and iron

Figure 9.5

Food Pyramid Servings

How much of each food group should you eat to achieve a balanced diet? You need to take into account both the number of servings and the size of servings.

Planning—The Way to Health

Each morning think about what you'll eat during the day. Ask the person who prepares the meals in your family what you'll be having for dinner. Then plan to get the other servings you need from the five food groups during breakfast and lunch. Suggested servings are shown in **Figure 9.5**.

Meat, Poultry, Fish, Dry Beans, Eggs, and Nuts Group
2 to 3 servings a day
- 2–3 ounces of cooked lean meat, poultry, or fish
- $\frac{1}{2}$ cup of cooked dry beans
- 1 egg
- 2 tablespoons of peanut butter

Fats, Oils, and Sweets
No recommended servings

Milk, Yogurt, and Cheese Group
2 to 3 servings a day
- 1 cup of milk or yogurt
- $1\frac{1}{2}$ ounces of natural cheese
- 2 ounces of process cheese

Vegetable Group
3 to 5 servings a day
- 1 cup of raw leafy vegetables
- $\frac{1}{2}$ cup of other cooked or chopped raw vegetables
- $\frac{3}{4}$ cup of vegetable juice

Fruit Group
2 to 4 servings a day
- 1 medium apple, banana, or orange
- $\frac{1}{2}$ cup of chopped, cooked, or canned fruit
- $\frac{3}{4}$ cup of fruit juice

Bread, Cereal, Rice, and Pasta Group
6 to 11 servings a day
- 1 slice of bread
- 1 ounce of ready-to-eat cereal
- $\frac{1}{2}$ cup of cooked cereal, rice, or pasta

MAKING HEALTHY DECISIONS
Choosing Healthful Snacks

*J*amie had put on 10 pounds during the course of the school year. None of her clothes fit properly, and she decided that the summer would be a good time to do something about it. She discussed the problem with her mother, and together they worked out a plan for eating healthful, low-calorie meals. She also decided to take the dog for a walk every day and to go swimming at least four times a week at the recreation center pool.

Jamie felt she was making some real progress toward her goal. Then her friend Suzanne called to suggest that they go to the movies with Brian and Felicia. Jamie wants to go, but she knows that they usually stop at a fast-food place after a movie.

Jamie doesn't know what to do. She wants to stay on her weight-loss diet, but she is afraid that if she chooses a salad they will make fun of her for eating "rabbit food." Jamie wonders whether she should

What About Snacks?

When you think about snacks, do potato chips, candy bars, and soft drinks come to mind? Snack foods such as these may be convenient and taste good, but they aren't very good for you. They contain fat and sugar, but few nutrients. They fill you up without helping you grow and stay healthy.

Snacks can be healthful and great energy boosters between meals. Some ideas for healthful snacks are provided in **Figure 9.6.**

Teen Issues

Switching Snacks

If the word snacks means candy bars and soft drinks to you, you need to rethink your snacking habits. Try to work nutritious snacks into your daily routine. For example, you might bring a bagel and juice to school instead of a soft drink.

Figure 9.6
Healthful Snacks

Healthful snacks such as these should be part of a nutritious diet.

A Milk, Yogurt, and Cheese Group
Low-fat or nonfat milk, yogurt, cottage cheese

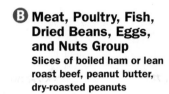

B Meat, Poultry, Fish, Dried Beans, Eggs, and Nuts Group
Slices of boiled ham or lean roast beef, peanut butter, dry-roasted peanuts

C Fruit Group
Dried fruits such as raisins, any raw fruits

D Vegetable Group
Carrot or celery sticks, tomato wedges, salad

E Bread, Cereal, Rice, and Pasta Group
Whole-wheat crackers, graham crackers, plain bagel, air-popped popcorn (without butter), instant oatmeal, rice cakes, tortillas

just say she is busy. Then she thinks about the step-by-step decision-making process she learned in school.

1. **State the situation**
2. **List the options**
3. **Weigh the possible outcomes**
4. **Consider your values**
5. **Make a decision and act**
6. **Evaluate the decision**

Follow-up Activities

1. Apply the six steps of the decision-making process to Jamie's situation.

2. Role-play the situation in which Jamie explains to Suzanne that she can't go to the movies.

3. Role-play the situation in which Jamie decides to have a salad at a fast-food restaurant.

4. List several healthful snack foods that might appeal to someone who is concerned about gaining weight.

Substances in Food

In addition to the six types of nutrients, you need to be aware of other substances in the foods you eat. Some of these substances are important to include in your diet, and some should be eaten only in limited quantities. Others should be avoided. Fiber is one food substance you need to eat plenty of for good health. Refined sugars, fats, cholesterol, salt, and caffeine are food substances you should limit to stay healthy.

Fiber

Fiber is *the part of fruits, vegetables, grains, and beans that your body cannot digest.* Fiber is not a nutrient, but it is very important to good health, helping to carry other food particles through your digestive system. A diet high in fiber can help lower your risk of colon cancer.

Most Americans have too little fiber in their diets. You need about one-third ounce (25 to 30 grams) of fiber each day. Whole-grain breads and cereals, raw fruits and vegetables, and beans are all high in fiber.

Sugar

It's hard to believe, but the average American eats about 100 pounds of sugar a year! Almost three-fourths of the sugar we eat is hidden in prepared foods (see **Figure 9.7**). Too much sugar can cause health problems. It contains only negligible amounts of nutrients, and it can promote tooth decay and contribute to added pounds. So avoid eating too many foods that are high in sugar, especially if you eat them in place of foods with more nutrients.

Did You Know?

Bran or Beans?

Not all foods proclaimed to be "high fiber" supply the same amount of this important food substance. For example, a single cup of cooked beans has the same amount of fiber as six bran muffins do.

Figure 9.7
Sugar in Common Foods

Can of cola contains 9 teaspoons of sugar

Sweetened cereal contains 8 teaspoons of sugar

Yogurt with sweetened fruit contains 7 teaspoons of sugar

Ice cream cone contains 3½ teaspoons of sugar

Hidden Fats

Most Americans choose diets that are too high in fat content. Fat in your diet should be limited to 30 percent or less of your total calories each day. The foods you eat probably contain more fat than you realize, because most fats are hidden.

It's easy to cut down on the fats you can see—don't butter your baked potato and avoid fried foods. It's harder to cut down on fats that are hidden, but it can be done. Read the labels on cans and packages, and learn which foods are high in fat. **Figure 9.8** provides some information about a few choices you can make to lower the fat content in your diet.

Cholesterol

Cholesterol (kuh·LES·tuh·rawl) is *a fatty, wax-like substance that helps your body make other substances that it needs.* Cholesterol also helps protect nerve fibers. There are two types of cholesterol: *serum cholesterol,* which is produced in your body and circulates in the blood, and *dietary cholesterol,* which comes from food. Cholesterol circulates through the blood in two forms. *LDL* is the bad form of cholesterol because it tends to leave deposits on the walls of the blood vessels. *HDL* is the good form because it carries excess cholesterol to the liver for excretion.

Foods, such as meats, eggs, and dairy products, that come from animals contain cholesterol. Dietary cholesterol is not an essential nutrient since the body produces its own. In fact, too much dietary cholesterol can increase a person's risk of heart disease. To keep your blood cholesterol levels low, you should avoid too much animal fat and choose foods that are low in cholesterol or cholesterol-free.

Your Total Health

Low-fat Choices ACTIVITY!

The best way to lose your taste for fat is not by replacing fatty foods with lower-fat substitutes. Instead, use naturally low-fat choices that will train your taste buds to prefer low-fat foods. Plan to select low-fat foods for two weeks. Keep a log of each time you replace a fatty food with a natural low-fat substitute. Record the fat content of the food you chose and the one you replaced. At the end of two weeks, calculate the amount of fat you didn't consume.

Figure 9.8
Fat Content in Foods

High-Fat Foods (grams of fat)	Moderate-Fat Foods (grams of fat)	Low-Fat Foods (grams of fat)
Fried chicken (3.5 oz.): 17.4 g	Roasted chicken with skin: 13 g	Broiled chicken without skin: 3 g
Whole milk (1 cup): 8 g	2% milk: 5 g	Skim milk: less than 1 g
French fries (14): 11 g	Baked potato with butter (1 pat): 4 g	Baked potato, plain: trace
Danish or donut: 12 g	Bagel with cream cheese (1/2 oz.): 7 g	Bagel, plain: 2 g

Fresh herbs are great taste boosters. Instead of adding butter, sour cream, and salt to your baked potato, try parsley or chives.

Sodium

Although *sodium* (SOH·dee·uhm) is a mineral nutrient, most Americans eat far more sodium than is healthful. You can get all the sodium you need by eating less than one-third ounce (3 to 8 grams) of salt a day. This amount is found in the natural foods you eat without adding any salt. However, the average American eats double or even triple that amount! Eating too much sodium can promote high blood pressure and make your body retain fluid.

Most of the sodium in our diets comes from processed foods. Some salt is added to foods when they are cooked or at the table with a saltshaker. To reduce the amount of sodium in the food you eat, read food labels and choose products with the least added sodium (see **Figure 9.9**). Don't add salt when cooking foods, and keep the saltshaker off the table.

Figure 9.9
Sodium in Common Foods

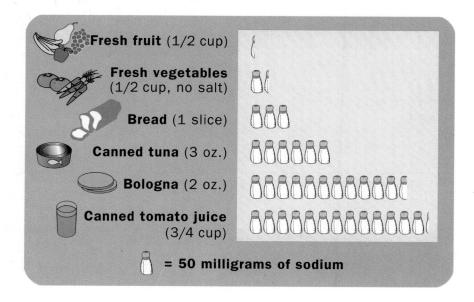

Fresh fruit (1/2 cup)

Fresh vegetables (1/2 cup, no salt)

Bread (1 slice)

Canned tuna (3 oz.)

Bologna (2 oz.)

Canned tomato juice (3/4 cup)

= 50 milligrams of sodium

Caffeine

Caffeine (ka·FEEN) is *a chemical, found in some plants, that can make your heart beat faster.* Caffeine can perk you up, but too much of it can make you tense. Like some drugs, caffeine can be habit-forming. For these reasons, you should limit the amount you consume. **Figure 9.10** shows the amount of caffeine in some common beverages.

History Connection

Caffeine Consumption

Coffee originated in Africa around 575 A.D. The beans were used as money and eaten as food.

Figure 9.10
Caffeine Count

To limit the amount of caffeine you consume, you need to know how much caffeine different drinks contain.

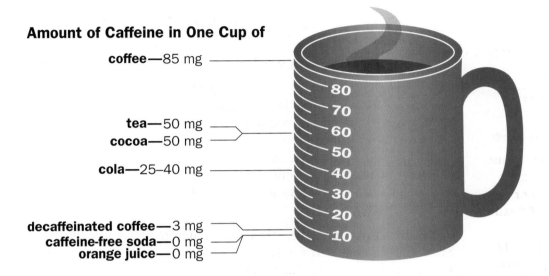

Amount of Caffeine in One Cup of

coffee—85 mg

tea—50 mg
cocoa—50 mg

cola—25–40 mg

decaffeinated coffee—3 mg
caffeine-free soda—0 mg
orange juice—0 mg

Review Lesson 2

Using complete sentences, answer the following questions on a separate sheet of paper.

Reviewing Terms and Facts

1. **Explain** Why is it better to broil rather than fry foods? Why is it better to steam vegetables than to cook them in water?

2. **Recall** What nutrients are found in the bread, cereal, rice, and pasta group?

3. **Give Examples** Suggest a healthful snack from each of the five food groups in the Food Guide Pyramid.

4. **Vocabulary** What is *fiber?* Why is it important to a healthy diet? List three sources of fiber.

Thinking Critically

5. **Analyze** Explain how the shape of the Food Guide Pyramid helps make it easier to choose a balanced diet.

6. **Explain** How can planning ahead help improve your daily food choices?

7. **Evaluate** Think about your own diet. What food groups do you need to increase in your diet? What food groups do you need to cut down on?

Applying Health Concepts

8. **Health of Others** Cut out pictures of snack foods from magazines and newspapers or make your own drawings. Use the illustrations to make a snack food "Do's" and "Don'ts" poster.

CON$UMER FOCU$

Improving School Lunches

At a recent meeting of the American Culinary Federation, chefs from around the country worked hard to make school lunches better. The lunches had to be inexpensive and appealing. They also had to meet guidelines proposed by the Agriculture Department concerning the amount of calories, fat, and sodium in the food.

Eleven chefs took part in the contest. The judges included a panel of food experts and a junior panel of children and teens—consumers of school lunches. Some students just tasted the dishes; others ate. As one of the officials remarked, "If the food doesn't taste good, the kids won't eat it."

The favorites with the junior panel were a bagel pizza and a taco salad. The adults agreed and declared the chef who had created those dishes the winner. The winning chef said he had spent a lot of time planning the meals because it was difficult to meet the cost and nutrition guidelines and still have a dish that tasted good. "But if the kids love it, then that's a success."

Teens Making a Difference

Weight-loss Counselor

Maria is a popular 14-year-old. At least that describes Maria now. A few years ago, however, things were very different. Then, Maria was a self-conscious loner. The reason? Maria was very overweight.

The change came when Maria's parents enrolled her in a weight-loss program at their local hospital. As the pounds dropped slowly but surely, Maria's self-esteem grew. After thinking of herself as a "fat kid" for as long as she could remember, she came to realize that she could finally conquer her weight problem. With each passing week, Maria became more self-confident and outgoing.

Today, Maria helps other overweight teens as a peer counselor in the same weight-loss program she went through. She's a great role model for teens who need to lose weight but are discouraged by failures in the past. Maria inspires them with her own success and her high spirits and self-confidence.

Myths and Realities

Margarine vs. Butter

Margarine is better for you than butter because it's lower in fat, right? Wrong! Both margarine and butter get virtually all of their calories from fat. Whether you butter your toast with butter or spread it with margarine, you're adding about 10 grams of fat per tablespoon.

So, which one is better for you? Butter contains more saturated fat than margarine. Saturated fat is the kind that leads to high blood cholesterol levels and increases one's risk of heart disease. However, margarine contains *trans fatty acids*. Trans fatty acids are produced when hydrogen is pumped into vegetable oil to make it solid. Like saturated fats, trans fatty acids also increase the risk of heart disease.

How can you tell if a food contains fatty acids? Look at the list of ingredients. If the product contains "partially hydrogenated" oils or fats, put it back on the grocery shelf. Like all fats, butter and margarine should be used sparingly for good health.

Health Update

Ready-to-eat Cereals

The next time you want a snack, you might want to reach for a box of cereal. In a new study at the Tulane School of Public Health, two groups of young people were surveyed—those who ate ready-to-eat cereals (pre-sweetened and unsweetened) and those who did not.

The two groups had similar amounts of calories, protein, carbohydrates, sugar, and fat in their diets. The cereal eaters, however, consumed significantly higher amounts of iron and vitamins A, B, and D.

Not only are ready-to-eat cereals nutritious, they're handy. Forty-two percent of the cereal eaters said they ate cereal for lunch, dinner, or snacks.

People at Work

Dietician

Tony Hererra has always loved good food. He also loves to cook. Now he has a job that gives him the chance to combine his flair for cooking with his desire to help others. Tony is a dietician.

As the food service manager of Hillcrest House, Tony plans and directs the preparation of the meals and snacks for more than 100 senior citizens. He loves the challenge of meeting the residents' diet restrictions with tempting dishes he creates for them. Tony also loves it when the people at Hillcrest House rave about his recipes.

To become qualified as a dietician, Tony graduated from college with a degree in foods and nutrition. This was followed by a six-month internship at a large hospital. Then he passed a test given by the American Dietetic Association and became certified as a Registered Dietician.

Managing Your Weight

This lesson will help you find answers to questions that teens often ask about weight management. For example:

► How much should I weigh?
► How can I lose weight without damaging my health?
► What can I do to keep my weight the same?

Words to Know

weight control
desired weight
overweight
obesity
calorie
nutrient density

What Is Weight Control?

We all want to keep our weight under control. **Weight control** means *reaching the weight that is best for you and then staying at that weight. The weight that is best for you* is called your **desired weight.** It's based on your sex, height, and body frame (small, medium, or large). People who stay at their desired weight tend to be healthier than those who are either underweight or overweight.

Weight control probably receives more attention than almost any other health issue. Fad diets are popular for short periods of time. Diet gimmicks are often expensive, unsafe, and ineffective. Check with your doctor before starting any weight-loss program and remember that there is no easy way to lose weight quickly and safely.

The Pressure to Be Thin

Many of us feel strong pressure to be thin. Most young people, however, don't need to lose weight. In fact, unwise dieting may interfere with normal growth and development.

HEALTH LAB
Counting Calories

*I*ntroduction: In this lesson you'll learn about the role of calories in weight control. Knowing your calorie intake is an important component of any weight-loss or weight-gain plan. Yet most people have little idea how many calories they take in.

Objective: In this health lab, you will learn how to keep track of the calories you eat and how to use this information to improve your food choices for successful weight management.

Overweight or Obese?

A person who is **overweight** weighs *more than the desired weight for his or her sex, height, and frame size.* This is not the same as being obese. **Obesity** (oh·BEE·suh·tee) is a more serious condition than being overweight. It means *having too much body fat.* Obese people weigh at least 20 percent more than their desired weight. Their obesity puts them at greater risk of disease and other physical problems. Unfortunately, obesity is a common health problem in the United States. **Figure 9.11** shows how excess weight affects the body.

Figure 9.11
How Excess Weight Affects the Body

Obesity places an extra burden on the body and increases a person's risk of developing certain disorders, such as diabetes and high blood pressure. It also affects a person's self-image.

A The body frame has to bear more weight than it should, putting stress on bones and muscles.

B The heart has to work harder to make blood circulate.

C Excess weight makes it more difficult to exercise, so weight gain continues.

Materials and Method: You will need a notebook, pencil, and calorie-counting guide. You will also need some measuring cups and spoons. In the notebook, record everything you eat and all serving sizes for at least one day and preferably for three or more days. Don't forget snacks, beverages, and meals eaten away from home.

Observation and Analysis: At the end of this period, look up the calorie content of each food you recorded. For prepared foods, see the calories-per-serving information on the package label. For foods made from scratch, consult a cookbook and estimate calories per serving from the ingredients. Many fast-food restaurants will provide you with calorie and nutrient content information for their products. Add up your daily calorie intake. If you have kept track of your calories for more than one day, calculate your average daily calorie intake.

Which food group is the largest single source of the calories in your diet? Do most of the calories come from the bread, cereal, rice, and pasta food group, or do many of the calories in your diet come from foods that contain a lot of fat and sugar?

The Role of Calories

A **calorie** (KA·luh·ree) is *a unit of heat.* Calories are used to measure the energy available in different foods. The more calories in a food, the more available energy it has. Calories are also used to measure the energy your body uses.

Whenever you eat, you take in calories. Growth and exercise burn up calories. When you take in the same number of calories that you burn up, your weight stays the same. When you take in more calories than you burn up, your body stores the extra calories as fat, and you gain weight. **Figure 9.12** shows how your calorie intake, physical activity, and weight are related.

Figure 9.12
Calories and Your Weight

Food Consumed (per day)	Energy Used (per day)	Effect on Weight
2,000 calories	2,000 calories	Same
2,000 calories	1,700 calories	Gain
2,000 calories	2,300 calories	Loss

However, planning your diet involves more than counting calories. You also need to consider the nutrient value of the foods you eat. For example, most high calorie foods contain a lot of fat or sugar but few other nutrients. A healthful diet is built around foods that have high **nutrient density.** These are foods that *contain large amounts of nutrients relative to the number of calories they provide.* The following are examples of nutrient-dense foods from each of the five food groups.

- **Meat group:** chicken and tuna
- **Milk group:** low-fat and nonfat milk, yogurt, and cheese
- **Grains:** whole-wheat pasta, whole-grain breads, and rice
- **Fruit group and vegetable group:** includes almost every fruit and every vegetable

Gaining or Losing Weight

Someone who is overweight or obese needs to lose weight. Someone who is underweight may need to gain weight. Although it is often difficult in practice, losing or gaining weight is simple in principle. To lose weight, you must take in fewer calories or burn up more calories than you usually do. To gain weight, you must take in more calories than usual. It is important to select foods that have high nutrient density.

Adjusting Calorie Intake

To reduce the number of calories you take in, eat smaller servings or lower-calorie foods. Switch from fried to broiled or steamed foods. They not only have fewer calories but also contain less fat. To increase the number of calories you take in, eat larger servings of complex carbohydrates such as bread and pasta. See **Figure 9.13** for sample menus.

Figure 9.13
Menus for Weight Loss and Weight Gain

Math Connection

Burning Calories

You have to use up an extra 3,500 calories to lose 1 pound of fat. To lose 5 pounds in a month, how many extra calories do you have to burn per day?

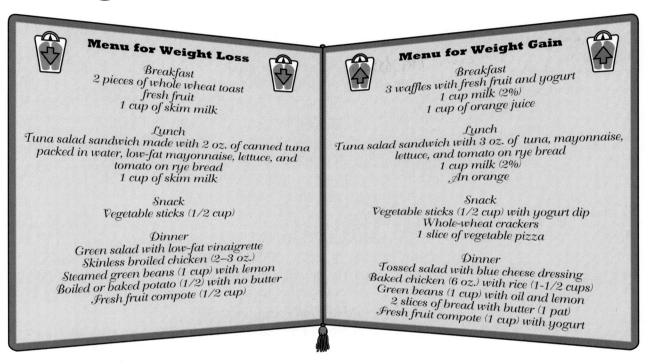

Menu for Weight Loss

Breakfast
2 pieces of whole wheat toast
fresh fruit
1 cup of skim milk

Lunch
Tuna salad sandwich made with 2 oz. of canned tuna
packed in water, low-fat mayonnaise, lettuce, and
tomato on rye bread
1 cup of skim milk

Snack
Vegetable sticks (1/2 cup)

Dinner
Green salad with low-fat vinaigrette
Skinless broiled chicken (2–3 oz.)
Steamed green beans (1 cup) with lemon
Boiled or baked potato (1/2) with no butter
Fresh fruit compote (1/2 cup)

Menu for Weight Gain

Breakfast
3 waffles with fresh fruit and yogurt
1 cup milk (2%)
1 cup of orange juice

Lunch
Tuna salad sandwich with 3 oz. of tuna, mayonnaise,
lettuce, and tomato on rye bread
1 cup milk (2%)
An orange

Snack
Vegetable sticks (1/2 cup) with yogurt dip
Whole-wheat crackers
1 slice of vegetable pizza

Dinner
Tossed salad with blue cheese dressing
Baked chicken (6 oz.) with rice (1-1/2 cups)
Green beans (1 cup) with oil and lemon
2 slices of bread with butter (1 pat)
Fresh fruit compote (1 cup) with yogurt

Exercising

The fastest way to burn up calories is to exercise more. You should also exercise when trying to gain weight to be sure the weight you add is muscle and not fat.

Ⓐ Exercise helps your heart and lungs to work better.

Ⓑ Exercise helps tone your muscles.

Ⓒ Exercise increases the rate at which your body changes nutrients into energy, making it easier for you to control your weight.

Exercise is a great way to control your weight because it has many benefits besides burning calories.

Keeping It Off ACTIVITY!

One of the keys to maintaining weight loss successfully is getting support from family, friends, a counselor, or a support group. Find out what counseling services and support groups are available in your school or community to support teens with weight-control problems.

Dieting Concerns

Many people want to lose weight fast. Dieting safely, however, is a gradual process. It requires eating a balanced diet and losing no more than 1 to 2 pounds a week. Every year a new diet that promises people amazing results becomes popular. In magazines, you can see ads of various pills and other "procedures" that promise quick weight loss.

Some of the popular fad diets are limited to a few foods or food groups. Some are extremely low in calories. There are also diets that consist entirely of a liquid formula. Any of these may lead to serious nutritional deficiencies. Furthermore, such diets do not deal with the main cause of excess weight, which are the eating and exercise habits of the individual. For this reason, they do not result in permanent weight loss.

Fasting, or not eating for a long period of time, is an extremely dangerous way of losing weight. Long-term fasting has the same effect on the body as starvation. It can result in loss of muscle tissue, heart damage, digestive problems, and stunting of growth.

Diet aids such as pills and body wraps may also be ineffective and harmful. Diet pills, which are supposed to reduce your appetite, can have serious side effects and may be addictive. Sweating in body wraps encourages water loss rather than loss of body fat.

To lose weight and maintain your weight loss, you need to change your eating behavior and exercise habits. Otherwise, you will regain the weight you lost once you return to your old eating habits. Moreover, quick weight loss can lead to a cycle of weight gain and loss called seesaw or yo-yo dieting, which can be even more dangerous than being overweight.

The following is a list of "Do's" and "Don'ts" that you can follow to achieve safe weight-loss dieting.

Dieting Do's

- Follow a diet and exercise program under the supervision of a doctor to ensure that the plan is safe.

- Set realistic goals (1 to 2 pounds of weight loss per week).

- Exercise to help burn calories.

- Change poor eating habits.

- Consider food preferences when planning your diet.

- Eat nutrient-dense foods.

- Eat mainly low-calorie foods from the five food groups.

- Eat slowly and wait before taking a second helping.

- If you are tempted to snack, try doing something else—take a walk or visit a friend.

- Weigh yourself only once a week at the same time of day.

- Focus on your progress.

in Your Journal

Do you eat "on the run" and gulp down your food, or do you eat slowly and chew each mouthful thoroughly? Eating too quickly can lead to indigestion and can contribute to weight gain. In your journal describe how you usually eat, and analyze your eating behavior.

Dieting Don'ts

- Don't be taken in by diets promising quick results.
- Don't rely on special formulas or products.
- Don't lose more than 2 pounds a week.
- Don't eat fewer than 1,400 calories a day.
- Don't skip meals.
- Don't weigh yourself every day.
- Don't reward yourself with food.
- Don't become discouraged if you have a setback.

Choosing healthful foods is an essential part of maintaining your desired weight.

Maintaining Your Desired Weight

To maintain your weight, plan your meals and snacks so that you take in the same number of calories you burn up. Keep track of your weight. If you start gaining pounds, eat less or exercise more. If you start losing weight, eat more. Your goal should be to develop good eating and exercise habits that keep you healthy.

Review

Using complete sentences, answer the following questions on a separate sheet of paper.

Reviewing Terms and Facts

1. **Vocabulary** Define *weight control*.
2. **Vocabulary** Who has a more serious problem, a person who is *overweight* or one who is *obese?* Why?
3. **Vocabulary** Define *nutrient density*.
4. **Recall** How does exercise help you to control your weight?
5. **List** Name four dieting "Do's" and four dieting "Don'ts."
6. **Review** Summarize the guidelines for maintaining your desired weight.

Thinking Critically

7. **Contrast** Explain how weight control differs from weight loss.

8. **Relate** Explain how calories are related to both diet and exercise.
9. **Analyze** Kevin went to a fast-food restaurant for lunch. He ordered a cola drink; a taco with chicken, cheese, shredded lettuce, and tomato; and ice cream. Which of these foods has high nutrient density, and which has low nutrient density?

Applying Health Concepts

10. **Consumer Health** Look through several teen magazines and count how many times you see thin models in an advertisement. Then walk through your local shopping mall or supermarket and note how many teens and adults you see who are as thin as the models in the advertisements. How do your two sets of observations compare? How do your observations relate to the pressure that many young people feel to be thin?

Eating Disorders

This lesson will help you find answers to questions that teens often ask about eating disorders. For example:

► Why do some people develop eating disorders?
► Can people with eating disorders do permanent damage to their bodies?
► Where can a teen with an eating disorder get help?

Words to Know

eating disorders
anorexia nervosa
malnutrition
bulimia

Teen Issues

Mind and Body

ACTIVITY!

Anorexia nervosa is a psychological disorder affecting the mind and the body. It is caused by outside pressures, high expectations, the need to achieve, or the need to be popular. People with anorexia nervosa have an irrational fear of becoming obese. Find out about famous people—singers, gymnasts, actors—who have had this disorder. Prepare an oral report on one of these people.

Taking Weight Loss to Extremes

There's no question that Americans spend a lot of time worrying about losing weight. An army of doctors and thousands of diet books prove it. Some people get carried away with losing weight and becoming thin. Others may have serious underlying psychological problems that require professional treatment. They develop **eating disorders**—*extreme and damaging eating behaviors that can lead to sickness and even death.*

Anorexia Nervosa

Anorexia nervosa (a·nuh·REK·see·uh ner·VOH·suh) is *an eating disorder characterized by self-starvation leading to extreme weight loss.* Anorexia means "without appetite," and *nervosa* means "of nervous origin." Most people suffering from anorexia nervosa are female. It's particularly common among teenage girls and young women. However, men and boys can also have the disorder. There are many theories about the specific causes of anorexia nervosa, but experts agree that the disorder is related to how an individual sees herself and to her ability to cope with the stresses of everyday life.

People with anorexia nervosa see themselves as fat even when they are thin.

People with anorexia nervosa may eat so little they develop **malnutrition,** the *condition in which the body doesn't get the nutrients it needs to grow and function properly.* Treatment for anorexia nervosa may include a stay in the hospital, where the patient is fed nutrients and receives counseling. Untreated, anorexia may lead to serious illness—and even to death.

Bulimia

Bulimia (boo·LEE·mee·uh) is *a condition in which people repeatedly eat large amounts of food and then try to get rid of the food they have eaten.* Like anorexia nervosa, bulimia is more common among young women and teenage girls than it is among men or boys. People with bulimia are extremely concerned about being thin and beautiful. The disorder grows out of their desire to control their bodies. For example, after they eat a gallon of ice cream and a bag of potato chips, they panic, thinking they are losing control of their bodies. They may force themselves to vomit the food, believing that this will put them back in control. They may also take laxatives (LAK·suh·tivs). Laxatives make food speed through the digestive system with little time to release nutrients. Other people who are bulimic may go on crash diets to make up for overeating. The result of any of these methods is that the person does not get enough nutrients. **Figure 9.14** shows the many ways that bulimia can damage the body.

Figure 9.14
How Bulimia Damages the Body

The behavior of someone with bulimia can do a great deal of damage to the body.

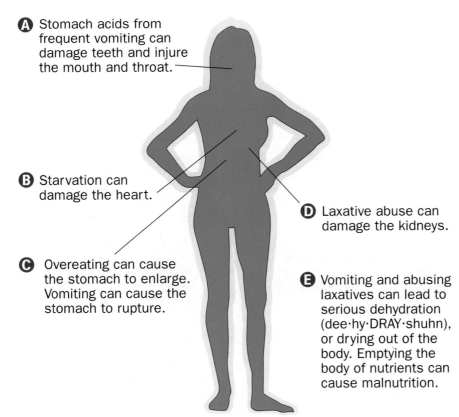

A Stomach acids from frequent vomiting can damage teeth and injure the mouth and throat.

B Starvation can damage the heart.

C Overeating can cause the stomach to enlarge. Vomiting can cause the stomach to rupture.

D Laxative abuse can damage the kidneys.

E Vomiting and abusing laxatives can lead to serious dehydration (dee·hy·DRAY·shuhn), or drying out of the body. Emptying the body of nutrients can cause malnutrition.

Overeating and Obesity

People overeat for a variety of reasons, including boredom, stress, and habit. Overeating is not as severe an eating disorder as anorexia nervosa or bulimia. However, if overeating leads to obesity—being 20 percent or more over your desired weight—it can result in serious health problems.

Excessive body fat puts a strain on the heart and lungs. The obese person may exercise less, resulting in more weight gain and increased health risks. These risks include high blood pressure, stroke, diabetes, heart disease, and even cancer. Obesity may also lead to low self-esteem or even to psychological and social problems associated with obesity. **Figure 9.15** shows the factors involved in adolescent obesity.

Losing excess weight is important to a person's overall health. Although heredity is a factor, overeating and a lack of exercise often cause obesity. The obese person needs to replace poor eating and exercise habits with healthful ones. Regular exercise, a diet approved by a physician, and a basic change in eating behavior are the keys to successful long-term weight loss.

Help for People with Eating Disorders

People with eating disorders rarely get better on their own. This is because they do not have a realistic view of themselves. Although family and friends can play an important role, professional help is usually required. In addition, many communities

Q&A

Recognizing Anorexia Nervosa

Q: I have a friend who is very thin. How can I tell if she has anorexia nervosa?

A: Your friend may have anorexia nervosa if she eats very little yet shows an abnormal interest in food, exercises obsessively, or thinks she's fat when she's actually thin. If you suspect anorexia, follow the steps in the diagram to get her professional help.

Figure 9.15
Factors Contributing to Obesity

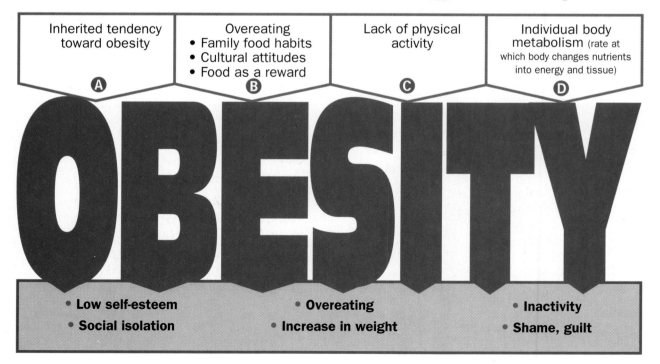

| Inherited tendency toward obesity **A** | Overeating • Family food habits • Cultural attitudes • Food as a reward **B** | Lack of physical activity **C** | Individual body metabolism (rate at which body changes nutrients into energy and tissue) **D** |

OBESITY

• Low self-esteem
• Social isolation
• Overeating
• Increase in weight
• Inactivity
• Shame, guilt

have clinics and support groups, such as Overeaters Anonymous, that can help. It may be difficult, however, to convince a person with an eating disorder, particularly someone with anorexia, to seek help. It is important that he or she get treatment, though.

Treatment and recovery is usually a long-term process. People with eating disorders need the support of family and friends to continue treatment and to remain healthy (see **Figure 9.16**).

Figure 9.16
Helping Someone with an Eating Disorder
To help a person with an eating disorder, follow these steps.

❶ **Convince the person to get help.** A person with an eating disorder may not be aware of the seriousness of the condition.

❷ **Tell an adult.** The school nurse, a counselor, parents, or another adult must know about the problem so that the person will get the help needed.

❸ **Get professional help.** A person with an eating disorder has psychological problems and requires professional help. Sometimes other family members are also encouraged to meet with the counselor.

❹ **Encourage the person to join a support group.** A support group can offer important support and encouragement to a person with an eating disorder.

❺ **Recommend a follow-up.** People who are treated for eating disorders may need to return for follow-up visits to be sure that the problem does not recur.

Review

Lesson 4

Using complete sentences, answer the following questions on a separate sheet of paper.

Reviewing Terms and Facts

1. **Vocabulary** What is an *eating disorder?*

2. **Vocabulary** What is *bulimia?*

3. **Review** Name the main factors contributing to obesity in adolescents.

4. **Outline** List the steps to take to overcome an eating disorder.

Thinking Critically

5. **Analyze** What are some characteristics of people who develop anorexia nervosa?

6. **Explain** Why are people who suffer from eating disorders at risk of dying from these disorders?

Applying Health Concepts

7. **Health of Others** Go to the library and find a biography or work of fiction about someone with bulimia or anorexia nervosa. Ask the reference librarian for help if you need it. Read the book and write a brief summary of it. In your summary, focus on the person's struggle with the eating disorder. Was this person able to conquer the illness? If so, how?

8. **Health of Others** Role-play a skit with a classmate in which one of you pretends to have an eating disorder and the other is a concerned friend. The friend should convince the person with the eating disorder to seek professional help.

Chapter Summary

▶ Eating a healthful diet can help you look and feel your best. (Lesson 1)

▶ A healthful diet provides the right amounts of each of six types of nutrients—carbohydrates, fats, proteins, vitamins, minerals, and water. (Lesson 1)

▶ Recommended Dietary Allowances, or RDA, tell you how much of specific nutrients you need each day. (Lesson 1)

▶ The easiest way to ensure a balanced diet is to use the Food Guide Pyramid, which shows how many servings of the five food groups you should eat each day. (Lesson 2)

▶ You need plenty of fiber in a healthful diet, but fats, cholesterol, sugar, salt, and caffeine should be limited. (Lesson 2)

▶ People who are overweight or obese are at risk of developing many more health problems than people of normal weight are. (Lesson 3)

▶ Losing (or gaining) weight depends on eating fewer (or more) calories in food than you burn up in exercise. (Lesson 3)

▶ In some people, an obsession with being thin leads to eating disorders. (Lesson 4)

▶ People with anorexia nervosa starve themselves until they are very thin; people with bulimia binge on food and then purge themselves by vomiting or by using laxatives. (Lesson 4)

▶ Anyone with an eating disorder needs professional help for the underlying psychological problems. (Lesson 4)

Using Health Terms

On a separate sheet of paper, write the vocabulary term that best matches each definition given below.

1. Eating the foods the body needs to grow, develop, and work properly (Lesson 1)

2. The substances made in your body and found in food that make up proteins (Lesson 1)

3. A fatty, waxlike substance that helps your body produce other substances it needs (Lesson 2)

4. A chemical found in some plants that can make your heart beat faster (Lesson 2)

5. The weight that is best for you based on your sex, height, and body frame (Lesson 3)

6. A unit of heat used to measure the energy available in different foods and the energy your body uses (Lesson 3)

7. A serious eating disorder characterized by self-starvation leading to extreme weight loss (Lesson 4)

8. The condition in which the body doesn't get the nutrients it needs to grow and function properly (Lesson 4)

Reviewing Main Ideas

Using complete sentences, answer the following questions on a separate sheet of paper.

1. Identify several factors that influence an individual's choice of foods. (Lesson 1)

2. Explain why RDA nutrient levels are set fairly high. (Lesson 1)

3. Why are grains found at the base of the Food Guide Pyramid? (Lesson 2)

4. Why should you limit your intake of beverages containing caffeine? (Lesson 2)

5. What happens when you take in more calories than you burn up? (Lesson 3)

6. What rate of weight gain or loss is considered to be healthful? (Lesson 3)

7. In which gender and age group do eating disorders most often occur? (Lesson 4)

8. What are some of the health risks of obesity? (Lesson 4)

Thinking Critically

Using complete sentences, answer the following questions on a separate sheet of paper.

1. **Explain** Tell why good nutrition is such an important factor in maintaining good health. (Lesson 1)

2. **Analyze** In selecting nutritious foods, why does it matter that some vitamins are water-soluble and some are fat-soluble? (Lesson 1)

3. **Apply** Explain the idea behind the Food Guide Pyramid and why its shape is so important. (Lesson 2)

4. **Distinguish** What are some steps you can take to lower the amount of fat in your diet? (Lesson 2)

5. **Synthesize** Explain how a person can be 20 percent over his or her desired weight without being obese. (Lesson 3)

6. **Apply** Why are nutrient-dense foods the best choices for a weight-loss diet? (Lesson 3)

7. **Analyze** How is advertising linked with the prevalence of eating disorders among teenage girls and young women in our country? (Lesson 4)

8. **Explain** Why does bulimia lead to health problems other than malnutrition? (Lesson 4)

Your Action Plan

Make an action plan to improve your diet. Look over your private journal entries for this chapter. What do they tell you about your diet? Based on your private journal entries and what you have learned about good nutrition in this chapter, draw up some guidelines to improve your food choices. Make sure your guidelines are reasonable for you. For instance, giving up all processed foods might be unreasonable. Choosing processed foods that are low in fat and sodium, however, might be a reasonable guideline.

Try your best to follow the guidelines you develop. Keep track of what works for you and what doesn't. Make adjustments to your guidelines so that your eating plan is nutritious, appealing, and practical.

Building Your Portfolio

1. Examine the nutrition labels on several food packages. Which product has the highest total fat content? Which has the highest percentage of total fat content from saturated fat? Which product is best for a low-fat diet? Why? Add this analysis to your portfolio.

2. Prepare an anonymous questionnaire for classmates on body size and weight. Include several open-ended questions, such as: "If you could change one thing about your appearance, what would it be?" Write a paragraph summarizing and interpreting the results of your survey to add to your portfolio.

In Your Home and Community

1. Work with several classmates to draw up a list of professional help available in your community for people with eating disorders. Look for hot lines, clinics, support groups, and psychologists who specialize in treating eating disorders. Distribute this list at your school and other places where teens go.

2. As a class, develop a skit for children in first through third grades that demonstrates the use of the Food Guide Pyramid. Have your teacher arrange for you to present your skit to a group of young children. After the skit, ask volunteers in the audience to choose food to make a nutritious meal.

Unit 4
Your Physical Health

Chapter 10
Wellness and Your Body Systems

Student Expectations

After reading this chapter, you should be able to:

❶ List eight major body systems and describe what each one does.

❷ Identify the parts of each body system and describe the job of each part.

❸ Describe how to care for each of your eight body systems.

❹ Identify problems that may affect each of your body systems and describe how these problems may be treated or prevented.

My sister just pulled up in her new car, and it's "loaded." It has a V-six fuel-injected engine, five-speed transmission, and a great stereo system. While I'm admiring the car, she tells me that if I help her take care of it, she might give it to me when I graduate from high school! Will I help her take care of it? You bet I will!

While I'm thinking about someday owning this fine machine, I remember the fine machine I already own and care for—my body. My body is made up of different systems that are more complex and finely tuned than those in the best automobile. These systems work together to keep my body working at peak efficiency day after day, year after year—and it's a good thing they do.

This machine that I already own has to last a lifetime. I cannot turn it in for a new model every few years. I want it to be working as well and looking as good on the day I get my sister's car as it does today.

in your journal

Read the account on this page. Do you also have a complex machine, such as a ten-speed bike or a computer, that you care for so that it works well? Do you care for your body as well as you care for this machine? Start your private journal entries on your body systems by answering these questions:

▶ In general, how well do I understand my body systems and what they do?

▶ Do I have any personal habits or activities that might harm my body systems?

▶ What changes can I make in my daily routine that will help me have a healthier, better-looking body?

When you reach the end of the chapter, you will use your journal entries to make an action plan.

Your Nervous System

This lesson will help you find answers to questions that teens often ask about their nervous system and how it works. For example:

► How are my senses connected to my nervous system?

► Why is damage or injury to the nervous system so serious?

► What can I do to protect my nervous system?

Words to Know

neuron
central nervous system (CNS)
peripheral nervous system (PNS)
brain
spinal cord
somatic system
autonomic system

The Control Center

What do brushing your teeth, riding a bicycle, and solving a math problem have in common? They all result from instructions from your body's control center—your nervous system. This complex group of specialized cells controls your thoughts and actions.

The specialized cells that make up the nervous system are called nerve cells, or **neurons** (NOO·rahns). Unlike other body cells, they cannot repair or replace themselves if they are damaged. Neurons carry messages to and from different parts of the body (see **Figure 10.1**). These messages are in the form of very weak electrical signals.

Figure 10.1
How the Nervous System Works

Neurons are more sensitive than other cells, and they work quickly. The action described here occurs in less than a few seconds.

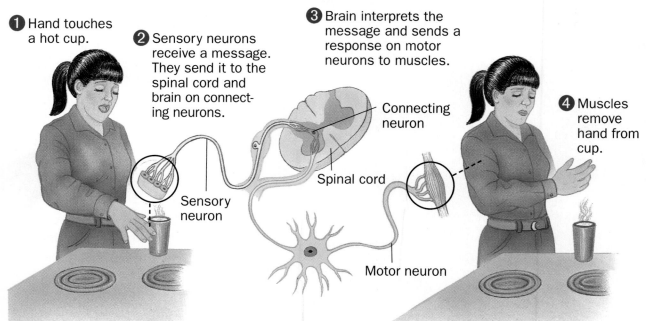

1 Hand touches a hot cup.

2 Sensory neurons receive a message. They send it to the spinal cord and brain on connecting neurons.

3 Brain interprets the message and sends a response on motor neurons to muscles.

Connecting neuron

Spinal cord

Sensory neuron

Motor neuron

4 Muscles remove hand from cup.

Parts of the Nervous System

Your nervous system consists of your brain, spinal cord, and many nerves. It is divided into two main sections (see **Figure 10.2**).

- The **central nervous system (CNS)** includes *the brain and the spinal cord.* It is your body's main control center.

- The **peripheral** (puh·RIF·uh·ruhl) **nervous system (PNS)** includes *the nerves that connect the CNS to all parts of the body.* It carries messages to and from the CNS.

Figure 10.2
The Nervous System

The nervous system controls all of your body's actions. The central nervous system (yellow) and the peripheral nervous system (blue) work together. Shown here are 31 pairs of spinal nerves that branch off from the spinal cord. Each pair serves a particular part of the body.

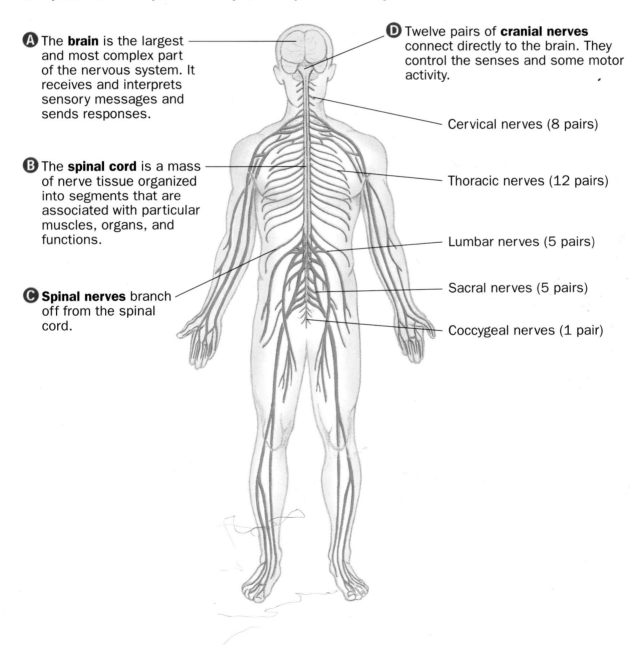

A The **brain** is the largest and most complex part of the nervous system. It receives and interprets sensory messages and sends responses.

B The **spinal cord** is a mass of nerve tissue organized into segments that are associated with particular muscles, organs, and functions.

C **Spinal nerves** branch off from the spinal cord.

D Twelve pairs of **cranial nerves** connect directly to the brain. They control the senses and some motor activity.

Cervical nerves (8 pairs)

Thoracic nerves (12 pairs)

Lumbar nerves (5 pairs)

Sacral nerves (5 pairs)

Coccygeal nerves (1 pair)

Taking Sides

The brain is divided into two halves, or hemispheres. The right side of your brain controls the left side of your body. The left side of your brain controls the right side of your body. The left side of the brain of a right-handed person is more dominant than the right side.

The Central Nervous System

The central nervous system (CNS) controls your body's actions. These actions are divided into two types—voluntary and involuntary. Voluntary actions are those that you control, such as walking and smiling. Involuntary actions are those that you cannot control, such as the beating of your heart.

The CNS consists of your brain and spinal cord. Neurons carry messages back and forth between the CNS and nerves found in all parts of your body.

- The **brain** is *the mass of neurons that controls all actions, emotions, thoughts, and memory.* It is made up of about 10 billion neurons and weighs about 3 pounds. Blood vessels cover your brain, carrying the food and oxygen it needs to work. Your brain is well protected. It is encased in the bones of your skull. It is also suspended in a fluid, which serves as a shock absorber.

- The **spinal cord** is *a long bundle of neurons that extends almost the entire length of the body.* It plays an important role. The spinal cord *relays messages from all parts of the body to the brain and from the brain to muscles and glands.* Your spinal cord, which is less than 2 feet long and about the same diameter as your index finger, is protected by your backbone.

Figure 10.3 shows the three main parts of the brain, the *cerebrum* (suh·REE·bruhm), the *cerebellum* (ser·uh·BE·luhm), and the *brain stem.* Each of these parts controls many important body actions. Also shown are the *meninges*, which protect the CNS.

LIFE SKILLS
Caring for Your Body Systems

*T*hink of your body as a complex machine made up of several simpler machines. In this case, the simpler machines are your body systems. For the body to function properly, all of its systems must be healthy and in good working order. You can play an important part in keeping the body systems at their best by making healthy choices.

▶ **Rest.** Get plenty of rest. Your body parts work hard, and you need the proper amount of rest to keep them in good working order.

▶ **Exercise.** Regular exercise strengthens your heart and muscles, and helps keep the lungs

working well. Exercise also helps bones grow properly.

▶ **Diet.** Food is the fuel that provides energy for all the cells in your body. Eat meals at regular times each day. Choose foods wisely. Eat a balanced diet and avoid foods that are high in fat, cholesterol, and salt. Keep your weight at a level that is right for you.

▶ **Stress.** Reduce your level of stress when you can. Stress that goes on too long or happens too often can harm your body. Try to think and plan ahead, and learn to relax.

Figure 10.3
The Brain

Ⓐ The **cerebrum** is the largest portion of the brain. It controls the senses, movement of muscles, thinking, and speech.

Ⓑ The **cerebellum** controls balance, posture, and coordination.

Ⓒ The **brain stem** controls such vital body actions as heartbeat, breathing, blood pressure, and digestion.

Ⓓ The **meninges** are membranes that cover the brain and the spinal cord.

Skull

Midbrain

Pons

Medulla

Spinal cord

Vertebrae

in your journal

Write two column headings in your journal—voluntary and involuntary. Define each one and list several activities that you carry out in the next few hours in each column. Find out which part of the brain controls each activity listed.

▶ **Smoking.** Say no to smoking. Cigarette smoke harms the nose, throat, and lungs. It reduces the ability of red blood cells to carry oxygen. Smoking can also lead to cancer and heart disease.

▶ **Drugs.** Don't use drugs, including alcohol. Drugs affect nerve cells and can damage or destroy brain cells. Damage to the nervous system cannot be undone.

Follow-up Activity

Nobody is perfect. We can all do better at making healthy choices. Which of the areas listed above do you need to work on most? Plan and carry out healthy actions in that area. Then tackle other areas on which you need to work.

Teen Issues

It's the Law ACTIVITY!

The number of people who enjoy bicycling, skateboarding, and in-line skating is large. Many state and local agencies have passed laws requiring the use of helmets and other safety gear. Organize a class debate to discuss the issue.

The Peripheral Nervous System

The peripheral nervous system (PNS) is made up of many nerves that connect the CNS to all parts of your body. Peripheral nerves carry messages to and from your muscles or various body organs. With this system, the brain is able to control the body.

The PNS has two main parts. One part, called the **somatic** (soh·MA·tik) **system,** *deals with actions that you control.* The second part, the **autonomic** (aw·tuh·NAH·mik) **system,** *deals with actions you do not usually control.* Such actions include your heartbeat, breathing, and digestion.

Problems of the Nervous System

Figure 10.4 describes several diseases and disorders of the nervous system. Some can be prevented; others cannot. However, treatment and therapy can help people who have these problems.

Figure 10.4
Diseases and Disorders of the Nervous System

Disease or Disorder	Description	Treatment or Prevention
Infections		
Polio	Caused by a virus; can result in paralysis (inability to use muscles)	Vaccination
Rabies	Caused by a virus transmitted by bite of infected animal; may be fatal if untreated	Series of shots; avoid contact with strange animals
Meningitis	Inflammation of the membranes that cover the brain and spinal column	Vaccine; antibiotics
Structural Disorders		
Brain tumor	Uncontrolled cell growth; may be cancerous	Surgery; additional treatment
Head injury	Caused by a blow to the head; blood collects in damaged area and may cause pressure	Rest; surgery if necessary
Spinal cord Injury	Results in paralysis of a part or most of the body	Physical therapy
Seizure Disorder		
Epilepsy	Brain disorder that causes uncontrollable muscle activity	Controlled by medication
Degenerative Disorders		
Cerebral palsy	Caused by damage or injury to the cerebrum; symptoms may vary	No cure; therapy can help victims live active lives
Multiple sclerosis	Caused by damage to protective outer coating of some nerves; symptoms may vary, but become progressively worse with time	No cure; medication and therapy can help somewhat in the early stages

Nervous System Injuries

Injuries are the most common cause of damage to the nervous system. Blows to the head can damage the brain. The most common and mildest form of brain injury is a concussion, which temporarily disturbs brain function. Injuries to the neck or back can cause spinal cord damage. Such damage can result in partial, or even total, paralysis. A pinched nerve happens when one part of the spine is displaced by a sudden movement or blow and presses on a nerve. Such injuries can be very painful.

Most injuries result from accidents or carelessness. You can prevent them by acting safely and wearing protective gear when necessary, as shown in **Figure 10.5.**

Figure 10.5
How to Avoid Injuries

Avoid neck and back injuries.
Be sure to take all necessary precautions and use common sense when diving and lifting.

Wear a helmet.
When you are bicycling, skateboarding, or playing a contact sport, always wear a helmet.

Wear a safety belt.
Whenever you are in a moving vehicle, fasten your safety belt.

Obey all traffic safety rules.
Whether you are in a car, on a bicycle, or just walking, obey all traffic rules.

Review  Lesson 1

Using complete sentences, answer the following questions on a separate sheet of paper.

Reviewing Terms and Facts

1. **Vocabulary** Define the *somatic* and *autonomic systems.*

2. **List** Identify four ways to avoid injury.

Thinking Critically

3. **Analyze** What takes place in the nervous system when you catch a ball?

4. **Hypothesize** Why do spinal cord injuries often result in paralysis?

Applying Health Concepts

5. **Health of Others** Volunteer to work at a hospital or clinic helping people with nervous system injuries or disorders. Give a talk to your class about your experiences and how they add to your understanding of the problems of the nervous system.

6. **Personal Health** Think about how many health choices involve forming good habits. In the library, read about the part played by the nervous system in habit formation. Then write an answer to this question: Why is forming a habit often difficult at first but easier as you keep trying?

Your Circulatory System

This lesson will help you find answers to questions that teens often ask about their circulatory system. For example:

▶ How does my heart work?

▶ Why does the doctor check my pulse and blood pressure when I have a physical examination?

▶ What is my blood type and why is it important?

Words to Know

circulatory system
cardiovascular
    system
arteries
veins
capillaries

The Transport System

The **circulatory** (SER·kyuh·luh·tohr·ee) **system** is your body's transport system. The circulatory system *keeps the body working well by delivering essential materials to body cells and removing waste materials from the cells.* This body system is also known as the **cardiovascular** (KAR·dee·oh·VAS·kyoo·ler) **system.**

How the Circulatory System Works

The blood carries various substances throughout your circulatory system (see **Figure 10.6**). Different organs of the body serve as transfer stations. At some stations, blood picks up needed nutrients and other materials and delivers them to the cells. Blood also picks up waste products and carries them to other transfer stations, where they are removed from the body.

Figure 10.6
How the Circulatory System Works

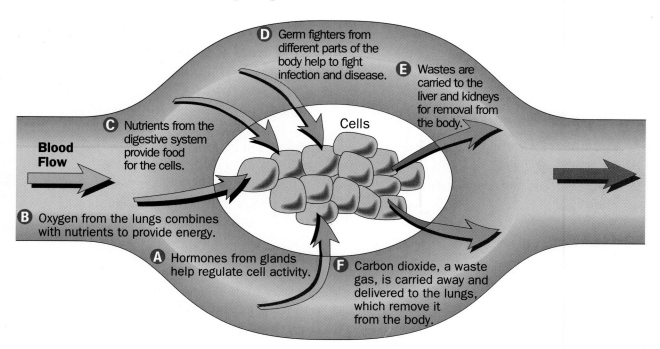

D Germ fighters from different parts of the body help to fight infection and disease.

E Wastes are carried to the liver and kidneys for removal from the body.

C Nutrients from the digestive system provide food for the cells.

Cells

Blood Flow

B Oxygen from the lungs combines with nutrients to provide energy.

A Hormones from glands help regulate cell activity.

F Carbon dioxide, a waste gas, is carried away and delivered to the lungs, which remove it from the body.

Parts of the Circulatory System

Your circulatory system includes your heart, blood vessels, and blood. Your heart is a pump that moves blood in two major pathways—pulmonary circulation and systemic circulation. **Figure 10.7** shows the two pathways.

Did You Know?

A Demanding Organ

The heart uses more nutrients and oxygen than any other organ in the body.

Figure 10.7
The Circulatory System

Systemic circulation moves blood to all the body tissues except the lungs. *Pulmonary circulation* is the flow of blood from the heart to the lungs and back to the heart. In these drawings, red represents oxygen-rich blood, and blue represents blood containing carbon dioxide.

A Your **heart** is divided into four chambers. Each upper chamber is called an **atrium** (AY·tree·uhm), and each lower chamber is called a **ventricle** (VEN·tri·kuhl). **Valves** open and close to control the flow of blood in a one-way direction through your heart.

B **Pulmonary arteries** carry blood containing carbon dioxide from your heart to your lungs.

C **Pulmonary veins** carry blood containing oxygen from your lungs to your heart.

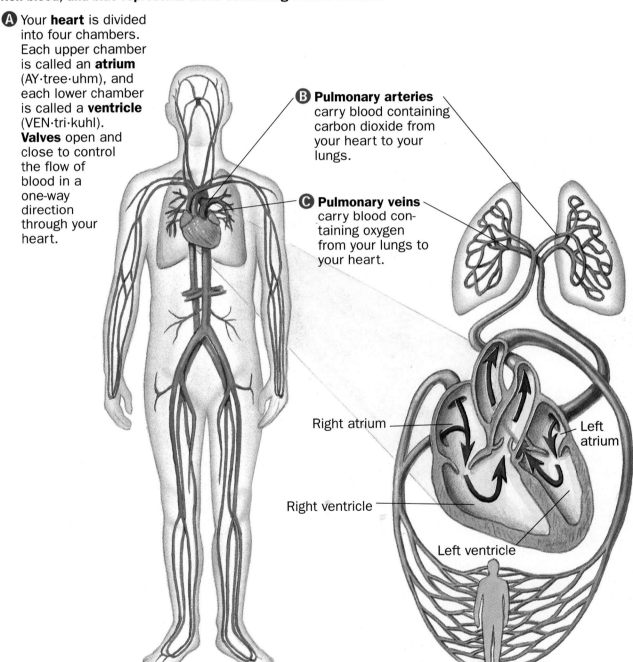

Right atrium

Left atrium

Right ventricle

Left ventricle

The Blood

Blood is a mixture of solids in a large amount of liquid called *plasma* (PLAZ·ma). Plasma is about 92 percent water. The solids are red blood cells, white blood cells, and *platelets* (PLAYT·luhts). **Figure 10.8** describes the role of each part of the blood.

Figure 10.8
The Parts of the Blood

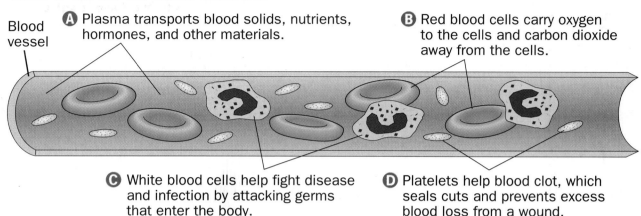

Blood vessel

A Plasma transports blood solids, nutrients, hormones, and other materials.

B Red blood cells carry oxygen to the cells and carbon dioxide away from the cells.

C White blood cells help fight disease and infection by attacking germs that enter the body.

D Platelets help blood clot, which seals cuts and prevents excess blood loss from a wound.

Blood Types

Blood is essential to life. Sometimes people lose some of their blood during surgical procedures or in accidents. If you lose too much blood, you will die. Fortunately, doctors can replace lost blood with blood from another person. Such a procedure is called a blood transfusion (trans·FYOO·zhuhn).

Your blood is not the same as everyone else's. In fact, there are four major blood types: A, B, AB, and O. Your type depends on the presence or absence of certain substances in the blood. For a transfusion to be successful, the blood from the person giving the blood, the donor, must mix safely with the blood of the person receiving it. Mixing certain blood types can have serious side effects. These include high fevers, difficulty breathing, and even death.

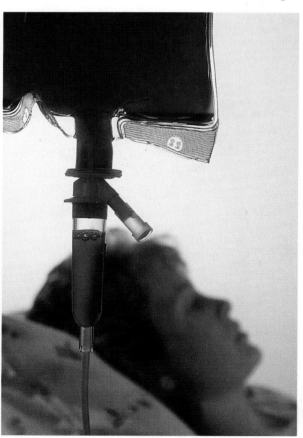

Before giving a transfusion, hospitals take extreme care in checking blood types.

Doctors must consider another factor, called the *Rh factor,* before a transfusion. Most people are positive for this factor, or Rh+, meaning that their blood contains the factor. The rest are negative for the factor, or Rh–. Their blood does not contain the Rh factor.

Adults who give blood usually receive a blood donor card that gives their name, blood type, and the number of pints donated.

Blood Banks

People who are old enough and in good health can give the gift of life—their blood. Every day, thousands of people donate blood to the Red Cross and other charitable organizations. This blood is stored in blood banks for use when needed.

Many people are concerned about the safety of blood stored in blood banks. Only people in good health are allowed to give blood. A new needle is used every time blood is taken and every time someone receives blood. All donated blood is tested for a variety of diseases, including HIV. Blood that fails the tests is discarded.

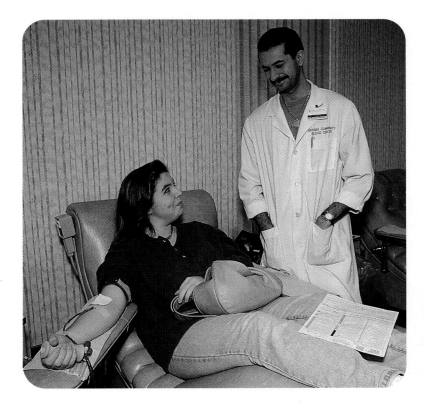

Adults who give blood are not at risk for contracting diseases of the blood.

Does someone you know have one of the diseases listed in Figure 10.10? In your journal, describe his or her symptoms and treatment.

Cultural Diversity

Sickle-Cell Anemia

Sickle-cell anemia is an inherited condition that affects the ability of blood to circulate properly. The condition is found mainly among people whose cultural roots are in Africa, India, and Mediterranean and Middle Eastern countries.

Your Blood Vessels

Over 80,000 miles of blood vessels move your blood throughout your body. There are three types of blood vessels.

- **Arteries** (AR·tuh·reez) *carry blood away from the heart.*

- **Veins** (VAYNZ) are *the blood vessels that carry blood from the body back to the heart.*

- **Capillaries** (KAP·uh·lehr·eez) are *tiny tubes that carry blood from the arteries to the body's cells and from cells to the veins.*

Blood Pressure

As blood moves through your body, it exerts pressure against the walls of blood vessels. This is called *blood pressure.* **Figure 10.9** explains how blood pressure is measured.

Health professionals use an instrument called a sphygmomanometer (sfig·mo·muh·NAH·muh·ter) to measure blood pressure. They wrap a soft, rubbery cuff around your upper arm and inflate it until it is tight enough to stop the flow of blood. The air is gradually deflated until, through a stethoscope, they can hear blood flowing through your arm. This maximum amount of pressure is called systolic pressure. The cuff is then deflated until blood flows steadily, giving a reading of the diastolic, or lowest, pressure.

Figure 10.9
Measuring Blood Pressure

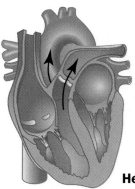

Heart contracted

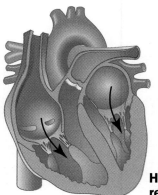

Heart relaxed

Ⓐ As the ventricles of your heart contract to push the blood into your arteries, the pressure is at its highest point (systolic pressure).

Ⓑ As the heart relaxes to refill, the pressure is at its lowest point (diastolic pressure).

Problems of the Circulatory System

Figure 10.10 gives information about some problems of the circulatory system. Those that affect the heart or blood vessels are known as *cardiovascular disorders.* Other circulatory problems affect the blood itself.

Figure 10.10
Diseases and Disorders of the Circulatory System

Disease or Disorder	Description	Treatment or Prevention
Hypertension (high blood pressure)	Blood pressure higher than normal for a long time; can lead to heart attack, stroke, kidney failure	Reduce stress; change diet to reduce intake of sodium, fats, and cholesterol; medication; regular checkups
Stroke	Cluster of blood cells blocks blood vessel in brain	Same as for hypertension
Heart attack	Stoppage in flow of blood to heart	Same as for hypertension
Arteriosclerosis	Artery walls harden; caused by diet high in fat and cholesterol	Same as for hypertension
Anemia	Lack of red blood cells or cells that do not carry enough oxygen; causes weakness, low energy	Iron supplements; rest
Sickle-cell anemia	Blood unable to circulate properly	Blood transfusions and medication
Mononucleosis	Viral infection; symptoms are sore throat, swollen glands, and fatigue	Bed rest and a well-balanced diet
Leukemia	Abnormal white blood cells	Medication; radiation
Hemophilia	Blood does not clot properly	Transfusions of blood-clotting factors

Review

Lesson 2

Using complete sentences, answer the following questions on a separate sheet of paper.

Reviewing Terms and Facts

1. **Vocabulary**   What are *arteries, veins,* and *capillaries?* Explain their functions.

2. **Recall**   Identify the three solids that make up blood. What is the liquid portion of blood called?

Thinking Critically

3. **Review**   What steps are taken to make sure that donated blood is safe?

4. **Suggest**   Why is high blood pressure called the silent killer? How can high blood pressure be detected before it leads to serious health problems?

Applying Health Concepts

5. **Consumer Health**   Do research to find out how the following substances in food affect your circulatory system: salt, fats, and cholesterol. Prepare a brief paper on the information to present to the class.

Your Respiratory System

This lesson will help you find answers to questions that teens often ask about their respiratory system. For example:

▶ Why is breathing so important to staying alive?

▶ What does smoking do to my respiratory system?

The Breath of Life

Did you know that you can live only a few minutes without air? Air contains oxygen, a gas your body needs to maintain life. Breathing—inhaling and exhaling—is carried out by your **respiratory system.** This system consists of *the organs that provide the body with a continuous supply of oxygen and rid the body of carbon dioxide.* **Figure 10.11** shows the important parts of the respiratory system and tells what each part does.

Figure 10.11
The Respiratory System

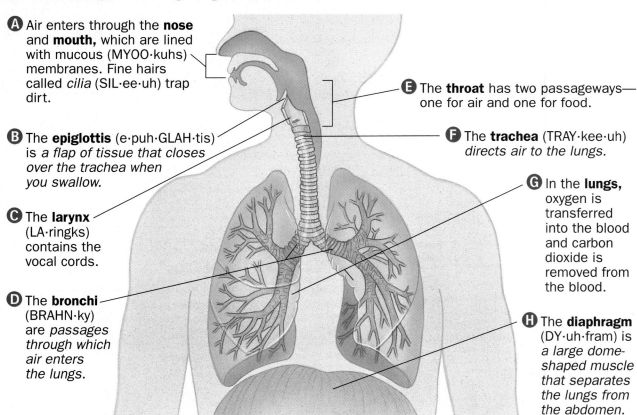

A Air enters through the **nose** and **mouth,** which are lined with mucous (MYOO·kuhs) membranes. Fine hairs called *cilia* (SIL·ee·uh) trap dirt.

B The **epiglottis** (e·puh·GLAH·tis) is *a flap of tissue that closes over the trachea when you swallow.*

C The **larynx** (LA·ringks) contains the vocal cords.

D The **bronchi** (BRAHN·ky) are *passages through which air enters the lungs.*

E The **throat** has two passageways—one for air and one for food.

F The **trachea** (TRAY·kee·uh) *directs air to the lungs.*

G In the **lungs,** oxygen is transferred into the blood and carbon dioxide is removed from the blood.

H The **diaphragm** (DY·uh·fram) is *a large dome-shaped muscle that separates the lungs from the abdomen.*

How the Respiratory System Works

The respiratory system has two important jobs. First, it supplies oxygen to the blood. This oxygen is carried to all cells of the body. In the cells, oxygen combines with nutrients to provide the energy the cells need to do their jobs. When oxygen combines with nutrients, the waste gas carbon dioxide is produced. The second job of the respiratory system is to remove carbon dioxide from the blood and release it outside the body.

How Breathing Works

Breathing consists of two actions—inhaling and exhaling. When you inhale, you bring in air from outside your body. When you exhale, you release air to the outside. The air you exhale contains more carbon dioxide and less oxygen than the air you inhale. **Figure 10.12** shows what happens when you breathe. The exchange of oxygen for carbon dioxide takes place inside your lungs. For this reason, the lungs are the most important organs of your respiratory system.

in your journal

Do you breathe more with your rib muscles or with your diaphragm? To find out, place your hand just beneath your rib cage and breathe normally. Can you feel your chest rise or fall? If so, you are mainly a rib breather. For more healthful breathing, strengthen your diaphragm muscle by using good posture and by exercising. In your journal, write a plan for doing so.

Figure 10.12
The Action of Breathing

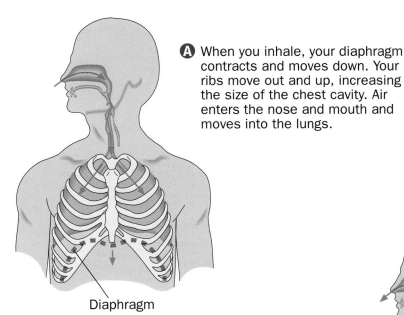

A When you inhale, your diaphragm contracts and moves down. Your ribs move out and up, increasing the size of the chest cavity. Air enters the nose and mouth and moves into the lungs.

Diaphragm

B When you exhale, your diaphragm relaxes and moves up into the chest cavity. Your ribs move in and down, making the chest cavity smaller. Air is forced out of the lungs and leaves the body through the nose and mouth.

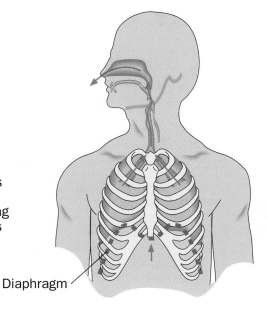

Diaphragm

What Happens in the Lungs?

Your lungs consist of clusters of *microscopic air sacs* called **alveoli** (al·vee·OH·ly). These sacs are at the ends of the smallest branches of the bronchi. **Figure 10.13** shows how oxygen and carbon dioxide are exchanged in the alveoli.

Problems of the Respiratory System

The respiratory system is a common site of infection because germs can easily enter the body through your nose and mouth. **Figure 10.14** lists some of the problems of the respiratory system. Bronchitis, emphysema, and lung cancer have been linked to smoking. The best way to prevent them is to not smoke.

Figure 10.13
The Exchange of Oxygen and Carbon Dioxide

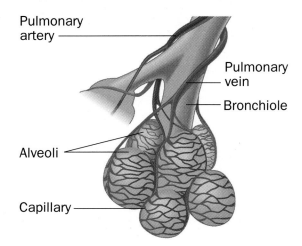

Pulmonary artery

Pulmonary vein

Bronchiole

Alveoli

Capillary

A Blood from the heart enters the lungs through the pulmonary arteries and capillaries. This blood contains carbon dioxide from the body's cells.

B Carbon dioxide passes from the blood into the alveoli where it is exchanged for oxygen.

C Oxygen passes from the alveoli into the capillaries, where it is picked up by the blood and carried back to the heart through the pulmonary veins.

MAKING HEALTHY DECISIONS
Choosing Health

*A*ll during Lenny's school years, he and several close friends did everything together. Then the unthinkable happened.

Last year, Lenny and his family had to move to another part of the country. The move was temporary, though, and after a year the family moved back.

Lenny now had a problem. His friends had taken up smoking. They urged him to smoke, too.

Lenny was confused. He enjoyed being with his friends. He knew smoking was bad for his health, but he felt uncomfortable being one of the non-smokers. He decided to use the step-by-step decision-making process to make up his mind.

❶ **State the situation**
❷ **List the options**
❸ **Weigh the possible outcomes**
❹ **Consider your values**
❺ **Make a decision and act**
❻ **Evaluate the decision**

Follow-up Activities

1. Apply the six steps of the decision-making process to Lenny's situation.

2. Along with several other class members, role-play a scene in which Lenny decides not to smoke. Have him use his refusal skills.

Figure 10.14
Problems of the Respiratory System

Disease or Disorder	Description	Treatment or Prevention
Flu/Colds	Caused by virus; cough, runny nose, aches, fever	Bed rest and fluids; flu vaccine can prevent some types
Tuberculosis	Bacterial lung infection; dry cough in early stages, chest pain later	Medication
Allergies	Sneezing, itchy eyes, runny nose, hives; caused by reaction to substances	Antihistamines may relieve symptoms; avoid contact with irritating substances
Pneumonia	Lung infection by bacteria or viruses; fever, chest pain, difficulty breathing	Antibiotics for bacterial type; bed rest for viral type
Bronchitis	Swelling of the bronchi due to infection; cough, fever, tightness in chest	No known cure; symptoms usually disappear after time
Asthma	Bronchial swelling and blockage; wheezing, short breath, coughing	No known cure; medication to reduce swelling
Emphysema	Alveoli destroyed; extreme difficulty breathing; often fatal	No known cure; pure oxygen to ease breathing
Lung cancer	Alveoli destroyed; often caused by smoking	No cure; surgery, radiation, chemotherapy

Review

Lesson 3

Using complete sentences, answer the following questions on a separate sheet of paper.

Reviewing Terms and Facts

1. **Vocabulary** Define the term *trachea*. Use it in an original sentence.

2. **Recall** Why are respiratory infections so common?

Thinking Critically

3. **Explain** What happens when you inhale? What happens when you exhale?

4. **List** Make a list of all the reasons you can think of for not smoking.

Applying Health Concepts

5. **Consumer Health** Conduct a survey of your class about smoking. Ask each student to give reasons why he or she decided to smoke or not to smoke. Present the results of your survey to the class.

6. **Health of Others** Record an interview with a person who has breathing problems, asthma, or allergies. Ask the person to tell what brings on the problem and to describe how he or she feels during an attack. Ask what actions he or she takes to bring the attack under control. Ask permission to present your taped interview to the class.

This lesson will help you find answers to questions that teens often ask about their skeletal system. For example:

▶ **Do bones have other jobs in the body besides supporting it and giving it shape?**

▶ **If bones are hard and inflexible, how is movement possible?**

▶ **What is the difference between a sprain and a fracture?**

Words to Know

skeletal system
cartilage
joint
ligament
tendon

The Body's Framework

All structures need some sort of framework to give them strength and shape. Your body's framework, which is called the **skeletal system,** is *a system made up of bones, joints, and connecting tissue.* **Figure 10.15.A** shows the skeletal system. In addition to supporting your body, it allows movement and protects your internal organs. It also produces red and white blood cells in the marrow, the center part, of your long bones. **Figure 10.15.B** shows two kinds of marrow in a long bone.

The Bones

Your skeleton consists of bone and **cartilage** (KAR·tuhl·ij), which is *a strong, flexible tissue that provides cushioning at your joints.* When you were a baby, your skeleton was mostly cartilage. As your body grew, the cartilage was replaced by bone.

Bones are living tissue composed of cells. Like all body cells, bone cells need food and oxygen to grow, strengthen, work, and repair themselves. Providing a framework for your body is just one job of your bones. They do many important jobs.

■ **Movement.** Bones provide points of attachment for muscles. Body parts, such as your arms and your legs, move when muscles pull on bones.

■ **Support.** Your backbone is made up of 24 bones called vertebrae (VER·tuh·bray). The backbone supports your head and upper body and protects your spinal cord.

■ **Protection.** The bones of your skull protect your brain. Your ribs protect your lungs and heart from injury.

■ **Blood cell formation.** Bones play a role in your circulatory system, too. Red and white blood cells are formed by tissue called marrow (MEHR·oh), which is in the center of some bones.

■ **Storage.** Bones store minerals, such as calcium and phosphorus, for use when needed by your body.

Teen Issues

Safe or Cool? **ACTIVITY!**

Medical and health officials recommend that you wear a safety helmet and other protective gear when you go skateboarding or in-line skating. Many teens ignore this advice. They think that wearing such gear is not cool. Write a paragraph to explain how you feel about this issue.

Figure 10.15A
The Skeletal System

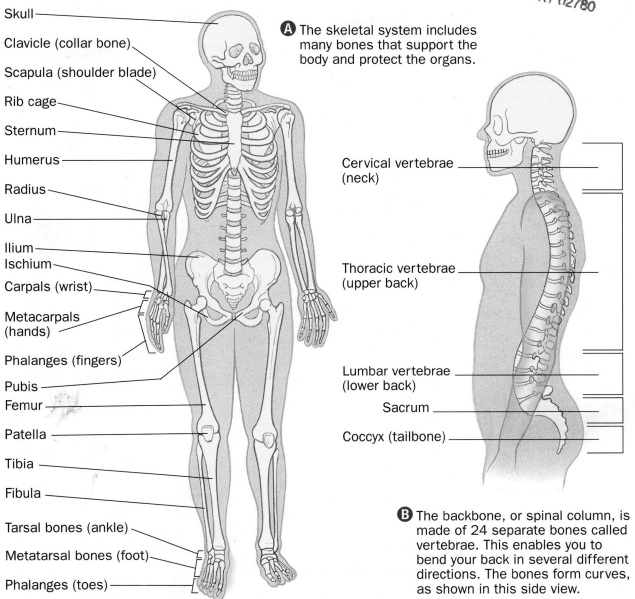

Skull

Clavicle (collar bone)

Scapula (shoulder blade)

Rib cage

Sternum

Humerus

Radius

Ulna

Ilium

Ischium

Carpals (wrist)

Metacarpals (hands)

Phalanges (fingers)

Pubis

Femur

Patella

Tibia

Fibula

Tarsal bones (ankle)

Metatarsal bones (foot)

Phalanges (toes)

Ⓐ The skeletal system includes many bones that support the body and protect the organs.

Cervical vertebrae (neck)

Thoracic vertebrae (upper back)

Lumbar vertebrae (lower back)

Sacrum

Coccyx (tailbone)

Ⓑ The backbone, or spinal column, is made of 24 separate bones called vertebrae. This enables you to bend your back in several different directions. The bones form curves, as shown in this side view.

Figure 10.15B
Cross-Section of a Long Bone

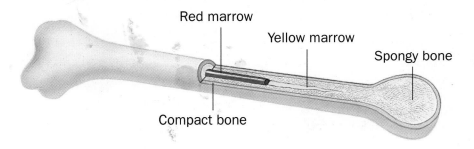

Red marrow

Yellow marrow

Spongy bone

Compact bone

The inner cavity of your long bones, such as the femur, contains yellow marrow, which is a fatty tissue, and red marrow at the ends. Red marrow produces red blood cells and most of the white blood cells in your blood.

Figure 10.16
Types of Joints

Each type of joint allows a certain kind of movement. What type of joint is in your fingers?

The Joints

Joints are *the points at which bones meet.* Joints differ from one another in the type of movement they allow. **Figure 10.16** shows the various types of joints in your body.

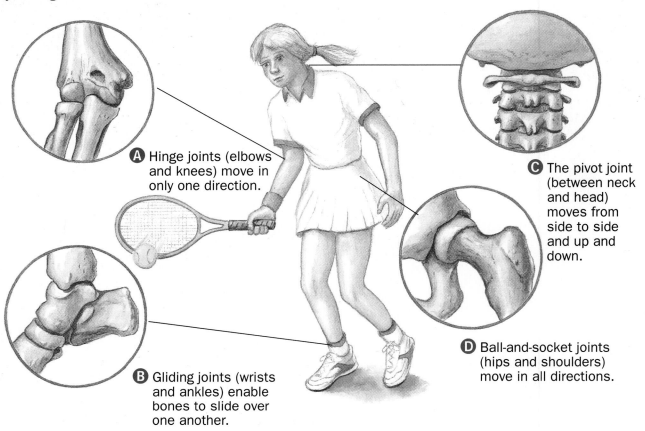

A Hinge joints (elbows and knees) move in only one direction.

B Gliding joints (wrists and ankles) enable bones to slide over one another.

C The pivot joint (between neck and head) moves from side to side and up and down.

D Ball-and-socket joints (hips and shoulders) move in all directions.

The Connectors

Movement is made possible by three kinds of tissues.

- **Cartilage** is a tough, flexible tissue that is similar to bone. It acts as a cushion between bones at a joint and protects the bones. Your nose and ears are made of cartilage.

- **Ligaments** (LI·guh·ments) are *strong cords of tissue that connect bones at the joints.* Ligaments hold the bones in place.

- **Tendons** (TEN·duhns) are *tough bands of tissue that attach your muscles to bones.* You can feel a large tendon called the Achilles tendon on the back of your leg just above your heel.

Problems of the Skeletal System

Problems of the skeletal system can result from accidents, viral infections, poor posture, and poor diet (see **Figure 10.17**).

in your journal

Look at snapshots of yourself taken when you were about six years old and at your present age. Which bones have grown longer? Which have changed shape in another way? Write your observations in your journal.

Figure 10.17
Problems of the Skeletal System

Disease or Disorder	Description	Treatment or Prevention
Fracture	Break in bone caused by falls or accidents; swelling, extreme pain	Bones are set and kept from moving, usually by enclosing in a cast
Dislocation	Bone pushed out of its joint, usually includes stretching or tearing of a ligament	Bones are reset into proper position and kept from moving
Sprain	Swelling of a joint caused by stretching or twisting ligaments	Rest; elevation of joint to reduce swelling
Arthritis	Swelling and stiffness of joints caused by wear and tear; usually affects older people	Pain relievers and exercise may help; if severe damage, may replace with artificial joints
Scoliosis	Curvature of spine	Exercise may help if mild; if severe, may need braces or surgery
Osteomyelitis	Bacterial infection of the bones	Medication
Osteoporosis	Bones become brittle and porous; associated with deficiencies of calcium, protein, and certain hormones	Regular exercise and a diet rich in calcium may prevent osteoporosis

Review — Lesson 4

Using complete sentences, answer the following questions on a separate sheet of paper.

Reviewing Terms and Facts

1. **Vocabulary** Explain the difference between *ligaments* and *tendons*.

2. **Identify** What two parts of your body are made up mostly of cartilage?

Thinking Critically

3. **Compare and Contrast** Describe the similarities and differences between fracturing, spraining, and dislocating your finger. Describe how each problem is treated.

4. **Give Examples** What are some ways you can act now to prevent osteoporosis later in life?

Applying Health Concepts

5. **Growth and Development** Working with a classmate, plan a way to construct a model skeleton. What materials would you use for the bones, cartilage, tendons, and ligaments? Describe the steps you would follow in making your model.

6. **Consumer Health** Do research to find out about artificial joints. Write a brief paper about these joints to present to the class.

Your Muscular System

This lesson will help you find answers to questions that teens often ask about their muscular system. For example:

▶ **How can I have stronger muscles?**

▶ **Why do my muscles sometimes ache?**

▶ **What causes muscles to cramp?**

Words to Know

muscular system
contract
extend
smooth muscle
skeletal muscle
cardiac muscle

Moving Body Parts

Your bones serve as a framework that gives your body shape and support. Your muscles allow you to move that framework. Your **muscular** (MUHS·kyuh·ler) **system** is *the group of tough tissues that make your body parts move.*

You control the muscles that move your body. However, your muscular system also includes muscles that you do not control. Many organs, such as your stomach and intestines, are lined with muscles that move without your being aware of them. Your heart is the strongest and, perhaps, most important muscle in your body.

How Muscles Work

You have over 600 major muscles in your body, and they all work the same way. Working in pairs, they **contract,** or *shorten,* and they **extend,** or *lengthen.* When one muscle in a pair contracts, the other muscle extends. This activity produces movement at a joint. **Figure 10.18** shows how your muscles work together to produce movement.

Figure 10.18
Muscles Working Together

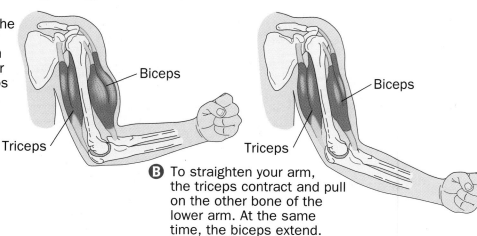

A To bend your arm, the biceps (flexors) contract and pull on a bone of your lower arm while the triceps (extensors) extend.

Biceps

Triceps

Biceps

Triceps

B To straighten your arm, the triceps contract and pull on the other bone of the lower arm. At the same time, the biceps extend.

The muscles in your body are responsible for moving your bones, pumping blood, moving food through your digestive system, and controlling the air that moves in and out of your lungs (see **Figure 10.19**).

in your journal

List your daily activities that include exercise. Identify the major muscles used in each activity.

Figure 10.19
The Muscular System

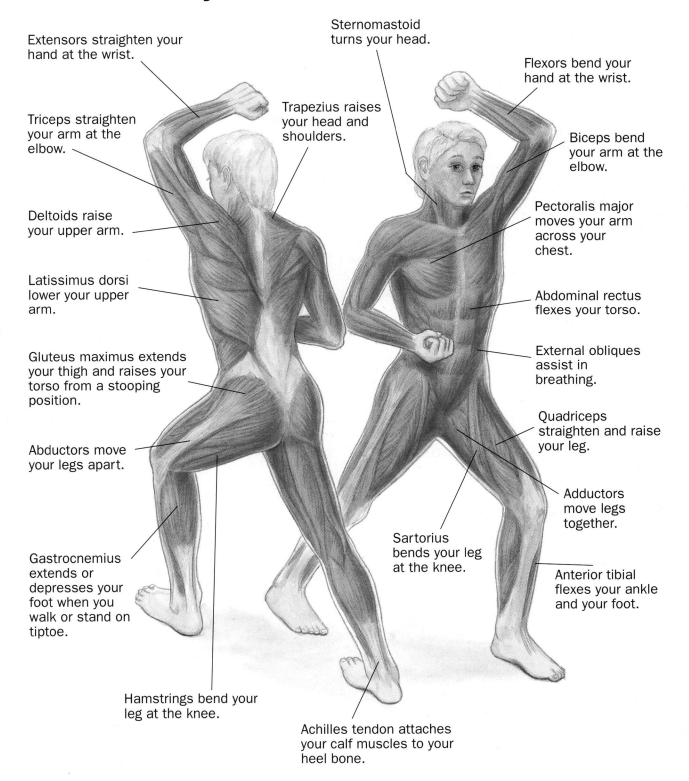

Extensors straighten your hand at the wrist.

Triceps straighten your arm at the elbow.

Deltoids raise your upper arm.

Latissimus dorsi lower your upper arm.

Gluteus maximus extends your thigh and raises your torso from a stooping position.

Abductors move your legs apart.

Gastrocnemius extends or depresses your foot when you walk or stand on tiptoe.

Hamstrings bend your leg at the knee.

Sternomastoid turns your head.

Trapezius raises your head and shoulders.

Flexors bend your hand at the wrist.

Biceps bend your arm at the elbow.

Pectoralis major moves your arm across your chest.

Abdominal rectus flexes your torso.

External obliques assist in breathing.

Quadriceps straighten and raise your leg.

Adductors move legs together.

Sartorius bends your leg at the knee.

Anterior tibial flexes your ankle and your foot.

Achilles tendon attaches your calf muscles to your heel bone.

Kinds of Muscle

Your muscular system consists of three different types of muscle tissue. Each type is designed to carry out certain tasks. **Figure 10.20** shows the three types.

Figure 10.20
Types of Muscle

Ⓐ Smooth muscles are *found in various organs in the body, such as the stomach and intestines.* You do not control these muscles. For example, once you have swallowed your food, smooth muscles move it through the digestive system.

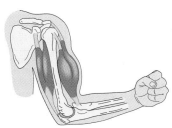

Ⓑ Skeletal muscles are *attached to bones.* They work with the bones of the skeleton to allow you to move. You control skeletal muscles. For example, you can make your arms and legs move whenever you wish. Skeletal muscles make up about 40 percent of your body weight.

Ⓒ Cardiac muscle is *a special type of muscle that is found only in the walls of the heart.* Controlled by your brain, Cardiac muscle constantly contracts and relaxes, causing your heart to pump blood to all parts of your body.

HEALTH LAB
Testing Your Strength and Endurance

*I*ntroduction: What kind of shape are you in? Perhaps you can easily lift a certain weight or do a few pull-ups. Such actions show that your muscles have strength, but how many times can you lift the weight before you are too tired? How many pull-ups can you do before you have to stop and rest? The length of time shows endurance.

The following activity will help you test your strength and endurance.

Objective: Determine the effects of regular exercise on your strength and endurance.

Materials and Method: You will need a horizontal bar and a sheet of paper. On the sheet of paper, prepare a data table like the one shown here. You will record the results of each exercise session in the table.

Grasp a bar with an overhand grip. Feet should not touch the floor and legs should hang straight. Begin by hanging with your arms straight. Pull your body up with a steady movement until your chin is over the bar and extend back down. Do as many pull-ups as you can. There is no time limit, and the pull-ups must be done with straight legs. Repeat this exercise twice a day, once in the morning and once in the afternoon, for five consecutive days.

Observation and Analysis: Compare your performance at the end of the five days with that of the first day. Do you see any improvement? Share your results with a group of your classmates. Think of an exercise routine to improve the strength and endurance of your legs and lower body. If you want to try your routine, get your teacher's approval before doing so.

DATA TABLE

DAY 1		DAY 2		DAY 3		DAY 4		DAY 5	
AM	PM	AM	PM	AM	PM	AM	PM	AM	PM

Problems of the Muscular System

Almost everyone has experienced sore muscles after overworking them. This is usually a temporary condition. With rest, sore muscles recover. Some muscular conditions are not temporary. **Figure 10.21** lists some of the disorders that can have an effect on the body's muscular system.

Teen Issues

No More Gym! **ACTIVITY!**

Some students think that physical education classes waste time. They want to be excused from them. Write an essay to explain what you think.

Figure 10.21
Problems of the Muscular System

Disorder	Description	Treatment
Pulled or torn muscle	Muscle torn from bone	Medical help
Strain	Soreness due to overwork	Rest; application of cold pack, then heat
Cramp	Muscle unable to relax; feels very tight and sore	Massage; application of heat
Tendinitis	Stretched or torn tendon; very painful	Varies according to severity; may range from rest and a cold pack to surgery
Muscular dystrophy	Most common type is an inherited disorder characterized by a weakening of the skeletal muscles; eventual inability to walk and stand	No known cure; muscle therapy as long as it is effective

Review

Lesson 5

Using complete sentences, answer the following questions on a separate sheet of paper.

Reviewing Terms and Facts

1. **Vocabulary** Define *cardiac muscle*. Use it in an original sentence.

2. **Synthesize** Explain how muscles help you move.

Thinking Critically

3. **Analyze** Why is the heart the most important muscle in your body?

4. **Evaluate** Why do muscles sometimes ache after you exercise?

Applying Health Concepts

5. **Growth and Development** Organize an exercise group. Have interested classmates meet at regular times to exercise. Ask your physical education teacher to suggest exercises to help the members of your group strengthen and tone their muscles.

6. **Consumer Health** Find out how aerobic exercises benefit your muscular system. If possible, observe or participate in an aerobics class at a local gym or health club. Write a report about the benefits of this popular fitness routine.

Teen HEALTH DIGEST

Teens Making a Difference

A Happy Ending

Anna Sun was ten years old when her five-year-old brother David was seriously hurt in an automobile accident. His legs were so badly injured that doctors feared he would never walk again.

David spent several weeks in the hospital, and Anna visited him every day. She was there when James Wilson, the physical therapist, came to talk to him. James described the different treatments and exercises they would be using to help David learn to walk.

Anna came to the therapy sessions every chance she had. At first, she just watched as James massaged David's leg muscles and bent and straightened the legs. As time passed, and David's legs got stronger, James encouraged Anna to help with David's therapy.

Finally, David was well enough to go home. He walked with a limp and needed a crutch, but he was walking! He returned each week for therapy sessions with James, and Anna helped him with his exercises at home.

The accident happened several years ago. Today, David plays on his school soccer team, running and kicking without pain. Anna is a senior in high school, preparing for college. You may have guessed her plans. She wants to become a physical therapist so she can help people in the same way that James helped her brother.

People at Work

A Labor of Love

Roger Washburn is a football coach at a small junior high school in Massachusetts. He doesn't coach for the money. He does it because there is no one else available to coach, and he thinks it is important to the students and to the school.

Roger was on the football team in high school and in college. He didn't play much, but he learned a great deal. Today he uses this experience to teach young people about the benefits of being physically fit and working with others to achieve a common goal.

He has some young people on his team who don't play much either, but they show up every day for practice. They do the calisthenics and the running. They, like their coach before them, know that what they are doing is important, and they are having a good time.

Look Before You Pay

One of the hottest businesses these days is physical fitness. It seems as if there is a health center or a "fitness" center on every block. People, including teens, are spending more and more time and money on equipment, clothing, and membership fees at health clubs.

Before you spend any of your (or your parents') hard-earned money to join a health club, there are a few features you should check.

- Are there any restrictions on the times when teens are allowed to use the club?

- Does the club have all the machines and equipment you need for the type of workouts you want to do?

- Are professional trainers on duty at all times during the hours of operation?

- Are there any "hidden" costs, such as towel rental or pool fees?

- If you are unable to get to the club for an extended period because of illness or other circumstances, will the club extend your membership to cover that time?

You may be able to think of other questions to be answered before you join a health club. The important thing is to get your money's worth and enjoy yourself.

No Bones About It

At the present time, about 25 million Americans suffer from osteoporosis. Most of them are women. This is a disorder in which the bones become porous and brittle. People with osteoporosis can break a bone simply by rolling over in bed!

Why should you worry about osteoporosis if it usually affects older people? Although osteoporosis shows up later in life, it could be starting in your bones right now, especially if your diet is lacking in calcium.

Once the bones start to deteriorate, the process cannot be reversed. Calcium supplements will not restore damaged bone. You need calcium all your life.

Studies show that young people between the ages of 12 and 19 take in about 900 milligrams of calcium each day in their diets. This is well below the daily recommended minimum of 1,200 to 1,500 milligrams a day. Check your diet, and be sure you get the calcium you need every day. The best source of calcium? Milk and milk products.

Myths and Realities

Doing It Naturally

Do you want to have a great-looking body? How would you like to double your muscle mass, maybe become the strongest person in your class or maybe the whole school? You can do it— and the best part is that you won't have to work all that hard!

Does this sound too good to be true? Well it is. Yet thousands of young people have been led to believe that taking anabolic steroids can help them meet these goals.

The truth is, taking steroids is dangerous. It is also illegal. The effects of steroid use on both males and females range from severe acne to serious liver and kidney damage. There is also increasing evidence that steroid use can become addictive and can lead to severe emotional problems.

So, if you'd like to be bigger and stronger and have a great-looking body, remember the old saying: "There's no substitute for hard work."

Your Digestive System

This lesson will help you find answers to questions teens often ask about their digestive system. For example:

▶ Why does my mouth water when I smell food cooking?

▶ Why does food have to be digested?

▶ What causes indigestion?

Words to Know

digestive system
digestion
saliva
stomach
small intestine
liver
gallbladder
pancreas
excretion
colon
kidney

The Body's Engine

Your **digestive** (dy·JES·tiv) **system** *changes the food you eat into nutrients that your cells can use.* Food is your body's fuel, or source of energy. The digestive system is something like a car's engine. The engine changes stored energy in gasoline into a form of energy that moves the car. The digestive system changes the energy stored in food into a form of energy the body can use to work properly and to grow and develop.

How the Digestive System Works

As food moves through your digestive system, it is chemically changed. It is changed into particles that can be absorbed into the bloodstream. *The process of changing food* in this way is called **digestion** (dy·JES·chuhn).

The Mouth and Teeth

Digestion begins in your mouth. There, your teeth cut and grind food into smaller pieces. At the same time, food is being mixed with **saliva** (suh·LY·vuh). Saliva is *a liquid produced by the salivary glands.* It consists of about 99 percent water and contains an enzyme that starts the digestion of carbohydrates. Saliva also moistens and softens food so it can be swallowed easily. **Figure 10.22** shows what happens when you swallow.

Figure 10.22
The Process of Swallowing

A **Before Swallowing**
Passages from the nose and throat to the trachea are open, allowing air to pass to the lungs.

B **During Swallowing**
Air passages are closed by two flaps of skin. The *uvula* (YOO·vyuh·luh) closes the airway to the nose. The epiglottis closes the opening to the trachea, or windpipe.

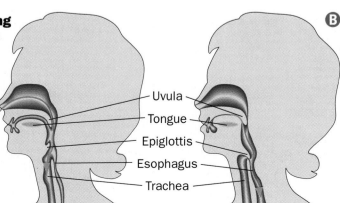

Uvula
Tongue
Epiglottis
Esophagus
Trachea

The Stomach and the Small Intestine

After being swallowed, your food enters your esophagus, a muscular tube that pushes food down into your stomach. The **stomach** is *a muscular organ in which food is held while digestion continues.* The muscular walls of the stomach churn the food and mix it with gastric juice, a mixture of acid and enzymes. Glands in the stomach wall produce gastric juice. The enzymes in the stomach begin the digestion of proteins.

Partially digested food moves from your stomach to your **small intestine,** which is *a coiled, tubelike organ about 20 feet long.* Most digestion takes place in the *duodenum* (doo·uh·DEE·nuhm), which is the first section of the small intestine. **Figure 10.23** shows the parts of the digestive system.

Figure 10.23
The Digestive System

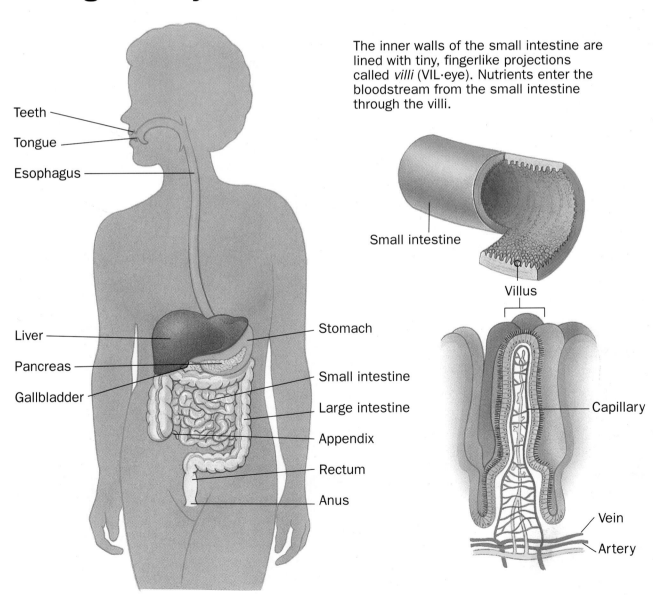

The inner walls of the small intestine are lined with tiny, fingerlike projections called *villi* (VIL·eye). Nutrients enter the bloodstream from the small intestine through the villi.

Teeth

Tongue

Esophagus

Liver

Pancreas

Gallbladder

Stomach

Small intestine

Large intestine

Appendix

Rectum

Anus

Small intestine

Villus

Capillary

Vein

Artery

Finger-Licking Good

Q: Why does my mouth water when I smell something good to eat?

A: Your smell sensors send a signal to your brain telling it that something tasty is nearby. Your brain then signals the salivary glands, telling them to get ready.

The Liver, Gallbladder, and Pancreas

Three other organs are included as part of the digestive system, even though no food passes through them. These organs—the liver, gallbladder, and pancreas—are shown in **Figure 10.24.** The pancreas is also part of your body's endocrine system (see the next lesson to learn more about that system).

■ Changes sugar into a form of starch that can be stored in the body until needed.

■ Helps maintain blood sugar levels.

■ Removes worn out red blood cells.

■ Changes toxic waste materials into less toxic substances.

■ Stores fat-soluble vitamins.

Figure 10.24
The Liver, Gallbladder, and Pancreas

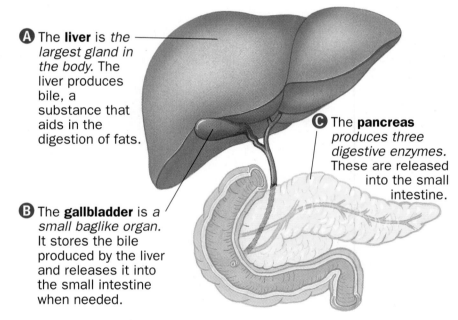

A The **liver** is *the largest gland in the body.* The liver produces bile, a substance that aids in the digestion of fats.

C The **pancreas** *produces three digestive enzymes.* These are released into the small intestine.

B The **gallbladder** is *a small baglike organ.* It stores the bile produced by the liver and releases it into the small intestine when needed.

Removing Wastes

Your body produces three kinds of wastes that need to be removed. Solid wastes are made up of foods that have not been digested. Liquid wastes and carbon dioxide gas are products formed by the activities of your cells.

Your skin removes some wastes through its pores when you sweat. Carbon dioxide is removed by your lungs when you exhale. The remaining wastes are removed by your liver, kidneys, bladder, and large intestine.

The Kidneys, Bladder, and Large Intestine

Many wastes produced in your body are dissolved in water. *The process of removing liquid wastes from the body* is called **excretion** (ek·SKREE·shuhn). **Figure 10.25** explains which parts of the body work together to remove these liquid wastes, which are called *urine,* from your body.

Water and undigested food that your body cannot use pass into your *large intestine,* which is also known as the **colon** (KOH·luhn). The lining of the colon absorbs almost all of the liquid. The solid wastes that remain are called *feces* (FEE·seez). When the large intestine is full, nerves signal muscles in the walls of the large intestine to contract. As a result, the feces pass out of the body through the *anus* (AY·nuhs).

Figure 10.25
The Process of Removing Wastes

in your journal

To have healthy kidneys you need to drink plenty of water—6 to 8 glasses a day. In your journal, keep track of the amount of water you drink each day. Are you getting enough?

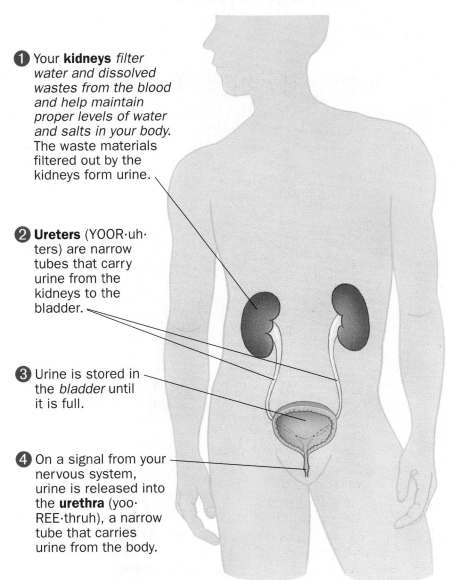

❶ Your **kidneys** *filter water and dissolved wastes from the blood and help maintain proper levels of water and salts in your body.* The waste materials filtered out by the kidneys form urine.

❷ **Ureters** (YOOR·uh·ters) are narrow tubes that carry urine from the kidneys to the bladder.

❸ Urine is stored in the *bladder* until it is full.

❹ On a signal from your nervous system, urine is released into the **urethra** (yoo·REE·thruh), a narrow tube that carries urine from the body.

Care of the Digestive System

The best way to care for your digestive system is to practice healthful eating habits. These include the following.

■ Eat a variety of foods from all food groups, especially foods that are low in fat and high in fiber.

■ Eat complete meals at regular intervals during the day. Eating breakfast is especially important.

■ Do not hurry through your meals. Take the time to relax and enjoy them rather than eating in a rush.

■ Eat enough food to satisfy your hunger. Do not stuff yourself.

■ Drink plenty of water. Your digestive system needs a lot of water to work properly.

■ Have regular dental checkups. Strong teeth are necessary to break food into smaller pieces to start digestion.

Problems of the Digestive System

Most digestive problems are related to eating habits and the kinds of foods eaten. They are usually temporary and minor. However, if the problems persist or if they are accompanied by a fever, a medical checkup may be necessary. **Figure 10.26** lists some of the problems of the digestive system.

Figure 10.26

Problems of the Digestive System

Disorder	Description	Treatment
Indigestion	Stomach too acidic, may be caused by eating too fast or too much or by spicy or acidic foods	Tablets to neutralize stomach acids
Diarrhea	Watery feces; caused by bacteria, virus, food poisoning, nutritional deficiencies	Usually clears up when cause has been eliminated
Ulcers	Sores on inner walls of stomach or small intestine	Medication, special diet, perhaps surgery
Cirrhosis	Destruction of liver tissue; caused by drinking too much alcohol	Medication and blood transfusions
Gallstones	Crystals in gallbladder; may block passage of bile to small intestine	Medication, special diet, perhaps surgery
Kidney stones	Crystals in kidney; may block passage of urine to bladder	Sound waves to break up large stones
Appendicitis	Inflammation of the appendix	Surgery
Hemorrhoids	Swelling of veins near opening of anus	Exercise, change in diet, perhaps surgery
Colon cancer	Uncontrolled growth of abnormal cells in large intestine	Chemotherapy, radiation, surgery

Review

Lesson 6

Using complete sentences, answer the following questions on a separate sheet of paper.

Reviewing Terms and Facts

1. **Vocabulary**   Describe the function of the stomach and what takes place in the stomach.

2. **List**   Identify six functions of the liver.

Thinking Critically

3. **Synthesize**   Trace the path of a meal through the digestive system.

4. **Analyze**   Why might a person take an antacid tablet for an upset stomach?

Applying Health Concepts

5. **Consumer Health**   In the past, it was assumed that the main cause of ulcers was negative emotions. Find a recent article in a magazine, health newsletter, or newspaper about the causes of ulcers. What is the current thinking about the main causes of ulcers? How are ulcers treated? Share your findings with the class.

6. **Consumer Health**   Do research on the role that water plays in maintaining health. Then survey your classmates about their water-drinking habits. Do you and your classmates generally drink the amount of water that is recommended?

Your Endocrine System

This lesson will help you find answers to questions that teens often ask about their endocrine system. For example:

▶ **Why does my heart beat faster when I am frightened or excited?**

▶ **Why am I shorter (or taller) than most of my classmates?**

▶ **Why do some people have diabetes?**

Words to Know

endocrine system
gland
pituitary gland

in your journal

Make a list of some of the major changes your body has undergone in the last year. Review the characteristics of adolescent growth on pages 211–213. Then, describe those changes that you consider to be secondary sex characteristics.

The Regulator

Your nervous system has been described as your body's control center. Your **endocrine** (EN·duh·krihn) **system** *works closely with your nervous system to regulate body functions.*

The endocrine system consists of several glands located throughout your body. A **gland** is *a group of cells, or an organ, that secretes a chemical substance.* The substances secreted by the endocrine glands are called *hormones.* Hormone comes from a Greek word that means "to set in motion." The endocrine glands secrete their hormones directly into your bloodstream, where they are carried to various parts of the body and activate these parts in specific ways. Some hormones are produced continually; others are produced only at certain times.

The Glands of the Endocrine System

Each hormone produced by the endocrine glands regulates one of your body's activities. **Figure 10.27** shows the locations of the endocrine glands and tells what each one does.

A gland in your endocrine system, the pituitary gland, controls your growth.

The endocrine glands work on signals from the brain or from other glands. The brain tracks the presence of substances in the blood. For example, when the brain senses too little thyroid hormone in the blood, it signals the pituitary. The pituitary, in turn, signals the thyroid, which releases more of the hormone.

Figure 10.27
The Endocrine System

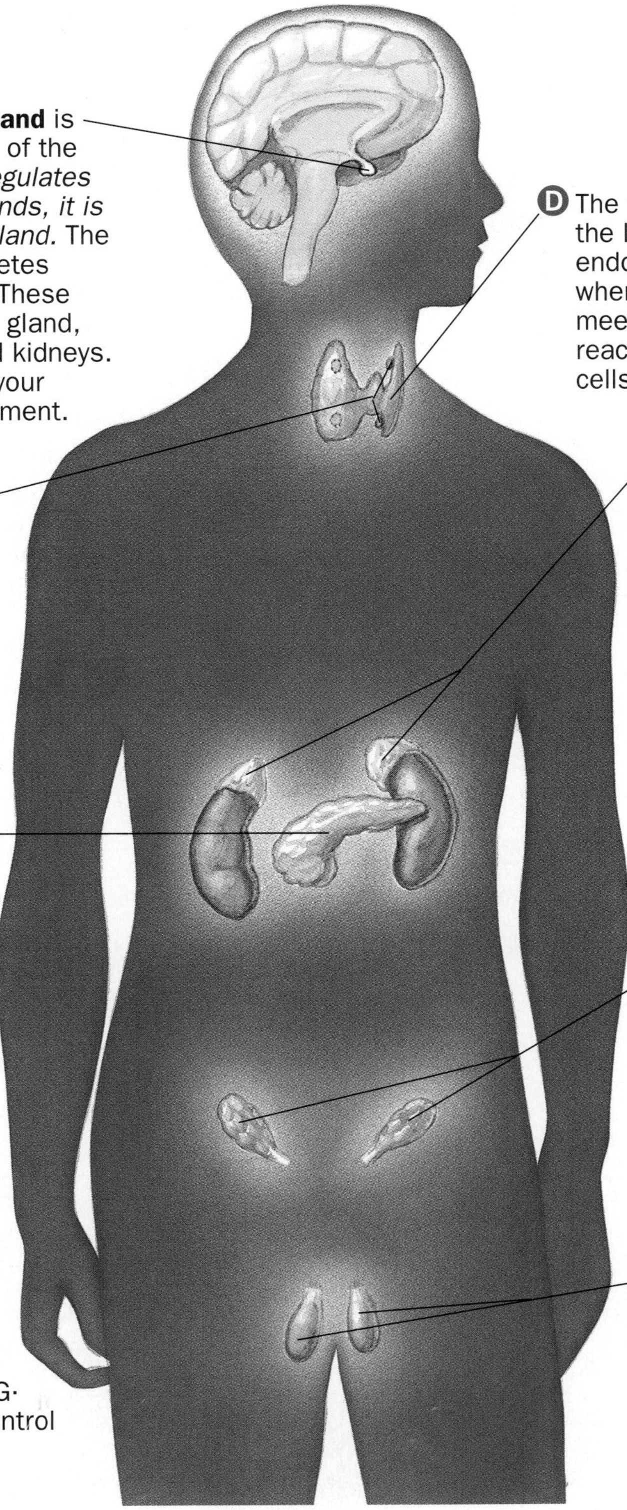

Small and Important

The pituitary gland is one of the smallest, but most important, glands in your body. It is about the size of an acorn.

A The **pituitary** (pi·TOO·i·tehr·ee) **gland** is located at the base of the brain. *Because it regulates other endocrine glands, it is called the master gland.* The pituitary gland secretes several hormones. These regulate the thyroid gland, adrenal glands, and kidneys. They also regulate your growth and development.

B The **parathyroid** (pehr·uh·THY·royd) **glands** regulate the distribution of certain minerals in your body.

C The **pancreas** (PAN·kree·uhs) is part of two body systems— the digestive system and the endocrine system. The pancreas is located behind the stomach and supplies the small intestine with digestive juice. The pancreas contains small clusters of cells called the **islets of Langerhans** (LAHNG·er·hahnz), which control blood sugar levels.

D The **thyroid** (THY·royd) **gland** is the largest gland in the endocrine system. It is located where the larynx and trachea meet. It regulates the chemical reactions of nutrients in the cells.

E The **adrenal** (uh·DREEN·uhl) **glands** are located on your kidneys. They secrete hormones that help the body maintain its levels of sodium and water, aid the digestive process, and control your body's response to emergencies.

F The **ovaries** (OH·vuh·reez) are the female reproductive glands. They control the development of secondary sex characteristics during adolescence.

G The **testes** (TES·teez) are the male reproductive glands. They control the development of secondary sex characteristics during adolescence.

Activities That Hormones Control

Medical experts are still uncertain about the functions of the pineal and thymus glands. The other glands do the following jobs.

- The pituitary gland controls physical growth; controls other glands; controls the movements of smooth muscles.

- The parathyroid regulates calcium and phosphorous levels.

- The islets of Langerhans regulate your blood sugar level.

- The thyroid gland controls the rate at which food is converted to energy in the cells.

- The adrenal glands control the body's water balance and use of carbohydrates, proteins, and fats; start the stress response.

- Ovaries and testes control secondary sex characteristics.

Good health habits are important for a healthy endocrine system, especially during the teen years.

The Stress Response

Whenever you are excited or anxious, your body is under stress. Your adrenal glands then release the hormone *adrenaline* (uh·DRE·nuhl·in). **Figure 10.28** shows how adrenaline prepares your body to respond to stress. This response ends when the cause of the stress is gone, or when your body slows down because it cannot maintain the high level of activity.

The stress response can be harmful if it goes on too long or happens too often. You can avoid harm caused by the stress response by learning to manage stress.

Figure 10.28
The Effects of Stress on the Body

Various changes occur as the body responds to stress. Some of them are listed here.

Body Part	Under Stress	After Stress
Brain	Blood flow to brain increases	Blood flow to brain decreases
Sweat glands	Sweat production increases	Return to normal
Lungs	Air passageways expand	Air passageways contract
Circulatory system	Heart rate increases; blood pressure rises; blood to skeletal muscles increases	Returns to normal
Digestive system	Digestion slows	Digestion increases
Adrenal gland	Releases adrenaline	Returns to normal
Liver and gallbladder	Gallbladder stimulates liver to release sugar	Return to normal

Disorders of the Endocrine System

Most endocrine disorders are related to the production of a hormone—too much or too little. **Figure 10.29** describes some disorders of the endocrine system.

Figure 10.29
Disorders of the Endocrine System

Disorder	Description
Diabetes mellitus	Loss of nutrients and energy due to inadequate insulin production by the islets of Langerhans; symptoms include lack of energy, extreme thirst, and frequent urination
Goiter	Enlargement of the thyroid gland; visible as a swelling of the lower neck; caused by too little iodine
Growth extremes	Caused by the release of abnormal amounts of growth hormones; too little growth hormone causes dwarfism (results in a very small person); too much growth hormone causes gigantism (results in a very large person)

Q & A ?

A Fishy Solution

Q: I don't think I eat foods that contain iodine. Why don't I have a goiter?

A: You don't need much iodine in your diet. Since seawater contains iodine, eating seafood can provide all the iodine needed to keep your thyroid healthy. Also, the table salt you use may have small amounts of iodine added.

Review

Lesson 7

Using complete sentences, answer the following questions on a separate sheet of paper.

Reviewing Terms and Facts

1. **Vocabulary** What is a *gland?* Explain the role of glands in the endocrine system.

2. **Identify** What gland is part of the endocrine system and also plays an important role in the digestive system?

Thinking Critically

3. **Explain** What is the largest gland? Where is it located? What is its function?

4. **Analyze** Why is caring for your endocrine system especially important during the teen years?

Applying Health Concepts

5. **Personal Health** Think of a situation when you experienced a stress response. Describe what caused the response, the changes your body underwent, and how the situation was resolved.

6. **Health of Others** There are two main forms of diabetes—juvenile and adult. Do research to find out how these two types of diabetes and their treatments differ. Make a chart comparing the two types. Share your findings in class.

Your Reproductive System

This lesson will help you find answers to questions that teens often ask about their reproductive system. For example:

▶ **What happens when a male ejaculates?**

▶ **Why do females menstruate and males do not?**

▶ **At what age do females begin to menstruate?**

Words to Know

reproductive
   system
sperm
menstruation
menstrual cycle

The Producer of New Life

Reproduction is the process by which life is maintained from one generation to the next. All human life results from the union of two cells, one from the mother and one from the father. These cells are produced in the **reproductive** (ree·pruh·DUHK·tiv) **system.** The human reproductive system *consists of body organs that are involved in the production of offspring.* **Figure 10.30** shows the cells produced by the male and female reproductive systems.

Unlike other human body systems, organs in the male and female reproductive systems are not the same. As a result, each system requires different care. In addition, the potential problems of each system are different.

Figure 10.30
Cells of the Reproductive Systems

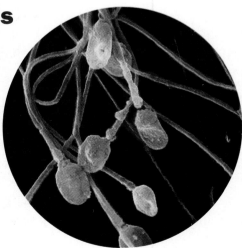

A The sperm in this photograph are magnified. Approximately 400 million sperm are present in the semen released during a single ejaculation.

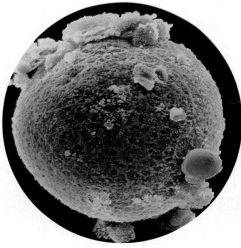

B The egg cell in this photograph is magnified. At birth, a female has hundreds of thousands of immature egg cells in her ovaries.

The Male Reproductive System

The male reproductive system produces **sperm.** Sperm are *male reproductive cells.* These cells join with female reproductive cells to produce new life. The union of male and female reproductive cells is called fertilization. Males begin to produce sperm when they reach puberty, usually between the ages of 12 and 15.

The male reproductive system includes the different organs involved in the production and storage of sperm and the release of sperm to the outside. **Figure 10.31** shows the male reproductive organs and describes what they do.

Sperm are produced in the testes and stored in the epididymis. When they leave the epididymis, they travel to the vas deferens. There they mix with seminal (SE·mi·nuhl) fluid produced by the seminal vesicles, the prostate glands, and the Cowper's glands. The mixture of sperm and fluids is called semen (SEE·muhn). The action that forces the semen through the urethra and out of the body is called ejaculation (i·ja·kyuh·LAY·shuhn).

in your journal

How might knowing the correct names for the parts of your reproductive system help when you have a medical checkup? Write your answer in your journal.

Figure 10.31
The Male Reproductive System

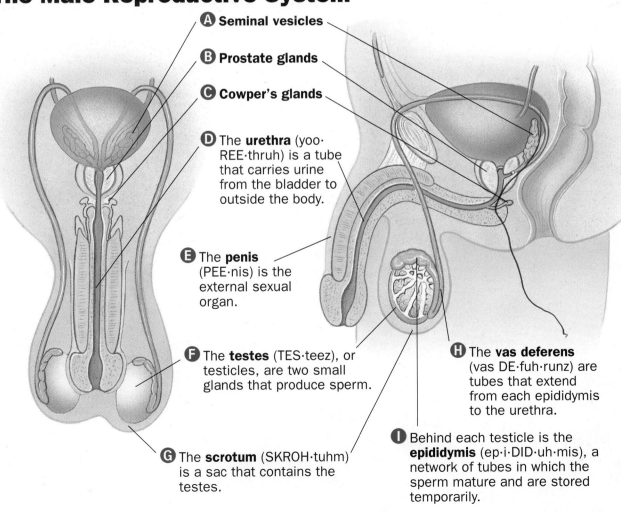

A **Seminal vesicles**

B **Prostate glands**

C **Cowper's glands**

D The **urethra** (yoo·REE·thruh) is a tube that carries urine from the bladder to outside the body.

E The **penis** (PEE·nis) is the external sexual organ.

F The **testes** (TES·teez), or testicles, are two small glands that produce sperm.

G The **scrotum** (SKROH·tuhm) is a sac that contains the testes.

H The **vas deferens** (vas DE·fuh·runz) are tubes that extend from each epididymis to the urethra.

I Behind each testicle is the **epididymis** (ep·i·DID·uh·mis), a network of tubes in which the sperm mature and are stored temporarily.

The Female Reproductive System

The female reproductive system has three important functions. They are to produce and store egg cells, to allow fertilization to occur, and to nourish and protect the fertilized egg until it is ready to live outside the female's body. **Figure 10.32** shows the female reproductive organs and describes what they do.

Figure 10.32

The Female Reproductive System

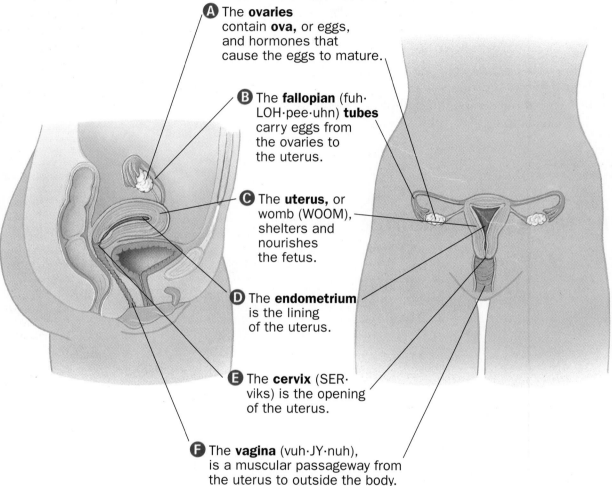

A The **ovaries** contain **ova,** or eggs, and hormones that cause the eggs to mature.

B The **fallopian** (fuh·LOH·pee·uhn) **tubes** carry eggs from the ovaries to the uterus.

C The **uterus,** or womb (WOOM), shelters and nourishes the fetus.

D The **endometrium** is the lining of the uterus.

E The **cervix** (SER·viks) is the opening of the uterus.

F The **vagina** (vuh·JY·nuh), is a muscular passageway from the uterus to outside the body.

The Menstrual Cycle

As a female reaches puberty, hormones cause egg cells to mature. The ovaries begin to release one mature egg cell each month. As a result of this process, called *ovulation* (ahv·vuh·LAY·shuhn), the uterus thickens in preparation to receive and begin to nourish a fertilized egg. If fertilization does not occur, the thickened lining breaks down. This material is then expelled from the female's body. *The flow of the lining material out of the female body* is called **menstruation** (men·struh·WAY·shuhn).

Menstruation usually lasts from 5 to 7 days. The **menstrual** (MEN·struhl) **cycle** is *the time from one menstruation to another.* A cycle usually is about 28 days, but it may vary from one female to another. In addition, stress or illness may affect the hormones that control the menstrual cycle. **Figure 10.33** shows what happens during the menstrual cycle.

Most girls begin menstruation between the ages of 9 and 16. For the first year or two, the ovulation and menstrual cycles may not be regular. That is not a cause for concern. The menstrual cycle normally varies greatly from one female to another. Some girls experience cramps, nausea, or dizziness when they menstruate. Some always have cycles of the same length. Others have irregular cycles.

Figure 10.33
The Typical Menstrual Cycle

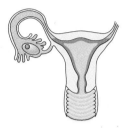 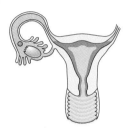 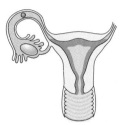 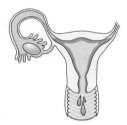

❶ On days 1 through 13 of the cycle, even while menstruation is occurring, a new egg cell is maturing inside the ovary.

❷ On day 14 of the cycle, ovulation occurs and the mature egg is released into one of the fallopian tubes.

❸ From day 15 through day 20, the egg travels through the fallopian tube.

❹ On day 21 the egg enters the uterus. After 7 days, if the egg has not been fertilized, menstruation begins.

Fertilization

When a male's sperm enters a female's vagina, it travels to a fallopian tube. Fertilization may occur, especially if there is a mature egg waiting. A sperm cell unites with an egg cell to produce a fertilized egg, and small hairs lining the fallopian tube move the egg through the tube into the uterus.

The fertilized egg attaches itself to the wall of the uterus. There it begins to grow and develop into a baby. The uterus has several layers of tissue and a rich supply of blood to nourish the baby during its months of development. The mother's body provides the baby with food and oxygen as it develops.

After about 40 weeks in the uterus, the baby is ready to be born. At that time, muscles in the wall of the uterus begin to contract. These contractions open the cervix. The baby is pushed out of the uterus through the cervix. It passes through the vagina until it is outside the mother's body.

Caring for Your Reproductive System

You can care for your reproductive system by taking the following actions.

Taking regular showers is one way to care for your reproductive system.

- Bathe or shower daily to keep your external reproductive organs clean.

- Males should avoid underwear or clothing that is too tight. They should wear protective gear when playing contact sports. Males should do self-examinations of their testes to check for lumps, swelling, or soreness and have regular physical checkups. **Figure 10.34** lists some problems of the male reproductive system.

- For females, cleanliness is especially important during menstruation. Sanitary pads and tampons should be changed often. Females should have regular checkups by a *gynecologist* (gy·nuh·KAH·lah·jist), a physician who specializes in the care of the female reproductive system. Females should also do breast self-examinations. **Figure 10.35** lists some problems of the female reproductive system.

Figure 10.34
Problems of the Male Reproductive System

Disorder	Description	Treatment or Prevention
Testicular or prostate cancer	Uncontrolled cell growth that destroys glands and surrounding tissue	Surgery is usually required; self-testing and regular checkups can identify these diseases in early stages
Inguinal hernia	Part of the intestine pushes into the scrotum; caused by improperly lifting heavy objects	Surgery to repair weak spot in the abdominal wall; avoid lifting heavy objects
Sterility	Inability to produce healthy sperm in sufficient numbers to reproduce; caused by exposure to certain drugs or illness	No known cure
Enlarged prostate gland	A common problem associated with aging	Surgery

Figure 10.35

Problems of the Female Reproductive System

Disorder	Description	Treatment or Prevention
Premenstrual syndrome	Physical and emotional changes before menstruation; headaches, moodiness, irritability	May be relieved by regular exercise and changes in diet
Toxic shock syndrome	Rare, but serious bacterial infection associated with tampon use	Change tampons every 4–8 hours; consult package instructions or physician about proper use of tampons
Infertility	Inability to reproduce due to blockage in fallopian tubes or failure of ovaries to produce eggs	May be corrected by surgery or hormone treatment
Vaginitis	Infection of vagina; pain, itching, and discharge	Medication
Ovarian cysts	Growths on outside of ovary	Surgery to remove large cysts
Cancer	Can affect breasts, ovaries, uterus, cervix	Surgery, radiation, chemotherapy; self-examinations and check-ups can spot it early

Review

Lesson 8

Using complete sentences, answer the following questions on a separate sheet of paper.

Reviewing Terms and Facts

1. **Vocabulary**   Define *menstruation.* Use it in an original sentence.

2. **List**   Identify common disorders of the male and female reproductive system.

Thinking Critically

3. **Compare and Contrast**   What happens if an egg is not fertilized? What happens if it is fertilized?

4. **Review**   What are the three important functions of the female reproductive system?

Applying Health Terms

5. **Consumer Health**   Pretend you are the author of a best-selling book about caring for the male or female reproductive system. Write a brief overview describing how the book can help improve the reader's chances for having and maintaining a healthy reproductive system.

6. **Health of Others**   With a partner, write a skit in which you describe a discussion you might have with a younger brother or sister about growing up. Include questions and answers about the body changes to expect when he or she reaches puberty.

Chapter Summary

▶ Your nervous system is your body's control center. It controls all of your body's actions. (Lesson 1)

▶ Your nervous system consists of your brain, spinal cord, and nerves. (Lesson 1)

▶ The work of the nervous system is done by neurons, which carry messages to and from all parts of your body. (Lesson 1)

▶ Unlike other cells in your body, nerve cells do not repair themselves. (Lesson 1)

▶ The best way to maintain your nervous system is to avoid head, neck, and back injuries. (Lesson 1)

▶ Your circulatory system is your body's transport system. It delivers essential materials to the body cells and removes wastes from them. (Lesson 2)

▶ The circulatory system includes the heart, blood vessels, and blood. (Lesson 2)

▶ The heart pumps blood through two major pathways. Pulmonary circulation moves blood from the heart to the lungs and back. Systemic circulation moves blood to and from all parts of the body except the lungs. (Lesson 2)

▶ Special white blood cells fight disease and infection by attacking germs that enter the body. (Lesson 2)

▶ Your respiratory system provides your body with the oxygen it needs and rids your body of the waste carbon dioxide. (Lesson 3)

▶ The lungs are the main organs of the respiratory system. (Lesson 3)

▶ Your skeletal system is your body's framework. It gives your body shape, structure, and protection. (Lesson 4)

▶ Various types of joints and connective tissue enable your body to move. (Lesson 4)

▶ Your muscular system works with your skeletal system to move your body. (Lesson 5)

▶ Working in pairs, muscles contract and extend to help you move. (Lesson 5)

▶ Muscles also help move food and nutrients through your digestive system and blood through your heart and blood vessels. (Lesson 5)

▶ Your digestive system changes the food you eat into nutrients your body can use. (Lesson 6)

▶ Your digestive system also removes solid wastes, or undigested food, from your body by a process called excretion. (Lesson 6)

▶ Most digestive problems are related to eating habits and the kinds of foods eaten. (Lesson 6)

▶ Your endocrine system controls and regulates many important activities of your body. (Lesson 7)

▶ Hormones released by the endocrine glands activate certain body processes. (Lesson 7)

▶ The organs of your reproductive system carry out the actions necessary for people to produce offspring and maintain life from one generation to the next. (Lesson 8)

▶ Unlike other body systems, the reproductive systems for males and females are different. (Lesson 8)

▶ Menstruation is the monthly process by which a mature egg and the lining of the uterus are discharged from a female's body. (Lesson 8)

▶ To care for your body systems, you should practice good health habits. These include eating a well-balanced diet, getting plenty of rest, exercising regularly, and avoiding activities that may put you at risk. (Lessons 1 through 8)

Using Health Terms

On a separate sheet of paper, write the vocabulary term that best matches each definition given below.

1. The body's main control center including the brain and spinal cord (Lesson 1)

2. The cells that carry messages to and from all parts of your body (Lesson 1)

3. The system that delivers essential materials to body cells and removes waste materials from cells (Lesson 2)

4. Another name for the circulatory system (Lesson 2)

5. The cells that help your body fight disease and infection (Lesson 2)

6. The smallest blood vessels (Lesson 2)

7. The system that consists of the organs that provide the body with a continuous supply of oxygen and rid the body of carbon dioxide (Lesson 3)

8. The tiny air sacs in your body where oxygen and carbon dioxide are exchanged (Lesson 3)

9. Your bones, joints, and connective tissue (Lesson 4)

10. The type of joint that allows movement in all directions (Lesson 4)

11. The tissue that attaches muscles to bones (Lesson 4)

12. The group of tough tissues that makes your body parts move (Lesson 5)

13. Muscle tissue that is found in the heart (Lesson 5)

14. The system that changes food into nutrients (Lesson 6)

15. Fingerlike projections in the small intestine (Lesson 6)

16. The organ that stores and releases bile (Lesson 6)

17. The system that works closely with the nervous system to regulate body functions (Lesson 7)

18. The gland that controls the body's response to emergencies (Lesson 7)

19. The group of organs involved in the production of offspring (Lesson 8)

20. The male reproductive glands (Lesson 8)

Reviewing Main Ideas

Using complete sentences, answer the following questions on a separate sheet of paper.

1. What are the two sections of your nervous system? (Lesson 1)

2. Which part of the brain—the cerebrum, the cerebellum, or the brain stem—controls each of the following actions: memory, breathing, speaking, balance, posture, digestion? (Lesson 1)

3. Which of the following are infectious diseases that affect the nervous system: brain tumor, rabies, meningitis? (Lesson 1)

4. Identify four materials transported by the circulatory system. (Lesson 2)

5. List the three types of blood vessels. (Lesson 2)

6. What happens when the flow of blood to the heart stops? (Lesson 2)

7. What function does the diaphragm have in the breathing process? (Lesson 3)

8. What substance is passed from the blood to the alveoli in your lungs? What substance is passed from the alveoli to the blood? (Lesson 3)

9. Describe the treatment and prevention for the most common respiratory diseases, flu, and colds. (Lesson 3)

10. What are two jobs of the bones? (Lesson 4)

11. What jobs do cartilage and ligaments perform? (Lesson 4)

12. List four types of joints and give an example of each. (Lesson 4)

13. What is the primary job of the tendons? (Lesson 4)

14. What are the three types of muscle? What does each type do? (Lesson 5)

15. What is a muscle strain? (Lesson 5)

16. What is saliva? What are two ways saliva assists in digestion? (Lesson 6)

17. How does gastric juice aid digestion? (Lesson 6)

18. In which part of your digestive system does most digestion take place? (Lesson 6)

19. Why is the pituitary gland sometimes called the *master gland?* (Lesson 7)

20. Which gland controls your physical growth? (Lesson 7)

21. How does adrenaline help the body deal with stress? (Lesson 7)

22. What are the islets of Langerhans and what do they do? (Lesson 7)

23. What causes dwarfism and gigantism? (Lesson 7)

24. What is the primary function of the uterus? (Lesson 8)

25. What happens during the menstrual cycle? (Lesson 8)

26. How can the risk of reproductive organ cancers be reduced? (Lesson 8)

Thinking Critically

Using complete sentences, answer the following questions on a separate sheet of paper.

1. Explain Why is it important to take special care of your nervous system? (Lesson 1)

2. Compare and Contrast Differentiate between the two parts of the peripheral nervous system. (Lesson 1)

3. Explain What is the difference between pulmonary and systemic circulation? (Lesson 2)

4. Analyze Why might inactive people have problems with their circulatory system? (Lesson 2)

5. Apply How does aerobic exercise help your respiratory and circulatory systems? (Lesson 3)

6. Classify Which of the following are parts of the respiratory system: cerebrum, trachea, alveoli, lymph nodes, bronchi? (Lesson 3)

7. Synthesize How would your ability to move change if your backbone was a single bone instead of 24 separate bones? (Lesson 4)

8. Hypothesize Which person is in greater danger of breaking a bone—an 8-year-old girl or an 85-year-old woman? Explain your answer. (Lesson 4)

9. Compare and Contrast How are smooth muscle and skeletal muscle alike and different? (Lesson 5)

10. Recommend Suggest some ways to avoid or relieve muscle cramps. (Lesson 5)

11. Hypothesize How does eating meals in a relaxed manner help digestion? (Lesson 6)

12. Synthesize Why are regular dental checkups an important part of maintaining a healthy digestive system? (Lesson 6)

13. Recommend Suggest some ways to care for your endocrine system. (Lesson 7)

14. Analyze What is the relationship between the brain and the endocrine system? (Lesson 7)

15. Recommend List some ways in which males can protect their reproductive organs. (Lesson 8)

16. Hypothesize Why does a female not have a menstrual cycle when she is pregnant? (Lesson 8)

Your Action Plan

Make an action plan to improve your physical health. First, set a goal. Review your journal entries for this chapter. What do they tell you about how well you take care of your body? Perhaps you don't eat meals at regular times or you don't get enough exercise. Select an attainable goal. For instance, becoming the strongest student in school is probably less realistic than increasing the amount of weight you can lift by 20 percent.

Once you have selected your long-term goal, choose short-term goals to help you reach it. If your long-term goal is to increase the weight you can lift, a short-term goal might be to join a weight-lifting class. Another might be to practice at home. Establish a schedule for accomplishing your short-term goals. For example, "By the end of the first week, I will be lifting weights five minutes a day." Check your schedule to keep yourself on track.

Building Your Portfolio

1. Clip articles from magazines or newspapers that discuss one or another body system. Possible topics include new medical treatments and people who lead active, productive lives despite a disease or disorder. Share your scrapbook with the class.

2. Do research on organ transplants. Find out which organs can be transplanted successfully and how problems of infection and rejection are handled. Learn about the availability of organs and how long people have to wait to receive a transplant. Find out about organ donor programs in your area. Write a report about your findings.

In Your Home and Community

1. Many hospitals provide lectures, classes, pamphlets, and other information about caring for your body. They also provide free preventive medical tests to check such things as blood pressure and cholesterol levels. Make a bulletin board to display the pamphlets, class listings, and other information.

2. Work with classmates at home to write a handbook or prepare posters that describe steps people can take on a regular basis to keep their bodies healthy. Include information about personal hygiene, the benefits of rest and relaxation, a healthy diet, and regular exercise. Get permission to distribute the handbooks to other classes or display the posters in the hallway. Share the information with your family, especially younger brothers and sisters.

Chapter 11
Communicable Diseases

Student Expectations

After reading this chapter, you should be able to:

1. Explain how to prevent the spread of disease.
2. Describe the body's defenses against germs.
3. Compare and contrast common communicable diseases.
4. Explain what sexually transmitted diseases are and the best way to avoid getting them.
5. Explain what AIDS is and how it can be prevented.

I'm a guy who really enjoys school. In fact, I haven't missed a single day of school this year. There are only two more weeks of school and, until last night, I thought I'd end up with a perfect attendance record for the year. That's when I came down with a cold. Mom said I should stay home from school unless I felt better in the morning. She said I needed the rest—and my friends didn't need my germs.

This morning, I feel worse. I'm hot, my throat hurts, and my nose is stuffy. Even though I feel rotten, I still want to go to school to keep my attendance record intact. On the other hand, what if I get worse and spread my germs? I wish I knew more about treating colds and preventing others from getting them.

in Your Journal

Read the account on this page. Has something like this ever happened to you or to a friend? Do you, too, wish you knew more about communicable diseases? Start your private journal entries on communicable diseases by answering these questions:

► What diseases do you think you can catch from others?

► What do you think you can do to help protect yourself from catching diseases when your friends are sick?

► What do you think you can do to help protect your friends from catching what you have when you are sick?

► When you are sick, what, if anything, do you do to get better?

When you reach the end of the chapter, you will use your journal entries to make an action plan.

Preventing the Spread of Disease

This lesson will help you find answers to questions that teens often ask about the spread of disease. For example:

▶ **What are germs?**

▶ **How are germs spread?**

▶ **How can I avoid picking up or passing on germs that cause disease?**

Words to Know

disease
communicable
  disease
germs
infection
bacteria
virus
rickettsias
fungi
protozoa
contagious period

What Is Disease?

When you are healthy, you feel good both physically and mentally. Sometimes, though, disease gets in the way of feeling good. A **disease** is *an illness that affects the proper functioning of the body or mind.* **Communicable** (kuh·MYOO·ni·kuh·buhl) **diseases** are *those that can be passed from one person to another.* Other diseases are not spread by contact with other people. Those diseases are caused by how people live, conditions they are born with, or environmental hazards. They are called noncommunicable diseases and are discussed in Chapter 12.

What Causes Communicable Diseases?

Communicable diseases are caused by *organisms so small you can see them only through a microscope.* These are called **germs.** When germs invade the body and its cells, they grow, reproduce, and often produce poisonous waste products. The result is an **infection** (in·FEK·shuhn), which damages or destroys body cells. **Figure 11.1** explains the difference between a communicable disease and a noncommunicable disease with similar symptoms.

Figure 11.1
The Difference Between Communicable and Noncommunicable Diseases

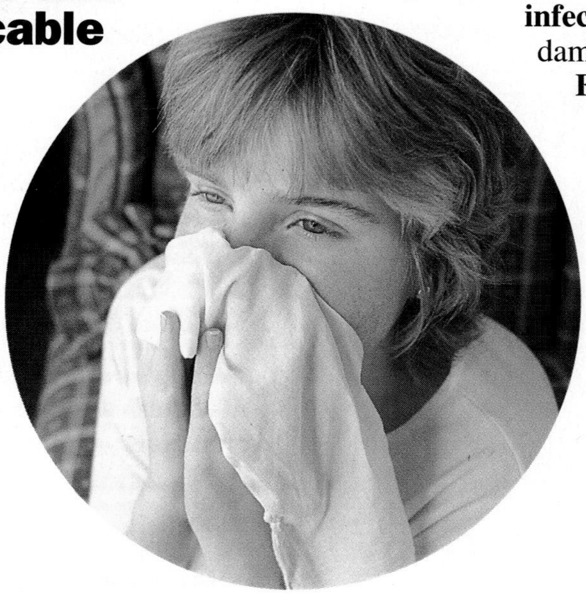

Ⓐ If your runny nose, watery eyes, and sore throat are caused by a cold, you have a communicable disease.

Ⓑ If your runny nose, watery eyes, and sore throat are caused by an allergy, you have a noncommunicable disease.

Types of Germs

The types of germs that cause communicable diseases include *bacteria, viruses, rickettsias, fungi,* and *protozoa*. Viruses are the most common cause of human communicable diseases. They cause such diseases as the common cold and the flu. They also cause some diseases, like AIDS, that can kill people. Viruses and bacteria together account for most illness in the United States. The following list describes the types of disease-causing organisms.

- **Bacteria** (bak·TIR·ee·uh) are *tiny one-celled organisms that grow virtually everywhere.* Bacteria can be harmless or harmful. There are three types of bacteria: cocci, bacilli, and spirilla.

- **Viruses** (VY·ruh·sez) are *the smallest and simplest form of life.* Many viruses are harmful to humans.

- **Rickettsias** (ri·KET·see·uhs) are *small bacteria that are spread by the bites of insects, such as ticks and lice.*

- **Fungi** (FUHN·jy) are *simple life forms that are unable to make their own food.*

- **Protozoa** (proh·tuh·ZOH·uh) are *simple, animal-like organisms.*

Countless bacteria live in the world around you—and even inside you. Most bacteria do not cause disease. In fact, many are helpful. Bacteria that live in your intestines help you digest food. Bacteria become harmful when they go places where they do not belong. Bacteria that is harmless in your mouth can enter your middle ear. Once there, they can cause an ear infection. To grow, bacteria need a food supply, warmth, and moisture. The body—which provides these three needs—makes an ideal home for them.

There are many different types of germs. Some common ones such as the bacteria *cocci* can cause such diseases as an abscess, gonorrhea, bacterial pneumonia, strep throat, and scarlet fever. *Bacilli* are responsible for botulism (food poisoning), diphtheria, tetanus, tuberculosis, whooping cough, and leprosy. *Spirilla* can cause polio, syphilis, and Lyme disease.

Viruses are very specialized. Some attack only certain kinds of animals. Some attack only certain cells of animals' bodies. The rabies virus, for instance, only affects the nervous system. Viruses are responsible for AIDS, measles, chicken pox, colds, the flu, mumps, polio, viral pneumonia, and mononucleosis.

Rickettsias are found in lice, mites, and ticks. They enter the human body when a person is bitten by an infected animal. Rocky Mountain spotted fever is caused by rickettsias. People who enjoy camping or hiking in the woods should guard against tick bites.

Fungi that attack the body often live in the hair, nails, and skin. Athlete's foot and ringworm are two diseases caused by fungi. Athlete's foot affects the feet. Ringworm appears on other body parts.

Many protozoa are harmless, but some cause disease. Malaria is caused by protozoa that live in certain kinds of mosquitoes. If an infected mosquito bites a person, the person will be infected.

Did You Know?

How Small Are Germs?

Most germs can be seen only with a microscope. In fact, viruses are so small they are visible only with a special microscope called an electron microscope. Until the electron microscope was invented in 1932, no one had ever seen a virus. Bacteria were first seen when the light microscope was invented. Do you know what year that happened?

Science Connection

Beneficial Bacteria

Many bacteria are harmless and some are even essential for life. Without intestinal bacteria, for example, we could not digest food. Even harmless bacteria, however, can cause infection if they go where they don't belong. Bacteria from the intestines, for example, can cause infection if they get into the urinary tract or the bloodstream.

How Germs Are Spread

Germs can enter the body in four ways. Each type of germ is spread in one of these ways.

■ **Close contact with a person who has the germ.** You can breathe in germs if someone coughs or sneezes near you. The germs travel in water droplets in the air, you inhale them, and they enter your body. Diseases such as colds, flu, measles, and tuberculosis can be spread this way. You also can get colds and other communicable diseases when you share eating utensils and drinking glasses.

■ **Direct contact with a person who has the germ.** You can pick up germs on your hands and skin through direct contact with others. You also can pick up germs through sexual contact. This is the way people get diseases such as AIDS, gonorrhea, syphilis, and herpes.

■ **Contact with animals.** You can get germs if you are bitten by some insects and other animals. Mosquito bites spread malaria, for example. Bites from animals infected by rabies spread that disease. Tick bites spread two serious diseases—Rocky Mountain spotted fever and Lyme disease.

■ **Other contacts.** Germs can enter your body if you drink water or eat food that contains them. Food that is improperly stored or undercooked is dangerous for this reason. Giardia (an intestinal infection) comes from contaminated water, for example, and botulism from spoiled food.

How to Prevent the Spread of Disease

Practicing good health habits keeps you strong and better able to resist germs. Practicing good health behaviors helps prevent the spread of germs between you and others.

Practice Good Health Habits

■ Eat a balanced diet.

■ Get plenty of rest.

■ Exercise regularly.

■ Bathe or shower daily to keep your skin and hair clean.

■ Avoid substances and behaviors that can harm your health.

Practice Good Health Behaviors to Protect Yourself

- Prepare food in safe ways. For instance, cook it thoroughly to kill bacteria.

- Store unused food quickly and properly.

- Do not use the same utensils or drinking glasses as someone else.

- Wear the right clothing and protective gear for your activities.

- Avoid having sex to prevent sexually transmitted diseases.

- Make sure your vaccination schedule is up to date for diseases that have *vaccines* (see Lesson 2).

Practice Good Health Behaviors to Protect Others

- If you are sick, find out about the **contagious period,** which is *the period of time when your illness can spread to others.*

- During the contagious period, stay home from school so you cannot spread your germs to others.

- Cover your mouth and nose when you cough or sneeze.

- Seek medical treatment so you can get over the illness more quickly.

- If a doctor prescribes medication, follow the instructions and take the full amount prescribed.

- Encourage your family and friends to practice the good health habits you have learned.

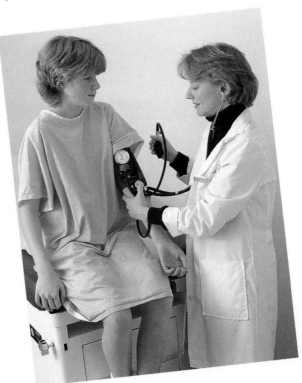

Personal Inventory

BEHAVIORS FOR GOOD HEALTH

Good health behaviors help you stay healthy, recover from illness faster, and prevent spreading germs. How healthy are your behaviors? To find out, write yes or no for each statement below on a separate sheet of paper.

1. I wash my hands after I use the bathroom and before preparing or serving food.

2. I cover my nose and mouth when I cough or sneeze.

3. I avoid sharing unwashed eating utensils or drinking glasses with others.

4. I avoid sharing combs, towels, or toothbrushes with others.

5. I make sure food is properly stored and cooked.

6. I avoid drinking water from streams and lakes.

7. When I'm sick, I stay home from school.

8. When I'm sick, I do not go out during the contagious period.

9. When I'm well, I avoid contact with people who have diseases that I could catch.

10. When I'm very sick, I get medical treatment.

11. I examine myself for ticks after being outdoors.

12. I have had all the necessary vaccinations.

To rate yourself, give yourself 1 point for a yes. A score of 10–12 is very good. A score of 8–10 is good. A score of 6–8 is fair. If you score below 6, you need to work on improving your health behavior.

Lesson 1 Review

Using complete sentences, answer the following questions on a separate sheet of paper.

Reviewing Terms and Facts

1. **Vocabulary** Define the term *communicable diseases,* using your own words.

2. **Recall** List four good behaviors to protect yourself from disease.

Thinking Critically

3. **Analyze** You have a friend who coughs and sneezes without covering his mouth and nose whenever he has a cold. What advice would you give him?

4. **Explain** Tell how exercise and a balanced diet can help prevent diseases caused by germs.

Applying Health Concepts

5. **Health of Others** Contact a local veterinarian or check out a library book to find out how ticks and fleas affect pets. Find out what you can do to help prevent a pet from getting ticks and fleas. Share your findings with your class.

The Body's Defenses Against Germs

This lesson will help you find answers to questions that teens often ask about how the body fights germs. For example:

▶ **If germs are all around me, why am I not sick all the time?**

▶ **What is immunity and how do I know if I am immune?**

▶ **What vaccines do I need and why do I need them?**

The Body's Defenses

Although germs are always around you, they seldom make you sick because of your body's defenses. Your body's first line of defense (your skin and body fluids) is described in **Figure 11.2.** If germs do enter your body, your body's main line of defense is activated. This is your **immunity** (i·MYOO·nuh·tee)—*your body's resistance to germs and the harmful substances they produce.*

Words to Know

immunity
lymphatic system
lymph nodes
lymphocytes
B-cells
T-cells
antibodies
vaccine

Figure 11.2
The First Line of Defense

Your body's first line of defense works to protect you from germs.

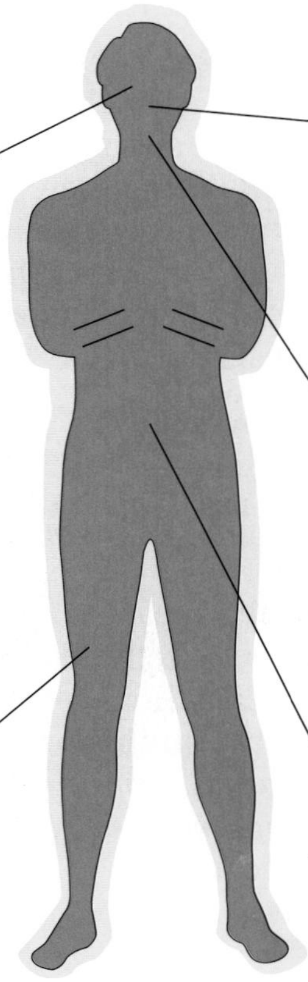

Tears
Tears wash germs from your eyes. They also contain chemical compounds that kill germs.

Mucous Membranes
These membranes line your nose, mouth, and throat and secrete a fluid called mucus (MYOO·kuhs) that traps germs. You get rid of the trapped germs when you sneeze, cough, or blow your nose.

Saliva
Saliva washes germs from your teeth and helps keep your mouth clean. It also contains chemical compounds that kill germs.

The Skin
As long as the tough, outer layer of skin is unbroken, you are protected. Germs can enter only when you have a cut, burn, or scrape.

Gastric Juice
Gastric juice produced by the mucous lining of your stomach destroys germs that enter through food or drink.

The Main Line of Defense

Sometimes harmful germs get through your first line of defense. Then your body's immune system takes over. Invading germs are attacked first in general immune reactions. Later, other immune responses occur that are tailor-made for specific germs.

General Reactions

■ When germs enter your body, blood vessels nearby release special white blood cells called *phagocytes* (FAG·uh·syts). These cells engulf germs and destroy them in a process called *phagocytosis* (fag·uh·suh·TOH·suhs), which means "eating up cells."

■ When certain body cells are invaded by viruses, they release a chemical substance called *interferon,* which stops the viruses from reproducing and infecting other cells.

■ Fever, or elevated body temperature, kills germs that cannot survive body temperatures that are higher than normal.

Specific Immunity

If germs survive the general immune reactions, *specific immunity* takes over. This involves immune responses to specific germs and the poisons they produce. Specific immunity often gives the body the ability to remember how to destroy the same germs if they invade the body again. The next time they invade, the body can respond quickly so the germs won't have a chance to multiply—and you won't get sick.

The Lymphatic System

Specific immunity involves the **lymphatic** (lim·FA·tik) **system**—*a secondary circulatory system of vessels and nodes that carry a fluid called lymph.* This system helps maintain the balance of fluids in the body and helps your body fight germs. Lymphatic vessels carry lymph to a vein near the heart, where it enters the bloodstream. **Lymph nodes** are *small lumps of lymphatic tissue located throughout the system that act as filters to keep germs from invading body tissues.* When the body has been infected by a germ, lymph nodes often become swollen. Have you felt them in your neck area when you have been ill?

Specific immunity is carried out by two types of **lymphocytes** (LIM·fuh·syts)—*special white blood cells that circulate in the lymph.* **B-cells** *produce substances that fight germs.* **T-cells** *attack germs directly and stimulate B-cells to work* (see **Figure 11.3**).

Lymphocytes react to *antigens,* which are the parts of germs that connect to body cells and harm them. With bacteria, these antigens are toxins, or poisons, that the bacteria release. To fight antigens, B-cells release **antibodies.** These are *proteins that attach to germs or to the toxins germs produce, thus preventing the germ or toxin from harming your body.* B-cells produce a specific antibody for each specific antigen.

Teen Issues

Fever Reliever · ACTIVITY!

If you have a fever, do not take aspirin or products that contain aspirin. In people under 18, taking aspirin for fever can result in Reye's syndrome, a potentially fatal disorder of the nervous system. Check the labels of fever-reducing medicines in the drugstore. Which ones should you avoid because they contain aspirin?

Figure 11.3
How the Immune System Responds to Viruses

B-cells and T-cells respond somewhat differently to bacteria in two ways. First, antibodies attack the toxins that bacteria release, killing those poisons. Second, antibodies force the bacterial cells to bunch together. Then they call on phagocytes to eat the bunches.

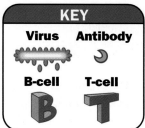

KEY

Virus   Antibody

B-cell   T-cell

1 Virus enters the body.

2 B-cells identify the virus. B-cells produce antibodies, which attach themselves to the virus cells.

3 Antibodies attract T-cells.

4 B-cells and T-cells multiply. Some become memory lymphocytes.

5 T-cells destroy virus cells by engulfing them.

6 Memory B-cells and T-cells remain in the bloodstream in case the same virus invades again.

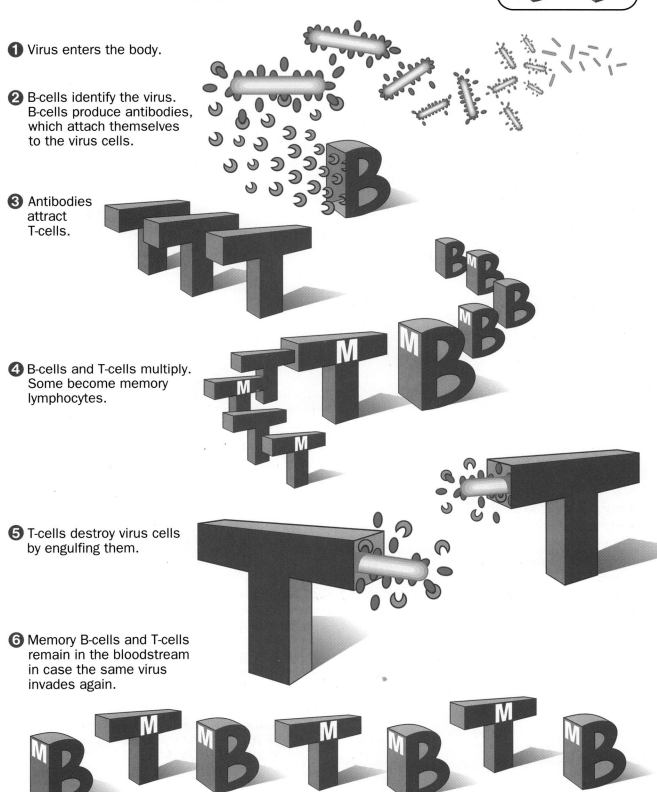

Immunity and Vaccines

Having a disease is one way you may become immune to it. Another way is through a **vaccine** (vak·SEEN). A vaccine is *a preparation of dead or weakened germs that is injected into the body to cause the immune system to produce antibodies.* Vaccines for each disease follow a specific schedule (see **Figure 11.4**). Some people have reactions to vaccines, such as rashes or fevers. Reactions usually are much less severe than the disease itself.

Figure 11.4
Vaccination Schedule

Vaccine	Recommended Ages for Vaccination
Diphtheria, whooping cough, tetanus	2 months, 4 months, 6 months, 12–18 months, 4–6 years
Polio	2 months, 4 months, 6–18 months, 4–6 years
Measles, mumps, rubella	15 months, 4–6 years (some experts postpone this dose to 10–11 years)
Influenza B	2 months, 4 months, 6 months (optional), 12–15 months
Adult tetanus and diphtheria	14–16 years, and every 10 years thereafter
Hepatitis	at birth, 1–2 months, and 6–18 months; *or* 1–2 months, 4 months, and 6–18 months

HEALTH LAB
Tracking Temperatures

Introduction: While the average body temperature in healthy people is 98.6 degrees Fahrenheit, temperature varies from person to person and even in the same person from time to time. If temperature is taken orally, a reading from 97.6 to 99.6 is considered normal. (The normal range for temperature taken under the arm is 96.6 to 98.6.)

Objective: Learning how to read and interpret body temperature is an important health skill. By taking the same person's temperature repeatedly for several days, you can practice this skill.

Materials and Method: Take your own temperature or that of a family member at least twice a day for a week. Body temperature may be measured by mouth (oral) or under the armpit (axillary). You may use a glass thermometer or a disposable thermometer. If the thermometer is glass, it should be wiped with alcohol after each use. This kills any germs on it. (You can also use a thermometer sheath. This paper sleeve covers the thermometer while the temperature is taken and is then thrown away.) Disposable thermometers are used only once and then thrown away. Here are the steps.

Using complete sentences, answer the following questions on a separate sheet of paper.

Reviewing Terms and Facts

1. **Recall**   Name the parts in the body's first line of defense.

2. **Recall**   How does fever fight disease?

3. **Vocabulary**   Which term refers to the lymphocyte that makes antibodies: *B-cell* or *T-cell*?

Thinking Critically

4. **Explain**   Tell how general immune reactions differ from specific immune reactions.

5. **Analyze**   Why does the law require vaccines for school-age children?

6. **Analyze**   Shawn became ill with a cold. His friend Jorge caught his cold, but another friend did not. Why do you think that happened?

Applying Health Concepts

7. **Personal Health**   Plan a vacation to countries in Africa, Asia, or South America. Ask your local health department what vaccinations are required to travel to those countries. Write a report explaining why each one is needed.

To read a mercury thermometer, hold the thermometer by the top. Twirl it in your fingers until you can see the column of mercury inside.

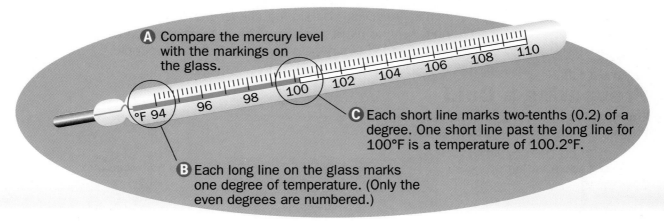

A Compare the mercury level with the markings on the glass.

B Each long line on the glass marks one degree of temperature. (Only the even degrees are numbered.)

C Each short line marks two-tenths (0.2) of a degree. One short line past the long line for 100°F is a temperature of 100.2°F.

1. Holding the thermometer by the top, shake it enough to put the mercury below 96 degrees.

2. Place the mercury end of the thermometer under the person's tongue with the rest sticking out of the mouth. Tell the person to hold it in place for three minutes with his or her lips. (To take axillary temperature, put the bulb end of the thermometer under the person's armpit and keep it there for three minutes.)

Remove the thermometer carefully and record the temperature. Note the conditions of each test. Record whether the person is well or ill; how warmly dressed he or she is; whether or not the person was sleeping, exercising, showering, or eating shortly before you took the temperature; and how warm or cool the room is.

Observation and Analysis: At the end of the week, add up all the readings and then divide by the total number of readings. The result gives you the person's average temperature. How much does each reading vary from the average? Look at your notes about each temperature-taking session. What conditions are associated with high and low values? How can you apply what you have learned to monitoring your own temperature the next time you are sick?

Common Communicable Diseases

This lesson will help you find answers to questions that teens often ask about common communicable diseases. For example:

▶ **What causes colds, and how can they be cured?**

▶ **What other common diseases are communicable?**

Words to Know

influenza
hepatitis
mononucleosis

The Common Cold

The most common communicable disease is the cold. Colds are caused by more than 100 different viruses. Symptoms of colds include mild fever, runny nose, itchy eyes, sneezing, coughing, mild sore throat, and headache.

Following healthy behaviors is the best way to prevent colds (see **Figure 11.5**). Get plenty of rest and drink lots of liquids. Some medicines can relieve cold symptoms. Even if they make you feel better, however, you should stay home for at least 24 hours after cold symptoms first appear. That is when your cold is most contagious, and you may pass the virus on to other people.

Figure 11.5
Preventing a Cold

Prevent colds by limiting your exposure to cold viruses and keeping yourself healthy enough to resist germs.

Ⓐ **Don't share eating utensils.**

Ⓑ **Exercise regularly.**

Ⓒ **Eat a balanced diet.**

Ⓓ **Wash your hands frequently.**

Ⓔ **Avoid smoking.**

Ⓕ **Get eight hours of sleep each night.**

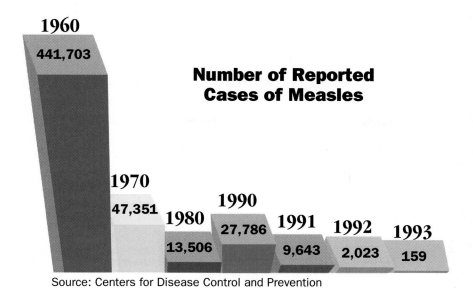

Number of Reported Cases of Measles

1960 — 441,703
1970 — 47,351
1980 — 13,506
1990 — 27,786
1991 — 9,643
1992 — 2,023
1993 — 159

Source: Centers for Disease Control and Prevention

Figure 11.6
Decline of Measles in the United States
Measles is an extremely contagious disease that usually affects children. However, people of any age may get it. Measles was once a very common disease. A vaccine first used in the early 1960s had sharply decreased the number of cases. Then, in the late 1980s, outbreaks of measles began to occur. Experts believe that these outbreaks were due to the failure to vaccinate many infants.

Other Communicable Diseases

Several communicable diseases—rubella, measles, mumps, polio, and whooping cough—were once fairly common childhood illnesses. Most of these diseases have been nearly eliminated by the use of vaccines. See **Figure 11.6** for measles statistics. Certain diseases that were once considered to be under control are making a comeback, however. Some communicable diseases are discussed in **Figure 11.7**.

Figure 11.7
Some Communicable Diseases

Disease	Symptoms	Contagious Period	Vaccine
Chicken pox	Rash, fever, headache, body ache	One to six days after symptoms appear	No
Pneumonia	Chills, high fever, chest pain, cough	Varies	For some types
Rubella	Headache, swollen lymph nodes, cough, sore throat	Seven days before rash starts to five days after	Yes
Measles	Fever, runny nose, cough, rash	Four days before rash starts to five days after	Yes
Mumps	Chills, fever, headache, swollen lymph nodes	Seven days before symptoms to nine days after	Yes
Polio	Fever, sore throat, muscle pain, paralysis	Several days before symptoms start to seven days after	Yes
Whooping cough	Fever, runny nose, sneezing, dry cough (with) whooping sound	From inflammation of mucous membranes to four weeks after	Yes
Tuberculosis	Fever, fatigue, weight loss, coughing blood	Varies	Yes

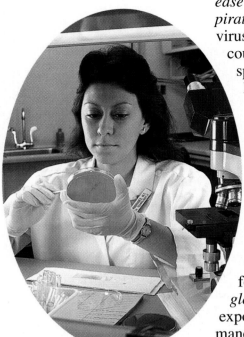

A blood test can determine if you have hepatitis.

Influenza

Influenza (in·floo·EN·zuh), or "the flu," is *a communicable disease characterized by exhaustion, chills, headache, body ache, respiratory problems, and fever.* There are three types of influenza virus, each with several different strains. Influenza is spread by coughing and sneezing. Vaccines cannot completely stop its spread. Because the virus changes frequently, a vaccine that kills an old strain may not harm a new one. Yearly vaccination is recommended for the elderly and for people who have chronic diseases. Treatment includes plenty of rest and fluids, a balanced diet, and medicines to help relieve symptoms.

Hepatitis

Hepatitis (he·puh·TY·tis) is *a viral disease of the liver characterized by yellowing of the skin and the whites of the eyes.* The two major types—*hepatitis A* and *hepatitis B*—are each caused by a different virus. Neither type has a cure, and treatment centers on complete rest. A new vaccine is available for hepatitis B. In addition, an infection-fighting agent, *gamma globulin* (GA·muh GLAH·byuh·lin), gives some protection after exposure, particularly for hepatitis A. Hepatitis B may lead to permanent liver damage.

Mononucleosis

You've probably heard of "the kissing disease," or "mono." These terms refer to **mononucleosis** (MAH·noh·noo·klee·OH·sis), *a viral disease that shows up as swelling of the lymph nodes in the neck and throat.* In addition to being spread by kissing, mono is spread by sharing eating utensils, drinking glasses, or toothbrushes with someone who has the disease. Mononucleosis is most common in teens and young adults.

in your journal

In your journal, make a list of behaviors that encourage the spread of mononucleosis. Do you ever practice any of these behaviors? If so, write down specific ways you could avoid these behaviors in the future.

LIFE SKILLS

Shopping for Cold Medicines

There are so many over-the-counter medicines for treating the symptoms of a cold that choosing the one that is best for you can be difficult. One important guideline to follow is to make sure the product you choose treats the symptoms you have and not those you do not have. Some medicines relieve runny noses, for example, whereas others relieve nasal congestion. Taking the wrong one for your symptoms may leave you feeling worse instead of better.

Most over-the-counter drugs have side effects or can cause allergic reactions, so it is important to read labels carefully. In addition, over-the-counter medicines may differ considerably in cost. Name brands are usually more expensive than generic brands.

Think about the last time you had a cold. Make a list of the symptoms you had when you felt your worst. Now, go to a drugstore and read package labels of cold medicines to find a name brand product that should help your worst symptoms. Then try to find a generic product that helps the same symptoms. Record the following information for each product:

Symptoms begin several weeks after exposure to the virus. They include fever, sore throat, swollen lymph nodes, and tiredness. Treatment is bed rest for three to six weeks. Symptoms gradually disappear after about six to eight weeks. The length of time the patient remains contagious is unknown.

Using complete sentences, answer the following questions on a separate sheet of paper.

Reviewing Terms and Facts

1. **Identify**   Cite four good health behaviors that reduce your chances of getting a cold.

2. **Vocabulary**   Which is a viral disease of the liver: *influenza, hepatitis,* or *mononucleosis*?

3. **Recall**   What has been the effect of widespread use of the measles vaccine?

Thinking Critically

4. **Synthesize**   Based on your study of contagious periods, describe how to protect others from infection with communicable diseases.

5. **Analyze**   Why is it difficult to develop a vaccine against colds and flu?

Applying Health Concepts

6. **Health of Others**   With a group of classmates, demonstrate to the rest of the class how germs on the hands can be passed from one person to another. Use a small piece of double-faced tape to represent a germ. Ask the rest of the class to point out ways the germ's spread could be interrupted.

7. **Health of Others**   Work with a group of classmates to write and illustrate a brochure informing other teens about mononucleosis. Include such topics as how it is spread, what ages are most at risk, what the symptoms are, and how it is treated.

▶ What symptoms is the product supposed to relieve?

▶ What are the product's side effects and warnings?

▶ How much of each active ingredient does the product contain?

▶ What is the recommended dosage for your age?

▶ How much does the product cost?

Follow-up Activity

Back at home or school, compare the two products. How are the products the same? How are they different? Which product would you choose if you had the same symptoms again? Why?

People at Work

Medical Laboratory Technician

Roberta Imann's mother is a nurse. Roberta's grandmother was also a nurse. When Roberta developed an interest in science in junior high school, she thought nursing was the career for her as well. That was until Roberta took biology in high school.

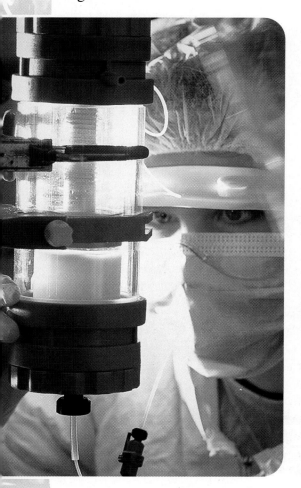

The first time she saw microscopic bacteria and protozoa swimming in a drop of pond water, she knew that the laboratory was where she wanted to be. Now Roberta Imann is a medical laboratory technician. To pursue her career, Roberta completed a two-year associate degree in medical laboratory technology at her local community college.

In a typical day in the lab at the hospital where she works, Roberta prepares samples of patients' blood and other tissues and performs analyses to diagnose disease and recommend courses of treatment. Roberta is quite sure she made the right choice. In the laboratory is where she wants to be.

Prescription Antibiotics and You

Suppose you have a sore throat and go to the doctor. After examining you, the doctor tells you that you have a cold. You ask for a prescription for an antibiotic, but the doctor says you don't need one.

When you go home, you decide to take some antibiotics that were prescribed for you when you had strep throat. If they took care of that, you think, they're bound to kill a cold. What you are taking, however, is an antibiotic that you do not need.

Prescribing and taking unnecessary antibiotics contribute to a growing medical problem—the development of strains of bacteria that resist antibiotics. Because of genetic changes, drug-resistant bacteria have evolved that are able to destroy the medications that used to destroy them. Researchers fear that an outbreak of a drug-resistant disease could kill thousands of people.

To avoid being part of the problem, take antibiotics only for conditions for which they were prescribed. Ask your doctor to test you before prescribing an antibiotic. Then you will get one only if you need it.

Sports
and
Recreation

Arthur Ashe: AIDS Awareness Advocate

Former U.S. Open and Wimbledon tennis champion Arthur Ashe died of AIDS in February 1993. After announcing his condition the previous year, Ashe, who was 49, had become an advocate for AIDS awareness. Ashe was infected with HIV through a blood transfusion. He remained strong in spirit despite being weakened by AIDS.

In addition to being a tennis champion, Arthur Ashe was an author and an advocate for racial equality. His dignified manner and positive attitude in battling AIDS serve as a model for many people.

Teens Making a Difference

Ben Bova—AIDS Counselor

Ben Bova has hemophilia. It is a life-threatening and incurable blood disorder that he inherited. Hemophilia prevents Ben's blood from clotting properly, so even the smallest cut can be a major medical emergency. Ben has been in the hospital so many times in his 14 years that he has lost count of them.

Several years ago, Ben was infected with the HIV virus during one of his many blood transfusions. AIDS symptoms began to show up a little over a year ago, just after Ben's thirteenth birthday.

Ben adjusted well to his new situation. He now works as a peer counselor for other teens with AIDS. Ben learned that the best way to deal with a difficult, life-threatening disease is by appreciating life one day at a time. He tries to get the teens he counsels to have this kind of outlook so they can enjoy life and better cope with their disease.

Recently, Ben received a letter from the mother of one of the teens he had counseled. The letter, written just after the boy's funeral, said that Ben had made a big difference in her son's acceptance of his disease and in the peace and happiness of his last days. Ben truly is a teen who has made a difference.

Health Update

Tuberculosis Returns

Since the 1880s, tuberculosis (TB) had been declining in the United States. By the 1960s, the battle against this highly contagious, bacterial disease seemed to have been won. In the second half of the 1980s, however, TB was once again on the rise. Today, TB is becoming an epidemic, with more than 25,000 new cases each year.

One of the major reasons for the recurrence of TB is that many new cases are resistant to the drugs that once cured TB. Other causes of TB's comeback include the reduction in government funding for screening and vaccination programs, homelessness, poverty, and drug abuse. Yet another reason the disease has begun to thrive again is the spread of HIV. People infected with HIV, who have compromised immune systems, are at especially high risk for contracting tuberculosis.

Sexually Transmitted Diseases

This lesson will help you find answers to questions that teens often ask about sexually transmitted diseases. For example:

▶ **Which diseases are sexually transmitted?**

▶ **How can I get a sexually transmitted disease?**

▶ **What is the best way to avoid getting a sexually transmitted disease?**

▶ **How can sexually transmitted diseases be treated?**

Words to Know

chlamydia
gonorrhea
genital warts
genital herpes
syphilis

Teen Issues

Planning Ahead

It is a good idea to have a quarter for a phone call when you go out on a date. If your date pressures you to have sex and you want to leave early, you can call home for a ride. Next time you go out, be sure to take your quarter.

What Are STDs?

STD is short for *sexually transmitted disease.* STDs are illnesses that pass from one person to another through sexual contact, but they can be prevented. Young people are at greatest risk of getting STDs because they lack knowledge about the diseases. See **Figure 11.8** for statistics about STDs. To avoid STDs, teens need to know more about them (see **Figure 11.9** on pages 360 and 361).

■ **STDs are dangerous.** Permanent effects can include sterility, blindness, deafness, insanity, and death.

■ **STDs may have no symptoms or some that come and go.**

■ **Most STDs can be treated.** Early diagnosis is important.

■ **STDs recur.** The body cannot build up an immunity to any STD.

■ **Most STDs can be spread only through sexual contact.**

Figure 11.8
Statistics About STDs

In 1992, more than 5,500 of the gonorrhea cases were teens. Teens also accounted for more than 3,000 of the cases of syphilis.

STD	Total
Trichomoniasis	3 million
Urethritis	1.2 million
Gonorrhea	501,409
Chlamydia	417,479
Genital Warts	171,565
Genital Herpes	166,796
Syphilis	112,581

Choosing Abstinence

Sexually transmitted diseases are different from other communicable diseases in two important ways. First, no vaccines are available to prevent them. Second, the body does not build up an immunity to any STD. Therefore, the only sure way to avoid getting most STDs is through abstinence—that is, avoiding sexual contact. It's as simple as that. Saying no to sex can be one of the most important health decisions you ever make.

Dates may pressure you to have sex, but they cannot decide for you. You must take responsibility for your own health. Here are some ways to help you stick to your choice of abstinence.

Smart Behaviors

- Choose your friends carefully—those who will support your decision to choose abstinence.

- Avoid being alone with a date.

- Seek advice from trusted adults.

- Say no through your words *and* your actions.

Smart Words

- If your date says, "You would have sex with me if you really loved me," you should say, "You would respect my wishes if you really loved me."

- If your date says, "Everybody's doing it," you should say, "Most teens *aren't* doing it. Anyway, it's my decision that matters to me and should matter to you."

- If your date says, "Sex can be safe," you should respond with, "Abstinence is the only sure way to be safe."

Group social activities are a good way to have fun while eliminating the pressure to have sex.

Did You Know?

The "Silent" STD **ACTIVITY!**

About 75 percent of females and 20 percent of males with chlamydia show no early signs of the disease. The lack of early signs of infection makes prevention crucial.

Write a public service announcement telling other teens the single best way to prevent getting chlamydia.

in your journal

In your journal, write down reasons you think STDs are more likely to go untreated in teens than in other age groups. Describe how you would feel and what you would do if you thought you had an STD.

Find out where in your community you can obtain information about STDs, including symptoms, testing, treatment, and prevention. Make a list of these sources in your journal.

Feeling Good About Your Decision

You may worry that by choosing abstinence, you may lose your boyfriend or girlfriend to another person. Dating should be fun. If it is full of tension over the pressure to have sex, it is no longer fun. If your date won't stop pressuring you, it may be best to end the relationship. This is a difficult decision to make, one that can hurt at the time. However, the alternative will hurt more when agreeing to have sex goes against your values. By sticking to your decision to say no to sex, you can live honestly and comfortably. You can still find company—and have fun without pressure—with other friends.

Help from Others

A parent or another trusted adult may offer some sound advice. In addition, people in government who are responsible for public health prepare and distribute brochures that explain the STDs and their prevention. Some public health workers give talks at schools and community centers to answer the questions teens have about these diseases. Others place public service announcements in the media—radio, television, and magazines—to explain that the safest way to avoid an STD is to say no to sex.

Common STDs

Each year, thousands of teens contract an STD. Many fail to seek medical attention because they are embarrassed or unwilling to take responsibility for their actions. Some ignore their symptoms. In some cases the symptoms are not obvious, and the teen doesn't know he or she has a disease. The symptoms and effects of many common and serious STDs are shown in **Figure 11.9** on pages 360 and 361. Another very serious STD, AIDS, is covered in Lesson 5.

MAKING HEALTHY DECISIONS
Helping a Friend Choose Abstinence

*L*illian and Tamara have been best friends since they were in elementary school. They spend a lot of time together on weekends and after school. Since the beginning of the school year Tamara has been dating a classmate, Tommy.

Tamara and Tommy are usually together at school activities and at parties. Tamara really likes Tommy and enjoys their dates together. She always talks about him to Lillian.

Today, however, Tamara is especially quiet. When Lillian asks her what is wrong, Tamara finally explains that Tommy has been pressuring her to have sex. Tamara says that her dates aren't fun anymore. She says she doesn't feel ready for sex, but she's worried Tommy will leave her if she doesn't give in—and that would "hurt too much." She asks Lillian what she should do.

What should Lillian say to her? Should she stress the dangers of sexually transmitted diseases? Should she urge Lillian to choose abstinence? Should she urge her to stop seeing Tommy?

Chlamydia

Chlamydia is one of the most common STDs in the United States. It is very hard to detect because signs of the disease may not show up until it is well advanced. **Chlamydia** (kluh·MI·dee·uh) is *an STD caused by bacterial microorganisms and affects the vagina in females and the urethra in males.* If left untreated, chlamydia can cause serious damage to other reproductive organs.

Chlamydia, shown here under a microscope, can lead to sterility (the inability to reproduce).

Gonorrhea

Another common and serious STD is gonorrhea. **Gonorrhea** (gah·nuh·REE·uh) is *an STD caused by bacteria affecting the genital mucous membrane and possibly other body structures such as the heart or joints.* The bacteria cannot live outside the body. Like chlamydia, the signs and symptoms may not occur until the disease is advanced, especially in females.

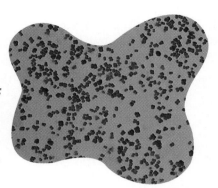

Gonorrhea can also cause sterility, as well as damage to the heart or other organs.

Genital Warts

Genital warts are *growths that develop in the genital area caused by the same virus that causes common warts.* They are generally harmless, but if left untreated they will multiply. They are easily transmitted to another person through sexual contact. Genital warts are sometimes a symptom of a more serious disease, such as syphilis or cancer. This STD is one of the major causes of cervical cancer in women.

Lillian uses the six steps of the decision-making process to help her come to a decision:

❶ **State the situation**

❷ **List the options**

❸ **Weigh the possible outcomes**

❹ **Consider your values**

❺ **Make a decision and act**

❻ **Evaluate the decision**

Follow-up Activities

1. Apply the six steps of the decision-making process to Lillian's story.

2. With a partner, role-play a conversation between Lillian and Tamara in which Lillian gives her advice.

3. What would you do if you were Tamara?

Genital Herpes

Genital herpes (HER·peez) is *an STD that is caused by a virus and produces painful blisters in the genital area of males and females.* The signs and symptoms of this disease may go away temporarily even though the virus remains in the body. The disease is contagious when the signs and symptoms are present, and it may be contagious for a period of time before they appear and after they disappear. At present, there is no cure for genital herpes.

Syphilis

Syphilis (SI·fuh·lis) is *an STD caused by bacteria. If untreated, syphilis may spread to the central nervous system, causing insanity, paralysis, and death.* Syphilis was once the most common

Figure 11.9
Basic Facts About STDs

Anyone who suspects that he or she has an STD needs medical help. The worst thing to do is to ignore the signs.

Disease	Cause	Signs and Symptoms	Treatment	Complications
Chlamydia	Bacteria	Pain, burning during urination; discharge	Antibiotics	Scarring of reproductive organs; sterility; infections of fetus in pregnant women
Gonorrhea	Bacteria	Discharge; swollen lymph nodes in groin; burning during urination; abnormal menstrual cycles in females	Antibiotics, although some strains are drug resistant	Sterility; permanent damage to joints, heart, and other organs; infection of fetus in pregnant women
Genital Warts	Virus	Warts in genital area three weeks to three months after sexual contact with an infected person	Antiviral drugs; surgery to remove warts	Cancer of reproductive system; obstruction of birth canal in females; can be passed to newborns during birth
Genital Herpes	Virus	Painful, itchy sores in genital area; fever; burning during urination	No cure; medications to relieve symptoms	Cervical cancer in females; brain damage or death in infants of infected mother
Syphilis	Bacteria	Reddish sores in genital area; body rash; flu-like symptoms	Antibiotics, usually penicillin	Damage to heart, blood vessels, liver, kidneys, nervous system; blindness; insanity; death

sexually transmitted disease. Although it is less common today, its incidence is increasing at an alarming rate.

Syphilis occurs in three stages. Between the stages, the signs and symptoms may disappear. As a result, the affected person may mistakenly think that he or she is cured. The second stage may not occur until months after the first stage. The third stage may not occur for up to 20 years after the second stage.

Other Sexually Transmitted Diseases

Several other serious diseases are transmitted through sexual contact. They are vaginitis, pubic lice, and scabies. *Vaginitis* is an infection of the vagina. Its symptoms include pain, itching, and a burning sensation during urination. It can be treated with antibiotics and proper hygiene. *Pubic lice* are insects that look like tiny crabs. They attach to the skin and hair of the pubic area and suck a person's blood. This causes severe itching. *Scabies* is caused by mites, tiny animals that burrow themselves into the skin and lay their eggs. They can live on clothes and towels for a short time and can infect another person who uses these items.

Disease	Cause	Signs and Symptoms	Treatment	Complications
Trichomoniasis	Protozoa	Yellowish discharge with strong odor; itching in females; males may have slight or no symptoms	Antibiotics	Infections of the bladder and urethra
Vaginitis	Bacteria, fungi, or protozoa	Itching; burning during urination; discharge in females; males may have no symptoms, but can transmit the disease	Antibiotics or fungicide creams	Urinary-tract infections
Nongonococcal Urethritis (NGU)	Bacteria	Discharge; burning during urination; abdominal pain	Antibiotics	Sterility
Pubic Lice	Small, crablike insects	Presence of lice and eggs in pubic hair; itching	Medicated shampoo; washing all bed linens and clothes	No lasting effects
Scabies	Tiny animals called mites	Rash; itching where mites have burrowed under the skin	Insecticide cream; washing bed linens and clothes	Scratching can cause bacterial infections

A Final Word

There are more than 30 different sexually transmitted diseases. Some have no cure, and all are serious, even deadly. STDs harm not only the person who has one, but that person's sexual partner.

In recent years, STDs have been spreading rapidly. According to the Centers for Disease Control and Prevention, more than 33,000 new cases occur every day. More than half of these new cases are occurring among teens and young adults.

> The most effective protection from STDs is to avoid sexual contact.

You can avoid getting an STD. Learn all you can about these diseases. Most important, remember that abstinence is the only sure way to avoid getting an STD. By putting off having sex for a while, you are protecting yourself and others.

Lesson 4 Review

Using complete sentences, answer the following questions on a separate sheet of paper.

Reviewing Terms and Facts

1. **Recall**   List four facts about STDs that teens need to know.

2. **Recall**   Cite two ways in which STDs are different from other communicable diseases.

3. **Give Examples**   Name six STDs.

4. **Vocabulary**   Which of the following STDs, if left untreated, may spread to the central nervous system: *syphilis, chlamydia,* or *gonorrhea*?

Thinking Critically

5. **Synthesize**   Why should you seek medical help if you think you have been exposed to an STD even though you have no symptoms?

6. **Explain**   Why is saying no to sex one of the most important health decisions you can ever make?

7. **Compare and Contrast**   Discuss how genital herpes and genital warts are similar and how they are different.

Applying Health Concepts

8. **Health of Others**   Make a poster that shows teens the potential dangers of STDs.

9. **Health of Others**   With another student, present a skit to the rest of the class in which one teen urges another to have sex. Ask the class to suggest convincing responses.

HIV/AIDS

This lesson will help you find answers to questions that teens often ask about AIDS. For example:

► **What is AIDS, and what causes it?**

► **Do I have to worry about being around someone with AIDS?**

► **What can I do to avoid getting AIDS?**

What Is AIDS?

AIDS, or **acquired immunodeficiency** (im·yoo·noh·di·FI·shuhn·see) **syndrome,** is *a deadly disease that interferes with the body's natural ability to fight infection.* The *virus that causes AIDS is* called **HIV,** or **human immunodeficiency virus.**

■ **AIDS is a deadly disease.** There is no vaccine to prevent infection with HIV, and there is no cure for AIDS; it is fatal.

■ **You can be a carrier of HIV without having AIDS.** A **carrier** is *an apparently healthy person who has HIV in the blood and can pass it to others.* People with HIV have the virus for an average of 11 years before showing any symptoms of AIDS. **Figure 11.10** shows how the number of AIDS cases has risen in the last eight years.

■ **AIDS is easy to prevent through abstinence.**

Figure 11.10
U.S. AIDS Cases in People 13–19 Years Old

What do these statistics say about AIDS among young people?

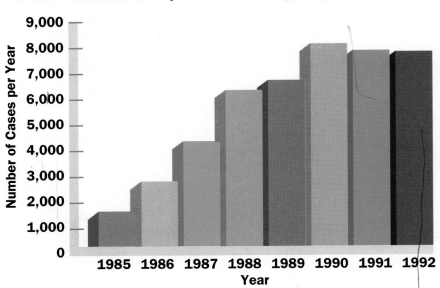

Source: Centers for Disease Control and Prevention

Your Total Health

Multivitamins Delay AIDS ACTIVITY!

According to a recent study, a healthy diet coupled with a daily multivitamin supplement may delay the onset of AIDS in HIV-infected people. Some scientists believe that good nutrition helps maintain the health of the body's immune system.

Make a poster showing what else we can do to keep our bodies healthy and our resistance up.

What HIV Does to the Body

AIDS is a relatively new disease. The first cases in the United States were reported in 1981. Currently, there is no cure for AIDS and no vaccine against HIV.

HIV attacks the immune system (see **Figure 11.11**), leading at first to swollen lymph nodes, tiredness, diarrhea, weight loss, and fever. Eventually, the weakened immune system cannot fight off the germs a healthy immune system could destroy. It is these other germs that usually cause the death of a person with AIDS.

HIV Lets Other Germs Attack the Body

A low T-cell count is one important sign of AIDS. Another criterion for diagnosing AIDS is the presence of certain other diseases. With an impaired immune system, a person with AIDS is susceptible to many *infections that otherwise rarely occur.* Such infections are called **opportunistic infections.** For example, a form of cancer called *Kaposi's* (KA·puh·seez) *sarcoma* was extremely rare until the AIDS epidemic began in the early 1980s. Another opportunistic infection that is common in AIDS patients is a rare form of pneumonia called pneumocystic pneumonia.

Figure 11.11
Comparing Healthy and HIV-Infected Immune Systems

Once in the body, HIV works differently than other viruses.

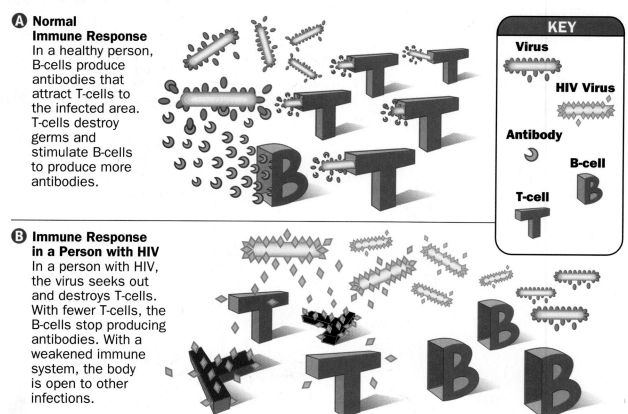

A **Normal Immune Response**
In a healthy person, B-cells produce antibodies that attract T-cells to the infected area. T-cells destroy germs and stimulate B-cells to produce more antibodies.

KEY
Virus
HIV Virus
Antibody
B-cell
T-cell

B **Immune Response in a Person with HIV**
In a person with HIV, the virus seeks out and destroys T-cells. With fewer T-cells, the B-cells stop producing antibodies. With a weakened immune system, the body is open to other infections.

Testing and Treating

A blood test can tell you if you are infected with HIV. A positive test result indicates the presence of HIV antibodies in your blood. However, it may take six months after infection before antibodies show up. If you think you might be infected, even though your test result is negative, have the test repeated at a later date.

Most of the treatments given to AIDS patients are for opportunistic infections, such as antibiotics for pneumonia. There is no drug available that kills HIV and cures AIDS. The drug AZT does delay the onset of AIDS symptoms in some patients by slowing the reproduction of the virus. AZT has serious side effects, however.

How HIV Is Spread

Because HIV is too fragile to survive in the atmosphere, it can be passed from one person to another only in body fluids—blood, semen, and vaginal secretions. Therefore, HIV infection can only occur in the following ways:

- **Sexual relations with an infected person.** People who have unprotected sex with multiple partners are at greatest risks.

- **Using the same needle to inject drugs that was previously used by an infected person.** Tiny amounts of blood that remain in the needle can be injected along with the drug. An accidental prick with a used needle is the main way health care workers get HIV infection.

- **Transfusions and other medical treatments using blood from an infected person.** All donated blood is tested for HIV. If it tests positive, the blood is not used. However, the tests are not 100 percent safe. The blood of a newly infected person may not yet contain the antibodies that indicate the presence of HIV.

- **Passing the virus from infected mother to fetus.** This occurs in about half of all pregnancies to HIV-infected women and usually leads to death of the child by age two.

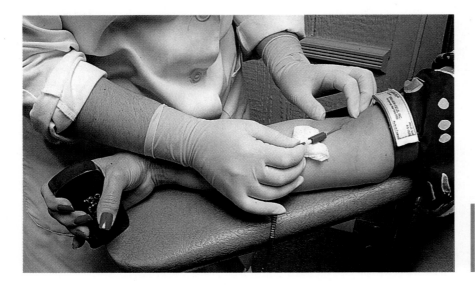

Biology Connection

T-Cell Gateway

Scientists have long puzzled over how HIV gets inside T-cells to destroy them. Researchers now think they have found the answer—a molecule on T-cells, called CD26, may provide the gateway the virus needs. This discovery could lead to a vaccine that works by blocking the CD26 gateway. Why would this prevent AIDS?

Teen Issues

Steroids and AIDS

Almost a third of Canadian teens who inject steroids to build muscles share needles. Sharing drug needles is a major cause of HIV infection, so it is only a matter of time before new AIDS cases start showing up in teen bodybuilders. If anyone you know injects steroids, make sure they know about the risk of AIDS as well as the serious consequences of steroid use. These dangers include sterility and impaired liver function.

Because clean equipment is used for each blood donor, you cannot get HIV from giving blood or plasma.

How HIV Is Not Spread

You have probably heard some myths about ways in which HIV is spread. Myths have led to unnecessary social isolation of people with AIDS. **Figure 11.12** lists six myths about how HIV is spread. Remember—HIV is *not* spread in any of these ways.

How to Prevent the Spread of HIV

Preventing the spread of HIV is simple. Here are the two important behaviors you must practice.

- **Avoid all sexual contact.** There is no way to be sure that another person is not a carrier of HIV. At your age, saying no to sex will protect you better than anything else you can do.

- **Avoid illegal drugs, especially those taken by intravenous needles.** Drugs impair your good judgment, making you less careful. Drug users who share blood-contaminated needles account for a large proportion of HIV infections.

HIV infection is incurable and AIDS is fatal. People who test positive for HIV will probably develop AIDS at some point. For these reasons, it is especially important to refrain from activities that place you at high risk.

in your journal

In your journal, describe how your knowledge of the spread of HIV has changed by reading this chapter. Will your increased knowledge affect how you would interact with a person with AIDS? Explain your response.

Figure 11.12
Exploding the Myths About HIV

Myth	Truth
HIV is spread through the air.	Breathing the same air as an infected person, even being coughed or sneezed on by an infected person, poses no risk of HIV infection.
HIV is spread through kissing.	"Dry" kissing (kissing with mouths closed) is considered safe. In theory, kissing in which saliva is exchanged can transmit HIV, although no cases have been proven.
HIV can be spread through casual contact with an infected person.	Although it is a likely way to pick up cold germs, shaking hands with an infected person or having other casual contact poses no risk of HIV infection.
HIV is spread by mosquitoes that have bitten an infected person.	Although some blood parasites can spread through mosquito bites, HIV is not one of them.
HIV is spread by sharing eating utensils with an infected person.	This is another way to catch a cold, but not HIV.
HIV is spread by donating blood.	The needles used to take blood are used only once, then thrown away. There is no risk of catching HIV by donating blood.

AIDS Research and Education

Millions of dollars are spent each year to find a cure for AIDS, to develop a vaccine to prevent HIV infection, and to educate the public about how to prevent its spread. Spearheading these efforts are the federal Centers for Disease Control and Prevention (CDC). CDC scientists gather and publish statistics on AIDS, support AIDS research, and help educate the public about AIDS.

Although we have learned a lot from this research, AZT is still the only FDA-approved drug for slowing the progress of the virus. Prospects for a cure or a vaccine are not yet in sight. Until a cure or vaccine is found, our only weapon against AIDS is prevention. To prevent AIDS requires knowledge of how it is spread. This means that education is still the key to preventing the spread of AIDS.

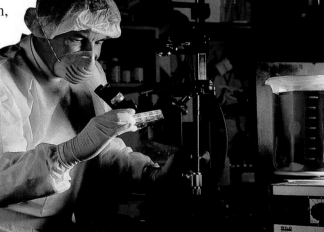

Scientists are working to find a cure for AIDS.

Review — Lesson 5

Using complete sentences, answer the following questions on a separate sheet of paper.

Reviewing Terms and Facts

1. **Vocabulary** Which of the following is a deadly disease that interferes with the body's natural ability to fight infection: *HIV, Kaposi's sarcoma,* or *AIDS*?

2. **Vocabulary** What is a person called who has HIV but has not developed AIDS?

3. **Recall** Cite three general facts about AIDS.

4. **Recall** Identify four ways that HIV infection can occur.

5. **Recall** List four ways that HIV infection cannot occur.

Thinking Critically

6. **Differentiate** Explain the difference between HIV and AIDS.

7. **Explain** Tell why AIDS cannot be spread through casual contact with an infected person.

8. **Synthesize** The campaign against AIDS is concentrated on education, because prevention is the only way to stop the spread of the disease. What would be the focus of the campaign against AIDS if there were a vaccine to prevent it?

Applying Health Concepts

9. **Health of Others** Write an essay describing how you think society's view of AIDS would change if an effective vaccine or a cure were found for this fatal disease. What other diseases could it be compared to? What effect do you think such a discovery would have on risky behaviors such as unprotected sex and shared IV needles?

10. **Health of Others** Do some library research on mandatory AIDS testing. Find out why some people are for it and others against it. Organize a class debate with other students and discuss both sides of the issue. Select one student to be moderator.

Chapter Summary

▶ Communicable diseases are caused by germs or viruses that enter the body and damage its cells. (Lesson 1)

▶ Many communicable diseases can be prevented by practicing good health habits that keep you healthy and prevent the spread of germs between you and others. (Lesson 1)

▶ Your body's own defenses against germs include your skin and body fluids, general immune reactions, and specific immune responses. (Lesson 2)

▶ Vaccines are available to prevent many communicable diseases. (Lesson 2)

▶ The most common communicable disease is the cold, which has no vaccine or cure; but its symptoms can be treated. (Lesson 3)

▶ Other common communicable diseases include influenza, hepatitis, and mononucleosis. (Lesson 3)

▶ STDs are dangerous because they can do great damage to the body, sometimes without noticeable symptoms. (Lesson 4)

▶ Although early treatment can cure most STDs, the most effective protection is abstinence, the avoidance of sexual contact. (Lesson 4)

▶ AIDS is a deadly disease caused by a virus called HIV. (Lesson 5)

▶ HIV weakens the body's ability to fight off other infections. (Lesson 5)

▶ There is no cure or vaccine for AIDS, but it can be prevented by avoiding sexual contact and shared IV needles. (Lesson 5)

Using Health Terms

On a separate sheet of paper, write the vocabulary term that best matches each definition given below.

1. Microscopic organisms that can cause infection (Lesson 1)

2. The period of time when your illness can spread to others (Lesson 1)

3. The condition of being resistant to certain germs (Lesson 2)

4. Proteins that prevent a germ or toxin from harming the body (Lesson 2)

5. A contagious disease causing exhaustion, chills, headache, body ache, respiratory problems, and fever (Lesson 3)

6. A viral disease common in teens and young adults that primarily affects the lymph nodes (Lesson 3)

7. An STD caused by bacterial microorganisms which, if left untreated, can lead to serious damage to reproductive organs (Lesson 4)

8. The virus that causes AIDS (Lesson 5)

9. Infections common in AIDS victims that rarely occur in people without AIDS (Lesson 5)

Reviewing Main Ideas

Using complete sentences, answer the following questions on a separate sheet of paper.

1. Define the word *disease*. (Lesson 1)

2. Identify the types of organisms that cause communicable diseases in humans. (Lesson 1)

3. What is your body's first line of defense against germs? (Lesson 2)

4. What causes colds? (Lesson 3)

5. List some communicable diseases that can be prevented with vaccines. (Lesson 3)

6. What is the only sure way to avoid getting an STD? (Lesson 4)

7. What are two common STDs? (Lesson 4)

8. How does HIV affect the immune system? (Lesson 5)

Thinking Critically

Using complete sentences, answer the following questions on a separate sheet of paper.

1. **Differentiate** Explain the difference between communicable and noncommunicable diseases. (Lesson 1)

2. **Synthesize** Explain how phagocytes help your immune system fight disease. (Lesson 2)

3. **Analyze** Explain how vaccines lead to immunity. (Lesson 2)

4. **Synthesize** Why are flu shots given every year, whereas diseases like measles and polio require just a few shots for life? (Lesson 3)

5. **Analyze** Why can a person get the same STD more than once? (Lesson 4)

6. **Classify** Which of the following body fluids transmit HIV: sweat, blood, semen, tears, saliva, vaginal secretions? (Lesson 5)

7. **Analyze** How do B-cells help physicians diagnose the presence of HIV? (Lesson 5)

Your Action Plan

Review your private journal entries for this chapter. Identify any behaviors you think you should change to reduce your risk of transmitting or picking up germs. Behaviors you want to change should be written as goals and recorded in your journal. For example, if you don't always wash your hands after you cough or sneeze into them, your goal should be to always do so.

Next, make an action plan to achieve your goals. In your journal, describe how you can encourage yourself to practice the behaviors you have identified as your goals. Another possibility is to post reminders around the house.

Review your action plan in a month. Do you consistently practice the behaviors you set for yourself as goals? If not, try to think of various ways to encourage yourself to practice the healthful behaviors in your action plan.

Building Your Portfolio

Make a list of common communicable diseases you have had. For example, have you had the measles, mumps, or chicken pox? If you cannot remember, ask a parent or guardian. Answer the following questions: How old were you? How long were you sick? What were your symptoms? What treatment did you receive to make you more comfortable? How long did the symptoms last? Did you spread it to anyone else? If so, to whom? (You could also ask your parent or guardian what vaccinations you have had.) Add the answers to your portfolio.

In Your Home and Community

1. Research sources of professional help in your community for people with HIV and AIDS. Then create a poster or pamphlet that tells the signs and symptoms of AIDS, how HIV is and is not spread and how to get tested for HIV. Ask permission to display your work in local hospitals, pharmacies, and other places.

2. Speak with family members about ways to improve health behaviors to protect themselves and others from disease. For example, you could remind a family member who routinely forgets to finish medication to do so. Work with family members to implement good health habits.

Chapter 12

Noncommunicable Diseases

Student Expectations

After reading this chapter, you should be able to:

1. Define *noncommunicable diseases* and *risk factors*.

2. Describe the main types of heart disease and list steps people can take to reduce the risk of heart disease.

3. Discuss how cancer develops and tell what people can do to reduce the risk of cancer.

4. Explain what allergies are and how they are treated.

5. Discuss the two main types of arthritis and the two main types of diabetes.

About six months ago, Dad had a heart attack. The doctor said it was not a major attack. Now Dad is back at work and he seems fine, but the way he lives is definitely different. Dad's doctor put him on a special diet and exercise routine. The doctor also told him to lose weight and quit smoking. Believe me, these are big changes for Dad.

Heart disease runs in Dad's side of the family, but he never seemed to take it too seriously. "Aida, one of these days," he would say, "I'm going to change my ways." Then he would wink as he took another helping of ice cream or lit up a cigarette.

Since his heart attack, Dad changed practically his whole way of living. Now he works hard to be healthy. The problem is he got on my case, too. Dad said that if he had started eating a healthy diet and exercising when he was young, he might never have had a heart attack. I appreciate Dad's concern, but good grief, I'm only 14! After all, it's my health and my choice. I'll have plenty of time later to change my ways.

in your journal

Read the account on this page. How often do you think about the effect of your lifestyle on your future health? Start your private journal entries on noncommunicable diseases by answering these questions:

▶ What long-term diseases are common in your family?

▶ Could any of your present habits or behaviors harm your health in the future?

▶ Are there any long-term diseases you are most interested in learning how to prevent and control? Why do you choose them?

When you reach the end of the chapter, you will use your journal entries to make an action plan.

Noncommunicable Diseases

This lesson will help you find answers to questions that teens often ask about noncommunicable diseases. For example:

► **What is the difference between communicable and noncommunicable diseases?**

► **Why do some diseases seem to run in families?**

► **Can anything be done to prevent noncommunicable diseases?**

Words to Know

noncommunicable
    disease
chronic disease
genetic disorder
birth defect
risk factor

Did You Know?

Leading Cause of Death

Accidents are the number one killer of children and young adolescents (5 to 14 years of age). The second leading cause of death among people in this age-group is cancer.

What Is a Noncommunicable Disease?

When you hear that someone you have recently been with has developed the flu—or some other communicable disease—you may worry about catching it. Your concern is understandable because most communicable diseases are caused by germs that are easily passed from one person to another. A second group of diseases, called **noncommunicable diseases,** includes all diseases that *are not spread through contact.* Asthma is one example. You cannot catch asthma by being with someone suffering an asthma attack. Heart disease, another noncommunicable disease, is the leading cause of death in the United States (see **Figure 12.1**).

The reason noncommunicable diseases cannot be passed to other people by contact is that most of these illnesses are not caused by germs. Instead, they are caused by a breakdown in body cells and tissues. The breakdown may begin because of the effects of certain traits a person has inherited or because of that person's lifestyle habits or environment. Some diseases cause further breakdown, or degeneration, in body cells and tissues as they progress. These are called degenerative (di·JE·ne·ruh·tiv) diseases.

Figure 12.1
Leading Causes of Death

In 1992, the four leading causes of death in the United States were noncommunicable diseases.

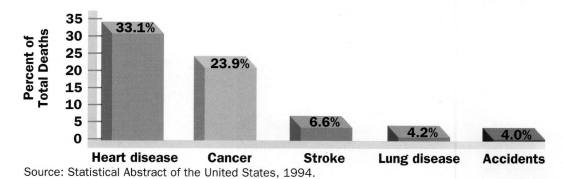

Source: Statistical Abstract of the United States, 1994.

Most noncommunicable diseases are **chronic** (KRAH·nik) **diseases,** which means they *are present either continuously or off and on over a long time.* A person may be born with the disease or a tendency to develop it. The disease may develop as a result of a person's lifestyle behaviors. Sometimes the disease develops because of substances in the person's environment. Some of the most common noncommunicable diseases are described in **Figure 12.2.**

Diseases Present at Birth

Some babies are born with serious health problems. If a baby does not have a communicable disease, the problem may be caused by a genetic disorder or a birth defect. A **genetic** (juh·NE·tik) **disorder** is *one in which the body does not develop or function normally because of an inherited problem.*

Math Connection

Changing Emphasis ACTIVITY!

The relative numbers of cases of communicable and noncommunicable diseases have changed over the years. Look in an almanac or encyclopedia to find the incidence of both types of diseases from 1900 to the present. Make a line graph that shows how the incidence of each type of disease has changed.

Figure 12.2
Common Noncommunicable Diseases

Disease	Description
Allergies	Bodily reactions to particular substances; common forms include hay fever, eczema, and allergic digestive problems
Alzheimer's disease	Affects the brain and causes increasing loss of memory and other mental functions; affects people 40 and over
Arthritis	Group of diseases that causes body joints to swell, making movement painful and difficult
Asthma	An attack that partially blocks the air passages and results in serious breathing difficulty
Cancer	Group of about 100 diseases; in all types of cancer, abnormal body cells multiply out of control and destroy healthy tissue
Cerebral palsy	Group of disorders caused by damage to the brain that occurs during birth or in the first few years of life
Cystic fibrosis	Causes certain glands of the body to produce large amounts of thicker-than-normal mucus; over time, mucus may damage body organs, especially lungs, pancreas, and liver
Heart disease (cardiovascular disease)	Group of diseases that affects the heart and blood vessels; includes hardening of the arteries, clogged arteries, and high blood pressure; can cause heart attacks and strokes
Multiple sclerosis (MS)	Affects the nervous system; can cause paralysis of limbs or some vision loss
Muscular dystrophy	Affects the skeletal muscles; four common types
Sickle-cell anemia	Blood disorder that causes tiredness and breathlessness

The term **birth defect** refers to various *disorders of the developing and newborn baby.* The causes of many birth defects are unknown. Others can be traced to harmful substances in the environment or to a combination of environmental and genetic causes. For example, if a pregnant woman is exposed to X-rays, the developing baby may be injured. Some serious birth defects are the result of unhealthy lifestyle habits of the mother-to-be. If a pregnant woman drinks alcohol, for example, it may cause fetal alcohol syndrome (FAS) in her developing baby. Babies with fetal alcohol syndrome may have malformed body organs or mental retardation.

In most cases, there is no cure for either genetic disorders or birth defects. However, many people born with health problems can be treated with drugs or surgery. In addition, people with some disorders can be helped by therapy and training.

Diseases Resulting from Lifestyle Behaviors

Generally, scientists are unable to predict who will develop a particular disease. For some diseases, however, they have identified *certain characteristics that increase a person's chances of developing the disease.* These characteristics are called **risk factors.** Environment, heredity, ethnic group, age, and lifestyle behaviors are examples of risk factors.

A person's lifestyle behavior has a significant effect on his or her health. Many diseases are the direct or indirect result of harmful lifestyle behaviors. Healthful lifestyle behaviors, on the other hand, can help prevent or control certain diseases and disorders. Six healthy lifestyle behaviors that can help you lower your risk of certain diseases and disorders are described in **Figure 12.3.** Which behaviors are part of your lifestyle?

LIFE SKILLS

Evaluating Personal Risk from Media Reports

*F*eatured news reports about health often contradict other reports. This is confusing. Some people throw up their hands and decide to ignore all health information. Others take every report seriously and try to change their behavior. Being able to evaluate health information that comes from the media is an important life skill.

Should you consider changing your behavior because of information in a health news report? Only if it meets four standards: Is the source reliable? Is the scientific research reliable? Is the

report or article reliable? Does the information have some relevance to you? To help evaluate these four factors, ask yourself the following questions.

1. The Source

▶ Does the newspaper, magazine, or program that is the source of the news have a high standard or reputation?

▶ Did you get the information firsthand, or did you hear it from another person? Can you rely on that person's understanding and memory?

Figure 12.3
Six Healthy Lifestyle Behaviors

Eat a healthy diet	Include plenty of whole grains, fruits, and vegetables in your diet. Avoid eating too much fat, salt, and sugar.
Exercise regularly	Regular vigorous exercise strengthens the heart and helps it do its job better.
Maintain your desirable weight	Keep your weight at the level indicated for your height and body frame.
Learn to manage stress	Get plenty of rest and learn to manage stress in your daily life.
Avoid smoking	Tobacco causes heart and lung diseases, cancer, and strokes.
Avoid using alcohol and other drugs	These substances harm your body, impair your judgment, and may cause permanent damage.

Following the healthy lifestyle behaviors described here is no guarantee that you will avoid developing noncommunicable diseases, but it can help. Even people who have a family history of a disease may get some benefit from these lifestyle behaviors. For example, if several members of your family have high blood pressure, you may be at greater risk of developing it yourself. Following healthy lifestyle behaviors may help you avoid the disease altogether or at least minimize its effects.

The Special Olympics provides an opportunity for people with disabilities to compete in athletic events.

2. The Scientific Research

▶ Is the research complete? Has it been repeated with the same results?

▶ Reliable research takes time and involves many subjects. How long has the study been going on? How many people were tested?

3. The Report

▶ Does the report focus on scientific facts rather than opinions? Does the report discuss other studies? Does it explain opposing views?

4. The Relevance to You

▶ Do you have the same characteristics—age, race, and gender—of the people said to be affected by the information? According to this report, can your behavior now affect your health in the future?

Follow-up Activity

Find a recent health news item. After reviewing the item, answer the above questions. If you cannot answer them all, find more information on the topic.

Diseases Caused by the Environment

Many diseases are caused by hazards in the environment. Lung cancer is an example. Although most cases of lung cancer are caused by smoking, some are caused by breathing in harmful substances such as asbestos. The environmental hazards listed below can cause health problems for some people or make existing health problems worse in others.

■ Fumes from chemical waste in landfills can seep into houses that have been constructed over them. Illness can occur years after the waste has been covered.

■ Gaseous wastes from automobiles create or add to air pollution that can cause serious illness.

■ Certain construction materials, such as asbestos and urea-formaldehyde insulation foam, cause disease after long exposure. They are now restricted.

■ Indoor air can be polluted by solvents, paints, and household chemicals.

■ Nonsmokers are exposed to dangerous secondhand smoke in restaurants, businesses, and homes.

■ The manufacturing of household items such as plastics and paint products can create dangerous air and water pollution.

■ Radon is a colorless, odorless gas produced by uranium. It can seep into homes from the surrounding soil. It can cause serious illnesses.

Nonsmokers must be on the alert to avoid exposure to secondhand smoke in restaurants and other settings.

Lesson 1 Review

Using complete sentences, answer the following questions on a separate sheet of paper.

Reviewing Terms and Facts

1. **Vocabulary** Using your own words, define *chronic disease.*

2. **Explain** What causes noncommunicable diseases? How does someone get a noncommunicable disease?

3. **Give Examples** Name five noncommunicable diseases.

4. **Recall** What is cancer?

5. **Vocabulary** What is the difference between a *genetic disorder* and a *birth defect*? Give an example of each.

Thinking Critically

6. **Compare** Point out similarities and differences between noncommunicable diseases and communicable diseases.

7. **Hypothesize** What are three harmful lifestyle behaviors?

Applying Health Concepts

8. **Personal Health** Do you engage in any lifestyle behaviors that are unhealthful? If so, what are they? Which, if any, of these behaviors would you like to change? What are some healthy behaviors that are part of your lifestyle as well?

Understanding Heart Disease

This lesson will help you find answers to questions that teens often ask about heart disease. For example:

▶ **What is a heart attack?**

▶ **Can I do anything to prevent heart disease?**

▶ **Can a person with heart disease get well?**

Number One Killer

Heart disease is the number one killer of adults in the United States. Someone dies as a result of heart disease about every 34 seconds. (See **Figure 12.4**.) Many people think this is a disease of the elderly, but about 17 of every 1,000 people with heart disease are under 18 years old.

The term *heart disease,* also called cardiovascular disease, includes any condition that lessens the strength or function of the heart or blood vessels. Healthy lifestyle behaviors can lower a person's risk of heart disease.

Figure 12.4
Frequency of Heart Disease

About 260 million people live in the United States. Roughly 1 out of every 4 of these people has some form of heart disease.

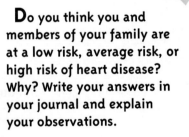

Words to Know

atherosclerosis
arteriosclerosis
heart attack
stroke
blood pressure
pacemaker

---

in your journal

Do you think you and members of your family are at a low risk, average risk, or high risk of heart disease? Why? Write your answers in your journal and explain your observations.

Atherosclerosis and Arteriosclerosis

Like other body cells, the cells of your heart muscle need oxygen and nutrients. These are carried by the blood. The arteries that supply your heart muscle with blood are called coronary (KAWR·uh·nehr·ee) arteries, as shown in part C of **Figure 12.5.**

When the coronary arteries are clear, blood flows freely through them. If the flow slows or stops, a serious health problem can result. **Atherosclerosis** (a·thuh·roh·skluh·ROH·sis) is *a condition in which fatty substances in the blood are deposited on the walls of the arteries.* Part B of **Figure 12.5** shows how atherosclerosis can clog arteries and reduce the blood flow.

One fatty substance that causes atherosclerosis is cholesterol (kuh·LES·tuh·rawl). Some cholesterol is produced by your body. Certain foods also contain cholesterol. Many people lower their intake of foods high in cholesterol and fats to lower their blood cholesterol level.

Healthy artery walls are elastic. As people get older, their arteries naturally tend to become less elastic. This *hardening of the arteries* is called **arteriosclerosis** (ar·tir·ee·oh·skluh·ROH·sis). Arteriosclerosis slows the flow of blood through arteries. It is also a major cause of high blood pressure. Atherosclerosis speeds up hardening of the arteries and makes its harmful effects worse.

When the flow of blood is reduced, blood clots may form within the blood vessels. These clots can block the flow of blood altogether. Blockage is especially likely to happen when a clot sticks in a part of an artery where there is a buildup of fatty deposits. When a coronary artery is blocked, the result can be a heart attack. When an artery in the brain is blocked, the result can be a stroke.

Figure 12.5
Heart Attack and Stroke

Healthy coronary arteries are clear and flexible. Enough blood flows to the heart tissue to keep it well supplied with the oxygen needed for life. *If the blood flow slows or stops, heart muscle tissue dies from lack of oxygen,* causing a **heart attack.** *If the blood supply to the brain is disturbed, part of the brain may be damaged.* The resulting body reaction is called a **stroke.**

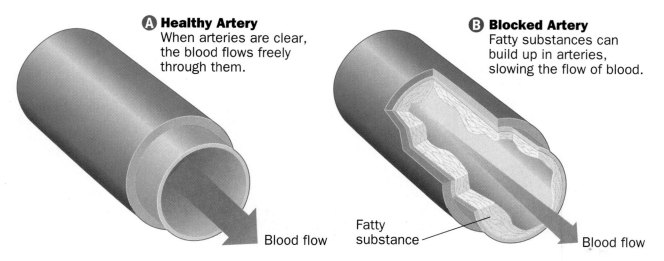

A Healthy Artery
When arteries are clear, the blood flows freely through them.

Blood flow

B Blocked Artery
Fatty substances can build up in arteries, slowing the flow of blood.

Fatty substance

Blood flow

High Blood Pressure

Your heart pumps blood throughout your body. **Blood pressure** is *the force of the blood on the inside walls of the blood vessels.* Blood pressure is expressed as two numbers. A typical blood pressure for a teen might be 110 over 70, often written 110/70. The top, higher, number is the measure of the pressure exerted when the heart contracts, sending blood throughout the body. The bottom, lower, number is the measure of the pressure when the heart relaxes between beats.

Your blood pressure is not the same at all times. When you are feeling stress or exercising, it may be higher than usual. When you are resting, it may be lower than usual. These changes are normal. When a *person's blood pressure is usually higher than normal* for his or her age, that person is said to have high blood pressure, or *hypertension* (hy·per·TEN·shuhn). High blood pressure can lead to heart attack, stroke, and kidney failure.

The cause of high blood pressure is often unclear. However, doctors know that four factors may increase your chance of having high blood pressure.

- Eating a large amount of salt

- Being overweight

- Feeling extreme stress for long periods of time

- Having a family history of high blood pressure

There are no outward signs of high blood pressure until it has caused serious damage. For this reason, high blood pressure is called the silent killer. A regular checkup can detect whether your blood pressure is too high.

ⓒ Heart Attack

A heart attack occurs when heart muscle tissue dies from lack of oxygen and nutrients because of reduced or stopped blood flow.

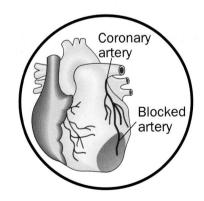

Coronary artery

Blocked artery

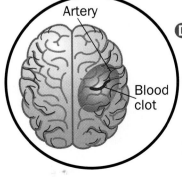

Artery

Blood clot

ⓓ Stroke

Most strokes are caused by a blood clot blocking an artery that supplies blood to the brain. The clot may develop in any part of the body and travel with the blood to the brain, or it may develop in the brain itself.

More About Strokes

Some strokes are caused by the breaking of an artery in the brain. This type of stroke is known as a *brain hemorrhage*. A stroke can cause a person to lose feeling or the ability to move. A serious stroke can result in death.

Treating Heart Disease

There have been many advances in the treatment of heart disease. If a patient's heart has been greatly damaged by heart disease, doctors may recommend a heart transplant. A heart transplant involves surgically replacing the patient's diseased heart with a healthy heart from a donor. In many more cases, three other treatments are used: bypass surgery, the dissolving of blood clots, and—as shown in **Figure 12.6**—angioplasty (AN·gee·uh·plas·tee).

- **Going around the blockage.** Surgeons create new paths for blood to flow around a blocked artery. They remove a vein from the patient's leg and attach it above and below the blocked area to form a detour through which the blood can flow freely. The procedure is called bypass surgery.

- **Dissolving clots.** Blood clots tend to form in blocked blood vessels where blood flow is affected. Medications are used to help dissolve clots and to keep clots from forming.

Figure 12.6
Clearing the Blockage in Arteries

Surgeons use instruments with tiny balloons attached near the end to clear blocked arteries. The procedure is called *angioplasty*.

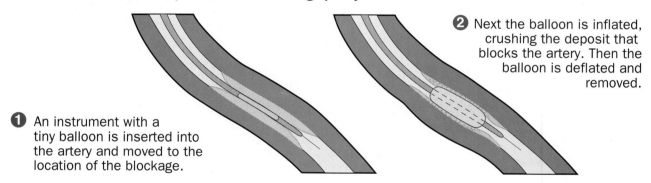

❶ An instrument with a tiny balloon is inserted into the artery and moved to the location of the blockage.

❷ Next the balloon is inflated, crushing the deposit that blocks the artery. Then the balloon is deflated and removed.

HEALTH LAB
Measuring Blood Pressure

*B*ecause blood pressure is an important health factor, many people check it regularly.

Objective: To learn how blood pressure is read.

Materials and Method: This activity should be done by a health practitioner and two or three volunteers. Each volunteer will be checked twice—once at rest and once after physical activity.

Both a stethoscope and a sphygmomanometer are needed to measure a person's blood pressure. A sphygmomanometer has three parts: a cuff, or wide rubbery band, that can be filled with air; a hollow rubber bulb used to pump air into the cuff; and a gauge with a glass tube filled with mercury.

First the health practitioner loosens the screw-valve on the rubber ball to deflate the cuff. The cuff is wrapped snugly, but not too tightly, around the arm of the volunteer. The cup of the stethoscope is placed between the cuff and the inner elbow.

The health practitioner uses the stethoscope to listen for the person's pulse. With the stethoscope in

Treating High Blood Pressure

People with high blood pressure may be given medicines to lower their blood pressure. In addition, researchers have found that certain lifestyle behaviors play an important role in lowering blood pressure. These include eating a balanced diet low in salt and fat and exercising regularly. Learning to manage stress and maintaining a healthy weight are also important factors. If someone with high blood pressure smokes, quitting is always his or her doctor's first recommendation.

Treating Other Heart Problems

Some people have problems with the valves of their hearts. The heart has four chambers through which the blood moves. Healthy valves open only one way and allow the blood to move in only one direction. Damaged valves allow blood to leak back into the chamber it has left. Doctors can correct some damaged valves with surgery, or they may replace a damaged valve with a mechanical one.

Irregular heartbeat is another common health problem. Healthy hearts beat at a strong, regular pace. If a person's heartbeat is irregular or weak, doctors may insert a **pacemaker** (PAYS·may·ker). This *small device sends steady electrical pulses to the heart to make it beat regularly.*

A person's blood pressure is an important indication of his or her health.

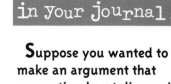

in your journal

Suppose you wanted to make an argument that preventing heart disease is wiser than trying to cure it. Write the major points of your argument in your journal.

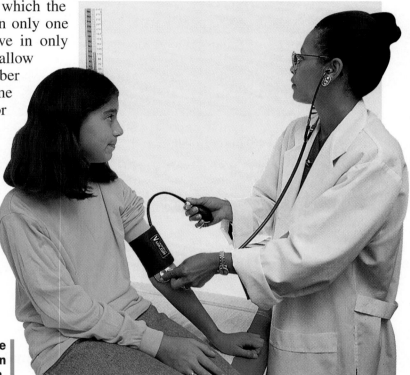

place, the screw-valve is tightened. The hollow ball is then pumped to fill the cuff with air until the mercury reaches about 130. Then the screw is loosened enough for the column to let air escape. The mercury starts dropping slowly. The health practitioner listens and watches the mercury as it drops, waiting until there is a steady thumping sound. The location of the mercury at the first thump is the top number of the volunteer's blood pressure—the reading when the heart is contracting to pump blood.

The thumping sound will grow faint and then stop. The location of the mercury at the last thump is the bottom number of the volunteer's blood pressure, when the heart is at rest.

Observation and Analysis:
Compare the readings of the volunteers' blood pressure before and after physical activity. What differences do you note?

Preventing Heart Disease

Heart disease can be a lifestyle disease—it can result from how a person lives. Doctors have identified nine risk factors for heart disease. Four of them are not within a person's control. These factors are age, gender, race, and a family history of heart disease. The other five risk factors are well within a person's control. They are matched in **Figure 12.7** with appropriate lifestyle behaviors.

Figure 12.7
Controlling Risk Factors

Risk Factor	Healthy Behavior
Weight	Maintain a desirable weight. Being overweight makes your heart work harder.
Exercise	Regular exercise strengthens your heart and helps you control your weight.
Diet	Follow a diet that is high in fiber and low in salt, fat, and cholesterol. Too much salt can lead to high blood pressure. A diet that is high in fats and cholesterol can contribute to the buildup of fatty deposits in arteries.
Stress	Learn to cope with stress in your life. Constant stress can increase your blood pressure.
Tobacco	Don't smoke. Even one pack of cigarettes a day doubles your chance of heart disease.

Lesson 2 Review

Using complete sentences, answer the following questions on a separate sheet of paper.

Reviewing Terms and Facts

1. **Vocabulary** Compare and contrast *atherosclerosis* and *arteriosclerosis*.

2. **Vocabulary** What is the difference between a *heart attack* and a *stroke*?

3. **Describe** Outline the course of a heart attack or stroke.

4. **Explain** What is angioplasty and what is it used for?

5. **Identify** What are six ways to reduce high blood pressure?

6. **Vocabulary** What is a *pacemaker?* What is it used to treat?

7. **Identify** What are four risk factors for heart disease that are not affected by changing your lifestyle?

Thinking Critically

8. **Analyze** Explain why a blocked coronary artery may lead to damage to heart tissue.

9. **Synthesize** Why is it a good idea to check your blood pressure regularly, even if you have no signs of high blood pressure?

Applying Health Concepts

10. **Personal Health** With a family member or friend, try some low-salt, low-fat versions of the foods you normally eat. For example, try low-salt soup, low-fat cookies, low-fat salad dressing, or low-fat frozen yogurt instead of ice cream. Try a variety of these foods. Which ones did you like and which ones did you dislike? Report your findings to your classmates.

Understanding Cancer

This lesson will help you find answers to questions that teens often ask about cancer. For example:

▶ **What causes cancer?**
▶ **How does cancer harm the body?**
▶ **What can I do to avoid getting cancer?**

What Is Cancer?

The second leading cause of death for adults in the United States is cancer. Cancer is actually a group of many different diseases. These diseases can affect most parts of the body, including the lungs, blood, skin, brain, and breasts. All types of **cancers** involve *abnormal body cells growing out of control.*

The human body has trillions of cells. Most cells, such as those that form blood, grow and reproduce all the time. The human body forms many trillions of new cells each year. Many thousands are abnormal, but most abnormal cells are destroyed by the body's defenses. However, sometimes an abnormal cell lives on and begins to copy itself at an out-of-control rate. This out-of-control growth of abnormal cells is cancer.

Benign and Malignant Tumors

When an abnormal cell survives and starts to reproduce itself, the cells grow much more rapidly than normal cells grow. *Groups of abnormal cells form in masses* called **tumors** (TOO·mers). There are two kinds of tumors—benign or malignant. **Benign** (bi·NYN) **tumors** are *not cancerous.* **Malignant** (muh·LIG·nuhnt) **tumors** are *cancerous.*

Words to Know

cancer
tumor
benign tumor
malignant tumor
metastasis
carcinogen
biopsy
radiation
chemotherapy

Cancer is a disease characterized by abnormal body cells growing out of control. Describe the difference between the cells shown in the two photographs—the normal cells (left) and the cancer cells (right).

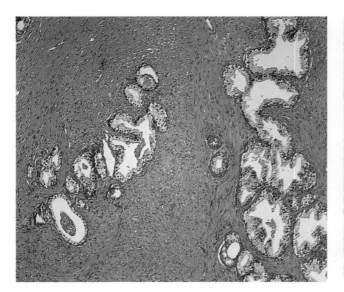
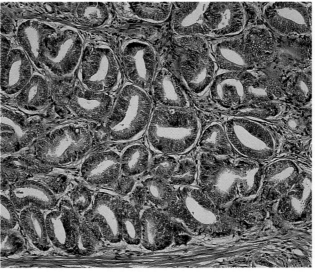

Cancer progresses in stages. In the final stage, cancer cells from malignant tumors may enter the bloodstream or lymph system and travel to other parts of the body and form new tumors. *The spreading of cancer cells* is called **metastasis** (muh·TAS·tuh·sis). Some types of cancer are described in **Figure 12.8.**

Figure 12.8
Common Types of Cancer

Cancer can affect almost any part of the body. Although different types of cancer may develop for different reasons, all types are caused by abnormal body cells growing out of control.

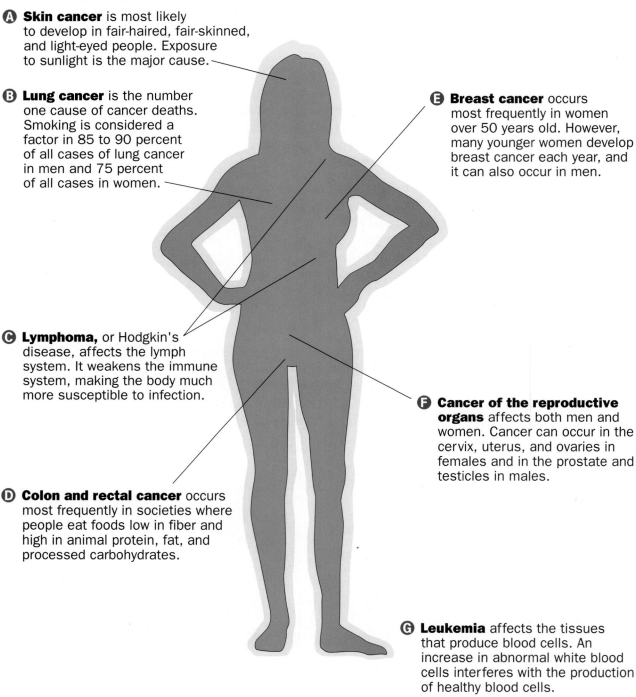

A **Skin cancer** is most likely to develop in fair-haired, fair-skinned, and light-eyed people. Exposure to sunlight is the major cause.

B **Lung cancer** is the number one cause of cancer deaths. Smoking is considered a factor in 85 to 90 percent of all cases of lung cancer in men and 75 percent of all cases in women.

C **Lymphoma,** or Hodgkin's disease, affects the lymph system. It weakens the immune system, making the body much more susceptible to infection.

D **Colon and rectal cancer** occurs most frequently in societies where people eat foods low in fiber and high in animal protein, fat, and processed carbohydrates.

E **Breast cancer** occurs most frequently in women over 50 years old. However, many younger women develop breast cancer each year, and it can also occur in men.

F **Cancer of the reproductive organs** affects both men and women. Cancer can occur in the cervix, uterus, and ovaries in females and in the prostate and testicles in males.

G **Leukemia** affects the tissues that produce blood cells. An increase in abnormal white blood cells interferes with the production of healthy blood cells.

What Causes Cancer?

Some types of cancer seem to be caused by factors that are inherited. Other types are related to lifestyle behaviors, such as smoking. Some types of cancer are caused by **carcinogens** (kar·SIN·uh·juhns) which are *substances that cause cancer.* Common sources of carcinogens are identified in **Figure 12.9.**

You can avoid some carcinogens. You can choose not to smoke or sunbathe. However, a few carcinogens, such as the chemical pollution from factories, are more difficult to avoid. This type pollution is monitored by government agencies. The Environmental Protection Agency (EPA), the Food and Drug Administration (FDA), and other agencies have regulations that are designed to protect the public from environmental carcinogens.

Diagnosing and Treating Cancer

Doctors can often find some types of cancer during a routine physical exam. They use tests to find others. A blood test, for instance, shows whether the blood cancer leukemia is present. If some tissue appears to be abnormal, the doctor may order a **biopsy** (BY·ahp·see). In this test, *a small piece of tissue is removed for testing in a lab.* The earlier cancer is found and treated, the better the chance of the person's survival.

Figure 12.9
Common Sources of Carcinogens

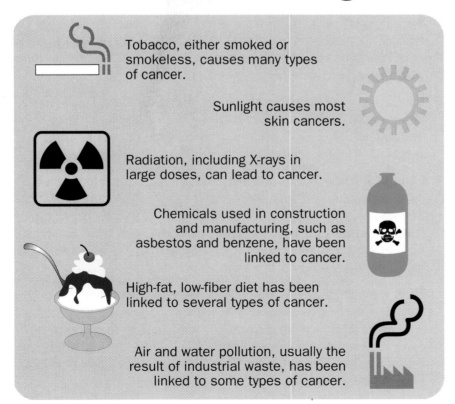

Tobacco, either smoked or smokeless, causes many types of cancer.

Sunlight causes most skin cancers.

Radiation, including X-rays in large doses, can lead to cancer.

Chemicals used in construction and manufacturing, such as asbestos and benzene, have been linked to cancer.

High-fat, low-fiber diet has been linked to several types of cancer.

Air and water pollution, usually the result of industrial waste, has been linked to some types of cancer.

Warning Signs of Cancer

People can play an important role in protecting themselves from cancer by watching for it. Females, for example, can examine their breasts for lumps, which may be a sign of breast cancer. Males can examine their testicles. Everyone can look for the seven warning signs of cancer identified by the American Cancer Society.

C Change in bowel or bladder habits

A A sore that does not heal

U Unusual bleeding or discharge

T Thickening or lump in breast or elsewhere

I Indigestion or difficulty swallowing

O Obvious change in a wart or mole

N Nagging cough or hoarseness

Treatment of Cancer

The key to treating cancer is finding it early. Once cancer spreads, treatment is more difficult. The main ways to treat cancer are surgery, radiation, and chemotherapy. Doctors often draw up a treatment plan for the patient. This plan may involve a combination of these methods.

■ **Surgery.** The goal of surgery is to remove cancer cells from the body. This method works best on cancers that have not spread to other parts of the body. Surgery is used for skin, breast, lung, colon, and many other types of cancer.

■ **Radiation** (ray·dee·AY·shuhn). In radiation therapy, *X-rays or other radioactive substances are aimed at a tumor.* These rays destroy cancer cells. Radiation may be used in combination with surgery to treat a number of different types of cancer.

■ **Chemotherapy** (kee·moh·THEHR·uh·pee). In chemotherapy, *chemicals are used to destroy cancer cells.* There are more than 50 anticancer drugs. Some cause serious side effects, including severe nausea and hair loss, but certain drugs may lessen the side effects. Chemotherapy can be used to fight cancers that have spread throughout the body.

Each type of cancer treatment has some disadvantages. All three can damage healthy cells along with the cancer cells. Radiation and chemotherapy used to treat one cancer may themselves cause a second cancer years later. The goal is to limit the number of healthy cells that are harmed while the cancer cells are being destroyed.

Preventing Cancer

Many factors that cause cancer are connected to lifestyle choices you make. You can lower your risk of developing some types of cancer by making certain healthy choices. These include avoiding tobacco, eating healthful foods—such as fruits, vegetables, and whole grain cereals—and avoiding high-fat foods, and limiting your exposure to the sun. Although making healthy choices does not guarantee that you will not get cancer, it does give you a greater chance of staying healthy.

Skin cancer is the most common form of cancer in the United States. To lower your risk, you should limit your time in the sun, wear a hat, and use a sunscreen with a SPF (Sun Protection Factor) of at least 15.

Review
Lesson 3

Using complete sentences, answer the following questions on a separate sheet of paper.

Reviewing Terms and Facts

1. **Vocabulary**   What is a *tumor*? Which type of tumor is a more serious health problem: a *benign* or a *malignant tumor*?

2. **Recall**   What is the major cause of skin cancer? What is the major cause of lung cancer?

3. **Vocabulary**   Define *carcinogen*. List two common sources of carcinogens.

4. **Vocabulary**   What is a *biopsy*?

5. **Identify**   List the seven warning signs of cancer.

6. **Recall**   What are the three main ways of treating cancer?

Thinking Critically

7. **Hypothesize**   What type of diet is best for reducing the risk of colon and rectal cancer?

8. **Analyze**   Why is it important to try to discover cancer in its early stages?

Applying Health Concepts

9. **Health of Others**   With a partner, role-play trying to convince a friend of the advantages of following the healthy choices for lowering the risk of cancer. Imagine the following situations: that your friend is a smoker, that your friend eats a high-fat diet, that your friend spends every possible moment outdoors without any protection from the sun.

Teen HEALTH DIGEST

Teens Making a Difference

Road to Remission

At Children's Hospital Medical Center of Akron, Ohio, a group of young cancer patients have developed a board game that helps them cope with the daily stresses of their illness. Sixteen-year-old Tim Snyder and other patients ranging in age from 7 to 17 created the game, called Road to Remission, to help them share their knowledge, feelings, and experiences with others.

Bandages, empty syringes, and pill bottles are used in the game. Players draw cards that present them with various cancer-related situations. Each card involves a move forward or back. Drawing a "You lose your hair" card moves you back. A card reading "You talk your doctor into putting off your hospitalization until after the prom," moves you ahead. The object is to reach the finish line, which is remission. Tim Snyder says, "You deal with cancer better if you can laugh about it. You can't be so serious all the time."

Health Update

Diabetes Genes

An international project to identify and chart all genes in the human body, the Human Genome Project, is producing some very interesting results. Scientists report that they have identified five genes associated with Type I diabetes. People who inherit certain combinations of these genes are likely to develop the disease.

The study, which was carried out in England, focused on 300 families in which two children had diabetes but their parents did not. Researchers took blood samples of family members and used new techniques to identify and locate gene patterns.

Ken Farber, executive director of the Juvenile Diabetes Foundation International, said the news was very exciting. "We now have a handle for determining who is at risk." This knowledge may make it possible to identify people who are at high risk of developing diabetes and to take steps to delay or lessen the effects of the disease.

People at Work

Doctors Just for Teens

Dr. Young Su Kim is one of a growing number of physicians who limit their practice to treating teens. In addition to the usual routine care for colds, flu, and injuries, doctors like Kim concentrate on educating teen patients about their bodies. These doctors also take time to counsel teens about health risks common to their age-group. These risks include drug and alcohol experimentation and sexual behavior.

Most of these doctors begin as pediatricians, doctors who specialize in treating children. One major difference between pediatricians and teen doctors is that parents are always included in the exam done by pediatricians. Teen doctors, on the other hand, usually ask parents to remain in the waiting room, at least for part of the visit, so that their patients can have privacy.

Sports and Recreation

Fastest Woman in the World

The place was Barcelona, Spain. The year was 1992, and Gail Devers was the fastest woman in the world. She had just won the 100-meter dash in the summer Olympic Games.

The road to her spectacular victory in Spain had been a tough one. In 1988, following the Olympic Games in Seoul, South Korea, Devers had complained of headaches, insomnia, and loss of vision. Despite her doctors assurances that she was in good health, her symptoms persisted. Then in 1990, Devers was diagnosed with Graves' disease, a thyroid disorder. The radiation treatment she received had serious side effects and, as a consequence, her legs were almost amputated.

With intense determination and the help of her coach, Bobby Kersee, Devers made a remarkable recovery. Gail Devers is currently training for the 1996 Olympic Games, to be held in Atlanta, Georgia.

CON$UMER FOCU$

Regulating Health Claims

Shopping for healthy foods has become easier. In 1993, the Food and Drug Administration declared that food manufacturers had to meet certain standards before claiming that a product was "low fat," "light," or a "good source of a particular vitamin." According to the new guidelines, a serving of a food must meet certain standards to use these labels.

- "Low in fat" must not have more than 3 grams of fat.

- "Light/Lite" must have half the fat of the regular product or half the salt.

Nutrition Facts
Serving Size 1/4 cup (40g)
Servings Per Container About 9

Amount Per Serving	
Calories 130	Calories from Fat 0

	% Daily Value**
Total Fat 0g	0%
Saturated Fat 0g	0%
Cholesterol 0mg	0%
Sodium 10mg	0%
Potassium 310mg	9%
Total Carbohydrate 31g	10%
Dietary Fiber 2g	9%
Sugars 29g	
Protein 1g	

- "A good source of" must contain 10 to 19 percent of the Daily Value for that particular vitamin, mineral, or fiber.

These guidelines should give consumers a more realistic picture of the food they buy.

Understanding Allergies and Asthma

This lesson will help you find answers to questions that teens often ask about allergies and asthma. For example:

▶ **Why do some people develop allergies and others do not?**

▶ **How can allergies be treated?**

▶ **What is asthma?**

Words to Know

allergy
allergen
pollen
histamine
hives
antihistamine
asthma
bronchodilator

What Are Allergies?

The human body has a natural, built-in defense system that fights germs that enter the body. This defense system is called the immune system. When germs enter the body, the immune system senses danger and starts a process to destroy or eliminate the germs. In some cases, the immune system also reacts to substances to which a person is sensitive. An **allergy** is *the body's sensitivity to certain substances.* A *substance that causes an allergic reaction* is called an **allergen** (AL·er·juhn).

For example, many people are allergic to **pollen,** *tiny grains from plants.* Pollen can cause sneezing, itchy eyes, and other disagreeable reactions in people who are sensitive to it. Although most allergies develop during childhood and youth, anyone can become allergic to practically anything at any age. **Figure 12.10** shows how allergens affect the body.

Figure 12.10
Allergic Reactions

Some allergens, such as poison ivy, cause allergic reactions in many people. Almost any substance, however, can set off an allergic reaction in a person who is sensitive to it.

❶ Contact with allergens happens in three ways: by breathing (pollen, dust, smoke, mold spores); by swallowing (milk, strawberries, aspirin); and by touching them (poison ivy, cosmetics, wool).

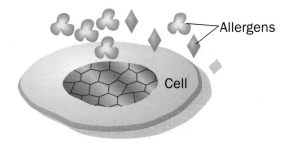

Allergens

Cell

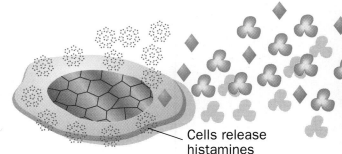

Cells release histamines

❷ When an allergen enters the body, special cells release histamines. These are chemicals that cause the symptoms of an allergic reaction.

Reactions to Allergens

The body's response to allergens is to release histamines. **Hista-mines** (HIS·tuh·meenz) are *chemicals in the body that cause the symptoms of the allergic reaction.* Two common symptoms are difficulty in breathing and a skin rash. Some people get **hives,** *raised bumps on the skin that are very itchy.* Common allergic reactions are shown in part 3 of **Figure 12.10.**

Diagnosing and Treating Allergies

Discovering the cause of an allergic reaction can be quite simple. Perhaps you break out in a rash when you eat strawberries, or your eyes begin to itch and water when you get close to a cat. If, however, the cause of an allergic reaction is not known, a doctor can perform various tests. In the most common test, the patient's skin is scratched and tiny doses of possible allergens are inserted. If the patient is allergic to one of the substances, the skin at that particular place will turn red and swell slightly.

There is no cure for allergies, but there are several ways of dealing with them. The first is to avoid the allergen as much as possible. When this is not possible, a person's symptoms may be relieved by taking **antihistamines.** These are *medications that work against the effects of the histamines,* which cause the symptoms of the allergy. In severe cases, treatment may involve exposing the allergic person to extremely small quantities of the allergen to build up immunity to it.

Math Connection

Pollen Count   ACTIVITY!

People allergic to pollen can monitor the amount of pollen in the air by checking reports in the newspapers and on radio and television. The daily pollen count is based on the number of ragweed pollen grains in one cubic yard of air.

In the library, check back issues of a newspaper for the pollen count on one day of each month in the past year. Make a graph. What time of year is the count highest? When is it lowest?

in your journal

In your journal, list any substances to which you know or suspect you are sensitive. (Don't forget about poison ivy.) Describe how your body reacts to these allergens.

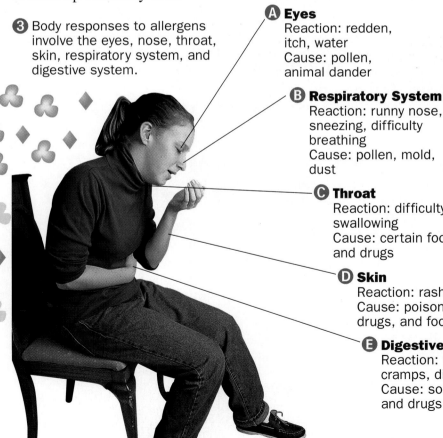

❸ Body responses to allergens involve the eyes, nose, throat, skin, respiratory system, and digestive system.

Ⓐ Eyes
Reaction: redden, itch, water
Cause: pollen, animal dander

Ⓑ Respiratory System
Reaction: runny nose, sneezing, difficulty breathing
Cause: pollen, mold, dust

Ⓒ Throat
Reaction: difficulty swallowing
Cause: certain foods and drugs

Ⓓ Skin
Reaction: rash, hives
Cause: poison ivy, drugs, and foods

Ⓔ Digestive System
Reaction: pain, cramps, diarrhea
Cause: some foods and drugs

What Is Asthma?

More than 10 million people in the United States have asthma. One-third of these people are under 18 years old. **Asthma** (AZ·muh) is *a serious chronic condition that causes tiny air passages in the respiratory system to become narrow or blocked.*

Periods when asthma symptoms are being experienced are called asthma attacks (see **Figure 12.11**). Substances or events that start the attacks are called asthma triggers. Something that triggers an asthma attack in one person may or may not affect another person with asthma. Common triggers of asthma include exposure to allergens, cold air, cigarette smoke, air pollution, certain foods or drugs, and strenuous exercise. Sometimes strong emotions or stress can trigger an asthma attack. This usually happens when other triggers are also present.

Figure 12.11
Asthma Attack

Symptoms of an asthma attack are wheezing, a high-pitched whistling sound made by forcing air through narrowed airways; shortness of breath; a gagging or choking sensation; and tightness in the chest.

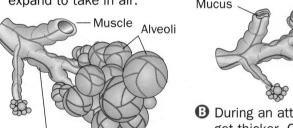

Ⓐ During normal breathing, air passes through the bronchial tubes. The alveoli expand to take in air.

Muscle — Alveoli

Mucus

Bronchial tube

> **Symptoms of an Attack**
> Wheezing, a high-pitched whistling sound made by air being forced through narrowed airways; shortness of breath; gagging or choking sensation; tightness in chest.

Ⓑ During an attack, the bronchial muscles tighten and the tubes get thicker. Cells in the airways make extra mucus, which blocks the airways. Without incoming air, the alveoli collapse.

MAKING HEALTHY DECISIONS
Managing Chronic Conditions

Jesse has asthma. He has worked out a treatment plan with his doctor, and as long as he follows the plan, Jesse manages fairly well. The plan includes taking preventive medication before exercise and using an inhaler at the first sign of an attack. Jesse also has to avoid exercise during times when there is a lot of pollen in the air.

Jesse started going to a new school this year and had trouble at first making friends. Now things are better. Jesse joined the track team and gets along fine with his teammates. His asthma has not been giving him much trouble, and for one reason or another, Jesse hasn't told the coach or his friends about his condition.

Today there is a major track meet. However, Jesse woke up this morning with some tightness in his chest, and he felt short of breath after walking to school. Jesse is worried. He doesn't want to let his team down. He doesn't want his new friends to think he is a quitter. Should he try to tough out the track meet or tell his coach that he may be experiencing the start of an asthma attack?

Learning relaxation techniques is also often helpful. People normally breathe faster when they are under stress or excited. This increase in breathing rate often worsens the breathing difficulties for people with asthma.

Several different types of medication are used for treating asthma. Some block swelling in the bronchial tubes and decrease the amount of mucus being produced. Others, called **bronchodilators** (brahn·ko·dy·LAY·terz), are used to *relax the muscles that have tightened around the airways*. When inhaled in a spray, bronchodilators can often bring relief within a few minutes. These different medicines may be taken regularly on a preventive basis or used during an asthma attack.

People who have asthma must learn how to manage the condition. Most of them are able to lead active lives.

Review

Lesson 4

Using complete sentences, answer the following questions on a separate sheet of paper.

Reviewing Terms and Facts

1. **Vocabulary**   Define *allergen.* List three examples of allergens.

2. **Explain**   Describe what happens when a person comes in contact with a substance he or she is allergic to.

Thinking Critically

3. **Synthesis**   What is usually the most helpful step in managing allergies and asthma?

Applying Health Concepts

4. **Health of Others**   Interview several people with allergies or asthma. Compile a list of how they manage their conditions. Display your list in your classroom.

Jesse remembers the step-by-step decision-making process.

1 **State the situation**
2 **List the options**
3 **Weigh the possible outcomes**
4 **Consider your values**
5 **Make a decision and act**
6 **Evaluate the decision**

Follow-up Activities

1. Apply the six steps of the decision-making process to Jesse's problem.

2. With a group of classmates, discuss who is responsible for managing Jesse's chronic condition.

3. With a partner, role-play telling someone about a chronic health condition.

Other Noncommunicable Diseases

This lesson will help you find answers to questions that teens often ask about arthritis and diabetes. For example:

► **Do only old people get arthritis?**
► **Is there any way to prevent arthritis?**
► **What is diabetes?**
► **Can diabetes be cured?**

Words to Know

arthritis
rheumatoid
   arthritis
osteoarthritis
diabetes
insulin
Type I diabetes
Type II diabetes

Did You Know?

How Many Are Affected?

About 31 million people of all ages in the United States are thought to have some form of arthritis.

What Is Arthritis?

Arthritis is not one disease, but many. A person with **arthritis** (ar·THRY·tuhs) may have *one of more than 100 conditions marked by pain and swelling in body joints.* About one person in seven suffers from one of these conditions. Many people think that arthritis affects only older people, but this disease can affect people of any age, from infancy on.

Rheumatoid Arthritis

The more serious of the two main kinds of arthritis is **rheumatoid** (ROO·muh·toyd) **arthritis.** In this condition, *body joints become swollen and painful, and cartilage that separates the bones is destroyed.* Affected joints often become deformed and stiff, and they no longer function normally. Joints usually affected are those of the hands, feet, elbows, knees, hips, and spine. Usually, the effects of rheumatoid arthritis are symmetrical—both hands develop the symptoms at the same time and in the same pattern.

The cause of rheumatoid arthritis is not known. It may follow infection or injury. A person's immune system may be reacting to and attacking the body's own tissues.

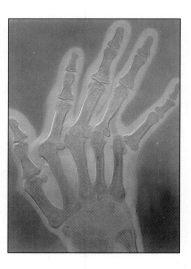

This X-ray shows the joints of a hand affected with rheumatoid arthritis.

Treating Rheumatoid Arthritis

There is no cure for rheumatoid arthritis. When a joint has been severely damaged, the joint may be reconstructed or replaced by surgery. For the most part, treatment centers on relieving pain and preserving or improving joint function. People with rheumatoid arthritis are often given the following advice.

Actions to Take

- **Rest.** Get plenty of rest to reduce stress on affected joints.

- **Medicine.** Take medication as prescribed.

- **Posture.** Develop good posture habits to maintain a healthful positioning of the body.

- **Heat.** Take hot baths or use a heating pad for pain.

- **Exercise.** Exercise daily to prevent further stiffness.

- **Diet.** Eat a healthy balanced diet, including foods that furnish protein and calcium to help prevent further loss of bone tissue.

Daily exercise can help prevent further stiffness.

Osteoarthritis

Osteoarthritis (ahs·tee·oh·ahr·THRY·tuhs) is a more common type of the disease. *This condition results from the wearing away of the body joints.* It affects the joints of the hip and knee most often. These are the joints that bear much of the body's weight. Osteoarthritis is a natural part of aging. Your risk of osteoarthritis increases with age, but this disease can affect people of all ages.

Pain and stiffness in the morning, pain or swelling in a joint, and pain and stiffness in the lower back or knees are warning signs of osteoarthritis. Early medical attention can help lessen its effects.

Treatment for osteoarthritis usually includes ibuprofen or aspirin to ease the pain and swelling. A doctor may also suggest specific exercises to prevent the damage from becoming worse. If the disease has severely damaged a patient's knee or hip joint, a doctor may recommend an operation to replace the diseased joint with a mechanical one.

in your journal

Arthritis often affects the joints of the hands. In your journal, write a list of the everyday tasks, such as writing, that require strong, flexible hands and fingers.

What Is Diabetes?

Diabetes (dy·uh·BEE·teez) is *a disease that prevents the body from converting food into energy.* About 14 million people in the United States have diabetes. Many of those affected do not know they have it. The tendency to develop diabetes can be passed along in families through the genes. Diabetes is caused by problems with the production and function of a hormone called insulin. **Insulin** (IN·suh·lin) *regulates the level of glucose in the blood.* **Figure 12.12** explains the role of insulin in the human body.

Types of Diabetes

Diabetes affects people of all ages and occurs as either Type I or Type II. **Type I diabetes** is *the result of little or no insulin produced by the pancreas.* Type I is also called insulin-dependent because the person must always take insulin to maintain life. This is the type of diabetes that usually develops in children and young adults and affects more males than females.

Type II diabetes is *the result of too little insulin produced by the pancreas or the inability of the body to use insulin.* About 90 percent of all diabetes cases are Type II. This type of diabetes usually develops in people who are overweight and more than 40 years old, although the age of developing it varies.

Did You Know?

Who Gets It?

Although in some families there is a tendency to develop Type II diabetes, another factor usually must be present for the disease to develop. Obesity is a major risk factor that can trigger Type II diabetes. Find out if anyone in your family has had diabetes.

Figure 12.12
Insulin and Diabetes

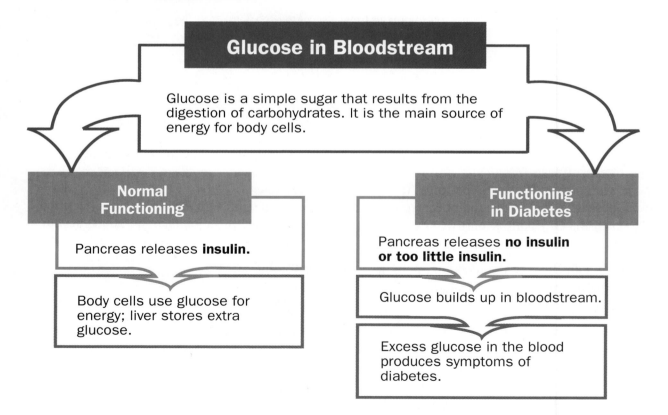

Glucose in Bloodstream

Glucose is a simple sugar that results from the digestion of carbohydrates. It is the main source of energy for body cells.

Normal Functioning

Pancreas releases **insulin.**

Body cells use glucose for energy; liver stores extra glucose.

Functioning in Diabetes

Pancreas releases **no insulin or too little insulin.**

Glucose builds up in bloodstream.

Excess glucose in the blood produces symptoms of diabetes.

Treating Diabetes

The symptoms of diabetes occur when a person's body cells are deprived of a source of energy. Anyone experiencing the following symptoms should be checked by a doctor.

Symptoms of Diabetes

- Excess production of urine
- Excess thirst
- Excess hunger
- Weight loss
- Shortness of breath
- Dry, itchy skin
- Lack of energy

Some people with diabetes need to give themselves insulin injections every day.

People with Type I diabetes need to take insulin every day. In most cases, they inject it with a hypodermic needle. These people must learn how to inject themselves and how to manage their diet. Some people with Type II diabetes take a medicine that helps them use the insulin their body makes.

Diabetes cannot be cured. If left untreated, it can lead to blindness, loss of feeling or severe pain in the feet and hands, kidney failure, and hardening of the arteries. In many cases, however, with medication and proper diet, people with diabetes usually can lead fairly normal lives.

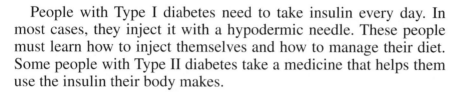

Review

Lesson 5

Using complete sentences, answer the following questions on a separate sheet of paper.

Reviewing Terms and Facts

1. **Recall**   Which is a more serious condition—rheumatoid arthritis or osteoarthritis? Why?

2. **Compare**   How are rheumatoid arthritis and osteoarthritis treated?

3. **Vocabulary**   What is *insulin*?

4. **Identify**   What are the symptoms of diabetes?

Thinking Critically

5. **Synthesize**   What do you think would be most challenging about having diabetes as a teen? Explain your thinking in a brief essay.

Applying Health Concepts

6. **Consumer Health**   Look in magazines and newspapers and on television for advertisements of products for people with arthritis. With several classmates, discuss the ads. Decide what the major point of each ad is. Decide which age-group the manufacturer is trying to appeal to. Do you think this is wise? Why?

7. **Consumer Health**   Look in magazines and newspapers and on television for advertisements of products for people with diabetes. Compare the number of these ads to the number of ads for arthritis products. Why do you suppose there is a difference?

Chapter Summary

▶ Noncommunicable diseases cannot be passed to other people by contact. (Lesson 1)

▶ Most noncommunicable diseases are chronic diseases. (Lesson 1)

▶ Heart disease is the number one killer of adults in the United States. (Lesson 2)

▶ Heart attack occurs when heart muscle tissue dies from lack of oxygen because of reduced or stopped blood flow. (Lesson 2)

▶ Healthy lifestyle behaviors can help prevent heart disease. (Lesson 2)

▶ Cancer is the name used to describe a group of many diseases. In all of them, there is an abnormal growth of body cells. (Lesson 3)

▶ People can reduce their cancer risk by making healthy lifestyle choices. (Lesson 3)

▶ Most allergies develop during childhood and youth, but anyone can become allergic to practically anything at any age. (Lesson 4)

▶ Asthma is a serious chronic condition that causes air passages in the respiratory system to become narrow or blocked. (Lesson 4)

▶ A person with arthritis may have one of more than 100 conditions marked by pain and swelling in body joints. (Lesson 5)

▶ Diabetes is a disease that prevents the body from converting food into energy. (Lesson 5)

Using Health Terms

On a separate sheet of paper, write the vocabulary term that best matches each definition given below.

1. A disease that is not spread through contact (Lesson 1)

2. Characteristics that increase a person's chance of developing a particular disease (Lesson 1)

3. The force of the blood on the inside walls of the blood vessels (Lesson 2)

4. A group of diseases caused by abnormal body cells growing out of control (Lesson 3)

5. Chemicals used to destroy cancer cells (Lesson 3)

6. A condition marked by a body's sensitivity to certain substances (Lesson 4)

7. Tiny grains from plants (Lesson 4)

8. Medications that work against the effects of histamines (Lesson 4)

9. One of many conditions marked by painful, swollen joints (Lesson 5)

10. A disease that prevents the body from converting food into energy (Lesson 5)

Reviewing Main Ideas

Using complete sentences, answer the following questions on a separate sheet of paper.

1. Give five examples of noncommunicable diseases. (Lesson 1)

2. What is a genetic disorder? (Lesson 1)

3. Explain the three ways that people get noncommunicable diseases. (Lesson 1)

4. Name and describe a major cause of reduced blood flow in people with heart disease. (Lesson 2)

5. What is the difference between a benign and a malignant tumor? (Lesson 3)

6. What happens when a cancer has reached metastasis? (Lesson 3)

7. How do people take allergens into their bodies? (Lesson 4)

8. Describe an asthma attack. (Lesson 4)

9. What are bronchodilators? (Lesson 4)

10. Which form of arthritis can affect body systems other than the bones? (Lesson 5)

11. What happens to the body when a person has diabetes? (Lesson 5)

Thinking Critically

Using complete sentences, answer the following questions on a separate sheet of paper.

1. **Apply** Joel was born with sickle-cell anemia. Could this disease have been prevented? Explain. (Lesson 1)

2. **Apply** Gita's uncle is suffering from cancer. She is afraid she may get it from him. Why is this an unrealistic fear? (Lesson 1)

3. **Analyze** Because both of Patty's parents have high blood pressure, she feels that she will, too, no matter what she does. Is she right? Explain. (Lesson 2)

4. **Analyze** The waiter at a restaurant offers you french fries or rice with your dinner. Which is the wiser choice for your health? Why? (Lesson 2)

5. **Explain** Why is it important to find cancer early? (Lesson 3)

6. **Apply** How can you protect yourself from skin cancer without staying inside all day? (Lesson 3)

7. **Evaluate** Ruth Ann avoids exercise because she has asthma. Is she managing her disease well? Why or why not? (Lesson 4)

8. **Analyze** Juan has diabetes for which he takes pills. What does this tell you about his disease? Why? (Lesson 5)

Your Action Plan

Make an action plan to choose healthy lifestyle behaviors so you can lower your risk of getting heart disease or cancer. First, set a goal. Look back through your private journal entries for this chapter. What do they tell you about your risk factors for these diseases?

The next step is to do research and write a list of goals—the behaviors and actions that are helpful in preventing your targeted disease.

Then think of a series of short-term goals that you can reach to achieve your long-term goals. For example, for the long-term goal of eating a balanced diet that is low in fat, a short-term goal might be to replace fast-food snacks with vegetable snacks. At the end of every month, look back to see how you are doing with your short-term goals.

Building Your Portfolio

1. Select a noncommunicable disease to investigate. Collect current magazine and newspaper articles about the disease. Read the articles and mark what interests you. Write a summary paragraph telling what you have learned. Explain how this information may affect you personally. Add the articles and summary to your portfolio.

2. Collect stories of people who have survived a serious noncommunicable disease. Clip articles from magazines and newspapers or record interviews with people you know. Based on these stories, tape-record the advice you would give to someone with such a disease. Add the stories and tape to your portfolio.

In Your Home and Community

1. One risk factor in many noncommunicable diseases is a family history of the disease. Does a member of your family have a non-communicable disease? Do research to find out what steps could be taken to lower the risk that other members of the family will get this disease.

2. Join with classmates to survey your community for environmental hazards that could contribute to the development of non-communicable diseases. Ask your teacher to help you arrange an appointment with the appropriate city official to share your findings.

Unit 5
Avoiding Substance Abuse

Tobacco and Your Health

Student Expectations

After reading this chapter, you should be able to:

1. Explain how tobacco affects your body and your health.

2. Describe how tobacco addiction develops.

3. Identify ways to avoid tobacco and ways to stop using tobacco.

I was reading my latest issue of a teen magazine when I saw the advertisement for the statewide poster contest called "Toward a Smoke-Free 2000." It was being held to get teens to think about the dangers of smoking and to help them aim for a tobacco-free society by the turn of the century. A few of my friends and I decided to enter the contest.

Karen drew a picture of a girl standing inside a giant cigarette pack, her head peeking over the edge. Her poster said, "Smoking's just a pack of trouble. Don't start." Paul drew a family at the dinner table, their heads covered by a cloud of smoke. His slogan was, "When one of us smokes, we all do."

My poster shows a New Year's Eve party and the slogan "Welcome to the Twenty-First Century . . . A Breath of Fresh Air." We all hope that one of our posters wins the contest. Of course, if we're tobacco free by the year 2000, we'll all be winners.

in Your Journal

Read the account on this page. Do you ever think about the dangers of smoking? Do you, or people close to you, use tobacco? Start your private journal entries on tobacco and your health by answering these questions:

▶ Have you ever tried tobacco? If so, what did you like and dislike about it?

▶ Have you ever felt pressured to smoke but resisted the pressure? If so, how did you do it?

When you reach the end of the chapter, you will use your journal entries to make an action plan.

What Tobacco Does to Your Body

This lesson will help you find answers to questions that teens often ask about using tobacco. For example:

▶ **What is in tobacco that causes health problems?**

▶ **Is tobacco harmful in all of its forms?**

▶ **What parts of my body would be affected by tobacco?**

Words to Know

nicotine
tar
carbon monoxide
cilia

Tobacco: Fact and Fiction

A single puff of smoke exposes the body to more than 3,000 chemicals. Some are deadly. Almost all make the body unable to work properly. At least 43 of the chemicals in tobacco smoke are known to cause cancer in smokers. Smoke also harms the health of nonsmokers. Even smokeless tobacco causes health problems in its users, including cancer. (See **Figure 13.1.**)

Figure 13.1
Smoking and Tobacco Use

Figure 13.1 on this page lists some questions and answers about smoking. In your journal, write some questions you have about smoking that do not appear in the chart. Ask your teacher or health care provider to answer your questions. Then write the answers in your journal.

Q:	A:
■ Can smoking for a few years as a teen hurt me?	■ Yes, any amount of smoking cigarettes will damage your lungs and affect your appearance.
■ If I don't inhale the cigarette smoke, can smoking still hurt me?	■ Yes, even if you don't inhale, some smoke enters your lungs.
■ Is the use of smokeless tobacco harmful to my body?	■ Yes, smokeless tobacco damages teeth and gums and causes cancer.

What Is in Tobacco?

There are three main harmful substances in tobacco smoke. **Nicotine** (NIK·uh·teen) is *an addictive drug in tobacco.* This drug also makes tobacco users crave more tobacco. It can cause the dizziness and upset stomach that many beginning smokers feel.

Tar is *a thick, dark liquid that forms when tobacco burns.* This tar covers the lining of the lungs where it can cause disease. **Carbon monoxide** (KAR·buhn muh·NAHK·syd) is *a colorless, odorless, poisonous gas produced when tobacco burns.* All three of these poisons are in tobacco smoke whether the user is smoking a cigarette, a cigar, or a pipe (see **Figure 13.2**).

Tobacco in Many Forms

Tobacco products come in several forms, which are smoked or chewed. The most commonly used form is cigarettes.

Cigarettes

The tobacco used in cigarettes is made from shredded tobacco leaves. Although filtered cigarettes reduce the amount of nicotine and tar released by a cigarette, they do not decrease the amount of carbon monoxide and other gases.

Special kinds of cigarettes are made using tobacco and other ingredients, such as spices. The spices make the cigarettes taste and smell sweet. Scientists believe that specialty cigarettes contain more cancer-causing chemicals than regular cigarettes.

Figure 13.2
Some Harmful Substances in Tobacco Smoke

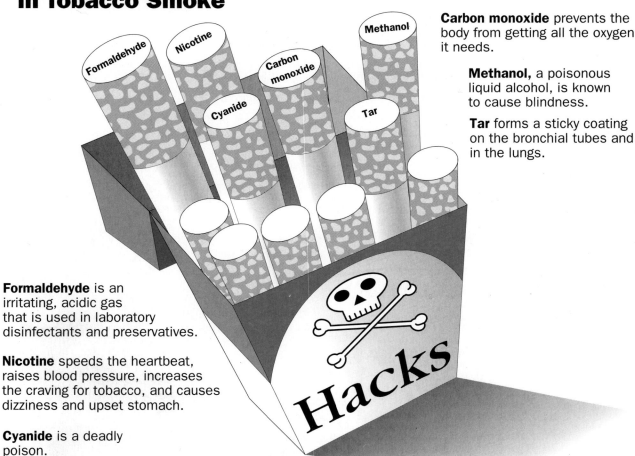

Carbon monoxide prevents the body from getting all the oxygen it needs.

Methanol, a poisonous liquid alcohol, is known to cause blindness.

Tar forms a sticky coating on the bronchial tubes and in the lungs.

Formaldehyde is an irritating, acidic gas that is used in laboratory disinfectants and preservatives.

Nicotine speeds the heartbeat, raises blood pressure, increases the craving for tobacco, and causes dizziness and upset stomach.

Cyanide is a deadly poison.

Why Embarrass Yourself?

Have you ever seen your favorite movie star spit? Spitting in public is not a cool or classy thing to do. In fact it is against the law in some parts of the country. People who chew tobacco, however, must spit out the tobacco juice that forms in their mouth. Keep this in mind if you think about chewing tobacco. Spitting is not going to win you any friends.

Smokeless Tobacco

Two forms of tobacco are placed in the mouth instead of smoked. Chewing tobacco is a form made from coarsely ground leaves that have been compressed. It is placed between the cheek and gum, where the wad is sucked and occasionally chewed. Snuff is smokeless tobacco that is finely ground into a powdery substance. It is placed between the lower lip and gum, where it mixes with saliva and is absorbed.

Smokeless tobacco may seem safe. Users feel that they are avoiding the tar and carbon monoxide in smoke. Although that is true, the nicotine in smokeless tobacco is just as harmful and addictive as nicotine inhaled in cigarette smoke. Smokeless tobacco is linked to an increased incidence of mouth cancer and cancers of the esophagus, larynx, and pancreas. Smokeless tobacco also causes red and inflamed gums, bad breath, yellow teeth, and it increases dental cavities.

Pipes and Cigars

Pipes and cigars are also used for smoking tobacco. They are filled with shredded tobacco leaves, some of which may be flavored. Smoking pipes and cigars causes health problems similar to smoking cigarettes. Pipe and cigar smokers develop lung cancer less often than cigarette smokers because they usually inhale less smoke than cigarette smokers. However, pipe and cigar smokers are more likely than cigarette smokers to develop cancers of the lip, mouth, and throat. That is because more tar and other chemicals are produced by pipes and cigars than by cigarettes.

Tobacco and Your Body

The drugs in tobacco are powerful. They affect the body in many unhealthy ways. Smokers have a greater chance than nonsmokers of getting lung and heart disease. Smokeless tobacco users are also at higher risk for getting certain diseases. **Figure 13.3** shows what using tobacco does to the lungs. **Figure 13.4** illustrates tobacco's effect on the whole body.

Figure 13.3
What Tobacco Does to the Lungs

Ⓐ This nonsmoker's lung is clear and healthy looking. There are no dark or diseased portions.

Ⓑ In this smoker's lung, chemicals in tobacco smoke coat the bronchi and alveoli in the lungs. This makes the lungs work less well and can cause serious diseases, such as cancer and emphysema. Smokers are ten times more likely to develop lung cancer than are nonsmokers.

Figure 13.4
What Tobacco Does to the Body

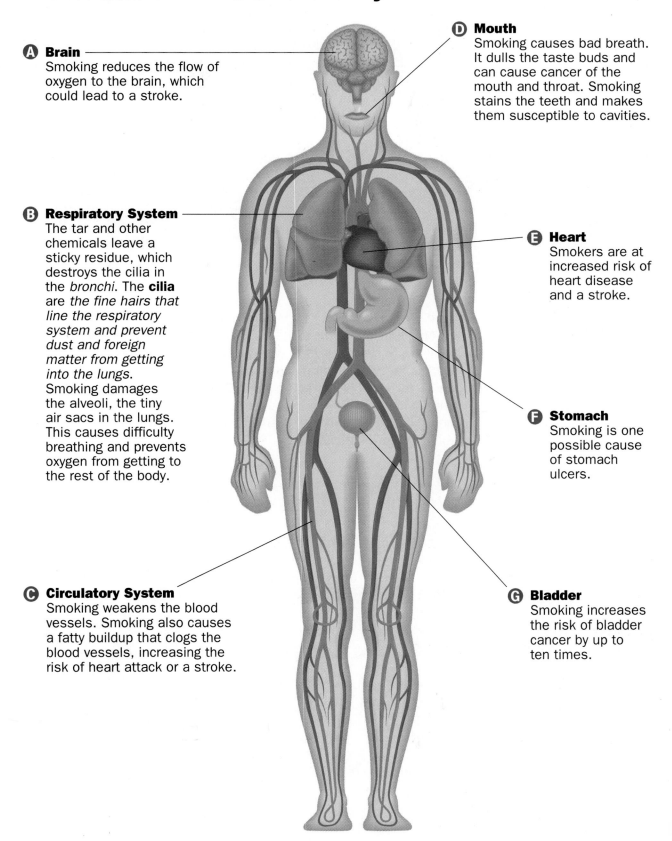

A Brain
Smoking reduces the flow of oxygen to the brain, which could lead to a stroke.

D Mouth
Smoking causes bad breath. It dulls the taste buds and can cause cancer of the mouth and throat. Smoking stains the teeth and makes them susceptible to cavities.

B Respiratory System
The tar and other chemicals leave a sticky residue, which destroys the cilia in the *bronchi*. The **cilia** are *the fine hairs that line the respiratory system and prevent dust and foreign matter from getting into the lungs.* Smoking damages the alveoli, the tiny air sacs in the lungs. This causes difficulty breathing and prevents oxygen from getting to the rest of the body.

E Heart
Smokers are at increased risk of heart disease and a stroke.

F Stomach
Smoking is one possible cause of stomach ulcers.

C Circulatory System
Smoking weakens the blood vessels. Smoking also causes a fatty buildup that clogs the blood vessels, increasing the risk of heart attack or a stroke.

G Bladder
Smoking increases the risk of bladder cancer by up to ten times.

Math Connection

The Price of Smoking ACTIVITY!

Calculate the cost of cigarettes over the course of one year, two years, five years, and ten years based on $2.00 per pack. Assume that you smoke one pack of cigarettes a day.

The Costs to Society

The effects of tobacco on those who use it have long been known. In 1965, health warnings began to appear on cigarette packs. In 1971, cigarette advertisements were banned from radio and television. Since that time, the percentage of Americans who smoke has steadily declined. As the number of nonsmokers has increased, public concern over the costs of smoking to society has increased dramatically.

HEALTH LAB
Smoking and Breathing

Introduction: Taking a deep breath of fresh air comes easily to people with healthy lungs. For people who smoke, however, breathing deeply can become a difficult activity. Tar covers their airways and lungs. This tar, along with the drying effect of cigarette smoke, paralyzes or destroys cilia, the waving hairlike projections that work to keep the respiratory tract clear. Without cilia, smoke that is inhaled into the lungs deposits harmful gases and particles in the bronchi and alveoli. Taking deep breaths of fresh air irritates these gases and particles and causes smokers to cough.

Objective: To recognize that chemicals produced by cigarette smoke damage the smoker's body as evidenced by the following experiment.

Materials and Method: You will be creating a smoking machine. To do so, you will need the following materials: a squeezable rubber bulb, rubber or glass tubing, a clean white handkerchief, cigarettes, and matches.

You will also need a sheet of paper for your observations. Divide the sheet into two columns: *Observation* and *Analysis.* In the observation column, write just the facts—what occurred as a result of the experiment. In the analysis column, write your interpretation of the experiment. Answer questions such as these: Do you think what happened to the handkerchief happens to the smoker's body, too? Where do you think the chemicals are deposited in the body? What harm might that do?

The cost to smokers is high. It includes the price of tobacco products and the cost of health care. The cost to nonsmokers—those who are exposed to the tobacco smoke of others against their will—is also significant. They are at increased risk for lung cancer and other respiratory diseases. The developing babies of pregnant women who smoke can also suffer serious effects.

Review

Using complete sentences, answer the following questions on a separate sheet of paper.

Reviewing Terms and Facts

1. **Vocabulary** Which of the following are poisons in tobacco smoke: *nicotine, tar, carbon monoxide?* Describe each one.

2. **Give Examples** List ways that smoking tobacco can harm your body.

Thinking Critically

3. **Explain** If you had a friend who used snuff, how could you persuade him to quit using it?

4. **Hypothesize** Why do you think it is difficult to quit smoking?

Applying Health Concepts

5. **Health of Others** Collect newspaper and magazine articles about the harmful effects of using tobacco. Use the articles and draw illustrations to make a bulletin-board display.

6. **Health of Others** Write to the local chapter of the American Cancer Society and request information about the effects of smoking or using smokeless tobacco. Use this information and what you have learned in this lesson to promote the health of a friend, neighbor, or family member who smokes or uses smokeless tobacco.

7. **Personal Health** With a classmate, write a pledge to never start smoking or, if you have started, to quit.

Now you are ready to begin the experiment. Attach the bulb to the tubing, placing a handkerchief between the bulb and the tubing. Compress the bulb and hold a lighted cigarette at the other end of the tube. Release the bulb, drawing the smoke through the tube and handkerchief into the bulb. Repeat this procedure three or four times, until tar accumulates on the handkerchief.

Observation and Analysis:
Share your analysis of the experiment with your classmates. Discuss the consequences of smoking on breathing.

Teen HEALTH DIGEST

CON$UMER FOCU$

Aids to Kicking the Habit

Some people use various aids and devices to help them quit the tobacco habit. One product on the market is a cigarette holder with a plastic cigarette that is filled with a peppermint-menthol flavored capsule. The former smoker is free to puff away—without harm—as often as he or she pleases.

Computer-minded smokers might prefer to use a new computer device to kick the habit. This computer, which is about the size of a credit card, is programmed to help the smoker gradually reduce the number of cigarettes he or she smokes. The computer is programmed to beep when the smoker is allowed to have a cigarette. On the smoker's predetermined quit day, the computer flashes a no smoking message. By this time the user should be sufficiently weaned from the habit to quit.

A physician can prescribe a treatment of nicotine gum. The amount of the gum chewed is gradually reduced until the user can quit and be nicotine free. Another aid that requires a prescription is a nicotine patch. The patch is placed on the smoker's body. It releases decreasing amounts of nicotine into the bloodstream. The former smoker gives up cigarettes while gradually withdrawing from the nicotine addiction.

Before deciding to use one of these aids, ask your doctor or pharmacist these questions:

- How much does the device or treatment cost?
- Does it produce any negative side effects?
- How long will it take to withdraw from nicotine using this method?
- What kind of success rate does it have?

Health Update

Taxes Save Lives

Teenage smoking in Canada decreased by two-thirds between 1979 and 1991. What was the motivation? Taxes, taxes, and more taxes. The price of cigarettes with all the taxes added came to more than $4 a pack—a 158 percent increase.

It is estimated that for every 1 percent increase in cigarette prices, 1 percent fewer teenagers would smoke. It is also estimated that in the United States a 15 percent increase in cigarette prices would stop 800,000 teenagers from starting the habit, which would eventually save about 200,000 lives.

The U.S. government is considering a large increase in taxes on cigarettes. The money received from the taxes could be used as a way of financing health care reform. How do you feel about such a tax?

Teens Making a Difference

Ending Vending Machines

The Drug Abuse Awareness and Life Skills (DAALS) committee was formed at Jackson Junior High School to encourage positive lifestyles and empower students to avoid negative lifestyles. The committee consists of student representatives from each grade level. These students plan activities throughout the year. At one committee meeting, Adam Jensen and Katie Montoya pointed out that the shopping mall near the junior high, where many of the students hang out, has several stores with cigarette vending machines. Katie explained that some of the student smokers she knows purchase their cigarettes from these machines.

The committee decided to see what they could do about having the vending machines removed from the mall. First, the committee obtained the support of the local police department. A police officer and several DAALS members approached the owners of the stores at the shopping center. They explained to the owners that some students from their school purchased cigarettes from unsupervised vending machines. They reminded the owners about the state laws governing the sale of tobacco to minors. As a result of DAALS's efforts, some store owners removed the cigarette machines. Others moved the machines to locations in their stores where the machines could be more closely watched.

Myths and Realities

No Smoke, No Problem. Not Really!

Today some teens are using smokeless tobacco. "Smokeless tobacco is okay to use. Since I'm not inhaling, it doesn't have the unhealthy effects that smoking tobacco has," declared Tom.

Unfortunately, the reality of using smokeless tobacco is not as "okay" as Tom wants to believe. Using smokeless tobacco causes nicotine addiction, mouth and gum cancer, stomach ulcers, and diseases of the small intestine and bladder. Other less harmful effects, yet certainly undesirable, include bad breath and stained teeth. Also, smokeless tobacco often contains grit and sugar, which can be damaging to gums and teeth. The grit can damage the outer surface of teeth and the sugar can cause tooth decay. Do you enjoy your healthy teeth? Then don't chew or dip tobacco.

People at Work

Addiction Counselor

Gloria Fernandez helps people who have addictions. "I like the variety of my job and the people I work with," she says. In addition to counseling recovering addicts in a halfway house, Fernandez also works in the outpatient clinic of the local hospital. Fernandez holds individual and group counseling sessions to help addicts cope with their problems. Sometimes she works with their families as well.

Fernandez works under the supervision of a physician and a psychologist. She regularly consults with these two health professionals about her cases.

Fernandez has an associate degree from a two-year college. Most of her training she received on the job. "Although the job is tough, the rewards are great. There's no greater satisfaction for me than seeing a former addict turn his or her life around."

Tobacco Addiction

This lesson will help you find answers to questions that teens often ask about tobacco dependency. For example:

▶ **Why do teens begin using tobacco?**

▶ **How do people become addicted to tobacco?**

Words to Know

addiction
physiological
    dependence
psychological
    dependence

Why Teens Begin Using Tobacco

Why do teens start to use tobacco? One of the main reasons is that their friends smoke. Many teens think smoking will give them confidence in social situations. Perhaps they believe that smoking will make them appear sophisticated and cool. Some teens use tobacco because their parents and other adults told them not to smoke. They become curious and experiment. Unfortunately, before they know it, they are hooked.

Other teens smoke because tobacco advertising on billboards and in magazines makes smoking look attractive. Teens also may think that the bad effects of smoking only happen after many years of smoking or when people are older. They do not realize that the negative effects on their health begin with the first cigarette.

Most young smokers believe they can quit at any time. Some do not realize how addictive smoking is. Others know about the addictive effects of nicotine but believe that they will not get hooked.

Did You Know?

Tobacco Tidbits

▶ The number of teenage females who smoke has doubled over the past 20 years.

▶ During this same time, teens began to smoke at increasingly younger ages.

▶ The Centers for Disease Control and Prevention—an agency of the U.S. Public Health Service—estimate that one billion packs of cigarettes are sold each year to people under the age of 18, although it is illegal in many states to do so.

Are you a part of these statistics?

Parents can serve as positive role models for their children by avoiding all tobacco products.

Reasons for Tobacco Use Among Teens

Every day, about 3,000 American teenagers begin using tobacco. Even though schools and the media send messages warning about the health hazards of tobacco use, teens are smoking and chewing tobacco in large numbers (see **Figure 13.5**). This is what they say:

■ Teens smoke because of peer pressure. As one teenager put it, "All my friends smoke, so I smoke too."

■ Some teens blame their smoking habit on their parents' habit. "Both my mom and dad smoke. I wanted to find out what it was like," explains a pack-a-day teen smoker.

■ "I tried cigarettes because I thought it would make me be more grown up and in control of my life," explained the teen who has since quit his habit.

■ "I wanted to look cool like the models I see in the cigarette advertisements in magazines and on billboards," rationalized another teen who was a smoker.

■ One athletic teen explained how his chewing-tobacco habit began. "I wanted to be just like my favorite pro baseball player. He's always chewing and spitting."

■ "It wasn't hard to get hooked. I could always buy cigarettes in vending machines," said one eighth grader.

Figure 13.5
Ages When People Begin Smoking

The total number of people surveyed for this graph was 6,388. According to the figures, the mean age of first trying a cigarette was 14.5 years old, and the mean age of becoming a daily smoker was 17.7 years old.

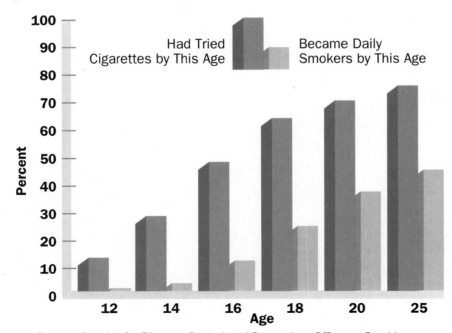

Source: Centers for Disease Control and Prevention, Office on Smoking and Health

The Nature of Addiction

Teens often wonder how people get hooked on tobacco products. The tobacco user forms an **addiction** (uh·DIK·shuhn). This is *a physical or mental need for a drug or other substance.* Nicotine has a powerful effect on the brain and nervous system. This is the reason a person becomes dependent on the drug and finds it difficult to stop smoking or chewing. Not only does tobacco poison the user, but the nicotine actually makes the user *want* the poison. This is addiction. For a person addicted to nicotine, it is extremely difficult to stop using tobacco. When tobacco users try to quit or reduce their use of tobacco, they usually become anxious, depressed, irritable, and tired. As an addictive drug, nicotine causes two kinds of dependence: physiological and psychological.

Physiological Dependence

Physiological (fi·zee·uh·LAH·ji·kuhl) **dependence** is *a type of addiction in which the body itself feels a direct need for a drug.* Nicotine affects many parts of the body, as shown in **Figure 13.6.** Moreover, nicotine addiction is strong. The tobacco user does not feel normal until he or she has another dose of the drug. Only by chewing tobacco or smoking is this need met. For instance, the smoker feels better after smoking, but the feeling does not last long. Soon the smoker must smoke again. As the smoker's body becomes more accustomed to the drug, he or she needs it more often to feel its effect. This same dependence is true of the nicotine effect in users of smokeless tobacco.

Take a walk or ride around your town or community. Notice every tobacco ad you see. In your journal, record the locations of the ads and descriptions of them. What are the messages in the ads? Why were those particular locations chosen? Write your answers in your journal.

LIFE SKILLS
Analyzing the Media's Message

What flashes through your mind when you see a cigarette ad that shows smokers having fun? Do you believe that smoking is a way to make friends and share a good time? This is the hidden message that the cigarette makers want you to get. They send this message to influence your decision about smoking. They show appealing pictures to make you feel good about smoking. They try to

Be Cool
Have Fun
Smoke *Flavor*

SURGEON GENERAL'S WARNING:
Quitting Smoking Now Greatly Reduces
Serious Risks to Your Health.

Figure 13.6
Nicotine's Negative Effects on the Body

Nicotine causes serious problems for many of the body's important organs.

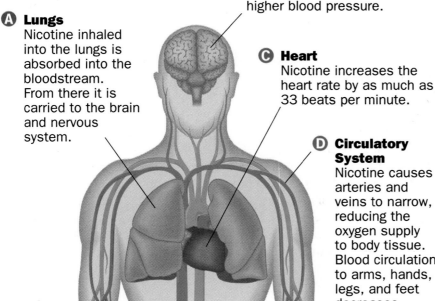

Ⓐ Lungs
Nicotine inhaled into the lungs is absorbed into the bloodstream. From there it is carried to the brain and nervous system.

Ⓑ Brain
Nicotine inhaled from a cigarette reaches the brain in about 20 seconds, causing the adrenal glands to produce adrenaline. This, in turn, leads to a faster heart rate and higher blood pressure.

Ⓒ Heart
Nicotine increases the heart rate by as much as 33 beats per minute.

Ⓓ Circulatory System
Nicotine causes arteries and veins to narrow, reducing the oxygen supply to body tissue. Blood circulation to arms, hands, legs, and feet decreases.

Cultural Diversity

Ban on Cigarette Ads

Thailand has placed a ban on all cigarette advertising. A smaller percentage of their population smokes than that of most western countries.

persuade you to smoke. The ad is concerned with "image," or the way things appear. This image is the media's message, but it does not tell the truth about smoking.

You can avoid being confused by this false media message. Just analyze any ad to see the hidden messages in its pictures and words. Look carefully at the ad on this page. To analyze the media's message, ask yourself the following questions:

1. What is the hidden message in the ad's picture? What is the hidden message in the ad's words?

2. After analyzing this ad, what decision about smoking would you make? Explain your choice.

The effects of nicotine from cigarettes or smokeless tobacco are felt quickly. **Figure 13.7** shows the speed with which nicotine is absorbed into the bloodstream and reaches the brain. Notice how quickly the "satisfying" effects of nicotine wear off. The first "rush" to the brain is followed by feelings of depression and fatigue. This causes the tobacco user to crave more nicotine in a short amount of time.

Because of their harmful effects, most cigarettes have filters to reduce the amount of nicotine and tar. However, filters do not reduce the amount of carbon monoxide and other gases that are inhaled by the smoker.

Figure 13.7
Nicotine in the Bloodstream

In less than two minutes, nicotine is absorbed by the blood and reaches the brain.

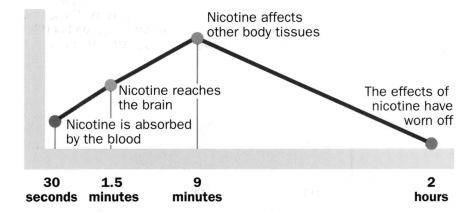

Psychological Dependence

Psychological (sy·kuh·LAH·ji·kuhl) **dependence** is *an addiction in which the mind sends the body the message that it needs more of a drug.* This kind of dependence can be caused by physiological dependence—the stimulation and depression caused by nicotine—as well as other factors. Psychological dependence can be created by the pleasurable experiences or rewards that smokers may associate with smoking. Tobacco use can be linked with daily routines. For example, a smoker may develop the habit of always smoking a cigarette after a meal, while reading the newspaper, or during a work break. Some people reward themselves with a cigarette after they have completed a difficult task. These habits, along with the physiological dependence on nicotine, make it harder for a person to quit using tobacco.

Psychological dependence may form as a result of tobacco's perceived effects. Some smokers feel they need the energy that cigarettes provide. Others say that cigarettes help calm them down when they are tense. Still others feel they need tobacco to keep their weight under control because smoking reduces their appetites.

Smokers also may develop rituals that create psychological dependence. For example, some smokers reach for a cigarette when they begin certain activities. Others talk with an unlit cigarette in their mouth before lighting it. These rituals can become as difficult to stop as the actual habit of smoking. One key to breaking the habit is to change the ritual—instead of reaching for a cigarette, think of something else to do.

Review   Lesson 2

Using complete sentences, answer the following questions on a separate sheet of paper.

Reviewing Terms and Facts

1. **Recall**   List five factors that influence teens' decision to use tobacco.

2. **Vocabulary**   Define the term *addiction.* Use it in an original sentence.

Thinking Critically

3. **Apply**   Describe an example of a magazine advertisement for cigarettes. How do the picture and the words of the advertisement encourage smoking?

4. **Analyze**   Which part of tobacco addiction do you think is more powerful—the physiological dependence or the psychological dependence? Give reasons for your answer.

Applying Health Concepts

5. **Health of Others**   Take a survey of teens who use smokeless tobacco. Ask them such questions as: Why did you start? Do you enjoy it? Would you like to quit? How much tobacco would you estimate that you use in a day? Do you think you are addicted to tobacco? Record the responses. Share your information with the class.

6. **Consumer Health**   Create an advertisement to discourage teens from smoking. Use the same hidden messages in the advertisement that the media use to entice teens to smoke.

7. **Personal Health**   With a classmate, write a short play about breaking a psychological dependence on tobacco.

Choosing to Be Tobacco Free

This lesson will help you find answers to questions that teens often ask about remaining tobacco free or quitting tobacco use. For example:

▶ **How can I remain tobacco free?**

▶ **What are some ways of breaking the tobacco habit?**

▶ **How can I defend my rights as a nonsmoker?**

Words to Know

withdrawal
secondhand smoke
sidestream smoke
mainstream smoke
passive smoker

Saying No to Tobacco

Saying no when friends pressure you to use tobacco can be difficult. There are ways to resist, however, as many teenagers know. The first line of defense is to be prepared for the pressure. Know ahead of time how you will respond to the pressure to use tobacco.

If the pressure is light, you can simply refuse. Say that you're not interested or that you don't like the taste or smell of cigarettes. If you need more help, refer to **Figure 13.8.** It will provide you with ten very good reasons to remain tobacco free.

Sometimes the pressure to use tobacco can be very strong. For example, peers may try to shame you into trying a cigarette by calling you names like "coward" or "chicken." If this happens, you should have responses ready that will help you stand your ground.

MAKING HEALTHY DECISIONS
Overcoming the Pressure to Smoke

*A*ll the science classes in seventh grade made a trip to Cape Henry every spring for four days. Tracy was looking forward to being with her friends away from home. The beach was her favorite place to visit, too.

Every evening after dinner, the students had half an hour of free time. The first evening, Tracy was returning to her cabin when a friend called her to come around back. Tracy was surprised to find two of her friends and two girls she didn't know smoking cigarettes. After Jill introduced Tracy to

Sally and Liz, Jill offered Tracy a cigarette and said, "Have a few puffs. It's a great way to unwind after following teachers' orders all day."

Tracy declined Jill's offer and said that she had to leave to help set up for that night's special program. The next evening she noticed that the four girls were behind the cabin again. Tracy could hear them laughing and thought about joining in.

Then the next morning, one of the girls, Sally, confronted Tracy. "Why don't you have a smoke with

You can ask them why they are so interested in sharing their habit with you. If you are an athlete, you can say that you want to keep your breathing healthy for basketball or swimming. You can simply say no and ask them to respect your right to make your own decisions. If the pressure continues, leave the scene. One way to resist the pressure to use tobacco is to choose friends who do not use it. If you stick together when the pressure is on, you may find it easier to refuse.

in your journal

Look at the reasons for quitting tobacco use. Review the list again. Are there any reasons you can think of that are not included in the list? If so, write them down in your journal.

Figure 13.8

The Top Ten Reasons to Be Tobacco Free

1 You will be healthier.
2 Your breath will not offend others.
3 You can save money.
4 Your senses of taste and smell will be sharp.

5 You will have fewer or no allergies.
6 You will not be confined to smoking areas.
7 You will have more energy and stamina for sports.

8 Your skin will be healthier.
9 Your hair and clothes will not smell like smoke.
10 You will not be polluting the air.

us after dinner? Are you one of those Goody Two-Shoes who thinks she is too good for us?"

Tracy was embarrassed by Sally's comments. She was torn between her desire to remain tobacco free and the pressure she was feeling to smoke. Tracy decided to use the step-by-step decision-making process to make up her mind about smoking:

1 State the situation
2 List the options
3 Weigh the possible outcomes
4 Consider your values
5 Make a decision and act
6 Evaluate the decision

Follow-up Activities

1. Apply the six steps of the decision-making process to Tracy's story.
2. With a classmate, role-play a scene in which Tracy resists the peer pressure to use tobacco.

Kicking the Habit

Many people who used tobacco in the past are kicking the habit. It is not easy. However, there are many ways to stop. There are also people and places to go to for help in quitting the habit.

Since the nicotine in tobacco is addictive, people who quit go through a period of **withdrawal,** which is *the physical symptoms that occur when someone stops using an addictive substance.* Withdrawal symptoms do not last long, but they include nervousness, moodiness, and difficulty sleeping. **Figure 13.9** shows how the body recovers after quitting.

Figure 13.9
How the Body Recovers After Quitting

Within 20 minutes of smoking the last cigarette, the body begins a series of important and beneficial changes. The changes and benefits continue for years as long as the person remains smoke free. All benefits are lost, however, by smoking even one cigarette a day.

Time Elapsed Since Last Cigarette	Health Benefits Gained
20 minutes	Blood pressure and pulse rate drop to normal. Body temperature of hands and feet increase to normal.
8 hours	Carbon monoxide level in blood drops to normal. Oxygen level in blood increases to normal.
24 hours	Risk of heart attack decreases.
48 hours	Nerve endings begin regrowing. Ability to taste and smell improves.
2 weeks to 3 months	Blood circulation improves. Lung function improves up to 30 percent.
1 to 9 months	Coughing, sinus congestion, fatigue, and shortness of breath decrease. Cilia in lungs begin regrowing, increasing the ability of the lungs to clean themselves and reduce infection. Body's energy increases.
1 year	Risk of heart disease is half that of a smoker.
5 years	Death rate from lung cancer decreases to almost half. Risk of stroke is reduced. Risk of cancer of the mouth and esophagus is half that of a smoker.
10 years	Death rate from lung cancer is the same as that for nonsmokers. Precancerous cells in the body are replaced. Risk of cancer of the throat, bladder, kidney, and pancreas decreases.
15 years	Risk of heart disease is the same as that of a nonsmoker.

Tips for Quitting Tobacco Use

- Make a list of reasons you want to quit smoking. Read the list whenever you get the urge to smoke.

- Set small goals. Try quitting one day at a time. Every year, the American Cancer Society sponsors the "Great American Smokeout," calling for all smokers to avoid smoking for one day. Wouldn't that be an ideal day to quit?

- Try to avoid being with people who smoke.

- Change your habits that are linked to smoking. For example, if you smoke when you walk to school, try chewing gum instead of smoking.

- Exercise when you feel the urge to reach for tobacco. Stretch, take deep breaths, go for a walk, or take a ride on your bike.

- Seek positive reinforcement from nonsmoking friends.

- Eat healthy snacks instead of reaching for tobacco.

Programs That Help

The "cold turkey" method of quitting tobacco is popular and recommended by many experts. In this method, the smoker simply stops using all forms of tobacco. Some people need support or assistance to quit. They should contact a group that has a program to help people quit. The American Lung Association, the American Heart Association, and the American Cancer Society are just a few of the many groups that offer such programs. You can contact these groups by telephone or mail to get more information.

Books, records, and cassettes can help people quit smoking on their own. Many can be borrowed from local libraries. There are also several products available to help alleviate withdrawal symptoms. They include over-the-counter drugs, nicotine-containing chewing gum, the nicotine patch, and sets of graduated filters designed to reduce tar.

People who are trying to quit need support and encouragement from family and friends. If you know someone who is kicking the habit, try to help. Praise the person for each day that he or she avoids smoking.

A person who is trying to quit smoking should find new activities that he or she enjoys to keep from thinking about smoking.

How Tobacco Affects Nonsmokers

Most restaurants provide separate nonsmoking sections for their customers.

Even if you are not lighting up and smoking, you may be breathing *air that has been contaminated by tobacco smoke,* or **secondhand smoke.** Each time a smoker lights a cigarette, smoke fills the air from two sources. *The smoke coming from the burning tip of the cigarette is* called **sidestream smoke.** It contains twice as much tar and nicotine as *the smoke that the smoker exhales,* or **mainstream smoke.** This is because sidestream smoke has not passed through the cigarette filter or the smoker's lungs.

Nonsmokers who breathe secondhand smoke become **passive smokers.** Passive smoking is harmful to your health because it contributes to respiratory problems. Passive smoking irritates your nose and throat, and it also causes itchy and watery eyes, headaches, and coughing.

A smoke-filled room has high levels of nicotine, carbon monoxide, and other pollutants. In such a room, a nonsmoker can inhale as much nicotine and carbon monoxide in one hour as if he or she had smoked a whole cigarette. Long-term exposure to secondhand smoke poses the same risk of serious illness for passive smokers as it does for active smokers. These risks include heart and lung diseases and respiratory problems. According to the U.S. Environmental Protection Agency, secondhand smoke is a human *carcinogen,* or cancer-causing substance, that is responsible for 3,000 lung cancer deaths each year.

Unborn Babies and Children

A woman who smokes during pregnancy seriously endangers the health of her unborn child. Cigarette smoking during pregnancy is associated with small fetal growth, an increased chance of miscarriage and stillbirths, and a low birth weight. The lower a baby's birth weight, the higher the risk is of complications in the baby's development. The effects of tobacco may affect the growth, mental development, and behavior of children for up to 11 years after their birth. In addition, the Coalition on Smoking and Health, a nonprofit group formed by the American Lung Association, the American Heart Association, and the American Cancer Society estimates that secondhand smoke accounts for 700 deaths a year due to Sudden Infant Death Syndrome (SIDS).

Rights of Nonsmokers

The facts are clear that secondhand smoke is as dangerous as smoking. Laws continue to be passed to restrict smoking in public places. In 1989 smoking was banned on all domestic flights. In 1994 more than 600 state and local ordinances restricted smoking. Congress is even considering a bill to ban smoking in all buildings except private clubs and restaurants. The Occupational Safety and Health Administration is considering banning smoking in all workplaces. Many employers are banning smoking, too.

What does this mean to you? As a nonsmoker, you have the right to breathe air that is free of harmful tobacco smoke. You have the right to express that you prefer people not to smoke around you. You also have the right to work for the passage of laws against tobacco smoke, especially in public places.

Because of the potential damage to children, both at birth and during their later development, women should not smoke while they are pregnant.

Review

Using complete sentences, answer the following questions on a separate sheet of paper.

Reviewing Terms and Facts

1. **Recall**   List four of the top ten reasons to be tobacco free.

2. **Vocabulary**   What is the difference between *secondhand smoke, sidestream smoke,* and *mainstream smoke?*

Thinking Critically

3. **Suggest**   Miguel went to a party with his friend Sam. Another friend offered them cigarettes, but Miguel did not want to smoke. What could he have done?

4. **Apply**   A friend of yours has asked you to help support her to quit smoking. What advice would you give?

5. **Analyze**   Although you enjoy bowling, the local bowling alley has no restrictions on smoking. You would like to exercise your rights as a nonsmoker. What would you do in this situation?

Applying Health Concepts

6. **Health of Others**   Organize a support group for students who want to stop using tobacco. Ask the school nurse to train some students to be peer supporters. Have the students who are former smokers keep a record of the days they have been tobacco free.

Chapter 13 Review

Chapter Summary

► There are more than 3,000 harmful chemicals in cigarettes, 43 of which are known to cause cancer in smokers. (Lesson 1)

► Smokeless tobacco, which contains nicotine, comes in two forms: chewing tobacco and snuff. Its use causes health problems, including deadly types of cancer. (Lesson 1)

► The harmful effects of smoking and using tobacco include addiction, high blood pressure, stomach ulcers, emphysema, several types of cancer, heart disease, bad breath, and stained teeth. (Lesson 1)

► The two main reasons why teens start to smoke are peer pressure and social pressure. (Lesson 2)

► Advertising in magazines and on billboards glamorizes smoking and uses hidden messages to encourage teens to start the habit. (Lesson 2)

► The nicotine in tobacco causes users to become physically dependent on tobacco. (Lesson 2)

► Psychological dependence on tobacco can be caused by the pleasurable experiences, rewards, perceived effects, and rituals that smokers associate with smoking. (Lesson 2)

► There are many ways to kick the tobacco habit and many people and places who are willing to help a user quit. (Lesson 3)

► Tips for quitting the tobacco habit include making a list of reasons why you want to quit, setting small goals, changing habits linked to smoking, exercising, and eating healthy snacks. (Lesson 3)

► Long-term exposure to secondhand smoke poses the same risks to passive smokers for serious illness as it does for active smokers. (Lesson 3)

► Nonsmokers have the right to breathe fresh air, speak out against smoking, and work to pass laws against tobacco smoke. (Lesson 3)

Using Health Terms

On a separate sheet of paper, write the vocabulary term that best matches each definition given below.

1. A colorless, odorless, poisonous gas produced when tobacco burns (Lesson 1)

2. Fine hairs that line the respiratory system and prevent dust and foreign matter from getting into the lungs (Lesson 1)

3. A type of addiction in which the body itself feels a direct need for a drug (Lesson 2)

4. The physical symptoms that occur when someone stops using an addictive substance (Lesson 3)

5. Air that has been contaminated by tobacco smoke (Lesson 3)

6. Nonsmokers who breathe secondhand smoke (Lesson 3)

Reviewing Main Ideas

Using complete sentences, answer the following questions on a separate sheet of paper.

1. List the forms in which tobacco is used. (Lesson 1)

2. How is using smokeless tobacco harmful to the body? (Lesson 1)

3. How does smoking harm the lungs? (Lesson 1)

4. List some parts of the body that are negatively affected by nicotine. (Lesson 2)

5. What kinds of dependencies do people form when using tobacco? (Lesson 2)

6. What kind of perceived effects of tobacco may cause psychological dependence? (Lesson 2)

7. What are three reasons to be tobacco free? (Lesson 3)

8. Describe how secondhand smoke affects passive smokers. (Lesson 3)

Thinking Critically

Using complete sentences, answer the following questions on a separate sheet of paper.

1. **Hypothesize** Do you think smokeless tobacco would be a safe alternative to smoking if the nicotine were removed? (Lesson 1)

2. **Analyze** Why do heavy smokers have difficulty inhaling clean, fresh air? (Lesson 1)

3. **Hypothesize** Do you think adults who start smoking do so for the same reasons as teens? If so, list some reasons they have in common. If not, list a few that differ. (Lesson 2)

4. **Synthesize** Which part of tobacco addiction do you think develops first—physiological dependence or psychological dependence? Explain your answer. (Lesson 2)

5. **Differentiate** In what ways are sidestream smoke and mainstream smoke different? How are they alike? (Lesson 3)

6. **Predict** You are in a restaurant enjoying your dinner when a person at the next table lights a cigarette. You cannot stand the smell of smoke, especially while you are eating. What could you do about this situation? (Lesson 3)

Your Action Plan

You can make an action plan to remain tobacco free or to kick the tobacco habit. First you need to set a goal for yourself. Look back through your private journal entries for this chapter. What do they tell you about your feelings toward tobacco use?

Once you have established what your long-term goal should be, write it down. Make sure your goal is realistic. Next, write down a series of short-term goals. If your long-term goal is to help your friend kick the tobacco habit, a short-term goal might be to get him or her to join a support group.

Plan a schedule for accomplishing each short-term goal. Check with your schedule frequently to keep yourself on track. When you reach your long-term goal, reward yourself (and maybe your friend too).

Building Your Portfolio

1. Clip magazine advertisements for cigarettes and smokeless tobacco. Analyze each advertisement by answering the following questions: What is the hidden message in the ad? What are you *not* told about smoking or tobacco use in the ad? Add the advertisements and your analysis to your portfolio.

2. Write a script about teens being pressured to use tobacco. The script can be based on a personal experience or the experience of a friend. Have some of your friends or classmates act out the script. Place a copy of your script in your portfolio.

In Your Home and Community

1. Action on Smoking and Health, or *ASH,* is a national organization working for a smoke-free America. Find out whether your community has a local chapter of ASH. If not, write to: Action on Smoking and Health, 2013 H Street NW, Washington, DC 20006. Ask how you can start a chapter in your community.

2. Write or call the American Lung Association or the American Cancer Society and ask if they can train you to work in classes to help your peers stop smoking. Once you are trained, ask an adult who does such work to help you begin a program in your school or through your community recreation department.

Chapter 14
Alcohol and Your Health

Student Expectations

After reading this chapter, you should be able to:

1. Explain how alcohol affects your health and safety.
2. Describe the stages of alcoholism and the steps that are part of recovery.
3. List ways to avoid using alcohol.

I'm really confused. I get so many mixed messages about alcohol that I have trouble figuring out what's true and what isn't. For instance, my parents tell me that drinking alcohol is bad for my health. That hasn't stopped them from sometimes having a drink before dinner.

Some of the guys on my basketball team say that there's nothing wrong with drinking at parties. They say that only certain kinds of people have drinking problems. Whenever I watch sports on television, I see lots of beer commercials. If beer was really bad for you, could they advertise it on television? The people in the commercials really look like they're having a good time. Drinking certainly doesn't seem to have affected their lives in a bad way.

I know that a lot of alcohol isn't good for you, but I don't see what's wrong with having a drink now and then. Everyone does it, and it's not as bad as doing drugs, is it?

in your journal

Read the account on this page. Does it sound familiar to you? Are you facing pressures to use alcohol? Start your private journal entries on alcohol use by answering these questions:

▶ How well do you know the facts about alcohol's effect on the body?

▶ What would you do if someone offered you a drink?

When you reach the end of the chapter, you will use your journal entries to make an action plan.

What Alcohol Does to Your Body

This lesson will help you find answers to questions that teens often ask about alcohol's effect on the body. For example:

▶ Why do people who have been drinking often act silly and have trouble walking and talking?

▶ Why do some people seem to tolerate alcohol better than other people?

▶ How much alcohol does a person need to drink before becoming drunk?

▶ Why is drinking alcohol illegal for teens but not for adults?

Words to Know

alcohol
depressant
cirrhosis
blood alcohol
   concentration
   (BAC)
fetal alcohol
   syndrome (FAS)
addiction

Alcohol and American Society

Alcohol (AL·kuh·hawl) is *a drug that is produced by a chemical reaction in fruits, vegetables, and grains.* It has a powerful effect on the body. In America, decisions about using alcohol are up to each individual. To make such important decisions, people need to know how alcohol affects their bodies and their judgment. Understanding these facts can help them make decisions that are right for them and for society.

Over 17 million Americans have physical, social, and psychological problems related to alcohol use. Drinking alcohol is illegal for teens—which is a good reason to avoid it. In addition, alcohol can seriously damage your body.

Alcohol and Your Body

Alcohol is a **depressant** (di·PRE·suhnt), *a drug that slows down the working of the brain and other parts of the nervous system.* **Figure 14.1** shows the short-term effects of drinking alcohol. Chronic, excessive use of alcohol can seriously damage nearly every organ and function of the body. It can even cause death. **Figure 14.2** shows the long-term effects of alcohol use.

Staying away from alcohol helps keep you mentally and physically healthy.

Figure 14.1
Short-Term Effects of Alcohol

Alcohol has many negative effects on the drinker's body and behavior. The short-term effects are those that occur within minutes of drinking an alcoholic beverage.

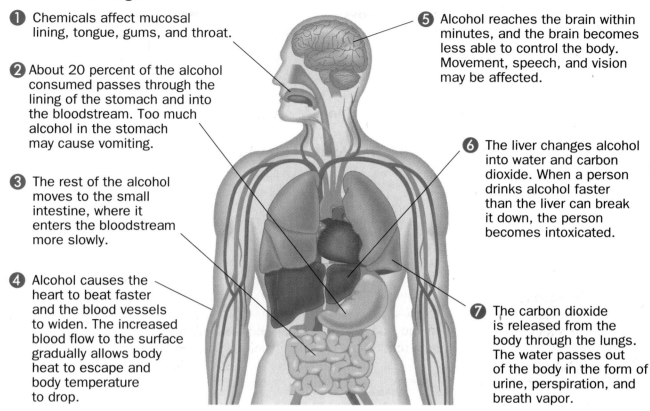

1 Chemicals affect mucosal lining, tongue, gums, and throat.

2 About 20 percent of the alcohol consumed passes through the lining of the stomach and into the bloodstream. Too much alcohol in the stomach may cause vomiting.

3 The rest of the alcohol moves to the small intestine, where it enters the bloodstream more slowly.

4 Alcohol causes the heart to beat faster and the blood vessels to widen. The increased blood flow to the surface gradually allows body heat to escape and body temperature to drop.

5 Alcohol reaches the brain within minutes, and the brain becomes less able to control the body. Movement, speech, and vision may be affected.

6 The liver changes alcohol into water and carbon dioxide. When a person drinks alcohol faster than the liver can break it down, the person becomes intoxicated.

7 The carbon dioxide is released from the body through the lungs. The water passes out of the body in the form of urine, perspiration, and breath vapor.

Figure 14.2
Long-Term Effects of Alcohol

The person who drinks excessively for a long period of time is at risk for developing serious health problems.

Brain	Liver	Heart	Stomach
Drinking alcohol for many years eventually destroys millions of brain cells. Unlike other body cells, brain cells cannot be repaired or replaced.	A person who has several alcoholic drinks a day, over a long period of time, is likely to suffer liver damage. He or she may develop **cirrhosis** (suh·ROH·sis), which is *scarring and destruction of liver tissue.* Cirrhosis can cause death.	Heavy drinking contributes to high blood pressure and may damage the heart muscle. It can even cause heart failure by putting extra strain on already damaged heart muscle.	Alcohol increases the flow of gastric juices from the stomach lining. Large amounts of alcohol cause a larger flow of these high-acid juices, irritating the stomach lining. Repeated irritation can cause open sores called ulcers.

Alcohol and the Individual

The effect that alcohol has on a person is influenced by a number of factors. They are listed here. **Figure 14.3** shows how the alcoholic content differs for some common beverages.

- **Speed.** Drinking a lot in a short period of time causes the alcohol to remain in the bloodstream longer.

- **Quantity.** The metabolism of alcohol takes place at a fairly constant rate. If consumption exceeds this rate, alcohol levels in the bloodstream will rise.

- **Food.** A person who has eaten recently has food in the stomach. This slows down the passing of the alcohol into the bloodstream.

- **Weight.** A lighter person feels the effects of alcohol sooner than a heavier person.

- **Gender.** Generally, females have more body fat and less body water than males. This means alcohol moves into the bloodstream faster in females.

- **Mood.** A drinker who starts off depressed usually finishes up more depressed.

- **Other drugs.** Mixing alcohol with other drugs increases the effects of the alcohol or of the other drug. Even aspirin makes a difference in how alcohol affects the body.

Figure 14.3
Alcoholic Content of Beverages

No alcoholic drink is a safe drink. Beer and wine contain a lower percentage of alcohol by volume than vodka or whiskey. However, a 12-ounce can of beer or a 4-ounce glass of wine contain the same amount of alcohol as 1.5 ounces of vodka or whiskey.

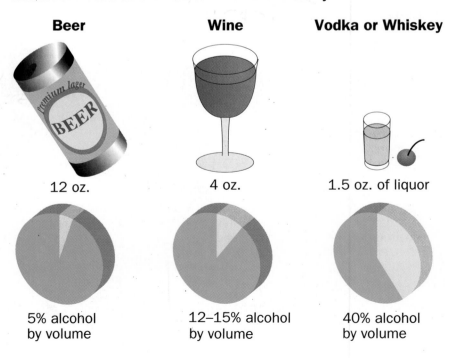

Beer	Wine	Vodka or Whiskey
12 oz.	4 oz.	1.5 oz. of liquor
5% alcohol by volume	12–15% alcohol by volume	40% alcohol by volume

Blood Alcohol Concentration

The amount of alcohol in a person's blood is expressed by a percentage called **blood alcohol concentration (BAC).** The person's BAC depends on the amount of alcohol consumed, body weight, and the other factors discussed on the previous page.

In most states, a person driving with a BAC of 0.1 percent or more is considered legally intoxicated and not capable of operating an automobile safely. A BAC of 0.1 percent means that $\frac{1}{10}$ of 1 percent of the fluid in the blood is alcohol. **Figure 14.4** shows how increases in the blood alcohol level affect a person.

Fetal Alcohol Syndrome

A woman who drinks alcohol when she is pregnant may cause permanent damage to her developing baby. The alcohol passes from her body into the baby's bloodstream. Because the baby's liver is not developed enough to process the alcohol, the alcohol remains in the baby's bloodstream for a long time. The baby may be born with a condition called **fetal alcohol syndrome** or **FAS.** Babies born with FAS suffer from *a group of alcohol-related birth defects that may include both physical and mental problems.* These babies may weigh less than normal at birth, be weak, and have facial deformities. They may be mentally retarded or have learning difficulties, and they may have behavior problems.

The tragedy of FAS is that the unborn baby has no control over what enters its body. The decision to drink alcohol or not is the mother's. Because even small amounts of alcohol may be harmful, the safe decision for a pregnant woman is not to drink any alcoholic beverages. FAS is entirely preventable.

Did You Know?

Fetal Alcohol Syndrome

During 1992, children with fetal alcohol syndrome were born at a rate of 3.7 per 10,000 births. This is three times the rate reported for 1979. Fetal alcohol syndrome is a leading cause of mental retardation.

Figure 14.4
Blood Alcohol Levels

Number of Drinks	Blood Alcohol Concentration	Effects
1–2	0.05%	Small decrease in reaction time; some loss of coordination, self-control
3	0.1%	Significant decrease in coordination, judgment, self-control, vision
6	0.2%	Drunk—serious loss of self-control, memory, muscle control, ability to think clearly, and depth perception
8–9	0.3%	Confusion, stupor, may pass out
12–plus	0.5%	Coma or death

Note: Calculations of BAC are based on drinks consumed by a 120-pound person in a two-hour period. Individual reactions will vary according to factors discussed earlier.

Drinking and Driving

Alcohol impairs a person's vision, reaction time, and motor coordination. When a person who has been drinking alcohol gets behind the wheel of a car, he or she is turning the car into a dangerous weapon.

Some people claim that having a drink or two does not affect them or their driving. In fact, the opposite is true. Even one drink slows reaction time and results in some loss of coordination. In 1992, drinking drivers were involved in nearly one-fourth of the fatal traffic accidents in the United States. Alcohol causes other accidents as well. The following facts paint a tragic picture.

Alcohol's Safety Record

■ About one-third of all bicyclists who die in traffic accidents have been drinking.

■ About half of all adult pedestrians who die in traffic accidents have been drinking.

■ More than half of all people who die from drowning accidents have been drinking.

■ About half of all deaths by fire involve drinking.

HEALTH LAB
The War Against Drunk Driving

Introduction: Each year alcohol-related traffic accidents cause thousands of deaths and an even greater number of injuries on highways in the United States. Drunk driving is the leading cause of death among teenagers over the age of 15. Government agencies and private citizens' groups have waged a forceful campaign against drunk driving.

Objective: To find out whether progress is being made in the campaign against drunk driving.

Materials and Method: You will need graph paper, a ruler, and a pencil. Study the following statistics from the National Highway Traffic Safety Administration. Then make a graph to illustrate the statistics. The percentages refer to the number of drivers involved in fatal traffic accidents who were legally drunk.

1982	30.0 percent	1988	25.0 percent
1983	29.0 percent	1989	24.5 percent
1984	27.0 percent	1990	25.0 percent
1985	26.0 percent	1991	24.0 percent
1986	26.0 percent	1992	21.9 percent
1987	25.0 percent	1993	21.0 percent

Alcohol and Teens

Right now, your body is going through some very important changes. Alcohol interferes with these changes. Furthermore, the use of alcohol by young people leads to some sobering statistics as shown in **Figure 14.5.**

Figure 14.5
Alcohol: A Danger for Teens

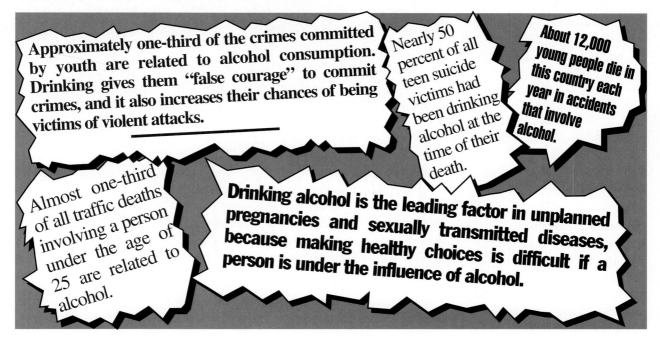

Approximately one-third of the crimes committed by youth are related to alcohol consumption. Drinking gives them "false courage" to commit crimes, and it also increases their chances of being victims of violent attacks.

Nearly 50 percent of all teen suicide victims had been drinking alcohol at the time of their death.

About 12,000 young people die in this country each year in accidents that involve alcohol.

Almost one-third of all traffic deaths involving a person under the age of 25 are related to alcohol.

Drinking alcohol is the leading factor in unplanned pregnancies and sexually transmitted diseases, because making healthy choices is difficult if a person is under the influence of alcohol.

Observation and Analysis:

After completing the graph, write a brief paragraph interpreting the statistics from the National Highway Traffic Safety Administration. Then discuss the following with a group of your classmates.

▶ By what overall percentage did the number of drinking drivers involved in fatal accidents change between 1982 and 1993?

▶ What does the graph indicate about the pattern of drunk driving in the United States?

▶ What do you think are the reasons for the change between 1982 and 1993?

Follow-up Activity

Research local (city or county) or state statistics on arrests for driving under the influence (DUI). Compare the figures for the number of people arrested for DUI last year and ten years ago. How have they changed? Find out what efforts are being made in your community or your state to combat drunk driving.

There are lots of ways to have fun without alcohol. In fact, alcohol can get in the way of having fun.

Social Studies Connection

Mothers Who Are MADD ACTIVITY!

An organization called Mothers Against Drunk Driving (MADD) is active in pushing for harsher penalties for drunk drivers. Check your school or local library to find out how MADD started. Find out what the penalties are in your community and in your state for drunk driving.

Alcohol Can Be Habit-forming

People who drink alcohol regularly need to drink more and more of it for the desired effect. After a while, this increased use causes the drinker to form an addiction to alcohol. An **addiction** (uh-DIK·shuhn) is *a physical or mental need for a drug or other substance.* Studies show that people who begin drinking at an early age have a greater chance of becoming addicted. This increases the risk of family problems, losing jobs, and poor health.

An addicted person who stops drinking alcohol will suffer withdrawal symptoms. Signs of alcohol withdrawal include sweating, inability to sleep, shakiness, and irritability. The person may experience unreasonable fears, seizures, and other disturbances of the nervous system. Withdrawal can be very painful.

Lesson 1 Review

Using complete sentences, answer the following questions on a separate sheet of paper.

Reviewing Terms and Facts

1. **Vocabulary** Define the term *alcohol.* Use it in an original sentence.

2. **Recall** List the factors that affect a person's blood alcohol concentration (BAC).

Thinking Critically

3. **Analyze** If alcohol is a depressant, why do people serve it at parties?

4. **Synthesize** Suppose a friend told you it is okay to drink, as long as you only drink beer. How might you respond?

Applying Health Concepts

5. **Personal Health** With a partner, plan a skit in which a young teen must decide whether or not to accept a ride from someone who has been drinking. Together, act out your skit for the rest of the class.

What Is Alcoholism?

This lesson will help you find answers to questions that teens often ask about alcoholism. For example:

▶ **How can you tell whether a person is an alcoholic?**

▶ **Can alcoholism be cured?**

▶ **If someone I know has a problem with alcohol, how can I help?**

Alcoholism: Problems and Disease

Alcohol can become addictive. In some cases, this *physical and mental need for alcohol turns into a progressive and chronic disease* called **alcoholism.** People with this disease are called alcoholics. They cannot keep from drinking. They cannot stop drinking once they have started. They drink even when they know they are harming their own health. **Figure 14.6** on page 436 describes the stages of alcoholism.

Alcoholics have a physical and a psychological addiction. In psychological addiction, the mind sends the body the message that it needs more and more alcohol. In physical addiction, the body itself feels a direct need for alcohol.

Many studies have been done in an effort to find out why people become alcoholics. It has been observed that the children of alcoholics are more likely to become alcoholics than children in general. One possible explanation for this is that children inherit the susceptibility to the disease from alcoholic parents. Another theory suggests that a child's environment—growing up in a home with alcoholism—has a greater influence on a person's chances of becoming an alcoholic than heredity. Researchers agree, however, that children of alcoholic parents will not automatically become alcoholics themselves.

Words to Know

**alcoholism
recovery
Alcoholics
    Anonymous (AA)
Al-Anon
Alateen**

Teen Issues

Ideas About Alcoholism ACTIVITY!

Write down some of the ideas you have about alcoholism. For example, do you think alcoholism is a disease or a personality weakness? Are certain types of people more likely to be alcoholics than others? After reading this lesson, look back on what you wrote. Have any of those ideas changed?

Alcohol abuse harms individuals' lives as well as society. More than one-third of the young people under 18 in juvenile institutions were under the influence of alcohol when they were arrested.

435

Figure 14.6
Stages of Alcoholism

Experts say that alcoholism develops in three stages. These stages occur over a period of time.

Stage 1
A person starts using alcohol to relieve stress or to relax. Soon the person needs alcohol to cope with the daily pressures of life. The drinker begins to make excuses about his or her drinking habits.

Stage 2
As the person continues to drink, the body develops a need for more and more alcohol. The drinker is often absent from school or work but continues to deny that there is a problem.

Stage 3
In the final stage of alcoholism, the problem is clear to other people. The drinker's body is strongly addicted, and the drinking is now out of control.

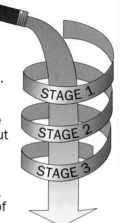

Help for the Dependent Person

A person who is addicted to alcohol is said to be dependent on it, but this addiction can be treated. With proper care, the majority of alcoholics who try to stop drinking succeed. After stopping, however, these people must never drink alcohol. Otherwise, they have a very high chance of becoming addicted again. Recovering from alcoholism is a difficult, lifelong struggle. It is much better not to get involved with alcohol in the first place.

MAKING HEALTHY DECISIONS
Helping a Friend Get Help

Katie and Jennifer had been best friends for years. Then, all of a sudden, Jennifer started to pull away. She told Katie that she didn't feel like going out or that she had too much homework to get together.

One Friday evening Katie decided to stop at Jennifer's house after a basketball game. She rang the doorbell three times before Jennifer finally answered. Katie thought that she looked flushed and confused. A few kids from school were in the living room. They all had beer and wine coolers.

Jennifer told Katie that she had invited a few friends over to work on a science project. When Katie asked where Jennifer's father was, she was told that he had gone to help her grandmother. Jennifer said they had to get back to work, and she would call Katie over the weekend. Katie thought she smelled alcohol on Jennifer's breath.

A few days later, Katie overheard two girls talking about what a great time they had raiding the liquor cabinet at Jennifer's on Friday. They said it was lucky that Jennifer's father had to spend so much time taking care of her grandmother.

When Katie told Jennifer what she'd heard, Jennifer got angry. She said that what she did was none of Katie's business and then stormed out of the room.

Treatment and Recovery

People recover from alcoholism at different rates and in different ways. *The process of becoming well again* is known as **recovery.** The recovery process generally includes the following steps.

- **Step One.** The dependent person admits to having a problem and asks for help in giving up alcohol.

- **Step Two.** The alcoholic goes through a process called detoxification to remove all alcohol from the body.

- **Step Three.** The alcoholic receives counseling on how to live without alcohol. This involves learning how to rebuild self-esteem and taking responsibility for his or her own life.

Some hospitals have medical detoxification units. There are clinics that offer treatment and counseling. Support groups play a vital role in recovery. One of the most successful *support groups for alcoholics* is **Alcoholics Anonymous** (uh·NAH·nuh·muhs), or **AA.** At AA meetings, people who are recovering from alcoholism help others who are struggling to stay sober.

Katie wants to help Jennifer, but she doesn't know what to do. She feels that she can't talk to Jennifer and get through to her. She doesn't want to talk to Jennifer's father because he might punish her for sneaking the liquor. Katie uses the step-by-step decision-making process to help her.

- ❶ **State the situation**
- ❷ **List the options**
- ❸ **Weigh the possible outcomes**
- ❹ **Consider your values**
- ❺ **Make a decision and act**
- ❻ **Evaluate the decision**

Follow-up Activities

1. Apply the decision-making steps to Katie's problem.

2. Along with a partner, role-play a scene in which Katie confronts Jennifer about her drinking.

3. Now role-play a scene in which Katie talks to her own parents about Jennifer's drinking.

in Your Journal

You don't need to be an alcoholic to benefit from a support group. Everyone needs to talk to people who have experienced similar problems and concerns. Who are the people in your support group? Write about them in your journal.

Because alcoholism is a serious disease that cannot be cured, recovery must be an ongoing process. People need to work at staying sober one day at a time for the rest of their lives. Without recovery, alcoholism results in irreversible harm to the mind and body, and premature death.

Help for the Family

The harmful effects of alcohol do not stop with the drinker. The family members and friends of heavy drinkers suffer, too. Alcohol abuse and addiction are major factors in marital separation and divorce. The children of alcoholics frequently have problems, such as depression and anxiety. In addition, many cases of spouse and child abuse are committed by people who have been drinking.

One in four families in the United States is touched by alcoholism. This means that a growing number of young people know or are living with a person addicted to alcohol. These people often need help for themselves as well as for the problem drinkers in their lives. The first step to take is to admit that the problem exists. The second is to reach out for help.

Individual or family therapy is often recommended for people whose lives are affected by alcohol abuse. There are also many support groups available to help the family and friends of alcoholics. Two support groups are described here.

■ **Al-Anon** is a *support group that helps family members and friends of alcoholics.* Al-Anon members learn how to help themselves as well as the person dependent on alcohol. The meetings are confidential and free.

■ **Alateen** is *a support group that helps young people cope with having a family member or friend who is an alcoholic.* Its members share their experiences and work together to recover.

Family programs are offered at many alcohol treatment centers. They provide a way for family members to learn about the disease of alcoholism and discuss how they have been affected by it. Family members of alcoholics work toward their own recovery and support others in the family during the recovery process.

Support is available to help teens who have family members or friends who are alcoholics.

How Can You Help?

Someone who has a drinking problem needs help. If a friend or family member has a problem with alcohol, you can try to help in several ways. To be helped, the alcoholic must admit that he or she has a problem. Your most important responsibility is to yourself. If you are close to an alcoholic, make sure that the person's drinking problem does not change your own behaviors and attitudes. Keep in mind, however, that some actions—no matter how well intended—will *not* help.

What to Do

- Talk calmly with the drinker about the harm that alcohol does. Discuss this when he or she is sober.

- Tell the drinker how concerned you are and offer to help.

- Help the drinker to feel good about quitting.

- Give the drinker information about groups that can help.

- Encourage the drinker to get help.

What Not to Do

- Do not argue with the person when he or she is drunk.

- Avoid using an "I'm-better-than-you" tone of voice when talking about the person's drinking problem.

- Do not make excuses to others for the drinker's behavior.

- Do not feel that you are responsible for the drinker's actions.

- Do not be afraid to seek help for the drinker if he or she won't do it.

Cultural Diversity

Talking Circles

Many programs for preventing and treating alcohol addiction among Native American children and youth are turning to Indian culture for inspiration. Traditional Indian ceremonies, rituals, and prayers help Native American youth develop a sense of belonging and self-esteem. One Indian tradition used in treatment programs is the "talking circle." Participants sit in a circle and share their feelings. Stones, feathers, or other symbolic objects are passed around the circle to absorb or release bad feelings.

Review — Lesson 2

Using complete sentences, answer the following questions on a separate sheet of paper.

Reviewing Terms and Facts

1. **Recall** Why are children of alcoholics more likely to become alcoholics than children in general?

2. **Vocabulary** What is the difference between *Alcoholics Anonymous, Al-Anon,* and *Alateen?*

3. **Review** Describe the three steps in the recovery process.

Thinking Critically

4. **Analyze** Is there a difference between a heavy drinker and an alcoholic? Explain your answer.

5. **Explain** Can alcoholism be cured? Why or why not?

Applying Health Concepts

6. **Personal Health** Read one or two magazine articles in which teens describe their problems with alcohol. Write a paragraph telling what you can learn from the experiences of these young people.

Teen HEALTH DIGEST

Sports and Recreation

Taking a Fresh Swing at Life

Mickey Mantle was one of baseball's greatest sluggers. As a New York Yankee from 1951 through 1968, he led the American League in home runs four times and hit a record of 18 World Series home runs.

Despite his power at the plate, Mantle struck out against alcohol. He began drinking at the age of 20 to ease the pain of his father's death. Alcohol became a habit during his years of playing baseball. After retiring from professional baseball, Mickey Mantle drank excessively to overcome frustration and boredom.

Although he suffered anxiety attacks, memory loss, and shakiness, he would not stop. In the early 1990s, Mantle's doctor warned him that if he took one more drink, it might be his last. Mantle finally admitted his alcoholism and checked himself into a treatment center.

Mantle had many regrets about his years of drinking. Most of all, he wished he had been a better father to his four sons. He also believed that alcohol shortened his career. In his autobiography, Mantle said, "The best time not to do drugs or alcohol is the first time. Don't end up over the hill before you even start to climb it."

Myths and Realities

To Be Sober, Stay Sober

Many myths surround the use of alcohol. One popular myth is that caffeine or a cold shower can make someone less drunk. Although they *can* make someone who has been drinking less tired, they *cannot* give the drinker's brain more control over the body. The result of drinking coffee, then, isn't a person who is no longer drunk, but a more-awake drunk. There is no way to speed up the body's process of removing alcohol.

People at Work

Police Officer

"The statistics say we're slowly winning the war against drunk drivers," said Sgt. Eva Carillo, "but when you see what I see every day, you know we've got a long way to go." Sgt. Carillo had just finished giving a breath-analysis test to a man who already had two convictions for driving under the influence.

Sgt. Carillo's present assignment is in the "drunk tank" at the downtown precinct, where she processes people picked up for drunk driving. She works many weekends, holidays, and nights, since drunk driving is more common during those times.

Before being accepted for training as a police officer, Sgt. Carillo had to score well on a written examination and pass a tough physical examination. The fact that she had two years of law enforcement training at a community college also helped her get an appointment to the police force.

There is one bright spot to her present job. Sgt. Carillo belongs to a team of police officers that goes into schools to talk about alcohol use. Sgt. Carillo feels she is helping students stay away from alcohol. She especially wants to get across the message that drinking and driving don't mix.

CON$UMER FOCU$

Health Headlines

You may have heard stories about the benefits of alcohol. Some recent studies indicate that drinking moderate amounts of alcohol—especially wine—can offer some protection against heart disease.

Should teens use this information as a reason to start drinking? Absolutely not! The research was based on the effects of alcohol in physically mature adults. It does not apply to teenagers, and no one has recommended that people should start drinking to have healthier hearts. In view of the many possible harmful effects of alcohol, adults may want to choose other ways to maintain a healthy heart.

Teens Making a Difference

Beating the Odds

Fifteen-year-old Willie often wondered why he felt jittery all the time and why he had trouble learning in school. Then he saw a television program about fetal alcohol syndrome (FAS). He recognized that many of the signs of FAS fit him. A school psychologist confirmed the diagnosis.

Willie grew up in a family troubled by alcohol. His mother admitted that she drank heavily during her pregnancy. FAS is the direct result of a woman who drinks alcohol while pregnant.

At first, Willie was angry with his parents and with his disability. A school counselor helped Willie channel his anger into speaking engagements. Now Willie tells teens and other groups about the causes and effects of FAS.

"One of my main messages," explains Willie, "is to tell kids that if you're going to create a life, be sure you don't mix in alcohol. Drinking never makes anything better."

Choosing to Be Alcohol Free

This lesson will help you find answers to questions that teens often ask about choosing to be alcohol free. For example:

► **Why do some teens decide not to drink?**

► **How can I refuse to drink and still have friends?**

► **How can I have fun and not drink?**

Word to Know

alternative

Why Some Young People Drink

There are many reasons not to drink. In spite of them, many young people still experiment with alcohol. At present, about 1,300,000 teenagers in the United States have drinking problems. Here are some of the reasons they give for drinking:

■ **"All my friends drink."** Some teens choose to go along with the crowd even if the crowd is drinking.

■ **"Alcohol makes me look grown-up."** Some young people want to look and act mature. They think drinking does that.

■ **"Alcohol helps me forget about my problems."** Alcohol is not an escape, though. The problems are still there when the alcohol wears off—with some additional problems.

■ **"Alcohol helps me relax."** The teen years are hectic. Some young people think alcohol will help them relax. Jogging or listening to music are much better ways to relax.

■ **"Alcohol helps me feel less shy around other people."** Most teens feel awkward in social situations. Some feel that alcohol puts them at ease. However, teens who rely on alcohol to boost their self-confidence may fail to develop effective social skills.

There are lots of healthy ways to have fun at a party. How many can you think of?

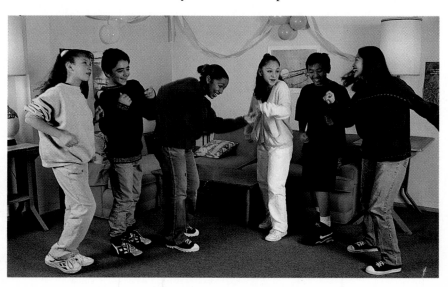

Some Reasons Not to Drink

One-third of the people over the age of 18 in the United States do not drink. Another one-third drink lightly and only occasionally. Many people who used to drink have stopped. As people are becoming aware of the physical and emotional damage that drinking can cause, fewer and fewer drink.

More and more young people are choosing not to drink. Here are some of the reasons they are giving.

■ **It is illegal.** Drinking is against the law in every state for anyone under age 21. Obeying the law makes your life easier and safer. It spares you expensive fines and a blot on your record.

■ **It gets in the way.** As a teen, your life is full of activities. You study, take tests, play sports, and try to be your best around your friends and family. Teens who choose not to drink will be more alert to meet these challenges. Athletics are especially difficult to pursue with a hangover.

■ **It is not fun.** Drinking can make people sick. It can also cause them to do something that may embarrass them. Drinking may even lead to injury or death. Many young people have decided that they can do without that kind of "fun."

■ **It is not smart.** Many teens know that they do not need to drink to be popular. They know that drinking does not make a person more mature. Acting responsibly is a sign of maturity.

■ **It does not solve problems.** Many teens understand that drinking does not solve problems. Instead, it creates them.

■ **It disappoints others and makes the user feel guilty.** Teens who drink alcohol live a lie because they have to hide their habit. Many young people would rather not have to sneak around and be dishonest with people they care about.

■ **It harms your health.** Drinking alcohol impairs development. It overworks the body system, particularly the liver. It also interferes with the absorption of nutrients from food.

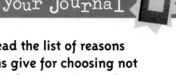

in your journal

Read the list of reasons teens give for choosing not to drink. In your journal, write your own list of reasons for saying no to alcohol.

Drinking can bring serious legal consequences to teens that can affect the rest of their lives.

Alcohol Advertising and Teens

Every day on television, in magazines, and on billboards, teens see good-looking, healthy people drinking alcohol. Entertainers promote the idea that it's normal, smart, and sophisticated to drink. Beer advertisements associate drinking with sporting events, fast cars, popularity, and fun. It is no wonder that teens are inclined to believe what they see.

Advertisers spend billions of dollars each year promoting alcohol. Their advertisements focus on how people act while using their products rather than the products themselves. The atmosphere is usually partylike with upbeat music or set in an outdoor environment that looks like fun, such as the beach. It's important to evaluate advertisements for the facts. Will that product make you more attractive or more popular? Will your relationships be successful and problem free as a result of drinking?

Promotion gimmicks are also popular. For example, at many sports and entertainment events you can buy T-shirts and hats that feature the name of the beer company sponsoring the event. When you wear the T-shirt or the hat, you provide free advertising for the product or company.

Few advertisements focus on the negative consequences of drinking. Those that do are usually public service announcements sponsored by organizations such as SADD (Students Against Driving Drunk) or MADD. Their advertising budgets simply cannot compete with those of major alcohol companies.

Some communities are trying to change the way alcohol companies advertise their products. They believe that promotions aimed at high school and college students, as well as sponsorship of sports and entertainment events, should be ended. They propose that billboard advertisements for alcohol should not be permitted near schools or hospitals. They know that alcohol causes problems for young people who use it.

Teen Issues

Raising Money

ACTIVITY!

Along with several other teens, hold a bake sale, car wash, or rummage sale to raise money for a "no-alcohol" publicity fund. Then use the money for posters, brochures, and other effective ways of getting your message to other teens.

Advertisers promote the idea that recreation is more fun when you are drinking their product. Name some of the health risks associated with drinking alcohol.

Many community groups sponsor dances and other social events for teens that focus on fun, healthy activities. Can you name some in your community?

LIFE SKILLS

How to Say No to Alcohol

*Y*ou know that drinking causes problems for you as well as friends and family members close to you. However, there will be times when you feel pressured to drink. How you handle such situations will affect your health and well-being for years to come.

There are many effective ways to avoid using alcohol. You need to find the technique that you feel comfortable using. Regardless of the technique you use, remember that no one has the right to pressure you to do something you do not want to do.

▶ **Choose a way that speaks the truth for you.** One teen might say, "I don't want to risk getting suspended from the team." Another might simply respond that the smell of alcohol makes her sick.

▶ **Avoid situations where people may be drinking.** Do not go to a party where you suspect there will be alcohol. If you attend a party and find that people are drinking, leave. Underage drinking is illegal. You could get arrested and have a record for the rest of your life.

▶ **Suggest alternatives.** Change the subject. You might ask if there's anything to eat, or say that you would rather dance instead.

▶ **Stick together with friends who support you.** You will find it easier to say no to alcohol if your friends also avoid it.

Follow-up Activities

1. Along with a partner, create a skit in which a teen is offered alcohol. Show the teen using one or more of the above techniques to refuse the alcohol. Act out your skit for the class.

2. Along with your classmates, think of more ways to avoid using alcohol. Publish your suggestions in the school newspaper, or prepare a flyer and distribute it to other students in school.

Steps for a healthy, productive life start with avoiding alcohol and other harmful substances.

Personal Inventory

HOW DO YOU FEEL ABOUT ALCOHOL?

The way you behave toward alcohol and your attitudes about drinking will affect the decisions you make throughout life. However, behavior and attitudes can be changed. Only you can decide if you need to make changes regarding alcohol.

On a separate sheet of paper, write "true" or "false" for each statement below. Your answers can help you identify and set goals to improve your behavior and attitudes toward alcohol. Total the number of true responses you have to the questions below. Then compare your score with the ranking at the end of the survey.

1. I have never had a drink containing alcohol.

2. My friends do not drink alcohol.

3. I avoid situations and places where I know there will be alcohol.

4. If I find myself in a place where others are drinking, I leave.

5. I have never ridden in a car driven by someone who had been drinking alcohol.

6. I think that alcohol is bad for the body and the mind.

7. I do not think drinking alcohol will make me more popular.

8. I do not believe the images I see in alcohol advertisements.

9. I do not believe that alcohol will make me more self-confident.

10. I believe that alcohol can ruin people's lives.

Give yourself 1 point for each true response. A score of 9–10 is very good. A score of 7–8 is good. A score of 5–6 is fair. If you score below 5 points, you need to set some goals for improving your behavior (if you answered false to the first five questions) or your attitudes (if you answered false to the last five questions) toward drinking.

Things to Do Instead of Drinking

Why do some teens simply give in when they are pressured to try alcohol? One reason is that they have not thought about alternatives. **Alternatives** (ahl·TER·nuh·tivz) are *other ways of thinking or acting.* There are plenty of alternatives to drinking. A few of them are suggested below.

- **Get good at something that requires a steady hand.** You could put together a model airplane, paint a picture, or practice calligraphy. Then remind yourself that a person whose senses are dulled by alcohol could not enjoy these activities.

- **Start a no-alcohol fund.** Every time you say no to alcohol put aside a small sum of money. At the end of a few months, treat yourself to a present with the money.

- **Join with other teens for alcohol-free fun.** You could plan an alcohol-free dance or have a basketball or volleyball game, keeping in mind that you will play better if you do not drink alcohol because you will be in control.

- **Volunteer to help others.** Teens who want to look mature can show their maturity by helping others. You could also volunteer at a hospital or nursing home helping sick or elderly people.

- **Learn a new sport or join a team.** Learn a sport you have never tried before, such as tennis or karate. You could practice your skills with a more experienced friend or relative.

- **Spread the word.** You could volunteer to teach younger children about the dangers of alcohol and the benefits of saying no. Younger children look up to teens as role models.

in your journal

Look at the alternatives to drinking shown on these pages. For each alternative, give an example of something you currently do or something you would like to do. Write your examples in your journal. What would you buy with the money you save in a no-alcohol fund?

Review

Lesson **3**

Using complete sentences, answer the following questions on a separate sheet of paper.

Reviewing Terms and Facts

1. **Vocabulary** Define the term *alternatives.* Use it in a sentence.

2. **Recall** List four reasons not to drink.

Thinking Critically

3. **Give Examples** How might drinking create more problems for a teen who is already troubled?

4. **Decide** You are at a party and someone offers you a drink in a glass with ice. You do not recognize the drink and suspect that it may contain alcohol. What would you do?

Applying Health Concepts

5. **Personal Health** Make a poster that shows healthy alternatives to using alcohol. Find or draw pictures that show young people taking part in worthwhile activities. At the top or bottom of your poster, write a headline that will persuade others about the importance of alternatives to drinking. Display your finished poster at school.

Chapter Summary

▶ Alcohol is a drug that depresses the brain and nervous system. (Lesson 1)

▶ Alcohol is a leading cause of traffic fatalities and other accidents. (Lesson 1)

▶ Drinking alcohol increases teens' chances of becoming involved in unsafe behavior. It also interferes with their emotional, social, and mental development. (Lesson 1)

▶ Drinking alcohol can be habit-forming. People who develop an addiction to alcohol risk family problems, losing jobs, poor health, and premature death. (Lesson 1)

▶ Alcoholism is a disease in which a person has a physical and mental need for alcohol. (Lesson 2)

▶ Recovery from alcoholism is possible, but it is a slow and often painful process. (Lesson 2)

▶ Many treatment programs and support groups are available to help alcoholics through the recovery process. (Lesson 2)

▶ Support groups are also available to help family members and friends of alcoholics. (Lesson 2)

▶ Despite the fact that there are many reasons not to drink, alcohol abuse is a serious problem for millions of American teenagers. (Lesson 3)

▶ The best way for teens to avoid problems with alcohol is to avoid using it. (Lesson 3)

▶ Teens can develop healthy alternatives to drinking. (Lesson 3)

Using Health Terms

On a separate sheet of paper, write the vocabulary term that best matches each definition given below.

1. A drug that slows down the working of the brain and other parts of the nervous system (Lesson 1)

2. A group of alcohol-related birth defects that may include both physical and mental problems (Lesson 1)

3. A physical or mental need for a drug or other substance (Lesson 1)

4. The physical and mental need for alcohol that turns into a progressive and chronic disease (Lesson 2)

5. The process of becoming well again (Lesson 2)

6. Other ways of thinking or acting (Lesson 3)

Reviewing Main Ideas

Using complete sentences, answer the following questions on a separate sheet of paper.

1. Describe alcohol's immediate effects on the brain and nervous system. (Lesson 1)

2. Name at least three ways excessive drinking over a long period of time might damage the body. (Lesson 1)

3. List at least four factors that determine alcohol's effects on a person. (Lesson 1)

4. Why is it dangerous to drive a car after drinking even a small amount of alcohol? (Lesson 1)

5. Why can drinking alcohol be especially harmful for teens? (Lesson 1)

6. What are three groups that can help people with drinking problems and their families? (Lesson 2)

7. Why do some teens choose to drink, even though they know about the harmful effects of alcohol? (Lesson 3)

8. List at least five reasons why teens should not drink. (Lesson 3)

9. What are some ways to say no to alcohol? (Lesson 3)

Thinking Critically

Using complete sentences, answer the following questions on a separate sheet of paper.

1. **Predict** How would you respond to parents who say, "Well, my teenage children may be drinking alcohol, but at least they aren't doing drugs"? (Lesson 1)

2. **Synthesize** Describe the stages in the development of alcoholism. (Lesson 2)

3. **Explain** What are the steps in the recovery from alcoholism? (Lesson 2)

4. **Analyze** Do you think alcoholism is the teenage drinker's greatest risk? Explain your answer. (Lesson 2)

5. **Analyze** How do advertisers try to convince young people to try alcohol? (Lesson 3)

6. **Give Examples** How can parents help teens deal with pressures to use alcohol? (Lesson 3)

Your Action Plan

Review your private journal entries for this chapter. Decide on a long-term goal you would like to achieve related to alcohol and health. For example, you might want to ensure that you remain alcohol free, or you might want to help a friend who has problems with alcohol. Once you have decided on a long-term goal, decide on several short-term goals or steps toward achieving your long-term goal. For example, if your goal is to remain alcohol free, you might develop hobbies and skills that would be alternatives to drinking.

One step that often helps a person achieve long-term goals is to tell family members and friends what he or she plans to do. These people then support the person in accomplishing the goal and often ask about his or her progress. This keeps the person working toward the goal. Try this technique to help you meet your goals.

Building Your Portfolio

1. Write a "Fact or Fiction?" quiz about alcohol use based on the information in this chapter. Make copies of the quiz and ask family members and friends to answer the questions. Put a copy of the quiz and the results of your survey in your portfolio.

2. Write a one-act play about two teens who attend a school where some alcohol is used by students. One teen tries to persuade his friend to stay away from the drinkers. If possible, act out your play for the class. Place a videotape of your play or a copy of the script in your portfolio.

In Your Home and Community

1. Interview your parents about the pressures they faced to drink when they were young. Tell them about pressures you may face and ask for their help. Together, write a list of "house rules."

2. Join a local chapter of SADD. If your school does not have one, ask a counselor or teacher to help you organize a group.

3. Attend an Alcoholics Anonymous, Al-Anon, or Alateen meeting and write about your reaction to the experience.

Chapter 15
Drugs and Your Health

Student Expectations

After reading this chapter, you should be able to:

1. Describe some of the uses for medicine.
2. Explain how stimulants and depressants can harm the body.
3. Describe the health risks associated with the use of marijuana, hallucinogens, and inhalants.
4. Identify ways to remain drug free.

Greg is my best friend. He used to be a star running back on the football team. His chances of getting a football scholarship looked good. Everything was working out for him. That is until some older guy offered to help Greg be a better player.

The guy gave Greg some pills called steroids. He told Greg that the pills would make his muscles stronger and bigger. He said that lots of football players use them to improve their performance. What he didn't tell Greg was that the pills were illegal and that he might get sick from them.

At first the pills seemed like wonder drugs and Greg was getting stronger and playing better than ever before. Then, all of a sudden after a couple of weeks, he started throwing up a lot. His skin broke out and he seemed real nervous and jittery.

Last week at practice, Greg started a fight with this new guy on the team. He lost control and beat the kid up real bad. Greg was crazy with anger. The coach guessed about the steroids and Greg couldn't lie to him. The result was that everyone lost. Our team lost a great player and Greg lost his chances for a football career.

in your journal

Read the account on this page. Do any people you know take drugs? Have you ever seen them get sick or violent because of the drugs? Start your private journal entries on drugs and your health by answering these questions:

▶ How do you think drugs affect the body?

▶ What can you do to avoid drugs?

When you reach the end of the chapter you will use your journal entries to make an action plan.

The Role of Medicine

This lesson will help you find answers to questions that teens often ask about medicines. For example:

► **What is the difference between drugs and medicine?**
► **How do medicines affect the body?**
► **What is the difference between prescription and over-the-counter medicines?**
► **How can I be sure I am using medicine properly?**

Words to Know

drugs
medicine
antibiotic
side effect
tolerance
prescription
    medicine
over-the-counter
    (OTC) medicine

Drugs and Health

In this century, medical discoveries and the development of more effective drugs have changed the overall health of the American people. Many drugs are now available to prevent, treat, or cure diseases, injuries, and medical problems. These drugs have helped millions of people live longer, healthier lives.

Not all of the changes brought about by modern drugs have been healthful, however. Sometimes drugs are not used the way they are supposed to be used. When that happens, drugs become dangerous. They can do great harm to people's bodies and minds, as well as to society as a whole.

Types of Drugs

Medicines are available in a variety of forms to prevent diseases, fight infection, and provide pain relief.

Drugs are *substances other than food that change the structure or function of the body or mind.* Most of the time, people use the term *drug* when they refer to medicine. **Medicines** are *drugs that are used to treat or prevent diseases and other conditions.*

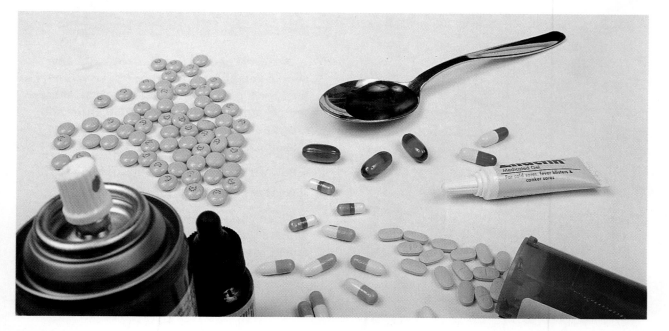

Medicines are usually grouped according to their effect on the body. Some of the most commonly used types of medicines include those that prevent diseases, those that fight infection, and those that provide pain relief. Each type of medicine is briefly discussed on the following pages.

Medicines That Prevent Diseases

Vaccines are medicines that prevent diseases. Made from preparations of dead or weakened germs, vaccines cause the immune system to produce antibodies. The antibodies then fight off the germs that cause the disease. The polio vaccine is one you probably had before you started school. It provides long-lasting protection against the polio virus. Other vaccines are for diseases such as diphtheria, tetanus, whooping cough, measles, mumps, rubella, hepatitis B, and influenza.

Medicines That Fight Germs

Many germs and diseases cannot be prevented with vaccines. Instead, medicines are used to restore people to health. A medicine commonly used to fight germs is an antibiotic. **Antibiotics** (an·ti·by·AH·tiks) are *medicines that reduce or kill harmful bacteria in the body.* Many types of antibiotics are available. They are usually sold in liquid or tablet form. Physicians also may give antibiotics to patients in a shot.

Each type of antibiotic fights only certain types of bacteria. For example, *penicillin* (pen·uh·SI·luhn), one of the most commonly used antibiotics, is highly effective in killing bacteria that cause strep throat and pneumonia. Unfortunately, antibiotics do not kill infections caused by viruses. Therefore, they are not effective in helping you when you have a cold or the flu. Some people are allergic to some of these medicines, but they can use others.

Medicines That Provide Pain Relief

Many people take medicine to relieve pain. With about 20 billion tablets sold annually, aspirin is the most widely used pain relief medicine available without a doctor's prescription. Aspirin and its substitutes (including acetaminophen) are used for headaches, toothaches, and muscular pain. They are also used to reduce fever and inflammation.

Prescription pain relievers are also available. Doctors may prescribe these when a person is recovering from a serious illness or to help a person manage the pain that accompanies a chronic disease, such as arthritis. Narcotics, one specific type of prescription pain reliever, are so powerful that they may cause physical and psychological dependence.

in your journal

What medicines have you used in the past three months? In your journal, list the medicines and explain why you used them.

Some types of penicillin are derived from natural molds or bacteria such as this. Others, known as synthetic penicillins, are chemically processed.

Other Medicines

A variety of medicines are available to treat people with certain health problems or conditions. Specific medicines are used by people with chronic conditions. These conditions include heart and blood pressure problems, diabetes, and allergies.

Some medicines have negative effects. Yet their use is essential for the health and well-being of some people. In those cases, additional medicine may be used to offset the negative effect of the first medicine. For instance, people who take certain types of blood pressure medicine may need to take another medicine to keep from retaining fluids.

Medicine in the Body

The effect of a medicine in the body depends on several factors. The type and amount of medicine a person takes are two important factors. The way you take medicine—by pill or shot—also has a lot to do with the effect of the medicine. Study **Figure 15.1.** Through which method are the effects of medicine more immediate? The shot is more immediate because it bypasses the digestive system going directly into the circulatory system.

You are different from everyone else. Your body chemistry is different from every other person's body chemistry. As a result, medicines can affect you differently from other people. For example, some people have reactions to certain medicines. This is why it is very important for medicine to be used only as prescribed and only by the person it is prescribed for.

Reactions to Medicine

One type of reaction to medicine is a **side effect,** which is *any reaction to a medicine other than the one intended.* Side effects include upset stomach, dizziness, and drowsiness. If you have any

HEALTH LAB
Home Remedies

***I*ntroduction:** Throughout history, and even today, people have used home remedies for a variety of ailments. Home remedies exist for illnesses, skin and hair care, and childbirth.

Many of these remedies have been handed down from generation to generation. Some of them may be useless, or even harmful. However, many others have been proven to work and, in fact, have real medicinal value. For example, one home remedy suggests using tea to dry up canker sores. This remedy is based on scientific evidence because the tannic acid in tea brings relief to the canker sore pain. On the other hand, the home remedy of applying butter to a burn can be harmful because there is a high risk of infection from the butter.

Objective: During the next week, identify and list home remedies that you have heard of or that you or members of your family use. Evaluate the effectiveness of the remedies.

side effects to medicine, talk to a physician, nurse, or pharmacist. Some side effects can be very serious. Both prescription and over-the-counter medicines list possible side effects on their labels.

Figure 15.1
How Drugs Enter the Body

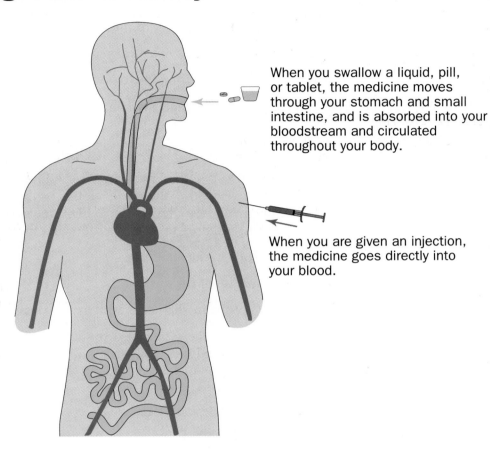

When you swallow a liquid, pill, or tablet, the medicine moves through your stomach and small intestine, and is absorbed into your bloodstream and circulated throughout your body.

When you are given an injection, the medicine goes directly into your blood.

Materials and Method: You will need a sheet of paper divided into three columns. Label the columns *Home Remedy, What It Is Used For,* and *How Effective Is It?* In the *Home Remedy* column, describe the remedy. In the *What It Is Used For* column, indicate what the particular remedy is supposed to cure or what condition it is supposed to relieve. In the *How Effective Is It?* column, evaluate the remedy's effectiveness. To get information for this column, you might need to do research at the library or interview people who have tried the remedy. If you cannot find any information on a particular remedy, write "undetermined" in this column.

Observation and Analysis: At the end of the week, share your home remedies and their effectiveness with your classmates. See how many different home remedies your class can identify. You could work with your classmates to make a bulletin board display of the most popular remedies.

Tolerance

When used over a long period of time, certain medicines can cause a person to develop a tolerance. **Tolerance** means that *a person's body becomes used to the effect of a medicine and needs greater amounts of it to be effective.*

Reactions to Mixing Medicines

When two or more medicines are taken at the same time, the effects may be dangerous. Any of the following reactions is possible.

■ Each medicine may have a stronger effect than if taken alone.

■ The medicines may combine to give unexpected effects.

■ The medicines may cancel out each other's expected effects.

Drug Safety and the Government

In the United States, the Food and Drug Administration (FDA) is responsible for regulating the use of drugs, or medicines. To make sure that all medicines are safe, the FDA requires any company that manufactures a drug to state the following facts:

■ The chemicals in the medicine

■ The medical use of the medicine

■ The effects of the medicine, as well as any possible side effects

Before any medicine is released for sale, it must be thoroughly tested by the FDA. **Figure 15.2** shows the process new medicines must go through. In some cases, it takes years for a medicine to be approved for use.

Keep Alert

Are you, or is anyone in your family, allergic to a medicine routinely administered, such as penicillin? People with such allergies need to wear a medicial identification tag. This tag provides important information that emergency caregivers need in case the person with the allergy has an accident that leaves him or her unconscious.

Figure 15.2
How the FDA Tests and Approves Medicines

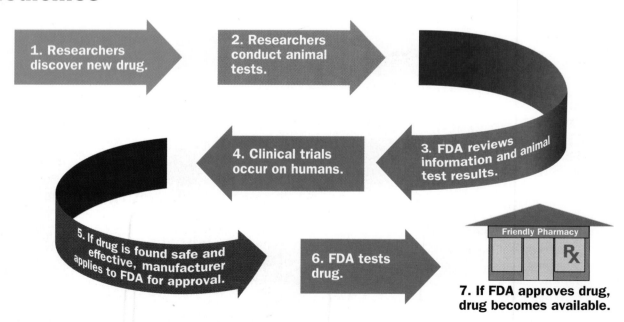

1. Researchers discover new drug.

2. Researchers conduct animal tests.

3. FDA reviews information and animal test results.

4. Clinical trials occur on humans.

5. If drug is found safe and effective, manufacturer applies to FDA for approval.

6. FDA tests drug.

7. If FDA approves drug, drug becomes available.

Prescription Medicine

Because some medicines are very strong and potentially harmful, physicians must write special orders for them. These **prescription** (pri·SKRIP·shuhn) **medicines** are *medicines that can be sold only with a written order from a physician.* **Figure 15.3** shows the basic information that must appear on a prescription label.

Figure 15.3
Prescription Medicine Label

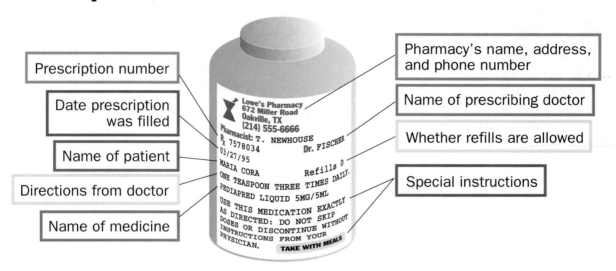

- Prescription number
- Date prescription was filled
- Name of patient
- Directions from doctor
- Name of medicine
- Pharmacy's name, address, and phone number
- Name of prescribing doctor
- Whether refills are allowed
- Special instructions

Lowe's Pharmacy
672 Miller Road
Oakville, TX
(214) 555-6666
Pharmacist: T. NEWHOUSE
Rx 7578034   Dr. FISCHER
03/27/95
MARIA CORA   Refills 0
ONE TEASPOON THREE TIMES DAILY.
PEDIAPRED LIQUID 5MG/5ML
USE THIS MEDICATION EXACTLY
AS DIRECTED: DO NOT SKIP
DOSES OR DISCONTINUE WITHOUT
INSTRUCTIONS FROM YOUR
PHYSICIAN.   TAKE WITH MEALS

Over-the-Counter (OTC) Medicine

Some *medicines are safe enough to be taken without a written order from a physician.* They are called **over-the-counter (OTC) medicines.** Although not as strong as prescription medicines, they still may be harmful if not used as directed.

OTC medicines can be bought at any store that sells medications. Aspirin and cold pills are examples. **Figure 15.4** shows what every OTC medicine should include on its label.

Figure 15.4
Over-the-Counter Medicine Label

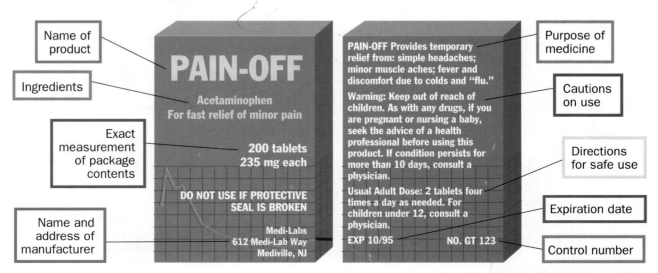

- Name of product
- Ingredients
- Exact measurement of package contents
- Name and address of manufacturer
- Purpose of medicine
- Cautions on use
- Directions for safe use
- Expiration date
- Control number

PAIN-OFF
Acetaminophen
For fast relief of minor pain

200 tablets
235 mg each

DO NOT USE IF PROTECTIVE SEAL IS BROKEN

Medi-Labs
612 Medi-Lab Way
Mediville, NJ

PAIN-OFF Provides temporary relief from: simple headaches; minor muscle aches; fever and discomfort due to colds and "flu."

Warning: Keep out of reach of children. As with any drugs, if you are pregnant or nursing a baby, seek the advice of a health professional before using this product. If condition persists for more than 10 days, consult a physician.

Usual Adult Dose: 2 tablets four times a day as needed. For children under 12, consult a physician.

EXP 10/95   NO. GT 123

Using Medicine Safely

Although consumers receive accurate information from the FDA, they still are ultimately responsible for using medicine properly. Some people use medicines in ways that are not intended. For instance, they may take four aspirins instead of two (hoping to get relief twice as fast) or use a medicine prescribed for someone else.

Misusing medicine is dangerous. Medicines have powerful effects on the body. If you are not sure how to use a medicine, ask the pharmacist or call your doctor. They can provide you with the information you need to use medicine safely.

Tips for Using Medicine

- Do not use OTC medicine for more than ten days without medical supervision. If an OTC medication does not help you, you may need something stronger. Call your physician.

- Do not share prescription medicine.

- Destroy medications that have passed their expiration date.

- Keep medicines safely sealed in childproof containers, and keep them out of the reach of children.

- Never take medication with alcohol.

- Never take two or more medicines at the same time without your doctor's approval.

Keeping medicines high above the reach of children is an important safety measure.

Lesson 1 Review

Using complete sentences, answer the following questions on a separate sheet of paper.

Reviewing Terms and Facts

1. **Vocabulary** Which of the following is a type of medicine: *antibiotic* or *tolerance?* Describe the medicine.

2. **Give Examples** List three possible unhealthy reactions the body can have to medicine.

Thinking Critically

3. **Contrast** What is the difference between prescription and OTC medicines?

4. **Analyze** Suppose you went to your local pharmacy to buy nose spray and the lid on the tamperproof box was open on the only bottle left. Would you buy the spray? Why or why not?

Applying Health Concepts

5. **Consumer Health** Make a poster showing the three main groups of medicines. Illustrate the poster to clearly show the differences between these groups.

6. **Consumer Health** Research the Food and Drug Administration. Find out when and why it was established and the types of services it provides. Present your information in a one-page brochure.

Stimulants and Depressants

This lesson will help you find answers to questions that teens often ask about drugs such as stimulants and depressants. For example:

► **Which kinds of drugs are misused or abused most often?**

► **How do stimulants affect the body?**

► **How do depressants affect the body?**

Drug Misuse and Abuse

People seriously harm their bodies by taking medicines or other drugs they should not be taking. In 1992, more than 7,000 people died as a result of misusing or abusing legal or illegal drugs. Some of them were teens.

People who harm themselves by using drugs are drug misusers or drug abusers. Drug misusers use a legal drug in an improper way. Drug abusers use substances that are against the law or are not supposed to be taken into the human body. Many of these drugs have no medical purpose and may be contaminated with lethal substances. The following are forms of drug misuse and abuse:

- Using a drug without following the directions

- Taking more or less of a drug than the doctor ordered

- Using a drug prescribed for someone else

- Giving your prescription medicine to someone else

- Using a drug for longer than a physician advises

- Combining medicines

- Using a medicine when you do not need it

- Using a drug for purposes other than medical treatment

- Taking a substance that was not meant to enter the body

Stimulants

Stimulants (STIM·yuh·luhnts) are *drugs that speed up the body's functions.* Stimulants cause the blood pressure to rise. They increase breathing and make the heart beat faster. A person using a stimulant feels alert and wakeful. Doctors may prescribe stimulants to patients who have physical or emotional problems. Other stimulants, however, are used illegally to prevent fatigue, increase alertness, and improve self-confidence.

Words to Know

stimulant
amphetamine
narcotic

Q & A

Overdosing Can Kill

Q: What does overdosing on a drug mean?

A: To overdose means to take too much. The term overdose usually refers to the abuse of illegal drugs. Only one overdose of some illegal drugs can cause death.

Effects of Stimulants on the Body

Many parts of the body are affected by stimulants. Stimulants

■ speed up the central nervous system.

■ cause the heart rate to increase.

■ cause respiratory rates to increase.

■ cause high blood pressure.

When stimulants are misused or abused, they can seriously damage the body. They are dangerous because the user cannot be sure of the purity, amount, or concentration of the drug. Furthermore, the user has no idea how the body may react. Even a first-time user could die. Another danger of stimulants is that they can become habit-forming. The more of them a person uses, the more the person needs to feel an effect. After a while, that person can develop an addiction to the drug, or a physical or mental need for it.

Some stimulants are so mild that people are unaware they are using a drug. *Caffeine* is a good example. It is found in cocoa, coffee, tea, and many soft drinks. The use of caffeine in moderate doses is a commonly accepted practice. However, other stimulants can be very dangerous. Stimulants such as amphetamines and cocaine often are abused by people who are trying to get "high."

Amphetamines

Amphetamines (am·FE·tuh·meenz) are *drugs prescribed to stimulate the central nervous system.* Doctors sometimes prescribe them to treat hyperactive children and *narcolepsy,* a disease that results in an uncontrollable need to sleep. However amphetamines are highly addictive. Users may become physically and psychologically dependent. Study **Figure 15.7** on page 462. In what other ways do amphetamines affect the body?

MAKING HEALTHY DECISIONS
Helping a Friend Who Might Be Abusing Drugs

*J*oanna and Martina have been best friends since they were in second grade. They were both in band, and they played on the school's soccer team. Whenever possible, they took the same classes. They also spent much of their leisure time together, going to concerts and attending many of the same parties.

In the past few months, Joanna has noticed a big change in Martina. For one thing, they have been spending much less time together. When they do spend time together, Martina often seems hostile toward Joanna. Martina's grades are slipping, and she is hanging out with a different crowd. Several times in recent weeks, Joanna has seen Martina exchanging pills with them. When Joanna questioned her, Martina said she was using the pills to help her get through some bad times at home. Joanna has tried to get Martina to talk through her problems, but she has refused.

Finally, Joanna told Martina that she thought Martina was abusing drugs and that she should get help. Martina denied having a drug problem and told Joanna to leave her alone.

Cocaine

Cocaine (koh·KAYN) is a powerful, illegal stimulant. Its abuse has become a major health problem in our society. Cocaine users come from many age groups. As **Figure 15.5** shows, however, cocaine's use is declining among high school students.

Cocaine creates a feeling of exhilaration and a burst of energy, followed by depression as the drug wears off. When users take more of the drug to relieve depression, they become dependent on it. Cocaine also makes the user crave more of it. In its most powerful forms, cocaine is injected into the bloodstream or smoked. People also sniff the powder up their noses.

in your journal

Many teens are joining the campaign to stop using drugs. In your journal, write phrases that you might use on a poster to explain why it is healthy to avoid drugs.

Crack Cocaine

Crack cocaine is a concentrated form of cocaine that is smoked. It produces an intense high in only a few seconds, followed by an intense low that leaves the user craving more. Crack is one of the most addictive and dangerous drugs used in the United States today. Because it is smoked, crack cocaine reaches the brain within ten seconds after it is taken. However, its effects last only a few minutes (see **Figure 15.6** on the next page).

Figure 15.5
Declining Cocaine Use Among High School Seniors

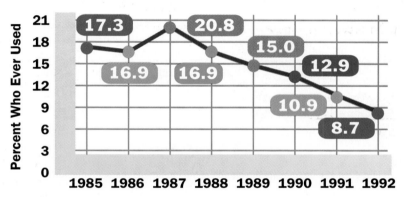

Source: *World Almanac and Book of Facts*, 1994

Joanna is torn. Should she leave Martina alone or try to get help for her? Joanna decided to use the step-by-step decision-making process to make up her mind:

❶ **State the situation**

❷ **List the options**

❸ **Weigh the possible outcomes**

❹ **Consider your values**

❺ **Make a decision and act**

❻ **Evaluate the decision**

Follow-up Activities

1. Apply the six steps of the decision-making process to Joanna's story.

2. With a partner, role-play a scene in which Joanna tells Martina that because she thinks Martina is abusing drugs, she doesn't want anything more to do with her.

3. Now role-play a scene in which Joanna tells Martina that she is going to find someone to help her with her drug problem. Think about suggestions Joanna can make to help Martina face her drug problem.

Figure 15.6
Crack-Craving Cycle

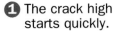

1 The crack high starts quickly.

3 The user then experiences a severe crash followed by a craving for more of the drug.

2 It gives the user an intense high, but it lasts only 15 minutes.

Smoking crack has the same effects on the body as using cocaine, only more intense (see **Figure 15.7**). Risks and side effects are also similar. In addition, users are at risk for getting emphysema from the smoke.

Figure 15.7
Stimulants

Drug	What It Is Called	How It Is Taken	What It Does
Amphetamines	Speed, crank, ice, uppers, pep pills, diet pills	Swallowed, by needle, inhaled, smoked	Causes uneven heart beat, rise in blood pressure, physical collapse, stroke, heart attack, and death
Cocaine	Coke, snow, toot, blow, lady	Inhaled, by needle, smoked	Damages nose lining, liver, and heart; causes heart attack, seizures, stroke, and death
Crack	Rock, freebase, ready rock, teeth	Smoked	Leads to seizures, heart attack, and death

Depressants

Depressants are drugs that slow down the body's functions and reactions. Commonly called sedatives, these medications reduce blood pressure and slow down the heart rate and breathing rate. Doctors may prescribe depressants to relieve anxiety, nervousness, and sleeplessness. However, depressants are frequently abused.

Main Kinds of Depressants

- Tranquilizers (TRAN·kwuh·ly·zerz), when used as prescribed by a doctor in small amounts, can help a person relax without making him or her less alert.

- Barbiturates (bar·BI·chuh·ruhts) are powerful sedatives that are used for medical purposes.

- Hypnotics (hip·NAH·tiks) are very strong drugs that bring on sleep and reduce anxiety.

Depressants are highly addictive. Over an extended period, they can cause physical and psychological dependence. Depressants should only be taken under a physician's supervision.

Abuse of depressants causes physical harm. When combined with alcohol, depressants are deadly. **Figure 15.8** shows some of the effects of various depressants on the body.

An amino acid (tryptophan) in milk, when heated, is a natural sedative. Drinking warm milk is one healthful way that a person can relieve sleeplessness.

Figure 15.8
Depressants

Kind of Depressant	What It Is Called	How It Looks	How It Is Taken	What It Does
Tranquilizer	Valium, Librium	Tablets or capsules	Swallowed	Reduces muscular activity, coordination, attention span, and anxiety Withdrawal can cause tremors and lead to coma or death
Barbiturate	Downers, barbs, yellow jackets	Red, yellow, blue, or red and blue capsules	Swallowed	Causes mood changes and excessive sleep Can lead to coma
Hypnotic	Quaaludes, Ludes, Sopors	Tablets	Swallowed	Impairs coordination and judgment Depresses the respiratory and circulatory systems

Narcotics

Narcotics (nar·KAH·tics) are *prescription medicines that are used to relieve pain.* Doctors may prescribe the narcotic *morphine,* an opiate, to treat extreme pain. *Codeine* (KOH·deen) may be prescribed to stop severe coughing. Although they are safe when taken under a physician's supervision, narcotics are so strongly addictive that their sale and use is controlled by law. In fact, pharmacists must keep records of all sales of narcotics.

Heroin

Heroin (HEHR·uh·win) is an *illegal drug that is made from morphine and is highly addictive.* Heroin users quickly develop a need for stronger and stronger doses of the drug. When users do not get the heroin they need, they feel severe pain. In addition, heroin depresses the central nervous system and can lead to coma or death.

Heroin is most commonly injected. Users of heroin and other drugs that are injected by needle run the risk of becoming infected by HIV. **Figure 15.9** shows what percentage of AIDS patients over 13 years old injected drugs.

Figure 15.9
AIDS Patients Who Inject Drugs (1993)

Drug abuse is an important risk factor in contracting HIV/AIDS and other sexually transmitted diseases. Because drug use impairs judgment, people under the influence of drugs are likely to engage in risky behaviors.

Males Over 13 Years Old

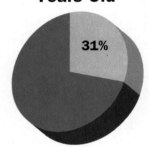

31%

Females Over 13 Years Old

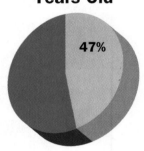

47%

Lesson 2 Review

Using complete sentences, answer the following questions on a separate sheet of paper.

Reviewing Terms and Facts

1. **Vocabulary** Which of the following terms refer to drugs that relax you: *stimulants, amphetamines, narcotics?*
2. **Give Examples** Name an example of misuse or abuse of each of the above.

Thinking Critically

3. **Contrast** How do the effects of stimulants differ from those of depressants?

4. **Synthesize** What advice might you give a friend who said she was going to try crack cocaine?

Applying Health Concepts

5. **Consumer Health** Choose two drugs that are frequently abused. Make a poster that warns of the dangers of both drugs.
6. **Health of Others** Read about a famous person who died from a drug overdose. Find out how the person's lifestyle and habits led to his or her death. Explain what you learned from the incident. Write a report on your findings.

Marijuana and Other Illegal Drugs

Lesson 3

This lesson will help you find answers to questions that teens often ask about street drugs. For example:

▶ **What are the side effects and risks of using marijuana?**
▶ **What are hallucinogens?**
▶ **What are the effects of using designer drugs and inhalants?**

Street Drugs

"If drugs do so much damage," some people have asked, "why not stop making them?" The answer is that many drugs have worthwhile uses. When drugs like morphine and Valium are used carefully and under a physician's supervision, they can help people who are ill or in severe pain.

Other drugs, however, have limited—if any—medical benefits. They are commonly abused and traded on the streets. These drugs are dangerous and illegal. Anyone who uses or sells them can be fined or sent to jail for a long time.

Marijuana

The most commonly used street drug today is *marijuana* (mehr·uh·WAHN·uh). Marijuana contains 421 different chemicals including THC (tetrahydrocannabinol), the main mind-altering ingredient. *Hashish,* a more powerful drug derived from the same plant, contains greater concentrations of THC. **Figure 15.10** provides information on marijuana.

Words to Know

hallucinogen
designer drugs
inhalant

in your journal

Imagine that you are asked to write a law that deals with users and sellers of illegal drugs. In your journal, write what the law would be and why you would write the law.

Figure 15.10
Marijuana

The common names for marijuana include pot, grass, weed, reefer, dope, joint, and mary jane.

Effects on the Body:
- Reduces memory, reaction time, and coordination
- Reduces initiative and ambition
- Increases heart rate and appetite, and lowers body temperature
- Damages heart and lungs
- Interferes with normal body development in teens by changing hormone levels
- May cause psychological dependence

Lesson 3: Marijuana and Other Illegal Drugs 465

Marijuana is usually smoked. Sometimes it is mixed with food and eaten. Although some people believe that smoking marijuana is safer than smoking tobacco, they are wrong. Marijuana contains as much as four to five times the amount of tar and other cancer-causing substances as tobacco.

The effects of marijuana are almost immediate, especially if a person smokes it. Most users feel mildly euphoric and relaxed, and they perceive sights and sounds more vividly. The exact effects of marijuana vary from person to person and are influenced by moods and surroundings.

Hallucinogens

Another group of street drugs is **hallucinogens** (huh·LOO·suhn·uh·jenz). These are *drugs that distort moods, thoughts, and senses.* Hallucinogens affect many parts of the body. Hallucinogens

- affect the cerebrum, the part of the brain that controls the intellect and perception.

- affect the nervous system.

- increase heart and respiratory rates.

Hallucinogens produce altered mental states that may last for several hours or several days. The effects are extremely unpredictable. Some people claim to have positive experiences, whereas others have very disturbing ones. Some people have even died while using hallucinogens because they believed they had super powers that enabled them to fly out of windows or walk on water.

PCP

Phencyclidine (fen·SI·kluh·deen), or PCP, is a powerful and dangerous hallucinogen whose effects last a long time. When the drug is used regularly, effects may come and go for as long as a year.

Many users have died from PCP. While overdoses of this synthetic drug can cause death, most deaths are a result of the strange, destructive behavior the drug produces in the user. **Figure 15.11** lists some of the dangerous effects of PCP.

- Common names are angel dust, lovely, loveboat, hog, and killer weed.

- Common forms are white powder, pills, capsules, and liquid.

- It may be swallowed, injected, or smoked when used with marijuana.

- It causes loss of coordination, as well as increases in heart rate, blood pressure, and body temperature.

Hallucinogens are dangerous substances that can seriously harm the body.

LSD

Another hallucinogen known by its initials is *LSD,* which is short for *lysergic* (luh·SER·jik) *acid diethylamide* (dy·e·thuh·LA·mid). LSD affects the areas of the brain that control vision and balance. This drug often distorts perceptions of sound and color. **Figure 15.11** shows how dangerous the effects of LSD are.

- Common names for LSD are acid, white lightning, sugar cubes, and micro dots.

- Common forms are tablets, liquid, squares soaked on paper.

- It may be swallowed, licked, or put in with eye drops.

- It increases blood pressure and heart rate, and causes chills, nausea, tremors, and sleeplessness.

Other Hallucinogens

The peyote cactus is found in northern Mexico and Texas. *Mescaline* is the hallucinogenic ingredient in peyote. Mescaline can also be synthetically produced and often comes in the form of brown disks, capsules, and tablets. The effects last 5 to 12 hours.

Psilocybin is the hallucinogenic ingredient that is found in the *Psilocybe mexicana* mushroom and a few other species of mushrooms. These mushrooms grow wild throughout the United States and other parts of the world. They are eaten in fresh or dried form, and their effects are felt for from 3 to 6 hours.

Designer Drugs

Designer drugs are *drugs that are made from chemicals that resemble illegal substances.* Street chemists make these drugs to avoid using illegal substances. *Ecstasy,* or MDMA, is one of the most popular designer drugs. The use of this drug can result in the destruction of brain cells.

Did You Know?

A Bad Flashback ACTIVITY!

People who use hallucinogens are in danger of having flashbacks. During a flashback, the effects of the drug may recur days, months, or years after the drug was used. Write a paragraph to explain why you think this could harm someone.

Figure 15.11
The Most Dangerous Drugs

Some drugs are so unpredictable that they are dangerous even to try once.

Drug	Dangerous Effects
PCP	• Convulsions, heart and lung failure, or broken blood vessels • Bizarre or violent behavior • Temporary psychosis • False feeling of having super powers
LSD	• Unpredictable behavior • Flashbacks • False feeling of having super powers
Injectable Drugs	• Possible HIV infection or hepatitis

Personal Inventory

You have learned that many types of drugs are misused and abused. The harm they do to the mind and body may happen after just one use. For that reason, and because your life depends on staying drug free, it is important for you to examine your behaviors and attitudes toward drugs.

On a separate sheet of paper, write yes or no for each statement below. Your answers can help you determine if you need to change your behaviors or attitudes toward drugs. Total your number of "yes" responses. Compare your score with the ranking at the end of the survey.

1. I avoid any type of illegal drug use.

2. I never take medicine that is not prescribed for me.

3. My friends avoid illegal drugs.

4. If I find myself at a place where people are using drugs, I leave.

5. I have never gotten into a car that was driven by someone whom I knew was under the influence of drugs.

6. I believe that using illegal drugs will harm my mind and body.

7. I do not like the thought of losing control of my thoughts or senses.

8. I think that people who use drugs are not smart.

9. I do not think I would enjoy the experience of getting high.

10. I believe that using illegal drugs once could ruin my life.

Give yourself 1 point for a yes. A score of 9—10 is very good. A score of 7—8 is good. A score of 5—6 is fair. If you score below 5, you need to look seriously at changing your behaviors (numbers 1—5) or attitudes (numbers 6—10). Your life may depend on it!

Inhalants

Anyone who uses or possesses drugs faces stiff fines and penalties, as well as having a criminal record.

Inhalants (in·HAY·luhnts) are *substances whose fumes are sniffed and inhaled to give a hallucinogeniclike high.* Inhalants include solvents and aerosols, such as glue, spray paints, gasoline, and other equally harmful substances. These substances are not meant to be taken into the body.

Inhalants also include *nitrites* and *nitrous oxide,* which are substances that have medicinal uses. *Amyl nitrite* is a prescription drug used to control *angina* (heart pain). It is a clear yellowish liquid that comes in ampules. When used illegally, the ampules are broken, and the fumes are inhaled. Nitrous oxide, which is sometimes called laughing gas, is used by dentists as an anesthetic. It is also used by manufacturers as a propellant in canned whipped cream.

Talking to young children about the dangers of drugs is one way to work to prevent drug abuse.

When inhalants are taken into the body, their harmful fumes go directly to the brain causing mental confusion, dizziness, lack of coordination, and hallucinations. Damage to the kidneys and liver is also common. Even worse, the fumes can kill brain cells and cause permanent brain damage or death.

Drug Awareness Programs

Drug use affects almost everyone. Consider the effect drug use has on crimes, accidents, and the rising costs of treatment. Drug use is a problem that takes its toll on society as a whole.

You can be part of the solution instead of part of the problem. You can work together with adults and other teens in your community to promote drug awareness. Your program could be targeted toward teaching younger children about the dangers of drugs. Your community would be a better place as a result of your efforts.

Review
Lesson 3

Using complete sentences, answer the following questions on a separate sheet of paper.

Reviewing Terms and Facts

1. **Vocabulary** Which of the following drugs distort people's senses: *hallucinogens, designer drugs, inhalants?* List some specific drugs that appear in each category.

2. **Explain** Why have designer drugs come into being?

Thinking Critically

3. **Analyze** Why is marijuana more dangerous for a teenager than it is for an adult?

4. **Synthesize** How can the feeling of having super powers make the use of PCP and LSD dangerous?

Applying Health Concepts

5. **Personal Health** Prepare a chart showing the risks marijuana poses to various body systems, such as the lungs, brain, and the immune system. Use library resources to find out what is currently known and being researched about marijuana and each body system.

6. **Health of Others** Design an advertisement for a teen magazine, warning readers about the dangers of using inhalants.

Teen HEALTH DIGEST

People at Work

Pharmacist

To know more about the medication you are taking, Miranda Ramirez is the person to help you. She is a pharmacist, a professional who is concerned with the preparation, distribution, and use of medicines.

Ms. Ramirez works in a pharmacy in the suburb of a large city. She fills prescriptions from doctors and dentists. An important part of her job is to prepare the labels on the medicines. These labels include directions about how to take the prescriptions. Although most medicines are supplied by pharmaceutical companies, Ms. Ramirez also prepares some herself, such as certain antiseptics and ointments. Ms. Ramirez's customers rely on her to give them information about their prescriptions and to give them help in selecting over-the-counter medicines.

Ms. Ramirez is a graduate of a college of pharmacology. She has completed a five-year program and one year of internship under the supervision of a practicing pharmacist. She took courses such as chemistry, biological sciences, and mathematics. After completing college, she had to pass a state board examination to get a license to practice in her state.

Ms. Ramirez says that her career brings her a lot of rewards. She is satisfied knowing that she is helping people maintain their health.

Being a Smart Medicine Taker

Do you ask questions about medications? An FDA study of more than 1,000 adults found that most of them never asked questions about the medicines prescribed for them. The American Pharmaceutical Association recommends asking the physician or pharmacist several questions about the prescribed medicine. These questions include:

- What is the medication supposed to do?
- Can it cause an allergic reaction?
- Should I avoid certain foods or activities while taking it?
- What should I do if I forget to take the medicine?
- Is there a cheaper alternative or an acceptable generic version of the drug?

It is also wise to establish a relationship with one pharmacy and even with one pharmacist with whom you feel comfortable. In doing so, one location will keep track of all your prescription medicines and you can avoid side effects and unhealthy interactions between them.

Health Update

Health Threat to Unborn Babies

When a pregnant woman is addicted to drugs or alcohol, her baby can be born addicted. During the early stages of pregnancy, each organ system in a baby's body is in an important stage of development. Any harmful substances used by the mother can cause birth defects, such as low birth weight and heart problems. During the later stages of the pregnancy, drug use by the mother can result in growth retardation and brain defects.

A baby born to a drug-addicted mother is sometimes born addicted and can suffer severe and long-lasting withdrawal symptoms. Even if the baby survives the withdrawal symptoms, in later life the child may experience behavioral and psychological disturbances.

Teens Making a Difference

Drug-free Homes

A new drug prevention program has taken hold in South Florida. The program, called "Drug-free Homes," is the brainchild of Ellen, a 14-year-old girl who wanted to start a volunteer program that focused on drug prevention.

To take part in the program, young people and their parents read a brochure about the effects of drugs. Once they have studied the brochure, they sign a pledge to remain drug free. The forms are then sent to Ellen, and the families receive special decals to place on their windows. Ellen also has T-shirts available that read "I live in a drug-free home and I am proud of it."

"I just wanted to find a way to help open the lines of communication regarding drug abuse," Ellen says. She hopes that will happen after family members discuss the brochure and sign the pledge. This is one way for family members to work together to help prevent drug abuse.

Sports and Recreation

Losing Out

Recently, drug abuse has occurred among athletes in many sports. The penalties for drug use vary among the many athletic organizations. However, in many cases the penalties for drug abuse are harsh. Despite the professional and health risks involved in taking drugs, some athletes still use them.

In 1994, Dwight Gooden, pitcher for the New York Mets, tested positive for drugs, was suspended from play, and was admitted to a drug treatment program. As part of the deal to return to play, he was required to complete the drug treatment program and submit to random drug testing. When he failed two random tests, he was suspended again.

Olympic sprinter Ben Johnson's drug abuse lost him his place in history. In 1988, Johnson was stripped of his Olympic gold medal when officials found traces of steroids in his urine.

"It's sad that people think a drug can make you a champion," said Florence Griffith-Joyner, who also ran in the 1988 Olympics and has won several gold medals herself. "Nothing replaces hard work, faith in God, and belief in yourself."

Choosing to Be Drug Free

This lesson will help you find answers to questions that teens often ask about ways to remain drug free. For example:

▶ How can I say no when offered drugs?

▶ What are some reasons for remaining drug free?

▶ What are some places where people with drug problems can turn for help?

Words to Know

anabolic steroids
detoxification

Avoiding Drugs

You have a responsibility to yourself to be the healthiest person you can be. With that responsibility comes the right to make choices. You have learned how dangerous drugs are and that drugs can harm your mind and body. You know that avoiding drugs is the right decision to make for your health. According to **Figure 15.12,** drug use among high school seniors has decreased steadily since 1981. The decision is yours, but avoiding drugs is the only sure way to avoid becoming "hooked" by drugs.

Figure 15.12

Changes in Use of Illegal Drugs Among High School Seniors

Some young people continue to experiment out of curiosity or because they do not understand the risks they take when they use drugs.

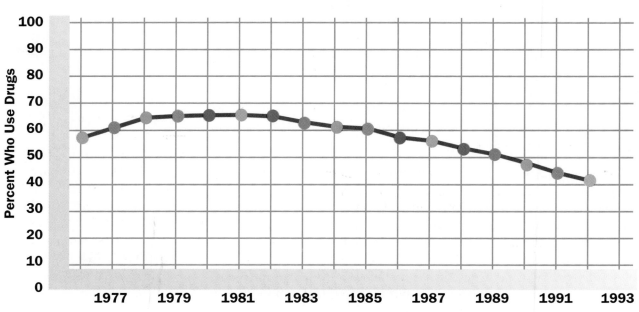

Reasons to Be Drug Free

- You will have better concentration and memory.

- You will have more natural energy.

- You will be in control of your feelings and actions.

- You will make better decisions.

- You will not impair your judgment and do something that you will regret.

- You will not be breaking the law or causing yourself legal difficulties for years to come.

- You will be able to focus on improving your talents and enjoying your interests.

- You will not ruin your mind or body, or your future.

- You will not harm yourself or others as a result of drugs.

- You will not waste money on drugs.

- You will not be afraid of possible flashbacks for years to come.

- You respect yourself too much to take drugs.

There are many reasons to choose to be drug free.

Athletes and Drugs

Some athletes take drugs illegally because they mistakenly believe that drugs can improve their performance. Athletes may take **anabolic** (a·nuh·BAH·lik) **steroids** (STIR·oydz), *synthetic derivatives of testosterone.* They may also take amphetamines or cocaine. They use the steroids to make their muscles bigger and stronger, and the amphetamines and cocaine to give them extra energy. They believe these drugs will increase their speed and endurance. All of these drugs harm their bodies in the long run, and the costs greatly outweigh any short-term benefits.

Furthermore, these drugs—and many others—are banned by many groups that oversee athletics. Users may even sacrifice their careers. Many national and international bodies governing different sports, such as the International Olympic Committee (IOC), have established strict rules on the kinds of drugs that competitors cannot use. The National Collegiate Athletic Association (NCAA) tests athletes for these drugs. Professional sports leagues help athletes recover from drug addictions, but if the athlete cannot kick a habit, he or she may be banned from playing in the league for a long time or even permanently.

Your Total Health

Drug Abuse and Sex

A government study of young adults found that, while abusing drugs or alcohol, teens are often put in situations in which they engage in sex—often unprotected—when they do not want to. Such behavior puts them at greater risk of pregnancy and exposure to sexually transmitted diseases, including HIV/AIDS.

Kicking the Habit

Kicking the drug habit is a lot harder than resisting pressure to start. The first step is for the drug abuser to recognize that a problem exists. From there, the road to recovery is an uphill one. If a user has become physically or psychologically addicted to a drug, then recovery involves withdrawal.

Withdrawal is usually a painful process and medications are given to ease the withdrawal symptoms. In addition to ridding one's body of the addictive substance, the recovering drug user must change his or her thinking and habits that led to the drug use. Although withdrawing from drugs is tough work, the benefits of becoming drug free are well worth the effort.

Getting Help

Drug abusers cannot recover from addiction on their own. They need help to recover. Most communities have a variety of treatment and support programs for drug addiction. The key is to find one that is right for the abuser. A good drug treatment program should have trained experts who provide education and support, and who help the abuser through the withdrawal period. This often requires **detoxification** (dee·tahk·si·fi·KAY·shuhn), *the physical process of freeing the body of an addictive substance.* "Detox" also involves helping the abuser overcome psychological dependence on the substance and regain health. Some programs include family members in the recovery process.

in your journal

Have you ever been in a situation in which you were pressured to take drugs? In your journal, describe how you handled the situation. If you have never been in such a situation, imagine how you would handle pressure from a peer to try marijuana.

LIFE SKILLS
How to Avoid Using Drugs

*T*eens often say that they tried drugs because they felt pressured by friends or people they respected. You need to be ready in case you feel pressured. The way to do that is to develop ways to deal with that pressure ahead of time.

The first way to avoid drugs is through your actions. Choose friends who do not use or approve of drugs. They will support you in your decision to remain drug free.

It is important that you and your friends stay away from situations in which people might have or use drugs. For example, if you know that the party you were invited to on Saturday night will not have a parent or adult present, do not attend.

Where to Go for Help

Counseling

Young people can start to get help by speaking to a parent, teacher, school counselor, or peer counselor—someone with whom they feel comfortable talking. They also could call one of the toll-free drug and alcohol hot lines or a drug and alcohol treatment center to find a counselor.

Support Groups

A support group is a group of people who share a common problem and work together to help one another cope and recover. Support groups are the most popular form of treatment for addictions. They provide the critical support that recovering addicts need to remain drug free.

Common support groups for drug addiction are Narcotics Anonymous, Cocaine Anonymous, and Nar-Anon, which provides help for those who have been affected by someone else's drug use. Support groups are usually confidential and free. Other support groups are listed in your local telephone directory.

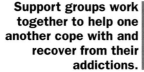
Support groups work together to help one another cope with and recover from their addictions.

If you are at someone's house or at a party where people begin using drugs, leave. That is the best way to avoid being pressured to take drugs. It is also a good idea to leave because people on drugs can be violent and dangerous. Also, because drug use is illegal, they may be arrested!

The second way to avoid drugs is through your words. Sometimes all you have to do is say no once. At other times, you might have to say no repeatedly.

You may find it easier to avoid drugs if you explain your reasons. For example, you might say, "Drugs are not good for me. I need all my strength to run track." You could also say, "If you were really my friend, you'd stop giving me a hard time." Do not be afraid to challenge people who are pressuring you by saying something such as "If you are really my friend, why are you trying to get me to do something that may hurt me?"

Finally, in some situations, there will be no easy way to get away from the pressure to do drugs. At those times, the best thing to say is "So long. I'll see you later."

Follow-up Activities

1. Review the suggestions for avoiding using drugs. Think of other ways and discuss them.

2. Illustrate your ideas in a brochure that you could share with younger students.

Alcohol and Drug Treatment Centers

There are a variety of centers available to help people who want to recover from drug abuse. These centers offer a wide range of services. **Figure 15.13** describes many of these services.

Figure 15.13

Specific Types of Treatment Centers

Type of Program	Description
Detox Units	These are located in hospitals and treatment centers. Alcohol and drug addicts remain under a doctor's care while being given medication to ease withdrawal symptoms.
Inpatient Treatment Centers	These are places where people stay for a month or more to fully concentrate on recovering from their drug problems.
Outpatient Treatment Centers	These are places where people get treatment for a few hours a day and then return to their homes and regular surroundings.
Continuing Programs	These are long-term support programs that are available to people who have gone through the standard short-term programs.
Halfway Houses	These are places where people who are recovering from addictions are offered housing, counseling, and support meetings. They learn the coping and living skills that they will need when they return to their regular lives.

Living Drug Free

When you choose to live your life drug free, you will find that there are many exciting ways to spend your time. The alternatives to using drugs are limited only by your energy and imagination. Why don't you get started by trying some of the suggestions listed below and on the next page?

If you are lonely, depressed, or bored:

■ Learn a new sport.

■ Join a club.

■ Start a physical fitness program.

■ Volunteer to help needy people in your community.

■ Exercise regularly.

■ Get involved in something new that energizes you.

If you want to do something adventurous:

- Take up an exciting sport or hobby like rock climbing, fencing, or white-water rafting.

- Read about adventurous activities you would like to pursue like skydiving or parasailing.

- Learn about far-off places that sound exciting, and plan a trip for the future.

If you need help solving personal problems:

- Talk to someone you trust and admire.

- Contact a hot line or support group.

- Read books about handling a problem such as yours.

If you are tense and anxious:

- Learn relaxation techniques.

- Get plenty of exercise.

- Do not overschedule yourself.

- Get enough rest and eat properly.

If you are looking for excitement or adventure, try a new sport, hobby, or activity instead of trying drugs.

Review

Using complete sentences, answer the following questions on a separate sheet of paper.

Reviewing Terms and Facts

1. **Vocabulary**   When does *detoxification* occur? Explain the process.

2. **Give Examples**   What might you suggest to a friend who asks your advice on where to go for a drug problem that he or she has?

Thinking Critically

3. **Hypothesize**   Why do you think many teens have decided to remain drug free?

Applying Health Concepts

4. **Personal Health**   With a partner, role-play a situation in which you need to deal with pressure to use drugs. You might use some of the techniques discussed in this lesson.

5. **Health of Others**   Find newspaper and magazine articles that deal with athletes who have problems with drugs. Choose one and write a report that tells about the athlete's problem and what was done to help him or her overcome it.

Chapter Summary

▶ Medicines are drugs that are used to treat or prevent diseases and other conditions. (Lesson 1)

▶ There are three main types of medicine: those that prevent diseases, those that fight germs, and those that provide pain relief. (Lesson 1)

▶ Medicines can affect the body in unhealthy ways. (Lesson 1)

▶ Prescription medicines are those that can be sold only with a written order from a doctor. Over-the-counter (OTC) medicines are those that can be purchased without a written order from a doctor. (Lesson 1)

▶ Stimulants are drugs that speed up the body's functions. (Lesson 2)

▶ Depressants are drugs that slow down the body's functions and reactions. (Lesson 2)

▶ Narcotics are prescription medicines that are used to relieve pain. (Lesson 2)

▶ Stimulants, depressants, and narcotics can be addictive. (Lesson 2)

▶ Marijuana, a commonly used illegal drug, harms users' health and can cause psychological dependence. (Lesson 3)

▶ Hallucinogens distort moods, thoughts, and senses. (Lesson 3)

▶ Inhalants are substances whose fumes are sniffed and inhaled to give a hallucinogenic-like high. (Lesson 3)

▶ You can avoid using drugs through your actions and through your words. (Lesson 4)

▶ Recovery from drug addiction involves withdrawal, a series of painful physical and mental symptoms that range from mild to severe, depending on the drug. (Lesson 4)

▶ Drug abusers need help to recover from addiction. Most communities have a variety of treatment and support programs for drug addiction. (Lesson 4)

Using Health Terms

On a separate sheet of paper, write the vocabulary term that best matches each definition given below.

1. Any reaction to a medicine other than the one intended (Lesson 1)

2. Develops when a person's body becomes used to the effect of a medicine (Lesson 1)

3. Drugs that speed up the body's functions (Lesson 2)

4. Prescription medicines that are used to relieve pain (Lesson 2)

5. Drugs that distort moods, thoughts, and senses (Lesson 3)

6. Drugs that are made from chemicals that resemble illegal substances (Lesson 3)

7. Synthetic derivatives of testosterone (Lesson 4)

8. The physical process of freeing the body of an addictive substance (Lesson 4)

Reviewing Main Ideas

Using complete sentences, answer the following questions on a separate sheet of paper.

1. What are three ways to use medicine safely? (Lesson 1)

2. What are two dangers of misusing or abusing depressants? (Lesson 2)

3. What are three dangers of using marijuana? (Lesson 3)

4. Why are hallucinogens so dangerous? (Lesson 3)

5. List three dangers of using inhalants. (Lesson 3)

6. Describe two ways, through your actions, to deal with pressure to use drugs. (Lesson 4)

7. List two places where people with drug problems can go for help. (Lesson 4)

Thinking Critically

Using complete sentences, answer the following questions on a separate sheet of paper.

1. **Synthesize** What are two questions you might ask a doctor who just prescribed a medicine for you? (Lesson 1)

2. **Suggest** Give three examples of how reading the label of an over-the-counter medicine can help you to use it safely. (Lesson 1)

3. **Synthesize** How might the use of cocaine affect the life of an adult? How might it affect the child of a pregnant woman who uses it? (Lesson 2)

4. **Compare and Contrast** How are the three main kinds of depressants similar yet different? (Lesson 2)

5. **Evaluate** Why is it dangerous to ride in a car with a driver who has been smoking marijuana? (Lesson 3)

6. **Synthesize** Why do you think people use hallucinogens if they are so dangerous? (Lesson 3)

7. **Evaluate** Why do you think recovery from drug addiction involves more than just recovering from withdrawal symptoms? (Lesson 4)

Your Action Plan

Remaining Drug Free

There are many reasons to become or remain drug free, and you can make an action plan to reach that goal. Look back through your journal entries for this chapter. What do the entries tell you about how you feel about drug use?

Identify your long-term goal and write it down. Next, think of a series of short-term goals, to help you achieve your long-term goal. Write these down. If your long-term goal is to find healthy alternatives to drug use, some short-term goals might be to plan specific activities.

Plan a schedule for reaching each short-term goal. For example, "By the end of the first week, I will take up a new and challenging hobby." When you reach your long-term goal of finding healthy alternatives to drug use, reward yourself.

Building Your Portfolio

1. Find out the techniques used in testing athletes and public employees for drug use. Give your opinion about the use of drug testing of these groups of people. Include your report in your portfolio.

2. Plan and design a two-panel mural. On one half, show images that suggest addiction to drugs. On the other half, show images that suggest recovery from the addiction. Use your design to plan an actual mural. Include your design in your portfolio.

In Your Home and Community

1. Find out about current statistics on illegal drug use in your local community. How do these statistics compare with those of five years ago in the same community? Make a graph to show the increase or decrease in use.

2. Research drug treatment centers and programs available in your community. Find out how they work for teen drug abusers. Do the programs involve just the drug abuser or the entire family? Include phone numbers and addresses of the centers and programs. Share your findings with the class.

480

Chapter 16
Safety

Student Expectations
After reading this chapter, you should be able to:
1. Explain how to break the accident chain.
2. Describe ways of preventing accidents at home and at school.
3. Explain how to reduce your chances of becoming a victim of violent crime.
4. Explain how to act safely on the road and when outdoors in general.
5. Describe ways of reducing risks during weather emergencies and natural disasters.

Some people say skateboarding ruined my whole summer, but that's not really true. What ruined my summer was not skateboarding safely. It's a long story, but it happened pretty fast. I ended up hitting a bump in the sidewalk, flying into a tree, hitting my head, and breaking my right arm. I wasn't wearing a helmet or any other safety gear for that matter. I thought I was too cool for that.

*I spent a few days in the hospital and the rest of the summer with my arm in a cast. It gave me a lot of time to think. I decided that maybe other kids could learn from my experience. That's why I started **Stacie's Safety School** for kids. It's almost like baby-sitting, but it's only an hour one day each week in the summer. I gather information from the fire department, the police department, the local Red Cross, and the local hospital about safe ways to enjoy different activities. Then I pass this information on to the kids. We talk about bicycling, in-line skating, swimming, and of course, skateboarding. I never knew kids could ask so many questions.*

in your journal

Read the account on this page. Do you, too, wish you knew how to stay safe from the dangers around you? Start your private journal entries on safety by answering these questions:

▶ What do you think are the greatest dangers to your safety?

▶ What steps do you take to reduce your risk of injury from the dangers around you?

When you reach the end of the chapter, you will use your journal entries to make an action plan.

Building Safe Habits

This lesson will help you find answers to questions that teens often ask about safety. For example:

▶ Why do accidents happen?

▶ How can I avoid being injured?

▶ How can I have fun with my friends and still "play it safe"?

The Importance of Safety

No doubt you learned many safety rules when you were a small child: don't play with matches, and look both ways before you cross the street. You probably know these rules by heart. However just knowing the rules isn't enough to keep you safe. You also need to be **safety conscious,** which means *being aware that safety is important and always acting safely.*

Accidents are a major cause of death among young people as shown in **Figure 16.1.** Although many accidents that young people have are not fatal, they can cause serious problems.

In 1993, there were about 37,000 reported injuries from in-line skating, one of the fastest-growing sports in the United States. These injuries range from minor scrapes and bruises to fractures, dislocated joints, concussions, skull fractures, and brain injuries.

Figure 16.1
Causes of Death Among Young People, Ages 15–24

Accidents are a major cause of death among young people. Acting safely helps prevent accidents and needless deaths.

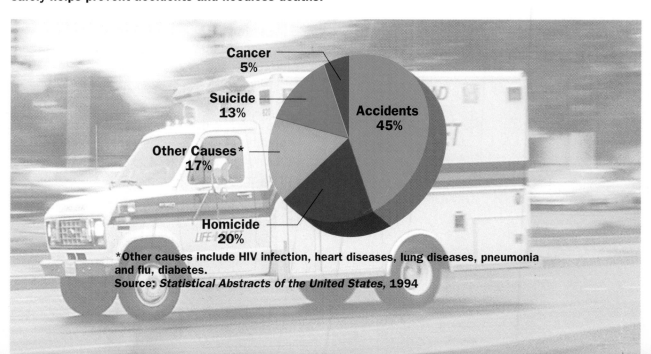

Cancer
5%

Suicide
13%

Accidents
45%

Other Causes*
17%

Homicide
20%

*Other causes include HIV infection, heart diseases, lung diseases, pneumonia and flu, diabetes.
Source: *Statistical Abstracts of the United States,* 1994

Acting Safely

An important part of acting safely means not taking needless risks. Risks—the chances that something harmful may occur—are all around us. When you walk in the woods, you risk touching poison ivy. When you cross a street, you risk being hit by a car. Avoiding such risks doesn't mean staying out of the woods or off the streets. It means learning to spot poison ivy and staying away from it. Avoiding risks means waiting for the light to change and looking both ways before you step off the curb. Study **Figure 16.2**. Do you follow these safety guidelines when riding a bicycle?

The greatest risk comes from being careless. To act safely, follow these guidelines. Your life may depend on it.

■ **Resist peer pressure.** You may know that riding in the back of a pickup truck or diving into unknown water is dangerous, but when your friends try to talk you into taking such risks, it may be difficult to resist the pressure. Remember, resisting peer pressure takes strength and courage, too.

■ **Always concentrate on what you are doing.** If you don't, you increase your chances of having an accident. Be extra careful when you are tired, excited, upset, depressed, or in a hurry. These are the times when accidents are most likely to occur.

■ **Know your limits.** Don't try dangerous activities that you aren't prepared for. For example, stay off the toughest ski slope when you are just learning how to ski, and don't swim farther out in the lake than you can manage comfortably. Staying within your limits is not being cowardly—it's being smart.

■ **Be prepared.** Think about the possible risks that a situation may pose *before* it's too late. If you're walking home at night, plan to use a well-lighted route. Being prepared also means using the proper safety equipment, such as a bicycle helmet, and using the equipment the way it was meant to be used.

in your Journal

In your journal, describe a real or imagined accident. Describe what led up to the injury. Then describe how the event could have been avoided by interrupting each link in the chain.

Figure 16.2
How to Act Safely

Following certain guidelines can help you be safe. How can these guidelines help you play your favorite sport safely?

A **Resist peer pressure.** Don't ride into on-coming traffic even if your friends do.

B **Concentrate.** Be aware of the traffic around you.

C **Know your limits.** Stay within a comfortable riding distance.

D **Be prepared.** Wear protective gear.

Figure 16.3
How to Break the Accident Chain
In many cases, accidents can be prevented by just being more careful.

The Accident Chain

❶ **The Situation**
Jared is in a hurry to take off his skates so he can get a snack.

❷ **The Unsafe Habit**
Jared's habit of leaving his skates on the porch creates an unnecessary risk of someone tripping.

Breaking the Accident Chain

❶ **Change the Situation**
If Jared had been in less of a hurry to get a snack he might have been more careful.

❷ **Change the Unsafe Habit**
Jared should have put away his skates where no one would be likely to trip over them.

Your Total Health

Use Your Head—Wear a Helmet ACTIVITY!

In-line skating is associated with more head injuries than regular skating, because in-line skates go faster and are harder to stop. Visit a sporting goods store in your community. Evaluate the ways store and manufacturers provide adequate information to consumers about the importance of helmets.

To see what can happen when you take unnecessary risks, consider the case of Jared and his nine-year-old brother, Toby. In-line skating always makes Jared hungry. When he finishes skating, he sits on the front porch, removes his skates, and goes inside for a snack. Yesterday Toby ran out the front door just after Jared came in from skating. Jared's skates were on the porch as usual, and Toby tripped over them, landing on the sidewalk and badly scraping his face and chipping a tooth.

Injuries like Toby's don't just happen. They are the result of a pattern known as an **accident chain,** *a series of events that include a situation, an unsafe habit, and an unsafe action.*

Figure 16.3 shows how the accident chain applies to the case of Jared and Toby. The accident could have been prevented by breaking the chain. In fact, any accident can be prevented by interrupting the accident chain in one of the following three ways.

■ Change the situation.

■ Change the unsafe habit.

■ Change the unsafe action.

If Jared and Toby had done any of those three things differently, they would have broken the accident chain and avoided the accident and the injury. Remember, when you act safely, you decrease the chance of accidents and injuries.

3 The Unsafe Action
Toby rushes out the door without looking where he's going and trips over the skates.

4 The Accident and the Injury
Toby falls down the porch steps to the sidewalk. He scrapes his face and chips a tooth.

3 Change the Unsafe Action
If Toby had been in less of a hurry, he might have seen the skates and avoided tripping.

4 No Accident and No Injury
If Toby had not tripped, he would not have been injured.

Review

Using complete sentences, answer the following questions on a separate sheet of paper.

Reviewing Terms and Facts

1. **Vocabulary** Define *safety conscious*.
2. **List** What are the three elements of the accident chain?

Thinking Critically

3. **Explain** Why might just knowing safety rules not be enough to keep you safe?
4. **Analyze** Why do you think teens are especially likely to take unnecessary risks?
5. **Interpret** There is an old saying that states, "An ounce of prevention is worth a pound of cure." How does this relate to safety?

Applying Health Concepts

6. **Health of Others** Find a newspaper account or take notes on a television report of an accident. Break down the description of the accident into the parts of the accident chain. Show the accident chain in the form of a chart. At appropriate points in the chart, include brief descriptions of at least two ways in which the accident could have been prevented.

7. **Personal Health** Choose your favorite sport. Then make a list of the protective gear needed to participate safely in that activity. Post your list with those of your classmates as a reminder for everyone to dress properly for the activities they enjoy.

Teen HEALTH DIGEST

People at Work

Swimming Instructor

Vinnie has always loved to swim, and he's always related well to kids. That's why he loves his job as aquatics director of his local YMCA. Vinnie spends most of his time on the job teaching children of all ages how to swim.

Vinnie first took swimming lessons at the same Y where he now works. He was only three then, and according to his mom, "he took to the water like a fish." After that, Vinnie signed up for progressive swimming classes at the Y each summer. By the time he was 17,

he was an assistant swimming instructor there himself.

Now Vinnie is an experienced teacher as well as a first-rate swimmer. The children he teaches learn to love the water as much as he does because of his attitude. Every time Vinnie gets into the pool with them, he shows them that swimming is not just important for safety and good health— it's fun!

Teens Making a Difference

Shelley Brandon— Red Cross Volunteer

In the summer of 1994, flood waters rose halfway up the walls of Maya Nardin's ranch house in Georgia. Disaster workers removed Mrs. Nardin, a 75-year-old widow, by boat to a nearby evacuation center. Mrs. Nardin was distraught at leaving her home of 55 years and losing a lifetime's accumulation of memories stored in photographs, books, and letters.

Then Maya Nardin met Shelley Brandon, a Red Cross volunteer at the emergency evacuation center. Although Shelley was just 16, she comforted Mrs. Nardin in a way that no one else could. The reason was that Shelley had been through her own disaster when she was 13.

An early morning fire had destroyed her family's home and all of their possessions. Red Cross volunteers were on hand to help the Brandons until they could put their lives together again. Shelley knew from personal experience that without Red Cross volunteers, many disaster victims might have no one else to turn to.

Shelley loves helping others, as she and her family were helped during their time of need. She knows firsthand how much the volunteers are appreciated, and that makes all the hard work worthwhile.

CONSUMER FOCUS

How to Buy a Bike Helmet

You know that bike helmets save lives, and you want to buy one. You've seen a blue one with yellow lightning bolts that looks pretty neat—but you wonder if appearance is the best way to choose gear to protect your head and your life. How do you know which helmet is best?

First, check for an ANSI (American National Standards Institute) sticker. This means that the helmet meets laboratory standards for absorbing severe blows. The helmet should have a rigid outer shell of polycarbonate or fiberglass that can stand up to scrapes and collisions with sharp, hard objects. It also should have a half-inch-thick liner of polystyrene foam to absorb the shock of a collision or fall.

Sponge rubber or fabric pads should hold the helmet firmly to your head. The pads allow ventilation—a necessity in hot weather. The helmet should fit securely with a snug-fitting strap that is fastened with a D-ring or buckle.

Myths and Realities

Go with the Flow? Yes!

Should bicyclists ride facing traffic? Some people think so, but they are wrong.

The safest way to bicycle is to ride with the traffic. The reason for this is that riding against traffic puts bicyclists where motorists least expect them. Because motorists cannot predict what bicyclists will do, many cyclists are hurt. In fact, more than one-fourth of all collisions between cars and bicycles are caused by bicyclists riding against traffic.

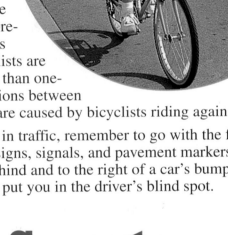

When bicycling in traffic, remember to go with the flow and to obey the same signs, signals, and pavement markers as the motorists. Stay behind and to the right of a car's bumper. Riding beside a car could put you in the driver's blind spot.

Sports and Recreation

In-line Safety

Many people who take up in-line skating buy the skates, but do not buy the safety equipment. If you decide to take up in-line skating, don't make this mistake. New skaters are the most likely to lose control and to need protective gear to avoid serious injury.

In addition to wearing the recommended safety equipment, follow these tips for safer in-line skating:

- Start on a flat, dry surface, such as an empty parking lot.
- Learn to stop by turning with your knees well bent.
- Master turning and stopping before you try any hills.
- Watch for rocks, sand, and other obstacles.
- Keep an eye out for cars as you skate against traffic.
- Skate at a safe speed so that you are in control at all times.

Acting Safely at Home and at School

This lesson will help you find answers to questions that teens often ask about safety at home and at school. For example:

► **What causes injuries at home and how can I avoid them?**

► **How can I keep safe at school?**

hazards
expiration date
smoke alarm

Safety at Home

You may think of your home as a happy and comfortable place. In reality, every home has many **hazards** (HAZ·erds), or *possible sources of harm*. Each year, hundreds of thousands of people are injured at home by such hazards as cleaning products, slippery bathtubs, and objects left on stairs. Like accidents in general, most injuries at home can be prevented.

Figure 16.4
Safety in the Home

Homes can be safe if people are careful to make them so. What are some ways of making a home safe?

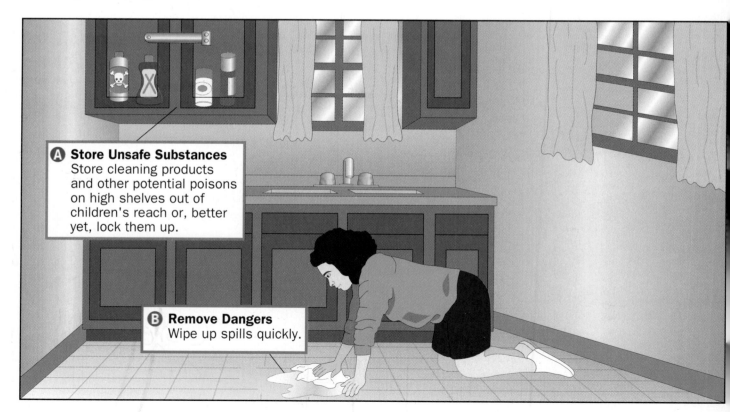

A **Store Unsafe Substances** Store cleaning products and other potential poisons on high shelves out of children's reach or, better yet, lock them up.

B **Remove Dangers** Wipe up spills quickly.

Preventing Falls

Falls are very common in the home and can lead to serious injuries. They occur most often in kitchens and bathrooms and on stairs. Falls account for many broken bones in older family members, whose bones may be brittle. Study **Figure 16.4.** In what two ways can falls be prevented?

Preventing Poisonings

Poisonings are a serious problem, especially for young children. Curious about everything but unable to read labels, toddlers and preschoolers may eat or drink toxic substances without knowing they are poisonous. Cleaning products and medicines are the most common causes of home poisonings. According to **Figure 16.4,** how can this type of poisoning be prevented?

Preventing Electrical Shocks

Electricity provides us with many of life's necessities, including heat and light. However, electricity can be deadly if misused. Most home electrical accidents involve problems with wires or outlets or misuse of electrical appliances. To prevent electrical shocks, never pull out a plug by its cord. Pull on the plug instead. Do not overload an outlet with too many cords. Make sure you keep electrical products away from water, and never use an electrical product when you are wet. Unplug appliances that are not working properly, and have them serviced.

in your journal

Look through the kitchen and bathroom cabinets in your home. In your journal, make a list of all the potentially dangerous substances you find. Are any of these stored within the reach of young children? If so, suggest better storage places for them.

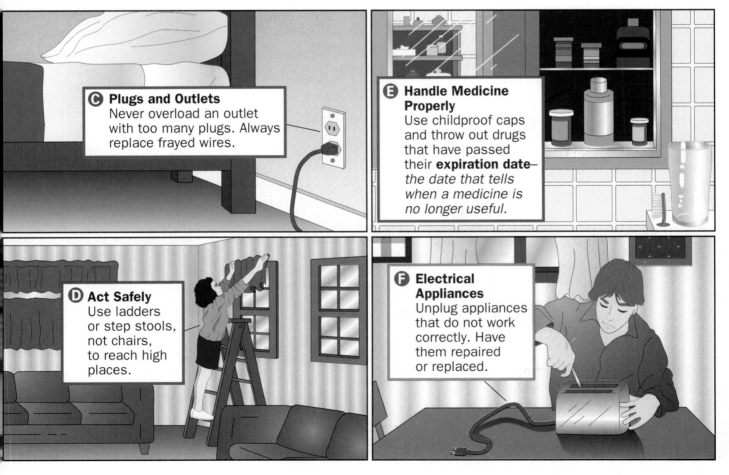

C Plugs and Outlets
Never overload an outlet with too many plugs. Always replace frayed wires.

E Handle Medicine Properly
Use childproof caps and throw out drugs that have passed their **expiration date—** *the date that tells when a medicine is no longer useful.*

D Act Safely
Use ladders or step stools, not chairs, to reach high places.

F Electrical Appliances
Unplug appliances that do not work correctly. Have them repaired or replaced.

Fire Safety at Home

Fire needs three elements: fuel, heat, and air. Fuel can be stored rags, wood, gasoline, or paper. Heat may be a match, an electrical wire, or a cigarette. Oxygen in the air feeds the flames. These elements are found in most homes. To prevent most fires that occur at home, follow these simple rules:

- Keep stoves clean to avoid burns and grease fires when cooking.

- Make sure that electrical wires, outlets, and appliances are safe.

- Make sure that no one smokes in bed.

- Keep flammable objects at least 3 feet from a portable heater.

- Throw out old newspapers and other materials that burn easily.

- Use and store matches properly, and keep matches and cigarette lighters out of the reach of small children.

The most dangerous home fires are those that occur during the night when everyone is asleep. By installing smoke alarms in your home, your family can reduce the risk of injury from fire. A **smoke alarm,** or smoke detector, is *a device that makes a warning noise when it senses smoke.* The sound is loud enough to warn your family to move to safety, even if everyone is asleep. A smoke alarm should be installed on each level of your home, especially outside bedroom areas. Be sure to test the smoke alarm regularly and replace the battery if needed. Another important step in preparing for a fire is to plan a fire escape route and practice using it. Agree on a place where everyone will meet outside.

Smoke alarms provide a warning system to alert your family in case of fire.

LIFE SKILLS
Acting Safely During a Fire

If your home catches fire, getting out quickly and safely should be your first priority. Most fatal home fires occur late at night, when it's easy to become confused. The best protection against confusion is to plan an escape route ahead of time and to practice using it often.

This exercise will help you develop a fire escape plan for your home. If your family already has a plan, use the exercise to try to improve that plan.

First, draw a floor plan of each level of your home. Include doors, hallways, and windows in your floor plan. Use arrows to point to two ways of escape, if possible, from each room in the house. Two escape routes are necessary in case one of the routes is blocked. A ladder or coil of rope is necessary for escape through upstairs windows.

Your escape plan should include these steps:

1. Turn on bedroom lights.
2. Arrange for a signal, such as a whistle, that will alert everyone to the fire.

What to Do if There Is a Fire

Even with safe practices, fire can occur. Your risk of injury from fire can be reduced if you know what to do when a fire does occur in your home. Here is what you should do.

- Leave the house quickly and call the fire department from a neighbor's house or a car phone.

- Never return to a burning house for any reason.

- Stay close to the floor so that you are below the smoke.

- Before opening a closed door, feel it to see if it is hot.

- If your clothing should catch fire, drop to the ground and roll around to put out the flames (see **Figure 16.5**).

- Leave firefighting to the experts; don't try it yourself.

Kitchen Fires

Small kitchen fires are the only house fires that are safe to extinguish by yourself. Grease fires can usually be smothered by a metal lid or by baking soda. If your family has a fire extinguisher, learn how to use it.

Figure 16.5
Personal Fire Safety

Stop, don't run.

Drop to the ground.

Roll on the ground to put out the fire.

3. Meet your family outside at a prearranged spot, and don't go back into the house.

4. Call the fire department from a neighbor's house or from a car phone.

Your plan also should include these safety tips for all the members of your family to follow:

1. When using your fire escape route, test closed doors for warmth before opening. If the doors are warm, do not open them. Use the alternate escape route.

2. Stay close to the floor in smoke-filled rooms. This will help you see better and will also help you have more oxygen for breathing.

Follow-up Activity

After making your escape plan, practice it with family members. Ask them for advice, and work together to improve the plan. Remember that the more you practice your escape plan, the greater the likelihood that you and your family will exit safely in the event of a real fire.

Safety at School

Safety is a concern in places where many people gather. Schools are such places, so they must meet certain safety standards.

Equally important for safety at school is the behavior of the students. The following list includes some of the ways in which students can help make school a safe place for themselves and others.

- **Industrial arts and home economics classes.** Wear appropriate safety gear and follow your teacher's instructions carefully.

- **Physical education class and after-school sports.** Concentrate on what you and those around you are doing.

- **Science labs.** Use equipment and chemicals only as directed.

- **Hallway traffic.** Walk, don't run, in halls and locker rooms.

Lesson 2 Review

Using complete sentences, answer the following questions on a separate sheet of paper.

Reviewing Terms and Facts

1. **Vocabulary** Define *expiration date* and use the term in an original sentence.

2. **Give Examples** List some ways in which students can contribute to making their school a safe place.

Thinking Critically

3. **Explain** Why might cleaning products be hazardous in the home?

4. **Synthesize** How would you convince a younger brother or sister not to leave toys or other objects on the floor?

5. **Discuss** How do smoke alarms help make a house or an apartment safe?

Applying Health Concepts

6. **Health of Others** Take a survey of your home to identify potential hazards that could cause falls, poisonings, electrical shocks, or fires. Describe each hazard, the type of accident it could cause, and a plan to remove or reduce the potential danger. Share your survey with family members, and work together to put your plans into action to make your home safer.

7. **Health of Others** Ask a physical education, art, home economics, or science teacher to identify the most important safety rule for his or her class. Then make a poster that states the rule and reminds students in the class to follow it. With the teacher's permission, display your poster in the room where the class meets.

Violence Prevention

This lesson will help you find answers to questions that teens often ask about violence. For example:

► Why is there so much violence in our country?
► How can I avoid becoming a victim of violent crime?

Violence and Victims

Violence is on the rise in the United States. There are more murders, rapes, assaults, and armed robberies than ever before. In 1991, for example, an average of 65 murders a day were committed in the cities and towns of America.

Violence occurs in our schools as well. In recent years, an average of 3 million weapons have been found in schools and 70,000 assaults involving weapons have occurred on school property. In fact, nearly all crimes committed by teens are on the rise.

Several factors that contribute to the growing violence have been identified. About two-thirds of violent crimes committed in this country involve drugs and alcohol. Other factors associated with violence include poverty, racial tension, possession of firearms, and the lack of economic opportunities.

Anyone can be a victim of a violent crime. For this reason, it is important to know what to do to prevent becoming a victim. Many acts of violence are not random acts. In fact, the victims of violence often know their attackers and may even have ongoing relationships with them. **Figure 16.6** shows that the most common cause of homicides, or murders, are arguments.

Figure 16.6
Factors Associated with Murders

Over 15,000 murders were committed in 1992. Arguments were the single greatest cause of murders.

Contributing Factor	Number of Murders
Arguments	6,843
Crimes involving drug trade	1,291
Fights resulting from alcohol use	426
Fights resulting from drug use	249
Sexual assault	171
Unknown	6,221

Words to Know

assertive
rape
acquaintance rape
date rape

Math Connection

How Much Violence Is There? ACTIVITY!

During a typical night in the United States, the following numbers of violent crimes are likely to be committed: 59 murders, 262 rapes, and 2,607 assaults. At this rate, how many murders, rapes, and assaults are likely to be committed in the United States in a week, a month, and a year?

Your Total Health

Drugs and Violence

Some people are more likely to display violent behavior when they use drugs. Alcohol, PCP (angel dust), cocaine, and steroids have all been shown to produce highly aggressive behavior.

Protecting Yourself from Crime

The best way to protect yourself from violent crime is to avoid situations that are unsafe. Stay away from a place that you feel is dangerous. Leave a situation that makes you feel uncomfortable. If you need help, find a police officer or other adult. If you are near a telephone, dial 911 or the police. Always carry important phone numbers and change for phone calls with you. Here are some additional precautions to follow.

DO'S

- Always stay in well-lighted public places at night.
- Walk by the curb and avoid doorways.
- Lock doors and windows when you are at home alone.
- Tell police the license numbers of suspicious cars in your neighborhood.

DON'TS

- Don't walk alone at night or in wooded areas or on deserted streets.
- Don't put your money in an easy-to-grab place.
- Don't open the door to anyone you don't know.
- Don't give personal information over the telephone.

In some areas, residents work together to watch over the neighborhood and to help reduce crime.

Neighborhood Watch Programs

Many areas have Neighborhood Watch programs. In these programs, neighbors watch each other's homes to ensure safety. Police officers train program participants to look for and report suspicious actions or people who look dangerous. In this way, the neighborhood residents protect their area and help reduce crime. You may wish to participate in a program in your neighborhood.

MAKING HEALTHY DECISIONS
Dealing with Violence

*E*mily's 16-year old sister, Sandy, has confided to her that she is feeling uncomfortable about her relationship with her boyfriend Jake. She told Emily that sometimes Jake gets really angry with her and yells at her. He has even slapped her a couple of times. Sandy used to look forward to her dates with Jake, but lately she worries about saying or doing things that might upset him.

Jake is a popular boy in school, and Sandy feels that no one would believe that Jake could behave so badly. She doesn't want to talk to Jake about his behavior, because she is afraid that this would make him angry. She also doesn't want to tell her parents, because she's afraid that Jake might get in trouble and that he would take it out on her.

Emily suggests that Sandy use the six-step decision-making strategy she learned in school to help her decide what to do.

Self-defense Strategies

Some people have learned to defend themselves against violent crimes by using physical strength and agility to stop attacks. However, this method is not the only way to defend yourself.

Many attackers look for easy targets—victims they can overpower quickly. You are less likely to be seen as an easy target if you are assertive. Being **assertive** means *behaving confidently*. It means speaking with conviction, standing straight, and walking with a determined walk. It's important to act assertively even when you don't feel that way. Some people find it difficult to be assertive. Assertiveness training classes help people feel and act as if they are more in charge of their lives.

Rape and Rape Prevention

Rape is *forcing another person to have sexual relations*. It is an act of violence, and it is illegal. According to FBI reports, over 100,000 rapes are reported in the United States each year (since 1990). Rapes occur among all age, ethnic, racial, and social groups.

Victims of rape often know their attackers. *When the attacker is known to the victim,* the act is called **acquaintance rape.** *When the attacker is a date,* it's called **date rape.**

The best way to prevent rape is to avoid situations in which an attack is possible. Going out with a group of friends, for example, will help prevent date rape. Here are some other suggestions.

■ Make it clear to your date that you're not interested in sex.

■ Respect and accept your date's refusal to have sex.

■ Don't drink alcohol or use other drugs or date people who do.

■ Don't enter an elevator alone with a stranger.

Teen Issues

Help for Victims of Rape

Victims of rape need two kinds of help. They need immediate medical help in case of injury, infection, or pregnancy. They also need emotional support and counseling. Telling a trusted family member or friend is the first step in getting both kinds of help.

① **State the situation**
② **List the options**
③ **Weigh the possible outcomes**
④ **Consider your values**
⑤ **Make a decision and act**
⑥ **Evaluate the decision**

Follow-up Activities

1. Imagine that you are in Sandy's situation. Use the six steps of the decision-making process to come to a decision.

2. Along with a classmate, role-play three scenes: one in which Sandy decides to confront Jake about his behavior, one in which she talks about Jake's behavior to an adult she trusts, and one in which she breaks up with Jake.

3. Sandy writes in her diary every night. Write a diary entry that Sandy might have written in which she evaluates her decision.

Preventing Violence in Your Relationships

Family violence is a growing problem in this country. Like other types of violence, family violence often involves alcohol or other drugs. If you live in a home where violence exists, you need to find help. Remember that the violence is not your fault and that nobody deserves abuse. You can help to end the violence by reporting it.

Brothers and sisters often play roughly and tease each other. However, no matter how close you are to someone, speak up if his or her behavior threatens you. Demand a change in behavior, or leave. Take all slaps and threats seriously. Remember that insults and yelling are sometimes followed by physical violence.

Violence is never the answer to anger and frustration. Talking over the situation will leave both people feeling better.

Lesson 3

Review

Using complete sentences, answer the following questions on a separate sheet of paper.

Reviewing Terms and Facts

1. **Identify**   What are some of the causes of violence in the United States?

2. **Give Examples**   List some precautions you can take to avoid becoming the victim of a violent crime.

3. **Vocabulary**   What is the difference between *acquaintance rape* and *date rape?*

Thinking Critically

4. **Hypothesize**   Why do you think violent crimes are on the increase in the United States?

5. **Analyze**   Explain how assertiveness is related to violence prevention.

Applying Health Concepts

6. **Personal Health**   Take a survey of friends to find out what they do that increases or decreases their risk of becoming victims of violence. Use the lists of Do's and Don'ts in this lesson to develop your questionnaire. Compare their responses to your own. Are there any changes you should make in your behavior to reduce your risk of becoming a victim?

7. **Health of Others**   Make a poster that highlights several ways to decrease one's chances of being raped. With your teacher's approval, display the poster in the cafeteria or another location where many students are likely to see it.

Acting Safely on the Road and Outdoors

This lesson will help you find answers to questions that teens often ask about safety on the road and outdoors. For example:

▶ **What are the traffic rules for bicycle riders?**

▶ **How can I skateboard without getting hurt?**

▶ **What can I do to avoid injuries in the water and outdoors?**

Traffic Safety

Knowing—and obeying—traffic signals, signs, and pavement markings is just as important for pedestrians and bicyclists as it is for motor vehicle drivers. The purpose of these traffic controls is to regulate the movement of all people who use the streets and highways. When you obey traffic controls, other road users can predict your actions. This helps prevent accidents from happening.

Traffic Signals

There are two types of traffic signals. One type is the *walk/don't walk* signal, which is found at crosswalks and controls pedestrian movement. The other type of traffic signal is the traffic light.

Traffic Signs

There are three types of traffic signs. *Warning signs* alert you to upcoming changes. *Guide signs* notify you of the roadway that you are on or are approaching. *Regulatory signs* control the flow of traffic. Here are some typical traffic signs.

■ **Stop sign.** Stop, check traffic in all directions, and proceed through the intersection if it is clear.

■ **Yield sign.** Allow traffic on the other road to pass, and then proceed through the intersection.

■ **One-way sign.** Proceed only in the direction in which the arrow on the sign is pointing.

■ **Do-not-enter sign.** Do not enter a one-way street incorrectly and signal other drivers who are about to.

■ **Directional sign.** In a given lane of traffic, go in the direction the arrows indicate.

■ **Road changes sign.** Use caution when proceeding. Be alert for changes in the road condition or direction.

Ⓐ Red Light
Stop at the intersection.

Ⓑ Yellow Light
Stop at the intersection. If you are in the intersection, continue through.

Ⓒ Green Light
Proceed through the intersection if it is clear.

Pavement Markings

Various markings are painted on the pavement to control the movement of traffic. Among the most important pavement markings are the lines that separate lanes of traffic (see **Figure 16.7**).

Figure 16.7
Pavement Markings

Knowing the meaning of pavement markings is very important for drivers. Why would knowing the difference between solid white lines and solid yellow lines be important?

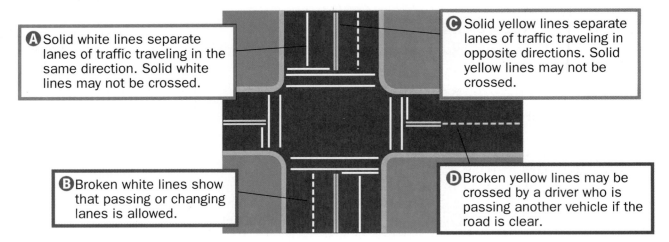

A Solid white lines separate lanes of traffic traveling in the same direction. Solid white lines may not be crossed.

C Solid yellow lines separate lanes of traffic traveling in opposite directions. Solid yellow lines may not be crossed.

B Broken white lines show that passing or changing lanes is allowed.

D Broken yellow lines may be crossed by a driver who is passing another vehicle if the road is clear.

Being a Safe Car Passenger

If you are on the passenger side of the front seat, sit back in the seat, and do not lean on the dashboard. This will prevent you from being injured if the driver needs to stop suddenly. Never distract the driver, who needs to concentrate on driving safely. Most important, wear a seat belt whenever you are a passenger.

Pedestrian Safety

A pedestrian is anyone who travels on foot. Pedestrian injuries are among the most common traffic accidents involving young teens. Follow these Do's and Don'ts to lessen your chances of being struck by a vehicle.

DO'S

- Cross streets at crosswalks and obey traffic lights.

- Look both ways before crossing streets and roads.

- Wear bright clothing in daylight; wear reflective gear and carry a flashlight at night.

- Where there is no sidewalk, stay to the left, facing oncoming traffic.

DON'TS

- Don't **jaywalk,** or *cross the street in the middle of the block.*

- Don't move into the street from between parked cars.

- Don't enter the street without first looking left, right, and then left again.

- Don't assume that a driver will see you just because you can see him or her.

Bicycle Safety

Bicycling is fun, good exercise, and a great way to travel. Bicyclists, like drivers, should practice **defensive driving.** This means not just obeying traffic laws but also *watching out for other road users.* Because you obey the rules yourself, you will not do things to surprise drivers or other cyclists. Surprises can be dangerous. Also, because you watch what other road users are doing, you can react safely when someone else makes a mistake.

You can also reduce the risk of bicycle accidents by making sure that your bike has the proper safety equipment. Which equipment in **Figure 16.8** do you feel is essential?

- Ride on the right side of the road with traffic, not against it.

- Obey all traffic signals, signs, and pavement markings.

- Use lights and reflective clothing when riding after dark.

- Avoid loose clothing, which could catch in the chain.

- Keep your bike in good working order.

- Avoid riding at night and in bad weather.

Even though you follow the safety rules, bike accidents do happen. A helmet can prevent serious head injuries. Three out of four fatal bike accidents are the result of head injuries. Wearing a helmet could save your life.

Figure 16.8
Bicycle Safety Equipment

This drawing shows bicycle safety features that are recommended. Why do you think reflectors are important?

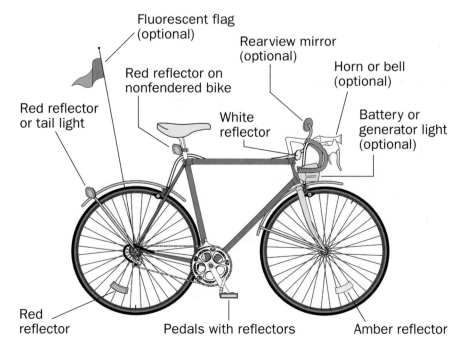

Fluorescent flag (optional)

Rearview mirror (optional)

Red reflector on nonfendered bike

Horn or bell (optional)

Red reflector or tail light

White reflector

Battery or generator light (optional)

Red reflector

Pedals with reflectors

Amber reflector

Skateboard and Motorbike Safety

For safe skateboarding, keep your speed down to a controllable level and watch for pedestrians. Avoid parking lots, streets, and other areas with traffic. Before heading downhill, practice the correct way to fall. If you do stunts, wear protective gear, including a helmet (see **Figure 16.9**).

Like bicyclists, motorbike and moped riders must follow all traffic rules. To be safe, they, too, should practice defensive driving. They also should wear the appropriate safety gear, which includes hard-shell helmets.

Hard-shell helmet

Wrist guards

Elbow pads

Knee pads

Figure 16.9
Safety Gear for Skateboarders

Safety Outdoors

You're not at home. You're not at school. You're not on the road. You're on vacation in the great outdoors. So you can enjoy yourself and forget about safety, right? Wrong! It doesn't pay to spoil a good time by taking risks. No matter what outdoor activity you prefer, it's better to do it safely. You can do that by following safety rules and using common sense. Here are two important tips to ensure your safety outdoors.

■ **Use the buddy system.** The buddy system is an agreement between two people to stay together. Always do outdoor activities with a friend—the two of you can watch out for each other's safety and help each other in case of an emergency.

■ **Be aware of the weather.** Use your common sense and try to avoid electrical storms, extreme heat, and extreme cold. If you are caught outdoors in an electrical storm, try to get into a car or house. If you cannot, take shelter under a group of bushes, or squat and put your head down. Do not stand under a tall tree. Get out of and away from water. If you are outdoors on a very hot day, keep your head covered from the sun, drink plenty of water, and don't exercise too hard. When it's very cold, dress in layers, stay dry, and warm up quickly if you begin to shiver. That way you will avoid **hypothermia** (hy·poh·THER·mee·uh), *a dangerous drop in body temperature.*

Safety in the Water

Whether your sport is swimming, diving, or boating, it's important to know about water safety. Between 4,000 and 5,000 people die from drowning in the United States each year. More than 1 million people have close calls. Drownings occur when boats overturn and when children wander off into unattended pools. They also happen if swimmers panic when they experience a cramp, swim farther out than they should, or get caught in a current. Most drownings and near-drownings are avoidable if people follow some water safety rules.

- Go in the water only if you know how to swim. Knowing how to swim not only helps keep you safe in the water, but it is also a lot of fun and great exercise.

- Always swim with a buddy and only in pools or at beaches that have trained lifeguards.

- If you ever feel yourself drowning, do not panic. Breathe slowly and tread water until help arrives. Thrashing about in the water only makes you tired and the situation worse.

- To prevent a cramp, or muscle tightening, avoid swimming when you're tired or right after eating.

- Dive only if you have had lessons from a qualified instructor. Always check the depth of the water and look for obstacles and other swimmers before diving in.

- When boating, always wear a life jacket. Don't stand up or move around in a small boat. If you're steering the boat, practice so you know how to handle it. If you plan to go boating regularly, take a course in boating safety.

- Learn the technique for drowning prevention (see **Figure 16.10**).

Your Total Health

Diving Disasters

Three-quarters of all diving injuries occur in rivers and lakes where the depth of the water varies from place to place. In swimming pools, 90 percent of diving accidents occur in water that is 6 feet deep or less. Consider the places where you swim. Where is it safe to dive, and where is it unsafe?

Did You Know?

Under the Influence

Operating a boat while under the influence of alcohol is just as dangerous as driving a car after drinking.

Figure 16.10
Drowning Prevention

This drawing shows a technique called *drowning prevention*. Both swimmers and nonswimmers can use this technique to save themselves from drowning. The main points to remember are do not panic and do not thrash around. Push down with cupped hands at the same moment as the walking motion takes place, to achieve more thrust.

1. Take a deep breath. Sink vertically beneath the surface of the water with only the back of your head above the surface. Relax your arms, legs, and neck until your fingers touch your knees.

2. Use a walking motion to raise your head above water. Breathe in; then, gently let your body relax and drop below the surface. Repeat these steps.

Figure 16.11
Getting Equipped for Safe Camping

Proper clothing for the weather

Backpack

Compass

Canteen of fresh water

Heavy shoes and socks

Safety When Hiking and Camping

Hiking and camping are popular ways to enjoy the sights and sounds of nature. Good preparation is the key to a successful hike or camping trip. Careful planning will ensure that you take the proper clothing and equipment. **Figure 16.11** shows some of the items needed for safe camping. Always tell someone where you will be and when you expect to return. Camping is more fun when you follow safety precautions. Unsafe behavior in and around campsites can lead to serious accidents. When you camp, follow these safety tips.

HEALTH LAB
Identifying Poison Ivy and Poison Oak

Introduction: Have you ever heard the saying, "Leaves of three, let it be"? It refers to poison ivy and poison oak. Both plants have leaves that are divided into three leaflets.

Poison ivy grows throughout most of the country, especially in the East and Midwest. Poison oak is less abundant, except along the Pacific coast, where it is often the most common small plant around. Both plants grow as vines, creepers, or low shrubs.

Sooner or later, almost everyone who spends time outdoors is going to come in contact with poison ivy or poison oak. Seven out of ten people are allergic to the oil in these plants, which causes a blistery, red rash that itches terribly.

Objective: Poison ivy and poison oak are toxic year round. To prevent an allergic reaction to these plants, you must avoid contact with them. In this lab, you will learn what poison ivy and poison oak plants look like. Then, when you are outdoors, you can stay clear of them.

Materials and Method: Study the photos of poison ivy and poison oak on page 505. Sketch the leaves by copying the pictures and read the descriptions of the plants below.

Poison ivy leaflets are usually shaped like arrowheads. The leaflets are a bright, shiny green. The leaves turn red in the fall, and the plant has white flowers and cream-colored berries in late summer. In the winter, the flower stems wither but still bear some berries.

Poison oak leaflets resemble oak leaves, with several lobes on each leaflet. Although most often there are three leaflets, there may be five or even more. The leaflets always have a shiny, oily appearance. They are deep green in the summer and then red or yellow in the fall. In late summer, poison oak has yellowish or whitish berries and greenish flowers that hang in loose clusters.

- **Shoes and clothes.** Dress for the weather and wear heavy shoes and socks to prevent getting blisters. Dressing in layers can ensure that you'll be ready for extremes in temperature and changes in weather. In some mountainous regions, you may be in danger of getting both sunburn during the day and **frostbite,** or *freezing of the skin,* at night. Be prepared with cold-weather, hot-weather, and wet-weather gear. Depending on where you will be, you may need to pack such items as sunscreen lotion, mittens and a ski mask, and waterproof boots.

- **Equipment and supplies.** Make sure you have a compass, a well-equipped first-aid kit, a flashlight with extra batteries, and an adequate supply of fresh water.

- **Campfires.** Drown your campfire with water, continually stirring it as you add water. If no water is available, use dirt that is free of twigs, leaves, and paper. Make sure the fire is out before leaving the area, or you could start a forest fire.

- **Poisonous plants and animals.** Learn which plants, snakes, and insects are poisonous and how to avoid them. Learn basic first-aid for treating reactions to poisonous plants, insect stings and bites, and snakebites. Don't eat berries unless you are sure they are not poisonous.

Biology Connection

Killer Bees

ACTIVITY!

"**K**iller Bees Invade the U.S." Does this sound like a science-fiction movie? It's not. The bees are a cross between common honeybees and African honeybees. However, they are not as dangerous as their name suggests. Their venom isn't any more harmful than that of common honeybees, though they are more aggressive and more likely to sting you. Read more about this variety of bee and give a brief report to your class.

Observation and Analysis:

If poison ivy or poison oak grow in your part of the country, try to find the plants growing outdoors. Look for them alongside roads, trails, and streams; in unused clearings; and climbing up tree trunks. Be careful to avoid touching the plants or stepping on them. If you have difficulty identifying the plants, try to find someone who knows what they look like to help you find them.

You can also follow these steps to minimize an allergic reaction.

▶ Remove the oil from your skin immediately, within five minutes if possible, by washing with plenty of soap and water, with rubbing alcohol, or with cool water and hydrogen peroxide or bleach.

▶ Apply calamine lotion or hydrocortisone cream to temporarily soothe the itch.

▶ Take an oral antihistamine to relieve itching if hydrocortisone cream can't control it.

▶ See your doctor if your symptoms are severe.

▶ Avoid breathing smoke in a fire where poison oak or poison ivy is burning.

Poison ivy |

Poison oak |

Safety When Enjoying Winter Sports

Ice skating, sledding, and skiing are all healthy ways to enjoy the outdoors in the winter. All of these activities can be dangerous, however, because of the cold and the risk of falls and collisions. Wear layers of clothing, a hat, and gloves or mittens to keep your hands warm. By following the safety guidelines below, you can increase your enjoyment of these winter sports.

When skating, make sure the ice is frozen solid before you go on it. It's safest to skate on supervised lakes or public rinks where the ice has been tested. When sledding, do so only on hills that are free of traffic or on streets that have been roped off. Before sledding down a hill, make sure it's free of people and other obstacles.

When skiing, wear appropriate gear, including goggles if snow is falling. Ski only on slopes you can handle safely, and check the condition of the snow before you head down the slope. Take lessons before skiing. If you know what you're doing, you'll have more fun.

Winter sports are more enjoyable if you dress properly to protect yourself from the cold.

<table>
<tr><td></td></tr>
</table>

Lesson 4 Review

Using complete sentences, answer the following questions on a separate sheet of paper.

Reviewing Terms and Facts

1. **Vocabulary**   How does *defensive driving* increase the safety of bicyclists?

2. **Recall**   What are some rules for skateboard safety?

Thinking Critically

3. **Analyze**   Why is it equally important for bicycle riders and motor vehicle drivers to follow traffic signals, signs, and pavement markings?

4. **Explain**   How does using the buddy system help keep you safe outdoors?

5. **Explain**   Why is it important to remain calm if you feel you're drowning?

Applying Health Concepts

6. **Growth and Development**   Design a poster that advertises a swimming program in your area. Include information that would encourage teens to learn how to swim.

7. **Health of Others**   Research car occupant restraints and seat belts, and make a video or brochure about them. Include information such as the number of lives seat belts save and the proper way to wear a seat belt.

Acting Safely in Weather Emergencies

This lesson will help you find answers to questions that teens often ask about weather emergencies. For example:

▶ **What should I do to stay safe in case of a severe storm in my area?**

▶ **How can I protect myself during a flood or an earthquake?**

Hazardous Weather and Natural Disasters

Hazardous weather and natural disasters can be devastating. A recent example of weather-related disaster occurred in Georgia in 1994. When the flood waters of the Flint River receded, 29 people were dead and 13,700 people homeless. The floods had damaged 10,120 additional homes and 89,000 acres of farmland.

The possibility of hazardous weather and natural disasters exists at certain times of the year and in certain parts of the United States (see **Figure 16.12**). You can reduce the risk of injury from hazardous weather and natural disasters by taking certain precautions to ensure your safety.

Words to Know

tornado
tornado watch
tornado warning
hurricane
blizzard
earthquake

Figure 16.12
Hazardous Weather and Natural Disasters in the United States

Tornadoes generally occur in the spring and early summer. Hurricanes usually occur between June and November, with most occurring in September.

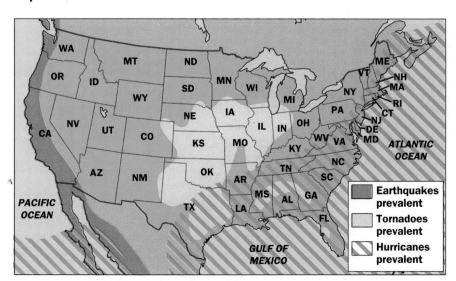

Tornadoes

A **tornado** is the most violent of all storms. It is a *whirling, funnel-shaped windstorm that drops from the sky to the ground.* The winds of a tornado—at speeds that can reach more than 200 miles an hour—are exceedingly dangerous. A tornado can destroy almost everything in its path. Although tornadoes occur mainly in the central part of the United States, they may also occur along the coasts after hurricanes. They are most frequent in the spring and summer.

Because tornadoes have such high winds and are so dangerous, the National Weather Service closely monitors the weather to see when a tornado may form. When the weather conditions indicate the possibility of a tornado, the Weather Service issues a **tornado watch,** which is *a news bulletin that tells people to stay tuned for further bulletins.* If conditions change and the tornado seems less likely to occur, the watch is removed.

When a tornado is actually approaching an area and the people living there are in danger, the Weather Service issues a **tornado warning** for that area. When that happens, people must take certain steps to protect themselves from harm. The safest action to take is to go to a cellar or basement that has no windows and to stay there until the storm passes. If you cannot do that, you should follow the steps listed below.

What to Do When a Tornado Strikes

- **Avoid places with windows.** Take cover in a hallway or bathtub. Stay as far away from windows as possible.

- **Cover yourself.** Duck down and cover your head with a mattress, blanket, or clothing to protect yourself from flying objects.

- **Lie down.** If you are outside, lie down in a ditch or other low ground.

Hurricanes

Another kind of hazardous weather condition is a hurricane. This storm can extend over hundreds of miles. A **hurricane** is a *strong windstorm with driving rain.* In the United States, hurricanes are most common on the eastern and southern coasts, where they may produce unusually high and destructive waves. They occur most often in late summer and early fall. **Figure 16.13** shows the wind patterns in a hurricane.

A hurricane is an area of low air pressure that forms over tropical regions near the Atlantic or Pacific Oceans. Hurricanes consist of storm clouds that circle around the eye, which is a calm area in the center of the storm.

Figure 16.13
Wind Patterns of a Hurricane
Hurricanes, like tornadoes, are dangerous weather storms. How are the two storms similar?

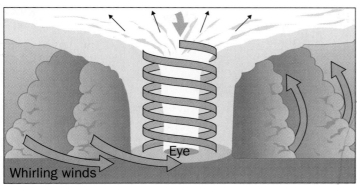

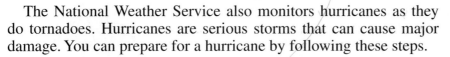

Eye

Whirling winds

The National Weather Service also monitors hurricanes as they do tornadoes. Hurricanes are serious storms that can cause major damage. You can prepare for a hurricane by following these steps.

- **Board up the windows and doors of your house.** This will prevent high winds from blowing them in.

- **Take inside any objects that may be blown away.** This means taking in any loose objects such as toys and lawn furniture.

- **Leave the area.** If you live on the coast, go inland. The farther inland you go, the safer you will be.

Blizzards

In winter months, some parts of the United States experience severe snowstorms called blizzards. A **blizzard** is a *very heavy snowstorm with winds of between 35 and 45 miles an hour.* The combination of strong winds and heavy snowfall results in poor visibility—usually less than 500 feet. It is very easy to get lost in a blizzard. Blizzards occur when a cold air mass from the Arctic moves into the temperate zone. Blizzards often follow periods of unusually warm winter weather.

What to Do When a Blizzard Strikes

Blizzards are dangerous. Snow piles up in great drifts, stopping traffic and disrupting life for several days. You can protect yourself from blizzards by following a few simple steps.

- **Stay inside.** The safest place to be during a blizzard is indoors. If you have to go out, follow the other precautions.

- **Keep your nose and mouth covered and keep moving.** These actions can keep you from freezing.

- **Avoid getting lost.** Find a landmark to walk along.

- **Wear protective clothing.** Wear thermal underwear, extra socks, and outer clothes that keep out wind and moisture.

Did You Know?

Lightning Strikes

You can avoid the dangers of lightning by doing the following.

- ▶ Stay in a house or in an enclosed car or truck.
- ▶ Use the telephone only in emergencies.
- ▶ Do not stand under or near a tall tree or other object.
- ▶ Stay out of and away from water.

Your Total Health

First Aid for Frostbite **ACTIVITY!**

Frostbite needs to be treated right away to avoid permanent damage of the injured body part. Bring the person indoors and cover him or her with a blanket. Give the person a warm drink. Place the frozen part in luke-warm, not hot, water or wrap it in blankets. Do not rub the frozen part. Get medical attention as soon as possible.

Figure 16.14
What Happens During an Earthquake

This diagram shows what causes an earthquake. On which part of the earth's surface do you think an earthquake is felt most strongly?

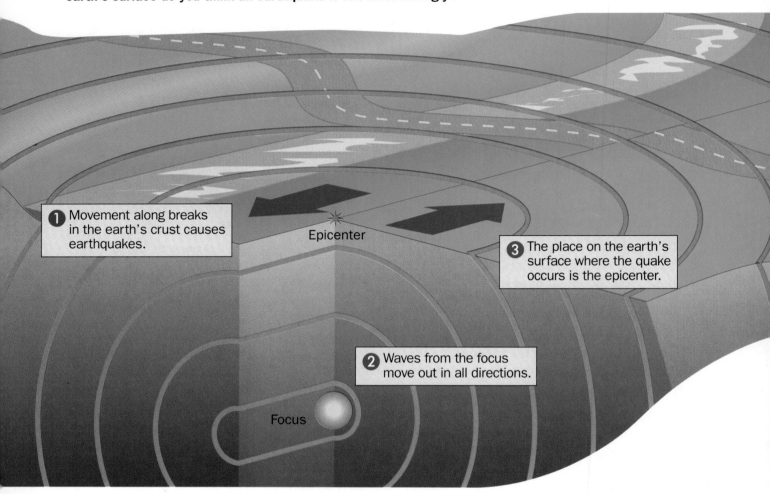

1 Movement along breaks in the earth's crust causes earthquakes.

3 The place on the earth's surface where the quake occurs is the epicenter.

2 Waves from the focus move out in all directions.

Epicenter

Focus

Earthquakes

Earthquakes occur often in some parts of the United States. California, for example, has about 5,000 weak but noticeable earthquakes each year.

An **earthquake** is *a shaking movement of the earth's surface.* **Figure 16.14** shows what happens during an earthquake. Small earthquakes cause little, if any, damage. Severe earthquakes can topple buildings. Most earthquake injuries are caused by falling objects and collapsing buildings.

What to Do When an Earthquake Strikes

■ **Stay inside.** If you are at home, remain inside. Brace yourself in an inside doorway or in a hallway, or crouch under a sturdy table. Stay away from objects that could fall or cave in and from windows or mirrors that may shatter.

■ **If you are outdoors, stand in the open.** Stay away from utility poles, chimneys, trees, brick or stone fences, electric wires, and buildings. These structures can be dangerous.

Teen Issues

Be Cool in an Emergency

Following these guidelines will help ensure your safety and the safety of others.

▶ Stay calm.

▶ Follow the directions of officials.

▶ Stay with your parents or another adult.

▶ Stay in your safe location until you hear official word that the danger is over.

Earthquakes can cause structural damage to roads, bridges, and buildings. In 1994, this California highway buckled under the pressure and took months to rebuild.

Did You Know?

What Is an Epicenter?

An earthquake occurs when there is sudden rock movement inside the earth. The site of the movement is the focus. The epicenter is the point on the surface just above the focus. This is where the seismic waves are the strongest.

Floods

Floods are another natural disaster that have caused severe damage and destruction. Floods may occur when rain falls too fast to be absorbed by the ground. Instead it runs off and fills rivers and streams until they overflow their banks and flood the surrounding land. Emergency barriers, such as sandbag levees, may keep a river from overflowing. You should leave the area for higher ground until the flood waters subside.

Review

Lesson 5

Using complete sentences, answer the following questions on a separate sheet of paper.

Reviewing Terms and Facts

1. **Vocabulary**   Differentiate between a *tornado* and a *hurricane.*

2. **Recall**   List three steps to take to prepare for a hurricane.

Thinking Critically

3. **Analyze**   Why is it important to stay indoors during blizzards?

4. **Synthesize**   Why should you stay out of damaged buildings after an earthquake?

Applying Health Concepts

5. **Health of Others**   Most communities have Civil Defense shelters to be used during weather emergencies and natural disasters. Find out where the shelters are in your community. What qualifies a place to serve as a shelter? What have they been used for in the past? Summarize your findings in writing.

Chapter Summary

▶ Acting safely will help you avoid accidents, which are the leading cause of injury and death during the teenage years. (Lesson 1)

▶ Acting safely means resisting peer pressure, concentrating on what you are doing, being prepared, and knowing your limits. (Lesson 1)

▶ An accident is the outcome of a chain of events; changing any one link in the chain can prevent the accident. (Lesson 1)

▶ Every home has hazards that can cause accidents, such as falls, poisonings, electrical shocks, and fires. (Lesson 2)

▶ Most home injuries can be prevented by being safety conscious and by taking a few preventive steps. (Lesson 2)

▶ By acting safely, students can help make school a safer place for themselves and others. (Lesson 2)

▶ Violence is on the rise in the United States. (Lesson 3)

▶ You can reduce your chances of being a victim of violence by avoiding unsafe situations and by acting assertively. (Lesson 3)

▶ Acting safely on the road means knowing and obeying traffic rules and riding your bicycle defensively. (Lesson 4)

▶ Being aware of dangers, following safety guidelines, and doing activities with a buddy will help you stay safe outdoors. (Lesson 4)

▶ By taking proper precautions and acting safely, you can reduce your risk of injuries from storms and natural disasters. (Lesson 5)

Using Health Terms

On a separate sheet of paper, write the vocabulary term that best matches each definition given below.

1. Being aware of safety rules and always behaving safely (Lesson 1)

2. A series of events that is likely to result in an accident (Lesson 1)

3. A possible source of harm (Lesson 2)

4. An indicator in a package that tells the user that the contents of a package are no longer useful (Lesson 2)

5. Unwanted sexual relations forced upon a person by someone he or she knows (Lesson 3)

6. To cross the street at a place other than the intersection (Lesson 4)

7. Watching out for other road users, such as drivers and pedestrians (Lesson 4)

8. A dangerous drop in body temperature (Lesson 4)

9. A whirling, funnel-shaped windstorm with speeds of more than 200 miles per hour (Lesson 5)

10. A storm with heavy snow, high winds, and poor visibility (Lesson 5)

Reviewing Main Ideas

Using complete sentences, answer the following questions on a separate sheet of paper.

1. List four general guidelines for acting safely. (Lesson 1)

2. What are the three components of an accident chain? (Lesson 1)

3. Why are accidental poisonings at home more likely to happen to toddlers than to older children? (Lesson 2)

4. What is the single best way to protect yourself from violent crime? (Lesson 3)

5. What is the difference between date rape and acquaintance rape? (Lesson 3)

6. Identify the types of controls that regulate traffic on roads. (Lesson 4)

7. What should you do if you are in the water and you feel you are drowning? (Lesson 4)

8. What steps can you take to protect yourself from blizzards? (Lesson 5)

Thinking Critically

Using complete sentences, answer the following questions on a separate sheet of paper.

1. **Evaluate** How can the idea of the accident chain be used to help prevent injuries? (Lesson 1)

2. **Analyze** Why is it especially important for teens to know safety rules and to be safety conscious? (Lesson 1)

3. **Analyze** Why are falls especially dangerous for older people? (Lesson 2)

4. **Apply** What are some ways in which you can reduce the risk of home fires? (Lesson 2)

5. **Explain** How can acting assertively reduce your risk of becoming a victim of a violent crime? (Lesson 3)

6. **Analyze** Why should you avoid dating people who drink alcohol or use other drugs? (Lesson 3)

7. **Evaluate** When a traffic light is yellow, is it safer to go through an intersection or to stop for it? (Lesson 4)

8. **Analyze** Why should you avoid swimming right after eating? (Lesson 4)

9. **Hypothesize** Why is a tornado warning more serious than a tornado watch? (Lesson 5)

Your Action Plan

Create an action plan to make your life safer. To set a goal, look back through your private journal entries for this chapter. How can you reduce your risk of injury from the hazards in your environment? Once you've identified your long-term goal, write it down.

Next, think of a series of short-term goals you must accomplish to achieve your long-term goal. Write these down. If your long-term goal is to reduce your risk of injury from bicycling, a short-term goal might be to put some safety equipment on your bike.

Create a schedule for accomplishing each short-term goal. Keep checking your schedule to keep yourself on track. When you reach your long-term goal, reward yourself. Do something nice to celebrate your achievement.

Building Your Portfolio

Survey several teens and adults about risky behaviors. First, prepare a questionnaire that addresses the types of risks they take, when they are most likely to take risks, and why they take risks. Keep the questionnaires anonymous to encourage honesty in the replies, but ask each person to write his or her age and gender on the questionnaire. After the questionnaires are completed, compare the risk-taking behaviors of teens with those of adults and those of males with those of females.

Summarize your findings in writing. Put a copy of the questionnaire, the survey results, and your written analysis in your portfolio.

In Your Home and Community

1. Prepare a fire-prevention checklist for your home. Then use the checklist to check your home for fire safety. If necessary, make suggestions on ways to make your home safer from fire.

2. Contact your local or state chapter of the American Red Cross to find out what, if any, emergencies or natural disasters are common in your community. If your community does not have a local chapter of the American Red Cross, find out who is responsible for handling disasters or emergencies, and contact that agency. Summarize your findings, and share them with the class.

Chapter 17

Handling Emergencies

Student Expectations

After you have read this chapter, you should be able to:

① List the steps in providing basic first aid.

② Explain what to do in a life-threatening emergency.

③ Describe how to handle some common emergencies.

I have this really great part-time job baby-sitting for my neighbor's son. I like this job because it gives me some extra money and a break from my regular routine. Stevie is a great kid and we do a lot of neat things together.

Last week, I was teaching him to ride his new bicycle. Since it has training wheels on it, I thought it was safe. Stevie didn't know how to use the foot brakes, though, and he panicked. The bike toppled and he fell, scraping his knee and elbow.

Now, here's the good part. I was prepared and knew exactly what to do. When I started this job, Mrs. Cahill showed me where the first-aid kit was kept and where the emergency phone numbers were posted. We learned about first aid in health class so I knew this was not a serious emergency.

The first thing I did was calm Stevie down. Then, I carefully washed the scrapes with warm, soapy water to remove the dirt. By the time Mrs. Cahill came home, Stevie and I were drinking chocolate milk and reading stories. It made me feel good to know that I could handle an emergency—even a not-so-serious one.

in Your journal

Read the account on this page. Have you heard of other emergencies in which people needed to react quickly? Start your private journal entries on handling emergencies by answering these questions.

▶ Do you know how to provide basic first aid?
▶ Do you know how to handle emergencies that are a matter of life or death, such as choking?

When you reach the end of the chapter you will use your journal entries to make an action plan.

 *(decorative — Lesson 1 tab)*

Basic Principles of First Aid

This lesson will help you find answers to questions that teens often ask about first aid. For example:

► **What are the basic steps to follow when someone needs first aid?**
► **How would I help someone who has stopped breathing?**
► **What would I do to help control severe bleeding?**

Words to Know

rescue breathing
shock

What Is First Aid?

First aid is the immediate care given to a person who becomes injured or ill. Knowing what kind of first aid to perform can prevent serious and sometimes permanent damage to the victim. In some cases, first aid can even prevent death.

You need to handle emergencies differently, depending on the severity of the illness or injury. A life-threatening emergency, such as occurs when someone is not breathing, requires a very fast, skillful response. A common emergency, such as a sprained ankle, usually is not as serious or as pressing. Because first aid can mean the difference between life and death, you need to know what to do in a variety of situations.

Regardless of the type of illness or injury involved, stay calm. In doing so, you will help the victim remain calm, too. Furthermore, getting scared or excited will only waste valuable time.

The First Things to Do

Figure 17.1 shows the sequence of steps to take when someone needs first aid. Each step is described in detail on the following pages. To be effective in any emergency, you must act quickly and carefully. Every second you take can make a difference. The Life Skills feature on the next page explains how you can use your senses to recognize emergencies.

Figure 17.1
First Steps in an Emergency

 **A** Recognize that an emergency exists.

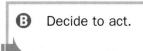 **B** Decide to act.

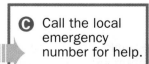 **C** Call the local emergency number for help.

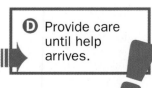 **D** Provide care until help arrives.

Decide to Act

Only you can decide whether you want to act. Do not be afraid to help emergency victims for fear that you will try and fail—or be sued by the victim or the victim's family. The Good Samaritan Law says that anyone who tries to help in an emergency cannot be sued unless he or she knowingly acted unsafely. If you know what you are doing and you use common sense, you cannot be sued and found financially responsible for the victim's injury.

However, do not put your own life in danger. For example, do not jump into a lake to save someone from drowning. Instead, throw the victim a life jacket or an inflated object. You will not be able to help anyone if you get hurt, too.

Call for Help

If no one has called for medical assistance, you need to do so now. You should call the police department, the fire department, or Emergency Medical Services (EMS). EMS can be summoned in many areas by dialing either 911, 0, or a direct number. Remember to provide the emergency operator with all the necessary information, such as the street address, nature of the emergency, and your name. Then stay on the phone until the operator has the necessary information and tells you that you can hang up.

LIFE SKILLS
Recognizing Emergencies

*E*mergencies are a combination of unplanned and unexpected circumstances that require immediate action. Everyone can be taught how to respond to an emergency. In order to do so, however, you must be able to recognize the signs of an emergency. Did you realize that you carry with you, at all times, tools that help you do this? They are your senses of hearing, sight, and smell. You can use these senses to help you recognize an emergency.

▶ **Hearing.** Unusual, sudden, and loud noises often are signs of an emergency. You may hear human noises that attract your attention, such as screaming or calls for help. Other noises that may be associated with an emergency include shattering glass, smashing metal, screeching tires, or a machinery noise that suddenly changes.

▶ **Sight.** You may also see something that does not look quite right. For example, a car may be located in an odd place. Broken glass, chemical spills, downed electrical wires, smoke, fire, or a person lying motionless are often indicators of an emergency.

Seeing a person behaving oddly may also be a sign of an emergency. For instance, you might see somone clutching her chest as if she were having a heart attack. Other unusual behaviors to investigate include slurred speech, unexplained confusion, unusual skin color, or facial expressions that show pain or discomfort.

▶ **Smell.** An odor that is familiar but is unusually strong may signal an emergency. For instance, you may be familiar with the smell of chlorine in a pool. If you notice that smell without being near a pool, there may have been a chlorine spill. Smelling an odor that you do not recognize can also indicate an emergency.

Follow-up Activity

Use your senses for one week to look for signs of emergencies. List all the "possible" signs that you heard, saw, or smelled. Were any of them actual emergencies? Share and discuss your lists with your classmates.

Provide Care Until Help Arrives

Providing care is a matter of learning the ABCs of first aid (see **Figure 17.2**). Move the person only if he or she is not safe. For example, move the victim if he or she is in danger from oncoming traffic or an explosion. A person should *not* be moved if he or she has a broken bone or if there seems to be damage to the head, neck, or spine. If the victim has to be moved for safety reasons, do so as gently as possible. Support the victim's spine to minimize movement.

When Rescue Breathing Is Needed

If the victim has stopped breathing but has a pulse, you can use rescue breathing. **Rescue breathing** is *a substitute for normal breathing in which someone forces air into the victim's lungs.* Rescue breathing for adults and older children is different from rescue breathing for infants and small children. **Figure 17.3** shows the steps to follow for adults and older children. As a general rule, children eight years or older qualify as older children. **Figure 17.4** shows the steps to follow for infants and young children.

Figure 17.2
The ABCs of First Aid

Ⓐ Airway
If the airway is blocked, it must be cleared. Gently roll the person on his or her back. Move the whole body at once. To open the airway, gently tilt the person's head back and at the same time lift up on the chin.

Ⓑ Breathing
Check for breathing. *Look* for the rise and fall of the chest. *Listen* for air moving out of the mouth and nose. *Feel* for exhaled air on your hand or cheek. If the victim is not breathing, perform rescue breathing as shown in **Figures 17.3** and **17.4.**

Ⓒ Circulation
Check the victim's *carotid pulse* on either side of the neck. If there is a pulse, you can continue doing rescue breathing until the person revives. If there is no pulse, the heart must be stimulated by someone who is trained in CPR. Call to passersby to see if someone has this skill. In the meantime, keep up the rescue breathing.

Figure 17.3
Rescue Breathing for Adults and Older Children

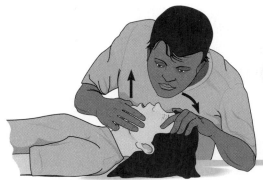

1 Tilt the person's head back by placing one hand under the chin and lifting up while putting the other hand on the forehead and gently pressing down.

2 Pinch the person's nostrils shut. Take a deep breath and place your mouth over the person's mouth, forming a seal. Give two slow breaths.

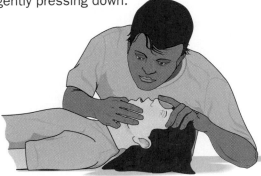

3 Repeat, giving about 12 breaths per minute or 1 breath every 5 seconds. After each breath, remove your mouth to allow the victim to exhale.

4 Keeping the head tilted, check the victim's breathing. *Look* and *listen* for air in the lungs. Check the carotid artery for a pulse. If the victim has not started breathing or there is no pulse, repeat steps 2 and 3.

Figure 17.4
Rescue Breathing for Infants and Young Children

1 Slightly tilt the head back— not as far back as you would an adult's. Gently support the child's head.

2 Take a breath and place your mouth over the child's nose and mouth, forming a seal. Give 1 breath and count to 3 (15 breaths per minute). The breaths should be *very* gentle.

3 After each breath, remove your mouth to allow the victim to exhale. *Look* and *listen* for air in the lungs. Recheck the pulse and breathing about every minute. If the victim has not started breathing, repeat step 2.

Lesson 1: Basic Principles of First Aid   **519**

How to Control Severe Bleeding

The next step is to control any severe bleeding. To stop or slow the rapid loss of blood, you can use one of the three methods presented in **Figure 17.5.** When you have stopped the bleeding, it is important to cover the wound to prevent infection.

Figure 17.5
Methods to Control Severe Bleeding

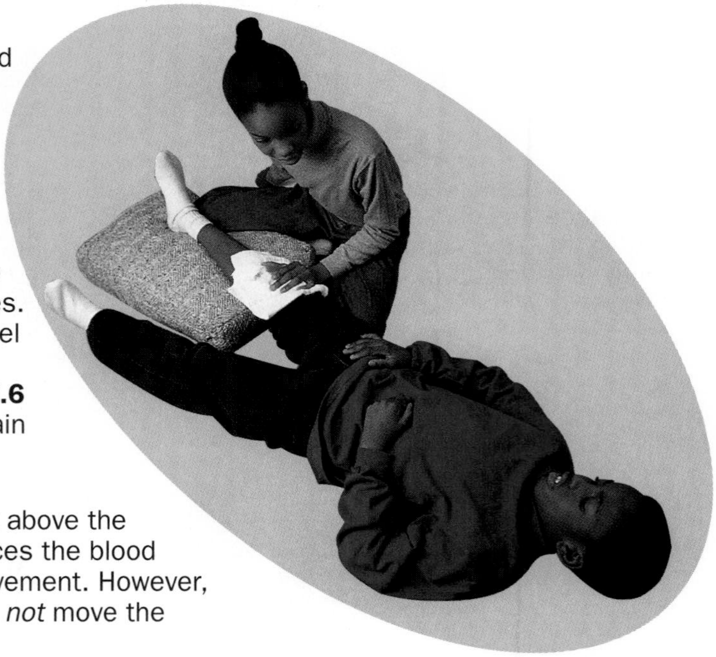

1 Apply direct and steady pressure to the wound. Place a clean cloth over the wound and press on it firmly. Add more cloth if the blood soaks through, but do not remove the first piece.

2 Combine direct pressure on the wound with pressure to a main artery leading to the wound. This is only done if you have tried method 1 several times. Push on the pressure point until you feel a bone. At the same time, apply direct pressure to the wound. (See **Figure 17.6** to locate the pressure points to the main arteries.)

3 Gently raise the bleeding body part above the level of the victim's heart. This forces the blood to travel uphill, which slows its movement. However, if the victim has a broken bone, do *not* move the body part.

Figure 17.6
Six Pressure Points

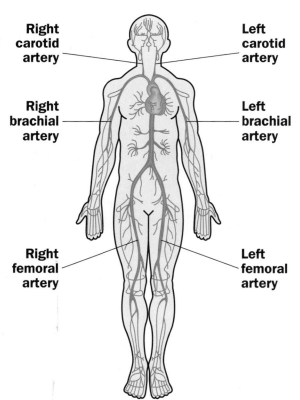

Right carotid artery

Left carotid artery

Right brachial artery

Left brachial artery

Right femoral artery

Left femoral artery

What to Do If the Victim Is in Shock

Shock can be caused by severe bleeding, heart attack, electricity, or poisoning. This is a *serious condition in which the circulatory system fails to deliver blood to all parts of the body.* Signs of shock include restlessness or irritability (after the person shows other signs of experiencing a significant problem); rapid, shallow, or uneven breathing; pale, cool, and moist skin; and rapid or weak pulse or no pulse. Cover the person with a blanket, coat, or other wrap to maintain body heat. Get help immediately.

First Aid for Poisoning

Many substances in homes, such as cleaning fluids and soaps, are *poisons*. Victims of poisoning need immediate treatment.

- **Call the 24-hour poison control center or a doctor.** The center's phone number is usually listed on the inside front cover of the telephone book. Listen for and follow all instructions.

- **Call Emergency Medical Services if you are told to.**

- **Remove any extra bits of the poison from around the person's mouth with a clean, damp cloth.**

- **Save the container of the poisonous substance.** Show it to the medical team and give them any details you are aware of.

in your journal

Take a survey of several adults you know. Ask them to name three signs of shock. Write down their responses in your journal. Compare and evaluate their responses with the signs listed on this page.

Review

Lesson 1

Using complete sentences, answer the following questions on a separate sheet of paper.

Reviewing Terms and Facts

1. **Compare and Contrast** Describe how the steps for rescue breathing for adults and older children are the same as and different from the steps for rescue breathing for infants and young children.

2. **Vocabulary** Define the term *shock.* Use it in an original sentence.

Thinking Critically

3. **Evaluate** List the four basic steps of first aid in the sequence in which they should be performed. Explain why the steps are in that order.

4. **Interpret** You are baby-sitting, and you find the child unconscious in the kitchen alongside an open can of cleanser. What has probably happened? What should you do?

Applying Health Concepts

5. **Personal Health** Use a book on health and first aid to make a list of first-aid supplies every home should have. Compare the list to supplies in your home.

6. **Health of Others** With a partner, plan a skit showing the use of basic first aid in one of these situations: you see someone fall off a bicycle and injure herself; a young child cuts himself and is severely bleeding; a friend goes into shock as a result of touching electricity. Together, act out your skit for the rest of the class.

Teen HEALTH DIGEST

Teens Making a Difference

First Aid Pays Off!

Jenny was 13 years old and starting her own baby-sitting service. She felt she should know how to handle emergencies while baby-sitting. She also believed that knowing first aid might help her get jobs. Jenny checked with her local recreation facility to see if they had a first-aid course she could take. Unfortunately, the only first-aid course the facility had was for people 18 years of age and older—so Jenny didn't qualify.

Jenny called the American Red Cross in her area. She asked them if they had a course she could take. The person Jenny contacted suggested that she find a place to hold such a course and invite other interested teenagers to take the course with her.

Jenny asked the head of the young adults section of her library if she could use a meeting room for the first-aid course. The librarian got permission for the course to be held at the library. Jenny coordinated all the arrangements for dates and times with the library and the American Red Cross. Then Jenny made posters to display in the library and at school explaining the first-aid course, where and when it would be held, and how to sign up for it.

As a result of Jenny's work, 17 teenagers passed the course. Jenny was able to tell her baby-sitting clients that she had taken first-aid training through the American Red Cross. Jenny was not only able to get numerous baby-sitting jobs but also to increase her hourly rate!

Health Update

Communicable Diseases and CPR

Many people are afraid to give first aid to victims because they fear contracting communicable diseases such as AIDS and hepatitis. However, there are no known cases of people who have contracted AIDS by giving rescue breathing or coming in contact with the victim's saliva. There is more of a danger if there is blood in the victim's mouth and the rescuer has an open cut in his or her mouth. The American Red Cross, however, encourages rescuers to use some kind of barrier between someone else's blood and other body fluids and themselves when performing rescue breathing or CPR or when controlling severe bleeding.

Professional rescuers use pocket masks when performing rescue breathing and CPR. This kind of mask can be placed over the mouth or nose and mouth area. The mask has a valve that allows the rescuer to perform rescue breathing without contacting the victim's saliva.

Latex gloves should be used when trying to stop bleeding or when putting a bandage or dressing on a wound. If you do not have latex gloves, wrap your hands in several sterile dressings or pieces of clean plastic. Wash your hands with hot, soapy water after treating injuries involving blood or other body fluids.

Sports and Recreation

Knowing When to Quit

Many sports and recreational activities are played outside. People often continue playing even though threatening clouds move in and thunder and lightning begin. Lightning kills about 100 people and causes about 300 injuries in the United States each year.

Lightning seeks anything tall—a tree, a tower, a person playing soccer in an open field—and uses it as a path for the electrical current. Lightning causes severe burns and causes the victim's heart to stop beating. Lightning also causes damage to the nervous system, broken bones, and loss of hearing and sight.

The National Weather Service advises sports enthusiasts to seek shelter in buildings or vehicles during thunderstorms. Stay away from tall trees. Instead, crouch down in a ravine or valley. If you are with a group of people, spread several yards apart from one another.

CON$UMER FOCU$

First-aid Kits

Everyone should keep a first-aid kit in his or her home and car. The American Red Cross suggests including the following items in each kit: gauze pads and roller gauze, adhesive tape, cold pack, plastic bags, disposable gloves, adhesive strips, hand cleaner, small flashlight and extra batteries, scissors and tweezers, blanket, triangular bandage, face mask for rescue breathing, and antiseptic ointment. The kit should also include emergency phone numbers and other items your physician might suggest for your individual physical needs.

You can buy a kit that is already prepared or you can make your own. Check your kit on a regular basis. Make sure the flashlight works, and replace used or out-of-date contents.

People at Work

Emergency Medical Technician

Frank was always cool under pressure. Even as a young child, if he was injured, he was more interested in what his body looked like under the skinned knee than in the amount of blood he lost. If friends hurt themselves, Frank would soon be there to help them home. He even gave advice to the victim's parents on how to handle the first aid.

It didn't come as a surprise to those who grew up with Frank that he chose to become an emergency medical technician. "I always knew that I wanted to help people in emergencies," explains Frank when asked why he went into this profession. "I am physically and emotionally strong enough for this kind of work. I function well under stress, and I enjoy driving an ambulance. The special medical training I received has helped me determine and provide correct emergency medical care to the accident and illness victims I care for. Helping save lives is the greatest job satisfaction a person can get."

Life-threatening Emergencies

This lesson will help you find answers to questions that teens often ask about helping someone in a life-threatening emergency. For example:

► Should I try to help someone in a life-threatening emergency?
► What should I do to help a choking victim?
► How do I know if someone needs CPR?

Words to Know

abdominal thrust
chest thrust
CPR (cardiopul-
monary resus-
citation)

Life-threatening Emergencies

In life-threatening emergencies, immediate first aid is essential. Its purpose is to prevent the injury from becoming worse, to maintain vital functions, and to reassure the victim until medical assistance arrives. Learning basic first-aid procedures for choking and cardiopulmonary resuscitation (kar·dee·oh·PUHL·muh·nehr·ee ri·suh·suh·TAY·shuhn) will help you deal with medical emergencies and save lives.

As in all emergencies, perform the first steps in first aid that you learned in Lesson 1. Although you need to summon help, you should never leave a victim with a life-threatening emergency alone. Instead, call out for someone to get help. Then provide the first-aid techniques described on the following pages.

First Aid for Choking

Over 3,000 choking deaths occur each year in the United States. Death by choking can be prevented, however. Choking occurs when a person's airway becomes blocked by an object. If the object is not removed, air cannot reach the lungs and the victim can die. **Figure 17.7** shows the universal sign of choking.

Figure 17.7
Universal Sign of Choking

A choking person who cannot talk will grab his or her throat. Other signs of choking include problems with breathing and turning reddish, then bluish. The person may also faint.

The hand is on the throat with the finger and thumb extended.

To help a choking victim, you need to remove the object that is blocking the airway. Strong force may be needed to do this. **Figure 17.8** explains first-aid procedures for choking in adults and older children. **Figure 17.9** explains the procedure in infants and young children. Practice the steps on a large doll.

First Aid for Choking in Adults and Older Children

If you suspect a person is choking, ask, "Are you choking?" If you do not get an answer and other signs of choking are present, use the method known as **abdominal thrusts.** This method uses *quick, upward pulls into the diaphragm to force out the substance blocking the airway.* Use the technique shown in **Figure 17.8.**

Figure 17.8
First Aid for a Choking Adult

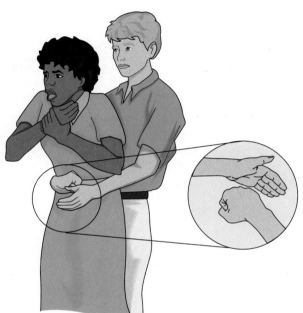

1 Stand behind the victim, sliding your arms under his or her armpits and wrapping your arms around his or her waist. Put the thumb side of your wrist against the midline of the person's abdomen, between the waist and the rib cage.

2 Grasp your fist with your other hand and apply pressure inward and up toward the person's diaphragm in one smooth movement. Deliver up to five rapid inward thrusts up toward the diaphragm. Once the object is dislodged, give rescue breathing if needed. Then monitor the victim.

First Aid for Choking in Infants and Young Children

If an infant or young child appears to be choking, use the first technique shown in **Figure 17.9** on the next page. If the blows between the victim's shoulder blades do not dislodge the object, try the second technique shown in **Figure 17.9.** This technique, which is called **chest thrusts,** uses *quick presses into the middle of an infant or child's breastbone to force out the substance blocking the airway.* Repeat both techniques if the victim does not cough up the object or start breathing on his or her own.

Figure 17.9
First Aid for Choking Infants and Young Children

1 Hold the infant or young child face down on your forearm with the head lower than the trunk. You must support the patient's head by placing a hand around the lower jaw and chest. Give the victim four blows with the heel of your hand to the spinal area between the victim's shoulder blades.

2 Turn the victim face up on your thigh, making sure that you provide adequate support for the head. Ensure that the head is lower than the trunk. Give four slow, distinct chest thrusts by pressing two or three fingers into the middle of the victim's chest, with the index finger placed just below an imaginary line drawn directly between the nipples.

HEALTH LAB
Locating Pressure Points

Introduction: If a person is bleeding severely, it is important to know where the main pressure points are located in the body. As you have read, if direct pressure on the wound does not stop the bleeding, you need to push on the main pressure point of the artery that provides the wounded area with blood. To do this, you need to know where these pressure points are located.

If a person stops breathing, you need to take the person's pulse to know if he or she needs more than rescue breathing. The pulse indicates whether the heart has stopped beating. If it has, you need to provide rescue breathing and stimulation to the heart.

Objective: Learn to find pressure points and take pulses by using the following steps.

Refer to **Figure 17.6** on page 520. Use your index and middle fingers on one hand to find each of the six main pressure points shown in the illustration. Locate the pressure points by gently moving your fingers around until you feel a regular throbbing known as a pulse. The pulse in the arteries is caused by the pumping action of the heart.

Next, decide which pressure point you would push to stop bleeding in wounds located in the following places: on the right calf, on the left forearm, on the right wrist, on the left side of the chest, on the right side of the head.

The best pressure points on the body to use to take a pulse are the carotid arteries in the neck. These arteries have the strongest pulse. Find a carotid artery on your neck.

First Aid for Choking If You Are the Victim

If you are choking, alert someone around you to the emergency. Use the universal sign of choking as shown in **Figure 17.7** on page 524. If no one is around to help you, use the technique described in **Figure 17.10** to give yourself an abdominal thrust. Simply make a fist and thrust it quickly into your upper abdomen to push free the object that is choking you. Another way to give yourself an abdominal thrust is to press your abdomen into a firm object, such as the back of a chair or sofa.

CPR

CPR, or **cardiopulmonary resuscitation,** is *a first-aid procedure in which another person breathes for a victim while pushing on the heart.* You cannot perform CPR unless you have successfully completed a CPR course and been certified. If CPR is done improperly, you could harm the victim by cracking a rib, puncturing a lung, or causing internal bleeding.

Figure 17.10
First Aid If You Are Choking
Make a fist and thrust it quickly into your upper abdomen.

Using your index and middle fingers, count the number of throbs or beats in the pulse in 30 seconds. Multiply this number by 2. This gives you your pulse rate per minute. For the next two days, you will be taking your pulse rate at various times of the day. Each day, take your pulse rate when you wake up in the morning, after you exercise or play a sport, and before you go to bed.

Materials and Method: You will need a sheet of paper for each observation. Divide the sheet into two columns: *Observation* and *Analysis.* In the *Observation* column, write the facts, such as which pressure point to use for which wounds. In the *Analysis* column, write your interpretation of the activity. Answer questions such as these: Why do you think pushing on a pressure point helps stops severe bleeding? When is your pulse rate the lowest? When is it the highest? Divide another sheet of paper into three columns:

Awakening, Exercising, Retiring. Log your pulse rate at various times of the day in the columns.

Observation and Analysis:
Share your observations and analyses with a group of your classmates. Compare pulse rates.

Now that you have read about some of the first-aid emergencies that could happen, would you consider taking a course in first aid or CPR? Why or why not?

In Lesson 1, you learned how to determine whether cardio-pulmonary resuscitation is needed. Even if you are not trained in CPR, there are several ways to help.

■ Gently shake the person to determine responsiveness. If there is no response, call for help.

■ Make sure the person is lying down on a hard surface.

■ Check for breathing.

■ If the person is not breathing, deliver two breaths at one and a half to two seconds each.

■ Check for a carotid pulse in the person's neck. If there is no pulse, CPR needs to be performed as quickly as possible.

■ If you are not trained to perform CPR, call out, "This person needs CPR. Is anyone trained?"

Learning how to perform CPR is a valuable skill that may help you save lives.

Lesson 2 Review

Using complete sentences, answer the following questions on a separate sheet of paper.

Reviewing Terms and Facts

1. **Vocabulary** Describe the following techniques and when they are used: *abdominal thrusts, chest thrusts.*

2. **Explain** Where is the carotid pulse located? How would you take your own carotid pulse?

Thinking Critically

3. **Compare and Contrast** How is first aid for choking in adults and older children the same as and different from first aid for choking in infants and young children?

4. **Draw Conclusions** You are at a recreational center. Suddenly an adult collapses. You think that CPR might be required, but you are not trained to perform it. What should you do?

Applying Health Concepts

5. **Consumer Health** Find out about first-aid and CPR classes taught in your community. Prepare a directory of the courses. Include the course name, a description of the course, where and when the course is held, any costs involved, and how to sign up for the course. Get permission to display the directory on a bulletin board in a public library or shopping center.

First Aid for Common Emergencies

This lesson will help you find answers to questions that teens often ask about first aid for common emergencies. For example:

▶ **How should I help someone who has a sprain, bruise, or broken bone?**

▶ **How do I determine what type of burn a person has?**

▶ **What is the best first aid for other common emergencies, including objects in the eye, fainting, nosebleeds, and insect bites and stings?**

Words to Know

fracture
first-degree burn
second-degree burn
third-degree burn

Common Emergencies

First aid for common emergencies usually involves treating injuries such as broken bones, sprains, burns, nosebleeds, and insect bites and stings. Medical assistance may not be required, but if you are in doubt, summon help. Proper treatment is essential for injuries to heal. For that reason, you should know simple first-aid techniques for handling common emergencies, and you should always have first-aid supplies on hand.

Broken Bones

Your body contains over 200 bones, many of which protect the organs of your body. Broken bones may put vital organs in danger. Breaks commonly result from falls or playing contact sports. A **fracture,** or *a break in a bone,* is usually painful. If someone around you gets hurt and you suspect a broken bone, do not try to straighten it. Doing so might force the bone to break through the skin. Instead, follow these steps.

■ Tell the person not to move the injured part.

■ Put a cold pack on the injured bone.

■ Summon medical assistance. If a leg is broken, have the medical help come to the victim. If an arm is broken, the victim can travel to a doctor's office or clinic. Take special care to keep the injured arm immobilized.

One way to prevent fractures is to take safety precautions, such as wearing protective gear when playing a sport.

Sprains and Bruises

A sprain results when a joint is suddenly and violently stretched. Wrists, knees, and ankles are the most frequently sprained areas. A bruise results from a blow to part of the body.

Both of these injuries are very common and usually not serious. The sprained or bruised part of the body is often painful, and it may become swollen. To relieve the pain and swelling, follow these first-aid steps.

- *Do not* use the sprained or bruised part of the body.
- Elevate the sprained or bruised part.
- Apply cold packs for the first 24 hours.
- If the pain and swelling do not stop, see a doctor.

Insect Bites and Stings

Sometimes an insect bites or stings a person, causing pain and swelling at the site of the bite or sting. Some people, however, have an allergy to insect bites or stings. If a rash develops or the person shows signs of shock, get medical help right away.

First Aid for Insect Bites

- Wash the bite.
- Apply a special lotion for bites.

First Aid for Insect Stings

- Scrape against the stinger with a credit card or fingernail to remove the stinger.
- Apply cold compresses or ice to relieve the pain.
- Watch for allergic reactions, such as a rash; difficulty breathing; swelling of the face, neck, and tongue.
- See **Figure 17.11** for instructions on removing a tick.

Figure 17.11
How to Remove a Tick

❶ Drop oil or petroleum jelly on the area where the tick is in order to suffocate it.

❷ Place tweezers close to the head of the tick and pull it away. Wash the area with soap and water. If the tick's head breaks off, seek medical attention immediately to remove it.

Burns

Burns vary widely in the extent of damage done to the skin and in the amount of discomfort that the victim feels. **Figure 17.12** shows how deeply the skin is damaged in each degree of burn. Burns may be caused by fire, hot objects or liquids, electricity, the sun, and chemicals. First aid for burns differs, depending on the degree of injury involved. See **Figure 17.12** for specific steps for treating each degree of burn.

A **first-degree burn** is *a burn in which only the outer layer of the skin is burned and turns red.* A first-degree burn usually heals quickly. A common type of first-degree burn is sunburn. A **second-degree burn** is *a serious burn in which the burned area blisters.* Although it may cause intense redness, pain, and swelling, this type of burn usually heals without scarring. A **third-degree burn** is *a very serious burn in which deep layers of the skin and nerve endings are damaged.* The burned areas may be white or charred, and pain may be intense.

Science Connection

Skin Banks? ACTIVITY!

To treat third-degree burns, doctors use a sheet of skin from another person. They place the skin over the burned area and remove healthy skin cells from elsewhere on the victim's body. These cells grow until there is enough to form new skin to graft to the burned area. Find out more about skin grafts for burn victims. Write a two-page report.

Figure 17.12
First Aid for the Three Degrees of Burns

Ⓐ First-Degree burns
1. Submerge burned area in cold water for 10 to 30 minutes.
2. Wrap burn loosely in clean, dry dressing.

Ⓑ Second-Degree burns
1. Submerge burned area in cold water. Do not pop blisters or remove loose skin.
2. Wrap burn loosely in clean, dry dressing.
3. Elevate the burned area.

Ⓒ Third-Degree burns
1. Call for medical help.
2. Cover the burned area with a clean dressing.
3. Elevate the victim's feet and arms.
4. If possible, have the victim drink small amounts of fluids.

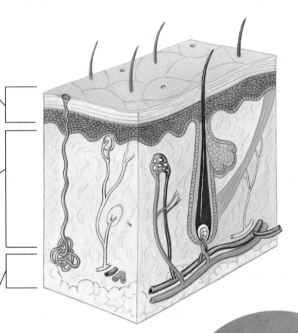

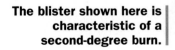

The blister shown here is characteristic of a second-degree burn.

Figure 17.13

First Aid for Someone with an Object in the Eye

Use a moist, clean corner of a handkerchief to gently remove the object. Then flood the eye with water.

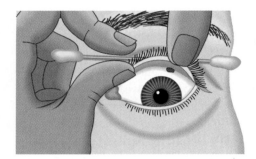

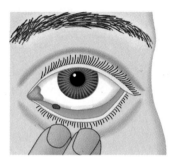

A If the object is under the upper lid, pull the lid over a cotton swab.

B If the object is under the lower lid, pull the lid down.

Objects in the Eye

A foreign object in the eye can cause pain and irritation. When this occurs, do not rub the eye. Doing so can cause further injury. Instead, follow the steps given in **Figure 17.13** to remove an object. If you cannot remove the object, or if the pain or irritation continues, cover the eye with a loose, dry, clean bandage and get medical help immediately.

Nosebleeds

Nosebleeds often occur without warning. They can be caused by an injury, by being in a very dry place for a long time, or even by a cold. Nosebleeds are usually not serious. Stopping a nosebleed is usually not difficult. The nosebleed victim should sit down, lean slightly forward, bow his or her head low, and firmly pinch the nose for about 5 minutes. If bleeding continues, get medical help.

MAKING HEALTHY DECISIONS
Should You Help Someone Who Is Hurt?

*B*ryan was taking his usual early morning bike ride. He approached his favorite part of the path—a one-way bridge over a small creek. The bridge was steep so he had to use most of the gears on his ten-speed to reach the top. Then he quickly made the descent.

As Bryan rode to the bottom of the bridge, he saw a large skid mark and some bent branches and he heard someone moaning. Bryan came to an abrupt stop. He saw a boy about his age lying to the left of the path beyond the bridge. His head was bleeding and he was motionless.

The sight of so much blood frightened Bryan. The boy was moaning softly, but Bryan could tell that he was not conscious. Although Bryan had taken a course in emergency first aid, he felt uneasy putting his knowledge into practice.

Many questions entered Bryan's mind while he was deciding what to do. I don't know this person, so why should I help him? Why don't I just go on and let someone else help him? What if he has a contagious disease? How do I know for sure what kind of injuries he has? I want to help, but what will happen to me if I do something wrong?

Fainting

Fainting occurs when the blood supply to the brain is cut off for a short amount of time. A person who faints temporarily loses consciousness. If someone faints, follow these steps.

- *Do not* lift the victim. Leave him or her lying down.

- Raise the victim's legs 8 to 12 inches.

- Loosen any tight clothing.

- Check the victim's breathing, keeping his or her airway open.

- If the victim does not regain consciousness, get medical help.

- Be aware that fainting may signal a more serious condition.

Review Lesson 3

Using complete sentences, answer the following questions on a separate sheet of paper.

Reviewing Terms and Facts

1. **Vocabulary**   Describe the extent of damage to the skin for each of the following: *first-degree burns, second-degree burns, third-degree burns.*

2. **Recall**   What is the procedure for stopping a nosebleed?

Thinking Critically

3. **Interpret**   How do you know when to get medical help for an insect sting?

Applying Health Concepts

4. **Health of Others**   Write a scenario for dealing with a common emergency. With a classmate, role-play your scenario for the class.

Bryan was confused. He decided to use the step-by-step decision-making process to make up his mind about responding to this emergency.

1. **State the situation**
2. **List the options**
3. **Weigh the possible outcomes**
4. **Consider your values**
5. **Make a decision and act**
6. **Evaluate the decision**

Follow-up Activities

1. Work in small groups and apply the six steps of the decision-making process to Bryan's situation. Have one person in each group record the members' thoughts as the group goes through each step. Have the recorder share the group's thoughts with the class.

2. With a classmate, role-play Bryan's situation, showing how Bryan decides to react to the emergency.

Chapter Summary

▶ Knowing the basic principles of first aid will allow you to help victims before medical assistance arrives. (Lesson 1)

▶ Rescue breathing is a substitute for normal breathing in which someone forces air into the victim's lungs. (Lesson 1)

▶ To control severe bleeding, apply direct, steady pressure to the wound; if you cannot stop the bleeding, at the same time push on the pressure point; raise the bleeding body part above the level of the victim's heart. (Lesson 1)

▶ A person can suffer shock from severe bleeding, heart attack, electricity, or poisoning. (Lesson 1)

▶ Use the abdominal thrust to dislodge an object blocking a victim's airway. (Lesson 2)

▶ To help a child or an infant who is choking, use a few sharp blows on the back between the shoulder blades or chest thrusts to dislodge the substance that is blocking the airway. (Lesson 2)

▶ If you are a choking victim, you can perform an abdominal thrust on yourself. (Lesson 2)

▶ If a victim has no pulse and is not breathing, CPR must be administered by a person trained to do so. (Lesson 2)

▶ Knowing simple first-aid techniques helps you handle common emergencies without the need for medical assistance. (Lesson 3)

▶ Get medical help for broken bones, burns, insect bites that create an allergic reaction, and other problems that persist. (Lesson 3)

Using Health Terms

On a separate sheet of paper, write the vocabulary term that best matches each definition given below.

1. Forcing air into the lungs of someone who is not breathing (Lesson 1)

2. A serious condition in which the circulatory system fails to deliver blood to all parts of the body (Lesson 1)

3. A first-aid method that uses quick, upward pulls into the diaphragm to force out a substance blocking the airway (Lesson 2)

4. Quick presses into the breastbone to force out a substance that is blocking the airway (Lesson 2)

5. A first-aid procedure in which a person breathes for a victim while pushing on the heart (Lesson 2)

6. A break in a bone (Lesson 3)

7. A serious burn in which the burned area blisters (Lesson 3)

Reviewing Main Ideas

Using complete sentences, answer the following questions on a separate sheet of paper.

1. What is first aid? (Lesson 1)

2. What are the basic steps of first aid in the order they are to be performed? (Lesson 1)

3. What are the ABCs of first aid? (Lesson 1)

4. What are the steps in rescue breathing for an adult? (Lesson 1)

5. What is the first step in treating someone who has swallowed a poison? (Lesson 1)

6. Explain how to administer back blows to a choking infant. (Lesson 2)

7. Why are the carotid arteries the best pressure points on the body to use to take a pulse? (Lesson 2)

8. What should you apply to a sprain or bruise—heat or cold? Explain your answer. (Lesson 3)

9. What is the first-aid procedure for first-degree burns? (Lesson 3)

10. How do you help someone who faints? (Lesson 3)

Thinking Critically

Using complete sentences, answer the following questions on a separate sheet of paper.

1. **Explain** How would you control bleeding if applying direct pressure to the wound does not stop it? (Lesson 1)

2. **Describe** How can you identify a shock victim? (Lesson 1)

3. **Deduce** Why do you think it is important to tell a medical team the kind of poison that a victim has swallowed? (Lesson 1)

4. **Organize** Renumber the steps for the procedure to help a choking victim. (1) Grasp your fist with your other hand and apply pressure inward and up toward the person's diaphragm. (2) Slide your arms under the person's armpits and wrap your arms around his or her waist. (3) Deliver rapid thrusts toward the diaphragm. (4) Stand behind the victim. (Lesson 2)

5. **Differentiate** How can you tell the difference between first-, second-, and third-degree burns? (Lesson 3)

6. **Hypothesize** Natasha was stung by a hornet. Now she is turning pale, sweating, and feeling faint. What kind of first aid does she need? (Lesson 3)

Your Action Plan

You can make an action plan to improve your reaction to emergencies. First, you need to set a goal. Look back through your private journal entries for this chapter. What do they tell you about first-aid techniques you need to learn or practice?

Once you have set a long-term goal, write it down. For instance, learning the first-aid procedures for broken bones, sprains, and bruises might be a realistic goal for you.

Next, think of a series of short-term goals that will help you achieve your long-term goal. Write these down. Then plan a schedule for accomplishing each short-term goal. Check your schedule periodically to keep yourself on track. When you reach your long-term goal, reward yourself and celebrate your achievement.

Building Your Portfolio

1. Cut out articles from newspapers that describe emergency situations. Highlight any first-aid techniques described. Then identify the emergencies that you feel you could have helped with had you been a passerby. Explain how you might have helped in each situation. Put the newspaper articles and your explanations in your portfolio.

2. You have read about the universal sign of choking. Make up your own universal signs for emergencies such as an insect sting, a poisoning, and burns. Write a caption next to each illustration explaining the emergency it shows. Add your work to your portfolio.

In Your Home and Community

1. Along with your parents, write a first-aid manual for emergencies that might occur at home. Be sure the first-aid steps are clear, concise, and accurate. Try to include illustrations that help explain the procedures.

2. Volunteer to help with a community blood drive. You could encourage people to donate, spread the word about the time and place of the blood drive, or serve juice and cookies to people after they have donated blood.

Chapter 18
The Environment and Your Health

Student Expectations

After reading this chapter, you should be able to:

❶ State the causes of different kinds of environmental pollution.

❷ Explain the importance of clean air and water.

❸ Explain how conserving energy helps the environment.

❹ Discuss the importance of finding safe ways to dispose of wastes.

oday is a very special day for me. My mother is going to take me fishing down at Beaver Lake. Mom says that when she was my age, there were no fish in the lake. People had been poisoning the water without knowing it. They used fertilizers and pesticides, which ran off into the lake. In addition, waste water from a car wash—carrying salt, wax, and detergent—drained directly into the lake. Over time, harmful materials built up in the water.

Each year, fewer and fewer fish were able to survive. Finally, there weren't any left.

Then people got to work, and things started to get better. Some local citizens realized what was happening and took steps to correct it. The car wash was hooked up to the local sewer system, and the use of fertilizer and pesticides on the land around the lake was strictly regulated. Every year, the lake water got cleaner. Finally, a local fish and game association stocked the lake with fish. Now Mom and I can look forward to a day of fishing on the lake.

in your journal

The lake in the account on this page is an important part of the environment. So, too, are the people and the fish. Start your private journal entries on health and your environment by answering these questions:

▶ How would you describe the living and nonliving parts of your environment?

▶ How do you interact with these parts of your environment?

When you reach the end of the chapter you will use your journal entries to make an action plan.

Earth As a System

This lesson will help you find answers to questions that teens often ask about their environment, its condition, and how their actions can affect it. For example:

▶ **What is the environment made of?**

▶ **Why is a healthy environment important to me?**

▶ **What is pollution?**

Words to Know

environment
ecosystem
groundwater
toxic
pollution

 in your journal

List the living and nonliving factors of your classroom ecosystem. Describe how you interact with each.

Enjoying outdoor activities in a clean, unpolluted environment is one of the great pleasures of life.

Health and Your Environment

In Chapter 1, the word *environment* was defined as the sum total of your surroundings. There, the focus was on your friends, your family, and your community. This chapter uses **environment** in a broader sense to refer to *all the living and nonliving elements around you.* Your environment includes the birds that fly overhead, the trees that grow along the street, the air you breathe, the water you drink, and the other people who live on this planet.

You interact with your environment in many ways. You depend upon it for the air, water, and food you need to live. You affect the environment when you plant flower seeds, cut down a tree, feed the birds, or use products that harm plants, animals, water, or air.

All life forms affect the environment, but the actions people take often have far-reaching effects. For example, for many years a chemical called DDT was used to kill insects that were considered harmful to crops. Unfortunately, DDT also killed many birds, fish, and animals. DDT is now outlawed. Understanding the effects our actions may have is an important step in protecting the environment and keeping it healthy. You should pay attention to the environment because your health depends on it.

Interdependence in the Environment

Different parts of the environment interact within an ecosystem. An **ecosystem** (EE·koh·sis·tuhm) is *all the living and nonliving elements in an area and the way they relate to each other.* Ecosystems can be just about any size, from a drop of water to a huge forest. In fact, the whole earth is a vast ecosystem. Each ecosystem includes everything needed for the survival of the plants and animals in it. **Figure 18.1** shows the parts of an ecosystem.

Science Connection

Climate and Environment ACTIVITY!

An area's climate affects its environment. Find out the climate in your area and how that affects your area's environment.

Figure 18.1
Elements of an Ecosystem

The living elements of an ecosystem can be divided into producers, consumers, and decomposers.

A Producers—make new resources
Plants use air, water, soil, and sunlight to produce food that is eaten by animals. They also produce oxygen, which animals need.

B Consumers—use up resources
People, animals, fish, and insects eat plants and other animals. People also use plants (trees, cotton), animals (leather, wool), and nonliving elements (iron, oil) to produce shelter, clothing, and energy.

C Nonliving Elements
Air, water, soil, and sunlight are needed by the living elements in ecosystems.

D Decomposers— break down plants and animals
Bacteria and fungi break down waste matter and dead plants and animals into materials that can be used by plants.

The health of an ecosystem depends on the well-being of its parts. If something damages one part of the ecosystem, all the other parts will be affected.

Air

Air is one of the nonliving elements in your environment. Almost all life forms need air to survive. You certainly do. When you breathe, you interact with the air around you. Your body removes oxygen from the air and releases carbon dioxide. Your body uses the oxygen to help produce energy. Plants use the carbon dioxide in air to help produce food, which you also need to live.

Water

Water is another important nonliving element in your environment. Like air, water is essential to all living things. Many plants and animals live in the lakes, rivers, and oceans of the world. They get the nutrients they need to survive from the water. These plants and animals in turn provide food for people.

About 70 percent of the earth's surface is covered by water. Most of this is the salty water of the oceans, but many plants and animals need clean, fresh water to survive. Streams, rivers, and lakes are the main sources of fresh water at the earth's surface. However, **groundwater,** which is *water below the earth's surface,* is a major source of fresh water in many areas.

The crops farmers grow to feed us are producers that need soil, air, water, and sun.

Soil

The solid part of the earth you live on—the soil—is a third nonliving element in your environment. Soil is the loose material on the earth's surface in which plants can grow. The plants get the nutrients and water they need from the soil. These nutrients must be replaced over a period of time by decaying plant and animal matter or the soil will wear out. Minerals in the soil, such as salt, phosphorus, and iron, have many uses.

LIFE SKILLS

Consumer Be Aware

*Y*our health depends on the health of your environment. For this reason it is important that you do your part to keep the environment healthy. When you go shopping, use the following guidelines to help you become an environmentally conscious consumer.

▶ **Containers.** Many items you buy are in containers you will throw away, so avoid wasteful packaging. Whenever possible, choose products packaged in materials that break down easily, such as paper and cardboard.

▶ **Labels.** Read all labels carefully. Many common household products, such as oven cleaners and

paint thinners, contain toxic substances. **Toxic** substances are *harmful or poisonous to humans or to plant and animal life.* If you must use a toxic material, follow label directions carefully for proper application and safe disposal of leftover material.

▶ **Recycling.** Select products made of materials that can be collected and used again in some way. Many materials, such as glass, aluminum, and some plastics, can be processed for reuse in other products. This saves energy and reduces the amount of solid waste being added to the environment.

Environmental Problems

Some actions that people take have a harmful effect on the environment and upset the balance of ecosystems.

■ **Pollution.** *Dirty or harmful substances in the environment,* called **pollution** (puh·LOO·shuhn), may affect the air, water, or soil. Most pollution is caused by burning fuels and disposing of waste materials.

■ **Demand for food.** Many activities carried on to increase the food supply harm the environment. Chemical fertilizers used on crops pollute the water supply. Cutting down forests for more farmland leads to soil being blown or washed away.

■ **Too many people.** The environment is also harmed by too many people living in an area. More people make more pollution and strain food and water resources. The world's population almost doubled between 1900 and 1960, and is expected to double again by the year 2000 (see **Figure 18.2**).

■ **Waste disposal.** What to do with solid wastes, or garbage, becomes more of a problem every year, especially in developed countries like the United States. As populations grow, they produce even more solid wastes.

Figure 18.2
Growth of World Population

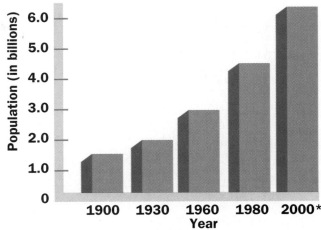

*Estimate
Source: *Statistical Abstract of the U.S., Encyclopedia Americana 1993*, Population Reference Bureau

---

Review

Lesson 1

Using complete sentences, answer the following questions on a separate sheet of paper.

Reviewing Terms and Facts

1. **Vocabulary**   Define *environment* and *ecosystem* and explain how they are related.

2. **Give Examples**   Name some steps you might take to reduce the amount of material you personally throw away.

Thinking Critically

3. **Analyze**   What is meant by the "health" of the nonliving elements in your environment?

4. **Synthesize**   Explain why efforts to increase the food supply often result in environmental problems.

Applying Health Concepts

5. **Consumer Health**   Read the labels on the cleaning products in your home. List the uses of each product and whether they contain harmful or toxic substances. Investigate substitutes for any products that are harmful. With classmates, make a poster that explains how to use these products safely and suggests replacements for unsafe products.

Teen HEALTH DIGEST

Teens Making a Difference

Operation Cleanup

Every day, students on their way to middle school had to pass a vacant lot choked with weeds and strewn with litter. One day in a social studies class, Julie asked her teacher why the lot was allowed to remain in such a run-down condition. Mrs. Warren's reply was, "Why don't we do something about it?" Thus began a class project called Operation Cleanup.

Julie, Saki, and Anita were chosen to go to city hall. There they learned that the city owned the lot, but did not have the money to maintain it. The class received permission to take responsibility for the lot. They drew up a plan to turn the lot into a small park and started to work. The city agreed to rototill the soil and provide shrubs and trees. Local businesses donated tools and materials. Over the next several weeks, the students cleaned up and worked on the lot. Today, the vacant lot is the pride of the community.

Buy Healthy!

At one time, "buying healthy" simply meant buying foods that were good for you. Smart shoppers checked food package labels for nutritional information, fat content, calories per serving, and added ingredients. To buy healthy today, you have to do a lot more. You have to shop with the health of the environment in mind as well. This means you need to:

- Make out a shopping list so you can buy only what you need and avoid waste.
- Bring your own shopping bags with you.
- Look for packaging that can be recycled or is made of recycled materials.
- Choose cleaning materials that are safe for the environment.
- If you go to fast-food restaurants, choose establishments that use paper or cardboard containers rather than plastic or plastic foam.

Your actions affect the health of the environment, your own health, and the health of others.

People at Work

Pioneers of Environmental Studies

Long before the environment was a popular topic, Joan and Hy Rosner recognized its importance. In 1968, as active members of the New York City education system, the Rosners conducted their first ecology workshop for teachers and students. These workshops offered people the chance to experience nature and to learn about environmental issues and concerns.

Today the Rosners are busy promoting environmental studies in the schools. They have developed environmental resource books that are used in schools around the country. In recognition of their tireless work and invaluable contributions, the Rosners were elected to the New Mexico Senior Hall of Fame in 1987.

Myths and Realities

No Free Rides

Nuclear energy was once considered to be the answer to the world's energy problems. Shortly after World War II, the advanced technology that produced the atomic bomb was directed toward peaceful purposes. Atomic energy had many advantages. It was much cleaner than the energy from burning fossil fuels. In addition, small amounts of atomic "fuel" could produce tremendous amounts of energy.

Unfortunately, the early expectations were too good to be true. First, building safe nuclear reactors proved to be very difficult and expensive. Second, many people came to feel that the potential dangers presented by a nuclear accident were too great. Finally, the problem of what to do with the poisonous radioactive wastes is almost impossible to solve. Thus, while nuclear energy is widely used, it has not lived up to its early promise.

Sports
and
Recreation

Sound Off!

Lake Hopatcong is the largest lake in the state of New Jersey. On a hot summer day, you will find hundreds of people at the lake, enjoying swimming, fishing, boating, and jet skiing. Over the years, New Jerseyans have been concerned about water pollution. Regular testing and treatment has kept the water safe for recreational use. However, a new issue has residents concerned—noise pollution. During peak periods of the year, people take to their power boats and jet skis in such great numbers that those on the shore cannot hear their radios or talk on the telephone.

Residents and local officials have held meetings to find ways to deal with this problem. One possible solution is stricter enforcement of laws requiring mufflers on the engines of boats. In the end, however, the best solution will probably be to educate people about the harmful effects of noise pollution.

Clean Air and Clean Water

This lesson will help you find answers to questions that teens often ask about the quality of the air and water and how their activities can affect that quality. For example:

► How clean is the air I breathe?

► Where does my drinking water come from and how clean is it?

► How can pollution affect my health?

Words to Know

fossil fuels
ozone
particulates
pesticides
acid rain
smog
greenhouse effect
sewage
biodegradable

The Air You Breathe

Air is a mixture of many different invisible gases. As you can see in **Figure 18.3**, nitrogen and oxygen are the main ingredients of dry air. Small quantities of carbon dioxide, argon, and other gases are also present. In addition, the air near the earth's surface always contains some water vapor.

When you breathe, your body interacts with the air in your environment. You breathe so that your body can get the oxygen it needs to function properly. The rest of the gases in clean air have little or no effect on your body.

Q & A

Natural Pollution

Q: Is all pollution caused by human activities?

A: No. Natural events, such as forest fires and volcanoes, can produce materials that make the environment dirty. At certain times of the year, pollen from trees and flowers can make the air unhealthy for some people to breathe.

Figure 18.3
Composition of the Air

You take in oxygen from the air when you breathe, and exhale carbon dioxide. Carbon dioxide is also released by the burning of oil, gas, and other fuels. Scientists are concerned that the level of carbon dioxide in the atmosphere is increasing. This could upset the balance of gases in the atmosphere and lead to climate changes.

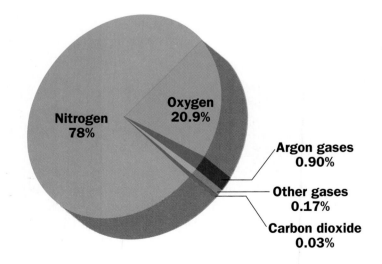

Nitrogen 78%

Oxygen 20.9%

Argon gases 0.90%

Other gases 0.17%

Carbon dioxide 0.03%

Unfortunately, the air you breathe is not completely clean. It contains all kinds of impurities (im·PYOOR·uh·tees)—things that make the air dirty. Every time you inhale, you bring these impurities into your body. They may include dust, pollen, smoke, chemical particles, and harmful gases. None of these substances are good for you. Some can be very harmful to your health.

Sources of Air Pollution

Air pollution consists of gases and particles. The major sources of air pollution are described below.

- **Burning fossil fuels.** The *oil, coal, and natural gas burned to provide energy* are called **fossil** (FAH·suhl) **fuels.** This energy is used to produce electricity, heat buildings, and run motor vehicles. However, burning these fuels releases toxic gases, such as carbon monoxide and sulfur dioxide. Another gas that comes from fossil fuels is **ozone** (OH·zohn), *a form of oxygen* that is harmful when produced by motor vehicle and industrial pollution. Burning oil or coal can also produce **particulates** (par·TIK·yuh·lits), *tiny particles that can remain in the air for a long time.* Many particulates are bits of soot or ash. Some particulates, such as lead or mercury, are poisonous.

- **Other sources of smoke.** Most kinds of fires produce smoke containing gases and particulates. Bonfires or burning leaves or trash contribute in a small way to pollution.

- **Chemicals.** Some common products found around the house contain chemicals that pollute the air. For example, many **pesticides** (PES·tuh·sydz), which are *products used to kill insects and other pests,* contain harmful chemicals. CFCs (chlorofluorocarbons), the cooling agents used in air conditioners and refrigerators, damage a layer of the atmosphere (the ozone layer) that protects the earth from dangerous solar radiation. CFCs are being phased out in an effort to stop this damage.

in your journal

Make a list of all your activities that use energy produced by fossil fuels. Beside each activity, tell which fossil fuel is used and if its use contributes to air pollution.

Increasing the use of electric cars will reduce air pollution from automobile exhaust fumes. California law requires that by the year 2001, 5 percent of the cars sold in the state must be electric or some other form of vehicle that does not contribute to air pollution.

Figure 18.4
How Acid Rain Occurs

When coal, oil, and other fossil fuels are burned, they produce sulfur dioxide and nitrogen oxides. These gases form sulphate and nitrate particles that mix with water vapor and form weak acids. The acids fall to the earth as **acid rain,** which is *rain (or snow) that is more acidic than normal.*

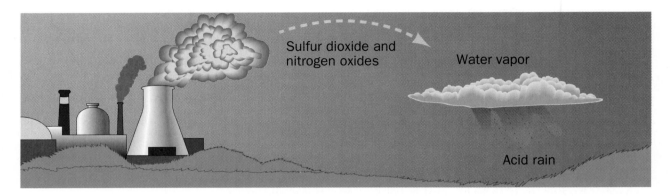

Sulfur dioxide and nitrogen oxides

Water vapor

Acid rain

Effects of Air Pollution

Air pollution has many harmful effects on the environment. Some of the effects are described in the following paragraphs.

■ **Acid rain.** Gases from burning fossil fuels may combine with moisture in the air to form acid rain (see **Figure 18.4**). Over time, acid rain can damage forests and destroy fish and plant life.

■ **Smog.** In cities with heavy traffic, a special kind of **smog** often develops. It is a *yellow-brown haze that forms when sunlight reacts with impurities in car exhaust.* The smog screens out sunlight, preventing it from reaching the earth.

■ **Greenhouse effect.** The burning of fossil fuels produces carbon dioxide, and this gas acts like a blanket holding heat near the earth's surface. *The trapping of heat by carbon dioxide and other gases in the air* is known as the **greenhouse effect.** Increased levels of carbon dioxide in the air may lead to a global warming, a rise in the earth's temperatures. This in turn could affect the water level of oceans and change weather patterns.

■ **Ozone destruction.** Although toxic near the earth's surface, ozone high in the atmosphere forms a layer that shields living elements on earth from the sun's harmful ultraviolet (UV) radiation. However, certain kinds of air pollution, especially from CFCs, may be destroying some of the ozone layer. This thinning of the ozone layer allows excessive UV radiation to reach the earth's surface, which can harm humans.

■ **Health problems.** Air pollution can cause a variety of health problems, including shortness of breath, sneezing, and itchy eyes. Air pollution can cause serious problems for people with such breathing disorders as asthma (AZ·muh) and emphysema (em·fuh·SEE·muh). (See Chapters 12 and 13 for more information on breathing disorders.)

Water: A Vital Resource

Like you, all plants and animals need fresh water, a resource that is in limited supply. In fact, one out of every five people in the world do not have an adequate amount of clean, fresh water. Even though the supply of this precious resource is limited, people still use water carelessly.

Water Pollution

The earth's water is polluted by various kinds of wastes, chemicals, and other substances. **Sewage** is *water containing wastes that are washed down people's drains.* Sewage includes food, human wastes, detergents, and other products. Harmful chemicals are another major cause of water pollution. Some enter the water from factories. Pesticides and chemical fertilizers can wash out of farms to pollute water.

Much human illness and disease is caused by harmful substances in water. Typhoid (TY·foyd) fever and cholera (KAH·luh·ruh) are caused by bacteria in untreated sewage. Hepatitis (he·puh·TY·tuhs), a disease of the liver, can be caused by eating shellfish taken from polluted water. Drinking water that contains lead or mercury can result in serious damage to the brain, liver, and kidneys.

HEALTH LAB
The Effect of Water Pollutants

Introduction: Detergents, fertilizers, and garbage in rivers and lakes can affect the health of the water. They may, for example, cause the amount of algae in the water to change. Algae (AL·jee), the green scum you see in ponds and other bodies of fresh water, are very simple plants that use sunlight to make their own food. Some forms of pollution can cause algae to multiply rapidly and form a thick layer that blocks the sunlight. Deprived of light, the algae below the surface die and decay, consuming large amounts of oxygen in the water. Deprived of oxygen, fish and other forms of life in the water also die.

Objective: To find out what effect detergents and garbage have on algae.

Materials and Method: You will need tap water that has been left to stand uncovered for three days; fresh water from a pond or aquarium with some algae; liquid detergent; some potato or carrot scraps; three clean glass jars of the same size with lids; and labels.

Label the jars D (detergent), G (garbage), and N (no additions). Fill each one halfway with the tap water. Add enough pond water to bring the level to three-fourths. Then add a tablespoon of detergent to Jar D and some vegetable scraps to Jar G. Do not add anything to Jar N. Put the jars on a windowsill for two weeks.

Observation and Analysis: Observe the jars every other day. Compare and note the color of the water in the three jars. In which jar was there the greatest increase of algae? In which jar was there the least increase of algae?

Working for Cleaner Air and Water

Anything you do that uses energy produced by burning fossil fuels contributes to air pollution. This includes such activities as using electric appliances, driving a car, and running a power lawn mower. Here are some ways you can help keep the air cleaner.

- Whenever practical, walk or ride a bicycle rather than having someone drive you in a car.

- Use public transportation. Buses, trains, and subways reduce air pollution by transporting many people at one time.

- Avoid outdoor burning of trash, leaves, and brush.

- Don't smoke! This advice is good for your health and good for the environment.

- Save electricity. Turn off lights and appliances when not in use. Don't overheat or overcool your house.

Here are some ways you can help keep water cleaner.

- Use detergents that are **biodegradable.** This means that they can be *easily broken down in the environment.*

- Discard all waste materials properly. Do not dump anything in the water or on the ground where it might get into groundwater.

Using your own power rather than riding in a car or bus helps you and the environment.

Lesson 2 Review

Using complete sentences, answer the following questions on a separate sheet of paper.

Reviewing Terms and Facts

1. **Vocabulary** What is the *greenhouse effect?*

2. **List** Name two sources of both air and water pollution.

Thinking Critically

3. **Synthesize** Explain how fossil fuels are connected to acid rain.

4. **Compare and Contrast** How can the same gas, ozone, be both harmful and necessary to people?

5. **Apply** You and three of your friends are going to meet at the mall. Each of you is going to have someone drive you to the mall in a car. What other arrangements could you and your friends make to reduce air pollution?

Applying Health Concepts

6. **Health of Others** Make a list of actions you or members of your family take that contribute to air or water pollution. Then draw up a second list of ways you could cut down on this pollution.

7. **Consumer Health** Find out the source of the fresh water used in your community. Visit the local water department to learn what measures are used to make sure that your water supply is kept clean. Write a brief report to present to your class.

8. **Health of Others** If you are concerned about your environment, you can do something about it. Write to a local political figure expressing your concerns and what you think should be done about them. Your efforts will be even more effective if you get a number of your friends and classmates to each send his or her own letter.

Reduce, Reuse, Recycle

This lesson will help you find answers to questions that teens often ask about conserving natural resources. For example:

▶ **What kinds of materials can be recycled?**

▶ **How does recycling help to save natural resources?**

▶ **What can I do to help conserve energy?**

Conservation

You use natural resources every day. A natural resource is any material from the earth that can be used: air, water, trees from the forest, and the fish from the sea.

Many natural materials are **nonrenewable resources,** which are *substances that cannot be replaced once they are used.* Fossil fuels are one example. Once a barrel of oil is burned, it is gone forever. **Figure 18.5** explains how energy is used in one manufacturing process. It's important that people learn to use nonrenewable resources wisely. **Conservation** is *the saving of resources.* The best way to conserve a resource is to use less of it. There are many ways to save energy at home.

■ Turn off lights and appliances when they are not being used.

■ In winter, put on a sweater instead of turning up the heat.

■ Repair all leaking faucets, especially hot-water faucets.

■ Seal air leaks around any doors and windows in your home to prevent heat from escaping.

Figure 18.5
Energy Used in Making an Aluminum Can

The diagram shows the steps needed to make an aluminum can. The energy is provided by fossil fuels.

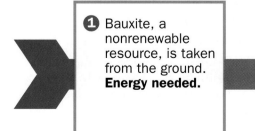

1 Bauxite, a nonrenewable resource, is taken from the ground. **Energy needed.**

2 This ore is processed to make a substance called alumina, which is then made into aluminum. **Energy needed.**

3 Sheets of aluminum are forced into molds of the desired shape to form aluminum cans. **Energy needed.**

Words to Know

nonrenewable
    resource
conservation
recycled
precycling

Q & A **?**

A Self-Renewing Resource

Q: Is water a nonrenewable resource?

A: No. The earth's supply of water is constantly being renewed, or replenished, through the water cycle. However, conservation of fresh water is necessary because it is always in limited supply.

Recycling

Imagine yourself in the school cafeteria. You have just finished lunch and are emptying your tray. You place a glass juice bottle in one bin and a foil sandwich wrapper in another. The banana peel goes into a third bin. In short, you have separated your trash into items to be thrown away and items that can be **recycled.** This means that they can be *changed in some way and used again.*

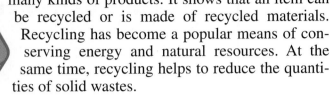

The symbol shown here is fast becoming a familiar sight on many kinds of products. It shows that an item can be recycled or is made of recycled materials. Recycling has become a popular means of conserving energy and natural resources. At the same time, recycling helps to reduce the quantities of solid wastes.

How does recycling help conserve energy and natural resources? As you saw in **Figure 18.5** on page 549, energy is needed to mine the ore that is used to make aluminum, to process the ore, and to manufacture the cans. When aluminum cans are recycled, they are changed back into sheets or blocks of aluminum. These sheets can then be used to make new cans or other aluminum products. No new ore is taken from the ground and much less energy is needed.

Not everything can be recycled. However, many of the items that people normally throw away can be recycled. The most common materials collected for recycling today are aluminum, glass, plastic, yard waste, and paper (see **Figure 18.6**).

MAKING HEALTHY DECISIONS
Deciding on Priorities

*L*arry belongs to a community environmental group. He believes that the group's work is very important and devotes a lot of time and energy to it. Because of his dedication, he has recently been appointed a junior member of the town's environmental commission.

The environmental group has been working on plans for a Highway Beautification Day on Saturday. A section of highway will be closed for the day, and volunteers will be cleaning up litter and planting thousands of spring bulbs, wildflower seeds, and grass seed. The day will end with a picnic.

Larry has been asked to bring his family and he would really like them to come. However, he knows that they have already planned an outing to the beach that day with some cousins. When he mentioned the problem to his father, his father suggested that Larry spend the day on his own and get a ride home with the group leader.

Larry doesn't know what to do. He loves the beach but feels he should be involved in the highway project. Should he participate in the project and miss the trip to the beach? Should he try to persuade his father and sister that the environmental project is more important than going to the beach that particular day? He uses the step-by-step decision-making process.

❶ **State the situation**
❷ **List the options**

Figure 18.6
What We Throw Away and Recycle

Material	What We Throw Away	Amount Recovered Through Recycling
Aluminum	2.7	1.0
Glass	13.2	2.6
Plastics	16.2	0.4
Yard Waste	35.0	4.2
Paper	73.3	20.9

Millions of Tons
10 20 30 40 50 60 70 80 90 100

Precycling

Some of the bother involved in recycling can be avoided by being a wise shopper and by **precycling,** *reducing waste before it occurs.* Here are some basic guidelines for precycling.

- Buy products in packages that can be reused or recycled.
- Buy products in glass, metal, or paper containers.
- Look for products in refillable containers.
- Bring a cloth bag to carry your purchases.

③ **Weigh the possible outcomes**
④ **Consider your values**
⑤ **Make a decision and act**
⑥ **Evaluate the decision**

Follow-up Activities

1. Apply the six steps of the decision-making process to Larry's situation.

2. With a partner, role-play a scene in which Larry tries to convince his family to participate in the Highway Beautification Day with him.

3. Now role-play a scene in which Larry explains to his environmental group that he will not be joining them. Think of suggestions he can make for finding other volunteers for the project.

Learning to repair items—large and small—is an important step in cutting down waste and protecting the environment.

in your journal

Review how your own habits and lifestyle affect the environment. Include your use of resources (such as water and energy), the items you throw out, and your efforts to reuse and recycle. Write a paragraph describing your habits and their effect on the environment.

Other Actions to Take

There are more things you can do to protect the environment.

■ **Reuse.** When you buy a product, think about ways it or its container can be reused. Store such items for use later.

■ **Repair.** If an item breaks or wears out, try to fix it instead of throwing it away.

■ **Pass it on.** Possessions that you don't want or can't use anymore can be donated to charitable groups that will give them to people who can use them.

■ **Be informed.** Get more information about environmental issues.

Lesson 3 Review

Using complete sentences, answer the following questions on a separate sheet of paper.

Reviewing Terms and Facts

1. **Name** What is a natural resource? Give three examples of natural resources that you use.

2. **Vocabulary** Give an example of a nonrenewable resource.

3. **List** Name four ways that you can conserve energy around your home.

4. **Identify** Which item that we throw away makes up the largest portion of our trash?

Thinking Critically

5. **Compare** What is the difference between recycling and precycling? Give an example of each.

6. **Apply** You have an old bicycle that you don't ride anymore. Instead of throwing it away, what can you do with it that will help the environment?

Applying Health Concepts

7. **Health of Others** Set up a recycling center in your home. Use cartons or containers to organize and collect recyclable materials.

Handling Environmental Hazards

This lesson will help you find answers to questions teens often ask about solid wastes and hazardous materials in their environment. For example:

▶ **What happens to the trash collected at my house?**

▶ **What kinds of waste materials can cause illness?**

▶ **What is radon?**

Solid Waste: The Leftovers

Every year, Americans throw out about 200 million tons of trash. That's enough trash to fill 5 million large truck trailers! This trash is known as solid waste.

Sometimes people just throw their trash anywhere. All across the country, paper bags, plastic wrappers, newspapers, cans, and bottles can be found cluttering roadsides and public parks. This waste is called litter. Litter is a type of environmental pollution. While it may not pose a health threat, it is wasteful and unpleasant to look at, and cleaning it up can be expensive.

Disposing of Solid Waste

Most solid waste is produced by businesses and households. Trucks haul it off to a **landfill,** a *place where wastes are dumped and buried.* At one time, everything and anything could be dumped in a landfill. As a result, these sites were dirty and unhealthy. Because some landfills had harmful waste, they were even dangerous.

Today, most landfills are strictly regulated, and only certain wastes can be dumped in them. The wastes are spread in layers and covered with layers of soil. However, no matter how hard landfill operators may try, landfills are unpleasant and unsightly places.

Words to Know

landfill
hazardous waste
nuclear waste
radon

Math Connection

Getting Rid of Trash ACTIVITY!

About 17 percent of the solid waste produced in the United States is recycled and reused. About 16 percent is burned. Most of the rest goes to landfills. Calculate the percentage of solid waste that goes into landfills.

Americans throw out about 200 million tons of trash a year. That comes to about 4.3 pounds of garbage per person per day.

553

Batters

Ordinary batteries—used for flashlights, toys, and portable radios and tape players—make up a sizeable portion of the hazardous household wastes in this country. Many types of batteries contain harmful chemicals that leak out and get into the soil and water supplies.

Another problem with landfills is that they take up tremendous amounts of space. As the human population increases, more land is needed for homes, schools, shops, and businesses. At the same time, more solid waste is produced. In some areas the problem is so great that wastes are being transported hundreds of miles to places far away that still have landfill space available.

One possible way to reduce the amount of solid waste dumped in landfills is to burn as much of our trash as possible. The energy produced by burning wastes in special furnaces, called *incinerators* (in·SIN·uh·ray·terz), can be used to heat homes or generate electricity. This cuts down on the use of fossil fuels.

There are disadvantages to burning wastes. Incinerators are very expensive to build and operate, and only certain waste materials can be burned safely. Many people argue that the smoke and ashes produced by burning solid waste are harmful to the environment. These people believe that recycling and reusing materials is a better and safer method of dealing with the problem of solid waste.

Personal Inventory

DO YOU PROTECT YOUR ENVIRONMENT?

You play an important role in the environment. For this reason, it is important for you to know how the products you use and the actions you take affect your environment. Many of the products found in your home are hazardous or contain hazardous materials. Some of these products can be found on the list below.

batteries	nail polish remover
bleach	oven cleaner
drain cleaner	paint, paint thinner
insecticides	rubber cement
motor oil, antifreeze	spot remover

Look over the list and pick out the items that you use. Write these down on a sheet of paper. Add to your list any other items you use that you think may be hazardous. Then answer the following questions for each item on your list.

1. What do you use it for?

2. Do you read the directions for the use of these products and follow those directions carefully?

3. Why or how is it hazardous?

4. What do you do with the remains of the product when you have finished with it?

When you have answered the questions, think about what you can do to help protect the environment from the hazards of these products.

Hazardous Wastes

Over the past 50 years or so, advances in science and technology have led to many changes. New industries have developed and thousands of new products have been introduced. These changes have led to a new problem—*waste products that may cause illness.* Such wastes are called **hazardous** (HAZ·er·duhs) **wastes.**

Hazardous wastes are dangerous in a number of different ways. Some are explosive. Some easily catch fire and can produce poisonous smoke. Some, called *toxic wastes,* are poisonous. When hazardous wastes enter and pollute the soil, water, or air, they can cause injury, illness, and even death (see **Figure 18.7**).

Hazardous wastes cannot be disposed of like other wastes. They need special handling. The government has a strict set of rules about how to get rid of hazardous wastes. The Environmental Protection Agency (EPA) has the job of enforcing the rules.

Many places in this country have been identified as toxic waste sites where hazardous wastes were dumped in the past. Millions of dollars are being spent to clean up these sites.

Chemicals

As the number of types of industries has grown over the years, the use of different kinds of chemicals has increased dramatically. Chemicals are used in the manufacture of hundreds of different products and materials. Many products, such as medicines, paints, fertilizers, and pesticides, can be dangerous if they are not used, stored, and disposed of properly.

Industrial by-products are chemicals left over from the manufacturing process. Careless disposal of these by-products in the past has produced many of the world's most dangerous toxic waste sites.

in your journal

Make a list of all the products in your house that may be hazardous or contain hazardous chemicals. Tell how each is used, stored, and disposed of. Make note of any unsafe practices and tell how those practices can be changed and made safer.

Figure 18.7
The Effects of Hazardous Wastes

Substance	Uses	Effects
Asbestos	Insulation, filler	Scars lungs, causes cancer
Benzene	Fabrics, detergents	May cause cancer
Carbon tetrachloride	Refrigeration, solvents	Can cause death or illness if inhaled
DDT	Pesticides	Kills fish, birds; toxic to humans
Lead	Paints, batteries	Causes brain, liver, kidney damage
PCBs	Plastics	Birth defects, liver damage, cancer
Vinyl chloride	Plastics	Causes cancer

Science Connection

Nuclear Energy

Nuclear energy is so named because the energy comes from the nuclei of radioactive elements. When the nucleus of an atom breaks down, energy is released in the form of radiation.

Did You Know?

Industrial Wastes

In one year, industries release more than 5 billion pounds of toxic chemicals into the environment. About half of this amount is released into the air.

Love Canal

Love Canal, a community in New York State, is a good example of the dangers of improper disposal of hazardous wastes. Love Canal was built on the site of an old chemical dump. After some years, it was noticed that many cases of birth defects, nervous disorders, and cancer occurred in the community. It was then discovered that buried chemicals had leaked from their containers and poisoned the soil and the water supplies. Nearly a thousand families had to be relocated. The site was closed to residents for more than ten years while it was being cleaned up.

Nuclear Wastes

Some industries use materials that are radioactive. These materials give off radiation, a form of energy that can be harmful to living things. Radiation has been linked to cancer in humans. Radioactive materials are used as fuel in atomic power plants. They are also used in weapons research and production and in medical research and treatment. The *harmful by-products of industries that use radioactive materials* are called **nuclear** (NOO·klee·er) **wastes.**

Nuclear wastes continue to give off radiation for hundreds or thousands of years. Therefore, the safe disposal of these wastes presents a very difficult problem. Scientists are working on it but still have not come up with a satisfactory solution.

Radon

In recent years, scientists have discovered a natural source of radioactive pollution. **Radon** (RAY·dahn) is *a colorless, odorless, radioactive gas.* It forms when radium (RAY·dee·uhm) breaks down. Radium is a radioactive element present in some rocks. Radon becomes a problem when it leaks from the ground and collects in the interiors of homes. Long-term exposure to high levels of radon can cause lung cancer.

Checking the radon level in your home is easy and inexpensive to do.

Dealing with Hazardous Wastes

Industry and government must find solutions to the major problems associated with hazardous wastes. Every individual can also help to reduce the problem and protect the environment.

- Use hazardous materials properly. Follow directions carefully when using materials such as pesticides, paint thinners, and oven cleaners.

- Follow the proper procedures in your community for disposal of materials such as motor oil, paints, batteries, and pesticides.

- Whenever possible, buy environmentally safe household chemicals.

- Form community action groups to clean up areas around local rivers and lakes.

- Support groups that work to get environmental laws passed and enforced.

Proper disposal of hazardous waste ensures a healthier environment for us and for future generations.

Review
Lesson 4

Using complete sentences, answer the following questions on a separate sheet of paper.

Reviewing Terms and Facts

1. **Vocabulary**   What is meant by the term *hazardous wastes?*

2. **Recall**   Name two methods of waste disposal and describe how each one works.

3. **Give Examples**   List at least three products that can be hazardous to the environment.

4. **Identify**   Explain what radon is and where it is found.

5. **Outline**   List four steps you can take to reduce pollution from hazardous wastes.

Thinking Critically

6. **Explain**   Why is the disposal of hazardous wastes more of a problem than the disposal of other solid wastes?

7. **Evaluate**   When you go to the store to buy a product for a cleanup job, you are offered two products. Product A is strong and will do the job quickly. However, it gives off dangerous fumes and you need to wear rubber gloves when you use it. Product B is safe to use but costs twice as much and will take longer to do the job. Which product would you use? Explain your reasoning.

Applying Health Concepts

8. **Health of Others**   Check with state or local health agencies to learn if radon gas is a potential problem where you live. Find out how you can check the radon level in your home and what can be done if levels are high.

9. **Health of Others**   Research alternative energy sources, such as solar power and wind power. Report on the advantages and disadvantages of each energy source.

Chapter Summary

► You are an important part of your environment, which includes you and all the living and nonliving elements around you. (Lesson 1)

► Air, water, and soil are the major nonliving elements in your environment. (Lesson 1)

► Pollution is the result of adding harmful substances to the environment. (Lesson 1)

► Your health and the health of all living things depends on having a clean environment. (Lesson 1)

► Burning fossil fuels—oil, natural gas, and coal—is the major cause of air pollution. (Lesson 2)

► Sewage and chemicals are the two main sources of water pollution. Harmful materials added to the land can eventually reach groundwater supplies and make them dirty. (Lesson 2)

► Conservation is one of the most important ways to keep the environment clean and to reduce the use of nonrenewable resources. (Lesson 3)

► Recycling and reusing materials are two important methods of conserving resources and energy. (Lesson 3)

► Most solid wastes are deposited in landfills. Some are burned in incinerators. (Lesson 4)

► Hazardous wastes are made up of materials that may cause illness. Most hazardous wastes are produced by industry. (Lesson 4)

► Hazardous wastes need special methods of disposal because they can't be recycled, placed in regular landfills, or burned. (Lesson 4)

► Many household products are hazardous or contain hazardous chemicals. (Lesson 4)

► Nuclear waste is a hazardous waste that is dangerous because it gives off radiation that causes serious health problems. (Lesson 4)

Using Health Terms

On a separate sheet of paper, write the vocabulary term that best matches each definition given below.

1. All the living and nonliving elements around you (Lesson 1)

2. Harmful or poisonous to people, plants, or animals (Lesson 1)

3. Chemicals that are used to kill insects and other pests (Lesson 2)

4. The trapping of heat by carbon dioxide and other gases in the air (Lesson 2)

5. Able to be broken down easily in the environment (Lesson 2)

6. The saving of resources (Lesson 3)

7. Changing materials in some way so that they can be used again (Lesson 3)

8. A place where wastes are dumped and buried (Lesson 4)

9. A colorless, odorless, radioactive gas (Lesson 4)

Reviewing Main Ideas

Using complete sentences, answer the following questions on a separate sheet of paper.

1. What are the main sources of fresh water on the earth's surface? (Lesson 1)

2. Explain the role of the ozone layer. (Lesson 2)

3. What does sewage include? (Lesson 2)

4. How does recycling help to conserve natural resources? (Lesson 3)

5. What is precycling? (Lesson 3)

6. How are most solid wastes disposed of? (Lesson 4)

7. What are hazardous wastes? (Lesson 4)

8. Why are nuclear wastes so dangerous? (Lesson 4)

Thinking Critically

Using complete sentences, answer the following questions on a separate sheet of paper.

1. **Explain** Rain and snow constantly replace fresh water in the environment, yet fresh water is in limited supply. Explain. (Lesson 1)

2. **Apply** How can conserving energy help to keep the environment clean? (Lesson 2)

3. **Synthesize** Explain how cutting down forests in one part of the world can affect the environment where you live. (Lesson 2)

4. **Analyze** How can using a hand-powered lawn mower instead of a gas-powered mower help to reduce the production of acid rain? (Lesson 2)

5. **Apply** What are some ways that being a smart consumer can help the environment? (Lesson 3)

6. **Synthesize** Describe several ways that the increasing world population affects the environment. (Lesson 4)

7. **Persuade** If you could write one law to protect the environment, what would it be? Explain your answer. (Lesson 4)

Your Action Plan

You are part of the natural environment of living and nonliving things in which you live. Anything that affects any part of this ecosystem affects you and your health. Make an action plan to promote the health of your environment. First, set a goal. Look back through your private journal entries for this chapter. What do they tell you about your awareness of the environment and your interaction with it?

Next, draw up a list of habits and actions that are helpful to the environment. Your list of habits and actions describes your long-term goals. Then think of a series of short-term goals, or steps that you will take to achieve your long-term goals.

As you practice habits that promote environmental health, the habits become almost automatic.

Building Your Portfolio

1. Take some photographs of a park or other open area in your community. Include as many different living and nonliving elements of the environment as you can. Arrange the photographs in a folder. Identify the elements in each and describe how they interact with each other. Add the folder to your portfolio.

2. Interview some older people who have lived in your community for a long time. Ask them to describe the physical changes they have observed over the years—the number of people, buildings, areas with plants and trees, and so on. Tape-record these interviews and add them to your portfolio.

In Your Home and Community

1. Find out about groups in your community that work on environmental issues. Then find out what local laws these groups have supported. Present a report to your class.

2. Call or visit a local factory or power plant. Find out what methods are used there to conserve energy and reduce environmental pollution. Find out the cost of such measures and how these costs are passed on to the consumer. Write a few paragraphs summarizing your findings.

Nutritive Value of Selected Foods

Nutrients in Indicated Quantity

Foods		Food energy (Calories)	Protein (Grams)	Fat (Grams)	Carbohydrate (Grams)	Calcium (Milligrams)	Iron (Milligrams)	Sodium (Milligrams)	Vitamin A value (IU) (International units)	Thiamin (Milligrams)	Riboflavin (Milligrams)	Niacin (Milligrams)	Ascorbic acid (Milligrams)
Dairy Products													
Cheese:													
Cheddar	1 oz	115	7	28	Tr	204	0.2	176	300	0.01	0.11	Tr	0
Cottage, lowfat	1 cup	205	31	4	8	155	0.4	918	160	0.05	0.42	0.3	Tr
Feta	1 oz	75	4	6	1	140	0.2	316	130	0.04	0.24	0.3	0
Mozzarella	1 oz	80	6	6	1	147	0.1	106	220	Tr	0.07	Tr	0
Pasteurized process (American)	1 oz	105	6	9	Tr	174	0.1	406	340	0.01	0.10	Tr	0
Milk:													
Whole	1 cup	150	8	8	11	291	0.1	120	310	0.09	0.40	0.2	2
Lowfat (2%)	1 cup	120	8	5	12	297	0.1	122	500	0.10	0.40	0.2	2
Nonfat (skim)	1 cup	85	8	Tr	12	302	0.1	126	500	0.09	0.34	0.2	2
Chocolate milk (commercial)	1 cup	210	8	8	26	280	0.6	149	300	0.09	0.41	0.3	2
Ice cream, vanilla:													
Regular	1 cup	270	5	14	32	176	0.1	116	540	0.05	0.33	0.1	1
Soft serve (frozen custard)	1 cup	375	7	23	38	236	0.4	153	790	0.08	0.45	0.2	1
Yogurt (made with lowfat milk):													
Fruit-flavored	8 oz	230	10	2	43	345	0.2	133	100	0.08	0.40	0.2	1
Eggs													
Eggs, fried in margarine	1 egg	90	6	7	1	25	0.7	162	390	0.03	0.24	Tr	0
Eggs, boiled	1 egg	75	6	7	1	25	0.7	140	320	0.03	0.22	Tr	0
Fats and Oils													
Butter	1 pat	35	Tr	4	Tr	1	Tr	41	150	Tr	Tr	Tr	0
Margarine	1 tbsp	100	Tr	11	Tr	4	0.0	151	460	Tr	Tr	Tr	Tr
Oils, corn	1 tbsp	125	0	14	0	0	0.0	0	0	0.00	0.00	0.00	0
Salad dressings (commercial)													
French:													
Regular	1 tbsp	85	Tr	9	1	2	Tr	188	Tr	Tr	Tr	Tr	Tr
Low calorie	1 tbsp	25	Tr	2	2	6	Tr	306	Tr	Tr	Tr	Tr	Tr
Mayonnaise:													
Regular	1 tbsp	100	Tr	11	Tr	3	0.1	80	40	0.00	0.00	Tr	0
Salad dressing (home recipe)													
Vinegar and oil	1 tbsp	70	0	8	Tr	0	0.0	Tr	0	0.00	0.00	0.0	0
Fish and Shellfish													
Fish sticks	1 stick	70	6	3	4	11	0.3	53	20	0.03	0.05	0.6	0
Haddock, breaded, fried	3 oz	175	17	9	7	34	1.0	123	70	0.06	0.10	2.9	0
Shrimp, fried	3 oz	200	16	10	11	61	2.0	384	90	0.06	0.09	2.8	0

Nutrients in Indicated Quantity

Foods	Food energy Calories	Protein Grams	Fat Grams	Carbohydrate Grams	Calcium Milligrams	Iron Milligrams	Sodium Milligrams	Vitamin A value (IU) International units	Thiamin Milligrams	Riboflavin Milligrams	Niacin Milligrams	Ascorbic acid Milligrams
Tuna, canned, drained solids:												
Oil pack, chunk light ...... 3 oz	165	24	7	0	7	1.6	303	70	0.04	0.09	10.1	0
Water pack, solid white ...... 3 oz	135	30	1	0	17	0.6	468	110	0.03	0.10	13.4	0
Fruits and Fruit Juices												
Apples, raw unpeeled ...... 1 apple	80	Tr	Tr	21	10	0.2	Tr	70	0.02	0.02	0.1	8
Apple juice ...... 1 cup	115	Tr	Tr	29	17	0.9	7	Tr	0.05	0.04	0.2	2
Applesauce:												
Sweetened ...... 1 cup	195	Tr	Tr	51	10	0.9	8	30	0.03	0.07	0.5	4
Unsweetened ...... 1 cup	105	Tr	Tr	28	7	0.3	5	70	0.03	0.06	0.5	3
Bananas ...... 1 banana	105	1	1	27	7	0.4	1	90	0.05	0.11	0.6	10
Cranberry juice cocktail ...... 1 cup	145	Tr	Tr	38	8	0.4	10	10	0.01	0.04	0.1	108
Grapefruit ...... ½ grapefruit	40	1	Tr	10	14	0.1	Tr	10	0.04	0.02	0.3	41
Grapes, green seedless ...... 10 grapes	35	Tr	Tr	9	6	0.1	1	40	0.05	0.03	0.2	5
Lemonade (from concentrate) ...... 6 oz	80	Tr	Tr	21	2	0.1	1	10	0.01	0.02	0.2	13
Oranges ...... 1 orange	60	1	Tr	15	52	0.1	Tr	270	0.11	0.05	0.4	70
Orange juice (from concentrate) ...... 1 cup	110	2	Tr	27	22	0.2	2	190	0.20	0.04	0.5	97
Peaches:												
Fresh ...... 1 peach	35	1	Tr	10	4	0.1	Tr	470	0.01	0.04	0.9	6
Canned, in syrup ...... 1 cup	190	1	Tr	51	8	0.7	15	850	0.03	0.06	1.6	7
Pears:												
Fresh ...... 1 pear	100	1	1	25	18	0.4	Tr	30	0.03	0.07	0.2	7
Canned, in syrup ...... 1 cup	190	1	Tr	49	13	0.6	13	10	0.03	0.06	0.6	3
Raisins, snack pack ...... 1 cup	40	Tr	Tr	11	7	0.3	2.0	Tr	0.02	0.01	0.10	Tr
Strawberries:												
Raw, whole ...... 1 cup	45	1	1	10	21	0.6	1	40	0.03	0.10	0.3	84
Frozen, sweetened, sliced ...... 1 cup	245	1	Tr	66	28	1.5	8	60	0.04	0.13	1.0	106
Grain Products												
Bagels ...... 1 bagel	200	7	2	38	29	1.8	245	0	0.26	0.20	2.4	0
Biscuits, from mix ...... 1 biscuit	95	2	3	14	58	0.7	262	20	0.12	0.11	0.8	Tr
Breads:												
Pita bread, 6½ in diam ...... 1 pita	165	6	1	33	49	1.4	339	0	0.27	0.12	2.2	0
Rye bread ...... 1 slice	65	2	1	12	20	0.7	175	0	0.10	0.08	0.8	0
White bread ...... 1 slice	65	2	1	12	32	0.7	129	Tr	0.12	0.08	0.9	Tr
Whole-wheat bread ...... 1 slice	70	3	1	13	20	1.0	180	Tr	0.10	0.06	1.1	Tr

Notes: *Tr* indicates presence of nutrients in trace amounts. All fruits and vegetables are fresh unless noted. Vegetables are fresh cooked unless noted.

Nutrients in Indicated Quantity

Foods	Food energy Calories	Protein Grams	Fat Grams	Carbo-hydrate Grams	Calcium Milli-grams	Iron Milli-grams	Sodium Milli-grams	Vitamin A value Interna-tional units	Thiamin Milli-grams	Riboflavin Milli-grams	Niacin Milli-grams	Ascorbic acid Milli-grams
Breakfast cereals:												
Oatmeal ... 1 cup	145	6	2	25	19	1.6	2	40	0.26	0.05	0.3	0
Cornflakes ... 1¼ cups	110	2	Tr	24	1	1.8	351	1,250	0.37	0.43	5.0	15
Crackers, snack-type ... 1 cracker	15	Tr	1	2	3	0.1	30	Tr	0.01	0.01	0.1	0
French toast (home recipe) ... 1 slice	155	6	7	17	72	1.3	257	110	0.12	0.16	1.0	Tr
Macaroni ... 1 cup	190	7	1	39	14	2.1	1	0	0.23	0.13	1.8	0
Pancakes, 4-in diam. ... 1 pancake	60	2	2	8	36	0.7	160	30	0.09	0.12	0.8	Tr
Popcorn:												
Air-popped, unsalted ... 1 cup	30	1	Tr	6	1	0.2	Tr	10	0.03	0.01	0.2	0
Popped in vegetable oil, salted ... 1 cup	55	1	3	6	3	0.3	86	20	0.01	0.02	0.1	0
Rice, white, cooked ... 1 cup	225	4	Tr	50	21	1.8	0	0	0.23	0.02	2.1	0
Tortillas, corn ... 1 tortilla	65	2	1	13	42	0.6	1	80	0.05	0.03	0.4	0
Legumes, Nuts, and Seeds												
Beans, dry:												
Cooked, drained, black ... 1 cup	225	15	1	41	47	2.9	1	Tr	0.43	0.05	0.9	0
Peanuts, roasted and salted ... 1 oz	165	8	14	5	24	0.5	122	0	0.08	0.03	4.2	0
Peanut butter ... 1 tbsp	95	5	8	3	5	0.3	75	0	0.02	0.02	2.2	0
Refried beans, canned ... 1 cup	295	18	3	51	141	5.1	1,228	0	0.14	0.16	1.4	17
Soy products:												
Miso ... 1 cup	470	29	13	65	188	4.7	8,142	110	0.17	0.28	0.8	0
Tofu (2½ by 2¾ by 1 in.) ... 1 piece	85	9	5	3	108	2.3	8	0	0.07	0.04	0.1	0
Sunflower seeds ... 1 oz	160	6	14	5	33	1.9	1	10	0.65	0.07	1.3	Tr
Meat and Meat Products												
Bacon ... 3 slices	110	6	9	Tr	2	0.3	303	0	0.13	0.05	1.4	6
Frankfurter, cooked ... 1 frankfurter	145	5	13	1	5	0.5	504	0	0.09	0.05	1.2	12
Ground beef, broiled ... 3 oz	245	20	18	0	9	2.1	70	Tr	0.03	0.16	4.9	0
Ham, cooked ... 2 slices	105	10	6	2	4	0.6	751	0	0.49	0.14	3.0	16
Poultry and Poultry Products												
Chicken:												
Fried ... 3.5 oz	220	31	9	2	16	1.2	74	50	0.08	0.13	13.5	0
Roasted ... 3.0 oz	140	27	3	0	13	0.9	64	20	0.06	0.10	11.8	0
Vegetables												
Broccoli, cooked ... 1 spear	50	5	1	10	82	2.1	20	2,540	0.15	0.37	1.4	113
Carrots:												
Raw ... 1 carrot	30	1	Tr	7	19	0.4	25	20,250	0.07	0.04	0.7	7

Nutrients in Indicated Quantity

Foods	Food energy — Calories	Protein — Grams	Fat — Grams	Carbohydrate — Grams	Calcium — Milligrams	Iron — Milligrams	Sodium — Milligrams	Vitamin A value — International units	Thiamin — Milligrams	Riboflavin — Milligrams	Niacin — Milligrams	Ascorbic acid — Milligrams
Cooked, sliced, drained ... 1 cup	70	2	Tr	16	48	1.0	103	38,300	0.05	0.09	0.8	4
Celery, raw ... 1 stalk	5	Tr	Tr	1	14	0.2	35	50	0.01	0.01	0.1	3
Collards, cooked, drained ... 1 cup	25	2	Tr	5	148	0.8	36	4,220	0.03	0.08	0.4	19
Corn, sweet:												
Cooked ... 1 ear	85	3	1	19	2	0.5	13	170	0.17	0.06	1.2	5
Canned (cream style) ... 1 cup	185	4	1	46	8	1.0	730	250	0.06	0.14	2.5	12
Lettuce, raw:												
Iceberg, pieces ... 1 cup	5	1	Tr	1	10	0.3	5	180	0.03	0.02	0.1	2
Leaf, pieces ... 1 cup	10	1	Tr	2	38	0.8	5	1,060	0.03	0.04	0.2	10
Onions, cooked, drained ... 1 cup	60	2	Tr	13	57	0.4	17	0	0.09	0.02	0.2	12
Peas, edible pod, cooked, drained ... 1 cup	65	5	Tr	11	67	3.2	6	210	0.20	0.12	0.9	77
Potatoes, baked ... 1 potato	220	5	Tr	51	20	2.7	16	0	0.22	0.07	3.3	26
Spinach, cooked, drained ... 1 cup	40	5	Tr	7	245	6.4	126	14,740	0.17	0.42	0.9	18
Tomatoes:												
Raw ... 1 tomato	25	1	Tr	5	9	0.6	10	1,390	0.07	0.06	0.7	22
Canned, solids and liquid ... 1 cup	50	2	1	10	62	1.5	391	1,450	0.11	0.07	1.8	36
Other												
Cookies:												
Brownies (home recipe) ... 1 brownie	95	1	6	11	9	0.4	51	20	0.05	0.05	0.3	Tr
Chocolate chip ... 4 cookies	180	2	9	28	13	0.8	140	50	0.10	0.23	1.0	Tr
Sandwich type ... 4 cookies	195	2	8	29	12	1.4	189	0	0.09	0.07	0.8	0
Corn chips ... 1 oz	155	2	9	16	35	0.5	233	110	0.04	0.05	0.4	1
Doughnuts, cake type ... 1 doughnut	210	3	12	24	22	1.0	192	20	0.12	0.12	1.1	Tr
French fries ... 10 pieces	110	2	4	17	5	0.7	16	0	0.06	0.02	1.2	5
Gelatin dessert ... ½ cup	70	2	0	17	2	Tr	55	0	0.00	0.00	0.0	0
Jam and preserves ... 1 tbsp	55	Tr	Tr	14	4	0.2	2	Tr	Tr	0.01	Tr	Tr
Pizza, cheese ... 1 slice	290	15	9	39	220	1.6	699	750	0.34	0.29	4.2	2
Potato chips ... 10 chips	105	1	7	10	5	0.2	94	0	0.03	Tr	0.8	8
Puddings:												
Chocolate, canned ... 5 oz can	205	3	11	30	74	1.2	285	100	0.04	0.17	0.6	Tr
Chocolate, dry mix ... ½ cup	155	4	4	27	130	0.3	440	130	0.04	0.18	0.1	1
Syrup, maple ... 2 tbsp	122	0	0	32	1	Tr	19	0	0.00	0.00	0.0	0
Taco ... 1 taco	195	9	11	15	109	1.2	456	420	0.09	0.07	1.4	1

Notes: *Tr* indicates presence of nutrients in trace amounts. All fruits and vegetables are fresh unless noted. Vegetables are fresh cooked unless noted.

Glossary

The Glossary contains all the important terms used throughout the text. It includes the **boldfaced** terms listed in the "Words to Know" lists at the beginning of each lesson and that appear in text, captions, and features.

The Glossary lists the term, the pronunciation (in the case of difficult terms), the definition, and the page on which the term is defined. The pronunciations here and in the text follow the system outlined below. The column headed "Symbol" shows the spelling used in this book to represent the appropriate method.

Pronunciation Key

Sound	As in	Symbol	Example
ă	hat, map	a	abscess (AB·sess)
ā	age, face	ay	atrium (AY·tree·uhm)
a	care, their	ehr	capillaries (KAP·uh·lehr·eez)
ä, ŏ	father, hot	ah	biopsy (BY·ahp·see)
ar	far	ar	cardiac (KAR·dee·ak)
ch	child, much	ch	barbiturate (bar·BI·chuh·ruht)
ĕ	let, best	e	vessel (VE·suhl)
ē	beat, see, city	ee	acne (AK·nee)
er	term, stir, purr	er	nuclear (NOO·klee·er)
g	grow	g	malignant (muh·LIG·nuhnt)
ĭ	it, hymn	i	bacteria (bak·TIR·ee·uh)
ī	ice, five	y	benign (bi·NYN)
		eye	iris (EYE·ris)
j	page, fungi	j	cartilage (KAR·tuhl·ij)
k	coat, look, chorus	k	defect (DEE·fekt)
ō	open, coat, grow	oh	aerobic (e·ROH·bik)
ô	order	or	organ (OR·guhn)
ȯ	flaw, all	aw	palsy (PAWL·zee)
oi	voice	oy	goiter (GOY·ter)
ou	out	ow	fountain (FOWN·tuhn)
s	say, rice	s	dermis (DER·mis)
sh	she, attention	sh	conservation (kahn·ser·VAY·shuhn)
ŭ	cup, flood	uh	bunion (BUHN·yuhn)
u	put, wood, could	u	pulmonary (PUL·muh·nehr·ee)
ü	rule, move, you	oo	attitudes (AT·i·toodz)
w	win	w	warranty (WAWR·uhn·tee)
y	your	yu	urethritis (yur·i·THRY·tuhs)
z	says	z	hormones (HOR·mohnz)
zh	pleasure	zh	transfusion (trans·FYOO·zhuhn)
ə	about, collide	uh	asthma (AZ·muh)

Abdominal thrusts Quick, upward pulls into the diaphragm to force out a blockage of the airway when someone is choking. (page 525)

Abscess (AB·sess) A painful tooth condition in which pus collects in the bone sockets around a tooth. (page 41)

Abuse (uh·BYOOS) Physical or mental mistreatment of another person. (page 138)

Accident chain The combination of a situation, an unsafe habit, and an unsafe act leading to an injury. (page 486)

Acid rain Rain that is more acidic than normal. (page 546)

Acquaintance rape A situation in which a person is forced to have sexual intercourse with someone he or she knows. (page 497)

Acquired immunodeficiency syndrome (AIDS) A deadly disease that destroys the body's ability to fight infection. (page 363)

Acrophobia (ak·ruh·FOH·bee·uh) An abnormal fear of being in high places. (page 87)

Active listening Receiving someone's message by hearing it, thinking about it, and responding to it. (page 107)

Addiction (uh·DIK·shuhn) A physical or mental need for a drug or other substance. (pages 204, 414, 434)

Adolescence (a·duhl·E·suhns) The time of life between childhood and adulthood. (page 208)

Adrenaline (uh·DRE·nuhl·in) A hormone that increases the level of sugar in the blood, which gives the body extra energy in response to emergencies. (page 82)

Advertising Creating and sending messages that are designed to interest consumers in buying certain goods and services; also called *ads*. (page 170)

Aerobic (e·ROH·bik) **exercise** Vigorous, rhythmic activity that aids the heart and increases the body's capacity to take in and use oxygen. (page 234)

Al-Anon A support group that helps anyone affected by close contact with an alcoholic. (page 438)

Alateen A support group that helps the children of an alcoholic parent. (page 438)

Alcohol (AL·kuh·hawl) A drug that is produced by a chemical reaction in some foods and that has powerful effects on the body. (page 428)

Alcoholics Anonymous (uh·NAH·nuh·muhs) **(AA)** A support group that helps alcoholics recover from their addiction. (page 437)

Alcoholism An illness caused by a physical and mental need for alcohol. (page 435)

Allergen (AL·er·juhn) Substance that causes allergic reactions in some individuals. (page 390)

Allergy An extreme sensitivity to a substance. (page 390)

Alternatives (ahl·TER·nuh·tivz) Other ways of thinking or acting. (page 442)

Alveoli (al·vee·OH·ly) Microscopic air sacs in the lungs in which the exchange of gases occurs. (page 306)

Alzheimer's (AHLTS·hy·merz) **disease** A disease that causes impaired thinking, memory, and behavior. (page 219)

Amino acids Chains of building blocks that make up proteins. (page 262)

Amphetamines (am·FE·tuh·meenz) Highly addictive stimulant drugs; may be prescribed to treat attention disorders in children or obesity. (page 460)

Anabolic steroids (a·nuh·BAH·lik STIR·oydz) Drugs that some athletes take illegally because they believe the drugs will build stronger muscles. (page 473)

Anaerobic (an·e·ROH·bik) **exercise** Intense physical activity that lasts a short time and involves great bursts of energy in which the muscles work hard to produce energy. (page 234)

Anorexia nervosa (a·nuh·REK·see·uh ner·VOH·suh) An eating disorder that is characterized by an intense fear of weight gain and that often leads to extreme weight loss from self-starvation. (page 282)

Antibiotic (an·ti·by·AH·tik) A drug that inhibits or kills microorganisms that cause disease. (page 453)

Antibodies Proteins in the blood that react to foreign bodies and destroy or neutralize them. (page 346)

Antihistamines Drugs that relieve the symptoms of allergic reactions. (page 391)

Anus (AY·nuhs) Excretory opening through which feces pass out of the body. (page 321)

Anxiety disorder The condition of feeling abnormally uneasy or worried about what may happen. (page 87)

Arteries (AR·tuh·reez) The largest blood vessels, which take blood from the heart to all parts of the body. (page 302)

Arteriosclerosis (ar·tir·ee·oh·skluh·ROH·sis) A condition in which the arterial walls thicken and harden. (page 378)

Arthritis (ar·THRY·tuhs) A disease of the joints characterized by painful swelling and stiffness. (page 394)

Artificial respiration (art·uh·FISH·uhl res·puh·RAY·shuhn) See *Rescue breathing.*

Assertive (uh·SER·tiv) Behaving with confidence. (page 497)

Asthma (AZ·muh) A chronic respiratory disease in which the bronchi swell and become blocked, causing the person to have difficulty breathing. (page 392)

Astigmatism (uh·STIG·muh·tiz·uhm) An eye condition in which images are distorted. (page 51)

Atherosclerosis (a·thuh·roh·skluh·ROH·sis) A condition in which fatty deposits build up on artery walls. (page 378)

Athlete's foot A problem caused by fungi growing in warm, damp areas of the foot. (page 57)

Atrium (AY·tree·uhm) Each of the two upper chambers of the heart. (page 299)

Attitudes (AT·i·toodz) Feelings and beliefs. (page 12)

Auditory (AW·di·tor·ee) **nerve** The network of nerves in the cochlea that carries messages to the brain. (page 53)

Autonomic (aw·tuh·NAH·mik) **system** The part of the peripheral nervous system that deals with involuntary body actions. (page 296)

Bacteria (bak·TIR·ee·uh) Tiny microscopic organisms that live everywhere. (page 341)

Barbiturates (bar·BI·chuh·ruhts) A type of depressant drug that is a powerful sedative; often prescribed as a sleeping aid. (page 463)

Battery The unlawful beating of another person. (page 139)

B-cells Lymphocytes that produce antibodies. (page 346)

Behavior The way a person acts in many different situations. (page 11)

Benign (bi·NYN) **tumor** A mass of cells that is not cancerous. (page 383)

Biodegradable A substance that is easily broken down by bacteria and other organisms. (page 548)

Biological (by·uh·LAH·ji·kuhl) **age** Age that is measured by how well various body parts are working. (page 218)

Biopsy The surgical removal of cells or tissue from the living body for purposes of examination and diagnosis. (page 385)

Birth defects (DEE·fekts) Abnormalities in a developing or newborn baby. (pages 203, 374)

Blended family A type of family that consists of a remarried parent, a stepparent, and their children. (page 112)

Blister A small, fluid-filled swelling on the skin, often caused by burns or rubbing. (page 57)

Blizzard A heavy snowstorm with high winds. (page 509)

Blood alcohol concentration (BAC) The percentage of alcohol in the bloodstream. (page 431)

Blood pressure The force of the blood against the walls of the blood vessels. (page 302, 379)

Blood vessels Tubes that carry blood throughout the body. (page 302)

Body composition The amount of body fat compared to lean tissue. (page 238)

Body language Messages transmitted through body movements and gestures rather than words. (page 108)

Brain An organ of the nervous system composed of neurons that control your actions, thoughts, and emotions. (page 294)

Brain death The result of oxygen being cut off from the brain. (page 221)

Bronchi (BRAHN·ky) The two passages through which air enters the lungs. (page 304)

Bronchodilators (brahn·ko·dy·LAY·terz) Medications that relax the muscles around the bronchial air passages. (page 393)

Bulimia (boo·LEE·mee·uh) An eating disorder characterized by extreme overeating followed by purging. (page 283)

Bunion (BUHN·yuhn) A painful swelling at the base of the big toe. (page 57)

Bypass surgery A surgical procedure to create a new path for blood to flow around a blocked artery. (page 380)

Caffeine (ka·FEEN) A substance found in coffee, tea, and some soft drinks that stimulates the heart and nervous system. (page 273)

Callus A hardened, thickened part of the skin. (page 57)

Calorie A unit of heat that measures the energy available in different foods or used up during exercise. (page 278)

Cancer A disease characterized by the rapid and uncontrolled growth of abnormal cells. (page 383)

Capillaries (KAP·uh·lehr·eez) The smallest blood vessels in the body. (page 302)

Carbohydrates Nutrients, such as sugar and starches, that are the main source of energy to the body. (page 262)

Carbon monoxide (KAR·buhn muh·NAHK·syd) A colorless, odorless, poisonous gas produced when a substance burns. (page 404)

Carcinogens (kar·SIN·uh·juhnz) Substances in the environment that cause cancer. (page 385)

Cardiac muscle The muscle of the heart. (page 314)

Cardiopulmonary resuscitation (kar·dee·oh·PUHL·muh·nehr·ee ri·suh·suh·TAY·shuhn) **(CPR)** A first-aid procedure to restore breathing and circulation. (page 527)

Cardiovascular (KAR·dee·oh·VAS·kyoo·ler) **system** The circulatory system. (page 298)

Carrier A person who has a virus and can pass it on to other people, but who may not show the symptoms of the disease. (page 363)

Cartilage (KAHR·tuhl·ij) Tough, flexible tissue that covers the ends of bones and supports soft tissue. (page 308)

Cell The basic unit, or building block, of life. (page 196)

Cementum (se·MEN·tuhm) Thin, bonelike material that covers the root of a tooth. (page 40)

Central nervous system (CNS) The part of the nervous system made up of the brain and spinal cord. (page 293)

Cerebellum (ser·uh·BE·luhm) The part of the brain that controls balance, posture, and coordination. (page 294)

Cerebrum (suh·REE·bruhm) The largest part of the brain, which controls the senses, muscles, thought, and speech. (page 294)

Cervix (SER·viks) The neck, or opening, of the uterus. (pages 200, 330)

Chemotherapy (kee·moh·THEHR·uh·pee) The use of chemicals to kill cancer cells. (page 386)

Chest thrust A technique used on an infant or child to dislodge a blockage in the airway. (page 525)

Chlamydia (kluh·MI·dee·uh) An STD that does great damage to the reproductive system. (page 359)

Cholera (KAH·luh·ruh) A disease caused by bacteria in untreated sewage and characterized by cramps, vomiting, and diarrhea. (page 547)

Cholesterol (kuh·LES·tuh·rawl) A waxy, fatlike substance found in the cells of all animals. (page 271)

Chromosomes (KROH·muh·sohmz) Threadlike structures in the nucleus of a cell that carry the codes for inherited characteristics. (page 202)

Chronic (KRAH·nik) **diseases** Illnesses that last a long time or that recur frequently. (page 373)

Chronological (krah·nuh·LAH·ji·kuhl) **age** A person's age measured in years. (page 218)

Cilia (SIH·lee·uh) Tiny hairlike projections. (page 407)

Circulatory (SER·kyuh·luh·tohr·ee) **system** The group of organs that transports blood throughout the body to deliver essential materials to body cells and to remove waste materials from the cells. (page 298)

Cirrhosis (suh·ROH·sis) Condition in which liver tissue is scarred and damaged. (page 429)

Clinical (KLI·ni·kuhl) **death** The result of the shutdown of a person's body systems. (page 221)

Cocaine (koh·KAYN) An illegal stimulant. (page 462)

Cochlea (KOK·lee·uh) A bony structure of the inner ear that is essential to the sense of hearing. (page 53)

Codeine (KOH·deen) A narcotic drug used in cough medicine. (page 463)

Colon (KOH·luhn) The large intestine. (page 321)

Commitment (kuh·MIT·muhnt) A pledge or promise. (page 127)

Communicable (kuh·MYOO·ni·kuh·buhl) **diseases** Illnesses that can be transmitted from one person to another. (page 340)

Communication The exchange of thoughts, ideas, and beliefs between two or more people. (page 102)

Comparison (kum·PEHR·i·suhn) **shopping** Judging the merits of different goods and services. (page 167)

Compromise (KAHM·pruh·myz) To settle differences by a mutual agreement. (page 102)

Conservation The saving of resources. (page 549)

Consumer (kuhn·SOO·mer) A person who purchases goods and services. (page 162)

Consumer advocates (AD·voh·kets) People or groups who help consumers with problems. (page 184)

Contagious (kuhn·TAY·juhs) **period** The period of time during which some diseases can be passed to another person. (page 343)

Contract To tighten or become shorter. (page 312)

Contraction (kuhn·TRAK·shuhn) A sudden tightening in the muscles of the uterus as part of the birth process. (page 200)

Cool-down A slow winding down of an activity, such as exercise. (page 249)

Cooperation Working together or helping someone to achieve a common goal. (page 103)

Coping strategy A way of dealing with a sense of loss when someone close dies. (page 224)

Corn A hardened, thickened growth of skin on a toe. (page 57)

Cornea (KOR·nee·uh) The clear outer layer of the eyeball. (page 48)

Coronary (KAWR·uh·nehr·ee) **arteries** Large blood vessels that carry blood away from the heart. (page 378)

Coupon (KOO·pahn) A piece of paper that offers savings on certain brands of goods. (page 169)

Crown The part of a tooth that is visible to the eye. (page 40)

Cuticle (KYOO·ti·kuhl) Nonliving band of epidermis around the fingernails and toenails. (page 37)

Dandruff (DAN·druhf) Whitish scales of dead skin that flake off the scalp. (page 37)

Date rape A situation in which a person is forced to have sexual intercourse with someone on a date. (page 497)

Decision making A six-step process for making up one's mind or resolving a problem. (page 20)

Defense mechanism (duh·FENS MEK·uh·nizm) Temporary way of dealing with stress. (page 86)

Defensive driving Obeying traffic laws and watching out for other road users. (page 501)

Degenerative (di·JE·ne·ruh·tiv) **disease** A noncommunicable disease characterized by the breakdown of body tissues. (page 372)

Dehydration (dee·hy·DRAY·shuhn) A serious loss in the body's water content. (page 283)

Dentin (DEN·tin) The hard, bony material surrounding the pulp of the tooth. (page 40)

Depressant (di·PRE·suhnt) A drug that slows down body functions, including breathing and brain activity. (page 428)

Depression An emotional state characterized by extreme sadness, inability to eat or sleep, and a loss of interest in life. (page 88)

Dermatologist (DER·muh·TAHL·uh·jist) A doctor who treats diseases of the skin. (page 34)

Dermis (DER·mis) The sensitive inner layer of the skin. (page 33)

Designer drugs Substances that are designed to be chemically similar to various controlled substances. (page 467)

Desired weight The weight that is right for a person based on his or her gender, height, and body frame. (page 276)

Detoxification (dee·tahk·si·fi·KAY·shuhn) The removal of harmful substances, such as drugs or alcohol, from the body. (page 474)

Developmental (di·vel·uhp·MEN·tuhl) **task** Something that must be accomplished in order for a person to continue growing toward a healthy, mature adulthood. (page 211)

Diabetes (dy·uh·BEE·teez) A disease in which the body cannot properly convert food into energy. (page 396)

Diaphragm (DY·uh·fram) The large muscle that separates the chest from the abdomen. (page 304)

Diet The combination of what one eats and drinks regularly. (page 261)

Digestion (dy·JES·chuhn) The process of changing food into substances that can be absorbed into the bloodstream. (page 318)

Digestive (dy·JES·tiv) **system** The organs that change food into nutrients for the cells to use. (page 318)

Discount store A store that carries regular merchandise at reduced prices. (page 169)

Disease An illness that affects the body or mind. (page 340)

Distress Negative stress that can prevent a person from doing something. (page 80)

Divorce The legal ending of a marriage. (page 128)

Drug A substance other than food that changes the structure or function of the mind or body. (page 452)

Earthquake A shaking or vibration of the earth's surface due to an underground shift. (page 510)

Eating disorder Extreme and dangerous eating behavior that can result in serious illness or death. (page 282)

Ecosystem (EE·koh·sis·tuhm) The various organisms and plants that make up a particular community or environment. (page 539)

Egg cell The female reproductive cell that joins with the sperm cell to make a new life. (page 197)

Embryo A developing organism in the period of its growth between fertilization and when its organs are developed enough to sustain life. (page 198)

Emotional need A need that affects a person's feelings and sense of well-being. (page 73)

Emotions Feelings, such as love, anger, or fear. (page 75)

Emphysema (em·fuh·SEE·muh) A lung disease in which the alveoli are damaged or destroyed. (page 307)

Enamel (ee·NA·muhl) The hard outer layer of the tooth. (page 40)

Endocrine (EN·duh·krin) **system** The glands that produce the hormones to regulate body activities. (page 324)

Environment (en·VY·ruhn·ment) All the conditions that surround a person and affect his or her development. (pages 11, 203, 538)

Epidermis (e·puh·DER·mis) The outermost layer of skin. (page 33)

Epiglottis (e·puh·GLAH·tis) A small flap of tissue that covers the trachea when a person swallows, keeping food out of the windpipe. (page 304)

Eustachian (you·STAY·shun) **tube** The tube from the nose to the inner ear that equalizes the air pressure on both sides of the eardrum. (page 53)

Excretion (ek·SKREE·shuhn) The act of removing liquid wastes from the body. (page 321)

Exercise frequency The number of times a person exercises in a specified period of time. (page 248)

Exercise intensity The amount of energy a person uses when he or she exercises. (page 248)

Exercise time The amount of time spent exercising during one session. (page 248)

Expiration date The date stamped on a package that tells when the contents are no longer useful. (page 491)

Extend To move muscles so they lengthen or stretch out. (page 312)

Extended family A nuclear family and other relatives living together. (page 112)

Eye contact The ability to look directly at the person to whom one is speaking. (page 108)

Fallen arches A foot condition characterized by flatness of the bottom of one's feet. (page 57)

Family The basic unit of society; a group of related people. (page 111)

Fatigue Extreme tiredness. (page 83)

Fats Nutrients that are a source of energy to the body. (page 263)

Fertilization (fer·til·i·ZAY·shuhn) The process of joining a male sperm cell and a female egg cell, which is necessary to produce a new life. (page 197)

Fetal (FEE·tuhl) **alcohol syndrome (FAS)** A group of alcohol-related birth defects. (pages 204, 431)

Fetus An embryo during the later stages of development in the mother's uterus. (page 198)

Fiber The part of fruits, vegetables, and grains that cannot be digested. (page 270)

First-degree burn A mild burn that affects only the epidermis and is characterized by reddening of the skin. (page 531)

Flexibility The ability to move body joints in certain ways. (page 237)

Follicle (FAHL·i·kuhl) A small opening or sac in the dermis, the deepest layer of the skin in which hair grows. (page 36)

Food Guide Pyramid A guideline to help people choose what and how much to eat from each food group in order to get the needed nutrients. (page 266)

Fossil (FAH·suhl) **fuels** Fuels taken from the earth, such as coal, oil, and natural gas. (page 545)

Fracture A break or crack in a bone. (page 529)

Frostbite Freezing of the skin. (page 505)

Fungi (FUHN·jy) Simple life forms that cannot make their own food and which can cause disease. (page 341)

Gallbladder A small organ beneath the liver that stores excess bile. (page 320)

Gang A group of people acting or staying together, often for some improper or unlawful purpose. (page 148)

Generic (juh·NEHR·ik) **product** A product sold in a plain package and at a lower price than a comparable brand name product. (page 169)

Genes Basic units of heredity; carry codes for individual traits. (page 202)

Genetic (juh·NE·tik) **disorder** A disease or disorder caused by a problem with the genes. (pages 202, 373)

Genital herpes (HER·peez) An STD that is caused by the herpes simplex II virus and is characterized by blisters in the genital area. (page 360)

Genital warts An STD characterized by warts in the genital area that multiply quickly if not treated. (page 359)

Germs Microscopic organisms that cause disease. (page 340)

Gingivitis (jin·juh·VY·tis) A gum disease caused by plaque or decaying food between the teeth. (page 44)

Gland A part of the body that produces a chemical substance. (page 324)

Goal Something to aim for. (page 23)

Gonorrhea (gah·nuh·REE·uh) A common STD caused by a bacteria, and, if untreated, results in damage to reproductive organs. (page 359)

Goods Products made for sale. (page 162)

Greenhouse effect An atmospheric condition caused by pollutants and characterized by warming climate trends. (page 546)

Grief Deep and painful sorrow related to the death of a loved one. (page 223)

Ground water Water that collects in the ground and supplies wells and springs. (page 540)

Group dating Going out with a group of male and female friends. (page 125)

Hallucinogen (huh·LOO·suhn·uh·jen) A drug that creates imaginary images or distorts real ones in the mind of the user. (page 466)

Hate crime Crime committed against a person or group because of racial, religious, or cultural differences. (page 146)

Hazard (HAZ·erd) A danger. (page 490)

Hazardous (HAZ·er·duhs) **waste** A waste product that can cause illness if not disposed of properly. (page 555)

Head lice Tiny insects that live in the hair. (page 37)

Health A combination of physical, mental, and social well-being. (page 5)

Health care facility A place where people can receive health care. (page 174)

Health care system The way in which people receive and pay for their health care. (page 172)

Health education Providing health information in a way that influences people to take positive actions regarding their health. (page 14)

Health insurance (in·SHUR·uhns) A program in which a person pays an annual fee to a company that agrees to pay certain health care costs. (page 174)

Health maintenance (MAYN·te·nuhns) **organization (HMO)** A group of many different types of doctors who provide health care for members. (page 176)

Heart and lung endurance How well the heart and lungs get oxygen to the body during exercise and how quickly they return to normal. (page 238)

Heart attack A serious condition in which heart muscle is damaged by a stoppage in the flow of blood to the heart. (pages 303, 379)

Hepatitis (he·puh·TY·tis) An inflammatory disease of the liver. (page 352)

Heredity (huh·RED·i·tee) The passing-on of characteristics from parents to their children through genes. (pages 10, 202)

Histamine (HIS·tuh·meen) A substance that causes the symptoms of allergic reactions. (page 391)

Hives A skin condition caused by an allergy and characterized by itching and raised, red patches. (page 391)

Homicide (HAH·muh·syd) The killing of one human being by another. (page 145)

Hormones (HOR·mohnz) Chemicals that are produced in the glands to regulate various body functions. (pages 75, 208)

Hospice A facility that cares for people who are terminally ill. (page 222)

Human immunodeficiency (im·yoo·noh·di·FI·shuhn·see) **virus (HIV)** The virus that causes AIDS. (page 363)

Hurricane A storm with heavy rains and high winds that usually begins in the tropical regions. (page 508)

Hypertension (hy·per·TEN·shuhn) High blood pressure. (page 379)

Hypothermia (hy·poh·THER·mee·uh) A sudden drop in body temperature. (page 502)

Immunity (i·MYOO·nuh·tee) The body's resistance to germs and other harmful substances that may be produced by those germs. (page 345)

Individual sports Sports people enjoy on their own or with a friend. (page 252)

Infancy (IN·fuhn·see) The first year after birth. (page 207)

Infection (in·FEK·shuhn) A condition that occurs when germs enter body cells and multiply. (page 340)

Influenza (in·floo·EN·zuh) A serious and contagious respiratory disease caused by viruses. (page 352)

Inhalant (in·HAY·luhnt) A substance that is inhaled to give a hallucinogenic high. (page 468)

Insulin (IN·suh·lin) A hormone produced in the pancreas that regulates the level of sugar in the blood. (page 396)

Interferon Substance produced by cells that stops a virus from reproducing and thus helps control infection. (page 346)

Iris (EYE·ris) The colored part of the eye that surrounds the pupil. (page 48)

Jaywalk To cross the street carelessly, without paying attention to traffic rules or lights. (page 500)

Joint A place in the body where bones are joined. (page 310)

Keratin (KEHR·uh·tin) A substance that makes nails hard. (page 38)

Kidneys The two bean-shaped organs that remove the body's water-soluble wastes. (page 321)

Landfill A place where garbage and other waste are dumped and covered with dirt in order to build up low-lying or wet land. (page 553)

Larynx (LA·ringks) The upper part of the respiratory tract that contains the vocal cords. (page 304)

Laxative (LAK·suh·tiv) A medicine that speeds foods through the digestive system with little time to release their nutrients. (page 283)

Lens (LENZ) The structure behind the pupil that focuses light. (page 48)

License Legal permission to do something. (page 185)

Lifestyle disease A disease that is caused by a person's health habits. (pages 14, 374)

Lifestyle factor A life-related habit. (page 13)

Lifetime sport A physical activity that can be enjoyed throughout life. (page 255)

Ligament (LI·guh·ment) A type of firm, strong tissue that connects bones at joints. (page 310)

Liver A gland with many digestive functions, including the breakdown of fats. (page 320)

Love Great affection for another person. (page 127)

Lymphatic (lim·FA·tik) **system** A secondary circulatory system that carries lymph. (page 346)

Lymph nodes Clusters of cells along the lymphatic vessels that filter out harmful matter from the lymph. (page 346)

Lymphocytes (LIM·fuh·syts) White blood cells that are the body's primary means of fighting germs. (page 346)

Mainstream smoke The smoke that the smoker exhales. (page 422)

Malignant (muh·LIG·nuhnt) **tumor** A mass of cancer cells. (page 383)

Malnutrition A condition in which the body does not receive the nutrients it needs to grow and function well. (page 283)

Malocclusion A condition in which the teeth fail to line up properly. (page 44)

Malpractice (mal·PRAK·tis) A failure to provide an acceptable degree of quality health care. (page 185)

Mediation (mee·dee·AY·shuhn) The process of resolving conflicts with the help of a neutral third person. (page 157)

Medicaid (MED·i·kayd) A government health insurance program that pays the medical care costs for poor people. (page 175)

Medicare (MED·i·kehr) A government health insurance program for people 65 years old and older. (page 175)

Medicine A drug that cures or prevents diseases or other health-related conditions. (page 452)

Melanin (MEL·uh·nin) The substance that gives skin most of its color. (page 33)

Menstrual (MEN·struhl) **cycle** The time between the beginning of one menstruation to the beginning of the next one; the process of menstruation. (page 331)

Menstruation (men·struh·WAY·shuhn) The process of discharging blood and tissue from the uterus. (page 330)

Mental health The state of liking and accepting oneself. (page 64)

Metastasis (muh·TAS·tuh·sis) The spread of cancer cells from a tumor to other parts of the body. (page 384)

Minerals A class of nutrients that are needed in small amounts for the body to work properly. (page 262)

Mononucleosis (MAH·noh·noo·klee·OH·sis) A viral disease that is common among young people and is characterized by an abnormal increase of white blood cells. (page 352)

Mucus (MYOO·kuhs) A fluid that moistens and protects the mucous membranes. (page 345)

Muscle endurance (en·DER·uhns) How well a muscle group can perform over a given time without becoming overly tired. (page 236)

Muscle strength The most work muscles can do at any given time. (page 236)

Muscular (MUHS·kyuh·ler) **system** The group of tough tissues that enables body parts to move. (page 312)

Narcotic (nar·KAH·tik) An addictive depressant drug that is used to relieve pain and can be obtained legally only with a doctor's prescription. (page 463)

Neck The part of the tooth between the crown and the root. (page 40)

Negotiation (ni·goh·shee·AY·shuhn) Process of reaching a solution by discussing problems face-to-face. (page 157)

Neuron (NOO·rahn) A nerve cell. (page 292)

Neurosis (noo·ROH·sis) A mental condition in which fear interferes with a person's ability to function. (page 87)

Neutrality (noo·TRA·luh·tee) Not taking sides in an argument. (page 157)

Nicotine (NI·kuh·teen) An addictive stimulant drug in tobacco that speeds up the heartbeat. (page 404)

Noncommunicable diseases Diseases that are caused by how people live, by conditions they are born with, or by hazards in the environment. (page 372)

Nonrenewable resource A resource from the earth that cannot be replaced once it has been used up. (page 549)

Nuclear (NOO·klee·er) **family** A family that consists of a mother, a father, and their children living in the same household. (page 112)

Nuclear waste Harmful by-products of atomic reactions. (page 556)

Nutrient (NOO·tree·ent) One of six types of substances in food that the body needs to grow and function properly. (page 262)

Nutrient density The nutrients in foods compared with the calories they provide. (page 278)

Nutrition (noo·TRI·shuhn) The process of taking in and using nutrients. (page 261)

Obesity A condition in which a person's weight is 20 percent or more above his or her desired weight. (page 277)

Obstetrician (ahb·stuh·TRI·shuhn) A doctor who specializes in the care of a pregnant woman and her developing baby. (page 203)

Opportunistic infection Any disease that attacks a person with a weakened immune system. (page 364)

Optic (AHP·tik) **nerve** A bundle of nerve fibers that carries messages from the eye to the brain. (page 48)

Organ A part of a living organism that is composed of tissue organized to perform a certain function. (page 197)

Osteoarthritis (ahs·tee·oh·ahr·THRY·tuhs) A chronic bone disease, common in elderly people, in which joints deteriorate and become painful. (page 395)

Ovaries (OH·vuh·reez) The two female reproductive organs that store egg cells. (page 330)

Over-the-counter (OTC) medicine Any medication that can be purchased without a doctor's prescription. (page 457)

Overweight Having more than the desired weight for a person's size, gender, and body frame. (page 277)

Ovulation (ahv·yuh·LAY·shuhn) The process of releasing an egg cell from an ovary. (page 330)

Ozone A form of oxygen present in the air, especially after a thunderstorm. (page 545)

Pacemaker (PAYS·may·ker) A small electrical device that sends pulses to the heart to make it beat regularly. (page 381)

Pancreas (PAN·kree·uhs) The organ that produces insulin and releases enzymes to digest carbohydrates, proteins, and fats. (page 320)

Parenting The raising of children. (page 129)

Particulates (pahr·TIK·yuh·lits) Tiny pollutants, such as dust and soot, found in the air. (page 545)

Passive smoking Inhaling the smoke of nearby people who are smoking. (page 422)

Peer A person of the same age. (page 119)

Peer pressure The pressure to go along with the beliefs and actions of your friends and classmates. (page 119)

Periodontium (pehr·ee·oh·DAHN·shee·um) The supporting structures of the teeth, including the jawbone, gums, and ligaments. (page 40)

Peripheral (puh·RIF·uh·ruhl) **nervous system (PNS)** The system made up of nerves that connects the central nervous system to all parts of the body. (page 293)

Personality The qualities and characteristics that make a person different from everybody else. (page 66)

Pesticide (PES·tuh·syd) A chemical used to kill or control animals and insects. (page 545)

Phagocytes (FAG·uh·syts) Special white blood cells that destroy germs. (page 346)

Phagocytosis (fag·uh·suh·TOH·suhs) The process of white blood cells destroying germs. (page 346)

Phobia A fear so great it interferes with reasonable action. (page 87)

Physical fatigue Extreme tiredness of the body. (page 83)

Physically fit A state of being in which the body is able to handle the demands placed on it. (page 230)

Physiological (fi·zee·uh·LAH·ji·kuhl) **dependence** A type of addiction in which the body feels a need for a drug. (page 414)

Pituitary (pi·TOO·i·tehr·ee) **gland** The gland at the base of the brain that controls other glands. (page 325)

Placebo (pluh·SEE·boh) **effect** Health improvement as a result of using a pill or preparation that contains no active ingredients. (page 181)

Placenta (pluh·SEN·tuh) The tissue that lines the walls of the uterus and that nourishes the developing baby. (page 199)

Plaque (PLAK) **1.** A thin film that forms on teeth. (page 41) **2.** Fatty deposits that build up on arterial walls. (page 378)

Pollen A powdery substance released by certain plants and grasses that causes allergic reactions in some people. (page 390)

Pollution Anything that dirties the environment or makes it unhealthy. (page 541)

Pores Tiny openings in the skin. (page 33)

Precaution Care taken beforehand to ensure good results or avoid bad ones. (page 19)

Precycling The process of reducing waste before it occurs. (page 551)

Preferred provider A physician who belongs to or has been approved by a particular health plan. (page 174)

Prejudice (PRE·juh·duhs) A negative and unjustly formed opinion, usually against people of a different racial, religious, or cultural group. (page 146)

Prenatal (pree·NAY·tuhl) **care** Steps taken to provide for the health of a pregnant woman and her unborn baby. (page 203)

Prescription (pri·SKRIP·shuhn) **medicine** Medication that may be purchased only with a doctor's written order. (page 457)

Primary care provider A doctor who provides general health care to patients. (page 173)

Proteins (PROH·teenz) Nutrients that are essential for growth and repair of body cells. (page 262)

Protozoa (proh·tuh·ZOH·uh) Single-celled organisms that sometimes cause diseases. (page 341)

Psychological (sy·kuh·LAH·ji·kuhl) **dependence** A type of addiction in which the mind feels a need for a drug. (page 416)

Psychological fatigue Extreme mental tiredness. (page 83)

Psychosis (sy·KOH·sis) A severe mental disorder. (page 87)

Puberty (PYOO·ber·tee) The period of adolescence when a person begins to develop certain traits of his or her sex. (page 209)

Public health Maintaining and improving community health, especially as a function of government. (page 186)

Pulp The soft, sensitive inner part of the tooth that contains blood vessels and nerves. (page 40)

Pupil (PYOO·puhl) The dark opening in the center of the iris that regulates the amount of light entering the eye. (page 48)

Quackery (KWAK·uh·ree) A fraud or scam. (page 180)

Radiation (ray·dee·AY·shuhn) A treatment used for some types of cancer. (page 386)

Radon (RAY·dahn) A radioactive gas formed by the decay of radium. (page 556)

Random violence Violence committed for no reason and against no one in particular. (page 145)

Rape A crime in which one person forces another person to have sexual relations. (page 497)

Recommended Dietary Allowances (RDA) A guideline for the amount of each nutrient that should be consumed daily. (page 264)

Recovery Returning to a normal state of being, usually after illness or addiction. (page 437)

Recycling The process of changing various materials so they can be reused. (page 550)

Refusal skills Effective ways of saying no. (page 109)

Relationship (ri·LAY·shuhn·ship) The connection one has with another person or group. (page 101)

Reliable Dependable and trustworthy. (page 118)

Reproductive (ree·pruh·DUHK·tiv) **system** The group of organs involved in the production of offspring. (page 328)

Rescue breathing A way of restoring normal breathing by forcing air into the victim's lungs. (page 518)

Respiratory system The group of organs that delivers oxygen to the body and removes carbon dioxide from the body. (page 304)

Responsibility An obligation. (page 130)

Responsible dating Being trustworthy, respectful, and careful about the other person in a dating situation. (page 126)

Retina (RE·tin·uh) The light-sensing part of the inner eye. (page 48)

Rheumatoid (ROO·muh·toyd) **arthritis** A chronic disease characterized by pain,

inflammation, swelling, and stiffness of the joints. (page 394)

Rickettsias (ri·KET·see·uhs) Tiny, disease-causing organisms that are spread by fleas, ticks, and lice. (page 341)

Risk behavior Acting in a manner that increases one's chances of being harmed. (page 19)

Risk factor A trait or habit that raises a person's chances of getting a particular disease. (page 374)

Root The part of the tooth that is beneath the gum. (page 40)

Rubella (roo·BE·luh) A contagious disease; also known as German measles. (page 205)

Safety conscious Having an awareness of the importance of safety. (page 484)

Saliva (suh·LY·vuh) The substance produced by the salivary glands; contains enzymes that start the digestion of foods. (page 318)

Sanitation (san·i·TAY·shuhn) The disposal of sewage and wastes to protect public health. (page 188)

Saturated fats Fats found in meats and some dairy products. (page 263)

Schizophrenia (skit·zoh·FREE·nee·uh) A serious mental disorder in which one loses touch with reality. (page 88)

Sclera (SKLEHR·uh) The tough outer layer of the eye. (page 48)

Sebum (SEE·buhm) An oily secretion associated with acne. (page 34)

Second-degree burn A burn that destroys the first layer of skin and damages the second layer, causing redness and blisters. (page 531)

Secondhand smoke Smoke nonsmokers inhale as a result of being around smokers. (page 422)

Second opinion After consulting one's regular physician, seeing another doctor to confirm the first diagnosis or recommend another course of treatment. (page 185)

Self-concept The view a person has of himself or herself. (page 68)

Self-esteem Confidence in one's own ability. (page 23)

Semicircular (SEM·i·SER·kyuh·ler) **canals** Three interconnecting, partially fluid-filled canals of the inner ear that are responsible for balance. (page 53)

Services Useful activities that are sold to others. (page 162)

Sewage (SOO·ij) Food, human waste, detergents, and other products carried away in sewers and drains. (page 547)

Shock A serious condition in which body functions are slowed down. (page 521)

Side effect A related condition that results from a treatment or medication. (page 454)

Sidestream smoke The smoke from the burning tip of a cigarette. (page 422)

Single-parent family A family with only one parent living in the household. (page 112)

Skeletal muscles Muscles that work with bones to facilitate movement. (page 314)

Skeletal system The bones of the body. (page 308)

Small-claims court A state court that handles civil cases involving small amounts of money. (page 184)

Small intestine The long, tubelike organ in which most digestion occurs. (page 319)

Smog An unhealthy mixture of pollutants and fog in the air, usually over cities. (page 546)

Smoke alarm A device that makes a loud noise when it senses smoke. (page 492)

Smooth muscles The involuntary muscles in the digestive system and circulatory system. (page 314)

Social age Age measured by a person's lifestyle. (page 218)

Social health One's ability to get along with the people around him or her. (page 100)

Socializing Being with and enjoying being with other people. (page 124)

Somatic (soh·MA·tik) **system** The part of the peripheral nervous system that involves voluntary actions. (page 296)

Specialist (SPE·she·list) A physician who is trained to handle particular kinds of patients or diseases. (page 173)

Sperm cell The male reproductive cell that joins with the egg cell to make a new life. (page 197)

Sphygmomanometer (sfig·mo·muh·NAH·muh·ter) The instrument used to measure blood pressure. (page 302)

Spinal cord A long bundle of neurons that relays messages to and from the brain and all parts of the body. (page 294)

Stepparent Someone who marries a child's mother or father. (page 112)

Stimulant (STIM·yuh·luhnt) A drug that speeds up body functions. (page 459)

Stomach A muscular organ in which some digestion occurs. (page 319)

Stress The body's response to changes. (page 80)

Stressor A trigger of stress. (page 82)

Stroke A serious condition that occurs when the blood supply to the brain is cut off, usually due to a blockage in the artery that goes to the brain. (page 378)

Subcutaneous (suhb·kyoo·TAY·nee·uhs) **layer** Fatty tissue under the skin. (page 33)

Suicide The taking of one's own life. (page 88)

Support system A network of people who are available for help and emotional support when needed. (page 91)

Sympathetic (sim·puh·THE·tik) Having and showing kind feelings toward another person. (page 118)

Syphilis (SI·fuh·lis) An STD that progresses through several stages and can cause death. (page 360)

Tar The dark, sticky substance that forms when tobacco burns. (page 404)

Tartar (TAR·ter) Hardened plaque on the teeth. (page 41)

T-cells Lymphocytes that fight germs. (page 346

Team sports Organized activities with a group of people playing on the same side. (page 253)

Teen hot line A special telephone number, usually toll-free, that a teen can call to get advice, information, or a referral to a counseling agency. (page 91)

Tendon Tough tissue that connects muscles to bones. (page 310)

Testes (TES·teez) The glands of the male reproductive system that produce sperm. (page 329)

Third-degree burn A severe burn that damages all layers of the skin and the nerve endings. (page 531)

Tissue A mass of similar cells that performs a specific function. (pages 40, 196)

Tolerance (TAHL·er·ens) **1.** Accepting and respecting other people's beliefs and customs. (page 103) **2.** A condition that occurs when a person's body becomes used to a drug's effect. (page 456)

Tornado A whirling, funnel-shaped windstorm that drops from the sky to the ground. (page 508)

Tornado warning A news bulletin announcing that a tornado is approaching. (page 508)

Tornado watch A news bulletin indicating that a tornado may be forming. (page 508)

Totally fit Physically, mentally, and socially ready to handle whatever comes along from day to day. (page 230)

Toxic Poisonous or harmful. (page 540)

Trachea (TRAY·kee·uh) The windpipe. (page 304)

Tradition (truh·DI·shun) The usual way of doing things. (page 170)

Tumor A swelling or abnormal growth of cells. (page 383)

Umbilical (uhm·BIL·i·kuhl) **cord** The tube that connects the fetus and the mother's placenta and through which the developing baby receives nourishment. (page 199)

Unsaturated fats The liquid fats that are generally found in vegetable oils. (page 263)

Uterus (YOO·tuh·ruhs) A pear-shaped female organ in which a fetus grows and develops until it is ready to be born. (page 198)

Vaccine (vak·SEEN) A preparation of dead or weak germs put into the body to cause the immune system to produce antibodies to certain diseases. (page 348)

Values Beliefs or ideals that guide one's actions. (pages 21, 67)

Veins (VAYNZ) Blood vessels that carry blood from various parts of the body to the heart. (page 302)

Verbal communication The exchange of ideas, opinions, and feelings through words. (page 105)

Vestibule (VES·ti·byool) The central cavity of the inner ear. (page 53)

Victim A person who has been physically or emotionally hurt or abused. (page 138)

Virus (VY·ruhs) Disease-producing agents. (page 341)

Vitamins Nutrients that the body needs in small amounts for proper functioning. (page 262)

Warm-up Body movements that stretch the muscles and prepare the body for physical activity. (page 246)

Warranty The manufacturer's written promise to repair a product during a specified period of time. (page 167)

Weight control Reaching and maintaining one's desired weight. (page 276)

Wellness Actively making choices and decisions that promote good health. (page 7)

Withdrawal A series of painful physical and mental symptoms associated with recovery from addiction to alcohol or other drugs. (page 420)

Glosario

Abdominal thrusts/presiones abdominales Presiones rápidas y hacia arriba que se hacen sobre el diafragma para forzar la salida de algo que esté bloqueando la tráquea de una persona ahogada.

Abscess/absceso Condición dolorosa de un diente, debido a la acumulación de pus en el alvéolo o hueso donde está implantado el diente.

Abuse/abuso Maltrato físico o mental que se da a una persona.

Accident chain/cadena de accidentes La combinación de una situación, un hábito peligroso, y un acto peligroso que pueden provocar un daño.

Acid rain/lluvia ácida Lluvia que está contaminada.

Acquaintance rape/violación por un conocido Situación en la cual una persona es forzada por alguien conocido a tener relaciones sexuales.

Acquired immunodeficiency syndrome (AIDS)/síndrome de inmunodeficiencia adquirida (SIDA) Enfermedad mortal que destruye la capacidad del cuerpo para combatir infecciones.

Acrophobia/acrofobia Miedo anormal de estar en sitios altos.

Active listening/audición activa El procesamiento de un mensaje el cual es escuchado, analizado, y respondido.

Addiction/adicción Necesidad física o mental de drogas u otras substancias.

Adolescence/adolescencia Periodo de la vida entre la niñez y la edad adulta.

Adrenaline/adrenalina Hormona que aumenta el nivel del azúcar en la sangre, y que da energía extra al cuerpo para responder a emergencias.

Advertising/propaganda La creación y envío de mensajes o anuncios diseñados para captar el interés de los consumidores con el fin de que compren determinados bienes y servicios.

Aerobic exercise/ejercicio aeróbico Actividad vigorosa y rítmica que ayuda al corazón y que aumenta la capacidad del cuerpo para inhalar y usar oxígeno.

Alcohol/alcohol Droga que es producida a través de una reacción química en algunos alimentos y que tiene efectos poderosos en el cuerpo.

Alcoholics Anonymous (AA)/ Alcohólicos Anónimos Organización que actúa como grupo de apoyo, para ayudar a los alcohólicos a recuperarse de su adicción al alcohol.

Alcoholism/alcoholismo Enfermedad causada por la necesidad física y mental de consumir alcohol.

Allergen/alergeno Sustancia que causa reacciones alérgicas a algunas personas.

Allergy/alergia Sensibilidad extrema a una sustancia.

Alternative/alternativa Diferentes maneras de pensar o actuar.

Alveoli/alvéolo Sacos microscópicos de aire ubicados en los pulmones en donde ocurren intercambios de gases.

Alzheimer's disease/enfermedad de Alzheimer Enfermedad que causa deterioro en el pensamiento, la memoria y la conducta.

Amino acids/aminoácidos Bloques de sustancias que forman las proteínas.

Amphetamines/anfetaminas Drogas estimulantes altamente adictivas; estas drogas pueden ser prescritas para tratar trastornos de la atención en los niños y para la obesidad.

Anabolic steroids/esteroides anabólicos
Drogas tomadas ilegalmente por algunos atletas debido a la creencia de que producen músculos más fuertes.

Anaerobic exercise/ejercicio anaeróbico
Intensa actividad física de corta duración, que demanda gran consumo de energía y en la cual los músculos trabajan duramente, para producir esa energía.

Anorexia nervosa/anorexia nerviosa
Trastorno caracterizado por un miedo irracional de ganar peso y que frecuentemente conlleva pérdida extrema de peso debida a autoinanición.

Antibiotic/antibiótico Drogas que inhiben o matan microorganismos causantes de enfermedades.

Antibodies/anticuerpos Proteínas de la sangre que destruyen o neutralizan los cuerpos extraños que invaden el organismo.

Antihistamines/antihistamínicos Drogas que alivian los síntomas de las reacciones alérgicas.

Anus/ano Abertura del intestino, a través de la cual las heces salen fuera del cuerpo.

Anxiety disorder/trastorno de ansiedad
Condición en la que se siente excesiva preocupación por las cosas que pasan.

Arteries/arterias Los vasos sanguíneos más largos, que llevan la sangre del corazón a todas las partes del cuerpo.

Arteriosclerosis/arterioesclerosis
Condición en la cual las paredes de las arterias se engruesan y endurecen.

Arthritis/artritis Enfermedad causada por la inflamación y endurecimiento de las articulaciones.

Artificial respiration/respiración artificial
Vea *Rescue breathing.*

Assertive/resuelto(a) Comportarse con seguridad en sí mismo.

Asthma/asma Enfermedad respiratoria crónica en la cual los bronquios se inflaman y bloquean, causando una dificultad en la respiración de la persona.

Astigmatism/astigmatismo Condición del ojo en la que las imágenes se presentan distorsionadas.

Atheroesclerosis/ateroesclerosis
Condición en la cual materias grasas se depositan en las paredes arteriales.

Athlete's foot/pie de atleta Problema infeccioso causado por el crecimiento de hongos en áreas húmedas del pie.

Atrium/aurícula Cada una de las dos cámaras superiores del corazón.

Attitudes/actitudes Sentimientos y creencias.

Auditory nerve/nervio auditivo Grupo de nervios de la coclea del oído que llevan los mensajes al cerebro.

Autonomic system/sistema autónomo
Parte del sistema nervioso periférico, que se ocupa de los movimientos corporales involuntarios.

Bacteria/bacteria Organismos microscópicos que viven en todas partes.

Barbiturates/barbitúricos Tipo de droga depresora, la cual es un poderoso sedativo y que, frecuentemente, se receta como una ayuda para dormir.

Battery/agresión Golpear a una persona, ilegalmente.

B-cells/células B Linfocitos que producen anticuerpos.

Behavior/conducta La forma en que una persona actúa en ocasiones diferentes.

Benign tumor/tumor benigno Masa de células no cancerosas.

Biodegradable/biodegradable Sustancias que pueden ser descompuestas fácilmente por bacterias y otros organismos.

Biological age/edad biológica Medida de la edad, por medio de la determinación del buen funcionamiento de varias partes del cuerpo.

Biopsy/biopsia La remoción quirúrgica de células o tejidos del cuerpo con el fin de examinarlos y obtener un diagnóstico.

Birth defects/defectos de nacimiento
Anormalidades en un feto o en un bebé recién nacido.

Blended family/familia incorporada Tipo de familia en donde uno o ambos de los padres es casado por segunda vez, hay un padrastro o madrastra, y hay hijos.

Blister/ampolla Pequeña inflamación acuosa de la piel, frecuentemente causada por quemadura o fricción.

Blizzard/tormenta Fuerte tormenta de nieve con grandes vientos.

Blood alcohol concentration (BAC)/ concentración de alcohol en la sangre Porcentaje de alcohol contenido en la sangre.

Blood pressure/presión sanguínea La fuerza de la sangre contra las paredes de los vasos sanguíneos.

Blood vessels/vasos sanguíneos Tubos que transportan la sangre a través del cuerpo.

Body composition/composición del organismo La cantidad de grasa del cuerpo comparada con la cantidad de tejidos magros.

Body language/lenguage corporal Mensajes transmitidos a través de movimientos corporales y gestos, más que con palabras.

Brain/cerebro Organo del sistema nervioso compuesto de neuronas, las cuales controlan las acciones, los pensamientos y las emociones.

Brain death/muerte cerebral La que resulta debido al paro total de suministro de oxígeno al cerebro.

Bronchi/bronquios Los dos pasajes a través de los cuales entra el aire en los pulmones.

Bronchodilators/broncodilatadores Medicamentos que relajan los músculos ubicados alrededor de los pasajes de aire bronquiales.

Bulimia/bulimia Transtorno que se caracteriza por un exceso en el comer, seguido del consumo de purgantes.

Bunion/juanete Inflamación dolorosa en la base del dedo gordo del pie.

Bypass surgery/cirugía de bypass Procedimiento quirúrgico que crea un nuevo camino para que circule la sangre alrededor de una arteria bloqueada.

Caffeine/cafeína Sustancia que se encuentra en el café, el té, y algunos refrescos y la cual estimula el corazón y el sistema nervioso.

Calorie/caloría Unidad de energía que mide la energía contenida en diferentes alimentos, o la energía usada después de hacer ejercicio.

Callus/callo Dureza que se forma en un lugar de la piel.

Cancer/cáncer Enfermedad que se caracteriza por el crecimiento rápido e incontrolable de células anormales.

Capillaries/capilares Los vasos sanguíneos más pequeños del cuerpo.

Carbohydrates/carbohidratos Nutrientes, como el azúcar y las harinas, que son la fuente principal de energía para el cuerpo.

Carbon monoxide/monóxido de carbono Gas venenoso, inodoro, e incoloro, que se produce cuando una sustancia se quema.

Carcinogens/carcinógenos Sustancias del medio ambiente que producen cáncer.

Cardiac muscle/músculo cardiaco El músculo del corazón.

Cardiopulmonary resuscitation/ resucitación cardiopulmonar Ayuda de emergencia para restaurar la respiración y la circulación.

Cardiovascular system/sistema cardiovascular El sistema circulatorio.

Carrier/portador Persona que tiene un virus y puede contaminar a otra persona, en algunos casos sin que los síntomas de la enfermedad se hayan manifestado.

Cartilage/cartílago Tejido fuerte y flexible que cubre las terminaciones de los huesos y soporta los tejidos suaves.

Cell/célula La unidad básica de la vida, que conforma la estructura de los seres vivientes.

Cementum/cemento Material parecido al hueso, que cubre la raíz del diente.

Central nervous system/sistema nervioso central La parte del sistema nervioso formada por el cerebro y la espina dorsal.

Cerebellum/cerebelo La parte del cerebro que controla el balance, la postura, y la coordinación.

Cerebrum/cerebro La parte más grande del encéfalo, que controla los músculos, sentidos, pensamientos y lenguaje.

Cervix/cervix El cuello o abertura del útero.

Chemotherapy/quimioterapia El uso de químicos para matar células cancerosas.

Chest thrust/presión torácica Técnica usada en niños para desalojar algún objeto que esté bloqueando el paso del aire.

Chlamydia/clamidia Enfermedad transmitida sexualmente y que causa graves daños al sistema reproductivo.

Cholera/cólera Enfermedad causada por bacterias en aguas no tratadas y caracterizada por calambres, vómitos, y diarrea.

Cholesterol/colesterol Sustancia semejante a la grasa y que se encuentra en todos los animales.

Chromosomes/cromosomas Estructuras filiformes contenidas en el núcleo de las células y que contienen los códigos genéticos de las características hereditarias.

Chronic diseases/enfermedades crónicas Las enfermedades que duran largos períodos de tiempo o que reaparecen con frecuencia.

Chronological age/edad cronológica La edad de una persona medida en años.

Cilia/filamentos Pequeñísimas estructuras parecidas al cabello.

Circulatory system/sistema circulatorio El grupo de órganos que transporta la sangre a través del cuerpo, con el fin de proporcionar materias esenciales a las células y remover materiales desechables de las células.

Cirrhosis/cirrosis Condición en la cual el tejido del hígado presenta cicatrices y está dañado.

Clinical death/muerte clínica El resultado del paro completo de todos los sistemas del cuerpo de una persona.

Cocaine/cocaína Un estimulante ilegal.

Cochlea/cóclea Estructura ósea del oído interno y la cual es esencial para la audición.

Codeine/codeína Droga narcótica usada en medicinas para la tos.

Colon/colon El intestino grueso.

Commitment/compromiso Una promesa u obligación.

Communicable diseases/enfermedades contagiosas Enfermedades que pueden ser transmitidas de una persona a otra.

Communication/comunicación El intercambio de pensamientos, ideas y creencias entre dos o más personas.

Comparison shopping/compras comparadas Las que se efectúan basándose en las ventajas de los diferentes bienes y servicios.

Compromise/transigir Solución de diferencias a través de un mutuo acuerdo.

Conservation/conservación El ahorro de recursos.

Consumer/consumidor La persona que adquiere bienes y servicios.

Consumer advocates/defensores del consumidor Personas que defienden a consumidores con problemas.

Contagious period/período de contagio El lapso de tiempo durante el cual algunas enfermedades pueden ser transmitidas.

Contract/contraer El movimiento de los músculos cuando se contraen o se hacen más cortos.

Contraction/contracción Encogimiento fuerte y repentino de los músculos del útero, que ocurre durante el proceso de dar a luz.

Cool down/enfriamiento Disminución progresiva de una actividad, como el ejercicio.

Cooperation/cooperación Trabajo conjunto o ayuda que se da a una persona, con el fin de obtener un objetivo común.

Coping strategy/estrategia de adaptación Forma de manejar el sentimiento de pérdida que se experimenta cuando alguien allegado muere.

Corn/callo Crecimiento y endurecimiento de un área de la piel, en algún dedo del pie.

Cornea/córnea La membrana transparente de la parte anterior del globo del ojo.

Coronary arteries/arterias coronarias Los vasos sanguíneos que transportan sangre fuera del corazón.

Coupon/cupón Papel que ofrece descuento en determinada marca de productos.

Crown/corona La parte del diente que es visible al ojo.

Cuticle/cutícula Piel muerta alrededor de las uñas de los pies y manos.

Dandruff/caspa Escamas de piel muerta que se forman en el cuero cabelludo.

Date rape/violación durante una cita Situación en la cual una persona es forzada, por otra persona con la que ha salido en una cita, a tener relaciones sexuales.

Decision making/toma de decisiones Procedimiento de seis pasos a seguirse para tomar decisiones o resolver problemas.

Defense mechanism/mecanismo de defensa Forma temporal de manejar el estrés.

Defensive driving/manejo defensivo El que ocurre cuando se obedecen las leyes de tránsito y se observa cuidadosamente a los demás conductores.

Degenerative disease/enfermedad degenerativa Enfermedad no transmisible en la cual los tejidos del cuerpo se destruyen.

Dehydration/deshidratación Pérdida del agua contenida en el cuerpo.

Dentin/dentina El material óseo que rodea la pulpa del diente.

Depressant/depresor Tipo droga de que disminuye las funciones del cuerpo, incluida la actividad del cerebro y de la respiración.

Depression/depresión Estado emocional caracterizado por extrema tristeza, incapacidad de comer o dormir, y pérdida del interés por la vida.

Dermatologist/dermatólogo El médico que trata enfermedades de la piel.

Dermis/dermis La capa más profunda de la piel.

Designer drugs/drogas sintéticas Sustancias que están diseñadas para ser químicamente similares a otras sustancias controladas.

Desired weight/peso deseado El peso apropiado para una persona, basado en su sexo, altura, y estructura del cuerpo.

Detoxification/desintoxicación La eliminación de sustancias dañinas, como las drogas y el alcohol, ya existentes en el cuerpo.

Developmental task/tarea requerida para el desarrollo Algo que se debe de hacer, para que una persona pueda convertirse en un adulto saludable y maduro.

Diabetes/diabetes Enfermedad en la cual el cuerpo no puede convertir los alimentos en energía.

Diaphragm/diafragma El músculo que separa el pecho de la cavidad abdominal.

Diet/dieta La combinación de comidas y bebidas que una persona consume con regularidad.

Digestion/digestión El proceso de convertir los alimentos en substancias que puedan ser absorbidas por la corriente sanguínea.

Digestive system/sistema digestivo Los órganos que convierten los alimentos en nutrientes, para que sean usados por las células.

Discount store/tienda de descuento La que tiene surtido de mercancías regulares a precios reducidos.

Disease/enfermedad Todas los trastornos que afectan el cuerpo y la mente.

Distress/angustia Angustia negativa que impide a una persona ejecutar determinadas actividades.

Divorce/divorcio La terminación legal de un matrimonio.

Drug/droga Sustancias diferentes a la comida, que cambian la estructura del funcionamiento de la mente o del cuerpo.

Earthquake/terremoto Temblor o vibración de la superficie terrestre debido a cambios subterráneos.

Eating disorder/trastorno alimenticio
Conducta en el comer, extremada y peligrosa, y que puede causar graves enfermedades o la muerte.

Ecosystem/ecosistema Los organismos y plantas que forman parte de una determinada comunidad o medio ambiente.

Egg cell/óvulo La célula femenina que unida a la célula espermatozoide forma una nueva vida.

Embryo/embrión Organismo en desarrollo, durante el período que comienza con la fertilización, hasta el momento en que los órganos están desarrollados para sostener una vida.

Emotional need/necesidad emocional Una necesidad que afecta el sentimiento de bienestar de una persona.

Emotions/emociones Sentimientos como el amor, la ira o el miedo.

Emphysema/enfisema Enfermedad de los pulmones en la que los alvéolos se dañan o destruyen.

Enamel/esmalte El material que cubre la parte externa o corona del diente.

Endocrine system/sistema endocrino Las glándulas que producen las hormonas que regulan las actividades del cuerpo.

Environment/medio ambiente Todas las condiciones que rodean a una persona y que afectan su desarrollo.

Epidermis/epidermis La capa exterior de la piel.

Epiglottis/epiglotis Cartílago que cubre la tráquea cuando una persona traga, con el fin de evitar que los alimentos entren a los tubos respiratorios.

Eustachian tube/trompa de Eustaquio Conducto que va de la nariz al oído interno y que equilibra la presión del aire en ambos lados del oído medio.

Excretion/excreción Eliminación de las secreciones del cuerpo.

Exercise frequency/frecuencia del ejercicio El número de veces, durante un lapso de tiempo determinado, en que una persona hace ejercicio.

Exercise intensity/intensidad del ejercicio La cantidad de energía que una persona consume cuando hace ejercicio.

Exercise time/tiempo de ejercicio La cantidad de tiempo que una persona gasta en una sesión de ejercicios.

Expiration date/fecha de vencimiento La fecha estampada en paquetes, que indica cuando ya no sirve su contenido.

Extend/extender El movimiento de los músculos cuando se estiran.

Extended family/familia extendida La familia nuclear y otros parientes que conviven bajo el mismo techo.

Eye contact/contacto con los ojos La habilidad de mirar directamente a los ojos de la persona con la que se habla.

Fallen arches/arcos caídos Condición del pie plano, que no tiene arco.

Family/familia La unidad básica de la sociedad; un grupo de personas relacionadas.

Fatigue/fatiga Cansancio extremo.

Fats/grasas Nutrientes que son fuente de energía para el cuerpo.

Fertilization/fertilización El proceso de juntar el espermatozoide masculino con el óvulo femenino, con el fin de producir una nueva vida.

Fetal alcohol syndrome/síndrome de alcoholismo fetal Grupo de defectos de nacimiento causados por alcoholismo.

Fetus/feto El embrión en sus últimas etapas de desarrollo en el útero de la madre.

Fiber/fibra La parte de las frutas, vegetales y granos que no puede ser digerida.

First-degree burn/quemadura de primer grado Quemadura leve que afecta solo la epidermis y que se caracteriza por el enrojecimiento de la piel.

Flexibility/flexibilidad La habilidad de mover de cierta manera las articulaciones del cuerpo.

Follicle/folículo La pequeña abertura o saco en la dermis, o capa más profunda de la piel, en donde crece el pelo.

Food Guide Pyramid/pirámide de alimentos Una guía para ayudar a la gente a elegir sus alimentos y a decidir cuánto comer de cada grupo de alimentos, con el fin de obtener los nutrientes necesarios.

Fossil fuels/combustibles fósiles Combustibles tomados de la tierra, como el carbón, el aceite y el gas natural.

Fracture/fractura Una ruptura o fisura en el hueso.

Frostbite/congelación Congelamiento de la piel.

Fungi/hongos Organismo viviente que no puede alimentarse a sí mismo y que puede causar enfermedad.

Gallbladder/vesícula biliar Pequeño órgano situado debajo del hígado y que almacena el exceso de bilis.

Gang/pandilla Grupo de gente que permanece junta o que actúa conjuntamente, a menudo con propósitos impropios o ilegales.

Generic product/producto genérico Producto que se vende en paquete sin marca y que a menudo cuesta mucho menos que los productos similares con marca.

Genes/genes Unidad básica que contiene los códigos de los caracteres hereditarios de cada individuo.

Genetic disorder/trastorno genético Enfermedad o trastorno causado por problemas en los genes.

Genital herpes/herpes genital Enfermedad transmitida sexualmente causada por el virus herpes simplex II y que se caracteriza por ampollas en el área genital.

Genital warts/verrugas genitales Enfermedad transmitida sexualmente, caracterizada por verrugas en el área genital y que se extiende rápidamente si no se trata.

Germs/gérmenes Organismos microscópicos causantes de enfermedades.

Gingivitis/gingivitis Enfermedad de las encías causada por placas o alimentos en descomposición, localizados en medio de los dientes.

Gland/glándula Parte del cuerpo que produce sustancias químicas.

Goal/meta Objetivo a ser obtenido.

Gonorrhea/gonorrea Enfermedad transmitida sexualmente, causada por una bacteria y que puede causar daños al área genital, si no es tratada médicamente.

Goods/mercancías Productos hechos para la venta.

Greenhouse effect/efecto de invernadero Condición de la atmósfera, causada por contaminación y que se caracteriza por una tendencia al calentamiento de la temperatura.

Grief/pesar Sentimiento de pesar, profundo y doloroso, relacionado con la muerte de un ser querido.

Ground water/aguas subterráneas Agua acumulada debajo de la superficie terrestre y que suple a pozos y manantiales.

Group dating/salidas en grupo Salir en grupo, con amigos o amigas.

Hallucinogen/alucinógeno Droga que crea imágenes imaginarias o que distorsiona las imágenes reales en el individuo que la usa.

Hate crime/crimen por odio Es el crimen cometido por una persona o grupo debido a diferencias raciales, religiosas o culturales.

Hazard/peligro Posibilidad de daño.

Hazardous waste/desperdicios peligrosos Desperdicios que pueden causar enfermedad, si no son eliminados en forma apropiada.

Head lice/piojos Insectos muy pequeños que viven en el pelo.

Health/salud La combinación de bienestar físico, mental y social.

Health care facility/servicios de salud Lugar donde una persona recibe cuidados de salud.

Health care system/sistema de salud La forma como una persona recibe y paga por sus cuidados de salud.

Health education/educación sobre salud Información sobre salud proporcionada de tal manera, que estimule a las personas a actuar positivamente en relación a su salud.

Health insurance/seguro de salud
Programa mediante el cual una persona se
compromete a pagar una suma anual a cambio
del pago de ciertos gastos médicos por una
compañía.

**Health maintenance organization
(HMO)/organización para el mantenimiento de la salud** Grupo de diferentes
clases de médicos que proporcionan cuidados
médicos a los miembros.

**Heart and lung endurance/resistencia
del corazón y los pulmones** La capacidad
del corazón y los pulmones de proporcionar
oxígeno al cuerpo, durante el ejercicio, y el
tiempo que se toman para volver a la
normalidad.

Heart attack/ataque al corazón
Condición seria en la cual el músculo cardiaco
es dañado, debido al paro del flujo de sangre
que va al corazón.

Hepatitis/hepatitis Enfermedad
inflamatoria del hígado.

Heredity/herencia La transferencia de
características de padres a hijos a través de los
genes.

Histamine/histamina Substancia que causa
los síntomas de reacciones alérgicas.

Hives/urticaria Condición de la piel causada
por una alergia y que se caracteriza por picazón
y erupciones enrojecidas.

Homicide/homicidio La muerte de una
persona causada por otra persona.

Hormones/hormonas Los químicos
producidos por las glándulas y que regulan
varias funciones del cuerpo.

Hospice/hospicio Lugar donde se cuida a
las personas con enfermedades incurables.

**Human immunodeficiency virus (HIV)/
virus de inmunodeficiencia humana (VIH)**
El virus que causa el SIDA.

Hurricane/huracán Tormenta con fuertes
lluvias y ráfagas de vientos y que con
frecuencia comienza en zonas tropicales.

Hypertension/hipertensión Elevación de la
presión arterial.

Hypothermia/hipotermia Disminución
repentina de la temperatura del cuerpo, por
debajo de lo normal.

Immunity/inmunidad La resistencia del
cuerpo a los gérmenes y a las sustancias dañinas
que puedan ser producidas por esos gérmenes.

Individual sports/deportes individuales
Los deportes que la gente disfruta indivi-
dualmente o con un amigo(a).

Infancy/infancia El primer año después del
nacimiento.

Infection/infección Condición que ocurre
cuando los gérmenes invaden las células del
cuerpo y luego se multiplican.

Influenza/influenza Una enfermedad
respiratoria seria y contagiosa, causada por un
virus.

Inhalant/inhalante Sustancia que al
aspirarse produce un estado de alucinación.

Insulin/insulina Hormona producida en el
páncreas y que regula el nivel de azúcar en la
sangre.

Interferon/interferón Sustancia producida
por las células que impide que un virus se
reproduzca y que, por lo tanto, ayuda a controlar
infecciones.

Iris/iris La parte coloreada del ojo que rodea
la pupila.

Jaywalk/caminar descuidado Cuando se
cruza una calle descuidadamente, sin prestar
atención a las reglas del tráfico o a las luces.

Joint/articulación El lugar del cuerpo en
donde se unen los huesos.

Keratin/queratina La substancia que
endurece las uñas.

Kidneys/riñones Los dos órganos que
remueven las aguas solubles desechables del
cuerpo.

Landfill/rellenos sanitarios Lugar donde la
basura y otros desperdicios son enterrados, con
el fin de rellenar terrenos bajoso húmedos.

Larynx/laringe La parte superior del tracto
respiratorio, que contiene las cuerdas vocales.

Laxative/laxante Medicinas que hacen pasar rápidamente los alimentos a través del sistema digestivo, sin que éstos tengan tiempo de liberar sus nutrientes.

Lens/cristalino La estructura debajo de la pupila que enfoca la luz.

License/licencia Permiso legal para hacer algo.

Lifestyle disease/enfermedad debida al estilo de vida Es la enfermedad causada por los malos hábitos de salud de una persona.

Lifestyle factor/factor del estilo de vida Hábito relacionado con el modo de vivir de una persona.

Lifetime sport/deporte vitalicio Actividad que se puede disfrutar durante toda una vida.

Ligament/ligamento El tejido firme y fuerte que conecta los huesos en las articulaciones.

Liver/hígado Una glándula corporal que tiene varias funciones digestivas, incluida la disolución de las grasas.

Love/amor Gran afecto por una persona.

Lymphatic system/sistema linfático Sistema circulatorio secundario que transporta la linfa.

Lymph nodes/nódulos linfáticos Grupos de células del sistema linfático, que filtran las sustancias dañinas del sistema linfático.

Lymphocytes/linfocitos Los glóbulos blancos, los cuales son las principales células responsables de defender el cuerpo de gérmenes.

Mainstream smoke/humo directo El humo que exhala el fumador.

Malignant tumor/tumor maligno Masa de células cancerosas.

Malnutrition/malnutrición Condición en la cual el cuerpo no recibe los nutrientes que necesita, para crecer y funcionar bien.

Malocclusion/maloclusión Condición en la cual los dientes no están alineados en la forma debida.

Malpractice/negligencia médica Cuando no se proporcionan cuidados de salud con un grado aceptable de calidad.

Mediation/mediación El proceso de resolver conflictos, con la ayuda neutral de una tercera persona.

Medicaid/Medicaid Programa de seguro médico del gobierno y que paga gastos médicos a la gente pobre.

Medicare/Medicare Programa de seguro médico del gobierno y que paga gastos médicos a las personas mayores de 65 años.

Medicine/medicina Droga que cura o previene enfermedades u otras condiciones relacionadas con la salud.

Melanin/melanina La sustancia que proporciona la mayor parte del color a la piel.

Menstrual cycle/ciclo menstrual El lapso del tiempo entre una menstruación y el comienzo de la siguiente; el proceso de la menstruación.

Menstruation/menstruación El proceso de eliminación de sangre y tejidos del útero.

Mental health/salud mental El proceso de gustarse y aceptarse uno mismo.

Metastasis/metástasis El proceso de propagación de las células cancerosas de un tumor a otras partes del cuerpo.

Minerals/minerales Una clase de nutrientes necesarios, en pequeñas cantidades, para que el cuerpo funcione bien.

Mononucleosis/mononucleosis Enfermedad viral, común entre la gente joven y que se caracteriza por el aumento anormal del número de glóbulos blancos.

Mucus/moco Fluido que humedece y protege las membranas mucosas.

Muscle endurance/resistencia muscular La cantidad de tiempo durante el cual un grupo de músculos puede funcionar, sin cansarse demasiado.

Muscle strength/resistencia muscular El máximo de trabajo que pueden enfectuar los músculos, en un momento determinado.

Muscular system/sistema muscular El grupo de tejidos fuertes que le permite al cuerpo moverse.

Narcotic/narcótico Depresor adictivo usado para suprimir el dolor y el cual se puede obtener legalmente, únicamente con una receta médica.

Neck/cuello La parte del diente entre la corona y la raíz.

Negotiation/negociación El proceso de llegar a una solución mediante la discusión de problemas, cara a cara.

Neuron/neurona Célula nerviosa.

Neurosis/neurosis Condición mental en la que el miedo interfiere con la habilidad de funcionar de una persona.

Neutrality/neutralidad El no tomar posición frente a un argumento.

Nicotine/nicotina Estimulante adictivo contenido en el tabaco y que acelera los latidos del corazón.

Noncommunicable diseases/ enfermedades no contagiosas Las enfermedades que son causadas por la forma en que vive la gente, por las condiciones con las que nacen, o por peligros en el medio ambiente.

Nonrenewable resource/recurso no renovable Un recurso de la tierra que no puede ser sustituido una vez que se gasta.

Nuclear family/familia nuclear La familia que consiste en el padre, la madre y los hijos que conviven bajo un mismo techo.

Nuclear waste/desecho nuclear Materias dañinas producidas por reacciones nucleares.

Nutrient/nutriente Una de las seis sustancias en la comida y que el cuerpo necesita para crecer y funcionar bien.

Nutrient density/densidad de los nutrientes Los nutrientes en los alimentos, comparados con las calorías que proporcionan.

Nutrition/nutrición El proceso de tomar y usar nutrientes.

Obesity/obesidad Condición en la cual el peso de una persona está en un 20 por ciento o más por encima de su peso deseado.

Obstetrician/obstetra El médico que se especializa en el cuidado de la mujer embarazada y de su futuro hijo.

Opportunistic infection/infección oportunista Cualquier enfermedad que ataque a una persona que tenga su sistema de defensas debilitado.

Optic nerve/nervio óptico Grupo de fibras nerviosas que transportan mensajes del ojo al cerebro.

Organ/órgano Parte de un organismo viviente que está compuesta de tejido y que ejecuta una función determinada.

Osteoarthritis/osteoartritis Enfermedad crónica de los huesos, común en la gente mayor, en la que las articulaciones se degeneran y se vuelven dolorosas.

Ovaries/ovarios Los dos órganos reproductivos femeninos que producen los óvulos.

Over-the-counter medicine/medicamento sin receta Medicamento que puede ser comprado sin una prescripción médica.

Overweight/sobrepeso El peso que es mayor al deseado para una persona, de acuerdo a su tamaño, sexo y estructura corporal.

Ovulation/ovulación El proceso mediante el cual se libera un óvulo del ovario.

Ozone/ozono Forma de oxígeno presente en el aire, especialmente después de una tormenta.

Pacemaker/marcapasos Pequeño aparato eléctrico que envia pulsaciones al corazón, para que los latidos sean regulares.

Pancreas/páncreas El órgano que produce insulina y libera enzimas para la digestión de carbohidratos, proteinas y grasas.

Parenting/crianza de hijos El cuidado y la educación los niños por los padres.

Particulates/partículas Pequeñísimas partículas contaminantes que se encuentran en el aire, tales como el polvo y el hollín.

Passive smoking/fumar pasivamente Cuando se inhala el humo del cigarrillo fumado por personas que están cerca.

Peer/contemporáneo Una persona de la misma edad.

Peer pressure/presión de contemporáneos La presión ejercida a través de las creencias y acciones de amigos y compañeros.

Periodontium/periodoncia Las estructuras que soportan los dientes, incluida la quijada, las encías y los ligamentos.

Peripheral nervous system/sistema nervioso periférico El sistema formado por los nervios que conectan el sistema nervioso central, con todas las demás partes del cuerpo.

Personality/personalidad Las cualidades y características que hacen a una persona diferente de todas las demás.

Pesticide/pesticida Químico que se usa para matar o controlar animales o insectos.

Phagocytes/fagocitos Las células blancas de la sangre, que destruyen gérmenes.

Phagocytosis/fagocitosis El proceso de los glóbulos blancos que destruyen gérmenes.

Phobia/fobia Un miedo de tal magnitud que interfiere con cualquier acción razonable.

Physical fatigue/fatiga física Cansancio extremo del cuerpo.

Physically fit/físicamente capaz Estado en el que el cuerpo es capaz de manejar las situaciones que se le presenten.

Physiological dependence/dependencia fisiológica Tipo de adicción en la cual el cuerpo siente la necesidad de una droga.

Pituitary gland/glándula pituitaria La glándula situada en la base del cerebro, que controla otras glándulas.

Placebo effect/efecto placebo Mejora en la salud, como resultado del uso de una píldora o preparación que no contiene ingredientes activos.

Placenta/placenta El tejido que cubre las paredes del útero y que alimenta al feto.

Plaque/placa La película delgada de sarro que se forma en el diente. Los depósitos grasos que se forman en las paredes arteriales.

Pollen/polen Sustancia en forma de polvo que es liberada por ciertas plantas y hierbas y que causan reacciones alérgicas a algunas personas.

Pollution/polución Cualquier cosa que ensucie el medio ambiente o que lo haga insalubre.

Pores/poros Aberturas pequeñísimas en la piel.

Precaution/precaución Cuidado que se toma con anticipación, con el fin de asegurarse buenos resultados o evitarse resultados negativos.

Precycling/preciclaje El proceso de reducción de la producción de desperdicios, antes de que los mismos se produzcan.

Preferred provider/médico preseleccionado Un médico que forma parte o que ha sido previamente aprobado, por un plan de salud específico.

Prejudice/prejuicio Una opinión negativa formada sin justificación y que, generalmente, es contra gente de un grupo racial, religioso, o cultural diferente.

Prenatal care/cuidado prenatal Pasos que se toman para cuidar la salud de una mujer embarazada y su futuro bebé.

Prescription medicine/medicamento con receta Medicina que solo puede ser comprada con una receta médica.

Primary care provider/médico de cabecera Médico que proporciona a sus pacientes cuidados de salud generales.

Proteins/proteínas Nutrientes que son esenciales para el crecimiento y reparación de las células del cuerpo.

Protozoa/protozoos Organismos unicelulares que, algunas veces, causan enfermedades.

Psychological dependence/dependencia psicológica Cualquier tipo de adicción en la cual la mente siente la necesidad de una droga.

Psychological fatigue/fatiga psicológica Extremo cansancio mental.

Psychosis/psicosis Trastorno mental severo.

Puberty/pubertad El período de la adolescencia cuando una persona comienza a desarrollar ciertas características propias de su sexo.

Pulp/pulpa La parte interna y sensitiva del diente, que contiene vasos sanguíneos y nervios.

Public health/salud pública Mantenimiento y mejora de la salud de la comunidad, especialmente, como una función gubernamental.

Pupil/pupila La abertura oscura en el centro del iris que regula el monto de luz que entra en el ojo.

Quackery/curanderismo Charlatanería, fraude.

Radiation/radiación Tratamiento usado para algunos tipos de cáncer.

Radon/radón Un gas radioactivo formado por la decadencia del radio.

Random violence/violencia al azar Violencia cometida sin razón y contra cualquier persona.

Rape/violación Crimen en el cual una persona fuerza a otra a tener relaciones sexuales.

Recommended Dietary Allowance (RDA)/ raciones dietéticas recomendadas Guía del monto de cada nutriente que debe ser consumido diariamente.

Recovery/recuperación Regreso del cuerpo a un estado normal, generalmente, después de una enfermedad o adicción.

Recycling/reciclaje El proceso de tratamiento de materiales para que puedan ser usados nuevamente.

Refusal skills/habilidad de rehusar Maneras efectivas de decir no.

Relationship/relación La conexión que una persona tiene con otra persona o grupo.

Reliable/confiable Digno de confianza.

Reproductive system/sistema reproductivo Grupo de órganos involucrados en la reproducción de la descendencia.

Rescue breathing/respiración de rescate Forma de restaurar la respiración normal, a través del refuerzo de aire que se dé a los pulmones de la víctima.

Respiratory system/sistema respiratorio Grupo de órganos que llevan oxígeno al cuerpo y que remuevan el dióxido de carbono del cuerpo.

Responsible dating/citas responsables Ser digno de confianza, respetuoso, y cuidadoso con la persona con quien se sale en una cita.

Responsibility/responsabilidad Una obligación.

Retina/retina La parte interna del ojo que es sensora de la luz.

Rheumatoid arthritis/artritis reumática Enfermedad crónica que se caracteriza por dolor, inflamación, y endurecimiento de las articulaciones.

Rickettsias/rickettsia Pequeñísimos organismos causantes de enfermedades y que son propagados por pulgas, piojos, y garrapatas.

Risk behavior/conducta riesgosa Manera de actuar que aumenta los riesgos de daño.

Risk factor/factor de riesgo Característica o hábito que aumenta los riesgos de una persona, de sufrir una determinada enfermedad.

Root/raíz Parte del diente que está dentro de la encía.

Rubella/rubéola Enfermedad contagiosa.

Safety conscious/conciencia de la seguridad Estar consciente de la importancia de la seguridad personal.

Saliva/saliva La sustancia producida por las glándulas salivales y que contiene las enzimas que dan comienzo a la digestión de los alimentos.

Sanitation/aseo público La eliminación de aguas residuales y desechos, con el fin de proteger la salud pública.

Saturated fats/grasas saturadas Las grasas que se encuentran en las carnes y algunos productos lácteos.

Schizophrenia/esquizofrenia Enfermedad mental seria, en la que la persona pierde su contacto con la realidad.

Sclera/esclerótica La membrana dura que está ubicada en la parte exterior del ojo.

Sebum/sebo Secreción aceitosa relacionada con el acné.

Second-degree burn/quemadura de segundo grado Quemadura que destruye la capa externa de la piel y que daña la segunda capa, causando enrojecimiento y ampollas.

Secondhand smoke/humo indirecto El humo que no fumadores inhalan de los fumadores que estén cerca.

Second opinion/segunda opinión Consulta que se hace a un segundo médico, después de la visita al médico regular de la persona, con el fin de confirmar el primer diagnóstico o de solicitar la recomendación de un tratamiento diferente.

Self-concept/autoimagen La imagen que una persona tiene de sí misma.

Self-esteem/autoestima La confianza que una persona tiene en sus propias habilidades.

Semicircular canals/canales semi-circulares Los tres canales interconectados del oído interno, parcialmente llenos de líquido, y que son responsables del equilibrio del cuerpo.

Services/servicios Actividades útiles que se ponen a la venta.

Sewage/aguas residuales Comida, desechos humanos, detergentes y otros productos, arrastrados por cloacas y desagües.

Shock/choque Condición seria en la que las funciones del cuerpo se vuelven lentas.

Skeletal muscles/músculos del esqueleto Los músculos que trabajan con los huesos, para facilitar el movimiento.

Skeletal system/sistema óseo Todos los huesos del cuerpo.

Side effect/efecto secundario Condición que se produce como consecuencia de un tratamiento o medicación.

Sidestream smoke/humo secundario El humo producido por la colilla prendida de un cigarrillo.

Single-parent family/familia con sólo la madre o el padre La familia que tiene únicamente uno de los padres viviendo en la casa.

Small claims court/tribunal de demandas menores Corte estatal que atiende los casos civiles relacionados con reclamaciones de pequeñas sumas de dinero.

Small intestine/intestino delgado El órgano semejante a un largo tubo, en donde ocurre la mayor parte de la disgestión.

Smog/niebla Mezcla insalubre de contaminantes y neblina en el aire, generalmente localizada sobre ciudades.

Smoke alarm/alarma de humo Aparato que emite un sonido agudo cuando detecta humo.

Smooth muscles/músculos lisos Los músculos involuntarios en el sistema digestivo y en el sistema circulatorio.

Social age/edad social La edad calculada de acuerdo al estilo de vida de una persona.

Social health/salud social La habilidad de una persona de relacionarse bien con la gente a su alrededor.

Socializing/socialización El disfrute de la compañía de la gente.

Somatic system/sistema somático La parte del sistema nervioso periférico relacionada con las acciones voluntarias.

Specialist/especialista El médico que está entrenado para tratar determinada clase de pacientes o enfermedades.

Sperm cell/espermatozoide La célula masculina reproductiva, que al unirse con el óvulo produce una nueva vida.

Sphygmomanometer/esfigmomanómetro Instrumento que mide la tensión sanguínea.

Spinal cord/médula espinal Una larga estructura formada de neuronas que lleva mensajes al cerebro y desde el cerebro a todas las partes del cuerpo.

Stepparent/padrastro o madrastra La persona que se casa con la madre o el padre de un niño.

Stimulant/estimulante Droga que acelera las funciones del cuerpo.

Stomach/estómago El órgano muscular en donde ocurre parte de la digestión.

Stress/estrés La respuesta que da el cuerpo ante algún cambio.

Stressor/estresante Un causante de estrés.

Stroke/embolia cerebral Condición seria que ocurre cuando se paraliza el flujo de sangre al cerebro, generalmente, debido al bloqueo de la arteria que va al cerebro.

Subcutaneous layer/capa subcutánea Tejido grasoso localizado debajo de la piel.

Suicide/suicidio El quitarse la propia vida.

Support system/sistema de apoyo Grupo de personas en el que cada miembro está a la disposición de los otros cuando se necesita su ayuda y apoyo emocional.

Sympathetic/compasivo La persona que tiene y demuestra sentimientos de compasión por otra persona.

Syphilis/sífilis Enfermedad transmitida sexualmente, que progresa a través de varias etapas y que puede causar la muerte.

Tar/alquitrán La substancia oscura y pegajosa que se forma cuando se quema tabaco.

Tartar/sarro Placa endurecida que se forma en el diente.

T-cells/células T Linfocitos que combaten los gérmenes.

Team sports/deportes en equipo Actividades organizadas en donde un grupo de gente juega para un equipo.

Teen hot line/línea telefónica para adolescentes Un número de teléfono especial, generalmente gratis, adonde un adolescente puede llamar para obtener consejo, información, o para ser referido a alguna agencia social.

Tendon/tendón Tejido fuerte que conecta los músculos con los huesos.

Testes/testículos Las glándulas del sistema reproductor masculino, que producen la esperma.

Third-degree burn/quemadura de tercer grado Quemadura severa que daña todas las capas de la piel y las terminaciones de los nervios.

Tissue/tejido Masa de células similares que desempeña una función específica.

Tolerance/tolerancia 1. La aceptación y respeto de las creencias y costumbres de otras personas. 2. Condición que ocurre cuando el cuerpo de una persona se acostumbra a los efectos de una droga.

Tornado/tornado Tormenta de fuertes vientos, en forma de torbellino, que gira en grandes círculos y que cae del cielo a la tierra.

Tornado warning/alerta de tornado Boletín de noticias que anuncia que un huracán se está acercando a una zona.

Tornado watch/aviso de tornado Boletín de noticias que indica que un huracán se puede estar formando.

Totally fit/completa buena forma El estar física, mental y socialmente listo(a), para manejar cualquier situación de la vida diaria.

Toxic/tóxico Algo venenoso o dañino.

Trachea/tráquea El conducto del aire del cuerpo.

Tradition/tradición La manera usual de hacer las cosas.

Tumor/tumor La inflamación o crecimiento anormal de células.

Umbilical cord/cordón umbilical El tubo que conecta el feto a la placenta de la madre y a través del cual se alimenta el feto.

Unsaturated fats/grasas no saturadas Las grasas líquidas que, generalmente, se encuentran en los aceites vegetales.

Uterus/útero El órgano femenino en el cual crece y se desarrolla el feto, hasta que está listo para nacer.

Vaccine/vacuna Una preparación de gérmenes débiles o muertos que se coloca dentro del organismo, con el fin de hacer que el sistema de defensas produzca anticuerpos contra ciertas enfermedades.

Values/valores Creencias o ideas que guían las acciones de una persona.

Veins/venas Vasos sanguíneos que llevan la sangre desde varias partes del cuerpo hasta el corazón.

Verbal communication/comunicación verbal El intercambio de ideas, opiniones y sentimientos, a través de palabras.

Vestibule/vestíbulo La cavidad central del oído interno.

Victim/víctima Una persona que ha sido herida o abusada física o emocionalmente.

Virus/virus Agentes productores de enfermedades.

Vitamins/vitaminas Nutrientes que el cuerpo necesita en pequeñas cantidades, para funcionar de forma apropiada.

Warm-up/calentamiento Los movimientos del cuerpo que estiran los músculos y los preparan para actividades físicas.

Warranty/garantía La promesa escrita de un fabricante, de reparar un producto, durante un lapso específico de tiempo.

Weight control/control de peso La obtención y mantenimiento del peso deseado.

Wellness/bienestar Decisiones y selecciones que promueven la buena salud y que son hechas de forma activa.

Withdrawal/retirada Una serie de síntomas mentales y físicos, asociados con la recuperación de una adicción al alcohol o a otras drogas.

Index

Note: Page numbers in *italics* refer to art and marginal features.

Fasting, 280
Fat, body, 238
Fatigue, stress and, 83
Fats, 263, 271
Fat-soluble vitamins, 262
Fear, 75
Feces, 321
Federal health departments, 187
Federal Trade Commission (FTC), 165
Feedback, listening and giving, 107
Feet, 56–57
Female reproductive system, 330–31, *333*
Fertilization, 197, 331
Fetal alcohol syndrome (FAS), 204, 374, 431
Fetal environment, problems in, 204–5
Fetus, 198
Fever, 346
Fiber, 270
Fight-or-flight response, 82, 86
Fights
    helping others avoid, 156–57
    preventing, 154–56
    reasons for, 152–53
Financial problems of teen parenthood, 133
Fire safety, 492–93
First aid, 516–21, 529–33
    ABCs of, *518*
    for broken bones, 529
    for bruises, 530
    for burns, 531
    for choking, 524–27
    CPR, *221, 522,* 527–28
    defined, 516
    for fainting, 533
    first steps in, 516–18
    for insect bites and stings, 530
    for nosebleeds, 532
    for objects in eye, 532
    for poisoning, 521
    rescue breathing, 518, *519*
    severe bleeding, controlling, 520
    for shock, 521
    for sprains, 530
First-aid kits, 523
First-degree burn, 531
First impressions, *66*
Fitness, physical. *See* Physical fitness
Fitness level, *239*
Fitness potential level, 232, 240
Flashbacks from hallucinogens, *467*
Flexibility, 237, *244*
Flexors, 312, *313*
Floods, 511
Flossing, 43, 44

Flu, the, *307,* 352
Fluids during exercise, drinking, 250
Fluoride, *263*
Follicles, 36
Food. *See also* Nutrition
    and alcohol's effect, 430
    as basic need, 260–61
    calming vs. stimulating, *87*
    demand for, 541
    nutrient-dense, 278
    substances in, 270–73
Food and Drug Administration (FDA), 165, *187,* 214, 456, 457
Food, Drug, and Cosmetic Act, *188*
Food Guide Pyramid, 266–67
    servings, *268*
Food Safety and Inspection Service (FSIS), 165
Foot problems, *56,* 57
Ford, Gerald, 164
Formaldehyde, *405*
Fossil fuels, 545, 549
Fracture, *311,* 529
Fraternal twins, 197
Friends, 117–21. *See also* Peer pressure
    and diet, *261*
    qualities of good, 118
    tips for making new, 117, *118*
    troubled, 92–93
Frostbite, 505, *509*
Fungi, 341

Gallbladder, 320, *326*
Gallstones, *323*
Gangs and gang-related violence, 148, 151, 153
Gastric juice, 319, *345*
Gastrocnemius, *313*
Gender, alcohol's effect and, 430
Generic products, 169, *170,* 352–53
Genes, 202
Genetic disorders, 202–3, 373
Genital herpes, *356,* 360
Genital warts, *356, 359, 360*
Geography, diet and, *261*
German measles, 205
Germs, 340
    defenses against, 345–49
    HIV and vulnerability to, 364
    medicines that fight, 453
    skin as defense against, *32*
    spread of, 342
    types of, 341
Giardia, 342
Gingivitis, 44
Gland, 324
    endocrine, 324–27
    reproductive, *325, 329, 332*

salivary, *320, 326*
sweat, 33, *326*
Glaucoma, 51
Gliding joints, *310*
Glucose, *396*
Gluteus maximus, *313*
Goals, setting, 23–27
Goiter, *327*
Gonorrhea, *356, 359, 360*
Gooden, Dwight, 471
Goods
    health, 162–63
    shopping for, 167–68
Good Samaritan Law, 517
Government
    consumer protection from, 165, *166,* 184
    and drug safety, 456–57
    insurance programs, 175
Government health departments, 186–87
Greenhouse effect, 546
Green light, *499*
Grief process, 223–25
Griffith-Joyner, Florence, 471
Groin stretch, *247*
Groundwater, 540
Group, belonging to, 104
Group dating, 125, *211*
Group health insurance, 175
Group practices, 176
Growth and development, 196–227
    adulthood, 216–20
    aging, 218–20
    beginning of life, 196–200
    birth, 200, 331
    from cell to system, *196–97*
    from childhood to adolescence, 206–13
    death and grief, facing, 221–25
    and environment, 203–5
    Erikson's stages of life, *208–9*
    factors in development, 201–5
    and heredity, *201,* 202–3
    measuring age, 218–19
    during pregnancy, 198–99
    inside uterus, 199
Growth extremes, *327*
Growth hormone, *208*
Growth spurt, 209
Gun-related deaths, *146, 147*
Guns, safety tips for, *146*
Gynecologist, 332

Hair and hair problems, 36–37
Hairstyles, *37*
Hair stylist, 46
Halfway Houses, *476*
Halitosis, 45
Hallucinogens, 466–67

Credits

PHOTOGRAPHS

Cover photo: Design Office/Curt Fisher.

Allsport: Mike Powell, page 471.

Boston Globe Photo: page 16.

CMCD Library: page 215 (left).

© Comstock Inc. 1995: Stuart Cohen, page 75.

David Crow: pages ii–iii, 136–37, 139, 141, 142, 144, 145 (left, right), 146, 150 (right), 151 (left), 152, 154, 155, 156, 157, 211, 219, 258–59, 265, 269 (all), 272, 275 (both), 276, 281, 282, 338–39, 340, 342, 343 (both), 353, 362, 365, 444.

Custom Medical Stock Photo: Delilah R. Cohn, pages 198 (right), 199 (both).

Duomo Photography Inc.: Ben Van Hook, page 215 (right).

© FPG International: C. Jose Luis Banus-March, page 166; Ron Chapple, page 145 (middle); Spencer Grant, page 222; C. Jeffrey Sylvester, page 509; Telegraph Colour Library, pages 224, 354.

Gamma Liaison: Jean-Marc Giboux, page 148; Brad Markel, page 408.

Ann Garvin: page 322.

General Motors: page 545.

H. Armstrong Roberts: Valbuena Chimps, page 207 (left); J. Nettis, page 200; M. Roessler, page 206 (right).

Richard Hutchings: pages ix (bottom), xiv, 17 (left), 77 (both), 86 (both), 88, 114, 228–29, 230–31, 232, 233, 234 (right), 236 (both), 237 (all), 238, 241, 242 (both), 243 (both), 246 (both), 247 (all), 249, 250, 251, 252, 253 (left), 255, 279, 435, 480–81.

Ken Lax: pages x (bottom), xii (bottom), 46 (top), 78 (left), 129, 178, 370–71, 375, 376, 381, 389 (both), 391, 393, 395, 397, 514–15, 520, 522, 523 (bottom, top right), 524, 527, 528, 529, 536–37, 538, 542 (right), 547, 548, 551 (bottom), 552, 553, 556, 557.

Medical Images, Inc.: Michael English, page 531; Frederick C. Skvara, pages 359 (bottom), 383 (both); Howard Sochurek, page 359 (top).

Cliff Moore: pages vii (bottom), 62–63, 64 (both), 65 (both), 69, 71, 72, 73, 74 (all), 76, 78 (right), 79, 80, 90, 92, 93, 208 (all), 209 (bottom), 214.

Peerless Photography: page 268.

Photo Network: Mark Miller, page 409.

© Photo Researchers, Inc.: Bachman, page 67; CNRI/Science Photo Library, page 202, 328 (right), 394, 453; Motta & Familiari/Anatomy Dept./University "La Sapienza," Rome/ Science Photo Library, page 328 (left); A. Glauberman/Science Source, page 406; Will and Deni McIntyre, page 367; Hank Morgan, page 388; Blair Seitz, page 543 (left); A. Sieveking/Petit Format, page 206 (left); Jim Steinberg, page 539 (right); Norm Thomas, page 540; Kent Wood, page 523 (top left).

PhotoEdit: Billy E. Barnes, pages xi (bottom), 410 (bottom), 417, 421, 450–51, 458, 463; Leslye Borden, page 223 (right); Robert Brenner, pages 25, 551 (top); Michelle Bridwell, pages 5 (right), 10, 24, 207 (right), 212; Jose Carillo, page 11 (bottom); Myrleen Ferguson Cate: page 217 (right), 218 (bottom); Paul Conklin, page 505 (left); Deborah Davis, page 103; Mary Kate Denny, pages 6, 194–95, 218 (left), 434, 437, 445, 446, 469, 473 (top), 475, 494, 496; Amy Etra: page 198 (left), 423; Tony Freeman, pages ix (top), 2–3, 13, 14, 15 (bottom right), 18, 19, 213, 220, 223 (left), 316 (top), 419 (right), 428, 470 (right), 473 (bottom), 484, 488, 492, 504, 505 (right); Robert W. Ginn, page 477; Richard Hutchings: page 218 (right), 221; National Center for

Atmospheric Research, page 508; Michael Newman, pages xi (top), 40, 189, 201, 290–91, 316 (bottom), 317, 410 (top), 419 (left), 422, 442, 465, 466, 468, 470 (left); Jonathan Nourok: pages xii (top), 12, 17 (right), 21, 297 (left), 324, 412, 452, 489 (left), 511; James Shaffer, page 441, 506; Rhoda Sidney, pages 217 (left), 295, 301, 438, 474, 498 (both); David Young-Wolff, pages vii (top), xvi–1, 4, 5 (left, bottom), 9, 11 (top), 15 (top, bottom left), 22, 27, 151 (right), 205, 209 (top), 288–89, 297 (middle left, middle right, right), 332, 402–3, 426–27, 482–83, 485, 489 (right), 502, 542 (left).

Phototake: Bob Schuchman, page 197.

Joan and Hy Rosner: page 543 (right).

Kathy Sloane: pages viii (bottom), 30–31, 32, 39, 45, 46 (bottom), 47 (both), 50, 54, 58 (all), 96–97, 160–61, 162, 163, 164 (both), 165, 169 (both), 171, 172, 173, 174 (left), 175, 179, 182, 183, 184, 185, 186.

Southern Stock Photo Agency: Tom McCarthy, page 260.

SportsChrome Inc. East/West: Rob Tringali, Jr., page 150 (left).

Sports Illustrated: Manny Millan, page 23.

Sports Photo Masters Inc.: Kirk Schlea, pages 192–93.

Stock Boston: Bob Daemmrich, page 253 (right); David Ulmer, page 234 (left).

SuperStock: BL Productions, page 35; Dave Preston, page 440.

Sygma: Brooks Kraft, page 355.

Tony Stone Images: Kindra Clinett, page 387; Daniel J. Cox, page 539 (left); Robert E. Daemmrich, page 352; Nick Gunderson, page 174 (right), Tony Henshaw, page 377; Jim Pickerell, page 300; Don Smetzer, page 357; Arthur Tilley, page 123 (top left); Bob Torrez, page 170.

Terry Wild Studio: pages viii (top), 26, 56, 66, 98–99, 100, 101, 102, 104 (both), 105, 106, 107, 108, 109 (both), 111, 113, 115, 116, 117, 118 (both), 119 (both), 122, 123 (bottom, right), 124, 126, 127, 128, 130, 132, 400–401, 411, 443.

Washington Convention and Visitors Association: page 187.

ILLUSTRATIONS

Bill Smith Studios: pages 188–89 (middle), 212, 216.

Ron Boisvert: pages 299, 310, 313, 325.

Max Crandall: pages xv, 20–21, 36–37, 57, 68, 82, 84, 120, 149, 180, 183, 214 (top), 215 (top), 277, 279, 290 (both), 347, 355 (bottom), 364, 377, 462 (top), 486–87, 493.

Hilda Muinos: pages x (top), 33, 36, 40 (top), 41, 48, 49, 52, 53 (top), 196 (both), 197 (both), 292, 293, 295, 304, 309 (all), 319 (all), 320, 321, 329, 330.

Network Graphics: pages 8–9, 14, 16, 38, 40 (bottom left), 42, 43, 53 (bottom), 55, 101, 106–7, 132, 133, 143, 170 (right), 179, 187, 210, 211, 235, 264, 267, 268, 283, 298, 300, 302, 305, 312, 314, 318, 331, 345, 350, 379, 380, 384, 390, 392, 405, 414, 436, 455, 490–91, 499, 501, 503, 520, 530, 546.

Parrot Graphics: pages 7, 24, 26 (top), 70, 83, 112, 113, 125, 131, 147, 162, 175, 183, 239, 245, 248, 270, 272, 273, 285, 301, 349, 351, 363, 372, 377, 385, 387, 413, 416, 430, 433, 456, 457 (both), 464, 472, 484, 500, 507, 541, 544, 549, 550, 551.

Precision Graphics: pages 34, 51, 306, 378, 407, 415, 429 (top), 509, 510–11, 518, 519 (all), 525, 526, 527, 531.